Libby Purves

Libby Purves is a broadcaster and journalist, who has presented the talk programme *Midweek* on Radio 4 since 1984 and formerly presented *Today*. She is also a columnist on *The Times*.

Her books *How Not to Be a Perfect Mother* and *How Not to Raise a Perfect Child* have been widely translated; *How Not to Be a Perfect Family* appeared in 1994 to complete the trilogy. She also wrote *One Summer's Grace*, an account of a voyage around mainland Britain with her husband and two small children in 1988. She lives in Suffolk with her husband, the broadcaster and writer Paul Heiney, and their two children.

∫

SCEPTRE

Casting Off
Home Leave

LIBBY PURVES

SCEPTRE

First published as two separate volumes:

Casting Off © 1995 Libby Purves
First published in 1995 by Hodder & Stoughton
First published in paperback in 1996 by Hodder & Stoughton
A division of Hodder Headline
A Sceptre Book

Home Leave © 1997 Libby Purves
First published in 1997 by Hodder & Stoughton
First published in paperback in 1998 by Hodder & Stoughton
A division of Hodder Headline
A Sceptre Book

This paperback omnibus edition 2000

10 9 8 7 6 5 4 3 2 1

A CIP catalogue record for this book is
available from the British Library.

ISBN 0 340 79418 6

Printed and bound in Great Britain by
Clays Ltd, St Ives plc

Hodder & Stoughton
A division of Hodder Headline
338 Euston Road
London NW1 3BH

Casting Off

To Paul

AUTHOR'S NOTE $\int$

All characters in this book are entirely imaginary and bear no relation to any living person. Apologies are due to the towns of Portsmouth, Torquay and Salcombe for various cavalier alterations to their harbour topography and tidal flow. The carpet tiles in the BBC Radio Drama corridor, however, appear as themselves.

Women can't throw overarm: every scornful cricketing school-boy knows that.

So Ray Brewer, in whose depths such a schoolboy still lingered, suffered a moment's irrelevant, open-mouthed surprise at the force with which a set of car keys hit his shoulder and bounced onto the quay with a sharp little jingle.

He had only just emerged into the cloudy late, August bright-ness from the tin-roofed boatyard shed in which he earned his living and was expecting no more diversion than the usual spectacle of the weekend yachtsmen fussing and huffing their way back to the car park from the boats which tinkled their masts aimlessly in his small marina. Then the keys hit him, impressively hard.

In order to do this, he calculated, they must have travelled fifteen feet upwards from the water below, and the same distance forwards. Not bad, to produce an impact like that at the end of it. Yet as he swung round, rubbing his shoulder, he saw that a woman had done the throwing. She was in the cockpit of a small boat passing the quay, and a pang of wistful admiration shot through him. Just his type, the dark woman on the blue-hulled yacht: big eyes, dark flying hair, not what you'd call fat, but nothing frail about her.

Ray Brewer had, in far younger days, seen land girls riding tractors past the school playground. He would be hanging over the gate, anxious for escape into the real world where men went to war or built boats, and women cooked their tea instead of nagging them to learn times tables. The girls on the tractors would come past and sometimes wave to him. The other lads had called the land girls names and laughed at their muscles and their canvas trousers; Ray had always secretly liked them. They were lithe, strong-faced, their curly hair all the more beguiling for its unselfconscious disarray. The war passed, Ray grew up, and conformed eventually with his peers by courting and marrying the blonde, giggling, home-making, sweetly dependent Mrs Brewer. He had, he would have said, no complaints. But once or twice, at dodgy moments in the boatbuilding trade, he had allowed himself to think that it might have been different if he had had a wife who – well, who maybe didn't set the tea as carefully or polish as much but who might have come down to the yard and done the job of the half-a-lad he could hardly afford. A woman who could hold the end of a deck beam while he joggled the other into place, who would have known which plane to pass up the ladder. A land girl of his own. One that got plenty of fresh air in her, not headaches from all that polish and Vim. For a moment, looking down at the woman on the blue-hulled yacht, his surprise turned to mellow appreciation.

She looked upset, though. Her arm was still half outflung towards him, her mouth a circle of shock. The flying hair, now he looked more closely, was very wild indeed; combined with the look on her face, it gave more an impression of Medusa or a Fury than the comfortingly steady land girl of his fantasies. Ray had not thought about Furies for years, not since the class teacher had a phase of reading *Tales From the Ancient World* at wet playtimes. Nor did he like the idea of them very much. Furies. Women running dog-mad. Not steady at all. Perhaps, he thought, if women did get too strong, they lost their steadiness. Mrs Brewer would, after all, do.

The dark woman's head went down, then up, and he could see her breathing hard. Crying, even. Tcha! Overwrought, thought the old boatman. Upset about something. Needs a sit-down and a cup of tea. Probably got hubby below decks having a sulk. She'll hit the quay in a minute if she doesn't concentrate.

But she looked forward again just in time, pushed the tiller across and let the boat slew round. Handy enough, Ray grudgingly admitted to himself. The boat shaved the end of the little pier, its exhaust coughing into the choppy grey water, and showed a flat stern bearing the words 'SHEARWATER, SOUTHAMPTON'.

Weekend sailor. Ray Brewer shook his head. Funny time to be going out, at six o'clock on the last evening of a Bank Holiday; most of the yachties were on their way home by now, their seagoing dream over for another week. The last few were visible at the end of his far pontoon, bickering over which of their sullen children should carry the empty, stinking cool boxes and drooping folders of charts up to the waiting car.

Besides – he was more alert now – the boat with the woman steering had still had two plastic fenders trailing from the guardrails, and the cover on the mainsail. It looked as if it had been tidied and stowed ready for another dull week in the marina berth. Odd, to see her going out now. He hitched up his trousers over a solid gut and gave his broad bottom an absent-mindedly affectionate scratch. Funny thing to throw your car keys at a stranger, too. Ah well, women.

Aware of someone behind him, Ray turned. A thin-faced man with receding sandy-brown hair, big worried eyes and very little breath left was reaching for the keys which lay in puddle of oily water near the edge of the quay. 'Sorry, they're mine. I think she thought – um – thought . . .' It was plain, reflected the boatman with the smugness of a man who still has all his breath, exactly what the woman had thought. The thin man's blue-and-white Norwegian sweater was identical to Ray's own. Identical, indeed, to those of half a dozen men to be found on any cooling evening in late August hanging around their boats in South Coast yacht marinas, reluctant to coil the last rope and go home to reality.

'Ah,' said Ray Brewer knowingly. 'She'll have thought I was you, like. Compliment to my figure, I'd say. Lucky she remembered your car keys. You'd be stuck otherwise. I had a chap last week, his crew sailed off with the car keys and his wallet and all.'

The thin-faced man, rather gratifyingly, clutched at his pockets on hearing this, only relaxing his look of panic slightly when he felt his own wallet.

'Anyway, no harm done,' said Ray comfortably.

The man went on breathing too hard, looking down at the maker's fob on the car keys as though he barely recognized it.

Ray Brewer was not much given to studying his fellow mortals' feelings but was moved at this point to take a closer, narrower look at his interlocutor. Faint coming on? Stroke? Heart attack? You never knew. Damn unfit, most of them. Worked all week in offices, drove down on a Friday in a right to-do, had a row with the wife over the price of some piece of chandlery in the shop, then set off racing to France. They thought they could put to sea in any weather and stand up to it like a fisherman. But a fisherman would have a quiet life at home, sleep regular, and keep a decent wife to look after him and give him a proper breakfast. Not one of these noisy bints in headscarves and high voices, shouting 'Jonno! Jamie!' and giving everybody orders. No wonder the men got heart attacks. Mrs Brewer drifted into the corner of his mind again, this time suffused with a rosy glow.

But this man didn't look ill, only shocked. Rubbing the back of his neck, Ray groped for an explanation. 'Not the wrong keys, is it?'

At last, the thin man seemed to gather his wits. 'No, these are my car keys all right. It's just – I wasn't expecting . . .' He tailed off, staring after the blue boat whose mast was slipping past the round tower at the entrance to the harbour. A fast spring ebb tide was chuckling round the stone quay and tugging at the moored yachts on the pontoons. It must have sped *Shearwater* faster than her engine could have done, out towards the ruffled open waters of the Solent and the English Channel beyond. She was, quite definitely, gone.

'It's my wife,' he explained inadequately. 'I ought to telephone . . .'

'Use the one in the office,' offered Ray magnanimously. 'Or, if it's the boat you want to talk to, you could call them up on Channel M.'

The man brightened. 'Yes, thank you, that's a thought. That *is* a thought. I ought just to tell my daughter, she's . . .' He glanced up at the dusty car park where a sullen streaked-blonde nymphet in abbreviated frayed denim shorts leaned on a grey estate car displaying, in every line of her body, eloquent contempt for the world. Her father's heart seemed to fail him. 'No, perhaps I'll try the VHF first, if I . . .'

The boatman, interested but despairing of this worried man

ever finishing a sentence, silently led the way to the office in the corner of his shed. Pushing aside half a mug of cold tea and a book of well-thumbed tide tables, he silently indicated the apparatus before retiring to open and shut a few drawers at random, well within earshot.

The man picked up the handset, listened a moment to make sure of silence on the calling channel, and began: '*Shearwater, Shearwater, Shearwater*. This is – um – Portsmouth new marina—'

'Brewmarine,' interjected its owner with a touch of asperity. Five years he had been here with his pontoons, a bit of private enterprise off a redundant naval pier. Five years of trading as a small marina and repair yard for weekend sailors, of keeping the toilet block clean, chasing up the shifty, newly-broke Lloyds' names and their suddenly penurious relatives for overdue mooring fees. Five years. A dozen cork tiles had already succumbed to gravity and fallen off the ceiling of his 'new' office. And still the yachties couldn't remember the proper trading name even if they did write their cheques out to it. '*Brewmarine*,' he said again, with bitterness.

'Thank you,' mouthed the man. '*Shearwater, Shearwater*, this is Brewmarine, over.'

The machine shashed and crackled, broadcasting silence. Urgently the man repeated, '*Shearwater, Shearwater, Shearwater*. This is Brewmarine. Keith speaking. Over. Over.'

More shashing, more silence.

'P'raps they're switched off,' offered Ray, hitching up his trousers.

'Well, one last time,' said his guest, trying unconvincingly for nonchalance. '*Shearwater, Shearwater*. Brewmarine. Over.'

Silence.

Then, leaning forward, the man suddenly almost hissed into the handset, 'Joanna. *You've made your point*. Over.'

More silence.

An incredulous smile spread over Ray Brewer's broad face. Made her point? Joanna? The wife, was it? Run off with the boat, had she, fenders dangling, chucking the keys at him, wooah! This'd be one to tell them! Fights he'd had on his pontoons, high shrill arguments, blows with boathooks, women storming off to the car; even one man pushed into the marina by an irate wife after a particularly badly bodged attempt at mooring and two large chips off the gelcoat on the bow (£65.17, plus VAT, plus labour, he could see the invoice now). He'd never had one hijack the boat, though. With the boy friend, perhaps . . . Now that'd be a thing.

The thin-faced man suddenly became aware of the entertainment he was providing and, pulling his anxious, disjointed silhouette more nearly into the semblance of a man in control of his world, was visibly seen to resolve that he would provide no more. 'Thank you very much,' he said crisply. 'Nothing I can't handle.' And he strode out towards the car park where his irritated daughter still lounged, kicking stones at pedestrian seagulls with vicious accuracy. One of his elbows hit the peeling doorjamb of the hut as he went.

Ray whistled, strode over to the drawer and, after some scuffling, pulled out a record card.

Yes. SHEARWATER: auxiliary sailing yacht, sloop, 30 foot length overall, hull colour navy blue, 18 hp Yanmar diesel. Property of Mr and Mrs K. Gurney, Old Vicarage, Bonhurst. Berthing fees paid up to date. No recent maintenance invoices.

None of his business, really. He took down his keys from the wall and reached over to switch off the VHF. Then something made the old boatman hesitate and pick up the handset instead. He had, after all, spent half a lifetime at sea before setting up as a boatbuilder and nursemaid for weekend yachties. Perhaps there wasn't a boy friend. Perhaps the lady was out there on her own, with the dusk coming on and the cold north wind rising. 'Shearwater, Shearwater, this is Brewmarine, over.' He tried a few times more, then sighed, shrugged, and switched off for the night. None of his business.

Joanna Gurney, pitching southward with a faceful of tears, drove the boat forward through the slapping waves, towards the looming Napoleonic forts outside Portsmouth harbour. She heard none of the calls. The radio was off. It had been off since Keith had tidied the cabin, carried up the three bags, and padlocked the hatchway doors. The cabin, come to that, still was padlocked. To get at the charts or the galley, or to switch on the radio or depth sounder, Joanna would have to turn the engine off for a few moments and remove the key in order to use its inseparable companion, the padlock key – unless she crouched down to fiddle the cabin key off its ring, which for the moment seemed unthinkable. Normally, one would unlock the cabin at the start of a trip, and that would be it. It wouldn't matter that the brass key of the cabin was dangling and vibrating the miles away on its ring attached to the ignition key.

Funny how one half-step away from normality could throw everything out of order. The winch handles for the sails were below too. *Shearwater* was really not ready for sea at all. Shouldn't be there. It should be just another modest fibreglass boat, lying idle alongside all the other weekend yachts as her owners drove, tired and glowing, up the motorway towards the Old Vicarage, the washing machine and the first drink.

And so it would have been, had it not been for a moment of particular and overwhelming emotional violence and a quirk of circumstance.

The violence arose from certain conversations, spread over two days – or perhaps ten years, she thought bitterly – with Keith. The circumstance was that when he went up to the car expecting her to lock up and follow, he took his own weekend clothes bag and sixteen-year-old Susan's. So Joanna was left aboard with her own bag, the cool box, the keys, and her anger. All she needed to do was to pick up the bags and follow him to the joint car and joint home, and on through another week of their lives, as she had a thousand times before.

But, shaken by a sudden violence, Joanna Gurney, aged thirty-seven and of hitherto sound mind, did something quite different. She stepped four paces forward on the pontoon and five back, throwing off the neat, plastic-sheathed mooring lines fore and aft; she started the engine, dragged the gearstick into reverse and steered the boat away from its berth (catching the bow a nasty thump as she did so). The defiant gesture did not buoy her up; she was already crying when she passed out of the marina and abreast of Ray Brewer's quay; already sorry, guilty, awash in hot, helpless, futile tears. Joanna was not, as a rule, a ready weeper. Certainly not since the children were born. It was, after all, a mother's duty to maintain a bright, optimistic, twinklingly brisk façade at all times. But there was nobody to see her now, no child to be worried, no husband to sigh. She had wept unhindered, seeing the harbour mouth far ahead through a fog of tears.

It was as she bent to dash her sleeve across her eyes that she suddenly saw the car keys lying on the cockpit seat. Had Keith, too, been rattled by the weekend's arguments? It was not like him to forget them. At the sight, she was instantly overcome by the restless maternal compulsion to avert family crises. The clouds of her own emotion fading, Joanna saw it all: Keith locked out of the car, Susan nagging about her train to London and having to meet Anneliese for the rock concert; Susan missing her train, snarling at Keith; he snarling back, having to find a garage on foot, not getting home until 1 a.m., with his Tuesday partners' conference to get ready for. She saw Susan flouncing off to hitchhike up the M3 and being picked up by a serial killer. While all the time the keys which could have prevented these crises would be lying on the cockpit seat on *Shearwater* under the weeping guilty eye of her mother.

Joanna could not bear it. On the quay she saw, through the mist of tears, Keith standing in his sweater, looking strangely old and fat. Sniffing, letting the boat sheer wildly about as she let go of the tiller, she accomplished the first and last classic overarm lob of her life, arousing Ray Brewer's land-girl memories and nearly crashing the boat into the quay.

And when the keys were safe ashore, the cloud of tears engulfed her again. Without thought or plan, Joanna turned the boat's head towards the sea.

2

'Mum's done *what*?' said the girl to her father.

'Taken the boat. Gone out of the harbour,' said Keith.

'What *for*?'

There was nothing but exasperation in Susan's voice. Sixteen she might be, a sophisticate, a frequenter of heavy metal concerts, a young adult prevented from driving, voting and staying out all night only by some laughable quirk of the law. But grown-ups were still as tiresome, unpredictable, unreasonable and weird in their ways as when she was four years old. These two had been sparring with one another all weekend, going on and on about the boat and the bills and Mum's loopy stuff about changing her life and selling the Bun. Hell!

'If Mum's not here, what about the Bun?' she began, then decided that this, too, was an adult problem. There was no way she could be forced to run the Bun herself. Not like she sometimes did in the holidays. With school officially starting tomorrow and the concert tonight, she was out of the Bun-running, and a good thing too. Susan hitched her shapely bottom off the bonnet of the car and decisively rattled the door.

'Look, I've got to get the train. I'm meeting Anneliese at Waterloo, OK? You said you'd drop me off.'

In times of utter bewilderment, any action is better than paralysis. There was something soothing to Keith in the action of unlocking the car, sitting down, adjusting his mirror, starting up, manoeuvring around the filthy, rusting Brewmarine travel hoist with its worn slings and flaky old chain, and driving through the Monday evening streets of Portsmouth towards the station. It was action. It put him back in control. For the moment, it would do.

Outside the dusty station, Susan jumped out smartly, banging her squashy bag against her tanned legs, and vanished with a dismissive 'Bye!' Then his paralysis descended again. Joanna, wife of Keith, mother of Susan and Lance, had gone to sea without them. Without warning or explanation she had vanished into a choppy, chilly, misty seascape. Alone. She had never even taken the boat out alone before. In their early sailing days she had been as keen to take command as he was; she had taken courses on navigation and seamanship and liferaft survival and two-cylinder diesel engines; she had talked of independence and the day when she would make a passage on her own. She had read the memoirs of the women singlehanders, Clare Francis and Nicolette Milnes-Walker and Naomi James, dreamed of a singlehanded Atlantic crossing and been grateful for Keith's mild encouragement.

But always there had been babies in baskets, crawling and staggering toddlers, children climbing onto the boom in life-jackets, teenagers wanting to learn to sail from Dad, who knew, not Mum, who cooked. There had been visiting friends of the children, too: saucer-eyed and nervous at the tipping and bounding of this strange weekend home, needing hot chocolate and benign reassurances. Somehow it had all drawn her eye away from the sailing of the boat across the sea, to the minutiae of the crew's warmth and wellbeing and cheerfulness. Keith noted, but never mentioned, that there had been less and less talk of her sailing one day alone. So she never had.

Perhaps she hadn't this time. Perhaps he dreamed it.

Slowly, he drove back to the marina and stopped by the gate to climb out and look down at the pontoons. *Shearwater* was definitely not there. Missing. Missing! Police, he thought. Missing person. Police. He drove off again, to look for some.

For the first time since the rage had struck her, Joanna Gurney had a decision to make. East or west? Battering straight ahead through grey waves, weeping, was all very well as a gesture, but the Solent is only a narrow sleeve of water between island and mainland. The Isle of Wight lay uncompromisingly in her way. East past Bembridge, or west toward's Egypt Point and Cowes Roads?

Or back the way she had come?

No, not back; not tonight. To turn against the sluicing tide, battle through the harbour mouth and into the marina, to tie *Shearwater* back with the same ropes and lamely telephone home – impossible. Until tomorrow. By then she would find, somehow, a form of words. Something beginning, 'Look, Keith, I'm sorry I gave you a shock, but you have to understand how serious I am . . .' Perhaps a bit of psychobabble would come in handy. Something about personal space, or assertive love, or family dynamics. Luckily, the Sunday papers were still lying below, full of useful phrases of this sort and exhortations to take up 'designer lesbianism', aromatherapy, colonic irrigation and a dozen other solutions to life's dilemmas. Hers, surely, would fit somewhere into the self-indulgent pattern. She didn't want much, after all. Couldn't he *see* that?

The boat snatched and bucked in the wake of a passing ferry, bringing her attention back to the present. Ahead lay the cramped anchorage of Fishbourne creek, in full sight of the mainland; round the point, at its eastern end, the intricate entrance to Bembridge harbour. *Shearwater* had visited both on innumerable picnic weekends. Even if the harbour charts were not stowed away behind the padlocked cabin door, Joanna did not want to revisit either harbour alone like this. She could not face the ghost of those happy picnics, that family contentment. But night was falling, the north wind still blustery, and she suddenly knew that she was bone-weary. She had to go somewhere and rest. Somewhere safe and hidden. 'Round the corner, out of sight,' she said aloud. 'Somewhere quiet. Quiet. Drop the anchor. I can do that. Quite capable. Done it before. Done the courses. No different being alone. Hundreds of singlehanded yachtsmen. Important thing is keep up your sleep. Anchor, sleep, then back to Portsmouth. Say sorry, sort it out. Sort – everything – out.'

With a jerk, she came upright again. Dropping off at the helm, under engine, crossing the Solent at six knots: it would not do, not at all. The shock of having fallen asleep – a second loss of self-control within an hour – woke her more thoroughly. She hauled the tiller towards her and slewed the boat's head south-eastward, to glide on the ebb tide round the island's green tip. Somewhere south of Bembridge Ledge, in Sandown Bay, there you could anchor. They had done it once years ago, waiting for a fair tide. There was a beach where small laughing Susan and serious nine-year-old Lance had made castles. Lance had measured out each side of his castle beforehand, and in the wet sand designed it in elevation and plan, like an architect. A wonderful child; all the more wonderful that he did not complain when Susan scuffed his design in one of her wild dances.

Sandown Bay. There were no rocks that she could remember, and a nice, obvious, easy approach. She could anchor far offshore and lie there unnoticed. That would do. She would be safe.

The forecast was for northerly winds, force 3 or at most 4: she had half heard it at ten to six while Keith packed his sailing bag and she wiped the galley and Susan sulked vaguely on deck in the poisoned atmosphere. Since they were not planning to go back to sea, she had missed the earlier synopsis with its deceptively casual talk of a low pressure area in the Western Channel moving rapidly across Europe and deepening 993. She had only by accident heard the forecast for area Wight during one of the silences. They were chilly, charged silences; for there still flowed, through their apparently practical conversation about who had turned off which seacock, an echo of the weekend's bitter marital argument about the Bun.

The Bun! Joanna was suddenly and horribly awake. The Bun in the Oven was Bonhurst's leading teashop. 'LOCAL WOMEN'S DREAM GREW TO AWARD-WINNING BUSINESS' the *Bonhurst Echo* had proudly reported, even though the award in question was only from the local Chamber of Commerce. 'JO AND MANDY'S SUCCESS STORY'. How was it going to open on Tuesday morning with its joint proprietress and weekday manager anchored sixty miles south of it, alone? Solicitude flooded through her. She could imagine shoppers standing puzzled outside the closed glass door, resenting the weight of their carrier bags, tapping and peering impatiently, wanting coffee and cakes. She could imagine the bakery order lying uncollected, going stale; the milk souring as the sun warmed the brick side wall where it waited in vain. She could imagine Zoë, the latest surly teenage waitress, arriving to find the place deserted.

True, Joanna had spent the entire weekend arguing with

Keith that she was sick of the Bun, had served her time with it, and wanted to sell up at any price, recession or no recession. She wanted to take another path through the second half of her life, as she had rather shyly put it. Keith had sighed, and clattered loudly with the washing-up; Susan had snorted. But a gradual, caringly managed divorce from the floury embrace of one's teashop was one thing; a heartless abandonment quite another. Mandy, of course, might step in. But then again, being Mandy, she might not bother. Perhaps Erika, if Keith asked her – which he might, of course, only he would have to explain, or make something up, and then it would be all round the town in ten minutes – Erika might . . .

Joanna bit her lip and shifted her feet uneasily as she stood, steering down the wind towards the tip of the island. Erika might step in. But the deal was that Erika handled weekends and holiday Mondays only, serving passion cake and scones to the tourists arriving to tick off Bonhurst Abbey (C14, notable clerestory) in their guidebooks; and tea to the homeward-bound Sunday travellers who knew enough to avoid the Fleet Service area and dive off instead down a B road for a decent brew. Erika did not work on weekdays. She had a husband to tend, and took her wifely duties seriously. Still, Erika might be willing to duck out of her Tuesday routines and come in, draggled blonde hair drawn back into her working bun, colourless and reliable. Keith could tell her some story.

Only Keith never told stories, did he? Keith was a model of righteousness. Perhaps he would tell everyone the truth, just like that. 'Joanna's run off with the boat, nobody knows where.' She giggled, the comedy of the situation striking her all of a sudden. 'Take life as a comedy, a romance, a melodrama if you like; not a tragedy,' Gabriel used to say to her in bed, years ago. 'You've got a choice, you know. It's in the eye of the beholder.'

Well, Gabriel was a bastard, turning other people's comedies into tragedies often enough and never staying for the last act. To hell with him. To hell with Keith, too, and his fussy desire to keep things what he called 'settled' and she called stagnant. Someone else would have to cope with the teashop for once and learn to take her defection as comedy, not tragedy. She had done Bun rotas for fifteen years. Sod the Bun.

She would, in any case, be home by lunchtime tomorrow. One night alone at anchor would give her time to think. Keith wouldn't worry. He would know she would be all right in this quiet weather on a familiar boat. She would call home on the VHF tonight, explain that it was an impulse and that she needed time alone.

As the light waned in the grey overcast western sky, Joanna patted *Shearwater*'s side deck affectionately. Who would have thought it? The old boat, scene of so many years of family trips, turning out suddenly to be a refuge and a means of fleeing them. An irony; part of the comedy, the oddity, the funny-five-minutes she was, after long sensible years, at last having.

Joanna's tears were dry now; the engine puttered on faithfully, bearing her on the tide round Bembridge Ledge.

Keith, far from comical in mood, sat on a tatty plastic-upholstered bench reading for the fifth time a pamphlet exhorting him to say No to Drugs. His clients, particularly the legal aid ones, had often told him how unnerving they found police stations. Something about the atmosphere, they claimed, caused them to say things they didn't mean and confess things they hadn't done.

He, being left to untangle the mess which this weakness engendered, usually replied to this rambling line of self-explanation with a sigh (in bad cases, a snort) of exasperated disbelief. Only the other week he had been summoned to represent a woman of transparent respectability who had been pulled in for shoplifting without a shred of evidence. An over-zealous store detective had accosted her before she had even reached the till, let alone the door. But within two minutes of arrival at the police station, she had begun weeping and saying to an embarrassed young WPC that she was a wicked, wicked woman and deserved nothing better than prison. This, the store detective triumphantly claimed, constituted a confession. Keith had spent days trying to unravel this one and resented the extra trouble – and the smooth barrister the silly cow's husband had demanded, down from the bloody Temple, not that it was ever going to come near a court – quite a lot.

But now he began to see the woman's point. Guilt hung around him like a bad smell. He no longer felt like the confident, reassuring, streetwise solicitor who came into such places to straighten things out. He felt felonious, a suspect layman in his grubby Breton red sailing trousers and snagged sweater. He had waited five minutes for attention although nothing whatever appeared to be going on in the half-glimpsed hinterland behind the desk apart from a desultory conversation between a stout dark WPC and a policeman with a straggling blond moustache; but the very delay made Keith feel unworthy and even more ill-at-ease. By the time PC Littlejohn sauntered over to his side of the desk, the unworthiness had become a desperate, defiant chippiness. Keith, in fact, was turning moment by moment into one of his own more difficult clients, metamorphosed from a frightened civilian needing help into an ill-tempered desperado by sheer atmosphere and circumstance.

PC Littlejohn saw a yachtie, and stifled a yawn of irritation. Lost something probably. Left his little rubber dinghy tied to the steps with a granny knot and a hundred quid's worth of oars and lifejackets lying loose in it, then acting surprised when they got nicked. Sod 'em all. Give him a good stabbing incident any day. 'Help you, sir?' he said, raising his eyebrows.

'Yes – erm – I'd like to report a missing boat,' said Keith. 'And a person. The person is on the boat.'

'I see, sir. Could you give me your own details first?'

'Keith Gurney. Old Vicarage, Bonhurst. Solicitor.'

The policeman looked up, even less inclined to care what happened to this pathetic twat. He did not like solicitors at all. His three years in the force had taught him that they always took the shine off the most triumphant arrest and bad-mouthed you in court afterwards. Twelve hours on duty, drunks all over the seafront, and now a twat solicitor. Still, back to business. 'Perhaps you could give me a description of the boat. Sir.'

Haltingly, Keith did so.

'And who is the person?'

'My wife, Mrs Joanna Gurney. She's thirty-seven years old, dark, medium height—'

'On the boat, sir?' said PC Littlejohn. 'With, er, anybody?' Serve the twat right if his wife had run off.

'No. Alone. We'd just got back, after the weekend, and tied

the boat up, and when I got back from taking some luggage, she was motoring out of the harbour.'

'So you want,' said the policeman, labouring, 'to report the theft of the boat?'

'No, er, yes – not theft, she's actually a part owner, legally – half owner actually . . .' Keith was sweating now. 'Look, probably better if we just – perhaps if you just took the details – it isn't theft, and she's not been gone long – it's just I'm worried . . .'

PC Littlejohn laid down his pen and looked with distaste at the thin, brown-eyed man opposite. God almighty, what was he on about? 'Can I get this clear, sir. Your wife's gone sailing, in a boat she partly owns. Do you want to make a complaint?'

'No, but I'm concerned. I don't know where she is or why she did it . . .' Floundering, wrong-footed, Keith realized with a small shock that he was acting more ineptly than he had done for years, as ineptly as the stupidest client, running headlong into some trouble he could not quite put a name or shape to. 'She may be in danger, she's never been out alone before.'

The policeman, ever alert for an opportunity to tear up paperwork, saw his chance. 'Perhaps you should contact the coastguard direct, sir. They can keep an eye out, then perhaps you could go to your local police station in a couple of days if there isn't any news. When we talk about missing persons we generally mean more than an hour or two, sir. Otherwise we'd all be missing, most nights, down the pub, wouldn't we, sir?'

Keith was suddenly angry. 'Look, I'm telling you, she could be in danger. She's been a bit – depressed . . .'

'You have reason to think she might do something foolish? You should have told us that, sir. Sergeant!'

An older, kinder-faced man appeared, led him inside the station, took over. The wheels revolved, forms were filled, notes taken. Sitting on a hard police chair, blue uniforms and brass buttons opposite him, Keith went further than he meant to.

PC Littlejohn listened in the background for as long as he needed. Then, half an hour later, he went off duty, made his way in plain clothes to the Spread Eagle on the corner of Nelson Street, took a drink off a young friend with a local newspaper job and national newspaper ambitions, and told him the whole picaresque story of the thin lawyer in the oiled-wool sweater and the wife who had run away to sea. The young friend, very pleased indeed, bought him another and left him to drink it alone. This was a lovely one for the end of the Bank Holiday. Yes!

He headed back to his bedsitter, his computer modem, and seventy-five quid's worth of professional advancement. He wouldn't get a by-line, sadly, since the local paper might ask why he hadn't saved it for them. Bastards. Why should he? Tasty little story. Littlejohn had stopped short of giving him the name, but one call to an ex-girl friend in Bonhurst identified the only sailing solicitor in the place. A cross-check with Ray Brewer – in which the journalist prudently became Joanna's brother – confirmed it.

'Portsmouth police and coastguards,' he wrote, 'were called in last night when a 37-year-old housewife slipped her moorings and took her husband's boat to sea alone. Joanna Gurney, a brunette Bonhurst mother of two, more used to navigating a trolley round the local shops, gave hubby Keith the yo-heave-ho and bolted for the briny . . .'

The young man paused and squinted at his work. Very nice. Just the stuff for the agency. Anyway, the local paper would only have checked with the police and got Littlejohn into trouble. The dirty dailies wouldn't bother. Make a good filler, they'd probably all take it.

'Yo-ho Jo, her husband revealed, had never sailed alone and came within inches of hitting a stone pier on the way out of the harbour . . .' Better put in a bit about how she might have been suffering from depression. All bloody women suffered from depression, nobody was going to sue over that. And the bloke did say it to the policeman.

'Fears are growing,' he typed in, 'for the safety of the woman, whose mental state is said to be unstable after a period of depression . . .' Even the broadsheets might like that. The feminist columnists could have a chew on it. Woman runs away to sea. The Grand Gesture. Great!

Twenty miles to the north on the roaring Monday evening motorway, Keith drove in the slow lane, feeling rotten. Low and lonely, and faintly disgraced. He shouldn't have talked about

Joanna like that. She would be fine. She was fine. Anchored somewhere, getting over the temper. She'd probably be home before Susan got back from her jungle-music concert. Fuss about nothing, and he shouldn't have made it. Might be best to ring the police when he got in, to call off anything they might be thinking of doing.

In Sandown Bay, with a rattle and a splash Joanna let go the anchor in five metres' depth of calm water. Crouching, she held onto the chain and felt the tug when *Shearwater* pulled back and the swing of the boat as the anchor bit into the ground. She paid out ten metres more chain, hand over hand, and, shivering, went back to unlock the cabin and light the lamp against the encroaching dusk. Below, out of the wind, the cabin felt warm, with the musty, tarry, woody, comforting boat smell Joanna had always loved. She pulled a box of matches out of the rack above the stove, struck one, plucked the glass shade off the little swinging paraffin lamp and lit it. Big shadows of her hands danced on the bulkhead. Turning the wick down a little, she slipped the glass chimney back into place and adjusted the lamp again until it shone, clear and bright, on the varnish and the red cushions which glowed like a sanctuary lamp. Pumping the galley tap, she drew herself a mugful of cold water and drank deeply.

Home tomorrow. One quiet night at anchor, alone. Things would seem clearer in the morning. She pulled out the down sleeping bag from its weekday stowage under the bunk and loosened the strings on its two bags, one nylon and one waterproof.

The bag puffed out, comforting and engulfing in the small cabin, and suddenly a great weariness came over her. Without tea or food, without washing, cleaning her teeth, or doing more than pulling off her jeans and sweater, Joanna climbed into the bag in her T-shirt, reached up to blow out the barely settled wick of the light, and lay down in the dank gloom of the gently rocking cabin. Within seconds she was asleep, blown out like a lamp herself.

3

Sometimes, in the small hours, the wind rises for a while unforecast and threatening. It rattles windows along the shore, makes trees clatter disquiet into the peaceful sleep of householders, and blows fretful dreams into the minds of sailors at anchor. At three o'clock, Joanna woke to the grinding of the anchor chain on its iron fairlead. Her cheeks were wet with the tears already soaking into the cotton lining of the sleeping bag, and a slick of sweat covered her shoulders. The Gabriel dream was back.

The strange thing, even to her distressed mind, was that it had hardly faded after years of being half forgotten; years when it visited only occasionally, on nights of fever. Perhaps bad dreams of old disasters are discouraged by the reassuring banality of family life. Maybe in the face of the equable, competent atmosphere that surrounded Joanna and emanated from her, the dream had been forced into retreat. Sometimes, after one of its brief, partial night visits, she liked to imagine it abashed; no self-respecting existential nightmare, after all, would like it known that one of its regular haunts was the pillow of a Hampshire teashop proprietress, mother of two and member of the Law Society regional ball committee.

Certainly the Gabriel dream had not been back so complete or so vivid since the very first married nights. Then, once a month or so, she had been woken sobbing and shouting by a kind, anxious, infinitely reassuring Keith. No Keith now; alone in the little cabin, her canvas trousers and smock the only huddled occupants of the bunk opposite, Joanna writhed herself awake, trying to escape the dream's renewed and horrible force.

She had been on Port Meadow again, shut out and shamed and lost. But time had somersaulted, and Emily was not dead, but dying; dying because she, Joanna, had run away. And a moment came, in the darkness of the meadow, when she knew from the distant bells that death had struck. The bells said death was not a rest but a misery, an endless bad dream of rot and shame which had swallowed Emily, through Joanna's fault.

Joanna wanted to be dead too, if Emily was. She was walking towards death, across the slippery tussocks of wet grass, when Gabriel turned from the door – a door on a meadow? – but it had always been there in the dream, the door of his bedroom with the painted Chinese symbols on it. Gabriel said, 'Oh, come on, Jo, you aren't the dying type. You'd look silly dead.'

And he laughed, and shut the door, and she was out on Port Meadow alone, and woke to the sound of his receding laughter and a crushing awareness of failure and shame.

Although the Gabriel dream had not come back for years, she knew what to do. Wake up properly. Don't slide back into more of it. Drink a glass of water, sit up, and run through things in the right order. Most of the things, anyway. The historical truth was bad enough; but nothing could be as bad as the guilt of the dream. In the truth there was less guilt.

Hugging her knees, leaning her back against the hard wood of the bulkhead, Joanna told herself the story as baldly and unemotionally as she could. It was an old recitation, practised years ago to push the Gabriel dream aside without lying outright. Or telling Keith. She had never so much as said Gabriel's name to Keith. It was a private ritual, although never yet more eerily private than aboard the little boat, rolling and tugging at its anchor in Sandown Bay in the small hours of a chilly August morning.

Aged twenty, in her Finals year at Oxford, Joanna – then Joanna Telford, scholar of Somerville, white hope of her tutors, confidently expected to bring home a First of the better sort – had indeed been found wandering alone at 2 a.m. on Port Meadow. The nervous breakdown, of which her silence and apparent amnesia were considered evidence, led first to her incarceration in the Littlemore hospital and then to her return home to Hampshire and bewildered parents. Finally it led to her implacable decision to take a menial clerical job in a firm of Southampton solicitors, where sandy-haired, serious Keith saw and immediately loved her.

The 'nervous trouble', as her parents to Joanna's irritation termed it, made her refuse to return to Oxford for an additional year as the college urged; even when the Principal offered to extend her scholarship grant, she politely and adamantly turned it down. Young Jo Telford had simply decided, after the Port Meadow night, not to take her finals, ever. Never to have anything more to do with Somerville, with Oxford, and most especially with Leckford Road or Gabriel O'Riordan.

For he, tormentor of the dream, was real too. So was the room with the Chinese symbols in the rundown house on Leckford Road where amid the brushfire smell of pot Joanna, a year before her disaster, lost heart and virginity together to Gabriel's laughing, bear-hugging, embracing, warm shaggy energy. Even now, eighteen years a wife and mother, she had only to see a Chinese letter or pass a hippie craft shop smelling of joss sticks and she would feel a stab of treacherous desire. It had long been unfocused desire; direct longing for Gabriel it certainly was not. That had died with Emily.

But it was a bitter thing, thought Joanna in the whistling, gurgling, chafing, clanking cabin of *Shearwater*, that you could reject a man with horror, see right through him, and still have his scorn haunt your dreams half a lifetime later. If anyone should be scorned, it was Gabriel himself. Because of Emily.

Who was also real. At this point, Joanna's stern recital to herself of the events of 1977 faltered painfully. It was all right to have an affair with an older, fascinating, lawlessly hip poet-academic at nineteen; to be rejected by him on your twentieth birthday with an injunction to 'hang loose, stay cool'. That sort of thing was part of life's experience. Such experiences were not uncommon in the backwash of the liberated sixties, when a great stroke of luck befell the type of man who would in a simpler age have been recognized as cad, bounder, villainous seducer with twirling moustachios. Such men's luck lay in coming to their doubtful maturity in an age when free, no-strings, pharmaceutically sterilized love enjoyed an unprecedented vogue.

Casanovas then had a lot of scope. They could play you countless songs about rolling-stone men leaving clinging women in
order nobly to follow their destiny. They could model themselves
on Bob Dylan singing, 'Go 'way from my window . . . I'm not
the one you want, babe, I'm not the one you need.' They could
screw you, win your flattering adoration, borrow all your spare
money and never return it, spin you any halfwit philosophy
they liked, and then get bored with you and chuck you out.
And when you protested, they could make you feel like the
fool. With one saintlike, patriarchal shrug they could convince
you that you were a narrow-minded little middle-class girl. It
was something, Jo often thought, to do with the beards; they
made you feel as if you had been offered a glimpse of Moses'
tablets, or a divine experience with Jove disguised as a swan,
and had responded by starting to book wedding caterers.

Such men were not uncommon in university towns; and for
a time nobody seemed to notice that they never did walk into
the sunset to meet their vaunted Destiny on the open road.
They stayed put, ushering a procession of adoring young girls
in and out of their dens in a cloud of fragrant fuddling smoke
until they saw the writing on the wall and allowed some
particularly strong-minded girl to lead them up the aisle and
into a nine-to-five job. Oh yes, Joanna had heard plenty of
women laughing sheepishly in their settled, domestic thirties as
they told stories of men who played the same tune as Gabriel:
'Someone to close his eyes for you, someone to close his heart?
It ain't me, babe, no, no, no, it ain't me you're lookin' for,
babe.' All this was just the embarrassing emotional juvenilia of
anyone's life.

But an awkward quirk had prevented Joanna from telling
her particular version of the standard seventies disaster story
to any friend. She had never made a healing joke of it, because
there was no healing to be had. Because of Emily. Because
Emily – sunny, dippy, laughing Emily, cheeky, kind, unstable
Emily – had died. Died of Gabriel, died of Joanna's failure to
keep her alive. Emily had wound herself into half a lifetime's
nightmares. The black, tolling, shameful nightmare of her death
was real.

Eighteen years on, Joanna huddled into the sleeping bag. The brief night gale was easing, the chain clanking more idly and intermittently, the roll and slap of waves abating. She did not need to think too much about Emily. Not now. Emily's death had driven her out into the rain, onto Port Meadow, to hear the clocks and bells strike night hours across the northern wastes by the river. It had driven her from friends, ambitions, city and university into another kind of life: a kindly, domestic, community-minded, parent-teacher-association, teashop life. A safe, decent life. Her wretched adolescent ancestress had seen the futility of Gabriel, and run for cover.

She need not think too much of Emily's end, but perfunctorily forced herself to run through the coda: the other, minor guilty admission. The truth nobody knew was that she had not been at all amnesiac that night on Port Meadow, nor 'confused' at the mental hospital. She had only been tired and angry. Too much so to speak to the police, or college, or psychiatrist, or parents. She had faked the breakdown, as far as it went, and refused the degree out of nihilism and rage. She was perfectly sane all the time. But hell, she was young and it was a rough passage. These days they would have called her depressed and given her Prozac, and not condemned anything, even her pretending to be madder than she was. The expression 'right to silence' drifted across her mind from some item of legal news. Jo Telford had a right to silence. So did Joanna Gurney.

Silently now, she lay down, closed her eyes, hardly aware of the quietening boat, and slid into a blank, flat sleep.

In the Old Vicarage, Keith tossed and threw an arm across the empty half of the bed. He whimpered slightly, knowing in his sleep that his wife was not beside him.

In South London, silent sleepy men threw bundles of newspapers into vans. From somewhere west of Ushant, to the south-west of *Shearwater*'s anchorage, the depression began to move stealthily, heading for Belgium. A light rain fell, and the boat shifted its heading, doubtfully, then swung back. No change yet.

4

Keith woke at twenty to eight from a vague dream of discomfort. He had been reaching vainly for his missing wife and rolled too far until his arm hung over her side of the bed and grew pins and needles.

Cursing, he sat up, and switched on the radio which he and Jo kept tuned to Radio 4 and the measured rhythms of waking middle England. An urbane newsreader was concluding the review of the morning's press, with the familar note of faint, kindly superiority befitting the senior service of British media: '. . . *Daily Express*, however, sees the minister's tough new line differently. With the headline: HOW TO HANDLE A VANDAL . . .'

Somehow, this morning, the tone jarred on Keith for the first time. What, he asked himself savagely, have they got to be so smug about? He jammed his arm into the sleeve of his wool dressing gown, catching his hand in the rolled-in cuff, then froze as the bulletin continued: 'Finally, several papers carry the story of the wife who, as the *Mail* puts it, staged a one-woman mutiny in Portsmouth harbour, slipping her moorings and heading out to sea while her husband's back was turned . . .'

Stiff with horror, Keith felt a blush mount from his shoulders to his hairline; such a blush as he had not felt since he hit a flat note in a school oboe solo in 1965. The blasted, blasted police station! How many times had he warned clients not to prattle, not to spill details irrelevant to the matter in hand, not while ears were flapping?

'. . . some concern at her inexperience and mental state. The coastguard, however, report calm weather conditions and no cause for alarm unless, said a spokesman, the woman does anything silly. Or, as the *Globe* condescendingly adds, anything else silly. Still, it makes a novel solution, says the paper, to the stresses of family life. The *Sun* sums it up with the headline MUM AHOY!'

A chortle followed from the studio pair; the man said, 'It used to be the boys who ran off to sea, now it's their mums.' The woman gave a contralto, Radio 4 giggle and added, 'Can't say I blame her, this end of the school holidays!'

Keith walked into the bathroom and, unable to look Jo's shampoo and toothbrush in the face, shaved hurriedly with the electric razor he despised and kept for oversleeping days. He did not trust his shaking hand. Disaster. Disaster. If Jo was awake, switched on the boat's radio – also tuned permanently to the long-wave for the shipping forecasts – if Jo heard that, she'd think . . .

Oh, God. She'd think he'd raised the hue and cry on purpose because they had had a row about her wanting to sell out of the Bun. It might have been all right if they were the kind of couple who had explosive public rows all the time, tipped spaghetti over one another in Italian restaurants, locked each other out and shrieked 'Bastard!' through upper windows. Like many of his clients. But they were not. They had never, either of them, cried public shame on the other. The most snarling private argument, the most crabby drive to a dinner party had never made either of them snipe or score points in public. Not like Mandy and Alex who appeared to get some obscure thrill out of bickering at other people's tables.

Joanna, he knew without asking, did not indulge in those 'Oh, men!' conversations with other mothers; at least, not in any private detail. Equally, he did not dish the dirt with the boys. Only with the children, during that golden, pre-adolescent stage of mutual understanding between ten and thirteen, had they giggled openly over one another's shortcomings, untidinesses, inadequacies over spiders, snoring habits, and the rest.

And, curiously, even during their most poisonous teenage rants, neither Lance nor Susan had betrayed or belittled these admissions of marital abrasion. Their marriage might be ordinary, passionless, rather routine, but Keith had lately felt that with the children nearly grown, some of its bloom might return. It had good soil to grow in; the warm privacy of their eighteen years' sharing of intimate life was intact.

Had been intact. Keith looked round wildly at the familiar high-ceilinged bathroom, the cork tiles, the missing bits of coving. He walked through onto the faded pink bedroom carpet beyond, looked at the rumpled bed and the pine chest of drawers bearing the silvered twig Lance had made at school for Jo to hang her gold chains on. Everything seemed odd, shabby, exposed, as furniture does when it stands in the street waiting for a removal van. This was their nest, their warm stuffy refuge; but some giant force had taken the roof off, and giant eyes were peering in. The press. Oh God.

There was one hope: that the blasted policeman had kept their names out of it. He must get the tabloids, instantly. Must know.

Keith stumbled down the wide oak staircase they had once loved for its dignity and now found dusty and noisy, and paused to smooth his sandy, greying hair in the equally depressing (now he looked at it with these startled new eyes) Victorian hall mirror. Damn being middle-class, he thought irrelevantly. Damn buying too-big vicarages from a dreary period and feeling honour bound to fill them with furniture from the same dire era. Why couldn't they have a cheap, cheerful bamboo mirror from a Third World catalogue, like they used to on Egg Terrace when he was an articled clerk and they drank terrible wine and sailed a leaky Mirror dinghy?

His hand was on the doorknob when the telephone rang. Four times, so the answering machine in the study must be off. He was a solicitor. He had to answer, it was bred in his bones.

'Gurney,' he snapped.

'Keith, it's Man-dee,' said the telephone, flirtatiously. 'Keith? It is you?'

'Yes, Mandy, I can't stop now—'

'Yes, I know!' Mandy could stretch the word 'know' to three syllables at least. 'I just wanted to say how awful about Joanna. Is she OK? I mean, it's such nonsense they print, Alex is ever so cross, says he'd sue. What are you doing?'

The question was rhetorical. Mandy twittered on, 'Honestly,

when I saw that bit about her being depressed and on tablets, I mean, you'd think they'd check. What Erika says is, they never think solicitors will sue because of the publicity. Like that man they thought buried his wife in the garden. Anyway, Erika's rung already, she's popping in to open the Bun just in case Jo doesn't feel up to it or . . .'

'Mandy, I'm sorry,' said Keith, seizing the opportunity provided by Mandy's brief, hopeful pause. 'That's good about Erika, because Jo isn't here, she's taking a couple of days' break to, er, sort out the boat. And I haven't seen any newspaper nonsense. I did hear something on *Today*, but I don't suppose it's anything to do with us—'

'Oh!' squeaked the telephone. 'Ooh, p'raps I'll get Alex to fax them from his study, 'cos you ought to see what they say in case reporters come and do a thingy, you know, *doorstep* on you. Like Mary Archer. You could answer the door in a dressing gown, dead cool. Do,' she added artfully, 'get Jo to call me!'

Keith could see her, the minx, putting the phone down, admiring her nails, pushing back her silvery-blonde hair in its stupid Alice band and doing a little shrug and pout of glee at having got to him first with the bad news. He had liked Mandy once. In early years, when he used to come home to find her and Joanna sprawled laughing at the kitchen table, Lance tricycling round it and the babies Susan and Anneliese propped in their plastic chairs, she was a welcome sight. She was good company for Jo, someone to be pregnant with. They had always made an odd couple: Joanna dark and practical and intellectual, Mandy an ebullient presence with her cloud of hair like, Jo said, an explosion in a marmalade factory; with her leopard-print leggings and repertoire of shriekingly blue jokes. But the friendship, ill assorted as it was, dragged Joanna out of the nervy depression which had followed Lance's birth. That alone was worth endless gratitude. In return, their home, he felt magnanimously, gave Mandy a more solid base. A house with a man in it. A refuge to supplement her precarious existence as a single mother in a council flat.

He had been pleased when, still pregnant, the two women borrowed £10,000 from him to start the Bun in the Oven. And comically astonished, according to his wife, when they paid it back in profits two years later.

He had dutifully tried to be pleased when Mandy abruptly married his widowed partner, Alex. He had tried not to think of Alex's first wife, a concert pianist who had died slowly and heroically of cancer only three months before. He tried to understand that Alex – big, lazy, conventional Alex – needed Mandy's vulgar vitality to warm himself at.

But a decade on from that marriage, he could no longer see Mandy as anything but a bad dream or hear her affected 'Bye-ee!' without a deep churn of rage. He absolved himself, with difficulty, of mere self-interest in the matter, but the fact was that his rage had lately deepened and become more personal. Mandy, Man-dee, pushy, artful bitch, had persuaded Alex to pull himself and his capital out of the comfortable smalltown legal practice which suited him. Actually, Keith admitted to himself, it suited him almost too well. Alex had been declining into pipe-and-slippers contentment so fast that it alarmed even Keith. The man had had leather patches on his elbows at twenty-seven. But Mandy had swung him too far the other way, dressed him in sharp suits, reformed his stringy taste in ties, cut his hair, and engineered him into friendships with property developers and contacts with hard, dodgy, backslapping builders who wanted a tame lawyer as a respectable front. Alex was leaving the practice for more and, in Keith's view, grubbier money. Mandy had made him into something more modern but nastier. When Alex left Heron and Gurney at Christmas, Keith would be alone except for Gus Terson, the former clerk who had only passed his last law exams, at the third try, in spring. Unless another partner could be found. The very thought was exhausting and depressing. Damn Mandy.

Moreover, thought Keith savagely, padding into the study to set the answering machine, the woman had gone strawberry-blonde and taken to Alice bands and a clipped, mewing delivery learned at the gate of Anneliese's new private school. She had inflated ideas of herself and, worst of all, she had used Alex's money to turn herself artfully into a sleeping partner in the Bun in the Oven. She had distanced herself from the work surfaces, the drains, the menu writing, the wiping down and cashing up and the compulsory smiling at arrogant tourists and dithering old ladies. Mandy had persuaded Jo that it was somehow fair that if she paid a girl to work her share of the hours and merely dropped by occasionally to discuss policy, she could still be an equal partner in the profits.

It was a diabolically cheeky move. Even though Jo had to find and train the part-time girls, Mandy had come to seem like everyone's employer; even Jo, in low moments, admitted that when she was sweaty and harassed and Mandy came in looking immaculate, she felt as if she and Zoë were both staff, respectfully making way for Lady Muck.

All this, thought Keith, and Mandy wouldn't give Alex a child. Or so he, Keith, suspected. Alex used to say, 'Just never happened for us, old boy,' in a manly, dismissive way; but Keith had his suspicions. Mandy had managed to get pregnant at nineteen fast enough, by some passing Swedish gorilla off a Whitbread race yacht. Hence that tarty little Anneliese, a bad influence on Susan – who ought to be home and changing for school, right now, and had no doubt missed the early train after a night of shrieking and bopping in London.

He felt curiously better for his flurry of dislike for Mandy. Had he paused to analyse the improvement in his mood, he might have found that it was a relief to despise someone more than, on this wifeless, shaming morning, he despised himself. He jabbed the button which set the answering machine and went out for the papers.

It was not, after all, such a big splash. No pictures, for one thing, and it had come in late. But as a grace note to the Bank Holiday, the Portsmouth stringer's story did well. He could see why the review of the papers on Radio 4 had picked it up. 'COME IN, MUM-BER 7, YOUR TIME IS UP,' said the *Sun*. The *Mail* wrote elegantly around the story, muting its amusement with the line about Joanna's 'depression'. Nothing about 'being on tablets', though; Mandy's imagination had provided those. The *Globe*, latest of the new challengers born of the technical revolution in newspapers, made most of it, printing his name and Joanna's and slanting the story well in to the sex war. 'The last bastion of male supremacy, an Englishman's boat, is no longer proof against mutinous wives . . . the solicitor left beached by his wife needed all his Dunkirk spirit . . .' Weak stuff, a fantasy spun round few facts and no quotes but, he had to admit, beguiling. Damn Jo. No, damn him, for being such a fool in the police station.

He read the papers in his study, before absently jabbing the replay button of the answerphone. It bleeped, hissed, and through a fuzz of VHF radio static, spoke in Joanna's voice. 'Keith. It's Jo.' He sat, frozen. The pause allowed him to hear the faint chattering breakthrough of other calls on the marine band VHF channels. Then Joanna spoke again from the grey plastic box.

'I want you to know that I heard the radio, and this is not funny. Sod you, Keith. I'll come back when I bloody well feel like it. I'm going for a sail. Tell Susan I'm fine. And good luck with her first day in the sixth.'

Keith played the message again, then sat silently as the tape ran into the next one, which began, 'Mr Gurney? My name's Kate Somerton, I'm a freelance journalist for the—'

He felt sick.

5

It was by sheer chance that Joanna discovered her new national fame. Waking stiff and tired at half past seven, she found her mind had formed a plan that was clear and plain and humble enough. She would call Keith on the VHF, making a link call through Niton Radio; then have a cup of tea, get the anchor up, and motor rapidly back to Portsmouth, home and duty.

Only, in the new wave of embarrassed gloom which now possessed her, she did not want any kind of conversation with Keith. He might sound avuncular, or headmasterly, or dry and legal, as he occasionally did these days. Better to be sure of the plan and its timing, briskly tell him, and ring off before he could gather his wits. But the timing of her return depended on whether there was enough diesel left in the tank; they had used the reserve five-gallon can on Saturday rather than face the Bank Holiday mêlée of boats round the fuel berth at Cowes. Last night, too wild and tearful to raise a sail, she had used a lot.

So, in yesterday's T-shirt and white cotton knickers, Joanna climbed on deck in the grey morning chill. Shivering a little at the damp northerly breeze, she pulled out the wooden dipstick notched in half-gallons, unscrewed the filler cap and slotted the stick into the tank.

It came out dry, except for its extreme tip. Less than half a gallon. An hour's running. Not enough for Portsmouth even without a headwind and foul tide. She might not ever have skippered the boat or been at sea alone, but fifteen years as a yachting wife made all these calculations automatic. She had known the wind was in the North the second she awoke and saw grey sea rather than green shore through the open hatchway. And now, the moment the dipstick emerged from the tank, she knew that motoring home was out of the question. With an exasperated 'Doh!' which sounded uncannily like one of the noises Keith made in such circumstances, she sat back on her cold haunches with one hand resting on the still-dewy canvas cover of the boom, considering.

She could sail back. A slant north-eastwards, a slow zigzag beat against the tide, maybe with the last bit of engine power, to get past Bembridge, then a tight fetch, just off the wind, to Portsmouth. It would be slow. She would have to tell Keith that. She wouldn't be home much before evening on the train. Unless he came to pick her up.

Suddenly, on the familiar boat, with Keith's old orange oilskins hanging in the wet-locker and his seaboots rammed under the step next to hers, Joanna wanted very much for him to pick her up and take her home. Which was perhaps why, returning dangerously damp-eyed to the little cabin, she switched on the radio before filling the kettle. A radio, as all the lonely know, is company. It had never, until this moment, been bad company.

'. . . how to handle a vandal. Finally, several papers carry the story of the wife who, as the *Mail* puts it, staged a one-woman mutiny in Portsmouth harbour . . .'

Stiffly, she listened to the end, to the last studio giggle, then made her cup of tea with a steady hand, as if the world had not just sharply tilted on its axis. The word 'alienated' floated into her mind, unbidden.

She was alienated now. An outsider. Her husband was not to be trusted. He had made the world laugh at her for a menopausal mutineer, laid her open to having coastguards calling her silly and impertinent whippersnappers speculating on her mental state in the *Daily* bloody *Mail*. Alienated. Beside the dismay, though, ran a light-headed sense of release. She owed nobody anything. The world had done badly by her. She was King Lear, noble in ruin, bayed by madmen, surrounded by ingratitude and betrayal.

These Shakespearian similes had always come easily to Joanna; she might not have a degree, but she had the cast of characters, all still there in her head, from Grendel's monstrous mother to J. Alfred Prufrock. All right then, Lear it would be. Off to the heath in rags and tatters, and to hell with the lot of them, most especially Keith.

As for Susan, she would be all right; she hardly spoke to her mother anyway these days without an exaggerated sigh of contempt. Somewhere in Joanna's mind this last year had tugged a set of memories: Susan small and loving, Susan eager at twelve, playing the clarinet in the school concert, dancing, hugging, laughing with her parents instead of sighing at them. But those dear vanished Susans seemed blurred and indistinct next to the awful clarity of the real, present, sixteen-year-old version. The only Susan she had now was the one who lay around on the bed with that slinky Anneliese, music blaring, cutting off in mid-giggle to stare up at an intruding mother with the cold, pretty impassivity of a pair of Siamese kittens. Susan had no need of her now. And Lance, clever kind Lance, who kept the family peace, was gone. He would be Inter-Railing round Europe thinking his great, straight-A thoughts for another two or three weeks at least. So she need not rush back. Keith could bloody well stew.

And Mandy – Joanna was surprised to find a harsh thought towards Mandy forming in her mind, because normally she banned such unsisterly thoughts, for ever defending her friend against Keith's visible dislike – well, Mandy could try running the Bun in the Oven herself for a change. To hell with them all. Howl, Howl, Howl, Howl, Howl, Howl, Howl, Howl! as Lear would put it.

The link call to Keith's answering machine took less than two minutes at that quiet morning hour.

When she rang off, Joanna went forward into the small heads compartment to clean her teeth, then frowned for a moment into the mirror. Normally she smiled into mirrors, but she rather liked the frown today. She tried a scowl. Not pretty, but striking. All those American feminists would be proud of her, running off on her own, scowling, like some woman in a bad-girl movie. Well, to hell with them too. There would be nobody but her on *Shearwater* today; no telephone, no customers, no welcome mat, no post, no newspapers. It would be, even if just for today, a boatful of Joanna Gurney, undiluted. Joanna Telford, even.

She finished her tea, pulled on the crumpled blue canvas trousers and smock, switched on the depth-sounder and electric log, and climbed out on deck. In a moment she had unlashed the tiller and freed the mainsheet rope, loosened the ties on the mainsail cover and sail, and pulled the blue canvas tube off the boom to stuff it tidily away. She ran forward to take the ties off the roller jib and, after fitting a brass handle to the winch on the mast, began to haul on the main halyard. The sail rose, fold by fold, its grubby white nylon gaining dignity as it took shape between mast and swinging boom. The boat rolled and tugged, feeling life coming back to it.

Finally she took two turns around the winch, tightened up the sail, pulled the kicking strap beneath the boom until it was taut, and went forward to fit the cold links of the anchor chain over the old-fashioned windlass and begin the long, to-and-fro pumping which would pull tight the chain which bound her to the sea bed. Then it would heave the anchor upright, trip its grip, and she would pull it on deck and be free.

The boat sheered around as she worked, its sail flapping. Her cold body warmed to the effort and blood began to flow more strongly in her. Years ago, when the boat was a new and shared adventure, she and Keith and the babies had always anchored, scorning marinas as no more than car parks on water. The tastes of growing children who needed to run along pontoons and fish for tiddlers and row rubber dinghies had changed their ways. Later, a kind of jaded lassitude and unthinking habit had made them haunt more and more marinas. It had been convenient but dull. She found herself enjoying the act of hauling in an anchor again.

When it appeared, dripping, at the stemhead she pulled it aboard and went quickly back to the helm, out of breath; kneed the tiller to her left and pulled in the sheet, bringing the sail under pressure from the wind. *Shearwater*, feeling the ancient stresses of sail, keel and rudder, swung obediently away from the shore and towards the gleaming green-and-grey of St Catherine's Point. West. She would go west.

Not crying this time, neither guilty nor shocked at herself, Joanna looked up at the sail, gave a strange little private smile, and bent down to release the rolled jib. The northerly wind, spun off the depression now tramping wetly over Brittany, caught the sail and heeled the boat onto a fast, graceful broad reach. Joanna reached below for a stale ginger biscuit from the night-watch bag and settled at the helm. 'Going for a little sail,' she murmured. 'Me and you. Bit of peace.'

6

'There's the Sussex child abuse thing,' said the Section 2 Features Editor, who was really the Women's editor, only smart tabloids no longer believed in such things.

'Sub judice,' said the star columnist of the *Globe*, a surly blonde in early middle age who wore rather too short a skirt and very much too tight a sweater. 'Besides, sod it.'

The Features Editor nodded, gloomily. Opinion pieces on child abuse were always a failure. Unless you were sure it was a fit-up by politically correct social workers, there was only one safe opinion to have: 'Shocking!' And this took up deplorably little space. So columnists always meandered off into half-baked, uninformed ideas about sentencing, therapy, pornography, and how it was all the fault of an insidious social rot dating from the 1960s. Or, alternatively, the legacy of the Thatcher government. The Features Editor turned a page of her notebook.

'OK, let's see: penis implants, Sharon Stone's bloke, the child prodigy – no, Dave's interviewing that. Bloody monster, its father wanted five K, I ask you.' She peered down the diary, pushing her enormous glasses up her nose. 'I know, what about the divorce figures? Up again.'

The star columnist winced. Her own second divorce, from the managing editor of the glossy magazine she also starred in, was reaching a noisy crescendo.

'I mean,' persisted the Features Editor, unwisely, 'you could do the personal pain, the guilt thing, the lonely moment when the decree absolute arrives in the post, the uncaring attitude of society and friends to what is basically a bereavement, OK?' She appealed to the rest of her staff, two thin pale young men and a bouncing blonde Sloane who was in charge of food and drink. 'Maeve did that terrific piece when the Princess of Wales—'

'That was about divorcing Ray,' cut in the star columnist (whose name was not really Maeve but who had decided in 1983 to become Irish as a career move). 'Divorcing Simon is not like a bereavement. More like having a haemorrhoid done. Anyway, if I write any buggery thing right now, his fat lawyer'll have me.'

'All the same,' said the Features editor, reasserting her authority with difficulty under the sooty terrorist glare of the ersatz Maeve. 'Marriage would be good this week. The Editor is very into marriage.' When the rude guffaws this remark engendered had died down, one of the pale young men stuttered into life.

'I mean – I thought – Jules and I thought – Maeve might be super on that Portsmouth woman, the one who ran off to sea in the husband's boat.'

'Yee-eess!' said the star columnist, the Voice of Wednesday. 'Dickie, that's *it*. Women's need for space.'

'Running away as therapy,' said the features editor.

'Why men deserve it!' said Dick. 'Bastards, we are. Jailers!'

'How every woman should do it!' said the food-and-drink writer.

'Except the Editor's nice new wife,' said Jules, and blew a lewd kiss at Dick.

Honour satisfied all round, the meeting proceeded. Maeve took the press cuttings from Dick and slipped off to her keyboard to begin pounding out her thousand pounds a week.

'Men on boats, as every sea wife knows, are tyrants. No, hold that. Men are tyrants anywhere, on land or sea. So it was refreshing . . .'

A mile away, in an older, more established newspaper office, the tail end of a similar meeting also focused on the Sailaway Wife story. Home news was scarce and political, foreign news depressing and monotone. The last two undeployed reporters, a chic bobbed blonde in leather trousers and a very young man with owl-like glasses, sat a little apart from their masters, wondering what their week held.

'She could be drowned,' said the news editor with relish. '*Tragic tiff that took a mother's life*. The agency's watching it, with the coastguard.'

'Nah,' said the Deputy Editor, who had a Moody on the Hamble. 'Calm as a millpond. She'll be OK. Turn up.'

'Then why hasn't she?'

'Engine failure, can't change a plug, drifts on the rocks?' said an Associate Editor.

'Sexist,' said another, of the opposite sex. 'There's a column in that.'

'Do we *want* a bloody think-piece?' said the news Editor. 'The *Globe*'ll have Maeve Mahoney on it, betcha. A woman's need to run away. Men are bastards. Every hubby is Cap'n Bligh at heart. No, tell you what,' he began suddenly to brighten, remembering that for once, thanks to an overenthusiastic training scheme, he actually had too many reporters – bloody spoilt graduate brats, they were – rather than too few. 'The *Globe*'ll run Maeve Mahoney's Wednesday woffle tomorrow. So we do nothing. Then on Thursday we do the interview. Scoop! Find the wife, exclusive pics on the boat, full story. Show up the *Globe* as the fluffy girly mag it is. We are a newspaper. We'll get the actual interview. Gordon, you go . . . No,' he cast around, 'Dinny, you go. Needs a girl.'

'*Where* do I go?' asked the sleekly groomed blonde reporter sulkily.

'Out,' said the News Editor. 'By the seaside. Go and see the coastguards. Show a bit of leg. Bung 'em a drink. Ring the boat parks.'

'*Marinas*,' hissed the Deputy editor.

'Find her, and get her story. If she turns out to be a silly cow, all the better, 'cos the *Globe*'ll be all over her with the feminist crap. If you don't get her by tomorrow, we'll run it on Friday. Go on, piss off. I pay you to be a reporter, so go and report something. Gordon,' his eye fell again on the youth, with disfavour – dear God, graduate trainees! 'You go to Bonhurst. Get the abandoned hubby and the rudderless teashop.' The News Editor smiled for the first time that day. He belonged to the old school, and hated to see reporters hanging around indoors rewriting news agency faxes. 'Go!'

Dinny, her pale bob flouncing, walked away down the long office, irritated. Gordon, younger and more excited, flipped through his Filofax to find Bonhurst on the railway map.

Out in the Channel, *Shearwater* left Shanklin and Ventnor behind and cleared St Catherine's Point to press past the island's less inhabited shore with the wind steady on the beam. Ahead, the clouds preceding the depression lay low and white, like a map or a mountain view of islands in a sky-blue sea. A sea-blue sky.

When she was a small girl, once, on holiday in an arid campsite in central France, Jo had seen cloud islands like these and imagined sailing a boat over the dull land horizon and up along the sky, round those white ragged headlands and into nebulous bays. These aerial Hebrides had stayed in her mind's eye ever since. When, on a school trip, she first saw the West of Scotland, she had recognized the dream landscape with a start and longed to sail the maze of blue between the cloudy islands. Later, on a summer trip to the Cyclades with Emily, they sweet-talked a fisherman into taking them for a day around the uninhabited islets. When Keith, hesitantly courting her in the solicitors' office at Southampton, diffidently told her that he sailed a dinghy and had dreams of a cruising boat, she had responded with such instant, eager joy that he had been charmed. Most girls talked of seasickness and men being tyrants on boats. Joanna, by contrast, immediately said, 'Could you sail to Scotland, or Ireland, really west, to all those islands, Aran and Inishvickillane? Or to Greece? You could, couldn't you, in a boat with a cabin?'

He had never thought of this; Channel crossings to Cherbourg or Dieppe were what the men at the Sailing Club talked of. But, in love, he said, 'Yes, one day. You could come too. We'll go on some courses together, get a bit of experience, then perhaps . . .'

Only once or twice since then had the dream seemed to near reality. For their honeymoon they had hired a little yacht and frightened themselves silly on a windy August tour of the inner Hebrides, nearly losing the boat (so they thought) in the whirlpools of the Dorus Mor while Joanna was doubled up with what turned out to be pregnancy sickness. Later, *Shearwater* had taken the family to Brittany. Between Houat and Hoedic islands, alone on deck with the children napping and Keith below decks, Joanna had entered the dream at last, alone, swinging between green blessed islands on a sea of ruffled, tender blue.

Then Lance woke, wanting to steer, and Susan needed changing, and Keith began fretting about whether they would get a berth at La Trinité. He put the engine on, sensibly, and it was over.

Now, hauling in the sails a little to fit the closer angle of the wind, Joanna saw headland after headland rolling before her towards the west. She had learned by heart once the lines from Frank Cowper's 1895 pilot book, and said them aloud now as the boat cut through the clean swell:

> Promontory on promontory, peak on peak, the varied coastline wanders away to the golden West. Headlands of many shapes, tossing their summits to the sea like wild waves driven before the roaring blast, grow fainter and fainter in the mellow light, sinking gradually to the lowland where Melcombe and Weymouth shimmer under the westering sun. But again, away in the South West, far out like a giant wedge, the long ridge of Portland rises like some half-submerged monster from the western sea . . .

The sun was not westering, but the clean northerly air gave her a view all the way to the ancient wedge, the crocodile head of Portland Bill forty miles away. Forty miles, say eight hours in this fast breeze. Under Portland, tucked up the armpit of the great granite limb, lay Weymouth. Yes, she thought. Weymouth. The easiest harbour on the coast to find, easy to enter in an offshore wind, full of holidaymakers to take a rope from a lone woman sailor and help her tie alongside. A creditable distance away for a first solo cruise. Easy to phone home from.

She would ring home, of course. She ought to speak to Susan about school. The sixth form suit they had bought together from the second-hand school shop – with much wrinkling of Susan's nose, and mutters of 'Gross!' – was at the dry-cleaners and needed collecting before the official Wednesday start of school at Angela Merici. Today Susan would be able to wear her own clothes for the sixth-form induction day. A very sensible idea, Joanna had thought. Really, Susan's implacable opposition to doing A levels at school would surely crumble in the face of Mrs MacEvoy's pep talk about the privileges and responsibilities of the sixth. Susan would settle. But it would be a bad start if she had forgotten about her uniform suit.

So she would ring Susan. And if she was, calmly and collectedly, speaking to her daughter, it would be easier for Keith to break in and take the chance to explain his appalling treachery, his telling—

She pushed that train of thought aside and consigned it to the wind. Weymouth would do nicely. Fair stood the wind for Weymouth.

She fiddled briefly with the elastic cords on the tiller which made the boat steer itself – more or less – on an easy course like this, and swung herself below to forage for a breakfast of cereal and UHT milk. There were three nectarines left in the cool box ready to go ashore last night. She pulled two into segments and put them in the cereal bowl, took it up on deck and sat eating and watching the coast slip by. The chuckling sound of the water and the thrum of taut rigging were company enough. Quite what the King Lear part of her would do next, or say to Keith, she did not want to know. For now, the boat was everything: refuge and occupation, escape and homecoming. She slipped the elastic cords off the tiller and took it in her free hand again, steering for the sheer pleasure of steering, balancing the cereal bowl on her knee.

Up among the deed boxes in his crowded, dark-beamed first-floor office, Keith was on the telephone to Mrs Repton. Mrs Repton was not a favourite client. She was old and she was imperious, and seemed to have some memories of the way her own elderly female relations of seventy years ago used to boss their 'man of business'. Either that, or she watched too many satellite television repeats of *Upstairs Downstairs*. Certainly it was clear that she had seen a documentary about medical research the night before. Keith nursed the receiver on his collarbone as he listened, flicking his desk drawers and making desultory notes.

'. . . but *if* I leave my body to science, Mr Gurney,' Mrs Repton was saying, 'do I have any *guarantee* over the kind of uses it will be put to? I should make it *quite clear*, don't you think, that there is no question of – ah – ovaries. Or eyes. Or hair. My late husband *worshipped* my hair and eyes – unforgettable, he used to say . . .'

Keith played with his pencil, picturing the scene at the medical school on the arrival of an 87-year-old cadaver with a list of prohibited areas pinned to its bosom. 'Perhaps if you could put a note in writing,' he attempted. But Mrs Repton's flow was unabated.

'. . . my nephew Dr Plomley,' crackled the receiver, stridently. 'If I could be certain he would supervise everything personally – only it might distress him, do you think?'

Keith did think. Dr Plomley would, he felt, be unlikely to make the round trip from Edinburgh Royal Infirmary just to stand guard over his aunt's withered ovaries and unforgettable hair. Especially as she was leaving the house and most of the money to the Sunny Paddocks Horse Rescue Trust.

A tart rejoinder to that effect hovered on his lips and, as usual, died. Mrs Repton was a client; more, she was a human being who had once been young and hopeful and now was old and irritating. She was as much a child of God as he was, or Susan, or Lance, or Jo. In his private musings he liked the expression 'child of God', which was curious, since he had grave doubts about God. Perhaps it was just that when you are an orphan of nearly forty, and a solicitor, and going grey, and losing your grip and your hopefulness, a paternal white-bearded God starts to have a secret attraction again.

Gus Terson, a younger member of the cosmic family and the Heron and Gurney practice, burst in without knocking, upturning a rubber plant left on the floor by the partnership secretary Aimée who was God knows where. Round at Alex's, probably, thought Keith, so he could 'work from home'. Ha bloody ha. Dance attendance on Mandy's latest interior decorator, no doubt. The pot rolled in a parabolic curve across the carpet, scattering topsoil. Gus failed to notice it. He was one of those pink, bouncing, chubby young men whose very hair seems to spring with misdirected energy.

'Keith, can I have a word? Only it's the conveyance on the brewery cottages—'

The phone chattered on. '. . . Another thing, of course, is that I *don't believe* in all this money being spent on homosexual diseases . . .'

'– Mowbray says, is the search invalid if the local government reform thing happens? God, sorry, did I kick that over?'

'. . . spread by *unnatural* practices, so that would have to go in. No AIDS research to be done on my remains, do you understand? It has to be in *the will*. Mr Gurney? Mr Gurney?'

Gus had seen the plant and was scooping up potting compost with his fingers, making the mess worse than ever and still talking. 'This is definitely my first chance to say I made the earth move for Aimée, hyuk! Oh, you're on the phone. Shall I . . .'

Keith drew himself together. 'Mrs Repton, I have your instructions,' he said loudly. 'The line is very bad, so I must hang up now and speak most severely to the telephone service.' Cutting off Gus's guffaw with a glare, he continued in the magisterial style he knew Mrs Repton preferred in her man of law. 'Our young Mr Terson,' another glare, 'will send you a note of the proposed codicil. Good day.' He put the telephone on its rest and, as an afterthought, took it off again and laid it purring on the desk. He fiddled his filing drawer open and shut, open and shut. 'Gus, will you kindly not barge in, chattering. Alex is doing the Brewery cottages. Bloody well ring him.'

'I did,' chirped Gus, unabashed. 'He said he was tied up, but that it was a point you could surely clear up. Oh, hey, I forgot. He also said – he said Mandy said – that if Jo wanted her to pop round this morning—'

Keith slammed the desk drawer shut with unnecessary violence, made a noise approximating to 'Kchut!' and stood up. 'I have a call to make on . . . on old Mr Palmer. Back at twelve or so.'

'But the thing is,' protested Gus, who never liked being alone in the office (in case, as he often explained, some woman might turn up blubbing about a divorce) 'Mr Palmer is actually, you know, we heard last week, he's dead.' But Keith was gone. Gus was talking to an empty room and his principal was walking down Bonhurst High Street, rapidly, to nowhere in particular.

Had he looked up as he passed the welcoming glass-and-gingham frontage of the Bun in the Oven, he might have seen Erika, a becoming flush brightening her sallow complexion, serving coffee and a Tropical Danish (the kind with the bits of pineapple in it) to ever such a nice young man who said his name was Gordon.

7

The last of the ebbing tide carried *Shearwater* round St Catherine's Point, but by noon it had slowed and turned eastward, against her. The boat's speed past the distant coast of the mainland hardly slackened; after the gentle morning, the wind was fresher every minute, pushing her forward in powerful, rhythmic lunges across the lumpy sea. The tiller, with its flaking dark-gold varnish, felt alive. It thrummed and throbbed, dragging against Joanna's hand as the dial of the electric log rose to six, seven knots. Once or twice, the plastic dial surged to eight in the stronger gusts, and the boat's bows tried to round up towards the coast to the north. The westerly course grew harder to hold.

The sails were set too closely. Sliding down from her perch on the wooden coaming of the cockpit, stiff from three hours' entranced and exhilarated sailing, Joanna loosened first the heavy mainsheet then the jib. The sails lurched gratefully out on the port side of the boat, ballooning and pulling hard. Joanna could point the bow back towards Portland now, but the purposeful plunging turned into a wild downwind roll. Below, in the cabin, plates and cutlery clattered against their locker doors. The boathook, not properly secured, rolled irritatingly to and fro. The two dangling plastic fenders she had not noticed in her precipitate departure brought themselves sharply to her attention by banging on the side and bouncing almost onto the deck. She reached forward and untied one with her free hand, throwing it into the cabin. The other, nearer to the bow, bounced and mocked.

Each roll shook the wind out of the jib. When it filled again it was with intermittent, jarring jerks and sharp cracks of nylon sailcloth. Joanna winced, freed it off further to flog uselessly and, using the thin line leading to the roller on the bow, reduced the big foresail's size by a third and tamed it again. Her hand hurt from the burn of the control line but the boat felt better. The wind was well in the east now and far stronger than it had been when it was in the North. So it had – veered? Backed? She made a clock face with her finger, frowning, trying to remember evening classes in her old enthusiastic days. It had veered. 'Veering and increasing, backing and decreasing.' That was the rule. Something to do with the approach and departure of a depression.

This one was clearly approaching, and rather rapidly at that. The day was still sunny and clear but the seas were shorter and sharper as the tide-piled water up in one direction, only to have it punched back by the wind. Wind over tide, the sailor's curse. Joanna leaned forward to adjust the mainsail, steering with the other arm twisted awkwardly behind her.

The boat's movement suddenly changed, warning her. Instinctively, Joanna leaned the tiller hard over towards the sail as the boom lifted dangerously, threatening to gybe violently onto the other side of the boat. 'Shit!' She hated sailing dead before the wind with this constant risk of gybing; once, on the Hebridean honeymoon trip, the boom of their modest little charter boat had slammed across with such violence that it detached itself from the mast. On *Shearwater*, it could easily break a wire stay and at worst bring the mast down.

'Shit!' She had come too far over; as she struggled to haul the helm back, a tall wave toppled the boat forward, snatching the rudder out of the water. A gust caught the mainsail and the boat's head pressed irresistibly round northwards in a terrifying, rolling broach. The rudder flailed for a moment helplessly in empty air and *Shearwater* leaned to port, gunwales under, water cascading into the cockpit and over Joanna's bare feet. Upright again, flapping, the boat hung as if suspended in time and space, waiting for orders.

'*Shit!*' With an effort, she pulled the boat's head round to point at Lulworth, further east than the distant root of Portland Bill but a safe course for the moment. The flogging sails quietened. Not easterly, that gust, more like south-east. Another veer. Things had changed quickly; but then, she had missed two shipping forecasts, midnight and dawn. Again, she made circles with her finger, plotting the way the winds blow anticlockwise round a depression. So it was – where? Moving across France?

With a sharp jab of self-knowledge, Joanna accepted that this academic theorizing was only a mechanism to stop her from telling herself the truth. This boat needed major attention, now. The mainsail, straining and dragging like a wild thing, threatening another broach every minute, would have to be reefed. Once wound down and reduced, the sail would be tamed, and no longer keep taking control. 'The time to reef,' Keith always quoted, 'is when you first think of it.' Joanna knew that Keith would have thought about it an hour ago. Now it would be harder than it would have been then; but it had to be done.

She would have to get some boots on, climb on the cabin top and reef. There was nobody else, and no choice. If she flew a whole mainsail much longer and the wind increased, the boat would become uncontrollable and something would get broken. 'Bugger!' she shouted, to give herself vigour. 'Bugger, bugger, bloody buggery wind!'

In Bonhurst, it blew Keith's jacket coldly open and lifted his thinning hair as he walked back from the Market Square towards the office. It was not an everyday summer wind. It felt nasty, a sharp little gale to mark the end of the warm days. It worried him, and wrapped him in his thoughts so that he did not see a dark young man with crumbs of Tropical Danish pastry on his jacket dart out from the ironmonger's doorway to accost him. 'Mr Gurney? If I could have a moment? Gordon Hawkings, I'm reporting the story of Mrs Gurney—'

'What?' Keith was on him, grabbing his arm. 'Has she been found? Is she OK?'

Gordon was wrongfooted. He took a moment to adjust from his vision of himself as one who sought news to Keith's conviction that he might be bringing it. 'Errm, not exactly. I was hoping we could have a quote, your point of view . . .'

Keith stared disbelievingly at Gordon. 'You're a reporter? Look, this is past a joke. My wife has gone for a sail, on her own boat, and you people fabricate some cock-and-bull—'

'With respect, Mr Gurney,' Gordon had got his composure back, 'you just asked me if she had been found and was OK. Presumably this means she is missing as far as you're concerned?'

'Certainly not. You jumped me, I had things on my mind. I'm a busy man. Good morning.' He turned away, up the step towards the Heron and Gurney brass plate and the sanctuary of his office.

Gordon felt his pocket for the reassuring whirr of the little tape and persisted, 'So you *are* able to contact Mrs Gurney? That's good, perhaps we could have a phone number, because my newspaper would like to offer—'

Keith swung round furiously. 'Look, do you know the first thing about boats? You can't bloody phone them! The whole point of going to sea is that pests like you can't ring up with a load of drivel. You don't break off in the middle of changing a sail or – or –' he looked at the racing clouds,' or shortening canvas in a gale just to answer the bloody phone!' He stepped into the front door of the office and slammed it shut.

Gordon, following the solicitor's glance, noticed the clouds and the wind whose significance he had up to that moment missed, and a beatific smile spread across his broad, handsome young face. For the first time it occurred to him that the annoying currents of air which were disarranging his hair, and the draughts he had suffered at the window table in the Bun in the Oven while pumping that blonde moron, were made of wind. Strong wind. That meant gales at sea. A tempest! Keith had escaped him, and appeared to have locked the door, but with only one more call he would have his story. All of it, all for him, unless that yellow-haired bitch had found the Gurney woman tucked up safe in some boat park and done a soupy girly interview. His brow furrowed, then cleared. Even if she was safe, not out in the gale thing, he had the worried husband, exclusive; plus the worried waitress and a couple of customers who said that Mrs Gurney was ever such a nice quiet lady. Now, with a bit of luck, he would get the best friend.

His back to the wind, Gordon flipped open his mobile phone – three weeks old, but it still felt pretty good, even if he had had to buy it himself – and punched in a number he had written on his wrist, courtesy of Erika.

'Mrs Heron? Amanda Heron? My name is Gordon Hawkings. I'm a journalist, passing through, and I'm terribly impressed by the Bun in the Oven, it's a really original, contemporary development of the traditional teashop idea. Is it right that you're the owner-manager?'

Possibly, he thought, he was laying it on a bit thick. But it seemed not. A series of ladylike squeals greeted his overture and acknowledged further compliments; finally the voice instructed him to come to an address in Market Street for a further audience and a bite of lunch. Gordon flipped open a small book he carried, dialled a number listed under 'PHOTO, agencies', and spoke briefly. Closing the telephone with a snap – it was, it really was, exactly like the *Star Trek* communicators of his boyhood TV idols – he headed up the road, more than pleased with his day so far.

Dinny Douglas, on the other hand, was having an appalling day. She had been frozen out by the police and grunted at by a noncommittal Ray Brewer who classified her instantly as a right little madam and would part with no information other than that the missing boat was blue. She had been laughed at gently by the coastguard service when she asked if any of their 'lookouts' had spotted the boat. There had been, they said, no lookouts in coastal huts since 1982. Had she been reading the *Famous Five* perhaps? She had met with outright derision from the eight marinas she had telephoned. It appeared that blue boats with sails were not scarce. Now, with her batteries running low, she had resorted to a malodorous telephone kiosk in Portsmouth in order to make a further appeal to the coastguard.

'Hi, Virginia Douglas here. I, er, rang earlier, about *Shearwater*.' She did not have much hope, but stiffened when she heard a small hesitation come into the voice which answered the enquiry. She had worked on that voice earlier with all the flattering, responsible sounding, woman-to-woman persuasiveness of her trade. It paid off.

'Oh – hold on – I spoke to you earlier, didn't I? We had a call ten minutes back. One moment.'

Holding her breath, Dinny traced circles with her neatly shod foot on the floor of the kiosk, holding the door open to dissipate the stifling smell of pee. The voice came back.

'Well, I maybe shouldn't tell you this, and it wasn't a distress call, I should emphasise that, but the old keeper went across to the Needles lighthouse this morning – it's automatic now, unmanned. But they had to take some photo or other for a magazine, and they went out with the magazine people in a fast motorboat. Anyway, they went out of the Needles Channel to do some pictures of the island from three or four miles south. And there *was* a blue yacht, out to the west. The old keeper rang in a few minutes ago, just to let us know, because they watched it for a bit and he wasn't sure it was all right. The sails were flogging, and there was quite a sea running, so they thought it might have problems. But the keeper says it could just have been having trouble reefing.'

The reporter wrote rapidly. 'Which way was it heading?'

'Well, they don't, do they? Boats, I mean. Not while they're doing things to the sails. They just sort of flap around. But they reckoned that when it settled down it was pointing towards Portland. West. Could be Poole, or Weymouth. Like I say, it's only a note we made. I'm not telling you this officially.'

Dinny stepped outside the box and considered, breathing deeply the clean air. Then she stepped back in to its smelly interior and rang a merchant bank in Leadenhall Street where a former boy friend worked.

'Jules? Dinny. Look, not much time,' she cut short his squawks of welcome. Annoying man he was, porky and self-important. 'Jules, sweetie, you go sailing, right? Tell me one thing. If you weren't very experienced and you were all by yourself and there was a lot of wind, would you go to Poole or Weymouth?'

Jules wanted to know where the wind was coming from. 'Oh, anywhere. You know, a gale sort of thing. But you're sailing west. Which would be the nicer harbour? For a woman, say, by herself.' She listened to the answer, wondered what a 'dodgy bar' might be in sailor speak and why a 'cross-tide' was a worry, but made her note accordingly. Then she adeptly brushed off his attempt to make a date and got back into her little car to find Weymouth on the map.

8

A hard wind behind you, pushing you along, disguises half its force. In a sailing boat, which seems to be borne up as well as along by the lift of the wind in the sails, it is easy to believe for a while in any rising wind that the force comes from the boat herself. She feels strong and proud and fast and commanding, as if she were flying like a bird and not, as is the truth, being blown along like a sheet of newspaper down a pavement.

The boat, of course, has more cunning than the newspaper. With the bite of her heavy keel and rudder and the aerodynamic trim of her sails, she exerts control. Her helmsman chooses her direction, down the wind or across it at a range of angles. But still, the boat or sailing ship is being blown. The wind is the prime mover. And the moment when the sailor best realizes this is when, to reef, he has to turn the boat's head into the wind and face its violence head on.

Joanna swung *Shearwater* round, hauling the mainsail in tight, lashing the tiller down and pulling the jib over to the other side so that the boat would heave to and cease its plunging forward motion. The full force of the east wind struck her like a blow. Her hair streamed back, her eyes closed involuntarily against it, and she gasped as her throat filled with blown spume. Opening her eyes again she saw several things that she knew she should have seen earlier: the whitecaps on the waves and the high, confused sea. Ten minutes ago she had been blithely riding it, not allowing herself to worry.

With sails secured, the boat lay relatively quiet, hove-to, prevented from sailing forward. It pitched up and down with a bearable seesaw motion and heeled away from the wind.

Bracing herself against the motion, Joanna pulled the hatch open and climbed into the cabin. She found boots, a harness, the winch handle for the lines which pulled the sail down onto the boom, and an oilskin jacket. Keith's. Her own hung next to it, but after a moment's hesitation she took his. Sticking the handle in her pocket, she clambered back out. She rolled up the jib until there was only a small triangle of steadying sail to hold the boat's head as near the wind as possible, then freed the wet clammy rope of the mainsheet from its jammer and gave it a few feet of slack to let the wind out of the big sail. This was always the worst moment, reefing; when everything first began to flog and shake and rattle uncontrolledly. Usually either she or Keith would hold the boat steady on the helm, sailing with the jib tight and the mainsail loose while the other clambered and hauled and fastened the big sail into its new, small shape. Their teamwork was automatic and unquestioning now; sometimes in the early years they had shouted at one another angrily, out of fright, but now such manoeuvres as this happened smoothly and without recrimination. Like an old-established double act of circus acrobats, they hardly noticed how good they were at co-operating and anticipating one another's moves on the deck.

Neither of them had ever had to reef *Shearwater* alone. The method Joanna was trying now was her best guess at the way to do it. She clipped the harness to the wire along the deck and began to creep forward, avoiding the murderous flogging of the boom. The noise, of rattling blocks and howling wind and whistling rigging, failed to drown her soft, deliberate, swearing.

Fifty miles NNE of Joanna, Keith was answering the telephone.

'Mr Gurney? Jane MacEvoy here, at St Angela's, sixth form centre. Susan has not arrived today, and has left no message. I hope there hasn't been any confusion. We do expect sixth-formers to register on induction day, you know.'

'I'm sorry,' said Keith who was at home, in the kitchen, padding around in yellow socks making himself a sandwich. The pub, with pink bouncing Gus, had proved an unbearable thought, and besides, Joanna might ring. He went back to the Old Vicarage because he had hopes of the answering machine, and wilder ones of Joanna being there in person, smiling sheepishly, arms outstretched to him.

Neither had materialized. Now he shifted, irritably, at the piercing authority of Mrs MacEvoy's tone. 'I thought Susan had gone in. She might be a bit late. She went to a rock concert in London last night, end of the holidays, celebration, sort of thing . . .'

'If she's missing, Mr Gurney, we ought to think of taking action.'

'No,' said Keith hastily, wincing at the associations this suggestion called up. 'She definitely came home.' He looked around at an African craftwork striped bag, a traffic cone with half a dozen signed messages on it in felt pen, a puffy pink jacket, and a pair of what appeared to be workmen's boots. These items were variously disposed around the kitchen floor; in the sink were two crescents of gnawed pizza crust, an apple core and a Diet Coke can. You always knew when Susan was home. 'I think she might be – I'll phone you back in a moment, if I may.' He put down the telephone and the piece of cheese he was clutching and crossed to the doorway, treading, as he did so, on a half-dead wasp. A stab of pain took his breath and it was hoarsely that he shouted 'Susan!' up the stairs. Through the hall window he could see branches moving, thrashing and bending in the wind. 'Su-san!'

Nobody answered. Keith climbed up the stairs, crossed the landing, and flung open the door of his daughter's room. Usually he knocked, according to the best modern principles of giving young adults respect, privacy and personal space. Now, on his painful foot, he limped right in. 'Susan, what the hell—'

Two heads rose from the tangle of bedclothes on his child's vast double bed. One bore the familiar striped, shaggy crop, blonde streaks on Joanna's black. The other, he noted with disfavour, was Anneliese's, with the all too familiar pixie features and sleek white-gold Nordic waterfall of hair. Susan yawned.

'S'all right, Dad, we've not gone lesbian. Stayed over with Annie's cousin near Waterloo. Jus' got in at nine, had a sleep. Where's Mum?'

'You are supposed to be at school. Mrs MacEvoy has been on the phone. This is the induction day for your sixth-form courses, and you are supposed to take it seriously. Anneliese, I'm surprised you haven't got anything better to do.'

'Annie isn't going back to Angela Merici. At all. She's going to the FE college. It doesn't start till Monday. If you'd let me go there, I'd be fine. School is lucky to have me.'

'Mrs MacEvoy—'

'Mrs Mac can wait. I'll be in tomorrow, won't I?'

The staccato truculence of his daughter was something, Keith felt, that he would never get used to. Lance had been argumentative and self-willed but had never thrown off such sharp, hot sparks of pure aggression. He was like his father and preferred not to fight. Susan seemed to thrive on it.

'Anyway, I asked you. Where's Mum? I need my sixth-form suit if I'm going to school.' She yawned again.

Keith had slept badly, made a fool of himself with the reporter, been needled by Mandy Heron, and trodden on a wasp. It was too much to expect him to notice that within his daughter's surly question could be heard, just, a perilous little wobble. *Where's Mum?* Or to reflect that she too might have hoped, on creeping into the silent house this morning, to find Joanna back. He erupted in fury.

'Mum has taken the boat to sea. The weather is not good; I have got a forecast and it is not one I would want to be out in. She may be in considerable danger. And you lie around in bed, dodging your responsibilities. Get up, get to school, and apologize to Mrs MacEvoy. Anneliese, you'd better go home. Your mother will be wondering where you are.'

He left the room where the two girls looked at one another, silent for a moment. Then, 'C'n I borrow your blue leggings, Suze?' asked Anneliese.

'Sure,' said her friend, and huddled back under the duvet. 'I'm not getting up yet.'

As Anneliese dressed, Susan curled gradually smaller under the covers and her thumb stole to her mouth. Anneliese paused by the door. 'D'you want to come round later? Have supper with us? Mum'll be cooking the fattened calf.'

'*Fatted*,' said a voice from under the duvet, whence only a tuft of blonde-and-black striped hair now showed. 'Yup, thanks. I don't want to be here.'

'We could work out,' said Anneliese, 'how you're going to tell your mum and dad about the big plan.'

'Yeah,' said Susan. 'Thanks, Annie. I'll be round.'

Anneliese slipped out, down the stairs, past the kitchen. Her father's partner, once 'Uncle Keef' to her when he did the playschool run, was eating a piece of cheese and staring out of the window. The first splatters of rain on the glass distorted the trees which swayed and thrashed in the chilly garden. She had been fond of Uncle Keef, even though he now seemed a creature from another era, probably Jurassic. Even worse than her stepfather, who at least wore jeans. She hesitated.

'Shall I ask Pops – Alex – to come round?' she said with rare diffidence.

'You could ask him,' said Keith without turning round, 'to go in to the office. I shan't be in this afternoon.'

'Okeydoke,' said Anneliese.

Standing by the mast, Joanna clung on with one hand against the bucking, rolling, senseless motion of the boat. She bent, undid the topping lift which would support the boom during the operation, and tightened it. Then she undid the main halyard and began to drag the sail downwards. The task was harder than she had ever known it. Gusts filled the sail and slapped it around, folds of harsh sailcloth skinned her knuckles and tore at her nails, and the boom, swinging out of control, crashed into her knees. Once, clawing for the sail with both hands, she slipped and struck her cheek hard against the cold metal curve of a winch. On her knees, she sobbed with the sudden pain and with fear. She could hit her head and die out here, alone on this bucking boat on the grey water, and nobody would know. But all the time she sobbed, she went on clawing and dragging until a good bight of sail was down and she could find the second big eyelet on the forward edge of the sail and manoeuvre it onto its hook to form a new, low tack at the corner of the sail.

Two hands again, one to hold out the hook, the other for the frantically kicking sail. Who said 'One hand for yourself and one for the ship'? What sort of ship had that many one-handed jobs? She balanced, one foot out behind, her knee bent, like a fencer.

At last the tack was down, the halyard tightened again. Stage one complete. Now all she had to do was select the return end of the deep-reefing line from the two which ran along the boom and out through blocks on its end, and use the small winch whose handle she had in her pocket to haul it in, bringing a bundle of redundant sail neatly onto the boom. Then make fast, tidy down the sail with its small cord reef-points, and get sailing again.

Fishing for the small brass reefing handle in her – Keith's – oilskin coat pocket, she inserted it into its hole and pulled at the reefing line. Her hand, she noticed detachedly, was shaking. The last time she had seen it shaking like that, like some object on a spring that did not properly belong to her, had been in the morgue, when Emily—

The boat, caught by a violent gust, staggered suddenly. A wave slapped hard against its leaning side, sending a thin, drenching salty shower ten feet above the deck. Behind her, a violent thump; as Joanna turned, startled, to see the forgotten white rubber fender dancing on the side deck, her foot slipped on the wet cabin top and she clutched the ropes along the boom for support. They gave, and she slithered down painfully onto the side deck, still clutching a festoon of rope. The small winch handle spun off, bounced on the side deck and somersaulted into the sea. Glancing towards the stern, Joanna saw the bitter ends of the reefing lines in the act of pulling through the blocks on the end of the boom, to flap uselessly over the stern.

Keith finished his piece of cheese, rang Mrs MacEvoy, and went slowly upstairs to Susan's room.

'Suze? You all right?' He no longer felt equal to the role of stern father.

'Yep,' said the duvet.

'Mum'll be all right, you know. Probably back for supper.'

'Yep.'

'I rang the MacEvoy, told her you'd had train problems and you'd be in tomorrow.'

'Yeah, OK. Thanks.'

He patted the foot of the bed in a small futile gesture its

occupant could not have felt, and went downstairs to where the silent telephone was.

Joanna, her dark hair flying in sticky salt strands around her eyes, was back in the cockpit. The loose reefing lines – or one of them – had to be threaded back through the block on the end of the boom, else the sail would not set. There was the alternative of taking it down completely and carrying on under jib, but without the full control which two sails gave, *Shearwater* would not go to windward. Suppose the wind veered further and drove her towards the shallows of Christchurch or Poole Bay? She had to be able to sail the boat efficiently. Besides, if she was in charge, alone, she wanted to be properly in charge. The bloody boat could learn who was boss. A new spirit crept into her. This was a fight, and fights could be won.

Sniffing, shivering slightly, she pegged the boom in tight, fixed the webbing line of her safety harness to the eye in the cockpit, picked up the dangling ropes and stood cautiously upright on the stern. The rolling was worse here, her hand shakier. After five minutes fiddling and threading, she crouched back, deathly sick, on the cockpit floor. The job was done. She dragged herself back, under the shaking boom, to kneel by the mast and haul the line tight. Without the winch-handle it took every ounce of her strength and made her palms raw.

When it was over, she came back to the cockpit, sat down, eased a little more jib out on its roller, and unlashed the tiller. The boat's head, pointing out to sea, was hauled round towards the dark snout of Portland again, the mainsheet eased, order restored, quietness and purpose recovered. Once again, although with half the frenzied energy of the morning, *Shearwater* tramped obediently westward.

9

Mandy Heron, Gordon decided, was pretty amazing for a teashop lady. Her ash-blonde bob and flat black pumps, the perfectly fitting white drill Bermudas, the pearl choker on her white neck, and the crisply upstanding shirt collar peeking from the expensive cotton sweater knitted with rosebuds – all these were the uniform of the provincial, upper-middle-class young matron. The look was familiar enough to him from his time on a local paper; plenty of women dressed like this had told him, in high, commanding, good-natured voices which always reminded him of Donald Duck, what to write about their charity do, or public school dance, or dinky interior design business called something like 'Suki's Stencils'.

But they were never sexy. They had an aseptic look, as if they washed too often, briskly, with a loofah. A chap never fantasised about leaving his fingerprints across their clean little tailored rumps or sliding a hand under their teddybear-patterned sweaters. They were bright and cheerful and self-assured and sexless. Whereas this one was seriously disturbing. He would be hard put to it to fault her Princess Di disguise, but disguise it clearly was. This woman was not, definitely not, what she dressed as. If the others were school prefects this was the school Bad Girl: grubby, wicked, and desirable. Not that she was grubby but . . . the way her breasts pushed out that sweater, the tilt of her hips as she led him into the house, the extra notch she had tightened her Gucci belt, the rounded babyish curve of her cheek and the Marilyn Monroe pout caused Gordon, who was still very young, to have some trouble with his breathing. He was glad that it was the draggled Erika, not Mandy Heron, who had served him his Tropical Danish earlier in the morning. He could not have choked it down otherwise.

As for Mandy Heron owning a teashop, that was another facer. He had visualized some cosy stout scone of a woman, bun-faced and greying at the temples. And Erika had told him she was married to a solicitor. That was equally improbable. This bimbo was never married to a lawyer unless – his thoughts were growing wilder – solicitors round here went in for black leather jeans and biker chains. She'd never let you out of bed, this one—

His thoughts were mercifully cut off by their arrival in a long, pale-gold, immaculately tidy living room. Anneliese was not allowed to spread teenage mess all over the house as Susan Gurney did. Her mother's domestic roots lay not in book-strewn intellectual Bohemia but in the cramped, fiercely guarded gentility of council estates. Nor did Mandy have the slightest wet-liberal compunction about slapping, threatening or shouting at children. Her house, therefore, was always tidy. There were two pale leather sofas in the room; on one, a handsome and prematurely grey-haired man of around forty was lying and dictating to a mousy secretary.

'. . . let me say again what a pleasure it has been comma over the years comma—'

'Alex,' said Mandy, 'leave that now. We've got a visitor. He's from the *Chronicle*, to write about the Bun in the Oven, isn't that fun?'

The silver-haired man sat up, feeling for his shoes with stockinged feet. His face, Gordon saw, was still young, creased with the lines of easy laughter, blue-eyed, relaxed and lazy. The flickering worry in those eyes now did not suit him. He did not have the look of a man who ever worried.

'Mandy, you are –' he said. 'Can I have a word? In private. Aimée, thanks, petal. You can get into the office now, Keith might need you.'

The secretary gathered up her things and left, with a curious glance at Gordon. The couple went through the end door, leaving the reporter to a lightning appraisal of the room. Money in evidence, fresh paint, over-ruched curtains – ritzy tastes but not a bottomless pit of money. Those leather sofas were not all they pretended to be. He moved cautiously towards the door they had gone through and was rewarded by a snatch of argument.

'. . . *obviously* about Joanna. Mandy, show him the door, it's not fair on Keith—'

'Alex, I shan't give anything away, and it's super publicity for the Bun, Jo will be thrilled, she's bound to be, it's good for business—'

Gordon leapt back hastily from the door as Mandy's voice grew nearer.

'– so anyway, Alex, I've said he can stay for lunch. OK?' Without waiting for an answer, Mandy reappeared alone, favouring Gordon with a naughty smile. 'Now. Drinkies? Kitchen's cosier.'

Alex met Anneliese in the hall as he was looking for his jacket. 'Annie, hello. Good concert?'

'Hi, Popsy,' said his stepdaughter, dumping a backpack. 'Yeah, triffic. We crashed out at Suzy's all morning. Her mum's vanished in the boat apparently.'

Alex, one arm trapped in the torn lining of his tweed jacket, stopped and looked at her.

'Annie, how much do you know? For sure? Joanna might just have gone sailing with someone down at that yacht club they go to. You can't believe the papers.'

'Well,' said Anneliese judicially, 'Uncle Keef came in, really wound up, and yelled at Sooze for not being in school, which she doesn't want to do anyway, she wants to come and do design with me at the college. Not my course, not fashion design, but magazine design. So anyway—'

She drew a breath and Alex, accustomed to having to prompt his womenfolk back to the point, patiently asked, 'What did Keith say?'

'He said,' Anneliese screwed up her pretty face, remembering, 'he said Joanna was in bad weather and considerable danger. So. That's what he said. And he said could you come into the office, because he wasn't going back.'

'Annie', said Alex seriously, 'I don't know what's going on, but your mother has got a bloody reporter for lunch, who pretends to be interested in the damn teashop. Will you do one thing? Just don't tell him what you just told me. Nothing about danger or Keith being worried. Please? Either Joanna really is in trouble and the press will make it worse for everyone, or she isn't and she'll be bloody livid. So *stumm*, OK? And if you could head your mother off saying anything, that would be—'

'Oh-oh-oh-oh no!' said Anneliese, shaking her blonde curtains of hair violently. '*Moi*? Come between Mum and newspaper stardom? With photo, *Hello Magazine* style, in Gracious Drawing Room? I would rather wrestle steaks off a man-eating tiger.'

'What photo? What d'you mean?'

'There's a smudger hanging around in a car out there, all the kit, big leather cases hanging off him, face like a baboon.'

Alex put on his jacket, tucked the ripped flap of lining up his left sleeve – Mandy was not a seamstress – grunted, and left the house. As he passed the open kitchen window he heard his wife's clear voice saying, '. . . absolutely my best friend. We started the business together when we were expecting. . .'

Joanna's teeth were chattering, but from cold rather than fright. *Shearwater* had settled now on her westerly course, and each rising sea behind her only lifted the stern, slid diagonally under it with a foaming hiss, and dropped her back harmlessly into the trough. The sailing was fast, but dry and controlled. The elastic cords on the tiller could hold the boat's head steady, for the moment. Thank God for a long old-fashioned keel and a balanced rig. Joanna watched the boat hold the course for five minutes before she decided it was safe to go below for a moment.

In the cabin, the motion seemed worse. She braced herself with her feet and rapidly pulled out from a locker a T-shirt, thick sweater, knitted hat, and dry towelling scarf. She stripped off to the waist, discarding a damp, salty bra without bothering to find another, and pulled on the dry clothes. Dry trousers could wait. She glanced up at the telltale compass set into the cabin roof: the course was still fine. She had looked after the boat; now she must look after herself.

She filled the kettle, lit the gas on the wildly swinging stove and clamped the kettle over it; put powdered soup into a mug and wedged that in the sink. No bread on board – they had thrown their last slice to the seagulls on the balmy sail home yesterday, which now seemed a month ago. There was a whole malt loaf, so she stuffed that in her oilskin pocket, together with the last nectarine.

A glance at the compass: still fine. The kettle whistled, and Jo poured the water onto the powder and noodles in the mug. A sickly, monosodium glutamate smell filled the cabin and seemed suddenly to be exactly what she had always dreamed of eating. With care she reached up to put the scalding liquid on the cockpit floor, praying no freak wave would make it slide and spill before she could climb out. Lastly, she took the portable long-wave radio, wrapping it in a rubbish sack against spray. A politician spoke, slightly muffled, through the grey plastic, promising a full inquiry about something or other.

Back on deck, all was the same. She almost did not hear the howling of the gale now, so familiar had it become. Seated by the tiller, only occasionally nudging it to correct the course, Joanna drank her soup, ate the whole malt loaf, and sucked at the squashy nectarine. She watched the seas rise and fall and hiss between her and the misty black shape of Portland Bill.

Normally, lunch would be a cup of the excellent filter coffee they sold at the Bun and a wholemeal ham salad bap from its menu. She would eat it in the small kitchen, listening for the 'ting!' of the door that announced a customer. Who was in that kitchen today? Erika would have been drafted in, no doubt, if that strict husband of hers agreed. She could hold the fort until the latest of Mandy's girls turned up to work the two-till-six shift. Joanna, biting consideringly into her malt loaf, hoped Erika would stay on to supervise young Zoë. She, Jo, had been doing just that for three months, since the comparatively reliable Donna had left. Zoë was not reliable. You could tell her what to do a dozen times – kindly, of course – and still she would not do it. So Joanna either stayed in the teashop or came back three times during the afternoon to check that all was well.

It never was. Once, Zoë had served a bowl of sea salt instead of sugar to a tired family off the motorway. Once, she locked herself out of the till. Once, she served cheese scones from the box which held yesterday's throw-outs, en route to a nearby piggery.

Sometimes, Jo wondered why she could not bring herself to

blame Mandy for these lamentable inroads into her free time. Mandy was meant to be in charge of the afternoons, not just to hire any passing moron and then turn her elegant back on the problem. She, Joanna, was unloading bakery orders at eight every morning; afternoons (and a share of lunch at busy seasons) were, immemorially, Mandy's responsibility. But all Mandy actually did now was to pay Zoë, or whichever girl was her current replacement. She did not even train them; indeed, so long was it since Mandy had served a customer herself that she probably would not know how to. No normal business partnership, and few normal friendships, would tolerate such an arrangement for two minutes, Jo knew. It was as if Keith or Alex were to stop solicitoring and put some halfwit articled clerk behind his desk and claim that this gave him the same rights as the remaining partner. It was nonsense.

Yet she had never complained. She was not remotely afraid of Mandy, nor of a quarrel – Mandy forgave quarrels in seconds. But somehow, whenever her friend had been selfish or otherwise appalling in their seventeen years' acquaintance, Jo had found herself oddly unmoved to protest. When Mandy dumped baby Anneliese on her for an hour and stayed out all night, she had coped, even breastfeeding Annie with her own Susan-milk. She had not even remonstrated, in the morning, when a hungover Mandy with marmalade hair in disarray had turned up demanding black coffee. When Mandy used to borrow her sweaters and give them back stretched and pizza-stained after shrieky nights out with the latest gang of lads, Jo merely washed them, without comment, and listened to the outrageous stories of how they got that way. When Mandy married Alex, the 'something blue' she wore was also something borrowed, Joanna's Janet Reger eggshell-blue silk teddy. It had not come back yet. Mandy got away with murder. She treated Joanna, Keith often thought, more as an indulgent mother than a friend.

Joanna did not see herself as a mother to Mandy. It was just, she reflected now, as if a voice always murmured at moments of exasperation, 'That's her, that's Mandy, that's the deal.' Mandy was a selfish, robust survivor. Someone who never needed to be worried about because she looked after herself. Mandy was a sunflower who always turned her face to the bright lights and the fun.

Joanna could never remember Mandy depressed or sheepish, self-doubting or apologetic. When her Swedish sailor left her pregnant, she called him every sort of bastard in the book but greeted baby Anneliese with gleeful pride. She took earnest young Joanna's proffered company and support as no less than her due, although in the small-town society of Bonhurst the friendship was widely seen as 'odd'. When the Social Security caught on to some undeclared earnings, Mandy only laughed and somehow came up with the £750 she owed in record time.

Jo never liked to think of that 'somehow'. 'Oh, I sold some stuff,' Mandy had said airily. But what, in her meagre flat, could have been worth £750? Nor, Jo reflected, did anyone but she know that the mysterious sale involved three nights away in Portsmouth while Jo babysat. Keith *certainly* didn't know. Nor Alex, God forbid. But Mandy, the debt paid, had laughed, winked, and turned towards the sun again. She was good to have around. If you were low, she goaded you until you, too, looked towards the light.

That must be it, thought Jo. Mandy cheers me up. By rights I should have spent those childrearing, school-gate years keeping company and talking babycare with nice middle-class girls like me, wives of teachers and solicitors and Waterloo commuters. My friends should have been women who regarded themselves as too grown-up to flirt, whose conversation was all of self-improvement and their children's education, who went to toddler groups and organized PTA coffee mornings and had hushed discussions about Prozac. But none of them ever made me laugh the way Mandy did.

Not since Emily. And Em had gone, into the darkness. With Mandy, you knew she was not going anywhere – not unless there was champagne on tap and plenty of admiring men with money. Em was a jewel, but the nettles grew on her grave. Mandy was a selfish tramp, with all the finer feelings of a rhino, but she was still here. Still laughing, and making her friend laugh. Even if, as years went by, the laughter Mandy provided seemed hollower, and thinner, and less nourishing to the spirit.

Out in the grey, foam-flecked Channel, Jo pushed her drying hair back and looked at the horizon, feeling suddenly very alone. She glanced at the clock, and switched on the radio. Nearly five to two. Shipping forecast.

'Thames, Dover. East or south-east, 5 to 7, increasing gale force 8, possibly 9, later. Rain later, good. Wight, Portland, Plymouth. South-easterly gale 8, increasing 9, later decreasing southerly 4. Rain showers, Good.'

Behind *Shearwater*, the seas still rose, and hissed, and slid forward, throwing her into a rollercoaster motion. The sails, well reefed, pulled obediently towards the west. Joanna listened to the reports from coastal stations, noting that Portland was already reporting force 8. She looked around the glistening wet deck and up the mast. All was secure and in order, the boat running freely and not overstressed. All was as it should be, tight and seamanlike.

Except that she was alone, quite incompetent to face such weather, unfit for command, pathetic. Once, years before when she had just passed her driving test and bought an old car with the profits from the Bun, she had driven to London to the theatre with an old Oxford friend. On the way back, she stopped for petrol and the car would not start again, or even turn over. It was as if the independence and competence she had been enjoying all evening had been a thin veneer that had cracked apart to reveal her as the fibreboard sham she was. A skinny youth in a tattered vest, stopping by on his motorbike, had whipped up her bonnet and condescendingly screwed the terminal back onto her battery, and she had driven home chastened and humbled.

She was only twenty-two then; and since that time the protective cocoon of early marriage had maybe kept her soft, and glad to be soft. She had recognized something about herself that evening on the garage forecourt while the hard young man was rescuing her. She saw that whereas in her little business, or in her kitchen with baby Lance, or hand in hand with Keith, she was competent and even tough, there might be a world outside where she would not seem so. Joanna was prone to these sudden self-doubts; there was actually a kind of stoicism in the fact that nobody else knew about them. Mandy, who suffered no self-doubt whatsoever, would probably have howled in public anguish and broken down utterly if she felt as bad about herself as Joanna quite often, quite routinely, did.

Joanna, alone in the cockpit of her small boat in the gale, felt humiliation well up in her now. *Mum ahoy . . . runaway wife . . . unless she does anything else silly . . .* Keith had been right to report her like a runaway child. Abashed, disgraced, a silly woman out of place, she felt the slow sad tears of self-abasement trickling down her face.

But she continued, mechanically, to steer safely down the wind towards the blackness of Portland Bill. Her cold arm on the tiller would not give up. 'Emily gave up,' said a small voice out of the howling grey waters. 'Emily let go.' Joanna did not. Under her hand the boat moved on, serious and steady, through the unforgiving waves.

10

Keith heard the forecast at home, in the vicarage kitchen. Susan had slammed out, muttering about 'going round Annie's', a turn of phrase he normally deplored but this time did not notice. He sat, head in hands, coffee cooling in front of him, thinking.

The coastguard had a description of *Shearwater*, knew that she was short-handed, and roughly where she could be. There was nothing more to be done in that direction. It needed a red distress flare, a drifting boat, wreckage or a radio call for them to act. That, or a firm report that the boat was in the charge of a dangerously irresponsible or ill person. He forced himself to work out what could be happening.

If the telephone call had been from the Solent, Joanna could well be in shelter by now, after sailing off her bad temper. But if she had gone further west, carried on the tide and the pleasant northerly wind of the morning, this gale would have caught her in Poole Bay and be pushing her towards the shore. She might, in that case, have the sense to head back through the Needles Channel on a narrow reach – only she would have to reef the mainsail heavily to do that, and do it alone, without a steadying hand on the helm. Neither of them had ever done that. People did, of course, all the time; singlehanders crossed oceans. But they were exceptional, tough people.

Maybe she would be sheltering in Yarmouth – an easy entrance – or up the Lymington River. But she would have rung. Wouldn't she?

So – Keith frowned, and drank a mouthful of coffee – suppose she was further west, heading, say, for Weymouth or the naval harbour at Portland? She would still have to reef to be safe;

and would need to make a decision about her landfall. Another two hours of this gale would pile big seas up in that corner of coastline, to bounce back with confused violence in toppling glassy mountains. It would be dangerous for anyone without a powerful engine and precise local knowledge to close the coast. One mistake and a boat could be swept ashore. Even with a fair wind like this, a sailing yacht could lose control in a very rough, confused sea, the power stolen from its sails by the wind-shadow of the waves themselves. An approach to Weymouth would be dangerous, even with the engine's help; and the engine was very low on fuel. It must be, the way she had been gunning it out of Portsmouth harbour last night.

But Joanna knew all that, didn't she? His wife had always been full of sense at sea. More than once a brief cabin door or chart-table conference with her – even when she had an armful of babies, in the early days – had saved him from doing something silly.

'Mmm,' she would say. 'How many hours of tide did you reckon we had? Then won't it be against us on the bar?' Or 'If we change course now, we could be in Cherbourg in three hours, and we can still get to Alderney tomorrow if it's a false alarm about the fog.'

She used her head, all right, but the boat decisions had always been, in the end, his. Sometimes he thought it might have been different if Lance had not come so quickly. She would have taken over more, maybe sailed alone with her own friends on weekends when he had to work. He would not have opposed it; welcomed it, rather. He had never understood his men friends and clients who clung stubbornly to power within their marriages and only ceded responsibility to wives or grown children after a fight. Boats, he felt, and families too, were safer for having more than one confident, competent person in them.

No, she was capable. There was not one job aboard *Shearwater* that Joanna could not do as well as he did. She could steer, navigate, and handle the sails. She had sense. She might make the right decisions today.

Only, in this kind of case, with no easy shelter to hand, the most sensible and seamanlike decision is to stay at sea, overnight if necessary, running before the gale in open water. That would be safer than risking the lethal conflict of land and sea near the coast. All the yachting advice magazines, all the Royal Yachting Association instructors would tell you that. The only trouble was that not one ordinary yachtsman in ten would follow such advice. Every time the wind blew hard in the Channel, people risked almost anything to run for harbour. They pleaded weak crews, seasickness, children, even work deadlines. Sometimes they made it; sometimes they were rescued by the lifeboat; some even sent up distress flares from yachts which, with a bit of resolution, could well have stayed at sea and ridden out the gale.

Keith sat, turning an almost empty coffee cup in his hands. There was no need to think of lifeboats. Please God, no. Jo had sense. He wished they had not quarrelled. It was a stupid quarrel anyway. She could give up the Bun in the Oven tomorrow and they would manage. Sixteen years was, he saw now, a long time to be shackled to a teashop. Maybe it was a long time to be shackled to a provincial law practice – the memory of Mrs Repton's telephone call made him shudder, and then grimace and, briefly, laugh. Perhaps he could get out too. Do something else. School fees? Susan hated Angela Merici and Mrs MacEvoy's brisk rule. She didn't want to do A levels. Wanted to do one of the new vocational courses, Media and Publishing Design, at an FE college with poxy Anneliese doing her fashion diploma. Wanted to live in a bedsit near college and come home at weekends.

And why not? He, who had opposed all Susan's plans and lectured her on the importance of a sound academic base, suddenly wondered: why not? At least she had a plan. And it was stupid to compare her with Lance who had never had a report below A or A+ all his schooldays, had had three universities fighting over him, and finally accepted a major scholarship to Cambridge. Why shouldn't Suzie choose? He remembered the tuft of black-and-gold striped hair sticking out from under the duvet and a tug of tenderness made him draw in his breath, deeper than he had breathed since the moment on Ray Brewer's jetty.

Why not, why not? Why not let Jo sell up the Bun and shake the icing-sugar out of her life? Why not take his capital out of the partnership, sell the Old Vicarage, get rid of the damn furniture, pool the money and go sailing for a couple of years? Perhaps, his lawyerly caution prompted him, buying a cottage first so they had a base to come home to. Somewhere like Egg Terrace, their first home: three up, two down, kitchen out the back. Back to basics. Do a bit of freelance legal work, just enough to feed the two of them. Read books, go for walks, never, *ever* go to Rotarian functions in the chilly corn Exchange. They could let the children have what extra they needed to survive on the attenuated state grant; otherwise tell them to get holiday jobs. *Why not?* If only Jo came back safe . . .

Adrift on a sea of new possibilities, his sails shaking, his hand for once off the tiller, Keith sat at the kitchen table and slowly, deliberately, emptied his coffee dregs onto the scrubbed wood. Just to see what shape the puddle came out.

At the other end of the small town Mandy Heron and Gordon were getting along famously, halfway down a bottle of Australian Chardonnay and going well. He had his notebook out and, admiring remarks about her kitchen completed, was down to business. She sipped, and smiled roguishly, and basked in the young reporter's attention.

'Joanna – like I said, she's absolutely my best friend. We started the Bun in the Oven together, while we were still expecting. So of course I know her better than *anyone*.'

Mandy paused, and leaned forward, carefully keeping her shoulders back so that her sweatered breasts would fuddle the boy even further. She loved to fuddle young men. And old ones. She was entitled to her fun with this one, anyway. Mandy was no fool, and had known all along that Gordon was not remotely interested in giving his readers a thrilling insight into the marketing of two-cup pots of tea and the freshness of Eccles cakes. She read the *Chronicle* and its rival the *Globe* with great enjoyment every morning, sipping her black coffee in her streamlined kitchen, shivering with happy *schadenfreude* at the misfortunes of the famous. It was obvious to her from the start that Gordon's need was for 'colour' details about Joanna, the Sailaway Wife.

'Jo's more involved in the cafe now, of course. I'm more

executive these days, planning, policy sort of thing.' His pen, which had hovered hopefully at the mention of Jo, fell limp. Mandy sipped and smiled. The boy was really desperate for his story, bless him.

Her need, on the other hand, was for company and diversion in the dull middle part of the day. Mandy, if truth be told, was bored to screaming point. When asked – usually by Keith – why she no longer personally worked her afternoon shift in the Bun in the Oven, she generally talked about being busy and entertaining Alex's new business contacts and 'charity commitments' – at which Keith audibly snorted. Sometimes she even said, rather piously, that she 'liked to give young girls a chance of a job'. This enraged Keith even further by its suggestion that Joanna, by struggling with cake boxes early every morning, fixing the plug on the hot-water boiler and making egg sandwiches for bossy old ladies, not to mention propping up dopey Zoë all afternoon, was somehow inconsiderately depriving the new generation of work.

The truth was that Mandy hated the Bun in the Oven. It had been fun at first, a kind of dare. When Joanna had suggested it, over a cup of vile bottled coffee and a stale hot cross bun on the oilcloth of the High Street's only daytime restaurant, it had fired Mandy's imagination. She could see Jo now, hugely pregnant, as she was too; and hear her saying, 'Mandy, this is foul.'

'It is. It's like mud.'

'And we come here twice a week to drink it, and I'll be down even more when Lance is at playschool. And there'll be clinics and stuff when the new babies come. Why do we pay these people money to feed us this disgusting liquid mud?'

'Because,' Mandy had said, 'it's here or the WonderBurger, and that's worse coffee. And you can't get a pushchair in.'

That was when Joanna had put forward the big idea.

'Why don't we have a café? Let's rent the old charity shop. We'll rake it in. All the women like us will come. Keith'll lend us the money from his dad's legacy. Do him good to have a flutter. Oh, come on, Mandy. Remember Julius Caesar: "There is a tide in the affairs of men, which, taken at the flood, leads on to fortune."'

It was one of the nice things about Jo, thought Mandy fondly now, that she never adjusted her conversation or her quotations just because Mandy left school at sixteen – well, fifteen actually, what with the three months' suspension. All the other mothers in their primary school-gate circle did. They said things like 'Opera – a sort of play with music', or 'Washington – in America, you know', which drove Mandy mad. Joanna just chatted on as if she was with one of her old student friends, and if Mandy didn't understand a reference, she would say so. And Jo would explain or lend her a book. She had read *Anna Karenina* that way, and been to the Shakespeare Festival. Once, Mandy had thought of doing Open University, but that was before Alex appeared. Marrying Alex was a much more straightforward project for self-improvement.

Anyway, Mandy and Jo and the Bun had taken the tide and made a fortune. By their unexacting standards, anyway. Everyone came to the Bun: shoppers, mothers, chaps on their lunch hour who wanted to avoid the pub, people off the M3. They never did hot food except Welsh rarebit or toast, but the baps were well stuffed, the cakes varied, everything fresh; there was leaf tea and fresh ground coffee from the beginning.

'It's a good café,' Mandy said now, to Gordon, 'because even when we were broke, just starting out, we did really classy things.'

'You ran the café together, at first? I mean, you worked with Joanna?' asked Gordon, steeringly.

'Yes. That's right,' said Mandy. 'It was good fun.'

At first it had been fun. Like a rolling party, only with money coming in. Jo laughed at Mandy for her fierce delight in cashing up every night, seeing all that earned money in the till. She would run it through her fingers, gloating. 'Well, you don't understand. In our street, money was stuff that comes from the Social. From the Giro.' Mandy's mother had left her when she was five, shouting at her father that he could have the little bitch since he was the one who spoiled her. Her father had taken it hard, and alcoholically.

The Bun opened from eleven till four at first; the women would wheel the two babies down while Lance toddled furiously alongside on reins. Susan and Anneliese were both champion sleepers, and Lance reliably happy with a small red plastic table and chair in the roughly screened kitchen area, pouring sugar and glue and poster paint on brown paper and muttering stories to himself. The café developed a homely, kitchen atmosphere, and early mistakes were forgiven by a charmed clientèle. The Environmental Health Officer was benevolent (she had a family of her own) and gave notice of her rare inspections. The Bun in the Oven flourished as the children grew.

'Do you, er, own or rent the building?' asked Gordon, deciding to approach the subject of Joanna obliquely, despite a nagging sense of deadline.

'We own it now. Since ten years ago.' That had been the first big change, in 1985. The owners, a charitable trust falling into disrepute and dispersal, refused to renew the lease because they had to sell. There was no other High Street site available in those boom years – Christ, thought Mandy, today we could take our pick – and the asking price was exorbitant. Mandy would have been happy to get out – by that time marriage to Alex was starting to look like a real prospect – but Jo was stubborn. She approached the bank, got a loan agreed for half the asking price on the freehold, and went back to the trustees of the ailing charity with a deadpan, take-it-or-leave-it cash offer, insisting on a decision within twenty-four hours. The charity's trustees were desperate to realize their few assets and the gamble paid off. They got the Bun for a song.

It gave Mandy, in particular, a malicious pleasure to have scored such a victory over the Mary Magdalen Reforming Foundation for the Rehabilitation of Unmarried Mothers. But it was the last pleasure the Bun was to give her. With a loan to pay off they had to abandon the pleasing amateurishness of their short hours, hire schoolgirl help on busy Saturdays, and keep professional accounts. They still flourished, and Jo appeared to enjoy it. To Mandy it was a bore, and gradually, after her wedding to Alex, she withdrew her interest until she devised the scheme of replacing herself with waitresses. She knew it was unfair, but if Jo put up with it, more fool her.

Gordon, watching her, saw a quite incongruous flicker of guilt on Mrs Heron's lovely face. He pressed home the advantage.

'What sort of person is your partner, Mrs Gurney? I'm terribly disappointed to have missed her, but I gather she's on holiday.

I'd have liked to get your different, sort of complementary, perspectives on running the teashop so successfully. But perhaps you could give me an idea of what she's like?' He took a gulp of wine and waited with deceptive casualness.

Mandy leaned forward and put a warm, delicately manicured hand over Gordon's, causing him to choke momentarily on his drink and whang the top of his ballpoint with his suddenly tensed thumb. It rolled, a little red cylinder like a doll's house bomb, across the vinyl floor. They both watched it for a moment. Then, 'Sweetie, you are such a bullshitter. I do know why you're here, you know. You're only interested in Joanna because of the story about her running away to sea. Give me one good reason why I should help you.'

It was said with such affectionate, flirtatious mockery that Gordon could not immediately absorb the challenge. 'No – I – er – honestly, it isn't that—'

'Bollocks. Course it is.'

'Well, all right. I'm only doing my job. I do want to know about Mrs Gurney. But the teashop is part of the story, isn't it? Good for business. That restaurant which Janey Paterson ran is coining it in.' He had hardly finished saying it before he bit his tongue, horrified.

Mandy looked at him, consideringly. 'Janey Paterson was murdered and cut up and put in the left luggage at Reading bus station,' she said. 'Nice one, Gordon. That's just the way to interview the worried friend of the missing woman. Did you get it out of a book on how to be a reporter?'

Gordon rose, stiffly, gathering his newspaperman's dignity around him. 'I'm sorry to have troubled you. Thank you for your help.'

'Any time,' said Mandy. Deftly, she scooped up his notebook with Erika's quotes in it and slid it into the front pocket of her Bermudas. There was barely room; Gordon could not have got it out without committing a prima facie sexual assault, and he had noticed a slinky teenage daughter crossing the hall a few minutes back. Moreover, this damned woman was married to a solicitor. He was helpless. The headline 'REPORTER ON ASSAULT CHARGE – HE WAS LIKE AN ANIMAL, SAYS WOMAN' danced before his eyes. Mandy offered him a pussycat smile. 'Hang on a tick and I'll make you a sandwich to take with you.'

And she did. Gordon, who hated cheese sandwiches, waited obediently for it in the hope of getting his book back, but only the foil packet was pressed into his hand at the end of the humiliating minutes. Mandy reached across, slipped an apple into his pocket, straightened his tie, and patted him on the shoulder. 'Don't you worry about Joanna,' she said. 'She'll be back. She knows her way around. We're almost old enough to be your Mum.'

When he had gone, Anneliese sauntered into the kitchen. 'Who's the guy throwing packed lunches into the hedge?' she enquired.

'A *nice* boy,' said Mandy. 'Friend of mine from Fleet Street.' She liked the feeling of the boy's notebook, fresh from his inside jacket pocket, nestling on her thigh. A girl was entitled to take her fun where she could find it.

11

It was ten miles off Portland that Joanna made her decision. The humiliating panic of the shipping forecast had passed and she had steered on westward for close on two hours with the tears drying on her face, hardly thinking. *Shearwater* rolled, and strained, and groaned, sometimes dipping the end of her outstretched boom into the water in the wilder racing waters off St Alban's Head. The boat leaned towards the land with a force that made Joanna instinctively keep her course offshore, pointing almost at the tip of Portland Bill as they passed the lesser headland. The south-easterly wind was sending a train of waves along, north and west of the boat's track, pushing her inwards. In less than two hours, surfing along these waves, she could be tied up in Weymouth, phoning home, eating fish and chips – the sickness past, Joanna was ravenous now – and cadging a shower off one of the bed and breakfast landladies. By nightfall, she could be home. And dry.

'Fairytale,' said Joanna aloud. Then, to the wave train, 'Bugger you.' It was strange; if Keith had been aboard, the decision to give up the idea of Weymouth would have been discussed, and mildly dramatized. The unpleasantness of the inevitable conclusion would have been cushioned by conversation and the simple consolations of human agreement.

Keith: Jo – could we have a word?

Joanna (appearing through hatch): Yup?

* * *

• Libby Purves

Keith: I've been thinking – this sea's getting up a bit. It won't be very nice outside Weymouth.

Jo (thoughtfully): No. Bit like threading a needle at speed. That narrow entrance. I bet south-easterly gales throw waves right over that pier where the anglers sit.

Keith: I'm afraid I don't fancy it.

Jo: Could we go back to the Solent? I suppose not, with so much east in the wind, it'd take half the night. What about Portland?

Keith: They've closed it to pleasure boats, remember? Since the bomb. Anyway, you'd still have appalling seas bouncing off the breakwater.

Jo: Oh, shit. We could stand on round Portland Bill.

Keith: Jo, I think the sensible thing is to stand on.

Jo: Then what?

Keith: Well – it sort of means we have to keep going. If this blows through we could turn back. Or try and get into Bridport or somewhere. Otherwise, Torbay. It's a short gale anyway, they reckon. Probably be right down by morning.

Jo: Well, that's a night sail, then. I knew we should have got up for the early forecast.

Keith: I should have woken up.

Jo: No, I should have. Never mind. I'll get some food made. (Vanishes below).

None of this could happen. She was alone. Nor did the conversation need to unroll at all: it would have been mere comfort-talk, the habitual exchange of old sailing companions. It had been obvious to Joanna for at least an hour that Weymouth would be far too dangerous an approach in these seas. Especially for an undermanned, virtually engineless small yacht with an inexperienced skipper and with even stronger wind forecast as the afternoon went on. She and Keith would have played the game of discussing it, but neither of them would have been doing more than getting their own judgement reinforced. Unless one of them argued for the rash, tempting course of running in regardless.

Once, pregnant with Susan and with a tiny, seasick Lance, Jo had done just that on a difficult sail up-Channel from Plymouth. Keith had caved in to her earnest requests, and to save two hours plugging against the tide up to Dartmouth they had run in across the Salcombe bar, notoriously deadly in strong onshore winds. They got in safely, with a cockpit full of water, but the look they gave each other when they had silently moored the boat was a look full of death. Their deaths, Lance's unbearable, pathetic small death; the unborn child's unconscious death.

They were subdued all evening. There was activity to seaward, lights and engines and ragged ends of shouts, while they cooked their risotto and settled the baby. That night on the radio news they heard a solemn report of the loss of two racing yachtsmen, swept overboard when their harness buckles snapped – on Salcombe bar, half an hour after them. Joanna had crept across to Keith's bunk and lain there with him, cramped and warm and silent. Neither apologized aloud, but Joanna knew she should not have asked, and Keith that he should not have given in. She thought of that night now, after sixteen years of survival and family life, and said aloud, just for the comfort of it, 'OK, Keith. On we go. Take no risks.'

Her head turned towards the seaward end of Portland, ten degrees closer to the wind, *Shearwater* sailed better. Joanna fixed the elastic cord, watched it for a while, then, satisfied, swung herself down through the hatch. She lit the flame under the kettle to make some more powdered soup, then lit the little swinging oven and grovelled under the bunks for a packet of part-baked, vacuum-packed rolls she had remembered earlier during her moment's reverie about the Bun in the Oven and how faithful Erika would be coping. Yes! Under the tinned peas and the spare kettle. *Two* packets. And a tin of Spam. A night's provisions. She stabbed open the sealed packs and put all six rolls in the oven, setting the little timer to ring in eight minutes. The timer reminded her of Susan who had bought it to time her hair dye, grown too expert to need it, and left it in the kitchen fruit bowl for weeks. Jo had annexed it for the boat.

A glance up through the hatch showed the boat steady on course, and no other vessels in sight. Joanna went forward to the cramped heads compartment, used the lavatory, and while she sat there rummaged briefly in the first aid box, steadying herself against the boat's pounding. Caffeine tablets. She had taken them at Oxford to help her sit up until four with essays; she had bought these on impulse in a chemist's four years ago while she was renewing the boat's emergency kit. Keith disapproved. 'For night watches? We hardly ever sail long nights now. And when we do, we need to be able to sleep off watch.' Joanna had bought them all the same. She supposed that they were still in date: caffeine, surely, could not lose its potency? The yellow phial went into her oilskin pocket, together with the glucose tablets.

On the way back to the main hatch, she stopped by the chart table and pulled out Stanford's *English Channel, Western Section*. The great curve of Lyme Bay was familiar, its eastern edge bounded by the sweep of Chesil beach and the rising snout of Portland Bill, skirted with wavy little symbols marking the dangerous offshore tide race where two streams fight southward for ten hours in every twelve. She must keep a distance from the Portland Race: five miles to be safe.

North and west of the Bill, Chesil beach itself streamed away, eerily straight, without shelter, graveyard of ships throughout history. Small harbours were marked: Bridport, Lyme Regis, Exmouth, Teignmouth, none of them of the remotest use in an onshore gale. She knew that without checking: the curve of this bay, all sixty miles' width of it, would fill with roaring water tonight. The proper, sensible place to be was out on the diameter of its semicircle, up to twenty miles from land, heading south-west towards Start Point.

Assuming she rounded Portland at six or seven o'clock and steered for Start, and assuming the forecast was right about the gale's abating, she could then come up the bay a little and make it into Torbay at dawn.

Torbay bulged out, a pimple of sea on the smooth buttock of

Lyme Bay, a bite of blue taken out of the white land to the west. If the wind went south as forecast – 'Wight, Portland, Plymouth. South-easterly gale 8, increasing 9, later decreasing southerly 4. Rain showers, good' – Torbay would be fine shelter by then. Torquay lay to the north of the bay, Brixham to the south. It would be dawn by then. Easy to go in, look round for masts, find a marina. Or anchor again while she gathered her wits for a solo approach. If the forecast changed at six o'clock, or midnight, and the wind blew on from the south-east, she could run round Start Point and anchor in Bigbury Bay. Or, by noon tomorrow, make the infallible, all-weather, ultimate shelter of Plymouth.

Joanna stabbed each harbour on the chart, noted down some compass courses on the back of her hand with Biro, and climbed back on deck. Whereon the wind hit her like a hammer blow and made the whole plan seem preposterous. Sail to *Devon*? Alone? In a gale? All night?

Yes. Either that or give up. Either head for Devon, under control, or send up flares here and now and hope to heaven that someone would see them. The watcher on the shore would alert the coastguard, radio for a lifeboat. Soon she would feel strong male hands reaching out to her, wrapping her in blankets, comforting her. She would be in an ambulance, then fetched from hospital by Keith, taken back to Bonhurst, put to bed with a hot-water bottle . . . the possibilities danced for a moment in the cold spray from the bow.

But *Shearwater*, all around her, seemed to shudder in distaste. Old voices from her learning days came back to her, from the days when she had no babies and dreamed of lone voyages. They were the voices of bluff old explorer-sailors in their understatedly British memoirs, of maverick singlehanders like Blondie Hasler saying, 'Every herring should hang by its own tail', and refusing to carry a radio. There was the voice of a sailing instructor telling the boatload of scared trainees not to worry about the yacht riding big seas, but to feed themselves and work on their own strength because 'we're the amateurs, the boat's a professional'. They were the bar-wise voices of dismayed yacht club members after the Fastnet Race disaster, when crews took to liferafts and some of them died even though their yachts were found days later, still afloat.

No. You stuck with your boat. Propped in the hatchway, watching *Shearwater* steer herself through the seas, Joanna decided. No surrender, no silliness. She would try to get this decent little boat decently to harbour, and risk nothing. If she called a lifeboat it would be *in extremis*.

The alarm on the timer went off and she slid below again, cut off the master gas tap, poured her soup into a mug and took two hot rolls from the oven. Provisioned, she settled back into the cockpit, took off the elastic cords, glanced at the scribbles on her hand and set a course of 255 degrees compass, 250 degrees true. *Shearwater* leaned a little more and tore along, hurling up spray, crashing into the sides of waves, aiming well south of the smoky bulk of Portland.

By mid-afternoon, the Bun in the Oven was winding down for the day. Erika and Zoë were serving their last customers, a couple of middle-aged women with a weakness for Mississippi Mud Pie. They were strangers in town who chatted to Erika after she had sternly banished Zoë to the kitchen to clear up her latest disaster with the sugar bag and the milk.

'Yes,' Erika was saying. 'I try to keep it homely. It's my own business, you see. It's more like a child than a job, really. You have to love it, else there's no soul in a place, is there?'

It was a game she often played, undetected, on her weekends and Bank Holidays in charge. Except in emergencies like this, she could only work on those days. On weekdays her husband, Ted Merriam the ironmonger, required his lunch and tea cooked and on the table by 1.00 and 6.00 p.m., respectively, not a minute later. He also required that the house should be clean, laundry done, and shopping put away. He could not abide a woman fussing about with housework when a man came in to sit down of an evening. It wasn't right. A man's home, Ted often said, was his home. It came of being fifty, thought Erika. She was barely thirty, but the ironmonger's wooing had been too much for his newest, shyest girl assistant to resist, so there she was, married in the old obedient style of his generation and not hers.

However, on weekends and Bank holidays, rain or shine,

Ted Merriam and three invariable companions took a packed lunch and went fishing. The four men had been doing the same thing since they were twelve. And strangely, on these days he seemed to become younger. He did not mind a late supper, or a scratch supper, or a tumbled house, and was – to Erika – quite good enough company to console her for the rather outdated (prehistoric, she privately thought) household standards he demanded most of the time. On fishing evenings, she had even got away with calling him, to his face, the name she had long given him in secret: Fred Flintstone.

On such days Erika was happy. She alone ran the Bun, with its pleasure-seeking proprietresses nowhere in sight. Wiping down cake trays, straightening tables, presenting thirsty customers with perfect trays of tea and toast gave Erika Merriam a joy so deep and serious and vocational that sometimes, as now, the only outlet was in fluent, harmless, wishful lies.

'I do use girls from the town as waitresses, but it's not easy training them to do things right. I'm thinking of reorganizing the kitchen a little, perhaps involving Zoë more – she's not a stupid girl, I just think she needs proper training – and I'm hoping to start doing hot lunches. But you have to think of all the contingencies, don't you, when you're running your own business?'

The two ladies (crop-haired artistic types, on a buying tour for their own small craft shop in County Cork) agreed enthusiastically. It was as well, really, that Erika had not played her fantasy game on Gordon that morning. That really would have muddled his line of research.

On the train to Waterloo, Gordon was fuming with lonely rage. Bitch! *Bitch!* Bloody woman! Stringing him along, wasting his time, nicking his notebook and putting it in her – aah, *bitch!* The scent of Mandy, the bouncy curves of Mandy, the tanned cleavage of her, the warm hand on his arm, the outline of his notebook against her thigh were all too vividly with him. He was glad he had thrown away her cheese sandwich or he would be, he knew, sniffing and biting into it even now, for reasons unconnected with his stomach. Well, not too closely connected, anyway; four inches to the south of it was where he angrily ached just now.

Hateful bitch! Women were in any case the bane of Gordon's life. Pushy little cows like that Dinny Douglas, sleeping with the managing editor (so he wrongly assumed) to get straight onto Fleet Street without the humiliations of local council reporting. Power bitches setting up women's networks to stop men rising – as they always had and obviously should – to their properly dominant position in newspapers! Women columnists, like Maeve Mahoney, earning a hundred thousand a year for scoring cheap points off men, making generalizations no man would ever get past the most Neanderthal Fleet Street editor.

And now, a suburban bloody vamp who stole your notebook and dared you to get it back. In the pub, he had sometimes listened respectfully to the big boys, back in their safari jackets from El Salvador or Bosnia, telling how news films or tapes had been taken from them by murderous thugs. 'I didn't argue,' they would say. 'He had a Kalashnikov, and I'm a devout coward!' And they would laugh, and bask in their peers' admiration.

But how could he ever admit to having his ring-backed notebook confiscated by a blonde in an Alice band who subsequently straightened his tie and packed him off with a sandwich? 'I didn't argue, she had a tight sweater on and I'm a devout wimp.' He stared out moodily at the bending trees and thrashing branches of Surrey in the gale.

Never mind. The office would never know what happened. Nobody would. He had a bit of Keith on tape anyway – handy that, him being a lawyer. At least he couldn't complain about the actual quotes, and any spin that got put on them was up to Gordon. He remembered plenty from the Erika bint in the teashop. As for Mandy-bitch-Heron, she of the hips – Christ, the hips! – and the mocking pout, she would be quoted all right. And described. Oh yes! She would get a surprise package from Gordon in the morning. So would her poxy friend Joanna, and Maeve Mahoney and the housewives' choice rag *Globe*. And Dinny Douglas, rot her. Unless, of course, Dinny had found the woman. Hell!

He would have felt better if he had known that Dinny was even now standing disconsolately on the end of Weymouth pier, looking at a rough grey sea and wondering whether to go into yet another reeking telephone box and plead to be recalled to the office. He would have felt even better if he could have seen his editor listening to the PM headlines on Radio 4 about two lifeboat searches and one yacht fatality in the Western Channel and saying, above the chattering of the faxes and keyboards, 'God, that's it. "FOR THOSE IN PERIL – Gales Strike Unwary Sailors as summer goes out like a lion." Run it under the Chancellor on the front page. Then human stuff on page three – do an RNLI appeal box, stuff on hero lifeboatmen, but big pics of the dead guy. And hang on, there's another page in it. Alan! We can do "Fears For Those Still Missing at Sea". Where the fuck has Gordon got to with the missing housewife?'

12

Night fell. The low pressure deepened and ran towards Belgium, its fronts shrieking the last of their short fury over southern England. Alone in the Old Vicarage, Keith watched the nine o'clock news which led on the yacht death in the Channel. A small boat in mid-Channel had been knocked down, dismasted and holed by its own falling mast. The helicopter had picked up two of her three crew from the liferaft, but a man of twenty-seven had not been seen since the dismasting. Terse rescuers in survival suits gave the bones of the story; the survivors appeared briefly, teeth chattering, talking about the suddenness of the gale and the hugeness of the seas. Reading between the lines, Keith deduced inexperience and that they had been carrying full sail at the time of the knockdown. Poor sods. Jo would have reefed early. Wouldn't she? She was always in favour of it in their discussions. Cautious.

The news went on, talking of lifeboat services fully stretched and cars flooded by waves on the seaside promenades of the south coast.

It was dark outside. Keith shivered, turned off the television, and went to his desk, looking for some work, any work, in which to lose himself.

Alex and Mandy sprawled on their leather sofa, watching their huge television. Mandy, thinking of young Gordon's furious, unwilling submission to her whim of the afternoon, giggled delightedly as she edged up to Alex on the smooth cushion, letting her kimono fall open to show more lightly tanned flesh.

'Mmmm?' she enquired, planting a kiss on his ear. 'Mmmm, Panda?'

'Hang on, I'm watching this. Look, it's obviously nasty out at sea. Hope Jo Gurney's all right.'

'She will be. She's not stupid.' Mandy had never anticipated a calamity in her life. Not her mother's defection, not her father's drunken death, not her Swede's vanishing back to sea, not her own pregnancy. Her way was to expect everything to work out all right. Generally, it did. When it didn't, Mandy found a way to wriggle out of the worst results. Alex's theory was that this was because she had not used up all her energy worrying. He had always thought, watching the Middle East hostage wives on TV, that if he were in a cell in Beirut Mandy wouldn't worry. She would expect him back any day. It made him, strangely, more fond of her than ever. She was nuzzling him now.

'Mmmm? Panda? Cuddleup?'

'Baby. You never worry about anyone, do you?'

'She'll be all right. Mmmmm.'

'Would you worry about me if I was in a boat tonight? Out at sea, in a gale?'

'Nope.'

'What would you do?'

'Come and get you, in my lifeboatman's gear, *if* I happened to want you. For anything. Mmmmm. You'd fancy me in yellow oilskins, wouldn't you?'

'Mmmmm . . .'

'With nothing underneath . . . look . . .'

Alex gave up on the news and his vague plan to finish the office letters, in favour of an early bed. Much later, ungluing herself from his sleeping form, Mandy rolled lazily onto her front and felt, under the mattress, the shape of Gordon's notebook. Hazy memories of Bible study came to her, something about committing adultery in your mind being just as bad as doing it really. Just as *good*, she always thought. Mrs Amanda Heron dropped off, smilingly, to sleep.

In the windowless newsroom of the *Chronicle*, Gordon read his story in page proof. Magic. His name, black and solidly satisfying. The picture of the Gurney woman with her teashop award, fished from the local paper's archives by a diligent picture desk. She looked tragic, big-eyed, hopeless. Brilliant! He had pulled every heartstring, stuck in every knife, made the most of every quote. At this rate, he'd get a staff writer job on the paper, or better himself, go to the *Daily Mail*, before the year was out. And Dinny Douglas was still stuck in Weymouth, bleating to be brought home. Magic, magic, magic.

He walked up and down the long room, holding the page proof casually, his name outermost. The back bench subs, who had seen it all and knew that it would be chip wrappings by tomorrow, failed even to lift their heads.

In Tedneric, the neat villa where Ted Merriam returned grumpily on each work night and cheerfully on fishing days, Erika was recovering from an evening of damage limitation.

'Potato and corn fritters,' she had said brightly when he got in, breathing deeply. 'And gammon and peas. Oh, Ted, you do look tired. I thought it would be nice if you sat on the patio with a drink first, unwind a bit. It said in my magazine you ought to relax before you eat, or you get an ulcer.'

'What you mean is,' said Ted flatly, 'you haven't *made* the tea. You been working in that caff.' But he had sat, and had a beer, and stared out moodily across the playing fields to the river. What profited a man if he had the best run ironmongery in south Hampshire, but had to wait for his tea? Erika, sweaty from rushing home, had flung the fritters (stored in the freezer for just such moments) in the deep-fryer, put the gammon under the grill, and tipped a kettleful of water onto the peas. Now, laying the table, she chatted brightly through the patio doors.

'See, Ted, won't be a minute. I think it's nice, us both working on the High Street. You could've popped in for your dinner – I know we don't do it for customers, but if I took in a pan I could do you a fry-up easy. That pub's ever so crowded, and those pies have got BSE in—'

'She back tomorrow, then? Mrs Gurney?' Ted stumped in and sat heavily on the chair.

'Well, I don't think so. Ted . . .' Erika hesitated, pitching her appeal as best she could. 'Ted, I oughter help. I wouldn't care if it was just Mrs Heron, snotty cow, but Mr Gurney was ever so polite. He came out from his office to see I was all right.'

The big ironmonger ate in silence for a while. He respected Keith Gurney, and that wife of his seemed a decent girl.

'You could get home earlier,' he said at last. 'You could get that waitress of theirs to lock up.'

Erika thought hard. Yes. Not worth pushing further. Zoë could lock up. She could always ask Mrs Heron to go in and help her, last thing. Wouldn't chip her nail varnish just to check round. And it *was* her business.

'Course I could, lovey. Got you a lovely pudding today, anyway. It's called Mississippi Mud Pie. I think that's a disgusting name, isn't it? Funny, how people give nice puddings these horrible names. Like blommonge.'

She chattered on, soothing, and Ted Merriam relaxed and ate bland sweetness and thought calm, peaceable, fluent thoughts of reeds and rods and fish instead of spiky, hard, awkward, jangling thoughts of ironmongery. Erika smiled secretly, and thought of crisp paper napkins, eager customers, a jingling till and the warm smell of floury baps and soup. Wrapped in their separate paradises, the Merriams settled for the night.

Anneliese and Susan were stretched out on Annie's black duvet, full length, relaxed as young cats. Anneliese, with all her mother's happy insouciance, had made Susan turn to the sunlight again and feel silly about her dark forebodings. Susan knew that as soon as she was alone again, the dark bits would come back, curling up the edges of her thoughts like tattered, rotten bits of old carpet. She needed Anneliese to keep her mood smooth and flat and bright.

Dad never understood that. He just thought Annie was a frivolous little tart, you could tell. Mum understood. Well, she always calmed Dad down about it. Susan, fleetingly, found herself wondering whether Mum felt like that about Mandy. At sixteen, her mother's feelings were a dangerous, taboo area to Susan. Sometime, she knew, she would have to face up to thinking of her mother as a person, another woman. Not yet. For the moment she could remain a grotesque. Another mad old wrinkly, put there to thwart teenagers. She put her mother aside, to concentrate on talking to Annie.

Right now, they were talking about sex. Anneliese, Susan knew, had Done It. She, Susan, had not. Love did not, for the moment, come into it; they had both had bruised hearts the year before, and agreed to give up love for the moment. Annie's episodes of Doing It, anyway, had not been with the loved one. It had been with Andy Carson. And, Susan suspected, one or two of his mates. Details were never discussed between them but general principles were, endlessly.

'Mum says,' began Anneliese after a pause, twisting her bright hair, 'Mum says sex is no fun at our age. She says it's only fun when you grow up a bit.'

'She prob'ly says that to stop you doing it and getting AIDS.'

'Nope. She says I can have the pill, and condom money, and just be careful. But she says it won't be any fun because boys aren't much fun compared to men.'

'Why not?'

'Well, 's obvious, innit? All the books say the woman's got to have her, you know, satisfaction, and that takes longer. And boys are ever so quick. So you don't get the, you know. Orgasm.'

'It said in *my* book, and in sex education,' the two doubled up in embarrassed merriment at the memory of Mrs MacEvoy's sex education talks, 'that the man ought to make the woman have a, you know, satisfy her, even if it was after he'd finished.'

'Yeah,' said Anneliese. 'But the thing is,' here she took on an air of authority, as the pair tacitly admitted that they spoke not as equals but across the gulf of Susan's inexperience, 'by the time they're finished, you sort of might not feel like any more fiddling about. I mean, you know, wet rubber things, and him all red and his eyes screwed up.'

'You mean your mum might be right? It's no fun at our age?'

'Unless we find an older bloke, I suppose.'

'Puh-leeze! Yuk! Some old wrinkly, like in that Melvyn Bragg thing on telly, or Lolita, some bank manager—'

'And he'd get bossy—'

'Sort of like your dad, all heavy, serious—'

'Then they get old, and you'd still be keen, and they're past it.'

'Judy Hopgood had it with a bloke who was *forty*.'

'Where did he park his Zimmer frame?'

The pair shrieked with laughter and their conversation passed on to less absurd ideas.

Along the corridor from his scornful stepdaughter, Alex – forty-three and counting – slept with his arm round the wonderful flesh of Anneliese's mother.

And further along the little town, Keith Gurney thought of going upstairs but stayed at his desk instead, because he could not bear the bed's emptiness.

The light was slower to fade at sea. Reflections of the day seemed to be held in the heaving, white-streaked surfaces around the boat, beaten to pewter in the troubled evening light. Gleams of sun shone onto dark grey cloud, sometimes illuminating the mast and sails like a spotlit prop on a dark stage. The whole effect, Joanna thought, was stagey: the wind too self-consciously howling, the light too artificial. Even the occasional spatters of rain were too wet and too brief to be real – some stagehand must have thrown a bucketful of water from offstage. A panicking stagehand, late on cue.

Joanna laughed aloud. There had been a nasty, twisting hour in the fringes of the Portland Race, when the helm seemed to fight her and the sails heaved great despairing flaps in the troughs of the waves, but that was over. The fading light found her clear of the Race, well out into the great bay and sensing something else which strangely raised her spirits.

The swell grows longer west of Portland. The English Channel, from being a mean and pinched waterway funnelling from seventy miles wide to twenty-one at Dover, suddenly becomes a hundred miles wide, and its sea bed swoops deeper towards the Western Approaches. Almost free from its constricting corset of land, the sea begins to breathe again with the rhythm of the deep Atlantic rollers. The squabbling, sandy abrasive meanness of the eastern Channel chop gives way to the clean, long rhythms of the west.

Joanna had felt this change before, sailing with the family; but never had the peace, the pleasure and freedom of the deep sea entered her spirit as it did now, alone.

Darkness came. Hours of night lay ahead, forty miles to landfall and an uncertain destination. But she was happy. The boat was under control, the seas manageable. Portland Bill lighthouse flashed astern on a bearing – she picked up the small compass to check it – of 065 degrees magnetic. That was as it should be. *Alles in Ordnung,* as her old German teacher used to say.

She tied the helm and slid below to light the masthead lamp: one switch to light one bulb, showing green to starboard, red to port, white astern. To save power, she also lit the small paraffin lamp over the chart table. Its low shielded glow would not disturb her night vision and would do to check distances and lighthouses without using the brighter neon light. Oh, this boat, this familiar boat! She felt a surge of love for it, for its compact practicality, its orderly shippiness, its dutiful precision, its homely solid shelter against the storm.

She sat a moment in the moving pool of golden light, sharpening a pencil and marking *Shearwater's* position line off Portland Bill. She estimated the distance by a glance at the log, and put the log reading – 19073.5 – with a neat naval triangle alongside her confident X on the chart. Thirty-two miles to Torbay, forty-five to Start Point and Salcombe, over sixty to Plymouth.

If Keith, or Mandy, or Alex could have seen her they would have been startled. There was a fit, calm decisiveness about the way she sat, one foot braced against the motion, hair pushed behind one ear, concentrating. Her air had nothing of the emollient, diffident or motherly in it. The way she looked now was at once very new and very old: Joanna had last looked like this when she was a student. Before Gabriel, and shattering ecstatic love; before Emily, and disaster.

A glance on deck: all well, flying westwards. She turned back, her dark form in the companionway suddenly irresolute, hesitant, anxious and feminine again, blurred by twenty years of compromises. The VHF radio telephone above the chart table was nagging her. Fair was fair.

Keith had been pig-headed and patriarchal, and failed to understand her cry of despair and her need to give up being a provincial teashop proprietress and be – something else, for God's sake. A student again; good God, she'd work part-time in someone else's teashop to finance it if necessary. Anything, anything to unbind her identity from that of fruit scones. He had not understood. He had reported her to the police and exposed her to being called silly on Radio 4.

But Keith did not deserve to be left wondering whether she was drowned. She, too, had heard the news about the dead yachtsman and the busy lifeboats, filtering out through the plastic bag wrapped round the cockpit radio. She ought to tell Keith where she was. And Susan ought to know. Funny, how little she had thought of her younger child today. It was as though Susan's course had veered away from hers months ago, off into a distant teenage land, so that they had to shout and signal to one another across a void. And today she could not be bothered to shout.

The link call was quick to get through. Twisting her hair nervously in her hand, moving her shoulders uneasily, Jo sat in the soft, lurching lamplight. Three rings, cosy sounds from another planet. Then the answering machine, saying that Keith and Joanna were unable to come to the telephone. A beep. Hesitantly, she spoke.

'It's Jo. Just to say I'm OK. Reefed the boat this morning. We had – I had to stand on round Portland for safety. I'll probably get in to Torquay or somewhere in the morning. The boat's fine. I think the wind's actually down a bit—' she glanced around, startled. The wind was indeed down a bit, but she had not realized that she knew this until she heard herself saying the words. It was odd, being alone. Perhaps nobody ever really knew anything consciously until they had the need to put it into words. 'So, should be fine. 'Bye. Talk to you tomorrow.' And flatly, uncertain again of everything, she climbed back on deck and stared ahead, into the darkness.

At his desk in the Old Vicarage, Keith slept on, his head pillowed on Underhill's *Law of Trust and Trustees*. He never heard the ringing telephone, nor the message, nor the beep. But something – 'I'm OK', or 'should be fine', or just the tone of his wife's voice – got into his dreams and quietened them. He slept on rather better until he woke with a start at one thirty, saw the winking light on the telephone, played back the message and went stiffly, gratefully, to bed.

By then, the presses had rolled and thundered under London and Manchester, spinning out long stretched skeins of paper bearing Gordon's half-truths and Maeve Mahoney's rantings. Vans in the livery of *Mail* and *Mirror*, *Globe* and *Chronicle* were screeching to a halt in wet empty streets, throwing out early bundles and speeding on.

Shearwater moved fast, too. At midnight, Joanna unrolled three inches more jib to keep the boat's speed up as the wind eased. At one o'clock, she clambered on deck in her harness, undid the deep reef with cold, stiff hands and hauled more sail up. The increase in power held the boat steady and fast through the darkness, across the rhythmic, twisting waves. To keep herself awake, she steered by hand, watching the compass. Two-seven-oh – two-six-oh – two-six-five. Mustn't sleep. Mustn't. *Nessun dorma*, none shall sleep. From *Turandot*, long before it was the 1990 World Cup song. That was better: something to think about.

Alice, almost the only friend from Oxford days Joanna still saw, had summoned her to London the year before for a night at the opera. Alice worked for the Royal Opera House and got occasional pairs of tickets; her husband Andy had decided dislikes, one of which, unaccountably to both women, was Puccini. 'You'd think,' said Alice, picking up Jo in her battered blue 2 CV at Waterloo, 'that a man who could sit through *Salome* could bring himself to come and see *Turandot*. But no. Says the Chinese references in the music are patronizing and tacky. Says Puccini is naff and speaks to the deep naffery of the British public, and should not be encouraged by taxpayers' money. But it's an ill wind—' Alice braked sharply and raised an unladylike finger at a taxi driver. '– It lets me have someone new to sit next to. I thought of our nights in the gods at the New Theatre in Oxford, weeping hot salt tears over Desdemona, not to mention yummy Welsh conductors with 1960s hairdos. Only you would do. I can't sit next to most people at the opera; they're either too clever or too stupid, or flap around with the sodding score. It's lovely to see you. And those who get to peep at rehearsals tell me this Turandot is *lush*.'

Jo was always absurdly shy and flattered when Alice remembered her. Alice had got her First, Alice had struck out across

Europe alone, come home and married the gloomily fascinating Andy, a junior don at Hertford College and later London University. Alice moved in chic intellectual circles, wore huge black glasses with panache, and drove her terrible car across London like a demon. Jo, beside her, felt the full inferiority of her provincialism, her teashop life and her scuffed heels. Only the subject of Lance's stupendous GCSEs – five As, three starred, three sciences and two languages – gave Jo any confidence. Alice, however, was unconscious of Jo's sense of inferiority and of her admiration, and rattled on all the way up to the Covent Garden balcony with the enthusiastic irreverence for grand opera which had made her a good companion years ago.

'Catharsis, that's why I can't resist it. Hardly costs more than primal scream therapy, and you don't get the sore throats 'cos Gwyneth Jones does the screaming for you. I love Turandot anyway, she's a sort of primitive Chinese-Italian Andrea Dworkin. All men are rapists, you know? That aria about how she'll never submit to one of the bastards, since her ancestress got ravished and murdered – that's probably why Andy won't come. And the set, they say you won't believe it – old Peking; severed heads everywhere, fab.'

On the boat, alone, Jo closed her eyes. She could see the *Turandot* set: Chinese balconies filling the stage, intricately latticed shutters so that patterns of light shone out from behind the central pagoda. The great cloudy moon rising, serenaded by the chorus; the pagoda where Calaf, the lover, sang '*Nessun dorma*' and the hackneyed World Cup song was made suddenly fresh again. She had sat rapt, shaken more deeply than the absurd and terrible fairytale deserved, thinking of the ruthless princess and her riddles. None shall sleep . . . 'within my heart my secret lies, and what my name is none shall know . . . a l'alba vincero!' Jo sang it, under her breath. 'At dawn I shall conquer!' The opera had stirred her as one sip of brandy stirs a teetotaller, dangerously. The death of Liu the slave girl, killing herself for love, made Jo shake; the closing chorus, echoing the '*Nessun dorma*', made her weep.

To Alice, Jo's silent pallor at the end of each act was a source of not unkind amusement. 'Got you, hasn't it? How's Keith gonna keep you down on the farm now that you've seen Paree?' It was a game to her, a joke, Jo realized. Alice had never left Oxford, not really; she had gone on reading, seeing, responding to books and art and music with undergraduate passion and freshness. She and Andy, for ever broke, were for ever buying pictures with the poll-tax money and having to sell others; they thought nothing of piling their clever children on a sleeper to Venice or driving to Glasgow in their rattling car to check out the newly built Burrell gallery.

Alice had no idea of how estranged you could become from that world and those responses. She could not conceive of how commonsensical life was in Bonhurst, how prone you got to deadening everything with cups of tea and saving your empathetic tears for satellite TV reruns of *Random Harvest*.

Shaken, she even said to Alice as they left, 'I don't know, it was just that Liu reminded me of Emily.'

A shadow of puzzlement crossed Alice's face. 'Emily – oh. Yes. You were pretty close. Awful business.'

'It was why I never took finals,' Jo had said, amazed at her own broaching of the long taboo subject.

'Didn't you? God, I forgot. Amazing how little a degree matters, after all these years.' Alice breathed an exaggerated sigh. 'I don't know when anyone last asked me if I had one.'

Amazing how *much* it matters when you haven't got one, thought Joanna sourly, and suddenly the gloss and splendour was off the evening. She had thanked Alice, refused her pressing offer of a camp bed in their living room, gone home, slipped in with the sleeping Keith and lain awake – *Nessun dorma* – until it was daybreak, with no chance of conquering anything, or doing anything but chase Susan to school and open up the Bun in the Oven. And there was no mystery about her name. Mrs Gurney, that was who she was. Nice Mrs Gurney at the teashop. The solicitor's wife. With that clever son and that, er, interesting daughter.

The splendour was back now, though. The clearing sky showed stars, bright patches behind the scudding black cloud shapes, pinpoints of light like the lanterns behind the lattices of old Peking. She sang, odd words linked by humming: '*Nessun dorma ... O principessa ... a l'alba vincero! Vincero!*' At dawn I shall conquer. Calaf loomed, magnificent, but behind him Princess

Turandot even more magnificent and unmerciful. Poor Liu faded in the shadows, eternal victim of her own loving weakness. Icy strength like Turandot or doomed sweetness like Emily; no third choice for women, was there?

Did Alice say that? What cynicism. Of course there was a third choice. You could run a sodding teashop in sodding Bonhurst, and be a good mother . . .

Her own sleepy giggle woke her; that, and the flap of the unguided mainsail. Her hand had fallen off the tiller. The lights of old Peking resolved themselves into the cold, impersonal flashes of the Berry Head and Start Point lighthouses, both suddenly visible. Joanna stood up in the swaying cockpit, stretched, and reached for the caffeine tablets and her flask of tea. At dawn she would conquer Torquay.

14

The travelling depression which had brought the gales slid away with the night, to lose itself in Eastern Europe. Behind its bright sharp winds and splatters of rain came a universal grey mugginess. There was no dawn to speak of on that Wednesday, only a gradual lightening of the sky from charcoal to a dreary slate. The clammy air found its way inside Joanna's clothes and made her shiver crossly. At ten past six, looking up at the great wedding cake of the Imperial Hotel, Torquay, she rolled the jib and made a hasty, untidy stow of the mainsail.

Her feet slithered on the wet plastic of the deck. She was tired now, almost mindless as she did these familiar jobs. On the way back to the cockpit she hung out two fenders either side and fixed a mooring line to the centre cleat on each side, in case. The red and green lights on the ends of the Princess and Haldon piers were still alight at six thirty when, the pilot book open on the damp cockpit seats beside her, she steered the last few hundred yards towards Torquay harbour.

Above the harbour hung damp trees and the sleeping town, teetering on its rocky outcrops and peering round wooded crags. She saw the bridge, the crinkly red church tower, and the absurd pavilion flanked by green domes. The distant whine of a milk float and the sputtering of *Shearwater*'s engine were the only sounds to break the indifferent silence. The piers had fishing boats alongside and no crews stirring; the marina looked fairly well filled, mainly with vast powerboats registered in Jersey or Guernsey but a few masts of sailing boats tinkled metallically in the remains of the breeze. She smelt that weedy, fishy smell which land visitors think of as the smell of the sea but which to sailors is, unmistakably, the welcome smell of the shore. Gulls whirled overhead.

Tie up, tie up; she must moor the boat, somehow, anyhow, and lie down. On the outermost pontoon lay a towering, solid motor yacht, a classic gin palace, its davits and hanging dinghy arrogantly blocking her way through to the only visible vacant berth. Joanna steered slowly towards it, the port-side mooring line in her hand. As *Shearwater* came alongside, gliding in neutral, she left the helm, dashed forward, and with a clumsy lunge got her line round a solid cleat on the big white boat's stern. Stepping aboard its pristine deck, she moved forwards to brace her boat against the larger one by taking the line forward, round a gleaming chrome samson post, then back aboard the little yacht.

At rest, tied up. God knows who to. She killed the engine and, with a deep, shuddering breath, stood upright, pushed back her hair, and began the familiar task of putting proper lines out. Bow and stern, springs and shorelines, one by one they came out of the stern locker, neatly coiled in some other harbour. She worked mechanically and mindlessly, capable only of the obvious, unable to think more than a step ahead. Long ago she had fed and changed babies at dawn in just this state, her mind wiped clear by weariness.

As the distant church clock struck seven, *Shearwater* lay secure and quiet. There was still no movement aboard the flashy motor yacht; something about its bland curtained windows convinced Joanna that it was untenanted. Relieved, she swung below and kicked off her boots. Ignoring the frowsy chaos of the cabin, she blew the lamp out, drank the cold dregs of her dawn cocoa, and paid a brief visit to the heads to wipe the salt out of her skin with a cold damp flannel. There were not enough words for weary, she thought, slithering into the sleeping bag. Tired, fagged, knackered, done up; exhausted, prostrate, dead beat, swinked, whacked, jaded; dog-tired, bone-weary . . . no, never enough. Drawing her knees up, yawning helplessly, Joanna Gurney slid into oceans of unconsciousness.

Erika was the first to see the paper. Ted liked a cooked breakfast and needed to leave the house at eight. He took the *Globe*, for the fishing column and the investment pages. Her small luxury was to have the *Chronicle* delivered and to read it while she made the breakfast. Eyes widening with alarm, she read Gordon's prose with all the gratifyingly close attention he could have desired.

Startled back into reality by the acrid smell of burning bacon, Erika leapt distractedly to her feet and used a most uncharacteristic string of expletives. Ted Merriam, emerging with senatorial dignity and slicked-back hair from his morning ablutions, was shocked to find her standing there, blackened pan in hand, wisps of blonde hair over her face, cursing like a fishwife with the newspaper scattered all around her on the floor. It was not the way, he thought resentfully, that a man ought to have to start a working day. Grunting, he sat down at the table and picked up his pristine copy of the *Globe*.

Mandy came down half an hour later, leaving Alex singing 'Ol' Man River' in the shower. Anneliese was deep in the *Chronicle*, reading the fashion pages first as she always had since babyhood, and barely looked up. Mandy took the *Globe* and a glass of orange juice into her corner near the Aga, and turned, as several million other women did on Wednesdays, to Maeve Mahoney for a dose of amused exasperation.

RUM, MATRIMONY AND THE LASH: Men on boats, as every sea wife knows, are tyrants. No, hold that. Men are tyrants everywhere. So it was refreshing to hear of Mrs Joanna Gurney, the Portsmouth woman . . .

'Ooh, they might have checked!' Erika was saying to Ted at that moment, peering annoyingly over his shoulder. 'I thought they had to. She doesn't live in Portsmouth.'

. . . who finally cracked, and sailed off into the wide blue yonder with the family boat – but without her bossy lawyer husband Keith. I hope she finds the Yo-heave-ho more to her taste on the other side of the briny, and enjoys her break from living with Cap'n Bligh. Most of us just have to hack it, Ma'am – but we're behind you all the way. Why should the men get to wear the peaked hat and the parrot through life, while we girls swab the decks and – once they're sick of us –

*get made to walk the plank when he fancies a second mate – or a
third, or a fourth?*

Mandy whistled, half delighted, half afraid, visualizing Keith's
embarrassment and Alex's loyal rage. Still, Alex couldn't blame
her for this one – different paper. But thank God she hadn't told
that boy from the *Chronicle* anything he could make anything
out of. She read on. Three hundred words of laboured nauticalia
later, Maeve concluded, '*One thing is for certain – Mrs Gurney won't
be wanting a husband in every port!*'

At this, reading over Ted's shoulder, Erika giggled. It was a
brief, high, nervous giggle – she was still unhinged by the
Chronicle report – but it had offended Ted who rose, gave her
a reproachful look and stalked off majestically to work.

Mandy did not giggle but shook her head, then sipped her
juice and let the newspaper lie for a moment unheeded.

Blinking feminists, always got it wrong. Keith wouldn't say
boo to a goose. Just like Alex. These middle-class men were
a doddle, in Mandy's expert view. Very biddable and quiet
compared to the ones down her street when she was a kid,
all pigeon racing and rough sex and cutting back your housekeeping. Middle-class men were easy. Alex was a saint around
the house compared to the kind of lad she would have married
if she hadn't luckily been up the duff and out of the running at
nineteen. Keith was a woolly lamb compared to someone like
Ted Merriam, who was practically Hitler as far as Erika was
concerned. If Jo ran off on an impulse, it wasn't because Keith
bullied her. Silly cow that Mavis what's-er-name must be.

For the first time, Mandy gave a moment to wondering quite
seriously why Jo *had* done it. Mandy was not given to considering
motives; people did what they did, and you dealt with it. Half the
time she didn't know why she did things herself. That business
with having the reporter round and teasing him, for instance.
She had no idea what possessed her. Bit of fun, really. She
supposed she must have just thought Jo ran off for a bit of fun.
To shake things up a bit. She had used the 'depression' and the
'tablets' to tease Keith with, without thinking, but would she
have even known if Jo was low? She hadn't seen so much of
her lately.

Mandy twisted uneasily in her chair. Jo was a good mate. She had been the only one who ever bothered with her in the old days, before Mandy married Alex, sent Annie to Angela Merici, and was more or less accepted as a middle-class Bonhurst wife. Jo was like, well, a sister. A big sister. The sort that's more sensible than you but not always telling you off all the time. In the years after her mother had gone, small Mandy often used to imagine a big sister, someone to look out for her on the dodgy walk home from school, when the boys called names. She had never found one. Not until Jo.

So, was Joanna upset now about some stupid thing? She used to get low and worry too much about the kids, specially Susan. Mandy used to know automatically when Jo was feeling down because she let her hair go straggly. That was the cue for a coffee and – before they both gave up – a fag. And for a bit of inspirational stuff from Mandy concerning the next holiday or some gossip about the assumed sex lives of their neighbours or the latest hilarity about how Ted Merriam got waited on hand and foot by poor old Erika.

But there hadn't been much coffee and chat lately. The kids were grown up now, nothing to worry about. Susan was sixteen, for God's sake, like Anneliese, virtually another adult in Mandy's tough view of the world. Even if the Gurneys were planning to make her stay at school, in a uniform, Susan was of an age to look out for herself.

But if Joanna was in trouble then she, Mandy, ought to do something about it. She would do something about it. A brief flicker of guilt crossed her mind concerning the Bun, but Joanna seemed to like the old Bun. Enjoyed running it. Surely . . .

Mandy paused in her train of thought, looking down at the insolent tousled picture of Maeve Mahoney. *Did* Joanna like the Bun? Did she like her life? Did anyone know if anyone else really liked their life? The thought would not have tormented Mandy for long – thoughts rarely did – but its short duration was cut even shorter by a squeal from Anneliese who still had the *Chronicle*.

'Bloody hell, Mum, look at this!'

Together, they looked. All over the town, people were looking. Gordon had got his audience at last, hanging on his words. The big picture was of Joanna, cut from the award photo taken when the Chamber of Commerce had honoured the Bun in the Oven with a Councillor Tranter Memorial Plaque for Community Business. The plaque, however, was artfully cut from this picture and the word MISSING, in stencilled red capitals, was angled across the bottom. Joanna's eyes looked haunted, her smile uncertain, but then that was how you tended to look after listening to a speech from the chairman of the Bonhurst Chamber of Commerce.

Lesser pictures were dotted around in boxes and over it all was the headline 'THE MOTHER WHO RAN AWAY INTO THE STORM', and the deep-black, really quite gratifyingly thick lettering which said 'BY GORDON HAWKINGS'. Transfixed, Mandy and Anneliese read on.

As death-dealing gales lashed the South Coast yesterday, one small town held its breath. In the dainty tea-shops of quaint old Bonhurst, there was only one topic of conversation. Was Joanna Gurney alive, or had the sea taken her? And what possessed a quiet, well-liked housewife who worked part-time in a teashop ('Oh, Gawd!' said Mandy) *to leave her bewildered, innocent children* ('Innocent? Lance? Hah!' said Anneliese, who had almost managed to seduce him at her fifteenth birthday party) *and grieving husband, and deliberately to sail out into the Channel, alone and inexperienced, with a severe gale warning?*

What made her so desperate, so uncaring of her little children's pain? ('How old exactly does this plonker think they are?' said Anneliese.) *What went wrong in this woman's marriage? people were asking. Why, in cosy middle England, was she so friendless? Were neighbourly doors closed to her agony? Why could she not care any more about her home, her husband, her little job?*

'That's a bit dodgy, legally,' said the envious woman's editor of the *Globe*.

'No, it isn't,' said her deputy. 'He's only saying people were asking it. He never says it's a reasonable question, does he?'

'Mmmph. Still wouldn't fancy his chances at the Press Complaints Commission.'

I walked the stricken streets of Bonhurst yesterday to find what undercurrents in an ordinary decent English market town can lead a gentle, conventional solicitor's wife to take such a desperate flight into danger.

'Oh, Jesus!' said Mandy. 'Do you think she is all right?'

'She will be till she reads the rest,' said her daughter uncompassionately. 'Your bit, Mum.'

Mandy noticed her own picture for the first time, taken as she was opening the door to Gordon. The bastard photographer must have been behind the Leylandii hedge. She looked OK. A bit Bardot, with the wind blowing her hair forward.

'Mum, read it,' said Anneliese. 'Apart from anything else, Susan'll be down in a minute. Get your story sorted out. Or get packed and go to Katmandu. Or something.'

Mandy read on.

Perhaps the best clues to Joanna Gurney's torment come from Mandy Heron, proprietress of the chintzy, old-fashioned Bun in the Oven café which employed her. In her luxury home behind a screen of trees at the better end of town, Mrs Heron sighed and admitted that she was not surprised the struggling older woman had cut and run. 'We all get depressed,' she said. 'Life can seem meaningless at our age. It is very hard for a woman to accept ageing, and the menopause. She was once absolutely my best friend, but as the years go by . . .'

'How old,' asked Anneliese again, 'do they think you two actually are? And if they think that, how do they work out the bit about the innocent little children?' But Mandy was not listening. Stricken, she was reading, seeing herself in a distorting mirror.

Mrs Heron blames herself for not seeing how disturbed life had become for her former friend and waitress. 'I'm more executive these days,' she explained ruefully. 'Jo . . . well . . .' It is not hard to fill in the gaps. Mandy Heron, attractive and ruthless, the quintessential 1980s Essex Girl made good, flying high with her business interests; Joanna Gurney depressive and mousy, always in her friend's shadow, with her arms in the washing up, feeling at a dead end down at the dingy café they used to run together long ago.

*   *   *

It had been the 'dingy cafe' which had caused Erika to burn the bacon as she stood horrified at her kitchen counter. Mandy, whiter than her daughter had ever seen her, went on reading.

Erika Merriam, a neighbour who is running the café during Joanna's crisis, showed me the pathetic evidence of dead-end despair the lonely woman felt, dealing out scones to an uncaring clientele as she planned her last flight into the storm. 'A lot could be done with this place,' said Erika. 'But Mrs Gurney isn't very go-ahead. She won't have a microwave, though we could make a fortune doing baked potatoes, and she won't use teabags.' It was as if the missing woman had turned her back on the twentieth century, turned her face to the wall.

Outside in the street, solicitor Keith Gurney (another snatched picture, of Keith looking windswept and burdened with the carrier bags in which he transported his law books home since his briefcase was appropriated by Susan) *struggled home with food for his two anxious children, and scanned the sky. Pathetically, he grabbed my arm as I appeared, a professional man caught up in the nightmare for which none of us are prepared, the nightmare of a quiet wife's aberrant behaviour. 'Has she been found? Is she OK?' Sadly, I had no answer. A few moments later, his composure restored, the stricken husband explained more quietly that he knew what his desperate wife must be going through at sea, alone. 'Changing a sail, shortening canvas in a gale . . . you haven't time to think.'*

But for the watchers on the shore, time hung all too heavily yesterday as hour after hour, the news from the Channel grew grimmer.

Mandy put down the paper and stood up. Tears were running down her face, smudging the sooty mascara she always put on as soon as she got up. She pulled her sleeve across her eyes, making things worse. 'Alex,' she said. 'Get Alex. I never said a word of it. We've got to sue.'

Alex, summoned, read it rapidly and shook his head. 'Never get anywhere,' he said. 'Two, three years, endless time and money, all to prove you never said something that doesn't damage you anyway. Hopeless. Jo could sue for being called a dead-end waitress, but I bet she won't. The only one I'd take a flier on is Keith. He could have a case over the Captain Bligh piece.'

'But Jo's gonna think – oh God, Alex, help me, I'm really upset. I never thought – I mean I never said *anything* to the boy.'

'You had him in the house. Without witnesses, and with his notebook.'

'But – hey, I even took his notebook off him, that's how much I wasn't helping.'

'You did *what*?'

'I took it off him. He was fishing for stuff about Jo, pretending he was interested in the café, so I whipped it into my pocket. Confiscated it. Like at school.'

'And?'

'Well, I straightened his tie and made him a sandwich. Sort of like a little boy. He stood there, you could see he felt caught out. It was a bit of fun.' She clasped her fists to her brow and wailed, wordlessly.

'I suppose,' said Alex, frowning, 'he could make a case against you for assault and theft.' He looked at his wife with affectionate exasperation. 'Knowing your idea of a bit of fun, probably sexual harassment by innuendo as well. Drop it, Mandy. It's chip wrappings. It's up to Jo and Keith whether they go to the Press Complaints Commission.'

'And that's the other thing,' cried Mandy, now really upset, pretty face distorted, tears in her usually untroubled baby-blue eyes, pacing the kitchen more out of control than Alex had ever seen her. 'With the picture and all that suicide stuff and the wind – where *is* Joanna? Is she all right? She could be bloody drowning, and we all sit here—'

Alex's warning gesture came just too late. Behind her, framed in the doorway, was Susan. Mandy turned, aghast and tearstained. The girl looked at her, expressionless.

'Can I see the papers?' she asked. 'Please?'

15

Port Meadow spread around her. Underfoot it was spongy between the hard tussocks, the sleek grass wet from the summer rains. It was dark, and the death bells were ringing. Dully, she looked towards the door with the Chinese symbols, waiting for Gabriel.

But when the door swung open, there was nobody there except Lance, making too much noise with his big boy's feet as usual, and she said, 'Ssh! Lance! You'll wake Emily. She's been sailing all night, she needs her rest.' There was comfort in that: of course Emily was only asleep. She was tired. But Lance kept clumping – on the roof now – and tapping, so that it seemed Emily might wake and something terrible happen. He was shouting, too. 'Er, ahoy! I say! Anyone there?' Perhaps he was looking for Gabriel who was in the fuel can all the time, complaining about the smell of diesel. What else could you expect in a fuel can?

The tapping became more insistent, dragging Joanna up long inclines of sleep. It was real tapping now, on the main hatch. Through the cabin windows she could see deck shoes and nubbly expensive socks. Sitting up, sweaty and creased in her T-shirt, she hopped awkwardly towards the hatch like a contestant in a sack race, with her sleeping bag clutched round her waist. Holding it up with one hand, she pushed the hatch open with another and peered through a curtain of sticky, salty dark hair at an immaculate young man dressed as if for Henley Regatta in white duck trousers, a monogrammed blazer, white open shirt and butter-coloured hair cut in public-school style with short back and sides and a long forelock which curled over his eyes as he bent to peer into the gloom of the cabin.

'I say, I'm terribly sorry, my skipper asked me to check who was here.'

'I came in very early. What's the time now?'

'Ten to eleven. Gosh, it was windy out there last night. Did you come far?'

'From Portsmouth.'

'Gosh, rough, I should think. The thing is, he doesn't usually like people mooring alongside.'

'Well,' said Joanna, feeling her scattered sleepy wits gathering fiercely around her again. 'He shouldn't moor up bang in the fairway so that his davits stop other people getting through to the other visitors' berths.'

'Gosh, well, that was me actually. Skipper went off in a hurry on Monday night, big business deal, we were late because of the wind. Only he can't drive, so I had to moor up and drive him, and it was dark. I thought the marina bods would sort it out, actually. Thing is, I can't move the boat now because he's got a satellite conference call, and he might lose the signal, so—'

'You want me to move? You're going out now?'

'Well, if it's no trouble. We're not going out until tomorrow, bit of a do in the town tonight, speeches to local businessmen, then we're off to Plymouth in the morning, but he really doesn't like—'

'All the other big boats on the outside visitors' pontoons have boats rafted outside them. It's what everyone does when harbours are full. I bet if I ask the marina they'll tell me to stay here.'

'Yes, but—'

'I haven't got any diesel left anyway. And you're still blocking the way to the only empty berth. And you say you can't move because your boss is working on board. I've got shorelines out, I'm doing no harm to anyone, I've slept precisely three and a half hours, and I want a shower. I'll be gone before you are anyway. So, no. Sorry. Maybe later.' Joanna smiled to soften her refusal.

The young man, whose name was Guy Pastern-Hopkins, shifted uneasily. This personal secretary job had sounded so attractive, perfect for a new, third-class graduate: learning about big business, yachting every weekend, meeting models ... Increasingly, though, the diplomatic demands of the role were wearing him down. His father, a bluff Cambridge veterinarian who thought the whole thing hilarious, said that he supposed Guy had been hired to be the acceptable face of Eddie McArthur but that, if so, it was as big a waste of money as putting a pink ribbon on a warthog. Sometimes, miserably, Guy thought that was not a bad description. He could have got a job as an MP's personal assistant, as several of his college friends had done. At least MPs had to *pretend* to be nice. His employer didn't.

'I don't normally say,' he attempted now, 'but my boss is actually Eddie McArthur'.

'Who?' Joanna was bluffing now. Even an intermittent, casual, provincial follower of the news knew who Eddie McArthur was. From frozen food to teenage fashion, from privatized railways to cable TV, he had interests in everything. He owned one newspaper outright – the *Chronicle* – and was rumoured to be surreptitiously collecting shares in two far more august titles. When Robert Maxwell died, Eddie McArthur bought great swathes of his empire (and, eerily, put on two stone in two months). He was reluctantly accepted by the establishment, and alternately bullied and flattered politicians. Sometimes he would fly them halfway round the world in his private jets only to insult them roundly on arrival. He gave parties of unspeakable lavishness and made only ten-minute appearances at them himself. He never gave interviews, but tales of his thin, nervy, cowed wife and sullen daughters filtered out into gossip columns from behind the electronic security gates of his mansion in Northamptonshire. Every financial journalist dreamed of finding the weak point in McArthur's armour, every young Fraud Squad officer of being the one to prove him a crook. But nobody had. He continued to kick his way through the establishment, to hire green graduate secretaries and drive them to nervous breakdowns, and to sate the sexual appetites thrown off by his intense, spinning egomaniacal energy.

Joanna was impressed. In the morning she had only focused on the mooring points of the big boat alongside, treating it as a wharf and seeing the rest as a vague irrelevant haze. Now she saw it whole: a great muscular wedge of a powerboat, forty feet long and almost as high with its flying bridge and forest of antennae. The name *Privateer* was gilded onto its stern, and she vaguely remembered reading that McArthur favoured a relatively small motor yacht so that he could come and go in yachting harbours without special arrangements. He had a number of coastal businesses. So this, she supposed, was the nearest any unconnected member of the public could get to the legendary tycoon: they lay only millimetres of fibreglass apart. She, in her battered family boat, was closer now than if they were neighbours in Egg Terrace.

An odd business, yachting. Some friends from Southampton had once found themselves anchored in a Scottish loch next to Princess Anne and Commander Tim Lawrence, and they had entangled their anchor buoy ropes and enjoyed an affable chat from their respective dinghies. On any weekend you might find yourself, an ordinary family boat, sandwiched between an evangelical prayer cruise full of chanting Dutchmen, a battered old fishing boat full of waterborne New Age travellers, a tycoon or two, and a TV personality having a weekend with someone else's wife. It was a very mixed society, boating. The thought had often cheered her up. But Eddie McArthur was something else again.

Guy was watching her. 'So, um, you see, there's the security aspect – there isn't anyone in the marina office, otherwise I'd—'

'Bollocks,' said Joanna. 'I'm not an assassin.' She felt a little light-headed, very hungry, and enjoyably stroppy. 'It's Mr McArthur's fault for being in the way. If he wants me to move he can come and ask me. And get out of the way to that empty berth. If he's a gentleman he might help me get some diesel.' She smiled at Guy, a smile which made him for a moment wistfully wish he was on her side, and blotted him out by firmly pushing the hatch shut.

Below decks, she dressed quickly in the same fetid clothes as yesterday, pulled out a clean cotton sweater and jeans from her bag, put them in a red canvas holdall and added a washbag, shampoo and towel and a pocketful of change for breakfast and the telephone. She hurried. If she was off the boat, they would hardly dare tow it away. Anyway, she doubted they had the manpower; she had read in some magazine – with much sexual innuendo – that in his summer tours McArthur whizzed around the coast with only a male secretary and the current mistress, finding his relaxation in driving his boat himself and summoning cleaners, caterers and the maintenance engineer to whatever harbour he was in by mobile telephone. If there had been crew, she reasoned, they would have been sent instead of the ineffective Guy. And they would have moored the boat properly in the first place. So battered blue *Shearwater* could lie alongside in peace for an hour or two. It would be a good story to tell Mandy. Mandy loved the idea of raunchy tycoons on big yachts. On the one occasion when the Gurneys had unsuccessfully taken her sailing, she had spent all her time at sea shivering in distaste in one corner of the cockpit, and in harbour had stared longingly at the biggest, most vulgar speedboats in sight. Mandy. The thought brought back home, Bonhurst High Street, Keith, the Bun in the Oven, Zoë, the milk to collect . . .

Joanna clambered out, putting it all from her mind like a puzzle too hard to solve. She locked the hatch and climbed across the extreme bow of *Privateer*, as politeness dictated, away from any accidental view into the cabins. Landing on the pontoon with a light bounce, she walked quickly up towards the office and the showers, her sea legs making her sway a little on the unmoving surface. Before anything, she must shower away the salt, the sweat, and the weariness. Then face the day. Ring Keith. Decide what to do. Somewhere, the reasonable and responsible part of her knew exactly what to do. Go home. But that part was shrinking and weakening. Other things in her were jostling for attention, and the sensation was odd, uncomfortable, but strangely exhilarating.

Keith, surrounded by newspapers, was in the office with Alex and a hovering, fascinated Gus. When traduced by newspapers, most lay people get over the shock by ringing their lawyers to say 'Sue the bastards!' The lawyer then bears the brunt of the hysterical complaining, and generally – if he or she is a calm, responsible, middling sort of lawyer – talks the traduced one out of it. Keith and Alex had no such outlet, being lawyers themselves. Made helpless by their own knowledge and caution, they raged.

In Alex's half of the cosy, untidy, dark-beamed office the two men sat together on chairs from which they had swept a muddle of documents. Alex, his customary languor kindled into animation, his greying hair ruffled above his square, handsome face, held the *Globe* in his fist as though he was planning to swat flies with it. Keith, his shirt untucked at the back, his tie lying at his feet like a discarded snakeskin, was resting his feet on the *Law of Tort* and staring at his wife's 'MISSING' picture in the *Chronicle*. The two men were communing more closely than they had at any time since Alex's announcement that he was leaving the practice to work for the Badstream Delauney property consortium.

Gus, who was pretending to tidy a shelf near the open door, thought that for the first time he could see how these two men had come to be partners in the first place. They had been at law school together, he knew, and gone straight into partnership – just like he and his fiancée Tiny meant to, one day – but for the past two years, since Alex started planning to sell out and work for Badstream, Gus had hardly ever seen them have a conversation that was not about work. They had gone all polite and formal. Now they were sitting together like friends. Keith looked ten years younger, far less stiff. Aimée, who had been equally agog in the doorway of her neat cubicle between the main offices, was unwillingly absent, having been despatched to the Bun for coffee and Danish pastries when Alex divined that Keith had not eaten since the failed cheese sandwich of Tuesday morning.

'It isn't the Captain Bligh stuff, I can take a joke,' Keith was saying.

'It's appalling,' said Alex warmly. 'Unfounded, mischievous extrapolation, no attempt made to speak to you, the whole thing based on a very skimpy agency report. At least a case for the Press Complaints Commission. You're *named*. And named as a solicitor.'

'No, it isn't that,' protested Keith, although in truth he felt warm towards his partner for caring. It took the burden of personal outrage off him and enabled him to concentrate on Gordon's contribution to public misinformation.

'It's Jo. She's being made out as a suicidal dead-end meno-pausal bad mother . . . Oh Jesus, Alex, what's she going to do? I started all this. Now the whole town's out there reading it.'

'She'll understand, I'm sure . . .'

'And Susan. Alex, I'm sorry you're landed with Susan. She rang up, you know. She says she won't come home, and she won't go to school. Said we'd made a mess of everything.'

'I know. Don't worry,' said Alex, who had heard Susan say a great deal more besides. 'She can stay with us. Give Mandy something to think about. I'm really sorry about Mandy. I saw the reporter, I should have thrown him out. But she swears she never said any of that. It didn't sound like her anyway.'

A silence followed. 'Yeah,' said Keith, only because it was growing into an awkward one. 'No, I'm sure she didn't.' He swivelled his chair a few degrees away from Alex and fiddled with a box of paperclips. There had been something a little too formal in his tone. Alex leaned forward and shaded his eyes with a hand, not looking at Keith either.

'Keith,' he said. 'I think she was crying. All these years, I've never seen Mandy cry.'

Still Keith said nothing.

Alex went on, 'I know you're not always so keen on Mandy, but she really, really is upset. She's genuinely very fond of Joanna. Keith . . .'

Gus, who had stood very still near the door, sidled out. With rare tact, he intercepted Aimée on the stairs and diverted her and the coffee into Keith's empty office. As he looked back, he saw the two men, both sitting as still as statues, not looking into one another's eyes.

The shower was hot and powerful, the relief of having clean hair and skin almost intoxicating. Joanna walked out into the quiet grey morning and smiled: at the spiky palms, the seagulls perched on the traffic lights, the pavilion and the seafront theatre. The moment was good. Moreover, in the marina office, the holiday-relief boy who took her berthing fee was not particularly interested in which boat she lay alongside. Displaying a smooth economy with the truth that rather surprised herself, Joanna had merely said that she was tied up to a motor yacht which was definitely not going out until morning; she had a hunch that if she said *Privateer* she would be forced to move immediately. Even the dumbest, most bored student temp would be afraid that annoying Eddie McArthur could lead to trouble. He might buy your boss's business and close it down out of sheer pique.

But she had got away with it. That, and the shower, and the deep inexpressible pleasure of landfall which still hung around her like incense made Joanna enter the telephone box in her clean warm clothes almost purring with contentment. All she wanted was breakfast and a quiet mindless browse through some undemanding newspaper; and that she would have, once she had let Keith know she was safe. That she must do. All these years of motherhood had taught her that the prime duty of the absent is to signal their safety, like satellites bleeping dutifully once per orbit.

Her heart, however, started to hammer as she dialled. She put the telephone down again, and rested her head against the cold glass. Hunger and apprehension suddenly made her dizzy and dispelled the cloud of euphoria. Since Monday's row, she had only spoken to the answering machine, twice. All she knew for certain was that Keith had somehow reported her defection to the authorities, in terms which made the review of the papers on Radio 4 speak of 'concern at her inexperience'. She had no idea in what spirit Keith had made his report. Concerned, or revengeful? Piqued and spiteful, or just untrusting of her 'inexperience'? One way meant he didn't think much of her behaviour, the other that he doubted her competence. Or sanity.

She knew Keith, had lived seventeen years beside him, borne his children. But now she could not call up his face or voice or anything about him other than his wronged husbandly status and the fact that he had gone to the police. Must have done. Unlike Mandy, who adored it, Joanna had always hated the word 'husband'. It stifled her. Keith himself was not stifling, far from it; but the word, the concept, was. Her mother had always said 'I must ask My Husband' in a voice of awful doom. Was she ringing an angry husband, a worried one, an uncomprehending one who thought she was going off her head? Would he, could he, somehow set in motion forces to capture her and counsel her, to wrap her in therapy and medicines and sit her in a room with a hissing gas fire as the college psychiatrist once did, years ago after the Port Meadow night? Well, if so, she wouldn't speak. That was her defence. Silence. Just like before. Say nothing, because nobody would understand.

Joanna's hand was damp on the receiver now. She wiped her hand on her cotton sweater and adjured herself to get a grip. She was not a troubled twenty-year old but a mother and business-woman pushing forty. Nobody could make her go to any doctor.

Maybe Keith would accept her flight as an aberration, hardly speak of it, and expect her to come home as if nothing had happened. Maybe they would sit down to supper tonight comfort-ably, go to bed after *News at Ten* and get up at seven thirty – checking the post hopefully for Lance's cryptic postcards – and make ready for another day. A day in the Bun, shopping on the way home; an evening's desultory chat in front of the television and a couple of small battles with Susan (must keep a united front, keep her nose down to work, get those A levels). And so to bed again, each reading on their own side, exchanging a friendly kiss before sleep.

Then there would be the Friday rush to get the café accounts done and Saturday orders ready for Erika; and down to the boat for a weekend pottering around the Solent creeks. Or a yacht club rally, with drinks on the biggest boat and a lot of chat about school fees and loose covers and how clever Edward and Hermione were to think of using a chicken brick in the boat oven, saves all that *mess*.

Maybe Keith expected, quite reasonably, that she would come back to all that with nothing changed at all. A settled, pushing-forty, middle-class, routine family life. The sort of life that if you were terminally ill, or unemployed and homeless, or bereaved, or a Middle East hostage would seem like a dream of comfort and freedom.

The kind of life that, from inside, could make you feel as if you *were* a hostage.

Only you couldn't complain or petition for release because you knew that in a dangerous and unfair world you were one of the lucky ones. So you worked your socks off collecting jumble and holding bazaars for Somalia and Bosnia, for Save the Children and cystic fibrosis research. And you still felt guilty. And even guiltier if, suddenly, seeing in the corner of some news film the spiky mountains of northern Iraq or the icy inlets of the Falklands, you forgot the sombre story you were meant to be concentrating on and longed to be on those distant mountains or frosty strands. Anywhere, as long as you could see the sun rise over new horizons and walk under a burden no heavier than the day's needs.

Then you would be overcome by shame and common sense, and blush from the neck of your warm Husky jacket to the roots of your discreetly streaked hair. Or, if you were really daring, you thought, 'Well, goodness, we do need a change, I wonder whether the holiday budget would stretch to a little adventure this year instead of dear old Benodet?' And then you qualified it: 'But of course the children do adore Brittany, and it's so good for their French, and the ferries are very reasonable, and the men love their golf . . .'

And you never changed a thing, in the end, but stayed on your rails. Mostly your husband carried on beside you; sometimes he didn't. Men seemed to have a lower tolerance of these decorous, dull provincial lives than women. They broke out regularly, even if they did rather lack imagination in the escape route they took, via the yellow brick road to bimboland. But with or without them, you the woman were always there: a rock, a pillar of the community.

Unless you suddenly blew a gasket, started shoplifting like Meriel Saunders, took to drink, got involved in a cult, or mutinously ran away to sea.

And then what became of you?

Not really wanting to know, Joanna at the third attempt managed with shaking fingers to dial Keith's office number, and put a pound in the box. Gus was in Keith's office, keeping out of the way, when the telephone rang. Motioning Aimée to her own desk, he picked it up. 'Oh, yes, great, Mrs G. I'll get him.' He put down the receiver carefully, as though it was made of glass, and walked past Aimée's hutch to the door of the office opposite. 'It's Mrs Gurney. For you,' he said. And Keith, without a word, stood up and walked stiffly through to his own office, closing the door behind him.

Joanna heard Keith's footsteps, moving across the boards of

the lobby outside Aimée's cubicle; the door closing; the footsteps soften and slow as he reached the carpet by the desk, and at last his breath.

'Jo? Joanna? Are you all right?'

'Yes, of course. I'm in Torquay. The marina. The wind's right down. Keith, I—'

'No, Jo, listen. Before anything else, I'm sorry. I wasn't sure what to do. I went to the police station. I should have gone to the coastguard, or just waited. Some little bastard of a reporter got told somehow. It just caught their eye, that's all. I'm sorry.'

Suffused with relief, hearing the old, boyish friend and confidant Keith instead of the looming problematical Husband of her fears, Joanna laughed and leaned back against the glass wall of the kiosk, grinning with relief. It was only Keith.

'Oh, Keith, don't worry. It's only a one-day wonder. I lost my rag, that's all. All we have to do is tell people the newspaper stuff was made up and that I was always supposed to take the boat to Torquay to get – I dunno, sea miles for the Yachtmaster certificate or something. They'll have forgotten it by now – it's only one day.'

There was a silence. Joanna looked out at the famous Torquay palm trees, gloomy against the grey sky. At last Keith spoke.

'You haven't seen the *Chronicle* and the *Globe*? Today's?'

'No. I just woke up, I'm only just about to have breakfast. Why?'

Keith's voice changed. 'Jo, I'm on my way. See you in Torquay. Two, three hours. OK?'

'I don't understand. The *Chronicle*?'

'No, no, I shouldn't have said anything. Stay put, I'm coming. Don't read them. I'll explain everything. I've talked it out with Alex.'

'Alex? What's Alex got to do with it?'

'Susan's staying with Anneliese. I've said she needn't go to school until the fuss has died down a bit.'

'Until what has? Keith, she was due back on Tuesday and you know how Mrs MacEvoy is.' The line bleeped.

'Yes, but – oh, Jo, look, we can't talk about this on the telephone. See you early afternoon. I'm leaving now, straightaway. And I do—'

She had not been watching the money tick away. Her pound ran out, and the line fuzzed and died. He had said, 'I do . . .' Do what? Do love you, miss you? Do wish you hadn't done it? Do need to be back tonight in time for the Law Society regional meeting? Do worry about asking Erika to hold the fort?

Slowly, Joanna walked out of the telephone box into the moist air and crossed the road to the newsagent next to the café on which she had set her sights. Within a minute she and her newspapers were safely installed in the window of the café, with a fried breakfast ordered.

Within three minutes she had moved to the very back of the café and a table invisible from the street, and was gazing disbelievingly at her own monochrome, haunted, 'MISSING' face. It was testimony to her hunger that, automatically and without tasting it, she ate her way through bacon, two fried eggs, a sausage, a round of black pudding and three triangles of leathery toast while she read. After the third time through the *Chronicle*'s account of her life and eagerly anticipated death at sea, she stood up, paid the waitress at the counter. She kept her head down and her hair hastily scraped back behind her ears to look as different from the photograph as possible. Burning with angry shame, she stepped out into the watery sunlight of noon and walked back down the pontoons to where, behind the absurd, towering bridge of *Privateer*, her *Shearwater*'s mast gleamed and rattled its halyards in the breeze.

Edward Warren McArthur was not in a good mood. His swoops around the coast were most satisfying when they were uninterrupted. Athough most of his time was spent in the usual ruck of haggling meetings with business-school suits and tiresome regulators, these maritime excursions enabled him to play the role he preferred, of old-fashioned merchant prince or Hollywood mogul. He loved to anchor in a bay, speed ashore in the launch, descend unexpectedly on one of his coastal companies, terrify the managers with his legendary black brows and vanish off to sea in a vapour trail of white foam.

To be penned by the gale into a public marina and then spend a scheduled, place-carded evening in the Imperial Hotel addressing West Country businessmen and councillors was a vexatious interruption to these pleasures. Since the West Country was his next target area, however, he needed to press a few hands extra hard in advance of some planning applications. His own staff would do the detail, but only a charismatic, almost archangelic descent by himself would have the necessary impact. He could already almost hear his own voice, booming out inane courtesies, insulting nobody for once, using his power to flirt instead of terrify. It bored him in advance.

Moreover, his latest mistress Therèse, a sleek Parisienne, had refused to come back to Torquay late last night after a furious row over his insistence on sleeping aboard after his meeting in Exeter. 'Eddie, *je t'adore*,' she had said. 'But not zis boating. *C'est affreux*. And zese marinas are very *petit-bourgeois*, it is a horror. The rough water make me sick when you go slow, and bump when you go fast. I will stay wiz you in a hotel. Or you come and visit me. *Au revoir.*' He had kissed her hand with all the ironic gallantry at his command, but inwardly seethed with irritation.

Eddie liked women. Needed at least one in the bed every night. His liking was strictly limited: he didn't like them when they argued or cried, hated having to meet them in a business setting, couldn't abide the grating conversation of his squeaky wife and daughters. He just liked popsies. Even as he kissed Thérèse's white hand, he decided to return to the commercial sector. He would hire a girl for this trip. No, two girls. It was a long time since he had that sort of expert attention. To hell with style and class. Thérèse had those, and they only led to trouble.

The escort agency had been, as ever, complaisant when telephoned by Guy at 11 p.m., but even they could not get girls from London to Torquay instantaneously. So he had slept alone and badly. The energy Thérèse should have dissipated was still crackling and fizzing through his dreams until dawn; then he woke to find some scruffy blue sailing boat tied to the gleaming flanks of *Privateer*.

He had told the elegant but unsatisfactory Guy to get the thing moved, but the moron had come back saying that he couldn't unless he could move *Privateer* forward along the pontoon to make space for it to get by. 'Later,' snapped McArthur. 'I've got calls to make. If you can't moor up properly in the first place, I'm not having you fannying about while I'm busy.' Guy did not dare point out that he had had to make the big boat fast in the dark and the gale while being shouted at, and then drive his employer and the sulky Thérèse to Exeter through the driving rain. Nobody ever pointed out things like this to Eddie McArthur. Instead they merely rose, as he liked to put it, to his high standards, and learned from the experience. He was doing them a great favour by bullying them.

And what gratitude did he get? Emerging now onto his flying bridge after an hour's curt telephoning, he saw to his fury that the shabby blue boat was still there, with a chic, poised blonde girl sitting on its roof as if she was waiting for somebody. 'Hoy!' he bawled. 'You have to move that boat! Can't you read?' The girl was, indeed, only inches from the large red sign 'NO MOORING

ALONGSIDE' which Guy had rather belatedly remembered to put up.

'It's not my boat, I'm afraid,' said the girl, looking up at the squat figure in sunglasses and peaked hat without recognition. 'I'm waiting for the owner.' She looked past him. 'I think she's coming now.'

Eddie turned. There were three women coming down the pontoon: two girls side by side, who by their immaculate big-haired, tight-legginged presentation could only be deliveries from the escort agency. Ahead of them was an older woman, dark and striking in careless cotton clothes, who walked rapidly with her head down. She had just overtaken the sweating Guy, who was staggering under the combined weight of two mock-Gucci holdalls in one hand and a five-gallon can of diesel in the other. Brief satisfaction flickered across Eddie's face. Guy could stow the tarts below, then move the blue boat, then go away while he looked over the girls. Raising a hand and cocking a thick black eyebrow in a practised satanic smile, he called down to them, 'Ah! Good afternoon!'

They giggled and waved. The dark woman was now, to his fresh irritation, climbing across the bow of *Privateer* as if it was some ordinary yacht in the middle of a Bank Holiday trot of family boats. She was carrying the marina's coil of hose, so her progress was impeded as she unrolled it, the end squirting water across his deck. At last she stepped onto her own boat whose mast jerked and swayed as her weight came on the side deck. Still carrying the spurting hose, she stopped dead, staring at the blonde in the cockpit.

They made a striking contrast in female types. The dark woman was wild-haired, flushed, strong-looking, dressed in canvas and cotton; the blonde immaculately bobbed and disdainfully dainty, the concave curl of her hair at the sides artfully arranged to show her earrings. She was made-up, red-taloned, chic in leather trousers and a loose but elegant green jacket. The dishevelled woman did not seem pleased to see the other one. From his high bridge Eddie could hear only snatches of their conversation, but something made him stay.

'. . . Virginia Douglas, Dinny Douglas . . . the *Chronicle* . . . very interested in your story . . . opportunity to put your side . . . authorized to offer . . .'

Eddie eased himself down the companionway steps as rapidly as his bulk would allow and slid open the window on the main wheelhouse deck below. This brought the conversation much closer. It was not every day that a proprietor got to eavesdrop on one of his own reporters at work. With a chequebook, too, by the sound of it. He was not very pleased with the *Chronicle* right now: too many libel payouts, slipping circulation, a general sense of demoralized freewheeling. The editor was a thug, which ordinarily would not have bothered Eddie in the slightest. He employed many thugs, although for his immediate entourage he preferred something a bit more Oxbridge, like Guy. The trouble was that he suspected this editor of being an incompetent thug. Why was this girl offering money to some tiresome yachtswoman, not even a pretty one?

The dark woman didn't seem co-operative. He craned to listen.

'. . . how you have the nerve . . . pack of lies . . . wouldn't talk to you lot for a million quid. Get off my boat. Go. Now! I mean it.'

'Mrs Gurney,' said Dinny, 'I do think you should reconsider. This is your chance to tell your story. If some errors have been printed, what better—'

'Go away.'

'It could help a lot of other women—'

Something moved, fast and shining, and there was a scream. Investigative chequebook journalism really works much better, thought Eddie with a chuckle of glee, if you first make sure your subject is not holding a running hose. The dark woman really did have an excellent aim and knew just where to put her finger over the nozzle to transform the tap's trickle into a thin, powerful stream. He watched as his distant employee first tried to fend off the water, then turned and ran, slipping, to the foredeck and swung herself across to *Privateer*. Careless of his territorial rights, the dark woman kept the water coming. Once or twice the blonde stopped, turned, and opened her mouth as if to remonstrate, but the cold water was playing on her face and she spluttered uselessly.

Eddie McArthur, thrice divorced, permanently angry, bored with toadies and intolerant of anyone who did not toady, had very few real pleasures any more. Sex was merely a need, business no more than an itch; the only times he really laughed were at private moments in his private cinema, watching slapstick. Chaplin, Laurel and Hardy, the Keystone Cops – these touched a depth in him that nothing else could reach. This furious woman with her hose, routing the chic spluttering journalist, made him laugh like that now, alone in his gleaming wheelhouse. He sat back on his pastel leather bench and his laughter rose high, cackling, whooping, choking.

Dinny Douglas heard it from the pontoon where she knelt doubled up, gasping and dripping and seeing for the first time with horror the name *Privateer* with its connotations of – oh God, oh God, oh proprietor, earthly god. Suppose he was on board? Gathering her soaking jacket around her, she fled up the pontoon.

Joanna, shocked at herself, reached mechanically to unscrew the top of her water tank and put the hose to its proper purpose. She heard the laughter as if from a long way off. Her hand was shaking. Perhaps she was mad, after all. Perhaps it was her own maniacal laughter she could hear.

Guy and the escort agency girls heard it from the cabin.

'Here,' said the younger of them nervously. 'He's not a loonie, is he?'

'No, no,' said Guy, hating his job even more than usual. The girl was very pretty, couldn't be older than his little sister, seventeen or eighteen, nothing like a tart. 'I'll mix you ladies a drink, and then we'll see about lunch.' He left them in the main saloon and went forward to the galley, his broad oarsman's shoulders in the blue blazer momentarily filling the narrow doorway.

'Nice, he is,' said the younger girl approvingly. 'I bags him, you can have the loonie.'

Her colleague, Marie, who had been on *Privateer* before, clucked in irritation at this naivety.

'He's the *staff*,' she said condescendingly. 'He doesn't get a sniff. No chance. You and me, Della, we are here to keep his Lordship happy. Both of us.'

Della stared at her, appalled. 'What, one after the other?'

'*No*,' said Marie, wishing the agency would not send out these new girls on special jobs. She normally went out on doubles, business doubles, with Inge, who knew her stuff. 'Together. You know. We do an act, fake it. He watches, takes pictures, joins in, or whatever he wants.'

'What, undressed? Wiv another woman? That's disgusting! I never done that!'

Guy came back with two brandy and gingers. Della appealed to him.

'She's having me on, in't she? She says we're both here for the boss, the bloke, Eddie? Three up? That's not right, is it?'

Guy squirmed, helpless. 'Well, he's very hospitable, and of course looking forward very much to seeing you both. I'm sure you'll have a super time.'

'Can I go on deck?' asked Della balefully. 'Think this one over?'

'I'll show you. This way,' said Guy. 'Got a small job to do myself.' He led her up the steps through the double door to the wide stern deck with its white leather chairs and awning. His diesel can stood incongruously on the floor.

'Just a sec.' He hefted it – nice muscly arms, thought Della, and ever so polite – and climbed over the rail to ease it down into Joanna's humbler cockpit. 'I say, *Shearwater* – I don't know your name – I brought you some diesel. Can I take that hose back for you, if you're finished? Then if you want a hand moving . . .'

Joanna, still numb but grateful for practical diversion, accepted his help with the hose, knelt to fill the diesel tank, and gave him back the empty jerrycan. 'Thanks. I will move. I may go out later anyway.'

'Are you all alone on that big boat?' asked Della. 'That's amazing. On holiday?'

'No,' said Joanna. 'I'm just – taking it somewhere.'

'I used to do yacht deliveries,' said Guy. 'That's how I met Mr McArthur, in the vac. He offered me a job as his secretary. I thought it'd be a terrific way to learn about business.'

'And is it?' asked Joanna politely.

'Funny business, more like,' said Della, less politely. 'Gets sent out to collect two of us girls at once, don't you, Guy, mate?'

'Delighted to meet you, Mrs Gurney,' said Eddie McArthur, reappearing on the stern deck with a folded-back copy of the *Chronicle* in his hand. He had fetched it from the pile Guy had dutifully put on board at dawn, because he was curious to know what the soaked reporter had been chasing. Since women had been running out on him with more or less violence and eccentricity ever since he was fourteen, sometimes cutting up his trousers, once setting fire to his car, he could not see much interest in one who merely sailed away. The story seemed to him feeble, gutless and overdramatized – all the things he most disliked about his newspaper. The thug would really have to go.

Meanwhile, there was this woman. He could bait her a little. Get her story. Phone the newsdesk, scoop his own staff, underline their incompetence, sack the thug. Eddie McArthur – who had actually, when he was up on the bridge laughing till the tears came, looked quite appealing, had anyone been there to see such a rare sight – now pasted on what he mistakenly thought to be an attractive smile and aimed it at her. 'A windy night you sailed through. Gave our readers quite a scare. Perhaps you would join us for lunch?'

Joanna felt the day running out of control. These things did not happen to her. She sailed decorously, with Keith and sometimes the children, had family evenings playing poker in the cabin and long bracing walks on cliffs. She was the kind of sea wife who met other nice couples on nice boats, and drank from wine boxes with them. The sea itself was the only adventure; otherwise, their sort of cruising was a homely pursuit. Why should it be that the mere absence of Keith plunged her into a chaotic world of storm survival, tabloid chases and hose attacks? Why was she suddenly involved with a Jilly Cooper cast of sultry call girls, demon-king tycoons and twits in blazers? Was there some magical quality in husbands that kept these things from happening to you?

Or was it just Torquay? Keith had always said that Torquay was too full of the ghosts of Edwardian swells and chorus girls for his liking, and give him Brixham any day, which at least smelt healthily of fishing nets. She should have gone to Brixham. She *would* go to Brixham. Right now.

'I'm sorry, I have to leave,' she said firmly. 'If you could throw me my shorelines, er, Guy?'

'Dear lady,' said Eddie, fiddling with his little black moustache and unconsciously strengthening her conviction that she had stumbled into a poor melodrama, 'you must at least do me the honour . . .'

Joanna could think of many things to say. She could have pointed out that this suddenly pressing host had been trying to get rid of her all morning, and none too politely; or that she did not feel equal to lunching with two overdressed girls, a caricature of an upper-class twit and a press baron, not in her diesel-stained canvas trousers. Or just that she had a need to go out to sea, alone, to think over certain problems related to the fact that his pet newspaper had just knocked askew her relationship with husband, best friend, teashop, neighbours, and self.

Instead, she said, 'No, I'm awfully sorry. I have to sail to – er – Brixham,' and took a shoreline from the obedient Guy. The other one could be slipped easily from the bow. She did that, then came back to the cockpit, started the engine, and began gathering in the other lines with the concentration of a child learning cat's cradle. She did not look up at the row of watchers: Marie interested, Eddie McArthur growing red in the face, Guy composing his face nervously into an expression which would neither breach his code of manners towards a lady nor enrage his employer; and next to him Della, with an unfathomable look on her face and a fierce grip on the rail.

'So, er, thanks. 'Bye, then,' said Joanna, bending to the gearstick and still not looking up. *Shearwater* edged forward, her fenders bumping against the big boat.

'Have a nice trip,' said Della, provokingly. 'Wish I was on *your* boat.'

Grateful for a direction in which to exercise unquestioned authority, McArthur turned on her. 'What do you mean, you stupid little whore?' he demanded. Della, quick as lightning, slapped his face, picked up her mock-Gucci holdall and threw a leg over the rail, her neat little foot groping for a moment then finding *Shearwater*'s moving deck. Joanna, preoccupied with turning the boat's bow outward, realized too late what was happening. As the stern of the smaller boat began to swing, just clearing the motor yacht, Della looked across the lifelines, full into Guy's astonished face. She ignored his open-mouthed, outraged employer and spoke to him directly.

'Pity,' she said. 'You could be such a nice boy.'

And Guy jumped.

Joanna, impeded by flailing flannelled legs and reaching hands, and rattled by the roar of fury from the master of *Privateer*, could see nothing for it but to kick the motor into full ahead and aim for the harbour mouth. Della thought she heard her say, under her breath, 'Things like this don't *happen*.'

17 ʃ

Shearwater's engine was not accustomed to have sudden, strenuous demands made on it. Jo's action in kicking the lever to full ahead was met first with a sort of startled obedience, then with outraged sputters of rebellion as the elderly machine gasped for air. Joanna, her whole being focused on not getting stuck in the middle of Torquay harbour, drifting helplessly while a black-browed captain of industry shouted abuse at her, bent to ease back the throttle. She hit Della's pretty ankle rather hard as she did so, and not entirely by accident.

'Owww!' cried Della, lurching sideways onto Guy's strong arm. Finding that she liked it, she kept a tight hold of that limb. 'Oww, watch out!'

'Steady,' said Guy chivalrously. And to Joanna, 'The poor girl's had a bit of a shock.'

Joanna could think of so many cutting ripostes to this pair of preposterous cuckoos that she found herself unable to say anything except, 'Well, at least sit down out of my way. I take it you don't want to be dropped off on the pier?'

The question was hardly more than rhetorical. Aboard *Privateer*, Marie was now screaming like a steam whistle and Eddie McArthur could be seen waving something which looked startlingly like a gun. Marie, in fact, was rather enjoying her scream. Years of police raids had convinced her that if a girl can't get away, her best recourse in a crisis is to be noisily distraught while keeping an eye on the route to the fire exit. The screaming threw men – generally, after all, the source of danger or embarrassment – off their balance. Seeing Eddie (who she remembered as an unnervingly cold and peremptory client even by her standards) thrown so very far off his balance was exhilarating. Besides, it was perfectly obvious it wasn't a real gun. Marie screamed on, happily.

Eddie discharged the pistol into the air with a violent report. High overhead, a ball of red fire described a parabola through the air, and then another, and another. Aboard the churning, scrabbling *Shearwater*, Guy reassured the two women. 'Verey pistol. He keeps it instead of distress flares. I had to renew the licence last week. He's only trying to scare us.'

'He's not doing badly,' muttered Joanna. Looking back, she could see a marina official running down the pontoon towards the disturbance. Elderly boat owners were walking down from the Royal Torbay Yacht Club and looking curiously at the big motorboat, some with dawning recognition. 'D'you know, I think it's that chap, McArthur, the multi-million newspaper feller.' On balance, Torquay looked a pretty poor habitat for Guy and Della right now.

'Er, if you don't mind,' said Guy, 'we'll sail with you until we get, er, clear.'

Della nodded, shining-eyed. Having made her own bravura, world-changing gesture she was content for the moment to be led. This was adventure: a man on her arm, young and so devastatingly handsome and kind; an unknown destination, an angry pursuer. A year ago she had left a dull house in a dull road on the edges of Leicester, hoping for adventure. Without a GCSE to her name, without so much as the word-processing course her mother had wanted her to go on, London in recession had not proved to be paved with gold. Or adventures. So there had been men, and escort work – because she really did know how to behave and how to look, and whatever her mum said, it was a real talent, that. And escort work had turned into something that the red-taloned ladies in charge called 'Realistic, dear. Giving them value. It's a service.'

But it had not been adventure. Once, coming out of a West End club with a hick American weighing all of twenty stone and bragging ceaselessly about his big Thing, dirty bugger, Della had been sure she saw Prince Andrew. But so far, until now, that was it. This adventure was therefore overdue, even if it did seem a pity to have this rather cross lady to thank for it. She rubbed her ankle.

Joanna steered past the piers and felt the boat rise again to the swell outside, a deep unsettled movement of the waters left over from the easterly gale. The wind now was a steady northerly breeze, so she bent to unroll the jib. It unfurled with the usual crack and flap, its full spread making the boat jerk and heel slightly.

'Oooh! said Della. 'We sinking, or what?'

'No, little one,' said Guy soppily. 'You're quite safe,' and added, 'I'll look after you.'

Joanna killed the engine's clatter with a sharp tug on the wire and turned the key with a click. Heading south slowly, with just her jib, *Shearwater* lost her bustling mechanical nervousness and became again a sane, balanced, graceful thing, an environment in which to think clearly. The relief of being clear of the land was intense. Ahead, the sea was grey-green, the shape of Berry Head reaching out and diving to the sea, the sweep of Torbay's white beaches falling into picture-postcard loveliness as the buildings receded and melted into the landscape. It was a calm but living place, that boat moving across that water; a place for reflection, for lovers to talk quietly or troubled hearts to be alone.

'So, all right,' said Joanna after the three of them had had a moment to contemplate the peace of the bay and the engineless silence. 'What – where do you – where shall I drop you?'

Guy had not worked six miserable months for Eddie McArthur without becoming adept at diplomacy and the soft answer that turneth away wrath. Sitting in the corner of the cockpit, his hand on Della's thin white arm, he framed one now.

'Umm, the first thing is that I really – we both really – must apologize for imposing ourselves on you and intruding on your holiday—'

'It's not a holiday!' said Joanna, violently pushing back her flying hair which was, in its new clean softness, being blown all around her face by the following wind. 'If you really want to know, I'm the mutinous runaway wife in the newspapers.' The hair whipped her eyes and gave her a desperate look, witchy, slit-eyed, ragged black.

'I thought you was her,' said Della. 'Me and Marie read the

paper with that really sad picture they took. You're ever so much prettier, though. Would you like a bobble for that hair?' She fished in the pocket of her holdall and proffered, with candid seriousness, a short piece of Lurex elastic with plastic crystalline bobbles at each end.

Joanna, touched in spite of herself by the simple feminine observation of her need, accepted it and, holding the tiller between her knees, swept back her hair into a ponytail. Now only a few wisps blew forward, giving her the air of a schoolgirl fresh in from hockey. She smiled at Della who, seeing the witch face softened and transformed, smiled back. Guy ploughed on.

'We really don't have any right to impose on you but the thing is I've worked for Mr McArthur for nearly six months now, and I know what he can be like – terrifically talented, of course, I really sort of admire him – only I don't think that Della ought to go back. Not now she's hit him. He's quite short-tempered and very keen to get even with people.'

'He's a fat pervert,' said Della. 'You're not catching me back there. And I'm not going in any bed with Marie. She's a cow.'

'I should think not!' said Guy warmly. 'He has no right to ask—'

'It was you that booked us,' said Della, turning suddenly on him like a kitten in a fluffy rage. 'You must'a known.'

Guy took this like a professional. 'I wasn't expecting anyone like you,' he said, bending his head towards her in a way which made Joanna, fifteen years older, suddenly and sentimentally wish those years away.

'What d'you mean, like me?' fluttered Della.

'Young. Pretty. Nice. A girl like you – how did you get tangled up with an escort agency? When I saw you at Paignton station I knew it must be a mistake.'

'It's a long story. I'm not what you'd call full-time. I've got modelling offers and that.'

'I'm not surprised,' said Guy warmly, gazing into her wide blue eyes. 'You'd be a stunning model.'

'Oh, I dunno. But I'm def'nitely not doing any more escort work. I only been there a couple of months, filling in.'

Joanna, on the helm, looked at her uninvited passengers with helpless incredulity. She should be irritated by them, she thought, and probably would have been if she had been going anywhere with a firm plan in mind. But numbed by a long night, a short sleep and a rude awakening, she had been existing, ever since breakfast with those terrible newspapers, in an emotional void. Whole areas of normal reaction seemed to have closed down in her. All she could do was the next thing, the obvious thing. It had been obvious that the water tank needed filling, as they always filled it in marinas. A brief focusing of her rage had made it equally obvious that the newspaper girl – Binny? Ginny? – must be hosed from the deck. Once that was over she had gone back to filling the tank up blankly. The invitation from the black-browed demon king and the little melodrama on the motor yacht's deck had been only a pantomime in which she really, really did not want to go on stage with the other children. And as she escaped it, it had taken a few moments to realize that she had acquired two of the cast in the form of this young couple.

For a couple they were indeed becoming, before her very eyes. The pantomime had switched from Beauty and the Beast to Cinderella, with this handsome young rowing-blue clearly willing to play Prince Charming to a slightly shop-soiled Cinderella. And, bereft of normal responses, she could only look at them with a kind of bemused acceptance and wonder if she had to play the fairy godmother. On the whole she thought not. They couldn't be more than two or three years older than Lance and Susan, they were sitting in her cockpit like Lance and Susan, and yet she was not responsible for them.

There was something comforting about that. She had been responsible for the young for so long, so long; ever since she was young herself. There were babies who woke and fretted, toddling children who might drown or be snatched, who had fevers and tantrums. There had been schoolchildren with sadnesses and worries and toothache and lost games socks; then teenagers in revolt against everything that nurtured them. Oh, teenagers! Full of the life force they had drained out of you over the years, but using that force to scorn and batter you for your emptiness. Irrelevantly, she remembered Susan ranting at her about not wanting to go into the sixth form. No weapon had been too dirty for her daughter to use against her.

'What's the point? You got A levels, you went to university, and you end up serving scones to old bags in Bonhurst High street. I'm not going to end up like that!' It would have been easy to give in, to shrug – as Mandy did over Anneliese's woeful GCSE results – and say, 'Let them make their own way.' Joanna could not. Susan's future was her responsibility, like so much else. Have a baby, and the responsibility never left you; not at midnight in the throes of your own rare bouts of marital passion, not when you slept exhausted with 'flu and woke ill and unrefreshed with a day's work ahead. Always, always, you watched over them. And if you deserted them, as she was now deserting Susan (oh God, Keith on the A303, heading for Torquay!) you felt alien from your own self, ill and afraid.

But she was not responsible for these two. They could go to hell their own way. Listening to them was almost a balm.

'Mr McArthur isn't my career. It's been my first job, after Cambridge,' Guy was explaining to Della. 'Bit of a false start. I always meant to go into something to do with sport really.'

'You are clever, going to university,' said Della. 'Me, I couldn't even get GCSE.'

'You don't have to be so clever,' said Guy. 'You go to the right kind of school, they practically force you in. I got a pretty bad third. I mainly played rugger and rowed and played tennis.'

'I like a man to be fit,' said Della. 'Sporty. I love Wimbledon, that Agassi.'

'I bet you'd play a terrific game of tennis,' said Guy warmly.

'I never played,' said Della, and looked up at him, full face, sweet as a flower. Joanna had seen Anneliese do that to boys; Susan had never quite learnt it. She ducked her striped head and stammered, surly from caring too much. Poor Susan. Anneliese's way, Della's way, worked every time. Guy came in on cue, his broad, handsome face alight.

'Tell you what, when we're back in London I could teach you to play tennis.'

'That'd be really nice.'

'You could come to my club. It's in Maida Vale, and we could go for a Thai meal.'

No, thought Joanna, this is not even Cinderella. Babes in the

Wood, more like. She would be hopping around scattering leaves on them any minute.

Steering on across the bay, she realized that they were already a mile out and felt her situation painfully coming back into focus. You really could not meander off to sea with no destination. Not two days running, anyway.

'Where exactly,' she asked, 'were you thinking of going? Now, this afternoon.'

'Well, er, what would suit?' asked Guy politely. 'As I say, we are very aware that this is putting you to a lot of trouble. We'll just go along with your plans. Tide's running south for a bit – nice wind. I presume you're going this way.'

'Yes, I think so,' said Joanna. 'Certainly no point going up to Teignmouth, and I'm not ready to go back round Portland yet either. Not tonight.'

'Well, south then. Drop us off at – I mean you're spoilt for choice round here. Up the Dart, Salcombe, Brixham—'

'Not Brixham,' said Della beadily. They turned to her in astonishment. What did this urban sparrow, this painted, dainty little blonde geisha, know about West Country harbours? Guy and Joanna suddenly saw themselves in contrast to her: big-boned, healthy, middle-class, yachting hearties.

''Cos we *said* Brixham, in front of him,' she explained. 'Your loony boss. So he'll come and find us.'

Joanna privately doubted whether McArthur would do any such thing, but the idea seemed to throw both her passengers into a frenzy of insecurity. She had noticed this before in people who worked for tyrants: they became nervous and diminished and looked over their shoulders to the point of paranoia. Like the year before Alice got her Royal Opera House job, when she had worked for a television executive, a terrible black-bearded prima donna with a taste for humiliating his staff. Alice used to stay odd weekends with them and baby Lance at Egg Terrace. Joanna remembered how she was seemed always to be half expecting her boss to burst in and shout at her, even at breakfast. Alice jumped out of her skin once when his voice came on the *Today* programme defending the BBC against the government. Guy and Della had the same hunted look; they were both clearly convinced that Brixham spelt disaster.

'Well, gosh, you never know,' said Guy. 'He can run that boat himself. I was there for the donkey work but he's actually quite a seaman, I'll give him that. And it's very fast.'

Della, unfamiliar with such ready use of the old word seaman, looked momentarily startled.

Guy went on, 'But of course the main thing is we've really got to fit in with your plans. This is your boat and we weren't exactly invited.'

'I have no plans,' said Joanna again, heavily. 'I was going to go home. I think. My husband is – oh, God, he's actually on the way to Torquay. What's he going to do?' The vision of Keith arriving in Torquay to find her flown was too much. She began to falter. 'I was going to go home, probably, but I read the paper and . . .' Tears treacherously welled up in her eyes. 'I can't . . . decide. Oh, shit!'

She was really crying now, jolted out of the surreal mood which had kept her going since breakfast. She sobbed on, adrift on the embarrassment and absurdity of it all. *Shearwater* ceased to be any comfort; she was oblivious to the boat's glad purposeful progress over the swell, to the gleams of sun on the grey-green sweep of the coast and the lazy circling of gulls. Bowing her head, steering without thinking, she wept.

Guy was not good at many things apart from sport, but weeping women were his speciality. His younger sister had been prone to weep over everything from sick kittens to Bette Davis films, and he had long ago grasped the vital point that understanding why women weep is not necessary to comforting them. Unhesitatingly, he stood up and put an arm round Joanna, and took the tiller from her.

'Here, sit down. I think you were jolly brave, sailing in on a night like that, all on your own. You can't have had much sleep because I went and woke you up, and I bet those papers printed a pack of lies. It's – it's – a damn shame.'

Joanna, curled up sobbing in the corner of the cockpit with one cotton jumper sleeve across her eyes and nose, said something she was later to think extraordinary and significant. She could not have told her own mother, or husband, or doctor such a thing but to this strange young man and this absurd little bimbo she said, muffled, 'It's not the lies. Lies are just lies. They don't matter. It was the true bit. About having no friends, and being desperate.'

She genuinely had not known this until she said it, but realized instantly that it was so. Being described as a dead-end waitress or an abandoner of small children did not matter. It was froth and nonsense, part of the gaudy fiction of daily journalism. What had struck to the heart, even as her busy, justifying brain had fulminated against Gordon's inaccuracies, was his entirely accidental flare of truth. Her own truth, the secret emptiness.

She was a respected, happily married, competent, prosperous, responsible businesswoman, wife and mother with a circle of friends. But she was also alone and desperate and meaningless. Gabriel had known that when he threw her out. Must have. He had laughed at her in the dream for thinking she could die like Emily. Emily must have known it too and gone away into death without talking to her because she could not have helped. Now Gordon, who was a stranger, a cubbish reporter of no great gifts, and who had never even met her, had by some chance guessed right.

Partly right. He was wrong to hint at suicidal intentions. Joanna had not sailed suicidally into the storm. A long instinct born of sailing, a moral sense born of fundraising for the lifeboats would have prevented such a use of the sea or the boat. But the flight from Mr Brewer's quay, she knew now, had been an impulse from the same bitter root.

'I wasn't running away,' she said now. 'I was *throwing* myself away.'

'But you didn't,' said Guy. 'Because here you are, and jolly good luck for me and Della, and this is a really nice boat. And the sun's coming out. Would it be all right if I made us a cup of tea?'

Joanna looked up and saw the bay, and the curve of the jib, and Guy steering, and Della offering her a heavily scented and slightly grubby lace handkerchief.

'Yes,' she said. 'Yes, do. There's longlife milk. Then we'll work out what to do.'

18

By the side of the A303, north of Yeovil, Keith Gurney bent struggling over the Peugeot's rear offside wheel. Cars buzzed like angry hornets and lorries thundered past him: taking bananas from Southampton to Somerset for ripening, car parts on a roundabout route via Wales for inscrutable Japanese quality-control reasons, and deliveries of Taiwanese table decorations to corporate functions in Minehead and Exeter. Each one brought its own gust of diabolical wind, making his sandy hair stream out sideways, sharpening his face to gawky youthfulness as he crouched over the stiff wheel nuts. 'Hell, hell, hell!' he murmured.

Back in the picturesque premises of Heron and Gurney, Solicitors, Aimée and Gus were sharing Keith's uneaten Danish pastry and discussing the morning's epic developments. Not since Mrs Cothill's shoplifting charge had there been such stirring doings afoot in the middle-class sector of the small town. Women did, of course, go missing, fleeing back to their mothers or off with men. Husbands absconded from family and community life as often here as anywhere else. But a particular lustre was cast over the present crisis by the involvement of the national press, the swashbuckling manner of Mrs Gurney's going and her comfortable familiarity to customers of the Bun in the Oven.

Gus and Aimée knew that if they were to walk through the small, red-gabled, proudly dull little town they would hear the matter discussed everywhere. In the wool-shop queue where fussy pensioners tormented the assistant with demands for taupe-and-amber double-knitting fleck; in the fish shop; amid the trendy kitchen gewgaws and fretwork chicken friezes of

Cuisine It All; in Ted Merriam's ironmongery which stood opposite the latter and glared at it from behind a fringe of no-nonsense aluminium saucepans. And most especially it would be discussed in the post office and the building society, where resigned queues built up nine or ten deep behind the imperious county ladies who drove their four-wheel-drive monsters in from the outlying farmhouses for the Wednesday afternoon bridge club meeting. The affair would be less avidly talked over, perhaps, in the big outlying Pricedeal supermarket at the edge of the council estate; but in the pretty town centre, there really was no other topic. So Gus, and more especially Aimée, felt a slight glow of pleasure in knowing that they knew more.

'Torquay, Mr Gurney said he was going to,' said Aimée after a long analysis of just how worried Mr Gurney had looked when he came off the phone. 'My mum had her honeymoon there. Palm trees, she reckoned. Ever so romantic. D'you think he'll bring her back tonight?'

'I suppose,' said Gus, 'they might want to sail the boat back. That'd take a day or two.'

'Do you think she's, er, actually coming back?' asked Aimée. 'I mean, are they all right, those two?'

Gus suddenly felt his position as qualified lawyer and incipient partner.

'Sure they are. Here, you take lunch now and I'll get a sandwich later when Alex gets back.'

Aimée departed, wondering whether to do the wool shop or the post office queue first with the news about Torquay.

Gus stood up, threw the rest of his pastry into the waste-paper basket, and swivelled round on Aimée's office chair, fiddling restlessly with her old Amstrad computer. He ought not to gossip with the secretary. It was a terrible habit in a man of law, as his father the Judge would no doubt tell him. Only there was nobody else to gossip with, and it could be a lonely life for a young man, underpaid in a provincial backwater run by bossy old tabbies and pompous Rotarian duffers. Mrs Gurney was different: younger in manner and outlook than any of the other senior wives of the town, who were in his opinion a poisonous pack of ex-head girls who went on and on about dog training and sank alarmingly into middle age at thirty-five. You could have a joke with Mrs Gurney. He had thoroughly enjoyed lodging at the Old Vicarage when he first came, before he got his own flat up the High Street. He had fond memories of evenings when he had not been able to bear another minute with Snell's *Equity* and had sneaked downstairs to watch *Bonanza* on satellite TV with Susan; or played Scrabble with Mrs Gurney and Lance (no chance of beating Lance) while Keith worked at his desk.

Mrs Gurney was really clever. Shouldn't be in that boring tearoom. He had hinted as much once while they washed up after a dinner party a year ago. He was meant to be guest of honour, having just announced his engagement to Tiny, but his old, lodgerly habits came back at times like these and he could not be kept out of the kitchen. Passing him a dripping meat dish, Joanna had surprisingly agreed with him about the Bun.

'Only, you see, when Lance and Suzy and Mandy's Anneliese were babies, the teashop was something Mandy and I could do as well as look after them, because we've always kept it dead easy, no hot food. It was our bit of adventure and independence. My own money. Something to be in charge of.' She had passed him a plate with the sudden flashing smile which transformed her rather stern, regular features. 'I always knew it was a rut. I was going to stop when Susan was at secondary school and do an Open University degree. Then it started making more money, when they put up the "HISTORIC MARKET TOWN ALL SERVICES" sign on the motorway. And Susan hated the High School, so we switched to paying fees, and I kept on. I was so much in the habit, and I'm not qualified to do anything else. And I do like to help out, financially. With Keith working so hard, and things being tough in the practice since the house market collapsed . . . you know.'

Gus knew. All around, in London as well as Bonhurst, he saw just such fossilized lives. The unemployed were not the only casualties of recession. People in work grew timid too, afraid to change and develop, abhorring risk, never making way for the next generation, standing stock-still for fear of slipping backwards. He had been extremely lucky to be taken on as clerk in 1992, considering that every law practice in southern England was reeling under the impact of the housing slump. At first, Keith used to joke about swings and roundabouts, saying,

'What we lose in conveyancing we pick up in divorce.' But as the recession bit deeper, it seemed that people around Bonhurst could hardly afford even divorces any more. The office telephone rang less often, except with the sad cases for whom kind Keith did not log a quarter of the hours he worked. The third partner, Ned Bandon, retired and was not replaced. Alex moved down into Ned's office, leaving Gus the sloping attic. Now Alex was going, and Gus guessed that if he took up his father's proffered capital to buy the vacant partnership, there would not even be a new clerk. The partnership income simply would not stand it. He and Keith would be alone with Aimée.

Still, it was one step nearer his real ambition: a husband-and-wife partnership: Terson and Terson. Him and Tiny. He glowed at the thought of Tiny. Prettiest, funniest law student of their batch, best beloved of Gus for five faithful years but currently languishing in a huge London firm. Tiny only wanted to marry him, move to some Hampshire farmhouse and commute to undemanding small-town work in between raising babies, dogs and chickens. That was the long-term masterplan.

The marrying bit was easy, and scheduled for December. Tiny, who was Hong Kong Chinese, was planning to look adorable in a white fur parka cloak. Her people had the capital to buy a partnership and would give it as a wedding present. If only Keith wanted two new partners instead of one, they could both move in at Christmas when Alex left. Tiny would be brilliant with the local clientele: a five-foot glossy Chinese doll might initially be a change from suave greying Mr Heron and trustworthy Mr Gurney. But, as Tiny had said, expertly demolishing a bowl of fried rice on his last visit to London, if the characters in *The Archers* could get used to an Asian woman solicitor called Usha, Bonhurst could get used to having their wills drafted by Li Pan Terson. And she would wow the Hampshire magistrates, all of whom she suspected of fantasizing about Suzy Wong (pause for Tiny's impression of an Oriental temptress striding into court with a whip and thigh boots). And if any clients did jib at her, Gus could compensate by being very male and very English indeed to provide protective colouring, couldn't he? (Pause for Gus to do his very brilliant impersonation of a fusty old judge failing to recognize an egg spring roll presented to him in evidence.)

Oh yes, Tiny and he would be a great team. Perry Mason and Tonto, Rumpole and Man Friday. With children and chickens. Lost in his daydream, Gus forgot about the disappearance of Joanna Gurney for a moment. They would have a dog, a really big red setter which could sleep in its basket in the office corridor. Clients who didn't like dogs could bog off. He was really, despite his proud new qualifications, still very young.

The telephone rang. 'Terson and – I mean Heron and Gurney,' said Gus. 'No. I'm sorry, Mr Heron's in court this morning.'

This was a euphemism born of habit. Alex was not in court. He had, at the fleeing Keith's behest, rung the coastguard to report Joanna's safety and cancel any watch for her, then driven home where he found Mandy alone in the kitchen rereading Gordon's report with those alarming rare tears running down her cheeks. He had taken her into his arms, limp and sad, but got no sense out of her beyond, 'Jo will think I said those things. I can't go out. I can't go to the caff, honestly. I'm a letdown, aren't I? Oh, Alex. I dunno what to do. I never felt like this before. I've done all sorts of naughty things, you know that, but never like this. I didn't even do it, but I feel worse than if I did. Alex, I wish I was dead. I really am a no-hope slag.'

He had reluctantly left her, instructing Anneliese to stay in the house and administer tea. As he passed the dining-room door, he half noticed Susan Gurney, that surly stripe-haired child, looking extremely busy filling in some sort of printed form.

Now he was downtown again, standing in the back kitchen of the Bun in the Oven with Erika Merriam. This, at least, was something he could do. Summoning up all his urbane smoothness, Alex set about charming this straggle-haired, beaky woman into solving at least one of the problems thrown up by Joanna Gurney's escapade.

'Mrs Merriam, first of all I'd like to say how grateful my wife is for the way you've taken over. She's not well herself—'

Erika sniffed. Alex took no notice. A lot of women in the town seemed to sniff at the mention of his wife; if she didn't mind, he supposed he must not mind either.

'– and you see Mrs Gurney's had to go away for – it might be another few days. I think you normally just do weekends and holidays for her, don't you?'

'That's right,' said Erika. 'My husband likes me at home.'

'Ah yes, Ted,' said Alex. 'Anyway, we do see how awkward it is for you, filling in—'

'Excuse me. A customer,' said Erika.

She left him leaning on a shelf of white-and-gold saucers, marvelling at the sudden crispness that could come over shy women when they had something to manage. She returned a moment later to catch him pulling a curl of chocolate from the side of a waiting gateau, and so cold was her stare then that he slammed the plastic visor down over it and smirked apologetically.

Erika began to assemble a tea tray for two with deft hands. 'You really shouldn't—' she said, and stopped.

'I know, I know,' said Alex. 'Sorry.'

'It's just that we're not supposed to let outsiders in the kitchen. Hygiene regs. Like you aren't wearing an overall.'

She herself was neat in pink gingham. Joanna's faded blue apron hung in the corner, and with it a smaller, grubbier one. On the back of the door hung a small pink gingham housecoat like Erika's, unworn by the look of it.

'I'll go. I'm very sorry. You're very good at this job, aren't you? All I wanted to ask—'

'You want me to come in, I'll come in. Till Mrs Gurney gets back. Ted can put up with it. Only I'm leaving Zoë on her own after the dinnertime rush, so it does need someone to lock up at five. Zoë's not fit to have a key, she'd lose it at some disco. If Mrs Heron could come in at four . . .'

'Either she will or I will,' promised Alex. 'She's not well.'

'There's cashing up, too,' said Erika, with the air of one who did not believe in any illness of Mandy's, and never would. 'And putting the takings in the night safe.'

'I can do that,' said Alex. 'I used to work in an ice-cream shop in the vacation. Keith and I ran the best ice-cream stand on Brighton beach.'

She looked disbelievingly at him, and put two scones, a bowl of blackcurrant jam and a jug of milk onto her tray alongside the teapot and cups. 'Yes. And there's checking to be done. Plugs out, work surfaces clean, floor swept, rubbish out the back, *sealed*.'

'I can do that. Or Mandy will. Mrs Merriam, we really are most grateful. I think Mrs Heron and Mrs Gurney would want me to say that this extra responsibility deserves extra, er, salary.'

Erika looked at him coolly as she turned towards the door with the fragrant, immaculate tray. 'It's not a problem. I don't think Zoë will be trouble. I'm going to stay on an hour today and get her into some routines.'

Alex watched her go, then heaved himself off the shelf and followed her through the door, into the prim tearoom. 'Thanks. Again.'

As he left, a thin dreadlocked child in a miniskirt, tube top, and cloud of sullen attitude came in through the door.

'Zoë. You're late,' he heard Erika say. 'There's a new clean overall for you behind the door, and a ribbon to tie your hair back. It's better if you look the part. Get a step on, now.' Alex escaped, marvelling.

In the dining room at the Herons' house, Susan Gurney finished her form, folded it, and put it in a heavy, expensive long lawyer's manila envelope brought to her by Anneliese from her father's desk drawer.

'I think you're really brave,' said Anneliese. 'There'll be a row.'

'Don't care.' Susan licked the flap and banged her fist down hard on the envelope. 'Mum's bogged off, Dad's chasing her round Torquay, Lance is poncing around on his personal Starship *Enterprise*, it's my bloody life.'

'What do you mean, Starship *Enterprise*?'

'Got a postcard the other day. From some crumbling observatory, Prague or somewhere. All it said was "Nothing matters except the laws of nature and the power of Love". Weird.'

'Weird.' Anneliese proffered a stamp, then changed her mind and put out a hand for the envelope instead. 'I'll take it in tomorrow. Mum's driving me to Southampton. I'll be going into the Purser's, no, whatsit, Bursar's office. I'll drop it in.'

'The bedsit all signed up?'

'Yup.'

'D'you think we'll be all right, sharing? Not have rows, all that?'

'Yup.' Anneliese shook her white-gold mane, with the lop-sided, wicked grin that lifted Susan's heart. With Annie, you couldn't always approve, but you did feel better for being around her.

'Will your mum mind you sharing?'

'Thrr-illed.' Anneliese rolled the word out with relish. 'I told her it was a schoolfriend I was sharing a flat with. She said thank God, I thought it was a Hell's Angel chapter. Anyway, we'll be back every Friday night. It's only to save getting on the early bus. And there's room for two drawing boards. We can even work.'

'I do want to work, Annie. It's not a skive. I'm gonna be an art editor. I'd do it the other way, do Art A level, only not with MacEvoy's Fusiliers. Besides, the college course gets me further in, and I need a head start. Publishing's really competitive. And I can't stay at school. I can't.'

'No way. Gross. It's your fault for getting so many GCSEs. I saw it coming. More than six and you're doomed to A levels. Scrape five Cs, like me, and all you have to do is bring home a few leaflets about trendy new GNVQs and even Alex caves in. Glad to keep me off the streets— ssh!'

Mandy was in the doorway, pale and quenched. With dexterity born of practice, Annie slid the envelope under the table, but her mother noticed nothing.

'I've a headache. I'm going to bed. Sue, if your mother rings . . . tell her I'd love to talk to her . . .'

Neither girl had ever seen Mandy so hesitant, but concern evaporated in the heat of their own needs.

'Mum, you are taking me to Southampton tomorrow? To college, for the signing-on thing?'

Mandy looked blank. 'Oh – yes. Of course.'

'Can Sooze come for the ride?' Anneliese held her breath. Would it occur to her mother that Susan was supposed to be a lower sixth student at Angela Merici in a bottle-green suit, not free like Annie to schlepp around a further education college twenty miles away? Mandy, as she had suspected, was too distracted by the morning's events for such ratiocination.

'Yes, yes. Fine.' Mandy turned away rapidly. Susan looked too like Joanna. The straight little features, the big eyes and full mouth were smiling at her, delighted at the prospect of delivering her own envelope. But Mandy saw only the ghost of Joanna's features; of her friend, the only friend who had always stuck by her, who might now be dead, who if alive would be disgusted with her. She saw those features distorted by disappointment and reproach. Without a word, she left, leaving the girls to face one another and, simultaneously, jauntily, put their thumbs up.

On the A303, Keith straightened up, wiped his hands, threw the jack and spanner back in the boot with the flat tyre, and climbed into the driving seat to wait for a gap in the relentless stream of lorries. He would be in Torquay by four. In time for a cup of tea, with Jo.

19

The cup of tea that Guy made did Joanna good. Her outburst of grief passed quickly and, strangely, seemed to leave no awkwardness behind it. Everything was too surreal for embarrassment: the boat composedly rocking southward across a glittering afternoon sea, the willowy elegance of Guy in his college blazer, the incongruous figure of the girl with her red talons and carefully made-up baby face. Della, who had begun to look queasy as the waves grew longer south of Berry Head, refused her tea and now sat silent in the corner of the cockpit, with an old Arran jumper of Keith's wrapped round her shoulders in their flimsy blouse. Guy patted her fake-tanned, goosepimpled knee occasionally. She seemed not discontented.

Joanna and Guy sipped their tea on either side of the helm as the north wind pushed *Shearwater* steadily down the coast towards the Mewstone Rock.

'He'll look for us in Dartmouth, for sure,' said Guy. 'Better not go there.'

'He probably won't look for us *at all*,' said Joanna, for the fourth or fifth time.

'You don't *know* him,' said the young man with a shudder. 'He's probably never been slapped and walked out on before.'

'Bet he has,' said Della, rousing briefly from her sick torpor. '*Bet* he has.'

'Well, not by a personal secretary. I'm his employee, the lawyers made me sign twenty sorts of contract stopping me from *breathing* unless he says so. If Della had come away alone, things might have been all right. But me coming has probably made things worse for all of us. He'll be angry.'

'He can't do anything if he does catch us,' said Joanna dampeningly. 'This isn't a James Bond film. If he does anything, it'll be to ring his lawyers, stop your money, all that stuff. Even Robert Maxwell didn't actually go around drowning people.'

But nothing would convince her companions that they were not fleeing for their lives. After a few minutes' contemplation of this thought, Guy even anounced, in a tone straight out of Hornblower, that they should 'cram on all sail'. With Joanna's amused permission, he raised the mainsail and dragged out the boat's worn and grubby spinnaker from its bag to hoist that as well.

It was an atrocious sail, orange and green and hideous, made twenty years ago for another boat and so ill cut that at the slightest provocation it twisted inextricably round the wire forestay. Joanna hated it. Keith and Lance had bought it in a boat jumble sale when Lance was fourteen and razor-keen on racing. The two of them used to rig it enthusiastically while Jo and Susan jeered from the cockpit. Once it had fallen off its halyard and dragged under the keel, just in the entrace to Poole harbour, causing the boat to veer out of control and almost hit the chain ferry. Watching Guy haul it up and steady it on its pole, Joanna could almost see Lance, her boy, her cheerful genius, on the foredeck again. Guy adjusted things to his satisfaction and swung back into the cockpit. Glancing at the log, Joanna observed that this rig gave *Shearwater* an extra three knots, raising their speed to seven nautical miles per hour.

'What top speed does *Privateer* do?' she asked unkindly as Guy admired his rig.

'Thirty knots.' Guy ducked his head a little sheepishly. 'I know. But he might not get out very quickly, and if we could just get round the corner . . .'

'What corner, exactly?'

'Look,' said Guy. 'Six miles beyond Start Point, just past where you'd turn up the channel into Salcombe, there's a little hole called Starhole Bay.'

'I know it. You stop there when the tide round Start Point is against you, going up-Channel. Steep cliffs all around. There's nothing there.'

'Right. Well, we could anchor there – if you agree – tonight.

Nobody would notice or expect us there. We could disguise the boat a bit. Then in the morning, very early, we could sneak just inside Salcombe harbour, Della and I could get a taxi, and you'd be clear of us.'

As a plan for foiling an imaginary pursuer, thought Joanna, it was not bad. There were enough bits and pieces of food, emergency tins under bunks and the like, for the three of them. There were three sleeping bags including Susan's. Della could have that. She would – she shamefacedly caught herself thinking – wash it before Susan had it again. Della was rather more extravagantly scented than was usual on board the boat.

'OK,' she said. 'Only I have to get on the VHF and leave a message for my husband. He thinks I'm in Torquay. He might even be there already.'

Guy took the helm, and once again Joanna sat below at the chart table, in a far calmer ship this time, and went through the rituals of a link call to the Old Vicarage. Just as she got through, an anxious face appeared in the companionway.

'Keith,' she began. 'I've had to leave Torquay. I'll be in—'

'No!' hissed Guy. 'It's a public airwave. He might be listening in. The Boss!' Joanna flashed him an irritated look and went on.

'I'll be in, er, on, er – safe harbour anyway. Don't worry. Tomorrow I'll go in to—'

'No, not even that!' said Guy, anguished. 'It's not safe!'

'Don't give us away!' squeaked Della. 'He's a pervert!' And threw up over the side, noisily. Guy turned to her, full of concern, and momentarily ignored the helm. The spinnaker seized its chance, collapsed with a rustle and a flap, and wound itself round the stay with an expertise born of long practice. The trapped jib cracked and shook.

'Shit!' yelled Guy.

'Owww . . . are we sinking?' said Della, raising a grey face, eerily streaked with blusher.

'It's going to rip!'

'Anyway,' persevered Joanna, shutting out the racket with her left hand on her ear. 'No, shut up, you two, it's too bad – Keith, I will ring – from Salcombe. 'Bye.'

Furious, she stamped back up the steps to the cockpit. 'No, *really*,' she said. 'What's he going to think?'

'You said the harbour!' wailed Della. Guy switched on his diplomatic heat-lamp again, full beam, and calmed her down with platitudinous soothings, most of them shouted from the foredeck as – skilfully, she had to admit – he freed the great orange and green sail.

'More tea?' he said at last, returning to a quieter cockpit.

'If,' said Joanna, 'you take that bloody spinnaker down first. Now.'

In the offices of the *Chronicle*, Gordon sat with a polystyrene cup of coffee, basking in the quiet glow of achievement. A shadow fell across his desk. Looking up, he saw the News Editor, massive in his grey ribbed cardigan, with a piece of scrawled paper in his huge hand. 'The Editor,' he said sourly, 'has had a call from the Proprietor. Were we aware, he says, that our pisspoor Page Three story omitted the most newsworthy aspect of the whole affair of the sailaway teashop lady?'

'Which is?' said Gordon, affecting a bravura he did not feel.

'That the lady has not in fact run off alone. That she is not some lonely desperate menopause victim, laddie. She has been sighted in Torquay, disporting herself,' he gave a really rather attractive Scottish roll to the 'r', 'on a ship of sin with a lesbian vice girl in suspenders and a toyboy of twenty-two.'

'He made that up!' blurted Gordon before he could stop himself. The News Editor looked at him with a pitying dislike. 'Know a lot about making it up, do you, laddie?'

'Well,' said Gordon, recovering, 'I'll chase it up, obviously.'

'Obviously not,' said the News Editor, turning to depart. 'Our Miss Douglas is there, on the spot, and will be filing shortly.' Gordon, left alone, crushed his polystyrene cup in his hand.

Eddie McArthur looked out across Torquay harbour and wondered briefly how good an idea his call to the thug had been. In the chilly Northumbrian minor stately home where he grew up, his nurse had been prone to say, 'Temper, temper never won a race; spiteful never won a pretty face.' Temper had stood him in pretty good stead so far in life, and pretty faces could be bought. The temper had been considerable, fuelled not so much by the humiliation of the slap as by the realization that without Guy, he might still be able to command and drive his boat but he had lost command of the rest of his life. He had no idea where anything was, nor how to find the telephone numbers of his other aides, lawyers, and employees; did not know where or when to appear for tonight's West Country business dinner. He had no clue as to where his portable telephone was kept. Guy had been briefed and trained by his last departing secretary who in turn had been instructed by the one before; Eddie did not believe in cluttering his mind with administrative trivia. He did not even know his own home telephone number.

The reappearance on the pontoons of Dinny Douglas, roughly towelled dry on the unabsorbent roller-towel in the Ladies', was a godsend. This woman worked for him; well, let her work.

'Hoy!' he cried 'You! Here!' She had come, babbling apologies for the earlier disturbance.

'Never mind that. You *Chronicle* staff?'

'Yes – staff reporter, six-month contract. Sir.'

'You are seconded. From this minute. To my personal staff.'

'Er, thank you . . . How long, er?'

'While you are needed. You have a mobile? No? There is one in the cabin. Get me your Editor.' It had been as simple as that. Miss Douglas had since then found out the details of his evening appointment, made half a dozen calls as they occurred to him, located his dinner suit, brushed it, unpacked a light lunch of Parma ham and melon left labelled in the vast galley's chill cabinet, and driven Marie to the station after Eddie had treated her to a brief encounter in his cabin. During this latter embarrassingly obvious interlude, Dinny had sat on the flying bridge, thinking that if ever she were to change alliances – say, topple that harpy Maeve Mahoney on the *Globe* – she would have some stirring memoirs to write.

On the way to Paignton station, Marie had bolstered this conviction with some scarifying detail and made Dinny decide that her secondment to Eddie's personal staff should end well before dusk, and certainly before it got too personal. 'I don't know why he's getting shot of me now,' grumbled the call girl. 'He said he'd be too busy tonight. Dunno who with.'

Dinny flinched slightly and pulled up at the station.

The next visitor to *Privateer* was Keith, hot and flustered.

The marina office had directed him vaguely towards the end pontoons, 'outside one of the big boats'. The lack of interest or precision, oddly untypical of the marina Keith vaguely remembered from other visits, was not unconnected with his own quest. For two days, the owners and management of a large chain of marinas had been immured in meetings connected with getting the best deal out of a takeover by McArthur Holdings. For several weeks the staff had been so unsettled that any of them with alternative possibilities of employment had left the chain. The result was a state of uneasy, unhappy chaos, such as almost always presaged a McArthur takeover. (Had the employees but known it, however, this was as nothing to the state of unhappiness which generally occurred after the deal was signed).

The takeover was expected to be given the final nod at tonight's glittering function. It would have been kind of Eddie to have told them he was planning to spend two days in their marina first; but then Eddie was rarely kind. He had sent Guy up to pay the dues, and the student had entered the boat as *Private Ear* and the owner as McMaster. So Keith, not an avid reader of gossip columns, arrived in all innocence at the end of the pontoon where *Privateer*'s great white bulk lay.

There was a blonde woman in leather trousers and a smart but oddly streaked and crumpled green jacket on the stern deck, hammering at a laptop computer. She did not look up until Keith's third tentative 'I say!' and then only to glare at him.

'I say, I'm looking for a boat called *Shearwater*,' he said. The woman looked up properly this time.

'*Shearwater*?'

Her tone made Keith's heart leap. She must have seen the boat, to use such a tone.

'Yes, have you seen her? My wife—'

'Your wife?'

Maybe, Keith thought in brief despair, she was foreign and didn't speak any English. In his defence it must be said that around Bonhurst you didn't get to hear many of the flat, dead cool, up-yours little London voices that Dinny and her friends affected. She did sound faintly as if English was not her first language.

'Yes, my wife – Joanna – we're supposed to meet here.'

Dinny closed her computer, glanced down at Keith's picture in the folded newspaper next to her, and came to the rail.

'Mr Gurney, I have to tell you I am a journalist, *Daily Chronicle*, and we are also trying to trace your wife. If we could work together—'

'But she was here!' said Keith. 'She rang me. She's fine. You printed a lot of irresponsible nonsense—'

'I know. I wasn't involved in that. We'll be printing the facts tomorrow. Meanwhile, do you have any idea of where they might be heading?'

'No! I mean – what do you mean, they?'

'Your wife,' said Dinny, 'and the bisexual London prostitute, and her so-called protector Mr Guy Pastern-Hopkins, aged twenty-two, who has a criminal record for drug offences and has absconded with his employer's credit cards.' She drew breath, slightly puffed. Older reporters in the scandal game had often advised her that if you're going to hit 'em with what you know, you should hit 'em hard and fast. Then shut up, listen, and take down the next thing they say. The drug offence was pushing it a bit, but Eddie had let her ring his contract lawyer who had helpfully come up with Guy's one venture into serious criminality, viz. possession of a half-smoked spliff after the 1991 Varsity match. Every little helped, when you were hitting 'em hard and fast.

Now she waited for Keith to react with a good quote. 'I knew it!' would be nice. Or 'We were so happy – I can't believe that she had a Secret Life.' Dinny cocked an eyebrow enquiringly at the silent, thin, dignified figure below her on the pontoon. Keith looked at this woman, avid and gloating with her sharp little teeth and plucked eyebrows and the moist, red glisten of her lips. With a surge of affection he thought of Joanna's straight intelligent gaze and self-deprecating smile.

'I'm not surprised she sailed away from you lot,' he said. 'I'm going home. If you are planning to print any more libellous material, your Editor will be hearing from me, as my wife's legal adviser. Good afternoon.'

And he walked up the pontoon, without looking back.

20

A filthy, battered, ripped and mended canvas holdall bumped up the Old Vicarage steps, scraping against the worn stones. It lay exhausted, gaping at one seam to reveal a fray of blue denim within, while its owner clinked and fiddled with his keys. At last, the door swung open and the disgraceful bag was borne into the silent hall where motes of dust circled in the autumn sunshine. A rucksack thumped down beside the bag, and – after a sigh and a fumble from above – was joined by a well-worn leather bumbag bearing the initials LKG. The bags lay in the shaft of sunlight from the leaded fanlight over the door, exotically scruffy against the cool dull tiles. They lay untouched while their owner could be heard stamping around the house, opening and shutting doors (including the metallically clunking ones of fridge and freezer), scraping chairs, clattering crockery, and eventually climbing stairs and running taps.

They were still there an hour later, unmoved, when the door opened again and Susan Gurney came in. Her striped, slicked-back hair and beaky little nose gave her the look of a small fierce foreign animal confronting a TV wildlife film crew. She wore the preoccupied and grudging air with which she faced the outer world these days, but at the sight of the bags her eyes widened with pure and spontaneous pleasure and relief. On a rising note, clear and joyful, she cried, 'Lance!'

She could not have borne it, she thought, if he had gone out again. 'Lance!' But a door opened upstairs and a sleepy, tousled figure, hair down to his collar and moustache to his chin, peered over the banisters. He was wearing Joanna's Chinese nylon kimono which made him look like a reluctantly pressed understudy for a budget production of *The Mikado*. To his sister, Lancelot Keith Gurney was, however, an entirely beautiful sight. He yawned.

'Eeuh. Babysis. Sooze. Hi.'

Susan ran up the stairs, and delivered a friendly blow to his dragoned midriff. 'Lance. The hair! The 'tache! Dad'll have a fit. How was Europe?'

'Large and various,' said Lance, his hand on her shoulder. Despite his height and his hairiness, nobody who saw the two together could mistake them for anything but brother and sister. Their small, hawk faces and big intense eyes faced one another, each echoing the other's expressions as he spoke. 'Various and mainly smelly. Beautiful women hurling themselves at me. Hideous men hurling themselves after the beautiful women. Rabid dogs biting the hideous men. Art treasures. Whistling trains. Canals. Spies in trenchcoats coming out of the sewers. Cathedrals. Coffee shops. Great.'

'Why are you back? I thought you had another week.'

'Dunno. There I was in the Galaxy Café in Amsterdam, smelling my own socks and watching various dorks smoking their heads off, including my new friend Rudi the Ludicrous, who is wanted by the police of seven countries, so he says. Only I doubt if any of them would still want him if they had shared a hostel with him for a week.' He took a breath. 'And I suddenly thought: even the chairs are uncomfortable, so why am I here? So I took the train to the Hook and the ferry to Harwich and the coach to Southampton and the thumb to here, dreaming of afternoon tea with cuke sandwiches at the Bun in the Oven.'

Susan turned away and began picking varnish off the banister.

Lance continued, 'So I went to the Bun, and there is Erika Merriam drilling some poor little waitress in hair extensions like it was the Foreign Legion in pink check pinnies. And she looks at me as if I was Jack the Ripper. So I head for home, and on the way I meet Mrs Colefax coming out of Cuisine It All with a wok in brown paper. And she says what a good boy I am, a lovely son to come home and be there for my Poor Father. And I think "What, what?" So I come home, and here's nobody. And I boil a curry in a plastic bag from my baby sister's personal store of disgusting foodstuffs, and I go to bed.'

He paused, and gave her a penetrating glare. His voice dropped to a less theatrical level.

'And I wake up and say, what is going on, Susan? Why am I a Good Son? Why is Frau Obersturmfuehrer Merriam running the Bun?'

During this spirited recital Susan had removed most of the varnish from the ball on top of the newel post and started on the curve of banister, where the flakes proved toughter to dislodge. She abandoned it and kicked the post instead.

'Mum has run off, basically. On the boat. And it's been in the papers.'

'Which papers?' asked Lance, rather stupidly, just to give himself time.

'Heaps of them, the first day, with a little bit each. Now it's big bits in just the *Chronicle*, and a feminist rant in the *Globe*, saying Dad must be like Captain Bligh.'

'You are joking. Sure it didn't say Captain Birdseye?'

'It's not funny.' Susan kicked the post again. 'Yesterday Dad was really worried, in the gale. I couldn't stand it, so I went and slept at Annie's. Now apparently Mum's all right. Gone to Torquay, Alex says, and Dad's gone to find her, and I came back to see that Dad was all right. When he gets back.'

'He's gone to get her?'

'Alex thought that. But I don't know if she'll come with him. She did sail off. And Dad went to the police, and now there's awful things in the paper about how she might be having a, you know, breakdown. And about her having no friends, and being desperate enough to leave her children. Actually, Annie says that bit shows they're talking crap, because they said "innocent children", and she thinks that definitely couldn't mean you.'

'Anneliese is a menace.' Lance considered this information, frowning. 'So, do we worry?' He rubbed his chin, then went back into his bedroom, emerging with a small pocketbook, like a missal, which Susan recognized as an anthology entitled *Scorn* by Matthew Parris. It had been in Lance's Christmas stocking, a habit which Joanna doggedly refused to abandon, and had been an inspired choice. Like many deeply kind and sensitive people, Lance adored literary insults and contumely. He flipped the pages now, frowning.

'Here we are ... yes ... Norman Mailer. He should know. He said, "Once a newspaper touches a story, the facts are lost for ever, even to the protagonists." See? Perfect. Thank you, Mr Parris.' He closed the little book with a snap and hurled it through the door and onto his bed. He had been prone to these inconsequential literary gestures all his life; once, made to eat his lettuce at the age of four, he had toddled off to fetch *Peter Rabbit* and produced it as printed proof that 'eating lettuce does kill you, like Peter's Daddy'. Joanna had told that story a lot, until the children stopped her.

'For God's sake,' said Susan, irritated. 'What's the point of that?'

'The point is that you're all going on too much about the newspapers. Bugger what they say. If Mum has gone, the question is why has she gone? We're more likely to know than they are. Reading newspapers will only fog up your mind. What do we actually know? About why.'

'I was on the boat all weekend, with them arguing,' said Susan slowly. 'But it wasn't worse than usual. It was about Mum wanting to pack in the Bun.'

'So? It's her caff, where was the problem? Captain Bligh, don't tell me – he threatened to chain her to the cake rack? Dad?'

'No, course not. I think she sort of wanted him to *agree* that giving up the Bun was a good idea. And he just kept sounding pompous and saying how you shouldn't sell a healthy business in the middle of a recession, and how useful it was to the family finances, and how things were dodgy for him with Alex leaving.'

'Oh, yeah, I forgot. Alex is leaving to be a capitalist bastard, isn't he? So Mandy-pandy can have more holidays. But Dad's got Gus raring to buy in to the partnership, hasn't he?'

'Yeah, but ... Mum said that. Obviously. Said she couldn't see what all the fuss was about, since Gus was keen to buy in. And Dad stopped being pompous and lawyery and shouted that Gus was a moron and would drive him mad within a year because his clients drive him mad anyway and only Alex makes it bearable. He said if Gus was all he had in the office, he'd be the next one to walk out of work, and then who would keep a roof over our head?'

Susan paused. 'I'll tell you what it was like. It was like, um, that thing Mrs MacEvoy's always going on about in English. A subtext. It was as if *Dad* sort of wanted to give up everything and he was angry Mum thought of it first. And he wanted Mum to have the Bun as security. Only she couldn't see what he had to be angry about, because all she could think about was getting rid of the Bun. And he couldn't see that she really was desperate.'

'You mean they both want to drop out? Change?'

'Well, they can't. They have to keep on working and getting angrier and angrier, because neither of them can bring themselves to let the other one drop out. And they can't drop out themselves without asking. Because the other one would be left with the responsibility.'

It was a long speech for truculent Susan. Two days ago she could not have made such an analysis, nor would she have bothered. A lot had been achieved over two days of mentally replaying those last conversations of her mother's. Lance considered her thesis gravely.

'Do you think they're both burnt out? At work?'

'Well . . . sort of. But they never both said it at the same time. When Mum was talking about getting rid of the Bun, Dad was being all righteous and lawyerish. When he said the stuff about how Gus would drive him mad, Mum went sort of superior and amused as if he was a little boy who didn't like his new teacher.'

'She was never like that!' said Lance warmly. 'When I didn't like Mrs Harris, Mum came in and sorted her out.'

'Well, anyway. I thought she was treating Dad like a silly kid. And he was a bit stuck up, too. And all the time—' She stopped, suddenly struck by the brilliance of her own insight. 'All the time, they actually both want the same thing!'

'Perhaps they should drop out,' said Lance, with all the tranquillity of new-found independence and achievement. 'Be New Age travellers. Old Age travellers. Wrinkly wanderers, on the boat. Sell this heap.' Seeing Susan's appalled look, he added kindly, 'Once you've left school, obviously.'

'Ah. Well,' said Susan, slightly relishing her turn to appal him. 'That's the other thing. I just have.'

*   *   *

Keith had not slept more than a few hours since Monday. He had not eaten his Danish pastry, nor drunk his coffee. He had changed a wheel by the roadside in the spray of lorries' wheels and driven a hundred miles only to find his wife gone and in her place a disdainful young woman accusing her of complex and unexpected vice. He had been, for him, rather rude to the young woman. Strangely, that added to the burdens of his troubled mind. Keith did not believe in rudeness and conflict. His clients mainly did, which was why they needed him. Sometimes he felt like a sponge whose only function was to soak up the aggression of others. To be aggressive and unreasonable himself felt alien, as if he had put on someone else's jacket. Or rather, as if he had no jacket at all but stood – as he sometimes did in his nightmares – in front of the magistrates' bench wearing only a string vest. His anger made him feel naked.

Now, just outside Exeter, he was suddenly so weary that none of it mattered next to the pressing need for sleep. He pulled into a lay-by, locked the doors and let his head fall back on the seat. Around him, the Devon darkness gathered.

Erika Merriam was making soup. Not for Ted, who had already supped and was listening to the angling programme on local radio; but in epic quantities, to serve tomorrow at the Bun in the Oven. They ought to do soup. And, later, microwave potatoes with dainty garnishes for a simple hot meal at lunchtime. Mrs Gurney had always vetoed the suggestion, saying, 'Let's do what we do, really well, and not try to be a restaurant.' But Erika was growing daring. Mrs Gurney was off doing God knows what, and Erika was doing her a big favour. And, after prolonged negotiation, she had persuaded Ted that it would be less trouble for him if he popped into the Bun for his lunch. She could look after him with soup and a special bap at the quiet table behind the door while Zoë helped with the real customers.

The thought of Zoë in close conjunction with hot soup made Erika flinch for a moment, but the child was making definite progress. All she needed was training. Mrs Gurney was far too soft on the girls. Erika sliced a carrot, purposefully. Her scheme would work. She knew it.

*   *   *

Mandy Heron shivered on her leather sofa, an empty glass between her hands. Even with the vodka warming the hollow inside her a little, she was cold. She had not spirit enough to turn on the coal-effect fire or to fetch a jumper. On the huge television, the inanities of a quiz show flickered unseen. Alex banged around uncertainly in the kitchen, trying to put together some supper. Anneliese was upstairs, sketching out the furnishings she intended for her tiny Southampton bedsit.

Mandy began, for the third time that day, to cry silently. How dreary, she thought, how drab and pathetic to be crying. She had better think of something to do. The first thing, obviously, was to have another drink.

Sprawled before the fire which Lance, in the first flush of appreciative domesticity, had made in the living room, Susan by nine thirty was finishing her exposition to her brother of the great, the glorious, the daring and outrageous steps she had in secret taken since he left for the summer. She told how, even as her mother was buying her bottle-green sixth-form suit from the second-hand shop at Angela Merici and her father was prosing on about UCAS forms and the importance of working flat out for good grades at A level, she had given up the argument which had poisoned family life for the past year.

'That must have been a relief,' said Lance in superior tones. 'I never heard anybody make such a fuss about staying on for the sixth.'

'*They* never heard me at all. They didn't listen,' said Susan. 'They'd've rather I had a baby or something than not do A levels. So I stopped talking and started arranging.'

'So what did you actually do?'

'Wrote to the FE College, applied for the two-year vocational course in Publishing and Periodical Design – it's like two A levels really – and sent a portfolio. I used Alex's computer to do some desktop publishing. He's got all these amazing programmes he doesn't know how to get into, but Annie and I worked them out. Used the colour printer from the IT room at Angela Merici—'

'How?'

'Nicked it. In a games bag, the last Thursday of term. Brought it back Friday.'

Lance whistled his appreciation.

'Anyway, I sent it off, with all the forms and a letter. I applied for an out-of-area travel grant which they give to particularly promising students whose parents can't afford it.'

'But yours could. If they weren't paying school fees.'

'Yes, well, I sort of used Dad's signature, which is,' she flashed defiance at Lance's shaking head, 'easy peasy. And it's his fault for not listening. I got the grant agreed. It'll cover my half of the rent on Annie's bedsit, then I don't have to travel and I can get on with working. I really, really want to do this, Lance.' She looked at him beseechingly, and this time he nodded. 'It's not a skive. There's art and design history, typography, a really tough Use of English module, and fantastic technical access. There are five student magazines, and you get to work on each of them, from the daily sheet to the monthly glossy. They get people onto national magazines, into big publishers, all the time. One girl did work experience at DK and got taken on that same summer.'

She was flushed and eager, her surliness gone. All summer, with the great plan burning through her days and half her nights, there had been nobody but Anneliese to talk to about it; Anneliese was a mate, a flatmate-to-be, but she had opted for the one-year Fashion Design course, a less arduous business altogether. She rapidly tired of ravings about any form of scholarship. Lance did not. He looked at his sister with affection, then said gently, 'What are you going to live on, Sooze?'

In the ensuing moment of silence, Susan looked bleak. The travel grant manoeuvre had been a bit of bravura. Really, although she never admitted it even to herself, the entire plan would founder if Keith and Joanna stood firm. They could not get her back home by force, but they could starve her out. Back to Angela Merici? Never. Die sooner! But there it was. When you were sixteen, your parents still held all the aces.

Lance broke the silence. 'If it helps,' he said, 'I think you did the right thing.'

'But you're the Grade-A academic Cambridge scholarship wizard. I thought you'd say I ought to do A levels first.'

'I,' said Lance, 'am doing what I want. I want to read Physics as much as you want to learn about typefaces and mastheads and

White Space. My life revolves round the laws of matter which are second only to the power of love.'

'Oh, for God's—' began Susan angrily. He broke in, grinning.

'I may be weird but I am happy. So should you be. If you need money, I shall post you half my scholarship and half my student loan.'

'And what will you do then, dumbo? Starve?'

'Sell my body,' said Lance smugly.

'What, just the once? To the Medical School?'

The two scuffled their feet in battle for a moment like siblings five years younger, then Lance said, 'What about Mum, then?'

'I was dreading telling her,' said Susan. 'I'd have had to this week, 'cos the course starts on Monday and Mrs MacEvoy has been ringing every day from Angela Merici as it is. But now Mum isn't here to have the row with, I feel sort of empty.'

'The house feels empty,' agreed Lance.

'It did even when Dad was here, yesterday.'

'The Bun felt funny, too. Old Erika running it in a different kind of pinny. She's moved the tables round and put Zoë in pink gingham and a hair ribbon.'

'Dad was in a state. He misses her. Alex was all dithery this morning about having to lock up the café. Even Mandy's looking terrible. It's as if,' Susan said judicially, 'as if she'd vanished out of a picture and left a sort of Mum-shaped hole. Like one of those cut-out dolls.'

Lance reached over and threw a knob of coal onto the fire, wiping his hand on the dark part of the hearthrug pattern.

'Well, no wonder she buggered off,' he said.

'What do you mean?'

'Can't be much fun living in a Mum-shaped hole. What would happen if you wanted to move to another bit of the picture? Or wave your arms about? Or grow a bit in one direction and shrink in another?'

'I didn't mean literally.'

'I bet it felt literal, sometimes. Being a Bonhurst mum. Like being a live jellyfish someone's put in a china jellymould. I'll tell you something else, too.'

'What?'

'Bet you that after all this fuss, she couldn't fit back into her exact hole even if she tried.'

It was in the lull following this insightful remark that a white-faced Keith walked into the room and straight to the drinks cupboard. He had gulped down a large tot of whisky before he even noticed, lounging in the firelight and framed in unfamiliar hair, his son.

21

Shearwater cut through the sunset sea, her bow to glowing west, her outstretched and reddened sails giving her a gentle slant to port. Under the shelter of Prawle Point the water was calmer, and Della roused herself from the sick torpor of the afternoon. She sat, still close to Guy, on the downhill side of the cockpit, looking curiously at the changing coast and firing off streams of observations and questions.

'Doesn't the land look funny from out here. All spiky.'

'That's Bolt Head.'

'What happens if you bang into it when there isn't a proper harbour?'

'You get wrecked,' said Guy, beaming at his pupil.

'That's why you have to have charts.'

'What, like hospital charts?'

'No, it just means maps of the sea.'

'Why not call them maps?'

'Because . . . it's tradition. A lot of things have different names at sea.'

'Yeah, like calling the lounge the cabin. And when you and her were going on before, about sheets, and it turned out to be ropes.'

'There are other ropes with other names. Halyards, reefing lines, the topping lift.'

Della snorted. 'Yeah, and this verandah thing, whassit? Cotpip?'

'Cockpit,' said Guy kindly. 'And the floor isn't the floor, it's the sole. And the walls down there are actually bulkheads, and the ceiling of the cabin is the deckhead.'

'Like dickhead, you mean?'

Joanna, watching them absently from the helm, thought that perhaps the immaculate, classy Guy was not going to find the conquest of this spirited creature quite as smooth and flattering a process as he thought. Something about Della reminded her of Susan, and brought back the vague discomfort and guilt that afflicted her whenever she thought about her daughter.

Why could she appreciate the life and spark in this red-clawed call girl and yet be irritated beyond anything at Susan's defiances? Why was Susan such a thorn? Susan in childhood had been a joy: affectionate and clever, good-natured and energetic. Even two years ago there was still pleasure in family suppers, family holidays. Lance at sixteen and Susan at fourteen had had the normal share of moods but remained true and recognizable inheritors of their wonderful baby selves. Their high spirits energized the household, as they had down all the years from hammer-peg toys to GCSE choices. They fulfilled the ideal of family life that Joanna had chosen. The life that she had *planned*, she thought with sudden, bitter passion. She planned it in that time of silence after Port Meadow.

Keith, Lance, Susan were the family she had dreamt of so fiercely when she turned her back on Oxford, Gabriel, Emily and all the muddled, yearning, suicidally unconfined passion of Leckford Road. She wanted none of it: no more late nights with *Lear* and *Troilus and Criseyde* and Wagner on the record player, no morning bike rides through the misty spires with a breast painfully, gloriously full of unimaginable surging hopes for something she could not even define. All that poetry had led her only to disaster. She had wanted prose. The muck and muddle, the laughter and banality, the relentless small practical demands of family life had been what she wanted. What she needed.

And now they were evaporating. Lance was a joy, but he had been gone two months, faded away leaving only postcards from Inter-Rail Europe to console her. And most of them were as enigmatic as smiles from the Cheshire Cat. Soon he would go to Cambridge and enter his own time of poetry and intensity, perhaps. She would not worry about him overmuch. Lance had sense. He was robust. He had even been proof against the wiles of Anneliese.

Susan? Susan was still home, but distant and sullen. These days, her scorn had a real edge to it, and family life was anathema to her. Joanna had wondered about drugs – the symptoms in the leaflets were all there: change in behaviour, evasiveness, loss of interest in schoolwork – but in her heart she knew this was unlikely. Lance had been caught smoking cannabis in the sixth form but had charmed his headmaster into not sacking him because, he explained, it was the first time and he only did it in order to contemplate Einstein's general theory of relativity when high, just to see if it was even more wonderful.

'But it wasn't,' he had said. 'So that's that, for me, with drugs.' The head had believed him. Susan had called him a dork, and Lance later told his mother that Susan was famous in her circle for scorning drugs, drink, and random snogging. 'She's more serious than any of us,' he said. Joanna could not see it that way, but had held her peace, watching her daughter with loving, anxious, but increasingly joyless attention.

'Do *you* get on with your mother?' she asked Della suddenly, this thought happening to coincide with a lull in the girl's stream of questions. Della considered, pouting slightly.

'Well, I didn't,' she said. 'I def'nitely didn't for a bit. But that was when I was leaving home. Now she's all right. She doesn't like me doing the escort work, obviously, but I do go home. Some weekends, you know.'

'Why did you leave?'

'Just boring. My mum never does anything different. Work, telly, bingo, and off to the library every week for two new Mills and Boons. She really likes her life. She thinks I ought to do a secretarial, then marry a Leicester boy from a nice white family where the Mum's just like her, and do just like she does.'

'And what did you want? Really want? When you decided to go?'

Della wriggled. 'Sounds silly if I say it.'

'No, it doesn't. Go on.'

'We're all a bit silly on this boat today,' said Guy, helpfully. 'I bet you had a jolly good idea what you wanted.'

'Well . . .'

'There's nothing wrong with wanting to be rich and famous,' prompted Guy. 'Like Dick Whittington. I sort of ran away when

I came to work for Mr McArthur. At least, my dad didn't like it.'

Della regarded him with surprised scorn. 'I didn't think of *that*,' she said, with all the grandeur of a duchess to whom someone has mentioned the market value of her ancestral silver tureen. 'I wasn't thinking of being *rich*, not just for the money, anyway. I just wanted to have adventures.'

'Adventures?' said Joanna, trying to keep her voice bland and not too curious.

'Yeah.' Della paused, but something in the hypnotic, swaying, confidential atmosphere of a yacht sailing down the sunset made her go on. 'I had this book, at baby school – I had it a long time 'cos I was a bit slow with the reading. My teacher said I might be dys-leckic but my dad said that was middle-class talk for thick, and he kept threatening to go round and thump the teacher. So she gave up about that. Anyway, the book. It had stuff in it about adventures.'

'What sort?' asked Guy.

'Giants,' said Della firmly. 'And fairies and princes and swords and caves with dragons in.'

Joanna stared at her, entranced. In her flimsy short skirt, strappy sandals and huge Keith sweater, Della looked like a ten-year-old, remembering.

'Do you remember any of the names of the people in the book?'

'Yeah – well, the monsters mainly. Grendel, with long green arms. And Giant Despair.'

'Did everyone get the book?' asked Joanna wonderingly. This child was Lance's age, or a year older. And from his childhood she remembered a dourly multicultural, inner-city, kitchen-sink type of school reader, with not a real adventure in them. Lance's primary teacher had chided her once for reading him *Beowulf* in a modern translation: too violent by far. She was curious that such an outmoded, heroic early reader should have survived into Della's Midlands childhood.

'No,' said Della. 'It was Miss Leckie's own one. She lent it me 'cos I was the only one in slow-reading group that year. I had,' said Della with regret, 'to give it back.'

'Do you mean you ran away to find dragons and things?' said Guy.

'Yeah. S'pose so.' Della huddled into Keith's jumper. 'I s'pose so. Big things, anyway. Adventures. Not just,' she shot an unfathomable look at Guy, 'not just blokes.'

'And you found Eddie McArthur,' said Guy. 'I'd say he was probably the nearest thing to a dragon around, these days.'

'Ahead,' said Joanna, 'is the entrance to Starhole Bay, I think. Guy, could you fetch the chart up?'

Dinny Douglas succeeded, at the fourth try and after reducing a receptionist to tears, in filing her copy by modem from the hotel. This entailed disconnecting the switchboard for five minutes, and was only made possible by the threat that she would bring Mr McArthur up personally. At last, the flickering acknowledgement from the *Chronicle* mainframe computer was on the screen of her laptop. 'Total sent 1500 wds,' it said. Dinny promptly switched off, unplugged her lead from the telephone socket, slid the machine into its flat grey bag, and walked away from the desk without turning her head or thanking the anxious girl behind it. She was unlikely to need any more help from the receptionist, so why waste smiles? The girl had been a pain.

Back on the marina pontoons, she began to phrase her speech to Eddie McArthur. 'Mr McArthur, I think I ought to get myself back to the paper. Perhaps I could call up London and organize you another personal secretary to come straight down, one of your staff there, perhaps, who knows the work . . .' She was not, definitely not, staying the night on that creepy boat with that creepy man.

On the other hand, the creepy man did own the *Chronicle*. And was moving in on other ailing newspapers. There were reporters – and editors – who would give their eye teeth to be where she was now, close and necessary to the Proprietor. Gordon, for one, the oily prat. But then it would be different for Gordon, wouldn't it? He wouldn't feel quite the same threat that she did, would he? She thought of Marie's disgruntled revelations, and shuddered. Bloody men. Nobody preyed on them, did they? They could take their chances without risking – that sort of thing. The laptop computer banged against her hip as she walked faster, more irritably.

Back aboard *Privateer*, Eddie sat smoking a small cigar in the big saloon. He was wearing a purple velvet dinner jacket which made him look like a large, Satanic plum. He raised his terrible peaked black eyebrows and greeted her as expansively as if he had guessed at her reservations.

'My dear. You got your copy filed. Excellent. I am glad your editor has got a few competent people around him. What contract do we have you on?'

'Six monthly, renewable but not rolling.'

The little man's eyebrows shot up, exaggeratedly. 'Six *months*? The man is more careless than I thought. You can't keep really good staff on short contracts. I shall,' he made a note on a silver-backed pad on which he had been scribbling earlier, 'speak to him.' He smiled wolfishly. 'Or, should I say, to his successor.'

Bravely, Dinny struggled on with her speech. 'Mr McArthur, your taxi is arranged for five minutes' time. Perhaps I should be getting back to the paper . . .'

He had stopped listening and was frowning at one of the preceding pages of his silver tablet. Her voice faltered and died. There was a silence.

'Splendid. Taxi back, from the Criterion, at ten thirty sharp. We sail early. You had better make yourself at home in the secretary's quarters. You may choose any clothes you need for sea, and throw the rest of his luggage overboard.' He rose, snapped his silver book shut, threw it onto the varnished table with a clatter, and was gone. He had learned, early in a buccaneering business career, that a good exit was worth five good entrances.

Starhole Bay was not such good cover as Guy had suggested. Anybody steaming across Salcombe Bar could see into it easily and make out any boat silhouetted against the towering cliffs. When *Shearwater*'s anchor was down, Guy fussed for a while over disguising the yacht's silhouette. He laid a dinghy oar out over the bow to look like a bowsprit, took the spinnaker pole and a collection of ropes and rigged the pole upright on the boat's modest after hatch, to mimic a second mast.

'He won't be looking for a yawl,' he said hopefully. The other dinghy oar, with the sail cover bundled round it, did service as a dummy boom. The sun was gone now, and in the dusk against the glimmer of the cliffs and the rising moon his work was moderately convincing. Below decks, Jo had lit the brass paraffin lamps for warmth as much as light, and was rootling under bunks for the emergency stock of food. Della huddled in the corner of the cabin, looking curiously around her at the strange, nautical shapes of things in the flickering lamplight.

'Put the anchor light up,' called Joanna to Guy. 'Side locker.'

'We mustn't.'

'It'll look more suspicious if we don't. Anyway, he won't come.'

'Well . . . all right.' Guy banged around, hunting for the aluminium lantern, filling and lighting it, hauling it up between the forestay and the real mast. Joanna, fumbling under a bunk locker with the lid balanced on her head, pulled out three steak pies designed to be baked in their tins once the top had been taken off, two tins of peas and a tin of carrots. 'That's it, I'm afraid,' she said to Della. Then she remembered something, clawed up a floorboard, and reached down into the boat's damp, cool, bilge. 'Aah! Thought so.' Triumphantly, she hauled out two bottles of white wine.

'I got some chocolate,' said Della unexpectedly. 'And some raisins. Marie said always go on a job with something to eat, you never know when you might feel faint.' She thrust her thin arm into the mock-Gucci bag and hauled out a pound slab of milk chocolate and a plastic bag full of miniature raisin packets, of the kind Joanna used to slip into Susan's lunchbox. Tears sprang unexpectedly to her eyes as she took them.

'Thanks. That's pudding, then.'

Replacing the cushions on the bunk, she straightened up in the small cabin and took one step to the galley. Behind it, stuffed casually upright in a cave locker behind a wooden bar, was an almost full bottle of Scotch, the last of the season.

'Drink?' she asked.

Guy came below. With the pies in the oven and the vegetables ready mixed up in the saucepan, the three sat together in the lamplight, the whisky warming them from within, the cliffs glimmering and swinging lazily across the portholes.

22

Not everybody is gathered, by nightfall, in the primitive safety of a firelit circle at the hearth. Not everyone is around a lamp with food and friends, or even (like Eddie McArthur at that moment) lapped in the tribal dignity of a banqueting suite, a Rotarian Valhalla.

Some are outsiders, prowling alone, free from the stifling warmth of human kinship. Some prefer it that way. Brief, jagged encounters will do for them, whether of battle or love. They will visit a fire, their wolf eyes gleaming white in the outer shadows. For a moment, maybe for a spell of days or weeks, they will sit, looking almost like the peaceable house-dogs around. But then they will go, without warning or apology, back into their formless darkness at the edge of things. They will be free and alone, available for the next kill or the next mating.

Just such a prowler was picking his way across the network of grimy streets to the north of Oxford Circus, stepping absentmindedly over the outstretched feet of the cardboard-box sleepers who were already settling for the night, propped like November guys in the doorways of wholesale clothing shops under the cold sickle moon. He had come from a lamplit circle, the lone walker; a circle in a cheerful restaurant on the corner of Tichfield Street where diving suits, trombones and stuffed fish hung wittily from the ceiling and every table had a clashing oilskin cloth. He had come from the circle because it bored him.

He had thrown down his share of the bill – or an approximation to it – and said abruptly that he must get back to the office to sort out a couple of things. His companions, all younger than he, had said, 'Oh, shame!' and 'stay for some tiramisu'. But they had been, he could see, secretly relieved at his going. He was prone to rant, these days, at the young. They were so *middle-aged*, with their earnest relationships, their new babies, their footling talk of primary education and play spaces, their bright aseptic clothes and bright boring ideas and their infernal, soul-killing political correctness.

At the moment when he left, they had been discussing a Potrayal Seminar which three of them in the department had been attending. Fascinating, the young ones agreed, to get in touch with the racism and sexism in oneself; even more fascinating to overcome it. They really appreciated the opportunity to learn how fruitful it could be to introduce characters into their work – for these were all, in some degree, peddlers of the Drama – characters which called the stereotypes into question. Jake had a marvellous script sent in, said Ellie, about a deaf-mute Asian storyteller whose pregnancy grew as her tale did, 'so that the childbirth moment and the legend's climax came together, you see, in blood'.

And he, the walker through the streets, had rudely interrupted and asked how the fuck were you going to make a decent radio play out of a bloodstained deaf-mute? And where would the pleasure of it be, anyway? Where the beauty, where the thrill?

They had stared at him uncomfortably. And, leaving, he had known that all the anti-stereotyping seminars in the world would not prevent those colleagues, after he left, from referring to him as an old fart, an ageing hippie, a bit of a throwback. They would say he was losing his edge. Hah!

He padded on through the dark streets in his canvas shoes, his greying hair curling over his collar, the crumpled carrier bag he used as a briefcase completing a trampish appearance. As he negotiated the street sleepers around his feet, he might almost have been about to sit in a doorway himself. Bugger his young colleagues! Bugger the whole lot in charge these days, with their seminars and prissy little workplace sexual harassment guidelines (he had fallen foul of those a good few times, which added greatly to his grievance and his sense of precariousness in employment). He did not belong to this tribe, not any more. The old ones, the good old ones, had gone or died or mutated horribly into supporters of the brisk new regime.

He would get out. Go somewhere clean and new, perhaps to the west of Ireland and the mountain which was his namesake. He would write a magnificent novel and raise two fingers to the Philistine bastards at the BBC.

For it was at Broadcasting House, the great battleship building into which he finally stepped, that he and his convivial colleagues worked. He waved a plastic identity card irritably at the security man and walked a long, wide corridor to the second set of lifts. Inside one of them, alone, he broke deafening wind as he rose six floors: an open, but safe, defiance of his surroundings. Finally he and the carrier bag travelled over a certain carpet – hideously spotted with carpet tiles bearing tragic and comic mask designs, to indicate that this was the Drama Corridor – and turned into his office.

He preferred to keep erratic hours, these days, ever since he had acquired an open-plan office to be shared with Neville and Ellie. Both were immensely talented, he had been told, but to him both were immensely annoying. In the old days, the 1970s even, a man could have his own cell, ten feet by six, in the great honeycombed building and tread his own path. Now the walls were swept down and memos were sent around about creative interpersonal interacting and God knows what, and a man had no privacy to make rather private telephone calls, which were usually to young women in need of a wise mentor. Neville, at the end desk, had a wife and new baby in Greenwich and a penchant for plays by women. No, he thought savagely. Not even women: wimmin, or womyn. Ellie was a total nightmare, dressed all in ragged black, with tight leggings, like a scarecrow witch. She took offence at the slightest thing, especially slight things to do with his fascination with her leggings. She went on and on about the depravity and inadmissibility of any work by dead white males. Which was fine; had he not himself in his day talked down the Shakespeare season, ridiculed the old buffers who wanted to put on Rattigan, and produced a savage parody of Noel Coward?

It was just that these days, even living white males seemed to be out of favour. He had heard Ellie saying Tom Stoppard was a closet fascist, and Samuel Beckett a phallocentricist. He had not argued. A mark of his depression, these days, was that he did not bother. He just drank a little more at lunchtime, and on one memorable occasion vomited, neatly, right onto the nearest fancy carpet tile to his office. The masks of comedy and tragedy looked up at him reproachfully through the pile of sick, and Ellie had refused to clean it up, even though she was the only woman in the office. One mask of tragedy still bore a hideous grey smirk.

Sitting down at his desk now, he listlessly turned over the latest project: a three-part poetic drama about Lilith, first wife of Adam and symbol of the old wild pre-Christian goddesses, dispossessed by demure and obedient Eve and haunting the world in anger down the centuries. He had thought he could sneak it past Ellie and Neville on the feminist ticket and so get some full-blooded politically incorrect poetry onto the air. About thighs, and milky clefts, and breasts. But already the project had run into trouble over the word 'whore'. Ellie felt it was 'being used in a negative way'. Irritably, he pushed it aside.

There was a copy of the *Chronicle* on the desk, left there no doubt by the secretary the three of them shared. He looked at the front – a lot of fuss about some windy night in the Channel – and turned the page listlessly. Then his eye lighted on a woman's face and the years fell away.

MISSING, it said. MISSING. She was missing, all right. She was what he had been missing. The wide eyes, the direct honest gaze, the slight melancholy around the mouth, the cloud of dark hair. Joanna Telford, by God! Joanna Gurney, they called her here, but there was no doubt. She looked hardly different from the girl he had known: still young, open-faced, but perhaps a little more secure, less clinging, than he remembered her. She could not have been more than nineteen then. Ten years his junior.

And women had all been clinging, then. Lord, how women had changed! They seemed to set the pace these days, take their piece of action with one eye still on their career and the safety of their own psyche, and move on with brisk antiseptic firmness of purpose, like nurses. Women in his young days used to yearn and worship and give themselves completely; they used to wash socks and serve meals and be like Ben Bolt's Alice, who wept with delight when he gave her a smile and trembled for fear at his frown. And they used to cling and weep and have to have it gently pointed out to them when it was time to move on. Now, girls seemed to move *him* on, ever more briskly. Women had definitely changed.

Unless it was he who was less clingable-to? He pushed the thought aside. Joanna Telford! Gurney. Who was Gurney? Some chap she had found who let her cling. Kids, it said here. He closed his eyes and imagined her breast-feeding. Nice tits, always had. Like Lilith's in the poetry-drama, 'bird-soft, bird-white, breathing with life's breath'.

Suddenly, he was awake and sober and purposeful. This would kick-start the novel. A great project was swelling within him. Pushing off his canvas shoes, he began pacing the room in his hairy socks. The BBC wanted rid of him, one of the last few staffers in his job. His head of department had hinted heavily at voluntary redundancy with a decent payoff. He would talk the payoff up by a few thousand, take it, and go to the far west of Ireland and rent a cheap cottage. But first he would find this older Joanna and – if her effect on him was anything like her picture's effect – he would rescue her from this blighted Hampshire existence of hers, of which quite clearly she had grown sick and tired. He would appear as the fulfilment of an old dream, change her meaningless life, and permit her, this time, to cling and serve and inspire him while he wrote.

He may not have been quite as sober as he thought. Nonetheless, it did not take him long to pad down to the newsroom where the national telephone directories lived, and find the only Gurney in Bonhurst. From their computer terminals, annoyed-looking young people glanced meaningfully at his socks. Taking no notice, he wrote the number on the back of his broad hand and padded back upstairs, deciding not to call the lift in case the waiting spoilt his purposeful, self-starting mood. On the way out of the long newsroom he saw a pile of early copies of the Thursday morning papers, on their way to the compilers of the morning news bulletins. He glanced around at the young people intent on their terminals, and neatly filched the *Chronicle*. Might be something else about Joanna.

Back in his silent office he spread it out and whistled softly through pursed lips. Even better. The photograph was the same, but to freshen it up the picture desk had cropped it lower down and brushed out the neckline of Joanna's jumper, to give a décolleté impression. Then someone had suggested cropping the hairline at the sides 'to bring out the lesbian theme a bit'. The result was, to the lonely reader in the drama office, even more appealing. As for the text, – headed 'SAILAWAY WIFE IN GAY HOOKER MYSTERY', it could hardly be more stimulating. He pulled down Neville's atlas and looked for a while at the south-west coast of Britain, then picked up the telephone and dialled the number written on the back of his hand. A young man answered.

'Mr Gurney? Sorry to trouble you. I'm an old friend of Joanna's. My name's O'Riordan. Gabriel O'Riordan.'

Lance, who had answered the telephone, had never heard the name before, nor the soft, cultured, faintly Irish tones. He had, however, just spent ten minutes with his father and sister, listening in increasing bafflement and worry to an incoherent answerphone message. More of a short radio drama, really, complete with sound effects: 'Keith . . . *ccrrrr, skcrrrr* . . . leave Torquay – I'll be in – *crrrk* – (cry of "No . . . the Boss!") . . . safe harbour anyway. Don't worry. Tomorrow I'll go in to – *scccrrrk* – *cchhhhh* – ("No . . . not safe – he's a pervert" – *cccrrr* – *thump, eugh* (sounds of vomiting, flapping sails, "Shit!" in a male voice . . . "Are we sinking? Aaaaah" . . . Shut up, you two – *crrrrrk* . . . *thump* – "Owwww . . . are we sinking . . . going to rip!" . . . *shhhrrrrrkkk* . . . too bad, Keith, I will . . . *crrrkkk* . . . Salcombe. 'Bye.'

After this, any coherent voice on the telephone seemed very welcome. Lance was a trusting boy, and was lulled by Gabriel's expressions of concern and the fact that he seemed to be able to put names with some confidence to the background figures on the tape – 'Gather that she's with some friends of ours, Della Jones and Guy Pastern-Hopkins . . . hoping to join them for a drink. Was it Dartmouth they were heading for?' So it was not many moments before Lance shared with Gabriel the one useful word in the answerphone message: Salcombe.

'That could have been the fucking *press*!' howled Susan as he put the receiver down.

'I never thought of that,' said Lance, a little crestfallen. 'I'm not used to all this suspicion, like you lot. Sorry.'

Keith looked up from the sofa where he had been lying with a frequently replenished whisky glass in his fist for the past half-hour.

'Dun't matter,' he said, slurring a little. '"M going to Salcombe in the morning. Sort it out. Sh'can decide if sh's bloody coming or bloody staying away. Sick of it. Whassat doorbell? Inna middle of the night?'

Anneliese stood on the doorstep, apologetic. Behind her trembled an almost unrecognizable Mandy, her hair limp, her eyes red with crying, her puffed-up pink jacket clashing horribly with green Bermudas and a flapping red T-shirt.

'Suzie, Mum can't drive us to college tomorrow,' she said. 'She's going to find your mum, she says.' Lowering her voice, she hissed, *Vodka*.'

'Got to say sorry, tell her I never said any of it,' said Mandy. 'Going to go to all the harbours, find her. Come to tell Keith it's all my fault. Before bed. Not let the sun go down on it. Wrath.'

'Where's Alex?' asked Susan, practically.

'That's the other thing,' said Anneliese. 'Apparently there's a fire, at the Bun. The fire brigade rang up. It's OK now, but things got a bit wet and muddled. Erika Merriam is there helping, and she rang us, said one of the owners should be represented, so Popsy went.'

'Just as well,' said Lance who was watching Mandy as she knelt by the sofa, clutching the hand of a dazed, complaisant Keith and weeping on it. 'Your ma's breath would probably have started the fire up again.'

23

The golden glow of *Shearwater*'s paraffin lamp sparkled off the wet cutlery piled up beside the tiny sink, sent gleams along the varnished cabin table and shone, unimpeded, through the clear glass of the empty whisky bottle. It blended prettily with the green of two wine bottles, also empty, which lay propped in the corner of the starboard bunk. Joanna had put them there to make more room for all their elbows.

'Amazing,' Guy said unsteadily, 'how much room elbows take up. Just six elbows.'

'They're ever so handy,' said Della, 'for keeping your head propped up when you go a bit floppy.' She leaned forward, elbows spreading, and was asleep.

Joanna flicked a crump of pie crust from her shoulder, ate her last square of Della's emergency chocolate and rose carefully to her feet, steadying herself on the pillar under the mast.

'I think,' she said, 'we had better have some coffee.'

'We're not *drunk* exactly,' said Guy. 'I've been a lot drunker.'

'Thassright,' said Joanna, ducking expertly under the low deck beam. 'I've had it before on boats. It's the fresh air. And the food. And reaction. Relaxing. It does for you. Not the same as really drunk.'

She leaned on the safety bar in front of the galley, remembering other times. Once, when Lance was a baby, she and Keith had come through a hard Channel crossing, tied up in Cherbourg marina and fallen asleep in their clothes at one o'clock in the morning, their two heads on the cabin table and their hair trailing in spilt cocoa. And that was after just one whisky, the one they had splashed in the cocoa. They had woken at six, miserably uncomfortable, to hear the baby whimpering for his morning feed. While Joanna fed Lance, Keith had fried them both a large breakfast. They ate it, made love while Lance played with his toes and gurgled himself back to sleep in the forecabin, then slept again until nine. It was only then that they had noticed the stiff spikes of dried cocoa in their hair. But they hadn't been drunk, exactly.

Now, her hands flickering around the familiar shapes of the galley, she filled the kettle and reached for the matches. Della was fast asleep on the far corner of the table, her hair spilling over her face, relaxed as a baby. Guy gazed at her.

'Don't you think she's terrific?' he said in a low voice. 'I've never met a girl quite like her.'

Joanna looked across at the sleeping girl. 'Mmm – yes,' she said. 'Guy, if I were you—' She stopped, and concentrated rather too hard on lighting the gas jet.

'What?' said Guy. 'I mean, I really would value your sort of view. There are obvious, sort of, problems—'

'You mean because she's an escort girl?'

'No, no. I mean, things are so different now, aren't they? I mean quite important people, MPs and all that, go out with, um, escort girls. It's not sort of Victorian . . .'

'No,' said Joanna. 'But I think you ought to meet each other in a more ordinary sort of place, perhaps, a few times. Everything might look different.'

'I know,' said Guy. 'I found that before. Round Mr McArthur everything seems kind of different, more sort of brightly coloured, if you know what I mean. You decide things faster. Apparently his last secretary but two went off and joined a sect. Actually,' he added in a burst of confidence, swinging the brass lamp rather irritatingly so that the mugs Joanna was filling with coffee grew long, wavering, menacing shadows, 'if you hadn't been here I think I'd probably have asked Della to marry me by now.'

'I don't think—'

'No, no, of course I won't. Frighten her off, for a start. I'll take her out a bit, back in London. But I'm absolutely sure she's up to it. My parents would love her, honestly.'

Joanna, filling the mugs, decided that Guy would not see her point at all, even if she could bring herself, *in vino veritas*, to be impolite enough to make it. The question was not whether Della was up to Guy's standards, but whether Guy could keep up with Della. Not socially; intellectually.

Good heavens, she thought, passing him his coffee with a guilty smile, is that really what I think? That this nineteen-year-old call girl without an exam pass to her name is more than a match, *intellectually*, for this Cambridge graduate, albeit a scraped one, four years her senior? For this man-of-the-world and aide to one of the most powerful magnates in Britain?

'Yes,' she said inwardly. 'Yes, I do think exactly that. Guy is limited. Always will be.' The Guys, she saw, run along the rails and do as they are told. They are happy inside the system. That is why McArthur chose him as a gopher, she thought. That is why MPs and stuffy institutions take on boys of his type. They run on rails. McArthur's real, cutting-edge workers would surely be more like barrow boys, streetwise kids, the type who turned up in City jobs in the 1980s: student rebels or school dropouts, lads with ideas of their own.

Whereas Della, dyslexic Della, who walked out on home and family to find adventure, who took one look at McArthur and did a pierhead jump, whose spiky little personality provoked Guy into his first ever derailment, Della was different. Joanna looked fondly at Della's tousled blonde head.

Guy had taken his coffee from her during this reverie and climbed unsteadily into the cockpit to drink it on the foredeck. 'Get a bit of air,' he explained, "f that's all right.' At the thumping sound of his progress across the cabin top, Della woke up, looked around wildly, and smiled when she saw Joanna holding out a mug towards her.

'Ta. Where's Guy?'

'On deck.'

'Can he hear us?'

'Nope. Not from the foredeck.'

'Can I ask you something?'

'Yes.'

'What d'you think I oughter do? About him?'

'How do you mean?'

'He's going on about tennis, and meeting in London, and my

staying at his flat while I get another job, and all that. D'you think he's, you know, serious?'

'Yes. I think he is. Are you glad?'

'Well, I was. I really fancied him this morning. But just, you know . . . he's sort of a bit of a bimbo, in't he?'

'Don't you want a bimbo man?'

'Not for always.'

'What do you want? Rhett Butler?'

'Nah. Actually, I'd like . . .'

'What?'

'A rest from blokes. Something else. Some new place. A proper job. *Then* I might fancy going out with Guy.'

'What's brought this on?'

'Well . . . this, actually.' Della gestured, taking in the cabin lamp, the bunks, the varnished lockers, the compact snugness of it all, the chart still lying on the chart table in a businesslike way. 'It's sort of . . . *dignified.*'

'You mean the boat?'

'Yeah, it's like a whole house, with food and everything, only going somewhere, and you steering it.'

'Normally,' said Joanna, 'I sail it with my husband, Keith. Not on my own. This is the first time on my own.'

'Is he the captain, then, when he's here? Not you?' Della looked disappointed.

'No . . . not exactly captain . . . we sort of share the decisions. But it is different when he's here. It's OK, though.'

'Why did you run away with the boat, then?'

'I was upset,' said Jo, slowly. 'I was upset, because Keith wouldn't listen to what I wanted. I wanted to give up my job and try to study again. Or something. I wanted to change my life.'

'And he wouldn't let you?'

'It isn't a matter of letting. I could have done it without asking him. It's my money, my investment. But I wanted him to agree. I wanted him to see why I wanted to change. Once you're married . . .'

She paused. Della hung, interested, on the beginning of that sentence, so immemorially fascinating to women who are not yet married but think they might be. Joanna looked at her and felt a sudden tug of responsibility. She must not mislead this child. She continued, carefully, thinking it out as she spoke.

'Once you're married, all sorts of decisions have to be joint decisions. Else things don't work. If one of you steamrollers the other, it feels bad, even if you're the winner. Feels worse if you're the loser. So you have to work hard at agreeing. You have to put work into thinking the way the other person thinks. Sometimes you feel as if it would be less bother if you each just ran your own life and met for bed, or to discuss the children. But really, that wouldn't work either.'

'You can't agree about everything, though,' said Della, sceptically.

'No. But even if the other person doesn't quite agree, they have to understand what makes you do things. Respect it. Otherwise, it's lonelier than if you weren't married at all.'

Della thought, frowning, her head thrown backwards to rest on the varnished bars of the bookshelf.

'I don't think I want to get married. Not for a long time. It'd really, really slow you down, all that discussing, fitting in with someone else, wouldn't it?'

'Yes,' admitted Joanna. 'It does. But there are compensations.'

'How old were you,' continued Della relentlessly, 'when you got married?'

'Twenty,' said Joanna. 'Too young.'

'So why did you?'

'Because . . . because . . . I don't know,' said Joanna. Again, that strange tug, that insistent voice making her find a truth to tell this girl. 'Yes, I do know.'

'Why then?'

'Because I met a good man. A good, ordinary man. And I wanted a good, ordinary, decent life. Children. Kindness. Ordinary family jokes. Knowing all day who you'd be in bed with at the end of it. I didn't want any more . . . chaos.'

'Did you have chaos before, then?' Della was wide awake now, peering curiously over the mug which she held like a chipmunk in both small paws. What sort of chaos could this grown-up lady, who steered her boat so surely, have ever been involved in?

'Chaos of love,' said Joanna, stretching out on the bunk. 'I was

– had been – terribly in love with a man who wasn't ordinary, and wasn't good either.'

'What'd he do?'

'He used women – girls – for a while and threw them over.'

'Well, lots of them do that. Even at school they did. You don't trust them, ever. It's stupid.'

'I did,' said Joanna. 'I trusted him with my life. But the bad thing, the real point wasn't just that he threw you over. The bad thing he did was that he made it feel as if it was your fault. He made people feel really silly, and small. Sometimes it hurt them so much they – well, very much, anyway.'

'And your ordinary bloke, your husband, he didn't go round hurting people?'

'He asks a lot of himself. He takes blame. He doesn't cause people pain unless he really can't help it, and then he stays awake all night worrying. I told you, he's a good man.'

'So you didn't just marry him to be ordinary and have kids?'

'N-no. I think he was the one,' said Joanna. 'Really, truly, the right one for me. I think he would have been anyway. But when we got married I'm not sure I knew that. I might have been thinking too much about the ordinary secure bit, and not really encouraging him to be anything else.'

'Is he boring?'

'No,' said Joanna, with dignity. 'Certainly not. We have a lot of laughs.'

'So,' said Della. 'Why'd you run away?' She paused, a puzzled frown spreading over her face. 'Oh. Sorry. I asked you that at the start.'

Joanna stared at her for a moment and then began to laugh, and laugh, until tears ran down her face and Guy, tipsily half-asleep on the foredeck, woke and realized that there was a mast cleat sticking into his back and that he would rather be below, cosily in a bunk. Leaving the moon and the cliffs and the cold night air, he came below to find Joanna and Della opposite one another, elbows on the table, heads touching, laughing together like children who have just understood a wicked, adult joke.

Eddie McArthur returned majestically to his boat at midnight, sated with sycophancy. The Rotarian Valhalla had been a fine one; he had kept his taxi waiting for an hour and a quarter while he circulated among the guests for an unprecedented length of time. He had enjoyed the gathering of provincial businessmen, finding that their admiring deference and slight fear, which usually would have rather bored him, on this occasion were balm to wounded pride. Thoughts of revenge on Guy and Della had almost faded from his mind. Life was good. Those who were not with him were against him, but those against him were negligible. Powerless. Barely worth a thought, let alone an undignified pursuit. His small, rotund form almost bounced down the marina pontoon towards the looming bulk of his ship.

The saloon was lighted; beyond its thin curtain he could see the shadowy form of young Miss Douglas, sitting very poised and upright on a chair, reading. In the shadows, he paused to admire her. The blonde hair fell, once again, in a perfectly symmetrical smooth bell; she had found a white shirt somewhere, tucked it in to her leather trousers, and cinched her waist with a broad red belt. She looked cool, elegant and unapproachable. She had put on careful make-up during the evening, a shield against her own uncertainty in this new situation. As he gazed, a memory stirred in Eddie, and a desire. He bent, fiddled with something at his feet, then carrying it he climbed the gangway steps and went along the side deck, moving with the lightness of a cat.

When Dinny looked up, startled, he was standing in the doorway in his dinner jacket, smiling what he no doubt thought was a Clark Gable smile beneath his thin black moustache. She opened her mouth to speak, but he put his finger, unexpectedly, to his lips.

'Ssssh. Don't spoil the picture. My dear, would you do a small thing for me?'

Eddie rarely asked for anything politely. When he did, the shock value was so great that he generally got his way. Dinny nodded and waited.

'Just step out onto the stern deck. It isn't windy. And sit, just as you were sitting. Cool and beautiful.'

Mesmerized, she rose. He stepped aside as she passed through the doorway. She sat down on the white padded chair, folded her hands, and stifled a violent, primitive urge to abandon this passivity and run like hell. She waited. There was a faint sound of running water, distinct from the lapping of the ripples around the harbour boats. Eddie bent down, pulled at a dark shape on the deck, then straightened up and cried 'So!'

The water hit her for the second time that day, icy cold in a thin, violent stream. She put her arms up, crossed, in vain protest, and turned her face away. Still the water came. Behind the hose McArthur watched enraptured as the perfect hairdo disintegrated into wet rat's tails, the crisp shirt shrank clinging round her body, and the mascara ran down her cheeks, which flushed pink beneath the ivory-pale foundation. Even better, she was not hurt or humiliated but comically, gloriously angry. She shrieked, furious as a fishwife. 'Stop it! Bloody stop it! For Christ's sake! You arsehole!'

And Eddie laughed and laughed, a peal of pure unadulterated joy which flickered black-and-white through his innermost heart. He was in his Mack Sennett world, at one with the Stooges, Laurel and Hardy, Keystone Cops and Crazy Gang. He was happy. At last, he let the hose drop and said, through his choking laughter, 'Thank you. That was wonderful.' And, wiping his eyes, he vanished into the interior of the big boat, leaving the hose writhing and pumping vainly across the deck.

The marina was quiet in that late season and middle part of the week, but when Dinny shook the wet hair from her eyes she saw a small, fascinated audience standing silently, in pyjamas and nightshirts, on the pontoons and in the cockpits of neighbouring boats. An elderly couple with white hair and wondering blue eyes; two young men with ragged beards; a child clutching a teddy bear; a naval-looking figure who had put on his reefer jacket and a peaked cap over a striped sarong and bare chest. He was the only one who spoke.

'Torquay,' he clipped, 'is going to the dawgs.'

It was left to Dinny to climb off the boat, turn the tap off, coil the hose, and, squaring her shoulders, march back aboard and into the saloon where Eddie McArthur sat, still giggling, in the bigger of the chairs. Dripping, she confronted him.

'Right' she said. 'I hope you enjoyed yourself.'

'I did,' he replied, shaking a little with remembered mirth. 'Far better than sex. Sex is overrated. You are unique. Wonderful girl. Such dignity.' He erupted again, snorting.

'I didn't exactly do much,' said Dinny.

'It's not what you do, it's what you are. Next time, you can wear pearls and a high lace collar, and I shall . . . I shall throw a custard pie.'

'Why do you think there's going to be a next time?'

'Because you want a very, very good contract with my newspaper.'

'I might not.'

'You do. The Editor is leaving. You want to be the Editor?'

'I'm twenty-three. This is my first reporting job, for God's sake.'

'So it is. So young, yet so regal.' His eyes travelled over her sodden person and a new giggle rose in him, irresistible. 'You will go a very long way. Faster if you stay with me.'

'There was a message,' said Dinny, 'from the London office. On the fax. You told me to check them. Do you want to know what it said?'

'Yes. What?' She pulled a sodden piece of paper from her pocket.

'It's unreadable now. Basically it said that there is a message from the PM's office. About the New Year's Honours. That you will be receiving, very shortly, an invitation. It said congratulations, and asked whether you had decided on what title you want. Lord McArthur of where?'

Eddie was silent. He had not expected this, not yet. A knighthood first, perhaps. But a peerage! Lord McArthur of Melton Mowbray? Of Clapham, where the *Chronicle* was printed? Of Fleet? He would think about it. Meanwhile, he could not bear to let the warmth, the Saturday-matinee childish laughter ebb away in such adult considerations.

'I suppose,' continued Dinny, 'that these things are all very delicate, between the offer and the Honours List. Vulnerable to any breath of scandal.'

He roused himself slightly from his happy euphoria. 'Are you threatening me, young woman?'

'Yes,' said Dinny. 'You've used me as a skivvy all afternoon, and humiliated me in public with a hosepipe in the middle of the night. I can tell this story to the *Globe*, to *The Times*, to the *Telegraph*, to *Private Eye*. I can sue you for harassment and constructive dismissal and assault. People ought to know what you are really like.'

'Or,' said McArthur, closing his eyes as if bored, 'you can pack up all that pompous bloody crap about your rights and look after yourself. You can be a star in your own right, with a direct line up past the Editor to me. And every now and then you can come sailing, and let me throw custard pies at you. And buckets of water. I would like that. I would, of course,' he smiled his worrying smile, 'warm the water first. And you need have no fear for your virtue. Any needs I have in that direction are more easily satisfied. What you can do for me is in another, more celestial, league.'

His eyes remained closed. Dinny, seeing that the audience was at an end, crept wetly into the secretary's cabin, turned the lock on the door, threw off her sodden clothes and slid thankfully into Guy's heavy linen sheets. Some days, she thought as she pulled the duvet over her head, needed a line drawing under them.

24

The Old Vicarage had been designed in a more spacious, optimistic age. Its builders had meant it to shelter a clerical incumbent, his wife, some half a dozen children, a curate, a visiting bishop, and a couple of exhausted, raw-faced skivvies in the attic.

It had, therefore, no difficulty in accommodating Keith (out cold on the sitting-room sofa), Alex and Mandy (in Lance's double bed), Lance himself (resignedly back in his malodorous trans-European sleeping bag, on his parents' bed), and Erika Merriam (tucked up in Susan's room, rather to Susan's dismay, after insisting that she must stay nearby so as to be in the Bun at crack of dawn, mopping). Susan and Anneliese dossed down in the official guest bedroom in a jutting spur of the house known as the Curate's Annexe, where the radiator had a habit of knocking and gurgling throughout the night. It was, according to family tradition, haunted by a long-gone curate, poisoned by a bad egg he ate to humour the Bishop.

Susan had tried to put Erika there when Alex brought her in. Erika, such was her state, would have gone anywhere. But an ill-timed crack from Lance about the ghost had caused Ted Merriam – up to that moment a silent looming presence, his hands blackened by moving scorched objects around in the wreckage of the Bun – to veto it. 'Erika's nervous of ghosts,' he rumbled. 'If she say she's got to stay here, that's up to her. But I 'ave to get home and feed my old dog, and I won't 'ave my wife shut up in some room with ghosts. She han't deserved that.' Susan rather admired him for it. Protective men appealed to her.

Now, huddled together in the double bed for warmth, with

the curate's radiator groaning and squeaking alongside, the two girls discussed the evening's events.

'Wasn't it amazing,' said Anneliese, 'when Pops was all set to blame the fire on poor little Zoë, going on about how she must have left a hotplate on or boiled something dry, and Erika—'

'Erika went really apeshit, didn't she? I always thought she wouldn't say boo to a goose, let alone a solicitor.'

'Calling him a typical employer, blaming the workers, swearing that Zoë wouldn't possibly have left anything on because she would have done everything she was told.'

'Because for once,' Susan did a creditable imitation of Erika's tremulous fury, 'the poor child had been properly taught her routine and made to take notice, and your wife, pardon my saying it, Mr Heron, does her no favours by letting her get slack.'

'And Pops going all red and furious and gobbling like a turkey, and your dad snoring on the sofa not hearing a word of it . . .' Anneliese paused. Something in Susan's glee had flattened at the last words, and Anneliese felt it. She searched for a tactful conclusion and managed, 'I've never seen Uncle Keef drunk before.'

'Me neither,' said Susan flatly. 'Dad never gets drunk. I suppose he was tired, more than drunk.'

'Yes,' said Anneliese diplomatically. 'Anyway, he was well out of it.'

'So was your mum,' added Susan, to even things up. 'Pretty out of it herself, crying on his arm, saying how she'd let her only real friend down and now Mum might be drowned.'

The momentary rift between the girls healed in mutual enjoyment of the unfolding, unprecedented drama of the evening. Anneliese did not bother to defend Mandy's alcohol levels or plead tiredness for her, but accelerated into the glorious reminiscence.

'Yeah, and Lance telling her your mum was OK—'

'And him trying to get her off Dad, and her clinging on, and your dad gobbling away at Erika, and her standing up for Zoë—'

'And then the fireman arriving!'

The two girls paused again, contemplating the electrical

moment when a knocking on the door had broken into this late-night bedlam, and the assembly had fallen silent as a large fireman stepped inside bearing news that 'the boys reckoned they had found the source of the fire' and that there was no need to worry about arson or vandalism or electrical faults.

'Straightforward careless beggar, sir,' he had said, gleaming in his blue and brass, brushing an invisible speck of ash from his lapel. 'Someone, it appears, threw a cigarette butt into the metal bin in the kitchen. There must have been some cardboard cake boxes in there, possibly bearing traces of fatty materials.' This was not, Susan had dreamily thought, really the most flattering epitaph for a Black Forest gâteau. 'So up went the bin, flames caught the cloths hanging overhead, there you go.'

'Well,' Erika had said into the ensuing deathly silence. 'Zoë doesn't smoke, and nor do I. And customers don't come into the kitchen.' Her eyes were on Alex whose omnipresent, elegantly dangling cigarette was drooping from his fingers at a more than usually perilous angle.

'It was me who locked up,' he said bravely. 'I did go round the kitchen. Stopped and had a look at the big tea urn boiler thing, never really seen one before. I'm not sure if I was smoking. Ummm . . . if that's the case, officer . . . sorry.'

'A very large number of fires and some fatalities,' said the fireman, 'are caused by carelessness with cigarette ends.'

'It was a metal bin,' said Erika, heaping coals of fire on his head. 'And perhaps you thought it'd be safe? Maybe you didn't want to stub it out on the draining board that Zoë left so nice and clean.' There was, Susan thought, a real streak of malice in that nervous-looking woman.

Keith, at this stage, had half woken and found himself being clutched by Mandy, his hand damp from her drunken tears. In a movement of convulsive horror, he threw up his arms and broke her grasp sufficiently for Lance, who was standing nearby shaking with silent mirth, to pick his mother's friend up in his arms and, with a man-to-man apologetic smirk at Alex, carry her upstairs to lay her out in his own room. The amateur dramatic air of the proceedings was heightened by the fact that Lance was still wearing nothing but his mother's Japanese kimono.

Upstairs, after a brief, calming conversation with Mandy,

he left her asleep diagonally across the bed, thumb in her mouth.

'Lance looks terrific with all that hair,' said Anneliese. 'I was quite jealous of Mum, actually. Lance can carry me up to bed anytime.'

'In your dreams,' said Susan rudely. 'God, I suppose we'll have a major breakfast party now. It's funny having everyone here. Bit like a party sleepover when you're all kids.'

'Extra funny having old Erika here,' said Anneliese. 'Didn't know she was allowed to sleep away from home. Who's going to fry Ted's bacon?'

'Well, I thought Ted was very gallant, the way he made her have my room. Hidden depths. He was a lot more gallant than Alex. He was going to push off home if Lance hadn't made him stay with Mandy in case she was sick or anything.'

'Lance,' said Anneliese dreamily, 'is rather taking over the world, isn't he?'

'No chance, Annie,' said Susan. 'He is after higher things. He isn't going to get involved with anyone here. He's off to the big wide world. 'Bye 'bye Bonhurst. 'Bye 'bye little sister's friends.'

'Right, so are we. No more mooning over friends' big brothers. Hoo-ray. I fixed how we can get to college tomorrow, by the way. Taxi. I took fifty quid off Pops while he was in shock over being caught out as King Alfred burning the cake boxes.'

'Serve him right for torching innocent teashops. What a vandal,' said Susan. 'I wouldn't fancy your mum's driving much, after tonight anyway.'

'She's going to Salcombe,' said Anneliese smugly.

'What?' Susan sat upright. 'She's what?'

'She is going to find your mum. Lance said he'd take her. That's how he got her to lie down and go to sleep.'

'What about Alex?'

'He is doing penance with Erika Merriam and a mop.'

'She wouldn't trust him,' said Susan, 'with anything as high tech as a mop. He'll be sent to the office to get on the phone to the insurance company probably. With Gus detailed to stand by with a bucket of sand in case he drops another fag.'

'So Mum and Lance are going to Salcombe. I suppose your dad too? Is Uncle Keef going?'

'Yeah . . . no . . .' Susan frowned. 'Look, I dunno. Nobody's talked to Dad. He's the only one who wasn't going around last night announcing what he wants. He might just be sick of it all.'

'But he'll want to go and meet your mum? On the boat?'

'Well,' Susan said. 'I dunno. He's done his bit. He drove down to Torquay, which is hours – got a flat tyre – got there and she'd buggered off with some woman and a bloke he doesn't even know, no message or anything. Then he's left with some journalist going on about lesbians and conmen. So he drives back. He told us he had a row with the police about falling asleep parked on the hard shoulder, and he obviously hated being told off by some young policeman. I think that's why he started drinking when he did get back. Then all this chaos in the house . . . that Gabriel bloke ringing up seeming to know all about it, and the names of the other people on *Shearwater*, and it is Dad's boat too, and he doesn't know anything.' Susan was sitting up, hugging her knees, talking to the far wall while Anneliese lounged, watching. 'It's all exactly what Dad hates, all muddled and undignified. And if you think about it, it's actually all Mum's fault.'

Anneliese considered. 'You think he might just decide to stay here, ignore her, and let her come back if she wants?'

'Why shouldn't he? He's having an awful time. All they had was an argument, just in the family, and poor old Dad's got landed with all this stuff – newspapers and tragic suicide bids and Captain Bligh and tarts and Alex burning down the teashop and your mum sobbing all over him and Erika Merriam turning up at breakfast tomorrow going on about Zoë when he's got a hangover. He's going to hate it. He's already hating it. He's a *solicitor*, for God's sake. He's about being respectable. I think,' said Susan, warming to her theme, 'I think he ought to stay here, get on with his work, and let her bloody well come back and explain herself. Not go chasing round Devon like a *Carry On* film.'

'My mum,' said Anneliese, 'says that daughters are always hard on their mothers and soft on their dads.'

'Yeah, well. Can see why.'

'So are you going to Salcombe to tell her off? I can take your form and stuff in to college, if you want to go with Lance and Mum.'

'No,' said Susan. 'No. I'm coming to college. I feel like Dad. I want to organize my own life in peace.'

'OK.' Anneliese hauled the duvet round her and curled into her favourite sleeping position. 'I wonder where your mum is now?'

'That Gabriel man who rang up told Lance she was with friends of his – what was it? – someone Jones and Guy Pastern-Hopkins. Whoever the hell they are. Probably having wild parties. I dunno. It's not like Mum. I'm not surprised Dad's out of his depth.'

The first train to Totnes on a weekday morning leaves Paddington station at 5.30 a.m., change at Didcot Parkway, arriving at 9.42 and connecting, God willing, with a bus to Kingsbridge at the head of the spreading Salcombe harbour.

Gabriel, who what with one thing and another was quite accustomed to spending nights without undressing or entering any kind of domicile, let alone his own chaotic flat near Putney Bridge, decided after a brief doze on the floor of his office that he would go to the station and be ready for it. He took a restorative slug from the whisky bottle in his bottom drawer and got up from the floor, unsteady but determined. The idea – nay, project – of finding Joanna, removing her from her pointless life and allowing her to look after him while he wrote his masterpiece in an Irish hovel had seized his imagination. It had haunted his brief sleep under the desk as few things did these days. 'My own Lilith, my primitive, my foreshadowing love,' he said aloud, peering into the cruelly lit mirror in the sixth-floor gents' lavatory. 'I am coming back. "Thy firmness makes my circle just, and makes me end, where I begunne."'

He pocketed the bottle and took the lift down, loudly belching this time in its bland Art Deco privacy, and greeted the disapproving commissionaire with a blast of Johnnie Walker fumes. Walking through the black London darkness to Paddington, he switched from Donne to Yeats. 'Time can but make her beauty over again/Because of that great nobleness of hers/ The fire that stirs about her, when she stirs /Burns but more clearly . . .'

By the corner of Praed Street he had persuaded himself that

Joanna, years ago, had dismissed him and charged him to wander the weary world proving himself worthy of her. A long and noble quest had led him to this place. By the top of the concrete station ramp he was a knight who had served eighteen years, faithful, for a lost mistress whose beauty burned ever brighter as she aged. 'Oh, she had not these ways, when all the wild summer was in her gaze!' The picture in the *Chronicle* was between his fingers as he fell asleep again, contentedly, on an uncompromising yellow plastic Railtrack seating-module on the station concourse.

Over Starhole Bay the moon shone full and golden, throwing long shimmers of light across the still water and whitening the cliffs which rose, absurdly romantic, around the disguised shape of *Shearwater* with her two masts and her counterfeit bowsprit. The anchor light glimmered, sending its own fainter track of light through the blackness of the water. The portholes were darkened; behind them Joanna slept, dreamless and deep, and Guy sprawled on his back, head on his hands, mouth slightly open.

A movement in the companionway, a darker shadow against the pale fibreglass, resolved itself into the silent creeping form of Della. Trying hard not to creak, she climbed on the cabin top dragging her sleeping bag, wrapped herself in it and sat with her back to the mast. Alone with the moon and the cliffs and the water, she stayed for a long, long time, worshipping and thinking. She made decisions: not hard plans, but nebulous, important statements of intent to herself. This night, this moon, the lapping water must not go out of her life entirely. Something of them, something like them, must stay with her and lap around the corners of her life always. While the others slept, Della watched and planned and resolved and shivered through a long, blessed, starry hour on the deck alone.

Then a movement in the hatchway startled her, and the silent figure of Joanna, wrapped in her own sleeping bag, moved into the cockpit.

'Hello,' it whispered. 'Stargazing?'

'Thinking about things,' said Della.

They sat together for a moment, then, shyly, Della said, 'Do you often sit up here, like this?'

'I used to,' said Joanna. 'Not lately.'

'What do you think about?' asked Della.

Joanna half turned to look at the girl who was staring at her with large, candid blue eyes in the moonlight.

'I think about Emily.'

'Who,' asked Della, 'is Emily?'

25

Under the pouring moonlight, under the cliffs and the stars, the two women looked at one another for a moment. Della's 'Who is Emily?' echoed innocently in the silence. Then Joanna hitched her sleeping bag round her shoulders and said quietly, 'All right. I'll tell you. I haven't told anybody, ever.'

Della was alarmed. 'Oh Gawd, I didn't mean to ask something private. Don't tell me secrets, I'm useless.'

'It's not really a secret,' said Joanna. 'Lots of people knew. It was in the papers, eighteen years ago, in Oxford where I lived. It's just that I don't talk about it.'

'You don't have to tell me, then,' said Della, still uneasy.

'I want to. Tonight, I want to. If you'll listen.'

'OK then,' said Della, settling herself down in a corner of the cockpit, out of the wind. 'Who is Emily?'

'Emily,' said Joanna, 'was my best friend. The best friend ever. She was funny, she made me laugh more than anyone else ever has.'

'What was she like?' asked Della, interested. Joanna seemed startled for a moment by the question, but then smiled.

'She was a bit dippy. She once jumped into the river with all her clothes on because she was annoyed with someone who was being pompous. She used to smuggle stray cats into college. Once she threw a rotten tomato at a lecturer who was rude about women students. She could argue down anybody when she got going. But she was very, very kind. She helped people who were down on their luck, even if they had been horrible to her. She never had any money after the middle of term because she'd lent it to all these hopeless people. She had a collection of lame ducks—'

'What?' said Della, startled. 'Like the cats?'

'It's an expression – it means people who can't quite cope on their own. She looked after all the oddballs who didn't have any friends. But if you'd said she was good, she would have made a rude noise at you. Emily was lovely. I loved her. She was,' Joanna repeated, 'my best friend.'

'So,' said Della. 'What happened?'

'Gabriel happened,' said Joanna.

'What, the chaos man? The one who mucked you about?'

'Yes.'

Gradually, in a low, even, emotionless voice, the older woman told the story to the young one. Five and a half months after Joanna was dismissed by Gabriel to the strains of Bob Dylan, Emily succeeded her in Leckford Road. Emily's passion for Gabriel was, if anything, more complete than Joanna's; she had never really noticed men before, other than as friends.

And so very 1970s were they all, so idealistically free-form about 'relationships', that Emily remained Joanna's best friend. Her friend, despite Joanna's long, sleepless, weeping nights and red-eyed days in the library; her friend, although they barely saw one another. Emily's days and nights were too near a copy of Joanna's lost idyll. They could not be close, not when Emily, encountered at lectures, even smelt of Gabriel's joss sticks and Gabriel's self. So, friends though they were, they did not talk any longer of anything below the surfaces of life. The gulf between them was that Joanna was unhappy, Emily happy.

'I almost hated her for being happy,' said Joanna, looking out over the water, along the setting moon's track. 'Isn't that terrible?' Della was silent. It sounded perfectly natural to her.

Emily stayed happy until the night six months on (early summer term, it was, with finals only weeks away) when Gabriel tired of her adoration and told her that, in the words of the invaluable Bob Dylan, 'It ain't me you're looking for, babe.'

Whereon Emily screamed – so the inquest later heard from Gabriel's flatmate, a chemist by the name of Biggis who had always hated him – 'Well, it bloody well ought to be you, because I'm four months gone with your bloody baby!' She then, said Biggis, slammed the front door, kicked over and broke several milk bottles, and ran off.

And there the comedy ended. Gabriel assumed she had run to Joanna's digs down by the canal; or so he said, in evidence given sulkily and without his customary charm. He did not attempt to follow her. But in fact Emily ran to the fifteenth floor of the newest college's newest hall of residence and, breaking more glass, threw herself and Gabriel's unfinished child out into the night sky.

'She died?' said Della's small voice out of the darkness.

'She died,' said Joanna.

College had rung her digs in the morning when Emily was tentatively identified by a shocked undergraduate on an early run. Standing barefoot on the cold cracked linoleum Joanna had heard the news and had shaken all over, cold and ill tuned as she was after months of hard work and heartbroken starvation on coffee and apples.

Over the succeeding eighteen years, the older, better-fed, rational adult Joanna had often, sternly and reasonably, told herself that poor, thin, sad Jo Telford did all she could that day. By noon she had identified the crushed face and matted hair (holding hands, incongruously, with a big fatherly policeman). She had rung Gabriel, waking him well before his accustomed hour, and told him to go to the police and explain whatever had passed before she did it herself. She had been interviewed by the Principal, and volunteered to assemble Emily's possessions and take them to her parents' home twenty miles away in Burford.

The parents were very distraught, warned the don. But, 'I know them. I've had lunch there,' said Joanna. Emily's mother was as blonde and sunnily engaging as Em; she had met her husband when she was working as a waitress, dressed as a lewd rabbit. He, trying to impress an upper-crust fiancée with his sophistication, complained that his salmon was undercooked and the candle not lit. Em's mother the rabbit had lit the candle with a flourish, striking the match on her suspender belt in the club's approved manner, and snapped, 'Hold your bloody salmon over that.' He had, so he said, threatened her with the sack if he reported her; she had retorted, 'It's probably the only sack you're any good in.' Mysteriously, they had been married in Scotland within the fortnight, leaving his enraged fiancée an apologetic note.

Em's parents had told this story, antiphonally, gurgling with laughter twenty years on, a pair of unreformed 1950s ravers. So Joanna had to go to Burford now. 'I'll talk to them,' she said. 'I'll tell them she wasn't unhappy, not until the last minute. That it must have been an awful impulse, and she wouldn't have known what she was doing. Don't they say that attempted suicides say they never remember the half-hour before?'

And so she had gone that afternoon to Burford and told her gauchely merciful tale, and comforted them a little with talk of how well liked Emily was, what a star of her year. She had tried not to think, either in Burford or at the funeral, about the slow fifteen flights up, the lonely sound Em's hard boot heels must have made. Or the determination that it took to smash through reinforced glass with a fire extinguisher. Or the waist-high concrete sill Emily had had to climb. Jo had done her best, put on as good a gloss as it would take and kept the deep horrors to herself. Then she came back, by taxi, to college alone.

'I think you did really well,' said Della, quietened by the bald recitation of all this. 'Going to see her mum and dad. I think that was brave.'

'I had to,' said Joanna. 'I hadn't been to see Em for weeks, had I? Never knew she was pregnant even. I owed her that much.'

Jo Telford, said the Principal to her shaken deputy on the day after these events, was a very thoughtful girl. 'Nice type. Brilliant, in her way. Her tutor spoke most highly of her Chaucer term. Surely a First for the college, if only . . .'

Both women gloomed, in their decorous senior common room, over the unfinished sentence. Student suicides were a tragic waste; unfortunately, their best friends often got wasted too. They abandoned or muffed their degrees, had stupid love affairs, and showed symptoms of shock all round. The college psychiatrist was a disaster, a testy old Freudian bigot who saw no point in anything short of five years' analysis. The counselling industry was barely born. So the dons were grieved, but not unduly surprised, to be called a week later by the City police to a wandering, amnesiac young woman found on Port Meadow barefoot, with a college diary in her pocket.

'And that was the end of Oxford for me,' said Joanna. 'I never took my degree – you know, final exams – at all. I wouldn't go back.'

The dawn was creeping up now, grey and pink over the eastern crags. Della fiddled with a piece of rope, tying and untying a half-knot in its soft white end. She looked up to see whether Joanna had finished telling the story. Jo was looking out to the east with tears in her eyes, but her face was calm. Della ventured to speak at last.

'Why don't you usually talk about it?' she said. 'If it was me, I'd tell everyone, so they knew I'd had something awful to get along with in my life. I would.'

'I suppose,' said Joanna, 'that I have always felt guilty.'

'Why?' asked Della, really astonished this time.

'Because I didn't know Em was pregnant. Because I didn't stay in touch with her for those five months. Because I knew perfectly well that Gabriel was bad trouble, and I knew that Em was too gentle to stand it, so I should have seen it all coming.'

'But you didn't know,' protested Della. 'You were still fancying him, you said. You were only eating apples and stuff, and being miserable. You couldn't have told her he was trouble. She'd have thought you were jealous or something.'

Joanna looked at the girl with affection. 'I don't know,' she said. 'I really don't know. I'm never going to know. It's eighteen years ago. But maybe it doesn't matter.' She stood up abruptly, and reached out a hand to Della. 'Come on. We'll get stiff. No more stars now; look, it's morning. Let's get some sleep.'

'Will you be all right?' asked Della.

'Oh yes,' said Joanna. 'Oh, definitely, yes.'

And one by one, they slipped down the companionway steps and back into the cocooning warmth of the cabin where Guy breathed evenly on, undisturbed. Della curled into the corner of her bunk; Joanna stretched out on hers, relishing the chill of its corners for a moment before hauling the downy layers up round her and closing her eyes.

26

Lance was up first, waking at six from a confused dream in which Rudi and Yelena, companions of his travels, were chasing Erika Merriam along the Amsterdam canals in a speedboat full of firemen dressed in Gouda cheese. Must be, he thought, the smell of his sleeping bag. Wriggling out, he looked at the kimono on the floor and decided against it. Rummaging in the chest of drawers, he found a pair of his father's underpants. On the chair, left over from the disastrous Bank Holiday weekend, was a pair of Keith's sailing trousers, so he annexed those as well and pulled on a blue cotton sweater. He supposed that his shoes were in his own room, but peering in to see Mandy and Alex enwrapped fast asleep on the bed, he shook his head and padded back to adopt a pair of Keith's deck shoes.

With these in his hand, Lance toured the house, checking on its inmates. Erika's door was firmly closed and, he liked to imagine, barricaded against any more terrible Gurney goings-on with a chair wedged under the doorknob. He smiled reassuringly at the blank door. There was no sound from the curate's room, the radiator having spent its force in the small hours. Downstairs, his father lay on the sofa in front of the fire's embers, the blanket Lance had put over him lying sadly crumpled on the floor. Keith looked cold, grey, and older than usual. His son tucked him up with deft gentleness, then went to the kitchen and fetched a tube of Alka-Seltzer, a small bottle of mineral water and a glass, all of which he placed on a low table close to what would presumably be his father's line of sight when he awoke.

The tall young man sat for a while in the kitchen, drinking coffee, lost in thought. Then, with a sudden brisk movement, he jumped up, crossed the hall, took the car keys off the hook on the monstrous Victorian hallstand, and silently let himself out of the front door.

Ted Merriam, answering the door of Tedneric half shaven and in the hope of seeing a ParcelForce deliveryman with his new reel mechanism, glared at the hairy figure before him. 'Yes?' he said austerely. 'What can I do for you?'

'Buy the Bun,' said Lance, without preamble. 'Erika deserves it. Put in a bid. You'll get a good price, I bet you. My mother and Mrs Heron have had it long enough. I would say it brings in £150 a week clear profit after Zoë's wages and what Erika gets for weekends. Could be a lot more if you do lunches. The insurance will pay to have it redecorated and some new equipment. It's a snip.'

Ted stared, open-mouthed, at Lance. The young were, he always said, the last word in cheek. He was deeply grateful to Erika for never having shown any interest in saddling him with young of his own.

'"Tain't yours to sell, my boy,' he said, heavily. 'I don't know what you're doing here, trying to sell your mother's things before breakfast—'

'Oh, come on,' said Lance. 'I'm not trying to flog you her jewels for cash. All I'm saying is that I bet if you offered – oh, I dunno – forty thousand for the Bun, you'd have a deal. And Erika would be a brilliant businesswoman. You could give up the ironmongery, after a bit. Take early retirement. Go fishing.'

Ted went on staring. At the word 'fishing' a spasm crossed his face; what sort of spasm, Lance could not divine. He went on, briskly, deciding that to wait for Ted's reactions would only slow and fuddle the issue.

'I think the time is right. I think my mother and Mandy Heron both want to sell it, and an offer would tip them into it. And I think Erika's the girl for the job. A natural. That's it, really. I won't come in, and I'm sorry to have disturbed you. But you're an ironmonger, and you know about striking while iron is hot. I think today is the day for the offer, I really do. It's what tycoons do. They get hunches. I am your hunch. I just have a feeling about today. You know that song, "I can see clearly now"? Look at the way the sunshine is on the leaves. You could see for miles, if it wasn't for the back of Tesco's. It's a day of destiny. Thank you for listening. Have a nice day.'

And he turned, with a little wave, and got back into his father's car – so Ted noted, with acid disapproval – to drive away. In the doorway of Tedneric, the big man stood, lost in thought, hardly noticing the approach of a ParcelForce van bearing his heart's desire.

When Lance got home with a loaf under his arm, a fistful of bacon and a flimsy drooping bag containing a dozen eggs from the corner shop, Keith was stiffly upright on the sofa, cradling his Alka-Seltzer and staring disbelievingly at the empty whisky bottle on the table.

''Lo, Dad.'

'Hello. Did I fall asleep on the sofa?'

'Yes.'

'Must have been the drive. Atrocious road, that. I fell asleep in a lay-by and some twelve-year-old policeman told me off and breathalyzed me.'

'I know. You told us all about it.'

'Did I dream it, or were there a lot of people here later on?'

'Yup,' said Lance, from the kitchen door. 'Come and have a cup of coffee and I'll fill you in.'

Keith rose, groaning, and turned to straighten the cushions. He forgot he was still holding the glass of fizzing water, and as his hand came forward he poured it inadvertently down the back of the sofa. 'Oh, shit. Oh, hell.'

Lance came back, deftly took the glass from him, mixed a new Alka-Seltzer and held it out. He wanted to take his father by the arm and lead him to the warmth of the kitchen, but they did not normally touch, had not for years, not since Lance was twelve or thirteen. Keith stood, not taking the glass, rubbing his eyes on the back of his sleeve. Lance made a decision, and took his father's arm after all. It did not feel too unnatural.

Keith allowed himself to be led to the kitchen and seated with his glass in front of him. He sipped.

'Sorry. To be honest, if it was me who drank all that whisky last night, I may have been a bit blotto.'

'Smashed out of your wits, I would say.' Lance began frying the bacon. 'You were well out of it.'

'Of what?'

'Well, there was a fire at the Bun.' Lance held up his fish-slice commandingly as Keith groaned. 'But it's all right now. Erika Merriam is staying here because she wants to get in there early and find an electrician and all that. She's got a crusading desire to reopen it by the weekend, which is mad. She's in Susan's room. Alex and Mandy are in my room—'

'What the hell are they doing here?'

'Well, Mandy had a bit of a wobbler about Mum. She did have a word with you about it—'

Keith sat upright, staring at his son. 'You mean it wasn't a dream? Her crying on me?'

'It was not. She cried all over you the whole time the fireman was here, and all through the row between Alex and Erika about Zoë. Mandy is not one to bottle her emotions up. She doesn't have a lot of them, but when she does, by God she unbottles them.'

'Do you mind,' said Keith, 'if we don't go into any more of this until I have eaten something?'

'OK. Only I need your car all day, to take Mandy to Salcombe.'

'*What?*' For a wild moment Keith wondered whether his son had contracted a relationship with his mother's friend and signed up as her toyboy. Anything seemed possible, this week.

'Whaddoyou mean, Salcombe?'

'To find Mum. Remember? The phone message? She was going to Salcombe.'

'And what the hell does Mandy Heron want with chasing after her?'

'She wants to say sorry. About the newspaper. She's in a terrible state of remorse.'

'Mandy Heron? Wants to say sorry?'

'That,' said Lance patiently, turning over the bacon, 'is why she was crying on you.'

'Well, I need the car,' said Keith, getting up. 'I need the car to go to Salcombe myself.'

'Are you sure?' asked Lance whose mind had been working

in much the same way as his sister's. 'I can have a chat to her. Wouldn't it be better if you stayed here and got some peace?'

'Certainly not.'

'Well, drive down with us then.'

'No. I am going to see Joanna.'

'Dad, you're not—'

'Not what?'

'Not going to say anything you'll be sorry about. I mean, Mum's caused you a lot of aggro, anyone can see that, but she probably had her reasons—'

'I am going,' said Keith with dignity, 'to meet Joanna. My wife. Alone. She and I have private things to talk about. Without anybody else, especially Mrs Heron. If you insist on coming, you'll have to borrow Alex's car. And keep away from us while we do talk.'

'OK,' said Lance more cheerfully. 'He owes us one, since it was him who burnt down the Bun. Alex,' over Keith's shoulder, 'I can have your car today, can't I? If I promise not to set fire to it?'

Keith turned to see Alex in the doorway wearing Lance's dressing gown from when he was fourteen. It did not quite close over his chest and revealed a pair of Dennis the Menace boxer shorts lower down.

'Is there no lock on your bathroom door?' Alex peevishly enquired. 'I was just decent – only just – when Erika Merriam burst in wearing some sort of striped shroud—'

'Can I borrow your car? Today?'

'The BMW might not be insured—'

'Mandy's car then?'

'You'd have to ask her.'

'It's her I'm driving.'

Keith watched his son as he bargained with Alex. The European tour had changed him; Lance had always been bright and volatile and kind, but now there was an ease about the boy, a new confidence. He seemed no more than amused by the happenings around him. Lance, he thought vaguely, would be a comfort if—

There would be no if. Joanna would come back. If she did not want to come back, then he, Keith, would go with her wherever it was she was off to. He drained his Alka-Seltzer, crossed to the stove, picked up a piece of bread and crushed two rashers of bacon in it. Clutching his improvised sandwich he headed for the bottom of the stairs.

'Is anyone asleep in my bedroom? No? Good. I'm off early. Alex, tell Gus to chase up the Rugely-Smith conveyance this morning. If you would.'

With the same determined, loping stride that had characterized his son as he approached Ted Merriam's front door that morning, Keith climbed the stairs eating his sandwich, swung along the landing peeling off his sweater as he went, and crashed into the bathroom.

A thin, wailing cry made the men downstairs look at one another with eyebrows raised.

'Ze unmistakable alarm call,' said Lance in the voice of a German professor, 'of ze lesser female Erika, disturbed on its nest.'

Moments later, with his last night's sweater back on inside out, Keith flashed through the hall, slamming the door and calling, 'I'll get breakfast on the way – must get going. See Joanna.'

His half-finished bacon sandwich lay on the hallstand where the car keys had been.

The scream had done its work and roused the house. At the top of the stairs, draped in Lance's dark-blue bedspread, pale and tragic as Lady Macbeth with tumbled hair and dark rings under her eyes, stood Mandy. Behind her, Susan and Anneliese, bright-eyed and curious. Erika Merriam emerged from the bathroom in a long striped nightshirt of Susan's and stood in a defensive attitude a little apart from the rest, with a look that suggested she would sell her virtue dearly. The effect, to Alex and Lance as they stood in the hall, was very much that of the climax of Act I of a particularly rowdy opera. Lance, looking at the abandoned bacon sandwich on the hall table, had a momentary, light-headed, happy conviction that his father, in some obscure way, had just sung the principal love aria.

Alex picked up the bacon sandwich and sank his teeth into it. Outside, Keith's car could be heard starting, jerking into gear, easing off the gravel of the drive and fading down the street with a dwindling roar. Susan broke the silence.

'He hasn't got any shoes on,' she said.

27

The train was warm and fusty, empty apart from a dozen grey-faced business travellers and a party of sailors with kitbags and, in their great ham fists, open cans of lager. In the early morning the smell of the beer made Gabriel's stomach churn; he sat as far as he could from their raw adolescent bravado and huddled himself into the corner of a seat with his jacket bunched between his head and the steamy window. After a moment, he kicked off his scruffy plimsolls so that his stockinged feet rested on the empty seat opposite, one toe poking out through the grey wool of his left sock.

He regarded the sock with sorrowful affection. Poor sod. Poor old sod. That really was a classic middle-aged bachelor's foot: uncared for by the ministering hand of a wife, grubby and unappealing. A music hall joke, he was. Poor old bachelor.

It was not, of course, that he minded being a bachelor. Indeed, Gabriel O'Riordan had chosen this high and free destiny with some firmness. He had decided early in life to cast aside clinging women and follow his own star. He had cast aside his homeland, too, fleeing from the cosy Catholic values of the rural west of Ireland by way of Trinity College, Dublin, and then Oxford. He had never gone back, even for a holiday, to the shadow of the mountain in the far south-west which bore his name; never written home to Ballydehob, never turned up at his own mother's funeral.

It had been a considerable shock to him, two years ago, when another boy from his own village appeared at Television Centre where Gabriel, under duress, was sulking his way through a course entitled 'A dramatic matrix for the bi-media age: Edge,

Bottom, and Spin'. This Kieran was a confident young man twenty years his junior and far better paid. The stripling – who, to add insult to injury, was actually one of the lecturers – had casually observed in the BBC Club bar that the far south-west of Ireland was, these days, 'humming with it', and a 'happening place'. He mentioned one-horse towns Gabriel had fled from in 1965 as now being 'amazing', one boasting an award-winning school with its own planetarium, of all things. He reported that the region was now settled by artists, studded with gourmet restaurants, sought after by bohemians. Gore Vidal lived there, for heaven's sake. Hip media rabbis and modish actors claimed it as their secret refuge. There was a fax bureau in Ballydehob.

'But the spirit of the place,' said the young man smugly, 'the ancient magic, has not gone. It's where we draw our strength, we exiles.' And he had laughed a fashionable laugh and Gabriel had had an uneasy sense of having, somehow, thrown away a winning lottery ticket by mistake.

But, he told himself, in his day he had been right. There had been every reason for an artist to throw aside clinging, cloying Ireland at the turn of the 1960s. And clinging women, too, come to that. He was a poet, a creator. He needed freedom, not children and puppydogs. And bloody women never would understand that; so they had had to be detached from his coat tails, as forcibly as need be.

Closing his eyes against the dreary West London suburbs through which the train was listlessly rolling, Gabriel remembered Joanna, eighteen years ago, at the moment when he detached her from his coat tails. He could see her, easily: her half-forgotten face had become vivid to him from the newspaper picture. It haunted him, as faces will when they return from long oblivion. By now he had forgotten the drunken night fantasy of his *belle dame sans merci*, sending him away to work his time for her. He remembered the real Joanna, saw her white face pleading with him, her dark hair in disarray as she knelt by the Leckford Road gas fire in her black faded jeans and filmy Indian cotton shirt.

'Gabriel, Gabe, I love you – doesn't that count?'

'Baby,' he had said, 'it's as difficult for me as it is for you.'

'But what have I done? You loved me, you know you did. We loved each other. Only yesterday—'

'Joanna,' he had deepened and roughened his voice for this line, 'don't make it hard for me. You know the deal. We're both free. I gotta be free. If you want a man to tie up, it ain't me, babe. It never was me. If you've made yourself an imaginary man in my image, I can't help that. I love you, the same way I love life, and light, and everything that is beautiful. But you can't own me, any more than the trees in the wood can own me.'

Joanna had not seemed to appreciate the beauty of his cadences. She had refused the comfort of the joint he offered her and kept on and on at him, hatefully clear-headed in her pursuit.

'Can't I just – stay with you? Look after you? Just be near you? I wouldn't be any – trouble. Oh Gabe . . .' She shed tears, then. Oh, God, yes. Boring tears. Eighteen years later, he suddenly felt irritation as fresh as if it were yesterday. He leaned sideways against the cold window, tugging at his improvised pillow, while the old scene played on behind his eyelids. He was speaking again.

'I'm not the one, babe. I wish I were. You're torturing me. One day you'll find the man you need. When you've had a chance to grow up a bit.'

He hadn't believed it, of course. Hell, no. Women who had been with him were pretty well bound to end up settling for a second best. 'We shall become resigned, and settle sadly/ For gentle husbands in bland suburbs/ And a lifetime of wistful dreams.'

A girl in love had written him that in a poetic letter once, and Gabriel had treasured the idea. All those birds fading into genteel domesticity by their Agas, rearing their pasty-faced, middle-class, cello-playing children, dutifully humping their commuter husbands on Saturday night; all of them remembering the lost paradise of living with him, angelic Gabriel. Amazing. Joanna, though, had shown no sign of being resigned to the end of her idyll.

'I don't want to be grown up,' she said. 'I don't want anybody else, not ever. I just want to be near you. I'll be quiet. I'll help with your typing, cook for you. You can have other girls around, I'm not jealous. Only don't send me away.'

She had looked so small, so pathetic, so embarrassingly eager that he had turned away and put on the Dylan record. Jesus, some girls had no idea of how to go gracefully. It didn't seem to matter how bright they were, they seemed to lose all their self-respect and abase themselves at such moments, so that he, who never lost control except by prior arrangement with himself, looked on appalled.

It never occurred to him that there was in these girls' self-abnegation a generosity worth valuing even if it was misguided. They just seemed pathetic. This one was intelligent; when he first met her she was a bright spark, full of wit and laughter. How did she come to turn into this snivelling, pleading, runny-nosed lump? People who disliked Gabriel thought that he enjoyed bringing women to this pitch of humility. Sometimes they accused him of that. But, he thought indignantly, nothing could be further from the truth. The sniffling bit was quite his least favourite phase of an affair.

That afternoon, he had turned in the doorway where his fine features (as he saw from the Indian mirror opposite) were half in shadow, heartbreaking and mysterious.

'Joanna. It would be better if you were gone before I come back. We'll be friends. When you're ready to be.'

He had not seen her again, except in the distance, a proud, gawky figure in her scholar's gown on her old green bicycle. He never saw her all that winter, never spoke to her until she rang him one morning her voice flat and grim, to tell him that Emily—

He consciously paused, changing a certain mental gear in self-defence at the thought of Emily. Emily was the most intractable part of the stories he told himself. Gabriel had no trouble, as a rule, in shaping his own past life into pleasing romantic twists and patterns, but the matter of Emily required more mental discipline than most. His leaving of other girls, including Joanna, had been for their own sake – they should not be shackled to a burning, demanding creative spirit like his, and it was out of his noble kindness that he let them go before his flame scorched them. Similarly his BBC career, initially brilliant and lately a precarious and ill-tempered liaison, could without much difficulty be fashioned into a story of the artist betrayed, the creator of great drama rejected by a Philistine influx in Armani suits.

His drinking, his personal disasters, his failure to click with any colleague or see any project through for five or six years past could all be reworked into lovable eccentricities in the tradition of Dylan Thomas. But the death of Emily was not so easily dealt with. It would have greatly surprised Joanna, during her years of tormenting Gabriel-dreams, to know how often Gabriel himself thought about Emily. Emily had not pleaded or abased herself; she had shouted angrily at him, and then gone up that damn building and . . .

Well, the girl must have been unbalanced all along. It stood to reason. His college, his housemate, his landlord should have understood that. The junior fellowship should have been his. The following months, during which he had been slowly frozen out of the university city, were an outrageous example of the basic prudishness and hypocrisy of the academic establishment. Women dons, he suspected, had spoken against him, rot their witch-black hearts. He was well out of it; a year after leaving he had attracted the attention of the BBC by his work in the London fringe theatre (thank God he fell in with that actress girl, and thank God she suddenly became the star she did, trailing him upwards in her wake). The rest was history. Nobody he ever met these days knew anything at all about Emily. And Joanna . . . absurd to think that Joanna, seeing him again, would even think of that brief painful episode. He would be her dream returning, lovelier the second time around . . .

His head fell back and his untidy limbs relaxed into baby sleep. When the train stopped with a resigned sigh at Reading, Gabriel was hard asleep. He slept through the green fields of Berkshire and on into the rolling kingdom of Wessex; once he half woke to see the word YEOVIL on a signpost. The sailors at the end of the carriage slept too, waiting for Plymouth to gather greyly round them and return them to duty. A lager can rolled empty from one end of the carriage to another, dribbling, as the train changed speed.

*　　*　　*

Keith Gurney, too, was heading westward and thinking of past encounters with women. He had no memories of girls weeping and pleading, for he never had been the kind of man women plead with. Various classmates, fellow students and secretaries down the decades had yearned for him, but such was his polite, chivalrous reserve that they would have found it absurdly bad form to throw themselves at his head. By the time you were close enough to Keith to hold any emotional conversation, he was so committed to you as to be equally vulnerable himself.

Before Joanna, only one girl had been that close: Maroussia, his three years' infatuation, who left his bed abruptly to go back to her Russian dissident lover the minute he was freed to the West. Keith's friends had watched, through those years, the impossible chivalry with which the young lawyer worked alongside Maroussia in the campaigns of the 1970s to free her beloved Vladi and other Soviet Jews. His more percipient acquaintances suspected that he had always known that she was only his on loan; Keith himself never spoke of it. If he had a dilemma, it was invisible and never reflected in his actions. Vladi's fare into the West was paid officially by the campaign, but really by Keith out of his own pocket. If he wept as he signed that cheque, nobody ever knew.

A year after Maroussia left to a new life with Vladimir in the USA, Joanna came to work in the office, a pale, sad, reserved figure. It was to her that Keith first told his story. Probably, he realized himself, he was impelled to do it by a need he had to match, and thus coax out of her, whatever the terrible, visible grief was that she carried around. She had told him a little: about a friend who died unexpectedly, and a love affair that didn't work out. They had sat together in the corner of wine bars and pubs, over curries and tacos and Thai meals tasting of peanut butter, and talked endlessly, never of the detail of their lost loves, but of the wounds, the longings, the scars.

'It's being afraid you've lost a bit of yourself. The bit that only came alive with her.'

'I know. Like having something amputated. You think it was the best bit of you. You feel crippled.'

'But then it turns out there are other bits you were suppressing all the time, so one side of you withers and drops off, and the other puts out shoots and you end up a different shape, going somewhere else. Like those things you do in botany.'

'I know. You mean, er, rhizomes?'

'Do I?'

They had begun to laugh; to take long walks over the Dorset cliffs, to steal away for brother-and-sister weekends together. Keith, deeply in love by this time, sensed the danger of hurrying her and carefully made no pass. He held her hand, hugged her, never went further. But on one of these weekends, exhausted by a long wet walk on the cliffs at Beer and a little drunk after a pub supper, they had fallen into one another's arms, jokingly, as if for support; and Joanna had raised her lips to his.

The night that followed was a revelation to them both and, to their surprise, an unspoken, unbreakable guarantee of commitment. For Joanna, lovemaking until now had meant adoring and total submission, rather on the model of St Teresa of Avila being pierced by a divine spear of ecstasy. With Gabriel you did not make demands; you received and applauded. For Keith, the memory of loving Maroussia was a memory of delirious, crazy adoration; to be permitted to touch her was to be admitted to a sacred place. Every encounter was granted as if it were a queen's favour. Maroussia did not like him to stay the night, never wanted him to sleep on her breast afterwards.

So to both Joanna and Keith, stretched on the narrow pub bed with the rain and wind outside, that first night was a miracle.

Love lay suddenly revealed as something equal, no favours being asked or received, no gratitude owed. Love was mutual hunger and shared energy; it was laughter, hugging relaxation, warm satisfied sleep and waking joy. It was reaching out, half drowsy, to feel a fresh longing and know with complete trust that it would be satisfied. For Keith, who had longed for Joanna physically for weeks, the surprise was that the moment should feel so warmly familiar, so little precarious. For Joanna, the amazement was that something she had never considered at all should turn out to be exactly what she needed.

Remembering that first night now, Keith slowed the car, overwhelmed all over again and shaky with desire. Marriage had been inevitable. Indeed, both of them felt married already; walking the next day hand in hand on the clifftop above the

Old Harry rocks, they talked unselfconsciously about the future. Joanna said she had never thought of marrying so young; he said that neither had he. But to both of them it was obvious that married they should be.

In the few weeks before their wedding, the only blemish to their unity would come when he tried to explain that Maroussia had been nothing: a madness, a delusion, at best a pale foreshadowing of this solid love. He had said it, of course, because it was true; but also because he wanted her to say the same about her nameless Oxford lover. She would not. Joanna would never speak of him at all, not even to say his name. Keith was not a man to push such a point, and gave up. Joanna never, in their closest moments, spoke of the old love again.

That one blemish, over the years, had faded into irrelevance. Nothing mattered compared to their unity, their familiarity, their glorious, terrifying sharings of childbirth, their gentle rediscoveries of one another's bodies during the weeks when each new baby lay snuffling alongside the double bed. Only now, during these few days' puzzlement and terror and exasperation and loneliness, did Keith see that the shadow was still there. Something in Joanna was not his, and never had been. A terrible jealousy clawed at him as he drove. At the long roadworks east of Exeter, a woman passenger in the car alongside saw his scowling intensity and shrank, tousled, startled, from the window. She might have shrunk even more if she had seen that he still had no shoes on.

Back at the Old Vicarage, Lance with some difficulty chivvied the ill-assorted houseparty through breakfast and into the proper direction for their day. Erika (strong tea, thin toast) had departed for the Bun with half the contents of Joanna's cleaning cupboard. Alex (bacon sandwich, fried egg, instant coffee, five cigarettes) had trailed behind her, humbly carrying the mop and two buckets. Susan (coffee, two bananas) had departed in a taxi with Anneliese (ginseng tea with a slice of lemon, followed in a moment of weakness by a hand-ful of peanuts and a slice of stale walnut cake). Mandy (three cigarettes, black coffee) now sat watching Lance as he tranquilly finished a fried-egg sandwich. Her hand, with the fourth cigarette dangling from it unsmoked, trembled slightly.

'We ought to go. Lance, we really ought.'

'No hurry. Dad ought to have a chance to see her first. He'll have to find her. Even so, she might not be there.'

'She must! You said that she said Salcombe on the phone.'

'Well, she did. But you don't always end up where you set out for in a boat. Did you know that the Navy never fill in the top of the log page with their destination? You can't say 'Torquay to Salcombe, 3rd September'. You can only say 'Torquay *towards* Salcombe'. Apparently, anyway. Isn't that interesting?'

'No. I want to see Joanna. I have to see Joanna.'

'Indeedy. And so you might. The point is, I'm not really going down to see Mum.' Lance looked across the table at Mandy in her fragile drooping blondeness. 'I'm going down in case Dad doesn't find her.'

'And you're going so you can take me.'

'Yes. And to take you. But if Mum and Dad are there, they'll have a lot to talk about—'

'I know! I know!' Mandy's voice rose shrilly. 'But Lance, you have to understand that I need to see her too. She must be thinking I said terrible things about her. She thinks I betrayed her—'

'*You* think you betrayed her,' said Lance, with the calm confidence of the teenage amateur psychologist. 'You blame yourself for what that reporter wrote. You think you oughtn't to have given him any chance at all.'

'Yes! Yes! I know! I am a show-off cow! I never even *thought* of Joanna, all alone in that gale. I just thought it was fun to have a hunky reporter dangling on my every word.'

'Well, so what?' said Lance, comfortingly. 'Mum will see that. She knows you aren't St Bernadette, doesn't she? She's known you years. There's not much you could do would surprise Mum, is there?'

Mandy bridled slightly. 'And I've known you, young man, since you were shuffling around on a ride-on plastic duck.'

'I remember Ducko. What happened to him?'

'Susan had him. But she liked Anneliese's red tractor better, so they swapped. We had Ducko until the wheels came off.'

Lance dipped the last crust of his sandwich into the remains of Alex's egg yolk, ate it neatly, and clattered the two last plates into the dishwasher.

'Come on then. On the road.'

'Can we go by the office? I ought to say goodbye to Alex.'

But when Lance pulled in to let her enter the tall, crookedly picturesque premises of Heron and Gurney, Mandy was stopped at her husband's office door by a hovering Gus.

'*Terribly* sorry, Mrs H. Thing is, he's in a meeting with Mr Merriam. I don't think I should barge in, he always hates it. If you'd wait twenty minutes or so . . .'

So Mandy had picked up Alex's mobile phone from the secretary's table and come straight out again to the waiting car. Mrs Hopgood, who in her dung-coloured padded jacket had been accompanying Mrs Colefax as she returned her new wok to Cuisine It All with a strong complaint about the quality of the non-stick finish, paused in the shop door to register the hairy, dangerous-looking young man driving Mrs Heron in her own car. Spotting a knot of her friends gathered outside the blackened façade of the Bun in the Oven, she hurried to join them with the news. It really had been a wonderfully interesting week; and it was only Thursday.

28

Joanna woke at half past eight, with the reflected sunlight rippling the cabin ceiling. No dreams, no fears, no unease had marred the last hours of her night. She felt wonderful. She rolled off the bunk, kicked the sleeping bag from her feet and threw it into the corner. Guy still lay opposite, snoring slightly, twitching like a retriever in a dream. In the quarterbunk she could just see Della's bright, tangled hair with the sun falling on it, betraying darkening roots.

She remembered everything: the gleaming *Privateer*, the terrible newspaper in the rancid-smelling breakfast café, the sleek woman reporter, the hose – here Joanna's hand rose to her cheek, feeling it heat at the very thought. She remembered the fat, black-browed tycoon with his bossy little moustache, the moment when Della had stepped onto her deck, the staggering (in every sense) descent of Guy a moment later.

Joanna Gurney, herself again, remembered it all and marvelled. Yesterday she must have been too tired and overwrought to take in the full import of anything. But she had got here, to Starhole Bay.

She emerged onto the deck and looked around at the cliffs and the green glinting water, and the ridiculous spectacle of *Shearwater*'s disguise, the fake mizzenmast and bowsprit lashed up by Guy in the moonlight. Both were now leaning at drunken and unconvincing angles, one oar threatening to fall into the sea any minute. Smiling, she began to move around the boat, leggy and tousled in her long T-shirt and knickers, and deftly untangled the spars and lines.

Yesterday, my God, yesterday! It ranked with those disjointed college Maydays when, after a night at a party and a dawn on the river, she would wake in some unknown room, among comparative strangers with red eyes, wearing unfamiliar clothing and still clutching an undelivered essay designed for the noon tutorial. On such days you would look at the clock and find that it was eleven, and not know whether it was eleven in the morning or evening, or who it was who had done the Morris dance on the pub table. Emily, probably. This day had the same feeling to it. Light-headed, unregretful, full of hope.

Thursday, was it? Must be. Half-day in Bonhurst. God knows what was going on at the Bun. Mandy running it perhaps? Now there would be a turn-up.

Joanna laughed. On this clear, clean, damp sea-morning there was nothing that could not be faced, cleaned up, sorted out and turned into gold. The first step was to get into Salcombe, ring Keith and Susan, offload the two cuckoos currently nesting below decks, draw an end to this crazy autumn cruise, and take up the reins of real life again.

The prospect no longer disturbed her. Some pressure had lifted itself from Joanna's spirit during the final hours of sleep while the sun came up. Three days ago she had been trapped in a narrowing tunnel, a hostage to her own life, emotionally half-dead but fit to cry at anything. Now, she looked closely and saw that there were no walls to the cell, no boundaries to her future unless she agreed to them. If she had to go home and run the bloody Bun until the economic recovery made it profitably saleable, or until Susan got her A levels from that expensive school, so she would. She would open the damned teashop for shorter hours, give Zoë some responsibility or sack her. She would stop fussing.

She would let standards drop if necessary. Somehow she had come to persuade herself that if she cut any corners at the Bun, permitted Erika to serve nasty microwaved potatoes, use teabags or otherwise compromise her early principles it would be a betrayal of the past. A betrayal of her carefully built family and community life, her wall against chaos; a betrayal of Lance and Susan's babyhood and her early happy years of marriage.

What a load of hogwash! It would just be one more small café which had dropped its standards because its proprietress was sick of it. So what? A teashop was not an intensive-care ward, was it? What had the twittering ladies of Bonhurst done to deserve pampering with real butter croissants? To hell with them.

She, Joanna, would take time for herself, sit down and work out what to do with the second half of her life. Ring Alice. Have a drink, a night in London with Alice and Andy. Talk to them about proper jobs and occupations for an educated woman not yet forty.

Some fog had lifted from her brain after what must have been, she wonderingly thought, years or at least many months. The prospect all around was clear, glittering, an endless vista of amusing choices. The nonsense in the newspaper was unimportant; if it made Mrs Hopgood and Mrs Colefax happy to gossip about her, so much the better for them. Everybody should be happy in their own way. She intended to be, so why not them?

Keith – she paused in her impetuous reverie of freedom. Keith could be free-hearted and happy, too. Of course he could. He must come with her to this exhilarating upland, see this view; it was only a matter of attitude. No longer would Keith have the power to depress her with his doubts and haverings and clingings to the status quo. Not her; no, sir. She would drag him up instead. He would come? Surely?

When she had coiled down the last rope, Joanna stood by the hatch and stretched her arms upward in the rippling sunlight, smiling beatifically at the sky and muttering 'Yes!' rather the way her son Lance used to when, sprawled with his A-level work at the kitchen table (he never would use his own room, preferring the company) he got another of his astonishing calculations right. 'Y-Yess!'

''Scuse me saying,' said a voice down near her groin, 'but you sound chirpy.'

Joanna stepped back, to allow the emergence of a dishevelled Della wearing one of Keith's T-shirts. 'Sorry, I borrowed this. I'll post it back.'

'Keep it,' said Jo. 'You look very fetching with those long brown legs. Do you wax them?'

'Yeah,' said Della. 'You don't, do you?'

'No,' agreed Jo. 'Life is too busy for that. I do have a razor.'

'Can't do the bikini line, though, can you?' said Della, confidentially. 'Wax is the only thing, really.' She looked around at the morning. 'But I can see why you don't bother. Lovely, innit? I was thinking a lot, last night. I'd like to live near the sea.'

'Why not? There's bound to be some way you could. If you want something, just go for it, because you probably deserve it.'

Joanna, even in her moment of morning euphoria, was just able to hear her last sentence hanging on the air, like some disreputable New Age garment in rainbow-striped and draggled velvet. She saluted it with a certain ironic amusement, but the reality of her happiness still glittered around her on the water. 'Yes. That's it. You go and live by the seaside.'

'Proper sea, not seaside. Proper wild bits, like this.'

'Scotland or Ireland then. Or bits of Wales. Nobody ordinary can afford to live in a wild bit down here, in southern England. Wildness is costed, rock by rock, by estate agents.'

'I always fancied Scotland. There was Robert Bruce, in that book, with the spider.'

Guy appeared through the hatch. 'I never fancied Robert Bruce. All that struggling away like a spider. Too much like hard work.' The women looked at his sleepy, unshaven mien with scorn.

'Go get the kettle on, slave,' said Della.

'Tea, toyboy,' said Joanna. 'Then we go into Salcombe, and off you get.'

So Guy made tea while the two women clambered onto the foredeck and Joanna taught Della how to haul up buckets of clean cold seawater and pour them over herself from head to toe with a thrilling fresh shiver. When he came up with three mugs, his blazer already on and his hair combed, Guy saw the back view of two naked women, one with a bucket over its head from the depths of which helpless laughter could be heard.

From the sea, Salcombe is a great harbour, a refuge since Viking days, a narrow-wristed spreading palm of an estuary guarded by Bolt Head and Prawle Point, the Mewstones and Eelstone and Poundstone and Wolf Rock. Once a ship has passed its pouring, swirling sandbar, the harbour lies there deep and safe and welcoming; the town lifeboat bobs reassuringly at its mooring, muddy creeks spread out ahead for exploration; great golden beaches unroll on the right hand side above East Portlemouth;

and the clinging town, pink and blue and grey, climbs the rocks to the west.

Approaching Salcombe from the sea is an occasion. As *Shearwater* crossed the bar and saw these riches before her, the crew's spirits soared even further. Guy sang 'Spanish Ladies' and rang the brass bell in the cabin, presented by Lance for Joanna's thirtieth birthday so that she could call him back from his rowing expeditions around anchorages. Della sat singing little wordless songs on the cabin top, her arms round her bare knees, damp hair streaming, looking at last more like a teenage girl than like Ivana Trump. Joanna steered past the Wolf Rock buoy and turned gladly to starboard, deeply content to be bringing her small ship to such a harbour, on such a morning, with all safe and shipshape aboard. Salcombe spread and glittered, welcoming them.

Keith, as it happens, had never approached any part of Devon from the land. He was tired before he reached Exeter, flattened by the niggling delays of the roadworks, feeling silly without his shoes on, worrying about shortage of petrol and hungry for lack of breakfast. Thankfully he headed south at last, but the road seemed to go on for ever. Christ, this promontory went down a long way! he thought. One never noticed from seaward. Around eleven o'clock he passed Totnes (where, unknown to him, Gabriel, the man whose name he had never known, was engaged in a furious altercation with the driver of the Kingsbridge bus).

From here the road wound interminably onward again until, at last, with signs pointing off to Kingsbridge at the head of the great estuary, he began to feel a sense of sea after his long inland drive. The sea was still invisible beyond the moors, but it reflected in the sky, or gave a smell to the air, or stunted the bushes – anyway, it was there. He put his foot down and traversed the great open fields, expecting a headland any minute. A bend, and to his left he could at last see the upper creeks of the harbour, the same blue water which bore his boat, his wife, his hopes.

The petrol lamp came on, yellow and accusing. At last a filling station appeared on the outskirts of Salcombe. To his relief a stand just inside the door sold beach shoes, translucent red plastic versions of the kind that tiny children wear for scrambling on the rocks. He bought a pair in an incongruous size 11, a chocolate biscuit bar, and a can of fizzy lemon and felt rather like a giant six-year-old out on a day on the beach. On an afterthought, he bought a *Chronicle*, flipped through until he found Joanna's picture, read for a moment and then began to laugh, alone in his car, until he spilt the rest of his lemonade over his trouser leg and ridiculous shoes, which made him laugh some more. Then, a little restored, Keith set off again down the steep descent into the town.

Salcombe was, he thought, far less impressive from landward; a labyrinth of narrow roads and no free parking spaces that he could see except in the forecourts of genteel hotels with spiky palm trees. He drove twice around the steep streets, past craft shops and art galleries and businesses called 'Deck Out' and 'Schooners', wild with impatience to find somewhere to stop and scan the harbour. Once, between houses, he saw a mast moving up the harbour and craned from the driver's window to see it; but a stout middle-aged couple in matching pink canvas fishermen's smocks stood square in the way, laughing and gesticulating and waving their anchor-patterned holdall in front of where the hull would be as it passed the gap in the buildings. A Volvo honked impatiently behind him and, cursing, Keith moved on. Unlike his wife, euphoric out on the demure rippling water, he felt stale and hungover and old. The hope he carried was fragile, and the only shaft of light in his cell was Joanna. Somewhere, on that harbour, she must be there. Close by, the only woman . . . Where?

In the great snakes-and-ladders race to reach the West Country, conducted year in year out between public transport and the motor car, you can never quite tell who will win. Gabriel, rocking rapidly along on the Inter City express, had beaten Keith hands down as far as Exeter, quite neutralizing the advantage his rival had in starting from Hampshire. But, due to his own ineptness at Exeter, Gabriel had missed the Totnes connection and been forced to get a bus, then change at Totnes for Kingsbridge. This second bus had lagged behind Keith a little, but arrived in Kingsbridge at the very moment when the car driver was waiting for his change and his red jelly sandals at the petrol station. Gabriel had been told, not without impolitely protesting at the news, that there was no bus to take him on to Salcombe. That was a snake. But by chance, arriving in the little town at the head of the estuary, he found a ladder.

There was a small excursion boat, *River Darling*, half full of late holidaymakers and clearly about to leave the quay at Kingsbridge as the bus swished past it. Gabriel, properly awake by now, saw the word SALCOMBE on its stern and opened the bus's electric doors (using a trick he had learnt from a left-wing Hampstead novelist who kept losing his driving licence but did not believe in the fascist rigidities of the bus stop system). Having done this, and set off a loud alarm in the cab in the process, he leapt from the moving bus, followed by the driver's loud reproofs. Yelling an oath in return, Gabriel ran towards the little boat at something between a sprint and a lumber, his grey locks flapping, and threw himself aboard just as its red-faced skipper was untying his stern line.

'Bit of a 'urry, moi lover?' said the man. 'Salcombe excursion, this be. Two pound sixty pee single.'

'Good. Yes. Here.' Gabriel sat down, fishing awkwardly for change, and moments later was chugging between green banks and mudflats towards the Salcombe anchorage, on the water already while Keith was only just beginning his search for a parking space.

Shearwater, meanwhile, was nicely anchored off the Marine Hotel, with Guy on the foredeck, his leg pumping up and down as he inflated the rubber dinghy with the boat's slightly leaky footpump. But it was neither Keith nor Gabriel who found Joanna first. It was the harbourmaster's launch which left its quay even as they were laying the anchor, and swished alongside minutes later with two grim-faced policemen standing in the well.

Joanna, who had been below turning off the engine, emerged to find herself face to face with a warrant card, listening in astonishment to a poker-faced request that she allow them to search the vessel for one Guy Amadeus Pastern-Hopkins who was being sought to help the police in their enquiries concerning a number of stolen credit cards.

29

Eddie McArthur, to do him justice, had entirely forgotten his quarrel with the private secretary. When he had seen to it that the police were told that Guy had gone off with his credit cards (not, of course, mentioning that Guy always carried them as part of his duties) he instantly forgot having done so. It had only been one of the half-dozen rapid orders he had, in yesterday's brief irritation, barked at Dinny Douglas. Dinny had complied with his wishes, described Guy and *Shearwater* with considerable journalistic accuracy to the police on the telephone, stopped the cards, and herself in turn forgotten the whole matter.

So, at the moment when the police fingered – metaphorically speaking – the collar of Guy's blue blazer in Salcombe harbour, Eddie McArthur had virtually blotted the secretary's existence from his memory. He was gliding up-Channel at twenty-five knots on *Privateer*, making for Southampton Water where, his fax machine informed him, time was running out for a struggling boatbuilder with several acres of prime undeveloped waterfront among his assets. His agents could pounce, haggle and buy quite adequately without him, but he always enjoyed making personal swoops from the sea in these cases. He hummed, contentedly, a nameless little tune.

Below decks, Dinny had woken at ten to find the engines throbbing discreetly behind the wall of what she defiantly persisted in calling her bedroom. She had pulled on a pair of Guy's white trousers and a heavy blue sweater from the locker under his bunk, and come out onto what she preferred to call the verandah (although its rise and fall and feline sway betrayed it to be, horribly, a deck). She leaned on the rail to find herself staring out, blankly appalled, at open water. Unsteadily she climbed the white-painted steps to the flying bridge overhead, and with a reckless lack of tact or prudence rudely addressed the broad back of the figure at the helm.

'Where the fuck are we?'

'Lyme Bay, thirty miles off Portland. You slept well, my dear.'

'No, I didn't – look, for God's sake! Where – I mean I ought to be at the office—'

'The new Editor, appointed this morning, knows that you are on special research duties. The features editor is drawing up some dummies for your new by-lined page. It begins either next Wednesday or the one after, as you wish. The new Editor feels that Wednesday is a very good day, as it puts you right up against,' he glanced down at the pad next to his mobile telephone, 'Maeve Mahoney of the *Globe*. Two researchers will be available to assist you. You will be in the office tomorrow to look at the dummies. A studio session has been booked with Kurt Anhart for the photographs.'

An Anhart picture? For a by-line? Hers? Up against Maeve Mahoney? Dinny, three years into her newspaper career, felt faint. Was it Jesus who was taken to a high, dizzy place by Satan and shown things he could have if he wanted? Did Jesus, at that moment, feel as sick as she did right now? She held onto the rail, and protested automatically.

'Yes, but—'

'Tonight,' continued Eddie, tiring of the wheel and punching in the self-steering course so he could turn to face her, 'you will accompany me to dinner in Kingsbois Lodge, the home of my good friend Edmund Weissbraun, in the New Forest. He has a very remarkable Art Deco private cinema and a large collection of early Hollywood comedy.' He gave a sly, unfathomable look at the rigid little figure in the blue sweater and seemed to shake with an inward laughter which Dinny found peculiarly sinister. 'He and I share many interests.'

'I am not a hook—' began Dinny, but found a pudgy finger, smelling faintly of lavender hand cream, laid disconcertingly across her lips. It was the first time McArthur had touched her, and accordingly it froze her into shocked silence.

'Not a hooker. Understood,' he purred. 'A nasty word. Not a word for a lady's lips. Never use it again. And I would prefer it,' this rather coldly, 'if you were to go below and pay some attention to your grooming. I prefer to see you . . . immaculate. The eventual contrast is then more stimulating. So I find.'

And Dinny had slunk below, washed her hair and set it on some efficient heated rollers she found in the enormous bathroom; she had shaved her legs, been seasick twice in the process, and finally dressed in a cream linen shift and strappy gold sandals from the wardrobe in the cabin, presumably the property of some bygone mistress. Grooming, which normally soothed and uplifted her spirits, was in that heaving environment a peculiarly hateful occupation. When she returned to the bridge Eddie, by then smoothly rounding Portland Bill, promptly sent her below again to replace the strappy sandals with 'something more ladylike'.

Equipped at last with chaste medium-heeled leather sling-backs, her mouth sour, her head spinning, Dinny accepted defeat. She sat through the afternoon on the stern deck, pretending to read and breathing deeply in the hope of averting nausea, while her tormentor spun and bounced the powerful boat towards the Solent and the calm of Southampton Water.

The Devon and Cornwall Constabulary, of course, were not to know how little the robbed citizen cared about his deprivation. All they knew was that an important personage, with contacts at the highest level, who had actually dined the night before in the same room as the Deputy Chief Constable, had been robbed of his credit cards by a fraudulent employee known to be aboard the yacht *Shearwater*, last seen proceeding westward round the Devon coast. On Thursday morning, one Sergeant Renfrew of Totnes remembered the previous day's alert as he ate his breakfast and studied the newspaper, and remarked to his wife that the case had even made the morning papers. She, taking the *Chronicle* from him, had been more interested in Dinny's florid account of the lesbian prostitute and the toyboy, and observed that she did not know what things were coming to, and hoped he would catch them and teach them a lesson.

Fortified by this evidence of the case's moral importance, the sergeant repeated his observation about the newspaper story when he arrived at the station and dropped some hints about the importance of the police force being seen, by the public, to clear up prominent cases. It was a quiet day; his remarks inspired one ambitious younger spirit to ring round his contacts among harbourmasters and other likely sea-watchers along the coast. No joy from Brixham, or Dartmouth, or Plymouth or Newton Ferrers; but shortly after 10 a.m. PC Dingwall hit the jackpot. Salcombe harbour rang back to say that if it was a sloop called *Shearwater* they really wanted, the boy had spotted one when he came home from fishing this morning, just off the bar and heading in, with a lot of people singing and acting a bit daft. Though the dear Lord knew there were enough yachties called their boats *Shearwater*, since they didn't have a lot of imagination, in the speaker's opinion; so it could all be a damn waste of time.

The sergeant, however, decided to give PC Dingwall's information a chance. Within minutes his nearest patrol car crew were at the harbourmaster's office on the front at Salcombe, and two policemen reached *Shearwater* within moments of her anchoring, before the dinghy was even half inflated. Joanna, speechless, merely pointed at Guy. The officers spoke impersonally, officially, of their need to question him regarding the theft of credit cards.

There was a moment's silence, then, 'No, well, I say, gosh,' replied Guy, feeling that some response was expected of him. He was still a little out of breath from pumping. 'I mean, you can – he can – have them back – look – they always live here – in my wallet – Mr McArthur won't carry a wallet, it's a thing he's got, like the, you know, the Queen. Not carrying money. I was going to send them back.'

'We'll see about that, sir,' said the older policeman. 'For the moment it's best you come along with us.'

Joanna, the lawyer's wife, thought rapidly. 'Officer, it seems clear there was no intent, um, permanently to deprive the owner of these cards. Any charge of theft would hardly apply—'

'Be that as it may, madam,' said the officer heavily. 'We must ask this gentleman to accompany us to the station. Er,' he corrected himself, 'to the harbourmaster's office, perhaps, in the first instance, so that he can give us a statement.'

Guy was white. He turned to Joanna and spoke under his

breath. 'Mr McArthur – is ever so – I mean, he just knows everybody – I think – he'll have me in prison.'

Joanna looked at him. 'I,' she said with sudden firmness, 'am coming too.' She turned to the officers. 'I will help him to make a telephone call to his solicitor.'

'I haven't got a solicitor,' said Guy, hopelessly.

'You have now. My husband or his partner will deal with it.'

A part of Joanna was irritated to find herself acting like Guy's mother, but she was unable to stop. Something about the way his mouth fell open as he stared at the policeman, the way his eyes widened and his shoulders hunched reminded her too forcibly of Lance, aged ten, too bright for his own good and a year too young for his secondary school. She had arrived late to pick him up one afternoon and happened on an unforgettable scene: her small boy facing three much larger ones who were waving his treasured new leather briefcase in the air. She had waded in then, and she waded in now. Joanna had not liked what she had seen of Eddie McArthur, still less what she had heard. God knew what mischief he could make for this nice dim boy unless someone stood up to him. Once a mummy, always a mummy, she reflected, and turned to the girl.

'Della, if I go ashore, you'll be OK? The anchor's fine. I'll be back. You can come if you like, but there's not much point you being involved.'

'Can I stay here?' The answer came fast. Della had wondered whether she ought to go with Guy out of politeness, since after all he had only made his pierhead jump because of her. But going off with policemen went against the grain. She had not been, so far, in trouble; but Marie had lectured her on the train in the ways of the world and the inadvisability of getting tangled up with police, ever.

Besides, she was entranced by this boat, this rippling water, by the gulls and the harbour smells and the pride of having come in from the open sea. She did not want to be ashore again and on the way back to the bedsit in London. Any delay was welcome.

So Joanna and Guy climbed into the launch with the amused harbourmaster and the two policemen, and Della stayed.

Which is how it came about that when Gabriel landed from the Kingsbridge ferry and stood staring out at the boat he had spotted bearing the label *Shearwater*, he was in fact only yards from Joanna on the shore and never knew it. Instead of walking towards her he walked away, down the hard, and offered a bored small boy in an outboard dinghy fifty pence to take him out to the yacht. The boy jerked his head to indicate that Gabriel should sit in the bow, pulled his oily Seagull engine into coughing life, and shot off across the harbour, describing a couple of fancy arabesques across the tide-rip which succeeded in soaking the seat of Gabriel's trousers. When they eventually came alongside *Shearwater*, Gabriel grasped the guardwires and climbed determinedly aboard, the damp weight of his trouser seat making itself unpleasantly known. Peering into the cabin he found only Della, alone and startled, looking through a book about the Western Isles of Scotland. They stared at one another in complete bafflement.

Leaning on the wall of the harbourmaster's little waterfront cabin, the telephone pressed to her ear, Joanna was doing her best to interpret to her husband's depleted office the position of a still gabbling, dumbstruck Guy. 'Look, Gus, listen. Mr Pastern-Hopkins resigned his position, in effect, yesterday afternoon. There was no opportunity to return the credit cards which he routinely carried as part of his duties— What? No, in his own wallet. It was a genuine mistake.'

She shifted the telephone to the other hand and wiped a damp palm down her canvas trousers. 'No, it isn't the same as if he drove off in a company car. It's completely different. Think about it. Oh God, can't you ask Alex to break off his other call? I think someone should tell these policemen that Mr McArthur is a violent and vindictive man. In the moments following Mr Pastern-Hopkins' resignation, he couldn't have given the cards back because Mr McArthur was trying to shoot a Verey pistol in our direction – that's V-E-R-E-Y, not a regular firearm but a signalling device, registered under the firearms legislation. Oh, for God's sake, Gus, look it up. The police surely must have discretion over whether they just caution our client. He really can do without any more problems, McArthur is a maniac— Oh my God, Keith!'

Pressed to the window, pale and determined, Joanna saw the face of her husband. Keith looked oddly bloodless behind the misty glass, his face unreadable. The telephone in her hand buzzed with Gus's earnest voice.

She snapped into it, 'No, I know Keith isn't in the office, he's bloody well here. Outside the window. Look, I'll get him to deal with this. Simpler. Alex? No, I really don't want to talk to Alex – I don't see how it can be urgent. Look, Gus, you have no *idea* – oh, all right, put him on.'

In the moments that followed Joanna stood motionless, listening to the telephone in her hand, looking into the eyes of her husband through the harbourmaster's damp window, oblivious of the fascinated harbourmaster's assistant, the two stony-faced policemen, and Guy, who was edging, shrinking, shimmying imperceptibly towards the door. Finally she said into the telephone, 'Yes. Yes, I see. Call back on the car phone and tell Mandy yes, I think it's the best thing too. If Keith agrees. OK, Alex. Say thanks to Gus for being such a – help – with this business here. Storm in a teacup. Keith will cope.'

Putting down the telephone, she turned to the policemen. 'Mr Pastern-Hopkins' solicitor is in fact here. I think you'll find he can explain everything. If you'd wait one moment, I will fetch him.'

She walked out onto the tarmac square outside the office where Keith was now pacing up and down, fiddling with the wing mirrors of parked cars. Seeing him there, with his odd socks, his scarlet jelly sandals, his dishevelled thinning hair and huge, troubled green eyes, her heart turned over.

'Sweetheart. I'm sorry.'

'No, I am. It was my fault.'

They stood, close, not touching, searching one another's faces. Each seemed at once to find the assurance they most wanted; Joanna ducked her head, embarrassed by the intensity of her feeling in that public place. Gently, Keith spoke again.

'Can we go into that café over there and have a cup of coffee and talk?'

'Oh God, yes. Yes. Very soon. Only there's something else first. There's someone – one of my stowaways – who's in trouble. Lawyer sort of trouble. I'm really sorry, but might you—'

'Would this,' enquired Keith, 'be the gay teenage prostitute or the upper-class dope fiend on the run with the boss's wallet? Just so I know.'

A commotion behind her made Joanna swing round. Guy, deprived of her steadying presence, seeing only the terror of McArthur lying behind and before him, had panicked. She should have known that he would. Before their horrified eyes he erupted through the door of the harbour office, leaving one policeman spinning off balance and the other sprawled hatless on the floor. Joanna started towards him with some inarticulate protest on her lips, but Keith, who had spent half a lifetime trying to prevent his clients from making their situation worse at moments like this, was faster. Before she could see what happened, both men were afloat in a small green dinghy which had been tied to a ring on the hard. Keith was standing in the stern, reaching out to remonstrate with Guy; Guy, still visibly trembling, was threatening Keith with an oar. The flood tide took the little boat in its grip and moved it inexorably up the harbour and into midstream, silent and smooth as a revolving stage in a musical. At first it travelled upright; then a moment later, when Guy's lunge and Keith's neat duck had worked their mischief on the equilibrium of the dinghy, upside down.

Joanna held her breath until she had seen two heads, one sandy, one glossy brown, bob wetly up from underneath the boat and two pairs of hands take a firm grip of it. Then she ran down the pontoon behind the harbourmaster's assistant and the two policemen to parlay her way onto the launch for the second time that morning.

Fifty miles away, Mandy Heron was fiddling with the aerial of the mobile phone she had borrowed from her husband's office and looking sideways at the imperturbable face of Lance as he drove across the border into Devon.

'That was a funny thing,' she said. 'I rang Alex, and he actually had Ted Merriam in his office, making an offer on the Bun.'

'Good,' said Lance. 'Erika deserves the Bun. And Ted deserves to take early retirement from snarling at customers about soldering irons and pan scrubs.'

'It just seems odd that he should suddenly offer now,' said Mandy. 'I suppose it must be the fire. Made Erika realize how much she wanted the café, and Ted realize how serious she was.'

'Probably.' agreed Lance. 'So, did you say yes?'

'You heard what I said.' Mandy's spirit was returning as the car forged westwards. 'I said yes, but only if it was what Joanna wanted. And I said that I shouldn't get the full half, because I haven't kept the goodwill going as much as she has, not for years.'

'And Alex said?'

'He said it was possible to make an apportionment of the value into goodwill, and that could go to Joanna.'

'Well,' said Lance. 'That was very generous of you.'

'Shut up,' said Mandy. 'I've got embarrassing stories about when you were a baby. I've never used them yet, but I might. I might tell all your new Cambridge friends about you peeing through the letterbox when you were three.'

Lance smiled, and patted her knee in a fatherly way, and kept on driving.

30

Della had originally gone below to fetch the last squares of chocolate from her scuffed mock-Gucci holdall, planning to eat them on deck in quiet felicity and watch the water and the squabbling gulls. The book on the Western Isles, sticking awkwardly from the shelf, had caught her eye in passing, leading her idly to pull it out and turn its pages. By the time Gabriel clambered on board, however, she was lost in it. The photographs, harsh black-and-white studies by a notable war photographer who had retired to Skye after a breakdown, showed her a world she had never considered before. This was not the chocolate-box Mediterranean 'scenery' of holiday brochures and travelogues, not the illustrations from a CSE geography book. This was what she had seen by moonlight in Starhole Bay, only larger and grander, wilder and more uncompromising. This was . . . wilderness.

She said the word aloud, looking at a study of Loch Hourn, the Mouth of Hell, with mist pouring down from the mountaintops and curling over the sea. 'Wilderness.' She said it again, this time pronouncing the 'wild' as if it were the adjective. Della wanted wildness, wilderness. Nothing in her family life behind the Leicester curtains, nothing in her education – except perhaps the Grendel book – certainly nothing in her London life had made it likely that she should want any such thing. Marie and the others, she thought fleetingly, would not see much point in it. You could get cold out there in wilderness, cold and bored and wet. Seasick, if you were on a boat, like she was yesterday. She could see that. But still, there it was: Della wanted cliffs and gulls, the drama of spiked rocks with the moon behind, of crashing breakers, gales and rain and great swollen clouds and apocalyptic shafts of sunlight. One of the photographs – she turned the pages impatiently – had a beam of sun coming through dark clouds, over something called Ard-na – Ard-na-something. She bent her bright head, searching for it.

This was how Gabriel, landing in the cockpit and peering through the companionway into the dim cabin, first saw her. He was irritated at the sight of her blonde hair: this was not Joanna. His rehearsed overture was useless. He had planned to say, 'I have come back. It's our time now, it has come.' No point now. He glared for a moment. Della raised her head and glared back.

Neither of them was particularly prone to social embarrassment; Gabriel had caused too much, in his time, even to notice awkwardness. Della was too young, and had too much of the insolent kitten about her, to be bothered. She spoke first.

'Whaddyou want? Joanna's not here. She's ashore.'

'So this is Joanna's boat? I wasn't sure.'

'Yeah. How did you get on here?'

'I thumbed a lift. What are you doing here?'

'I,' said Della with dignity, 'sailed here. I was a crew. Now I'm minding the boat, for Joanna. I dunno what you think you're doing.'

'Searching,' said Gabriel grandly. 'I am searching for a woman I once knew, to make amends and take her to the Kingdom of the Blest.' That really sounded rather good. Since Joanna was not here for the moment, he might as well impress this one. 'The Kingdom,' he went on, 'of my ancestors, in the far, far west, under the mountain called by my name, where the sea of faith meets the land of saints and heroes.'

That, perhaps, was a bit over the top. He had spent too much time with that poet who wrote the Lilith plays. Certainly the line did not seem to be working on the little blonde; she was staring at him like someone about to pull the communication cord. She could make a lot of trouble if she yelled and screamed, and create quite the wrong atmosphere (he saw with a sinking heart) for his lyrical reunion with Joanna. She had better be soothed. He noticed the book on her lap, and took his line from that.

'Nice pictures, those. I know the man who took them. We used to drink together, when he first came back from Vietnam. He lives on Skye now. I told him he ought to go to Ireland. The Hebrides aren't a patch on south-west Ireland. Not to my way of thinking.'

'Whassat like, then?' asked Della. 'Ireland?' She too felt that perhaps she should humour this shaggy, craggy, grey old man. Another loony, she thought parenthetically; funny, how many you met around these yachts. Poor old Joanna seemed to know a lot of loonies. 'You from there?'

'Long ago,' said Gabriel. 'Long, long ago, I came from Ireland, from the holy western islands.'

'Did you live on an island, then?'

'No. I lived in a village on the mainland. But if you looked out to sea you could see Cape Clear and Sherkin, Castle Island and Horse Island and Illaunbeg. The sea is blue there, and the land is green and rocky, and the gulls cry over the peat moors and the grey seals dive among the rocks—'

'Real seals? Like, swimming, furry ones?' Della squeaked excitedly. 'Did you get close?'

Gabriel was not accustomed to being interrupted in his Yeatsian flow of ideas, polemic, and somewhat inaccurate descriptions. For years girls had listened to it entranced, sometimes daring to rest their heads on his knee as they sat literally at his feet. Lately, colleagues had merely ignored it, tuning it out as they did the builders' radios on the scaffolding outside the windows of Broadcasting House. He glared, now, at Della. He had, in fact, never actually seen a seal, being notoriously the least observant boy in West Cork and terrified of the water. Abruptly, he changed tack, plumping himself down in the corner of the seat opposite her.

'Never mind that. Where's Joanna? I need to see her.'

'She went ashore with the police, 'cos they got Guy, for stolen credit cards. She was going to ring her husband, the solicitor bloke, and get it sorted out for him. She's ever so kind to Guy.'

'Is he . . .' For once, Della caught Gabriel's meaning instantly. 'Nah. He's too young for her. He's a berk, really, but ever so sweet. He came because of me.'

'He's your lover?'

'Do you mind!' said Della indignantly. 'I only said he fancied me. I quite fancy him, too, but like I said, he's a berk. If he was an escort customer, like, you'd think you was really, really lucky. He's a gentleman, and ever so good-looking, like Hugh Grant, sort of. But if you were *choosing* – no. Not my cup of Horlicks.'

She giggled, with a certain unnerving coarseness, and appeared to be looking Gabriel over in much the same critical spirit. Suddenly, unusually, he was aware of his grubby plimsolls, his wrinkled, slept-in flannel trousers and stained jacket. This girl might well not recognize an intellectual bohemian when she saw one. He pushed back his dishevelled, greying mop of hair, felt how it was receding from his forehead, and hastily pulled it forward again. The seat of his trousers was still uncomfortably damp from the dinghy.

'Did Joanna say how long she'd be?'

'Don't think she knew,' said Della. 'Shall I give her a message?'

'I'll stay. I can't get ashore anyway. I came out in some child's dinghy, and he's gone.'

'Where'd you come from?'

'I came from London. When I saw the newspaper. I used to know Joanna. Years ago.'

A look of terrible comprehension came over Della's sweet little kitten-face, sharpening it, widening her eyes, bringing an incredulous smile to the pretty pink lips. Gabriel wished he had not spoken.

'I know who you are! I *bet* I know! You're the bad man, aren't you? You're the chaos man!'

She watched him, still as a cat. Gabriel could have denied it. There was no way she could be sure. He could have said, 'Don't be ridiculous, I'm a family friend.' Somehow, under the headlamp gaze of those big eyes, he failed and blustered.

'I – did – once, long ago. We were close friends, er, lovers, yes – before she was married—'

'And you're the one that chucked her?'

'Er, we broke up. She was very young at the time . . .' Oh Christ, why was he saying all this? On this damn claustrophobic boat, in this chilly harbour, to this little cow?

'Yeah,' said Della. 'You made it look like her fault. That's what she said. You screwed up her poor friend Emily, too, didn't you?'

Gabriel was silent.

Della paused and continued, 'What you come for, anyway?'

Still he did not speak. Instead, he pulled his quarter-bottle of Scotch from his jacket pocket and drank from it, wiping his mouth on his hand with a panache which took much of the sordidness from the gesture. Della peered at him, at the handsome ruin of a face, the still-dark brows, the high unhealthy colour on his cheeks where the drink had broken the veins, and the not entirely clean mane of greying hair. Bit of an old hippy. Nothing to be afraid of, this one. She ventured a guess.

'You haven't,' she said, 'come to get her back, have you?'

Gabriel was never short of a swashbuckling plot for long. He decided to make the most of this uncomfortable situation.

'Yes,' he said. 'She has run away from a pointless life. I have come to take her to the west, to the islands. We are going to start again, together, and make beautiful things, poems and pictures, in Ireland.' He was quite pleased with that. It had a certain simple grandeur.

Della gave him a long, penetrating, faintly satirical look. 'She won't come, you know. She really, really doesn't like you.'

'She will. She will understand that things have changed between us. Our moment has come, really, this time.'

'Yeah, but she likes her husband. Keith. You can tell.'

Gabriel, more incautious by the moment, the whisky burning in his gut, took issue. 'No, she doesn't. She ran away from him. He is just a shadow. I am the real thing.'

Della's laughter was a glad, young sound in the dim cabin. 'Ooh,' she said. 'You're just like the telly, aren't you?' And before he could bridle at this, she added, 'But go on, tell me more things about Ireland. Is it really *wild* where you're going to live? Rocks and caves and stuff?'

'Yes,' said Gabriel sulkily. 'I shall rent a small, ruinous cottage on the side of Mount Gabriel and draw water from a stream. I shall gather wood and cut peat to keep me warm, and walk miles for food and human company by a pub fire. I will write poetry by candlelight, and hear the sea crashing on the rocks below all winter. I shall live alone, a hermit above Dunmanus harbour, and die alone by the western shore. It will be better than laying waste my powers, getting and spending, in the shallow meretricious charade that is the BBC.'

He was quite pleased with that, too. So was Della, for different reasons. After a long, considering look she said, 'Tell you what. She's not going to come, is she? Be reasonable. But I will. I'd like to see seals and mountains and things. I could cook.'

Gabriel had never thought that anything could startle a conventional reaction out of him, and was horrified to hear himself say, 'But we hardly know each other.'

Della, who did not mind conventional reactions at all, merely nodded. 'Yeah, but I want to do somethin' different, and so do you, and you're a bloke, and I bet you can't look after yourself. And I'm a girl, and I'm not fussy. I just know what I want, right? And I want to live somewhere wild, with seals and cliffs. For a bit, anyway.'

Gabriel opened his mouth, and shut it again. Della, perhaps misunderstanding his hesitation, blithely continued, 'I won't be like that silly tart in that *Castaway* film, you know, that Lucy one who went off to a tropical island and then wouldn't do it with Oliver Reed. I'm not stupid, I know blokes all want a shag now and then. You prob'ly couldn't live with a girl without that. Well, that's all right. It's all the same to me. So is that a deal, then? 'Cos I can tell you, Joanna won't go anywhere near your Irish ruins. Bet you anything. She likes her husband really.'

Gabriel, for the first time ever, had nothing to say to a girl. All his life he had seduced, he had persuaded, he had elevated the sexual act into realms of symbolism and spiritual union, into a token of intellectual freedom; into anything at all that would get a hesitant, idealistic female undergraduate into his bed. Women had, of course, sometimes offered first. But they too had always dressed it up in a similar glittering gown of fine words. Nobody had ever classified him with whistling builders and randy bikers before, nor included him in the cheerful phrase 'blokes all want a shag now and then'. He did not know what he felt. When he examined it closely, though, he discovered that it was, in fact, relief. But he still had no words.

It was just as well for Gabriel that in that instant a commotion from just uptide of the anchored *Shearwater* brought this astonishing negotiation to a close. There was too much shouting and splashing to ignore. Both of them made for the companionway, colliding momentarily in the narrow entrance, and climbed out into the cockpit. Looking down at the upturned dinghy swirling past, Gabriel unknowingly saw for the first time the man who had succeeded him in Joanna's life, a dank, flailing figure clinging to an upturned dinghy which bumped its way along the yacht's side. Keith shot out an arm to grip the folded stern ladder, let the dinghy float away lopsidedly with Guy holding on to the other side, and began to struggle to reach the catch on the folding ladder so he could climb aboard.

Meanwhile, as the harbourmaster's launch drew alongside, Gabriel found himself, after eighteen years of forgetfulness and a night of tropic fantasy, looking straight at Joanna herself. Flushed, tousled and pretty, anxious and solicitous, there she was, jumping over the rail and hurrying to the help of another man. She was saying, 'Sweetheart! Hang on! Careful – OK, love. Oh Keith, oh God – there!' and then standing on the stern deck, laughing and crying as she embraced a thin, streaming wet man.

Gabriel stood stupidly, his hand raised towards her. She had not even recognized him.

Guy was picked up by the launch and returned, after some hesitation on the part of the policemen, to *Shearwater* since, as the elder of them put it, 'That's where his solicitor is.' After a confused conversation, it was, however, not Keith but Della who solved the problem. She suggested that the harbourmaster's assistant, on his portable phone, should ring up Eddie McArthur and let Keith ask him directly whether he wanted to pursue the case. ''Cos I bet he's forgotten it by now.'

The call reached Eddie on the gleaming, leaping, eastbound *Privateer* just as Dinny Douglas emerged for the second time, wearing the ladylike shoes he had demanded. Keith, to his surprise, found himself met with a bonhomous, expansive assurance that it had all been a misunderstanding, that the cards were cancelled, and that Mr Pastern-Hopkins would be hearing from his contracts people about the formal termination of his employment. Keith, still dripping, asked McArthur to repeat these assurances to the senior of the two policemen, which, with some impatience, the tycoon did.

So that was that, and the police departed in the harbour launch after the formality of taking Guy's address and Keith's. Guy, his teeth chattering, sat wrapped in Joanna's sleeping bag thanking everybody over and over again. Della, with a kind of annoyed pity, helped him off with his soaking socks and trousers.

Gabriel, during these exchanges, remained on the foredeck, his back to the company. He was severely shaken by the sight of Joanna, not only by her demonstrated affection for the bloody Keith man, but by a certain air of competence, a swiftness of movement, a lack of tremulousness and a womanly determination which did not match his memories and which dismayed him greatly. The whole thing had been, he saw, a silly idea. He must have been more drunk than he thought. This was not his woman. Not what his mate the photographer used to call a 'Ben Bolt woman'. The old song curled mockingly again through his mind, satirizing his own now visibly futile and contemptible desire:

> Oh don't you remember sweet Alice, Ben Bolt?
> Sweet Alice whose hair was so brown
> Who wept with delight when you gave her a smile
> And trembled with fear at your frown . . .

This damn woman had brought this cramped little boat halfway along the English Channel, alone, in a gale, on the sort of horrible sea which used to make him sick when he went out on his cousin's fishing boat from Dunmanus. She had even taken passengers. She had been the captain. She would not come with him to his dreaming new life; even if she did, she would wreck the dream. It wasn't her. *It ain't me, babe.* Jo Telford no longer existed. Probably hadn't for years.

Della, on the other hand, was no Ben Bolt girl either. Her offer, made so coolly, both fascinated and appalled him. No trembling submission, no seduction, just a business arrangement? Board and lodging in return for cooking, company and sex if and when required – was that what the great dream had come to? It was with blustering reluctance, but still that sense of relief, that Gabriel admitted to himself that the idea struck him, above all, as restful.

He wished he could get off the boat, but the launch had gone without him and the dinghy on which he was sitting was only half inflated. When the police had left, with enormous reluctance he turned to face Keith and Joanna where they stood together in the cockpit. Joanna was rubbing Keith's hair dry with a towel and laughing a little. She glanced sideways at the movement from the foredeck, and at last realized who the other presence on the deck had been for all this time. She stopped rubbing. Keith, without thinking, took over, his head covered, seeing nothing.

'What are you doing here?' asked Joanna, levelly. She barely knew what she felt except for an absurd anger that moments like this, in plays and novels, never occur in front of a ludicrous audience of husbands with towels on their head and shivering idiots in sleeping bags having their wet trousers pulled off, with difficulty, by strange blondes. Reunions of old, angry lovers after eighteen years ought to happen on mountaintops and moorland, in parked cars, on quiet trains or in the corners of restaurants where mournful gypsy violinists drown confidences with their wailing. The scene was badly set, and she herself miscast. She could feel nothing for Gabriel, nothing at all. He was a scruffy middle-aged man who was in the way.

'I came to see if you were all right,' he replied now, meek and lame. 'I got talking to your friend there, and the time just passed. I am,' he added hastily, 'actually on the way to Ireland. To find somewhere to live. I'm leaving the BBC.'

'Didn't know you were in the BBC,' said Joanna. It was a lie; she had heard his name more than once on the credits of plays and readings, and each time had seen the Chinese letters, smelt the joss sticks, felt her self-esteem plummet and the old rejection throb. None of this, however, was happening now. The real Gabriel was less impressive than the dream had ever been. Experimentally, she allowed herself to think of Emily in his presence; only a faint ghostly sorrow touched her, gently, without rancour. Alas, poor Emily.

'Well,' she said. 'We'd better get you and these two ashore.'

Keith emerged from his towel, hair sticking up in ginger tufts. He seemed to Joanna twice as vital as Gabriel, a solid active presence rather than a wispy grey ghost. Gabriel shrank further into himself as Keith said, 'I'm wet anyway – I'll finish off that dinghy and run you all to the quay.'

This, however, was not necessary. A buzzing heralded the fresh approach of the pasty-faced child and his outboard dinghy, this time bearing Lance and Mandy.

'Hello! Hi! Mum! Jo! You OK? Oh, Jo, I am so sorry,' shrieked the dinghy.

Joanna sat down suddenly. 'Keith. I've had it. Get them all ashore, for God's sake.'

'Mum,' said Lance, bobbing alongside at knee level, holding the wire. 'Mandy just needs to know that you aren't furious with her.'

'About what?'

'Talking to the newspaper. She never said it. The thing is,' he hissed, *sotto voce*, 'she's been very upset.'

'Mandy,' said Joanna, 'I am not remotely annoyed about anything. I'm fine. And I told Alex, yes, we'll sell the Bun, if Keith agrees.'

Mandy looked up at her from the dinghy and smiled stiffly.

'Sure? Really sure?'

'Yup. Only do one thing for me: just go back ashore. I'll see you there. This boat is too crowded. You can take this gentleman.' She gestured at the cockpit, abruptly.

'The gentleman with the trousers,' enquired Mandy, much revived, 'or the one without?' Guy had now emerged, leggy in his neat white designer-label jockey pants, to stand blinking behind Gabriel.

'Both,' said Jo firmly. Standing up, she reached into the cockpit locker, extracted a faded towelling bag with snorkels and the straps from rubber flippers sticking out of it, and rummaged. Finding a pair of garish beach shorts belonging to Lance, with ALOHA OHE! down the side, she held them out to Guy. 'These are decent enough to go uptown and buy something dry. I gather,' she added nastily, 'you have a lot of credit cards.'

Lance, Gabriel, Mandy and Guy were ferried back to the shore in the first load by the pasty child. Keith, freed from his towel, looked surprisedly at the shaggy grey figure climbing down into the dinghy.

'Who was that?' he said as they puttered away.

'That was Gabriel O'Riordan,' said Joanna. 'Someone I used to know. I want to tell you all about Gabriel, later.'

Keith nodded, smiled at her, and vanished forward to search for some dry clothes. Joanna and Della were left looking at one another.

'I'm sorry you got invaded by Gabriel,' began Joanna.

'It's all right,' said Della. 'He's a sad old bugger, isn't he? I'm going to try living in Ireland with him. On a mountain.'

Joanna sat down again. 'Della, you can't!'

'I can. Give it a whirl, anyway. I might get a job out there. He'll do, meanwhile.'

'Della, you're nineteen. He has to be – oh, forty-three, more. He's evil. He wrecks women's lives—'

'Only,' said Della, 'if he gets a chance. If they let him. I've got a big advantage. I'm not in love, am I?'

'But you might be. You might get pregnant.'

Della looked at her in amazement, as if at a creature from another age. Joanna gave up that tack.

'Well,' she said, 'stay in touch. Keith and I might sail out and see you. Take you away.'

'Yeah, maybe,' said Della.

EPILOGUE ∫

Ray Brewer hitched his trousers, scratched his ample stomach and thought about lunch. Knock off in ten minutes, maybe. First, he took a deep breath of warm spring air and stood back from the job he had all but finished. For an hour he had been slapping brown anti-fouling paint on the belly of the blue yacht and thinking about the day, six months earlier, when he watched *Shearwater* butting angrily out of the harbour, with the Fury – he remembered thinking about Furies, and land girls too – at the helm. Six months since the woman threw the keys at his chest.

There had been newspaper nonsense about it, which had upset the wife and annoyed him. *Roy Brewster*, indeed, and the yard not named right either. He had wondered, more than he told his wife, about the Gurney girl. But she had come back, mild as you like, with her husband, sailing into Brewmarine in the middle of September just as he was wondering about re-letting the berth and the lay-up space ashore. They had asked for an early launching, on the first of April, because they were taking a long cruise.

'Bit of extra holiday?' he had asked, and they had both laughed. 'Between jobs, really,' the husband said, and the wife giggled, said something about spending the school fees and seeing what happened next. So Ray Brewer probed no further. Redundant, probably. A lot of his clients had taken extra long holidays in extra scruffy clothes during this recession. Probably did some of them good.

Emerging from Cuisine It All, Mrs Hopgood met Mrs Colefax,

which was fortunate because together they could stand for as long as they liked, pretending to talk idly but watching all the time the door of the solicitors' office across the road. The new brass plaque had caused a small, pleasurable stir: Terson and Terson. Terson One they knew, of course – the stammering young man who had been clerk to Mr Gurney. Terson Two was his wife, newly arrived, without even a honeymoon, and rumour had it that the lady solicitor – fancy! – was actually *Chinese* as well. Fancy!

The watchers were rewarded. Tall, bespectacled Mr Terson appeared, hand in hand with tiny, dark-headed, white-skinned Mrs Terson. Together they turned to gaze raptly at their brass plate, then crossed the road – waving at Mrs Hopgood, hardly like lawyers at all, really, *very* informal – and vanished into the Snappy Snack.

At least it was supposed to be called the Snappy Snack, but to Mrs Hopgood and Mrs Colefax and the older generation of Bonhurst women it would, for many years yet, be the Bun in the Oven. Nor could they, without some pursing of lips, contemplate the changes wrought by Mrs Merriam: the microwave, the filled (but stony-hearted) baked potatoes, the tomato soup, the burgers, the catering-size fruit loaf. Thinking about the fruit loaf, Mrs Colefax shuddered. Still, the Tersons seemed more than happy to eat their lunch there. Young love!

In the kitchen of the Old Vicarage, a scratch lunch of bread and cheese and rather better soup was being washed down with convivial draughts of beer from a box balanced on the sideboard. Lance had bought it from a traditional brewery some distance east of Cambridge, a place of pilgrimage for the physicists of his year. He had insisted that it stand undisturbed for twelve hours before tasting.

Susan, clad in what looked to her mother like loose black curtains but which was in fact a set of separates designed as Anneliese's first-term project ('You can wear them inside out and upside down, it's a *Comme des Garçons* revival'), was drinking the beer and screwing up her face. 'Total horse piss, Lance, it's foul.' Keith liked it and was engaged in debate with his son over whether or not a couple of boxes would work on the boat, provided they were only broached after twelve hours stillness in a totally calm harbour.

'There'll be a lot of times when we stay a few days in harbours in Ireland and Scotland. We could wait until the second day to have the beer.' Lance was wondering aloud whether the preceding rough sea might not damage the molecular structure of the real ale.

Joanna said she would prefer wine boxes and had to that end ordered two dozen from the off-licence, because apparently wine costs a lot in Ireland and they would be two or three months sailing round its more remote coasts while Susan grafted away at college and stayed with Annie, and Lance drank his disgusting beer in Cambridge. She added that having her share of the Bun money in the bank was causing her to do some unconscionably extravagant things and that she would regret it. But at least there were no school fees, thanks to Mandy's daughter so sneakily corrupting her daughter out of doing A levels and into the dubious new GNVQ system.

At this point, she looked across at her daughter with love. Her capitulation to the college scheme had been as complete as it was sudden. Returning from Salcombe on the day of their reunion, Joanna and Keith had been confronted by a defiant, determined Susan prepared to make her last stand for sixth-form freedom. Joanna, thinking of Della's bold striking out into the far west, of her own casting-off of the Bun and the discussion she had just had with Keith about the chances of him wriggling free from Heron and Gurney in time for the spring, had surprised her daughter considerably by hugging her and saying it was a good idea, well thought out, and that she was proud of her.

Lance said she was out of date about GNVQ, that Susan would end up richer than any of them because early vocational training was the thing now; and that besides, there was no need to load the boat to its waterline with cheap booze because he and Susan could always bring some out, in the car, to West Cork in the summer vacation. Provided Dad sent them some money.

Mandy, who was five months pregnant, said it would be a miracle if Lance's terrible car made it to Fishguard, let alone West Cork. Alex, eating soup, said he didn't know, it wasn't a bad little car. Might buy Annie one of the new ones, to tootle around in. If and when she passed her first-year exams by designing some even more fetching black shrouds. The only mystery to him was that Anneliese, the fashion designer, only ever wore jeans and T-shirts these days, while Susan went around in Annie's bad-dream outfits. Susan could be very pretty, said Alex gallantly, if she allowed her mother to choose her clothes instead of letting Anneliese dress her like a doll. A voodoo doll, actually.

Susan, looking at her mother with tolerant affection, said that Joanna's clothes wouldn't suit her, and that hers wouldn't suit Joanna because every woman was different. Even mothers and daughters. There had been a really good piece about that in the *Chronicle*, by what's-her-name, Dinny Douglas. It was really good, that column; not nearly as spiteful as all the others. A girl at college had cut it out and stuck it on the board; something about how women shouldn't judge each other harshly for how they led their lives, because everyone had to find her own route to success, however odd it might look to other people. It was true, that, wasn't it?

Joanna said yes, it was. She leaned back, drinking her wine, while Lance took each plate away in a motherly fashion, and ladled out more soup.

Home Leave

To Dorothy Bednarowska
with love and gratitude

AUTHOR'S NOTE

It would be idle to deny my family background, as a travelling diplomat's child and one of four siblings. I have pillaged our common past for all manner of details and foreign postings: however, every character and significant incident in this book is purely fictitious. I am not in there, and nor are any of my relatives!

PROLOGUE ∫

1950–1996

At the mid-point of the twentieth century, amid the stiff gilding and blowsy classical façades of Vienna, Robert Gratton met his only and enduring love.

It happened at a New Year's Eve ball given by a group of city merchants to impress upon foreign visitors and officials that post-war austerity and humiliation would not for long keep Austria down. The once private ballroom, though tatty, still wore its operatic gilding with a swagger, and enough pressure had been put on rural apiarists for the candles to be of soft beeswax. Between their scented flickering and an emotional rendering of the "Gold and Silver Waltz" by a scratch orchestra, a pleasing illusion of unruffled nineteenth-century splendour was maintained.

Nobody noticed the shaky state of the great hall's stairway, floor and above all its drains; certainly not a tipsy young British diplomat on his first posting and wearing his first tail-coat. As the evening wore on, gatecrashers swelled the crowd: students in improvised evening-dress, old men with white hair over their collars and coats of greenish antiquity, ladies of not much virtue and musicians released from the opera house and seeking – not champagne, for that had more or less dried up by ten o'clock – but conviviality.

Most of the diplomats left early, oppressed by the romantic atmosphere and the shortage of drink. But Robert Gratton stayed

1 •

on, wandering alone but quite happy through the jostling crowd. Just before the stroke of midnight, he came face to face with a tall fair girl in a white dress. Around them, emotional Viennese embraced and seized one another's hands. Without thinking he seized hers.

"I am Diana," she said.

"Yes," he replied. "I can see that."

And that, more or less, was that. Diana Martin, daughter of a Hartlepool doctor, unpromising music student, had no need to play the huntress. Robert Gratton hunted her thereafter with concentrated care, and six weeks later central Europe had one fewer bad violinist, and one more bride.

Back at the Embassy this caused some consternation. The Ambassador was not impressed by this haste and his wife – who saw herself as a mother to all the young men of the mission, particularly the handsome ones – remonstrated most strongly with him on the day before his brief civil marriage.

"You know so little about her – about one another," said Lady Ford, plaintively.

"I know everything," said Robert firmly. Faced with his dark good looks and romantic determination, she fluttered a little, gave in, and made the Ambassador buy the young couple an unsuitably expensive silver tray.

They honeymooned at an inn near the Czech border, where Robert borrowed langlauf skis and Diana would trudge up through the snow to watch him sliding erratically along the high forest tracks. In the evening they ate their way through a dozen local variants on potato and sausage, drank steins of pale beer, watched the snow falling and marvelled at their luck.

Despite Lady Ford's misgivings, Diana proved to be the very model of a young diplomatic wife: unambitious for herself, deferential to the senior wives, eminently teachable when it came to the decorous conventions of entertaining and being entertained. "Never worry about *placement*," an elderly French chargé d'affaires told her in a comforting aside one day. "Diplomats are like circus horses. They always find their own places." Best of all, she was unhampered by any unfortunate tendency to attach herself emotionally to hearth and home. Moving on was never a problem to Diana as it was to other wives; almost alone among her peers she would greet each new posting with escapist glee, and regarded packing up house every two or three years to cross the world as a positive perk of the job.

Hartlepool, after all, had been dull: so dull she had frequently wept with rage and frustration from the age of thirteen onwards. The Martin parents, GP and district nurse, had been unswervingly dedicated to their humane callings, and baffled and irritated by their only child. At first they had seen her as a successor, and plied her from childhood with Little Nurse kits and books full of colourful cross-sections of intestines and diagrams explaining the Miracle of Skin. Diana had ignored these and crayoned dresses, flounced and princessy, on every blank end-paper. She demanded dance classes and saved her pocket-money for big, stiff wire curlers.

The child's delicate, fair prettiness seemed to annoy her mother in particular every bit as much as Diana's open dislike of the messy and arduous parental professions. It was with a certain guilty relief that the Martins sent her out of the vulnerable port area to spend the war on a Pennine smallholding with some cousins. Here Diana learnt that there was indeed a life worse than being a provincial doctor's daughter: a life spent farming. Here too, however, through a village schoolteacher's gramophone she encountered good music: a discipline so blissfully unconnected with either bandages or pig pens that she begged prettily for lessons. To her parents' further bewilderment, she showed enough swift shallow talent on the violin to win a place at Leeds, and to cap it, by November 1949, with a six months' exchange scholarship to Vienna. Of which, as we now know, she served only one month before New Year's night revealed her true vocation as a diplomatic wife.

Robert Gratton, still dizzy at his luck in love, struck lucky again in 1952 with a posting to Venice. It was not customary for diplomats always to come home between postings, and he took the pregnant and excited Diana by the night sleeper through the Alps, waking her with a kiss as the train trundled across the causeway towards the towers of Venice in the morning mist. Here Diana wandered for two blissful months through churches and galleries and piazze, determined to feed her unborn on beauty, on Bellini madonnas and Canaletto views. Here, at the height of Carnival, the first Gratton baby opened her eyes on the white apron, blue habit and pendent rosary of a midwife nun.

"I shall call her Catherine," said Diana dreamily. "She is going to be beautiful. My Venetian baby."

Soon, however, Catherine was merely Cat, and not particularly beautiful either. A stout, fair, stolid, practical child, she was very different from the dark elfin Venetian babies around her. Diana was almost embarrassed by her offspring's smiling pudding face and lack of mystery. Catherine grew fast, was never ill, turned the pages of her rag books with plump concentration, adored her father and merely tolerated her increasingly edgy mother. It is hard to know how these mismatches occur: how a baby not yet two can have a personality dangerously at odds with its own mother's. But it can happen. Somehow the practical, doctorly, Hartlepool inheritance had forced its way through Diana's defences. Hijacked by her own genes, she looked on her small daughter – already so painfully, obviously suitable to be a district nurse – with something like distaste. The grave, quirky, flaking romantic beauty of Venice was a daily reproof, a contrast to the child's blandly grinning fat pink Anglo-Saxon face.

An early onward posting moved the three Grattons to Tel Aviv in the newborn state of Israel. For Robert it was an important promotion, and the young nation's birth pangs excited and fascinated him. His reports to the FO were widely noticed and praised, his network of acquaintances and contacts discreet and effective. He was marked for stardom and knew it. To Diana, after Venice's dim velvet glamour, Tel Aviv was an atrocity: the buildings were concrete slabs, the landscape alien, alternately dusty and overbrightly green. Life within the diplomatic corps was tolerable but the intrusive, noisy, plain-speaking, prickly warmth of the Israelis offended both her natural reserve and recently acquired diplomatic poise.

However, she still worshipped Robert, despite the dough-faced baby girl he had so inconsiderately given her. Eventually, Diana resigned herself to making the best of it. She thankfully handed Cat over to Rachel, a stout teenager with a faint moustache. Cat's first whole sentence was "Rachie gimme Torah story", and her first naughtiness was cutting off, with craft scissors, the hair of a very expensive doll that Robert had ordered from Harrods for her second Tel Aviv Christmas. "Dat doll was *Samson*," she explained indignantly. "Dat doll was getting *too strong*."

Diana's doldrum ended in 1954 with the birth of Toby. This son, dark and saturnine like his father, provided all the romantic mystery and infant glamour which Cat so woefully lacked. He rarely slept but never cried; his black glittering eyes were everywhere, his smile devastatingly crooked, his demands on her breasts constant and strangely flattering. Cat had sucked happily but dully, eyes closed, so easily satisfied that she often fell asleep with her mouth open halfway through a feed, dribbling. Toby hung on Diana's breast as purposeful as a little vampire, feeding every two hours, punching her with his small perfect fists and watching, always watching her face through open, long-lashed dark eyes. At night, giddy and euphoric with sleeplessness and the released hormones of frequent feeding, Diana would gaze at her baby mesmerized, and wish she had not let Robert name him so boringly after a recently dead uncle. Toby! Bah! This baby should be a Giovanni, a Maximilian, or an Horatio; not that dull jug of a name. But never mind. He was here. She was, at last, complete.

It never occurred to placid Cat to be jealous. She adored Toby with baby passion, watched over him with care, and endlessly picked up the toys he hurled from the pram when Rachel – who was rather less enamoured – grew bored of his demands. Two years later, when the family was posted back into the heart of old Europe, to Berne, it was the four-year-old Cat who packed Toby's toys and worried whether there would be enough clean nappies for the long journey by ship and train. This time, Robert flew home for briefing at the Foreign Office and Diana was left alone, with a weeping Rachel, to pack up the Tel Aviv house.

She had the grace to be fleetingly glad of Cat's stolid helpfulness, and to call her a "good girl". The departure itself was rushed. Cat looked back at Rachel as the overloaded taxi drew away from the gate, but said nothing beyond "Bye-bye". She was not quite sure, and did not like to ask her mother, but expected Rachel would probably come on later. Nobody had explained the permanence of the separation.

"They just accept it, at that age," the Ambassador's wife had sagely told Diana. "The rule is, don't for heaven's sake make a big thing about the children saying goodbye to local help. They soon settle in the new post, and forget. Dimpy never even talks about his old ayah, though he had her for three years when we were on the Viceroy's staff."

Berne is no Venice. But the buildings are old, satisfyingly ornate and richly permanent, surrounded by a fine city wall. On each hour strutting figurines march out of the Zeitglocke in the centre of town and bang hammers for the chimes. There are parks, not deserts or irrigated plantations. Other wives at the Berne embassy grumbled about the stodginess of Swiss society, but for Diana, back from the horrid brash sandiness of the Bible lands, it was something to be revelled in: formal, safe, understated, *European*. Best of all, from Cat and Toby's points of view, there was a great concrete pit on the edge of the city with trees growing up the middle and real, live brown bears in it who served as the patrons and symbols of Berne. Sometimes they had baby bears with them, who crept from the caves below the roadway to glare up at the ring of visitors' faces above. Sometimes they climbed the biggest tree, and glared across the pit from eye level. Any level of good behaviour – in Cat, at least – could be instantly summoned up by a promise to go on the tram and see the bears; any bad behaviour quelled in a second by a threat to withhold this joy.

After a few months of settling in, a nanny-governess was engaged to teach Cat to read and keep Toby from falling into the bear-pit. The day of her arrival found Cat oddly excited, up early in her best dress, waiting. When Helge came, fair and formal and obviously not Rachel, she made no complaint but picked up Toby, hugged him briefly, then unaccountably went upstairs and changed into an everyday dress before returning dry-eyed to greet her new attendant.

"Cat could go home to school," said Diana, two years later and grumpily pregnant for the third time. "Most families do send children home to board. That's what the allowances are there for. It's stupid not to take the chance."

"Poor Pussy, she's only six," said Robert, who had a particular tenderness for his tubby little daughter, and loved to see her politely handing round bridge rolls and vol-au-vents at the compulsory cocktail parties. "Home is here. She's never even been in England, come to think of it."

"But she really ought to go to school. If we put her in school here, she'd have to do lessons in German. Switzedeutsch, too, not even real German."

"Other children do. I think it's rather broadening for them. She actually speaks it quite a lot, with Helge, I can't understand a word either of them are saying. It is a villainous accent, I grant you."

"You're changing the subject."

For the first time, a rift seemed to be opening between the two elder Grattons; but in the nick of time, just as Cat was about to be shown glossy prospectus photographs of a convent school in Wiltshire, Robert was posted to Washington. It was another showy promotion, second-in-command to a distinguished Ambassador. Accordingly, he flew to London for more prolonged and deeper briefings than before, then briefly back to Berne for Diana's confinement.

The baby was too late for the exigencies of the posting, however, and Robert was already on the train to Geneva airport at the moment when Mark was born, with some difficulty, in a spotless Swiss nursing home. Cat and Toby stayed for a week with Helge and her family in the mountains while Diana and the baby recovered from the long and frightening labour; the house was already relet and the family furniture and baggage crated in Pickfords' store, awaiting a freight 'plane. "Poor you," said the Vice-Consul's wife to Diana. "Isn't it hell, really, this life!" But Diana did not care at all about the furniture or her limbo of homelessness; only about Robert's not being there nor – apparently – much wanting to be.

So Cat went to school in Washington DC, and learnt to spell *color* and *labor* American style at school and English style at home, to salute the Stars and Stripes and – to Diana's dismay – to chew gum. At seven, even under the liberal regime of the chic private prep Diana chose, she was painfully aware of lagging behind her well-drilled contemporaries from Ivy League families. Toby, at four, was initially indignant at leaving the bears but before long found himself revelling in the American atmosphere of carefree wealth, TV cartoons, and the curious acceptability of cheekiness in small children. When his father, helpless with laughter, tried to check some of his wilder excesses of Yankee lip he would say, "I'm not a children now. I'm a kid."

Diana desultorily cared for Mark (another stolid, fair, dull sleepy baby) with much help from a Mexican maid, and longed for Europe. At one stage – Cat always remembered, with an uneasy sinking at her heart – there were many afternoon visits from one particular European, in a sitting room banned to children. Toby, smaller and less censorious and more in his mother's confidence, told Cat this visitor was a real live Count, like in fairy stories, from the Bavarian forests. "It's called a Graf, in Germany." The Graf had shot actual boars, with a blunderbuss. Cat would hear raised voices echoing up the broad stairway of their tall, brownish-yellow house on the rare evenings that Robert and Diana were not going out in cocktail party clothes. Eventually the Graf no longer came. Perhaps the raised voices were only because Robert's starry diplomatic career seemed unaccountably to have stalled in the New World. Or perhaps the career stalled because of his wife's too visible indiscretions. At any rate, he no longer felt himself to be inevitably on the fast track to Ambassador. Those who had described him as "brilliant" in Tel Aviv and Berne had scaled it down to "sound enough". When a posting to the industrial city of Lille in Northern France came, it was seen by his colleagues as a demotion. To Robert, who saw Diana's joy and relief at leaving the brash New World, it was equally a relief.

Europe did indeed seem to cure whatever malaise had affected Diana. As for the children, at nine years old Cat was at last free of the bewildering informality of American education, taken out of unflattering blue jeans and safely enwrapped in a dark-blue pinafore ("No, *tablier*, Dad, it's different"). Enrolled with the nuns of the Sacré-Coeur on the Rue Royale, joyfully she forgot her faltering Swiss-German and learned French at a speed which impressed even her mother. So did Toby, in the junior class and looking prettier than ever in a little pale-blue pinafore of his own. At four, Mark went into the *jardin d'enfants* and in his very first term was awarded a *prix de politesse* for his ps and qs.

Convent life, impeccably orderly behind the great oaken street door, brought Cat to a deep contentment she had not known since parting so many lands ago from Rachel. *Tenue*, manners, the look of things were respected; teachers greeted their class with a formal "*Bonjour mesdemoiselles*", expected a "*Bonjour Madame*", or "*Bonjour, ma mère*" in the corridors. The world of "Hi!" and "Hey, kids!" and acres of bare leg was safely an ocean away. There were dark-blue tunics for gymnastics and white ones for eurythmic dancing, homework about exports of the Côte d'Ivoire, lists of *Départements de France* with *chefs-lieux* and *sous-préfectures* to learn parrot-fashion, and La Fontaine's fables about crows and cheeses and foxes to memorize nightly. There were gold stars and linen napkins at lunch and a white-gloved ceremony on Saturdays in which you curtseyed to the Reverend Mother and received your "note" of whether you had been *très bien*, just *bien*, *assez bien* (a yellow card and a bit of a disgrace) or *médiocre*.

This latter, a white card, was given only once in Cat's three years at the convent, to one Marie-Claire Lapomelle. Her crime was only whispered, but had something to do with something *sale* she had done. All her life, Cat regretted that since this came early in her Rue Royale career, she never found out exactly what sort of dirtiness Marie-Claire had performed. She wanted to know; not least because she suspected that in America it would not even have been remarked upon.

Diana too loved France. The house that went with the consul's job was part of a palatial old merchant house ten minutes' walk from the Place Général de Gaulle; it overlooked a cobbled courtyard with worn stone lions and a wilderness which had once been an ornamental garden. The *grand salon* was shabby but widely gilded, and furnished in the style Robert described as "Ministry of Works Louis Quinze". Chopin had once played there. There was a small cosy sitting room beside the salon, a sweeping wrought-iron banister on the staircase, dusty shuttered bedrooms and half an acre of assorted attics in which to lay out Toby's train set and Mark's doll's house. Social life was easy and lively, less frighteningly smart than Paris would have been; Diana made close friends among the wives in the Dutch and Italian consulates. There were walks in the Bois, long Sunday lunches with prosperous banking families at their country seats, and for the children, countless tea parties for which bourgeois parents sent out neat copperplate invitations, in the third person. The Catholicism of the children's education did not bother Diana for a moment: their convent seemed to her to have considerably more *ton* than the *lycée*, and she thoroughly approved of Cat's formal little friends with their aprons and neat hair ribbons.

Robert did not repine at coming so suddenly from Washington to such a backwater, but took to consular work with vigour and humour and discovered in himself a taste for rescuing Distressed British Subjects. Sometimes he would bring them home for the night; once, a sailor who had followed a girl onto the train from Calais slept in the spare room before being returned to the Mission to Seamen on the coast; once Cat shared her bedroom with an indignant stripper from Manchester who had been lured to France under false pretences and found she was expected to provide services beyond mere dancing. Diana – who was in London on a shopping trip with the Dutch vice-consul's wife – made heavy weather of this incident on her return, but Robert only laughed.

"I don't think she'll have corrupted Cat into wanting to dance naked with a python," he said. "Toby, now that might have been a worry. But not Cat." Diana pressed her lips together, but said no more.

Cat continued to love the Sacré-Coeur with cosy passion, Mark was reading in French and English and even Toby appeared to be kept under reasonable control by soft-voiced nunly sternness. It was agreed by envious friends that the Gratton policy of keeping the children in local schools was paying off; so when, out of the blue, the news came of his posting to Johannesburg, Robert persuaded Diana that even now, with Cat twelve and Toby ten, all three children might just as well travel out there and find schools instead of being shipped home.

Listlessly, his wife agreed; she was pregnant again, and depressed at the thought of another brash, new, difficult, chippy, cheeky country after the emollient *politesses* of provincial French life. Toby, growing up and wriggling free from his mother's romantic devotion, was no longer the constant delight he had been. She had had a most difficult interview with Révérende Mère after he had stolen one of the litre bottles of beer which was served between each table of eight schoolchildren, hidden it in the shrubbery and absconded from a game of *ballon prisonnier* to down the lot and arrive, visibly drunk, for Benediction. He bit the nun who carried him out, although she shrugged this off with a promise to pray for his soul. At least Mark, a prosaic child rising five, was little trouble and spent most of his home-time in the attic with scissors and cardboard and a hundred battered toy aeroplanes, designing airports.

So the whole family sailed south, by Union Castle mailship, and arrived under Table Mountain at the end of 1964.

In later years, Johannesburg was one of the few things Cat and Diana and Robert all agreed about: the worst post ever. Despite the fact that Robert was fully in charge as Consul-General, despite the swimming-pool, tennis court and pomegranate trees in their Northern Suburb garden, despite the fascination of their holidays in the game reserve, a pall of fear and unhappiness hung over the Grattons during their brief sojourn in South Africa. Cat went to another convent, but her French education placed her at twelve in a class with fifteen-year-olds. Their teenage preoccupations mystified her, their bullying filled her with terror, and her emerging naïve sense of justice was affronted by the casually brutal racial attitudes of both her classmates and – more shockingly – the nuns. "Until you have heard a Reverend Mother referring to 'kaffirs'," she used to say in later life when arguments blew up about ANC terror tactics, "you can't understand what it was like, having to live there."

Toby, meanwhile, said little about his boys' school but returned most days with new red weals across his hands or the back of his calves; his monks, Cat suspected, were as free with the wooden ruler as her nuns.

Mark could not be found a school, and so stayed at home with Diana and became violently possessive of her. This did not make for harmony when Caroline was born. Toby later used to drive Mark into furies by taunting him that he had sulked for a whole year. He himself merely took advantage of the disruption to run away from school one lunch-time on his roller-skates and remain missing for twenty-four hours, which nearly killed his mother.

He was found in Alexandra Township, so grubby that with his dark hair he had passed for a "Cape Coloured". He was playing with a goat, and reluctant to leave. A few months later Cat was beaten and kicked by a group of bigger girls at her school. Robert, preoccupied by a prolonged visit from some troublemaking British MPs, seemed unaware of all but the very worst crises in his family, and would leave home hastily in the morning saying to Cat, "Look after the madhouse, darling, we all rely on you." Cat took him at his word, forged letters from her mother about medical appointments, and ducked out of school on average one day in three to help with the babies. Diana accepted this, and eventually wrote some of the letters herself, but banned her from telling Robert. "They're not teaching you a damn thing, anyway, darling," she said. "You know you'll have to go home to board, soon, don't you?"

"Yes," said Cat. "Let's carry on like this for a bit, anyway. Better for Toby and Mark." So they did.

Yet Diana was not entirely unhappy. Caroline, born in Jo'burg, made up for all its shortcomings. The mother knew, from the first moment she saw the exquisite baby with her soft swathe of gold hair, that this frail, small, and last infant was all she could want. Practice, it seemed, had made perfect. Where Cat had been strapping this baby was delicate, with long, elegant legs; she was as beautiful and long-lashed as Toby, but fairer and less fierce; as tractable as Mark but less dull.

Gazing at her in the hospital, Diana said dreamily to Robert. "I'm going to call her . . . Catherine. I always wanted a daughter called Catherine." The silent beat of horror which followed this, the universal turning of eyes toward stout, pink Cat at the bed's foot, made her instantly colour and babble: "I mean, I meant to say, *Caroline*." The incident became a family joke. It was better that way. And, after all, in 1964, hospitals were still very heavy-handed with the pethidine: there was every excuse to be fuddled. And Cat was not usually present when, in further unguarded moments, Diana would coo to women friends about the pleasure of having "a girl at last".

In the English autumn, with her father to escort her, Cat came "home" to the country she had only ever fleetingly visited. Everything looked like a film about England, an Ealing comedy: the square black taxi from Heathrow airport, the policemen's helmets, the serge-grey London buildings trimmed with red buses, the small, mean fields and woodland vistas melting through the raindrops on the train window as they travelled down into Sussex. Robert handed her to Miss Ilton, the Senior Mistress, and hurried away, head down, tears in his eyes, to pick up Toby from his sister's house in Highgate and take him in his turn to prep school deep in Devon. Three thousand miles away in Johannesburg, Diana lay beside the pool and watched Mark flabbily kicking around in his water wings and Caroline cooing on white cushions under a lace parasol.

"You be missing dem," said her maid, Mariona, who tempered deference with kindness. "Madam, I miss my kids too, off in de Township." She put down a tray with iced lemonade and biscuits, and stood half-expecting a reply.

But Diana ignored the girl's remark entirely, as a white Madam may do. The truth – which she had no intention of sharing with Mariona – was that she was not missing either of them, not at all.

Cat boarded at Abbey Grange for four years. Once she went home to Johannesburg for the holidays; then it was home to Venice while Robert was seconded to an arm of the UN. She never forgot those journeys from school, crossing Europe on the rattling, whistling night train with Toby. Then the kaleidoscope was shaken, and home became Los Angeles: Robert Gratton's last post.

This time, Diana loved America. She had reached a time of life when sunshine meant much to her: she loved the wide, easy Spanish-style house in Las Palmas Avenue, with its bougainvillea and lemon tree outside. Its marble and polished wood floors soothed and delighted her. She walked with her small beautiful daughter in Hancock Park and drifted coolly around the LA County Museum of Art. She shopped at Saks and, for the first time, became a relaxed and easy driver in her air-conditioned automatic.

It was to LA that Cat travelled in her first university vacation, gaining great credibility among her peers for this (although San Francisco would have been even better). By then Mark had joined Toby at Radley, after two unforgettably terrible years alone at Toby's old prep school.

They were not schoolmates for long, however. Toby was

expelled from the Lower Sixth for driving a master's car into the river. Caroline, golden Caroline, the image of her mother only more beautiful, polished to a bright sheen by a harmonious and cultured childhood in Venice, was never sent home to board. She stayed with her parents and attended a Californian progressive school where she covered herself with glory at the age of eight by invariably recognizing the old master reproductions pinned up on the wall to encourage Positive Attitudes. "She's the Madonna of San Giobbe," she would say. "Only they've cut off the arch bit that should go over her head. We used to go and see her quite a lot."

Her beauty, tractability and gentle manners made her an envied and adored child in their circle, diplomatic and local; which did much to make up to Robert and Diana for the spiky embarrassment of Toby's permanent presence in the area. For a senior diplomat's son to be working illegally in a Long Beach beach burger stand run by an equally illegal immigrant Mexican family was, to say the least, awkward. Still, as the family saying went, that was Toby. "I've found him much easier to bear," said Robert wistfully once, "since I gave up hope."

Surprisingly, Toby was not the first child to plunge the Gratton parents into real shock. In 1973, out of the blue, Cat wrote home from Bristol to say that she had married Tim Lorrimer, a fellow student, and was living with him in a squat and expecting his baby. She was sorry, she said, not to have organized the kind of wedding her parents would have liked to fly home for; but everything happened so quickly. The great thing, she wrote, was that Toby had turned up the night before just by chance. Moreover, he had borrowed a motorbike and nipped up to Radley to get Mark – ("A hundred miles at least! Each way!" moaned Diana. "And we thought he was on the burger stand – where did he get the money to fly home? That boy, that boy!"). So both brothers, continued Cat, were there and had bopped all night at the wedding; and they all sent all love to Caroline, and hoped to see her soon. There was masses of room at the squat.

The suggestion that their ten-year-old princess, their perfect golden Caroline, should go anywhere near the shambles of their elder children's lives filled both elder Grattons with horror. They need not have worried. Although in the following year Robert retired and brought his wife and younger daughter home to damp little England, by that time there was no squat and no marriage either. The unseen son-in-law Lorrimer had vanished from the scene leaving Cat with twin babies. He left them nothing more useful than the names he had chosen to have them registered by: Daybreak and Mooncloud. Cat left the squat to move in with her husband's mother Noreen in Hounslow, and refused steadfastly to join her parents in their retirement cottage in Sussex for more than the occasional weekend. "There's no room, and besides, Mum, you've had enough babies."

She did, however, make some acknowledgement of her return to their world by referring to her children always as Dave and Marianne. Caroline, by now an uncomfortable pupil at a Sussex comprehensive (the boarding allowances no longer applied) rather wished her nephew and niece had kept their exotic names. Mooncloud, in particular, she thought very beautiful. Mark, starting at business school, entirely approved of his elder sister's discarding of embarrassing names and hippie ways.

Diana lived for eight years of retirement; long enough to see Cat remarried to a young gentleman farmer called Gervase Hartley, Mark launched on a career in supermarketing ("A *grocer*, darling? Gosh!"), Toby in and out of successive curious occupations including the writing of punk rock lyrics, and Robert unexpectedly emerging as the author of an acclaimed political treatise on the state of Britain in the world.

This book proved so remarkable, so powerfully analytical and (it turned out) prophetic that it won him a worldwide reputation, an international lecture tour and, in 1987, a life peerage at the request of the Leader of the Opposition. Toby at this time was at his peak as a lyricist: the press had considerable fun with the ennoblement of the man who had fathered the author of "Snot Hard Rock I want its Hard On, Baybee" and "Jack and Jill they kill for thrill".

But Diana knew nothing of that. She was only Lady Gratton of Kilmore for three days before her death: she faded fast and unexpectedly before her sixtieth birthday. Her lord sat by her side in the hospice during those last days and nights, talking gently, vaguely, sorrowfully about the past. Sometimes he would feel the squeeze of her claw-like hand when she too remembered scenes and countries they had known together.

But her last look, her final struggling smile, was directed towards the other side of the bed where Caroline sat in a soft blue jumper, her pale beautiful face inclined, merging for Diana at that last moment into every Bellini Madonna and idealized maiden in every gallery, church and glowing city of the past.

1

1996

Catherine knew how tired she was when, looking towards the exit from Great Portland Street underground station at dusk, she mistook a bus for a building. London these days! she thought hazily. Imagine painting a whole façade as bright a red as that!

Upon which the building drove away and no longer filled the dingy frame of the Tube station's exit. Catherine shook herself, gave an embarrassed inward laugh and trudged with her overnight bag onto the winter street whose buildings were not red at all, but streaky London grey. Ahead of her, high overhead through the drizzle, she could see the illuminated name of her hotel. Eden Central. Its starburst logo proclaimed it an outpost of the Eden empire, and Catherine Hartley had seen that starburst often enough on cheques for its very shape to cheer her. Good old, boring old, Eden PLC.

She walked towards the misty glow, and turned left as the drizzle intensified. Her coat was wet across the shoulders before she reached the shelter of the hotel's concrete canopy. She dodged the puddles along the ramp where taxis with beating engines stopped to disgorge their cargoes of tourists and business travellers, and stepped thankfully through the smoked-glass doors. Holding the flap of her soft old leather shoulder bag open with her teeth, she dug distractedly in its messy interior in search of the Eden hotel voucher (*Accommodation only, not including breakfast, dinner, telephone services or minibar*). She did not stop walking towards reception as she rummaged. Catherine rarely did fewer than two things at a time. She had been known to correct page proofs in the dentist's chair, rather to his annoyance. Sometimes, she was so anxious to get ahead of herself that she would pull out her entry card to Eden Headquarters before she reached its glass doors, and have tidily put it away again before she got near the commissionaires' desk. So she would have to get it out all over again.

"Mrs Hartley," she said to the girl behind the desk. Her voice was muffled by the flap of handbag between her teeth as she hauled out the crumpled voucher. She dropped the flap and pushed the paper across. "It's a courtesy booking, head office, OK? Non-smoking—"

"One moment please," chirped the receptionist. She leaned forward, jabbing at a computer, her glossy blonde chignon wobbling slightly. "I'm sorree, Mrs Hartlee, we have no record of a booking—"

"Every Wednesday," said Catherine, tiredly. "I come every Wednesday. I have a meeting at Eden head office on Thursday mornings. I'm a freelance. I work for your company magazine and internal staff communications. They put me up here. Every week since last June."

There was, had anybody been there to appreciate it, a note of half-shameful triumph in the guest's voice when she said this. Even though the chain owned nine London hotels in addition to its shops and insurance business, it had been hard work to get Staff Communications to persuade Eden's tight financial establishment that if they insisted on a 7.30 a.m. London meeting every Thursday with a freelance who lived on a Northamptonshire farm, they owed that worker a bed for the night. It had been almost as hard for Catherine to persuade her husband Gervase that she would function better in every way, and come home sweeter, if she did not have to drive twenty miles to catch the Northampton milk train on winter Thursday mornings.

He had finally agreed, with his usual controlled politeness but without enthusiasm. At first, so as not to disrupt his day, she made a habit of postponing her Wednesday departure until after the six o'clock communal supper with the farm boys.

Recently, pleading the uncertainties of winter travel, she had taken to putting a large macaroni cheese in the oven and leaving, shamefacedly, in the afternoon before the chickens were even shut up for the night. Amongst themselves in the barn, the boys would josh about this.

"Mrs Hartley's off on the tiles again, up 'n London," Gary would say, and Duane would chortle, "Good on 'er, p'raps there is a bit of life in the old boiler." Luckily, perhaps, no such coarse suspicion occurred to Gervase. He would merely see her from the fields, and straighten up from his task to raise a hand in solemn farewell as she passed in her old blue Renault. Guiltily, Catherine would raise her hand in return and drive on.

On the train, she would read through the papers Eden PLC had sent, note down a few ideas which might sound convincing at the 7.30 meeting, and fall into a deep refreshing sleep in anticipation – not of any dissipation such as Gary and Duane might dream of – but merely of the bland, blessed anonymity of a hotel bath and a night in a featureless room, alone and responsible for nobody.

Today, however, she had not slept on the train, even though she much needed sleep. The tension of a long day was on her. Just before dawn sixty-three ewes, restless in the late stages of their pregnancy, had broken out of the field through a badly fastened gate and begun bleating stupidly under the bedroom window. Catherine lifted her head, soggy with fatigue: she had been up until two, answering letters and going over accounts. She remembered that Gervase was away addressing a social work conference in Bedford, and Gary staying the night with his mother in Midmarsham village. There was nobody there on that black winter morning but herself, inefficiently assisted by Duane, to get them back. In nightdress and waxed jacket, Catherine routed out the aged sheepdog and chivvied the foaming, bounding mass of sheep back down the lane into their field. There had been a heart-stopping moment when it seemed that the flock, under her inexpert guidance, would veer right instead of left and break onto the fast dual carriageway, but the old dog had reached the corner just in time to turn them.

Afterwards, heart pounding at the thought of the catastrophe averted, she could not sleep. How did people ever think that counting sheep could be soporific? The smell of lanolin and panic was still strong in her nostrils, and each time she nearly drifted off to sleep she would jerk awake to escape a vision of stupid faces and bulky, fleecy bodies, a jostling river of sheep flowing towards the headlights of the main road.

She was up early, to telephone for a replacement part for the electric fence; Gervase was not back until the afternoon, which left only time to tell him briefly of the crisis before she hurried out of the house to a later train than usual. She was by then too tired to relax on the journey. Now, at the hotel reception, Catherine's back and neck ached and a sniffle of self-pity rose in her as she leaned on the imitation marble desk amid the sleek business customers checking in. *Show me*, she thought savagely, *show me just one of these sodding corporate smuggos who could round up a flock of sheep in the dark with a half-dead dog and a drooling moron . . .*

The receptionist, who had a long, worried face not unlike a sheep herself, was prodding the computer console under the desk. "Sorree, we're in fact fully booked at the moment . . . we are implementing a refurbishment programme, which could be the reason . . . did you reconfirm under our SureBook system?"

"No," said Catherine shortly. "I never have before."

"It's a new system, if you look at your voucher – see—"

And indeed, printed in the corner of the voucher was a notification of booking condition alterations as from 13.12.96. Today was the fifteenth.

"It's not very big," said Catherine grumpily. "I couldn't be expected to see that."

"Ye-hes," said the girl, stretching the syllable out sympathetically. "We have had some misunderstandings previously, since the implementation date—"

"So there's really no room?"

"I can try and rebook you at our Islington hotel," offered the girl. "That's on the same grade as this. Or—" she consulted a leaflet. "The Eden Dockland."

"Oh, hell," said Catherine angrily. "Just forget it. I'll go to my sister's."

"Sorree for any inconvenience," said the girl automatically, to Catherine's retreating back. And to her colleague: "That's another of the SureBook ones, Nadine."

"Oh," said Nadine blankly, as if she didn't very much care.

Catherine trudged back into the Underground station, stood shivering on the platform for a while, then caught the Circle Line train to Notting Hill Gate. Her tiredness, briefly dispelled by fury at the hotel, returned as she walked on southwards through the rain towards the overgrown but exclusive square where her sister lived in a tall, imposing townhouse with her tall, imposing town husband. A husband who, pray God, by some glorious chance would be out. She might have visited Caroline more often on these London nights if she could only have been sure that Alan would not be there. Caroline asked her to, often enough. But Alan was always stressful company. So was Caroline, come to that, but she was family.

It suddenly occurred to Catherine as she turned into Moreton Square Gardens that Caroline herself might be out. She should have telephoned. But no: the light was on. Better, it was on in her sister's small studio, not in the long and formal sitting room favoured by her husband. Catherine, her hair streaming wet now, lying in brown rats' tails down her back, pressed the bell, rested her forehead on the stained-glass panel beside the door, and waited.

"Cat! Oh, Cat, come in – poor you – soaking – how lovely!" The wet visitor slid thankfully inside, gingerly kissed her sister's smooth cheek, and dropped her shoulder bag on the marble flagstones of the hallway.

"Can I stay? There's a cock-up with the hotel, and I got furious and flounced out. I should have rung."

"Oh yes – yes – that's wonderful," said Caroline, sweeping the wet coat away to a curly rococo hook on the marbled wall. "Alan's away, we can have a really good chat!"

Catherine flinched, hoping Caroline did not see her do so. She longed more than anything to sleep. Now, straight away, without food or even tea. Just to lie down in a dark room and drift away in the blessed urban night, where there was no risk whatsoever of sheep alerts. If her sister had been closer, a more familiar confidante, she might have said so. But there were twelve years between them and the older woman still felt a certain responsibility for not upsetting the younger.

"For a bit," she compromised. "I have an early meeting, so not late. Where is Alan, anyway?"

"Brussels. No, Stockholm. Drumming up co-production money. Or something."

Catherine looked sharply at her sister, wondering at the tone of her voice, but only said: "You're looking wonderful. Suits you, being pregnant. I looked terrible."

"Well, yours *was* twins," said Caroline graciously, leading the way into the small studio, ignoring the panelled door of the big sitting room on the far side of the hall. "How *are* my niece and nephew?"

"Horrifyingly adult," said Catherine. "Marianne got her psychiatric nursing ticket, you know – she's staying on at the London for a bit, though. She's on her way."

"And Dave? Did he get his postgraduate place? Brilliant. You are lucky, they're so marvellous, your children – come on, sit down. I'm in the snug, much nicer. Food? No? I've got a surprise for you—"

Caroline walked across the little room. She was graceful despite her pregnancy and her fair hair swung forward in a perfect bell as she bent to pick up a video cassette and put it momentarily on an angled drawing-board by the window.

"We can watch this. I taped it. On the news magazine thing, the new six o'clock. They did a report from the National Social Forum Workshop or whatever it's called, and guess who—"

"Oh God. I know what you're going to say."

"—Gervase was on! Yes! He was so, so good, honestly Cat. I just dived, hit the button and got all of it more or less, because luckily there was a long bit at the beginning and they said his name in that. So I *hit* the button, obviously. I think I've wiped Alan's rugby."

Catherine smiled a little crookedly. "That was really sweet, Caro. Thanks."

"So it's just right that you turned up. Isn't it?"

Catherine looked at her sister with affection. So kind, so beautiful, so anxious to please, so apparently unspoilt by a lifetime of being treated like precious porcelain. There was always an effortless air about Caroline, a comfortable sense of privilege. You could tell that she had been accustomed to being held as a rare and wonderful thing: first by their parents, then by a series of mentors at art college and the Courtauld Institute, and lately by doting – generally elderly and often gay – gallery owners in her various jobs. Now presumably the rich and influential Alan had taken over the role of curator of the porcelain. Nobody, thought Cat as she watched her, would leave Caroline to bring up newborn twins alone, or expect her to round up sheep, or turn up at 7.30 in the morning in ghastly boardrooms to write reams of rubbish about prioritizing interpersonal communication strategies. Nobody would expect Caroline to read stupid little notices in the corner of hotel vouchers, or indeed to check into a hotel alone.

This might have made other women – including her sister – resent Caroline; but strangely, it hardly ever did. Cat, although she was tired and conscious of her own worn, dishevelled, lined, workaday appearance, looked at the smooth lovely face and smiled. Dear little Caroline. Fancy her recording Gervase on the news.

Caroline bent again, grunting a little, and pushed the tape into the slot. Returning to a chair next to her sister's with the remote control, she said anxiously:

"But would you like tea, first? Or a drink?"

"Scotch. No, on second thoughts, don't bother going through to raid Alan's stuff. You've got a bottle of wine open."

Caroline took a glass from the shelf and poured white wine into it from a bottle which – Catherine noticed with a slight twinge of concern – was half-empty. Her sister caught her eye as she turned, and gave something like a laugh.

"I do normally stick to one glass a day, like the books say," she said, "only . . . with Alan away . . ."

"Anyway," said the older woman, breaking into the awkward moment. "I'll need most of the other half, if I've got to watch Gervase."

The programme was a chatty news round-up, the second half-hour of it devoted to the softer magazine stories. Caroline's tape began half-way through an item on young offenders.

"*—told the conference that there are other ways to return these troubled young men to a valuable life in the community. On his small organic farm in Northamptonshire, ex-offenders work and live for six* *months as part of a family, and, for the first time, get a chance to develop a real relationship with the natural environment. This, says Mr Hartley, can change their lives. Like the old song they plough and sow and reap and mow – using old-fashioned carthorses. Netta Harkess reports.*

The scene changed to a long shot of green fields and a red-tiled farmhouse, with two horses plodding across the foreground pulling a plough. The tune of "To be a Farmer's Boy" swelled on the soundtrack.

"God," said Catherine. "I forgot they did that filming. They were there on Monday. Someone picked up on the advance text of Gervase's conference speech. They kept Gary for two bloody hours, so Gervase had to ring up Mr Badsley to come and help load the pigs."

The music was faded. *"Seventeen-year-old Gary – we can't give his surname or show his face – has been in and out of trouble since he was thirteen,"* said Netta Harkess sententiously on the television, over a picture of Gary, his head turned from the camera, hauling a bale out of the barn in a self-consciously manly fashion.

"I wondered why there were two bloody bales left out in the rain in the middle of nowhere," said Catherine, swigging from her glass. "Props, of course."

"Sssh!" said her sister. "Gervase is on now!"

"But – as Gervase Hartley told the conference – Gary's six months at Knoll Farm, living in a purpose-built bunkhouse but sharing meals and work with the farming family, will give him, as it has dozens of others, a chance to learn a different set of attitudes."

Now the screen filled with Gervase: a strong, weathered but refined face, greying temples, broad shoulders, a keen eye: the very model of a leader and philanthropist. He was speaking:

"There are three things they learn straight away, and these are things which society has failed to teach them elsewhere." He began to tick off points on his fingers. *"One: they learn that work is something necessary, something basic: the animals obviously must be fed, the weeds must be kept down, or there will be no food for any of us. Two: they learn what responsibility is: if they don't feed the horses and the sheep, those animals will suffer and the suffering will be their fault. Three: most important of all, they learn that they have the capacity to be useful, and respected, and loved. Out in their own communities people may fear them and brand them as young thugs*

and tearaways to be punished, but here they are trusted and relied on, both by the animals and the people they work with. The animals don't know they're young offenders. They just know they've brought the food."

"But there must be risk," interrupted the reporter. "These are young men who have been convicted of serious offences."

"Well, they've been burglars," said Gervase, frowning judicially. *"And they've been in fights and affrays outside pubs, and usually stolen a car or two. But we don't take sex offenders, or kids involved in serious violence, because I have had my own family to think of. I wish we could take the challenge of more serious former offenders, and perhaps one day we will."*

"Super," said Catherine, with an edge of sarcasm that made her sister turn, in silent wondering query, before looking back at the screen.

"I don't want to sound precious," Gervase was saying, with a slight self-deprecating laugh. *"But I seriously believe that there is a healing element in the way we farm here. We respect and nurture the soil and the animals, and in return they feed and nurture us. It's an ancient cycle of birth and death and regeneration, and a lot of the problems we have in society stem from the fact that most people have lost touch with that reality. Here, we help the worst casualties of that disjointed society to come right back to the centre – to the root of all our being, if you like."*

The scene cut again to Gary, pulling out another bale of straw. Netta Harkess spoke in the background, this time more reverently.

"The Prince of Wales has expressed an interest in visiting Knoll Farm to see its work. Meanwhile, for Gary – it's time to feed the stock."

"On *rye straw*?" said Catherine. "Give me strength."

"I thought it was hay," said Caroline. "For the, you know, sheep and things."

"So did the reporter," said her sister. "No, it's actually wet straw. What's more, it's still there. I fell over that bale at four o'clock this morning." She reached forward and snapped the television off.

"Anyway, it's amazing about the Prince of Wales," said Caroline. "Is that true?"

"I dunno," said Catherine morosely. "Might be. Gervase met him at some organic conference, got introduced, he's really into young offenders, isn't he? The Prince's Trust, all that? Except they're not offenders, most of them. Besides, I can't see Gary starting a business. Not a legal business, anyway." She lost the thread of her thoughts, took a slug of her drink and yawned.

"It's *wonderful* work," said Caroline warmly, her beautiful, calm face lit up like a saint in a Renaissance painting. "I love the way he talks about it. It's so unassuming, so ordinary, but really valuable. Do most of the boys do OK afterwards?"

"Yes, actually," said Catherine. "I have to admit, they do. Gervase quite often finds them local work, and gives them references. There's one working at Harkeston Zoo, in the elephant house. A model citizen."

"Well, there you are!" said Caroline. "And" – suddenly the Madonna vanished and she took on a coquettish tone: "Didn't your husband look seriously dishy?"

Catherine laughed and poured the rest of the wine into her glass. "Oh God, yes, all right. I admit it. Gervase is wonderful. He's a saint." She swigged it, without refinement. "Have you ever tried being married to a saint?"

"No."

There was an odd moment of silence, and Catherine glanced sharply across at her younger sister. Caroline sat absolutely still, looking down at the swell of her pregnancy but not touching her stomach, her hands in her lap, her lips pressed tightly together. Again she said: "No, I haven't tried that. Being married to a saint is not something I know much about."

Catherine shifted in her chair, drained her second glass of wine, and asked gently, "Alan's at a sales thing, you said?"

Caroline continued looking bleakly at her belly.

"I don't know," she began slowly. "And it's disloyal to say, but . . ."

"But I have started the ball rolling by casting doubt on Gervase's canonization," said Catherine comfortingly. "So . . . ?"

The words began to tumble, the lovely face to distort, tears to roll down Caroline's cheeks. She was talking, sniffing, wiping her nose on her sleeve, out of control.

"I don't think he's on his own, I think he's been seeing an old girlfriend again, I'm sure of it, actually."

"Quite sure? I mean, everyone imagines disasters when they're pregnant, it doesn't usually mean a thing."

Another brief, awkward silence fell as both women became conscious of the infelicity of this remark. Catherine's first husband did, after all, walk out on her without warning when her twins were six weeks old. Therefore any premonitions she might have had during pregnancy would have been totally accurate. Caroline avoided her sister's eye as she said: "Quite sure. I asked him, weeks ago. He said—"

She could not go on, but bowed her head so that her beautiful pale hair swung forward over her face and parted, leaving the nape of her neck white and defenceless. Catherine looked at it with pity and affection.

"Go on. What did he say?"

"He thinks – it doesn't count."

"Why?"

"Ex-girlfriends. He said it wasn't as if it was someone new. Cat—" She stopped, and kicked out viciously with her foot so that the glass by her chair fell over and spilt an unregarded rivulet of white wine across the floor. "—Cat, he really thinks that. I suspect he's been sleeping with two or three of his old girlfriends ever since we got married. As a matter of course."

Catherine was silent. Her sister straightened up and stared at her for a moment, her face reddening.

"Cat, you're – not surprised, are you? You're not even surprised."

"No," agreed Catherine. Suddenly a great wave of fatigue overcame her. This, she thought suddenly, this was why she had avoided staying or lunching or even talking privately with Caroline in the year since the wedding. She had seen her only at wider family parties. The last had been at Easter, and a difficult gathering it was, too. Caroline's husband was anathema to Cat, and even more loathsome to the upright Gervase. Alan Halliday was handsome, charming, devious and cold. He had probably, the family concurred, married Caroline as a trophy: a beautiful, well-spoken, sweet-natured girl whose father sat in the House of Lords. Any child could see that Alan was an out-and-out pig. Only Caroline, apparently, couldn't. Nor was her sister close enough to challenge her on the subject.

So now she was in Alan's power, in his house, about to have his baby; and there was nothing anybody could do to save her from the acres of approaching pain. And all Catherine could do, could not help herself doing, was yawn.

"I'm really, really sorry. But I've got to get some sleep. Last night, we had the sheep out—"

Strangely, this change of tack seemed not to affront the stricken Caroline, but to come to her as a relief. She swung abruptly into another social gear, sprang to her feet and smoothed down her skirt.

"Of course, poor you – and there I am going on about all this nonsense, there's probably nothing in it – you do imagine things when you're pregnant, don't you? Anyway, poppet – hot-water-bottle?"

"No thanks." Catherine now felt inadequate: lumpen and boorish and ungrateful and ungraceful. It was an old, familiar feeling. Her younger sister led the way upstairs, smoothed already immaculate pillows, chattered brightly, and left her alone in a chaste, restful white room smelling faintly of lavender. Sadly, with a sleepy sensation of shame, Catherine set her pocket alarm for 6.30, shrugged off her clothes and fell into bed.

2

Under the window, in the afternoon sunshine, Gervase and Gary were bringing in the sheep. When he heard about Tuesday night's escape Gervase had decided that they should come in until their January lambing a few weeks away; he had set the boys to strawing the yard after breakfast and now was ushering a huddled woolly mass of ewes out of the home paddock and along the rough track below the front lawn. Cat looked out from her attic study as her husband, with measured step, followed his flock towards the sagging metal gate and the end of the red brick barn.

On the cork board above her desk, half-obscured by an untidy jumble of papers and sticky notes, was a sketch-map of it all: the track, the barn, the home paddock and the rest of the farm beyond. In a frame on the wall, fading slightly, hung an aerial photograph of the whole fifty acres. Years before, newly married and in love equally with Gervase and a new life, Cat had guiltily paid twenty pounds for this picture when an amiable young photographer came to the door on a cold autumn day. He had, he explained, hired a pilot friend, and from his plane had taken speculative pictures at the height of summer.

Gervase was a little shocked at such waste – the farm, after all, was where he had always lived, he needed no pictures of it, it was in every fibre of his body – but he had laughed at her enthusiasm and paid her back the money.

In the picture, the trees and hedgerows were in full buoyant leaf, the grass green. The pale, trodden-down ring in the meadow, made by the horses' cantering, stood out as clear and incongruous as a corn circle. The house and barns looked like toys, their shabbinesses hidden by distance: sheep were peacefully grazing, the flock scattered into white blobs. With a magnifying glass (provided by the salesman that day on the doorstep) Cat could just make out one of the black-and-white sows, snoozing outside her tin-roofed arc with a suggestion of piglets around her. Her favourite among the cows, redpoll Molly, was clearly visible next to a hedge, the others hidden by branches as they rested in the shade of an oak-tree. There was a half-built June haystack, where Gervase, Catherine and one of the boys of the moment (Jerry? Leroy? a decade on, their sharp young faces blurred in her memory) were forking sweet yellow bundles of hay off a waggon.

This tranquil moment, caught from high above, as perfect as a child's toy farm in a Christmas stocking, had hung imprisoned behind glass by Cat's desk for over ten years now. She no longer noticed or even saw it. Turning back now to her dusty old Amstrad 8256 word processor, Cat focused on the more immediate problem of concocting a lively, appealing, 750-word read on the subject of *Eden PLC and the Challenge of Portable Qualifications*.

"TRAINING DIVISION," typed Cat. "COPY FOR JAN 97, ex CJ HARTLEY."

That was the easy bit. She looked dispiritedly down at the notepad she had brought back that morning from the 7.30 meeting, picking out the words "National Vocational Quali-fication", "NB Transferable" and "Take risks\Win Loyalty".

What the hell had that been about? And why had she done the slash backwards in her notes? Usually, it was a device to remind her of something. She closed her eyes, and visualized the keen young personnel officer in the dark suit, his woman divisional boss in a cherry-red one, and the pale-grey decor of the conference room. She hated writing copy for the Training and Personnel divisions. It was far easier to be snappily convincing about new hotel construction, or the importance of diversifying into high-street life assurance outlets, or the future of retail display. Next to "the challenge of Europe" her most difficult pieces were the ones about middle-management motivation or assisted creative career planning. Having had a chaotically unplanned and unassisted career herself – prize scholar, single mother on benefit, school library assistant earning undeclared income from toshy magazine stories, freelance copywriter – Cat found it hard to throw herself into these corporate lives with any enthusiasm.

Still, the stuff had to be in by Monday. She flicked over the page. "Junior staff, sense of belonging" she read. That would do. Sighing, she began to address her invisible reader, yawning in some Eden staff canteen: *Eden PLC is where you work. Sure. But is it where you belong?*

Outside the window, some kind of commotion was brewing. There were shouts, and more baa-ing on a wider range of notes than was usual for minor stock movements. Cat looked out of the window on her left, and saw Gary running and Gervase trying to get the old sheepdog to head the flock off from the gateway. Voices floated up to her.

"Duane, shut the other gate – the OTHER one."

Ah. That must be it. Duane, the elder of the teenage ex-offenders currently in residence, must have left the far gate open, so that the first flood of sheep could flow straight into the yard and out again onto the barley stubble. Oh dear.

Cat had a fondness for Duane: he was so terribly dim that all his past misdemeanours could be, had to be, forgiven him. The joy-ride which had landed him in custody had ended ignominiously when he drove up a cul-de-sac and could not manage to get the unfamiliar car into reverse gear in order to get out again. Then he had locked himself in with the remote-control key, and could not get out without setting off the car alarm. The police had been laughing when they picked him up. He was a sweet boy, Duane, touchingly unconfident and anxious to please. They were not, under Gervase's rules, supposed to talk about their convictions ("it only makes them brag, and normalizes bad behaviour") but he had privately told Cat over the washing-up one night that he only nicked the motor for a friend who'd been "a bit down, like. To give him a laugh". Dear boy. Gervase would try and find him a mentally untaxing job for low pay, and he would most likely go straight. Especially if he could find an equally dim, good-natured girl to go with.

She had more problems with young men like Gary: bright wide-boys who had, it seemed to Catherine in her more unfor-giving moods, played the system deliberately from the start.

Garys exploited their mothers' weakness, idled at school, got girls pregnant and ignored them, got jobs because they were bright and lost them because they stole or lied or never turned up. Then – being bright – they made the most of their family problems in successive courtrooms. Gary knew how to be angelic when it suited him, and how to sound like an inarticulate victim, worsening his syntax to show that he "never had no chance". He knew when to speak, and how haltingly, about his disrupted and fatherless family.

Cat, however, had met his mother often enough to have a shrewd idea of how much of that disruption Gary had himself caused, and how very unkind were his hints at a childhood maltreated by a succession of brutal "uncles". Poor, meek, buck-toothed Mrs Bird, so Cat knew from her innocent chatter while she waited for Gary on Friday evenings, had only achieved one boyfriend since her husband's departure. By that time Gary was fifteen, six foot two, and up for his second burglary. Try as she might (and usually she succeeded in seeing the good or at least the funny side of what Gervase's mother called his "pet thugs") Cat could not like Gary. She was grateful that he was in the fourth month of his stint at Knoll Farm.

He would be gone by February, and there would be another boy. Winston somebody: cannabis, was it? Gervase had been on the phone to the probation service about it. Then Duane would be off in summer, and some other lad would turn up, sullen and defensive, in a tattered t-shirt and baseball cap and trainers quite unsuited to farmwork; and Gervase would talk to him, and Cat would find him boots and feed him up, and on it would go for another half-year of all their lives.

Sometimes, Cat wished there could be girls just for a change. But girls did not seem to commit the kind of crimes which made probation officers think that six months' simple farmwork would tone them up morally. Girls just got pregnant, perhaps? With a twinge of misery, she thought of Caroline.

Beneath the window the sheep, penned in a tight knot by the dog, had begun to move towards the end of the barn again, and turn through the gateway. She watched Gervase walk behind them, whacking the occasional fleecy back gently with his crook, and thought what a good, what a very good man he was. She turned back, with a sigh, to the computer screen, and so missed seeing him glance up at her window and hesitantly raise his stick in greeting.

At Eden Personnel, Jack Hardacre would like to know. As Senior Director with Board responsibility for Onward Training, so would Joanna Raschid—

Or was it Rashid? Cat had not been at her best, during that morning meeting. She had yawned several times. Not a good move. At Eden PLC HQ nobody dared yawn. One disaffected departing secretary had been heard to remark, as she viciously stuffed her possessions into a carrier bag in the corner of an office where Cat was waiting for an appointment, "Talk about tight-arsed. Eden makes Marks & Spencers look like San Francisco in 1975." Anyway. *Joanna Raschid (sp?)* it would have to be. The great thing about filling a corporation with frightened, neurotic, obsessive people in a strict and nervous hierarchy was that after a while nobody in such an organization was any longer capable of writing clear, cheerful, upbeat prose. So they had to hire freelances, and pay them, and let them work at home not far from their stoves and families.

Which, in turn, could lead to unsuspected social good, balancing the social evils perpetrated elsewhere by the company. In this case, thought Cat benevolently, stabbing at her keyboard, the absurdities of Eden meant that a man with an idealistic but unremunerative mission could follow his calling and do good in the world without a moment's anxiety about how to finance his own family life. For although Knoll Farm was Gervase's inheritance, and the boys' keep was notionally covered by £25 a week from a rehabilitation charity which also paid them a low wage, there were costs of seed and feed, of vets and transport to be met. Farm produce sales could only just cover farm costs in a good year; no nett income whatsoever had resulted from Gervase's long, arduous working days since 1990.

That was the year when Gervase's mother sold off an adjoining, and profitable, hundred acres in order to recoup her Lloyds' losses. That this hundred acres represented Gervase's income did not occur to Artemis Hartley at the time.

As a result the widely unrecognized fact was that for nearly seven years – despite the patrician and philanthropic appearance of Gervase and the general knowledge that he had taken on "poor little Catherine" as a divorcee with two children – Cat had supported him. The daily spending of the Hartley household, their council tax and petrol and food and clothes and reading matter, was met entirely by what Catherine earned alone in that scruffy study high over the lawn. Her income derived mainly from the profitable if unedifying task of writing – for the staff paper and a dozen departmental newsletters – some semblance of a human face onto the stiff corporate mask of Eden PLC. It was, in its way, a good joke.

Catherine looked out of the window again, to where Duane and Gary were engaged in acrimonious arm-waving debate over the matter of who told whom to open which gate, when. Gervase stood by the gate, looking back at the sheep. Unhurriedly he turned, walked over to the boys and said something. Cat did not need to hear. It would be "Cut it out, fellers", and an instruction. Sulkily, the two moved away, Duane towards the feed store and Gary to the stable barrow. Gervase looked up again at the window, and this time Catherine leaned sideways from her desk, and waved. A smile broke across her husband's face, and he carefully kissed his hand and blew the kiss up to her. Laughing, she drew back into the room and ran her hand across the static crackle of the green computer screen, chasing a veil of dust.

For what the neighbours, and most of the family, would not have understood was that Cat did not mind being the lone financial support of this absurdly quixotic enterprise. It seemed to her, and had always seemed, a central part of Gervase's nature: a brave stab at social cohesion and natural healing. It was a small gallant struggling plant with its roots in all the most deeply held beliefs of the decaying gentry class he came from: in guilt and pride and patriotic philanthropy and inarticulate public-school idealism. It had nothing to do with the worlds of Eden PLC or Alan Halliday. Nor with the elderly socialite world of Artemis, the hippy world of Cat's first husband Tim, or the argumentative Westminster world in which her own father seemed increasingly to live. Keeping Gary and Duane off the streets and usefully employed and smelling of dung instead of lager for six months might be ultimately pointless, given that there were not that many jobs for them to go to when they left. It might be true that, as her brother Mark had once argued at a difficult Christmas dinner, big international business deals and the chasing of profit did more for jobs and therefore for youth than toy farms could ever do.

But when the barricades were up, Cat said at the time, she would rather be on the losing side with Gervase at Knoll Farm than out there winning with the others. So when the money dried up in that same year, Catherine had said to Gervase that of course the farm and the work with the boys must go on. They could manage. That was the only conversation they had ever had on the subject. Catherine paid her Eden earnings into the joint account; most years she made between ten and twelve thousand pounds after tax. Without holidays or indulgences, and with her own children now grown, it proved enough. Just.

The sun had gone behind a low black cloud on the horizon. After a last glance out of the window at the suddenly grey and spiritless scene, Cat turned back with a sigh to the screen.

Joanna Raschid (sp?). The three letters on her mind at the moment are NVQ – National Vocational Qualification. "Its important," she says, "that young staff know we care enough to offer them not just internal progress, but a portable qualification—"

"Mrs H!" called a voice up the attic stairs. "Is there any bandages? Only Gary's cut his hand on the barrer."

3

"I'm not happy with the island SKUs," said Mark Gratton, for the third time since the meeting began. "To some extent yes, you do gain space. But I think psychologically—"

"*Psychologically*," chimed in Dean Harwood, with a ghost of a sneer. Mark pressed on, pretending not to notice.

"—there's a sense of unease, of disorientation. And shoppers lose sight of children, and anxiety levels rise. It isn't like aisle-end display, where there's a natural flow-past."

"It's geometrically more efficient than aisle-end," said Melanie Hayes, tapping her reading-glasses menacingly on her leather-bound folder. "In Esher we've proved that on the computer simulation."

"With the EasiTroll data fed in. How many R2 stores are going to get EasiTroll this year?" Suddenly, mysteriously, the treacherous Dean Harwood seemed to be batting on Mark's side. Some private feud with Hayes, probably. Mark seized the advantage.

"As you know, I've got doubts about EasiTroll too. The whole point of the traditional trolley design is shopper-pace degradation—"

"What?" This was the PR Director, newly arrived from the Hotels division. Mark smiled, to show that he did not despise this ignorance (although he did, rather) and smoothly said: "A bit of unwieldiness, not too much, obviously – slows the shopper down and gives her time to notice the mid-stack premium product."

"Peaches in brandy," said Harwood, sneering again. Mark winced at this direct hit, and unwisely let his foe see it. He flushed.

"So – we all make mistakes. The price was bloody good, and as a promotion—"

"As a promotion, cheapo Romanian bottled fruit that ends up by *fizzing* and getting exposed in the *Daily Mirror*," said Melanie Hayes scathingly, "is not ideal."

"We were talking about insular and peninsular stock-keeping unit trials," said Mark, recovering himself. He caught the Chairman's eye and thought he detected a ghost of an approving nod. So did the ever-vigilant Dean Harwood, who swung once again, effortlessly, to Mark's camp.

"Yes – *peninsular* – we ought to remember that's included in the trial. Perhaps if we compromised—"

Mark smiled, and relaxed a little. Though not much. It did not do to relax too much at EdenFoods inter-regional liaison meetings. The business of supermarketing today, as he often told his smiling admiring wife Lindy, was not just a matter of hiring people to stack up tins and waiting for other people to come and buy them. Customers were fickle and spoilt for choice. You had to pull 'em in, treat 'em clever, light and decorate and entertain and soothe and flatter, all so you could sell, sell, sell, and stay alive yourself. It was more than salesmanship: it was showbiz, it was bloodsport, it was – when you thought about Tesco, always out to wipe you off the map – yes, Lindy, it was war! Lindy would smile, and admire, and massage Mark's shoulders.

He thought of her now, with a pang of needy affection. The meeting wound through its circuitous course: underlying the discussion of display and branding, bakery aroma-reach and chill-area temperatures, there moved other shapes, other themes. Like monsters beneath ice, the half-visible politics of a large mistrustful corporation writhed: alliances and betrayals, rivalries and revenges all seething below the bland businesslike surface. Mark left the meeting at 12.22 to walk back to his own office for a 12.25 briefing concerning loyalty cards. He had compromised on insular shelving, won a tactical victory over trollies, and been badly caught out in the matter of the Romanian peaches in brandy. Fifteen all. Not bad.

Except that the humiliating small moment of the peaches would not leave him. Two years ago, dammit! He sat at the round marble table in his office and talked rapidly and clearly to his three immediate subordinates about the problem of computer-wise and cunningly fraudulent customers fiddling the barcode on their smart loyalty cards. He was well-briefed and succinct and usually a friendly enough manager to deal with; but today Mark cut short their questions and shooed them out faster than they had expected. Suddenly, uncharacteristically, he needed ten minutes to himself before facing a lunch-time meeting with a group of discontented suppliers.

Ten minutes, not much to ask. He stabbed the privacy button on his intercom so that there should be no calls, and moved round to the far side of the desk. Here he would be out of the line of sight of anybody passing the glass panel in his office door. Mark sat down in his heavy leather chair, shrugged off his jacket, and folded his thin arms on the desk. His head sagged forwards onto his forearms and he exhaled a long, self-pitying sigh. Peaches! For God's sake! It had been a bloody good idea, a bloody good price, an experimental way in to the new Eastern Bloc markets. Not his fault the quality control was crooked. Old Manders had never blamed him. Deering didn't, either, he was sure. Why Harwood and Hayes had ganged up in that brief exchange, when they normally avoided one another – why it had taken a snipe against *him* to unite them – why they did it so publicly, felt so safe doing it, in the middle of a discussion about bloody *trollies* . . .

His eyes were shut now, pressed against his arms on the desk, his floppy brown hair trailing forwards onto the neatly aligned leather-framed blotter. Old Manders had liked his senior executives to have gentlemanly-looking desks, and even if they never used a fountain pen from one year's end to the next, each had had a blotter. Mark had kept his when Eden – not a leather-blotter corporation, not gentlemanly at all in its instincts – absorbed the supermarket chain into its diverse empire. Normally its presence comforted him in a tiny, unacknowledged way. It showed that a small part of him was secretly resisting Eden, holding out against new sods like Harwood and syco-phantic bitches like Melanie Hayes. When office life oppressed him, Mark would, without really noticing what he did, stroke the soft leather edges of the blotter, running his finger over the old gold logo of ManderFoods.

Now, however, a stronger discontent than usual seized hold of him and he shuddered, clenching his shoulders, digging his forehead savagely into the flesh of his forearms. Bastards! Always the same – any chance to make him feel small. All of them. Just like Toby, telling Révérende Mère about the *pain-chocolat*. Just like when Piet the gardener called him – that word – and Caroline laughed, stupid baby, and said it again and Mum thought he had taught her the word, as if he bloody knew bloody Afrikaner obscenities – and sent him to his room – just like Purvis at school about the underpants – and what Toby said to the housemaster, trying to be so funny – and *"a grocer, darling? Gosh!"* – from Mum, cocking her head on one side, big-eyed, flirting as usual. But not, never, with him. And Toby's poem that Christmas about Grocer Gratton—

Knotted up, angry, head down on his big desk, Mark Gratton hunched his shoulders against the torrent of confused memory. He did not know why, nor want to, but it happened quite often these days: this sudden and total recall of every humiliation of his life.

Of life until Lindy. Mark raised his head from his shirt-sleeves, which were damp with tears or perspiration, and glanced at the clock. Ten to one. He could ring home and still be down in the marble reception hall on time to meet his lunch guests. Lindy! He picked up the private line and dialled rapidly. It was the only number he ever dialled himself, by hand, without the secretary's intercession. Nor was the number of their home stored in the machine's memory.

She was home. He could picture her straight away, her pale hair springing away from her vivid little face, leaning on the bright-red kitchen worktop against the bright yellow paint, one hip out, in her little high-heeled red boots, perhaps looking at her bright fingernails as she answered. He sighed with relief as Lindy's high enthusiastic Birmingham voice rang down the line.

"Marky! Ooh, lovely! You never ring at lunch-time, lovely to hear you!" And as an afterthought, for she was not a morbid girl but a naturally blithe one – "Is everything all right?"

"Yes," said Mark. The venomous cloud of humiliation receded, like smoke sucked through an unseen extractor-fan. It left the air around him clear. He blinked, and looked around the office. It was a big office, an important man's office, with a solid desk and walnut panelling. The very blotter showed him to be no corporate tool but an individual, with his own views and his own history.

"I just rang to see how your day was going." Against her vivid warm accents, his own voice sounded to him a bloodless and chilly thing, an effete and piping public-school whine.

"S'going lovely, thanks. Aerobics, shopping, library – I'm doing citizens advice this lunch-time, there's a meeting." He smiled, loving the hard g she sounded on the end of *meeting*, loving her upward inflection for its optimism. He was going to speak again, but could not think what to say, only wishing to hear her and bask in her unselfconscious enthusiasms. Before he could think what to say to prompt her, Lindy rushed on.

"Oooh . . . actually it's good you rang. Your sister's been on."

"Which sister?" Mark sounded defensive. "Why?"

"Catherine. She wanted to know about Christmas."

"Oh God. Did you tell her, no?"

"Well, no. Don't be cross, Marky—"

"Never cross, Lindy-Lin. Never ever. But you mean, you said yes? We have to go there for Christmas?"

"Well, I really like Catherine, she's not—"

"Not snooty like the rest of my bloody family?"

"Oooh, don't be chippy. They're all right. Only, it's your Dad. She just worked out he's going to be seventy, on Christmas Eve, OK? Seven Oh, the big one! Three score and thingy! So Catherine thought it would be really, really nice if we were all there, all his kids and that. I think it's a really nice thought!"

Mark smiled, in spite of his dismay. Lindy moved through a world of nice thoughts and kind people and fun ideas. Life to her was a laugh. It was what had first drawn him to her three years ago across a crowded supermarket: her laugh. Shrill, some would say; vulgar, unrefined, unsubtle; but it cut like a school bell through the tangled unhappiness of his first thirty-five years, and let Mark out, at last, to play.

"Oh, all right," he said now. "Who's going to be there? How much of the dreaded tribe?"

"Well, your Dad, obviously. And Catherine and Ger – Gervis,

her old man. And your other sister, the one I've hardly met, cos you didn't want to go to her wedding, you old misery – Caroline, that's it. So I suppose her hubby'll be there. And Dave and Marianne. And she's got both her mothers-in-law, she said. Would that be her mother-in-law from the first time, I thought that was years ago?"

Mark glanced at the clock. Two minutes, and he must go. Trying to keep his voice inconsequential, he said: "Well, it was, but old Cat's ever so faithful. She has the old trout every year. That's all, is it? She didn't say anything about Toby?"

"She's trying to get him. Only he's not in Glasgow any more, apparently. That's why it's good you rang. She thought you might know where he's staying."

"Doesn't Dad know?"

"He's in Zag – Zagreb, she said. Doing a fact-finding thingy. So shall I tell her you don't know where Toby is?"

"No. I do know. I'll call her tonight. Sweetie, I must go—"

"Kiss kiss."

Lindy made loud, chirruping kisses down the wire. Mark returned the endearment more cautiously, put the receiver down and went to lay down the law to his suppliers over an unappetizing, low-fat salad in the boardroom. It was a nasty lunch for a dank December day, and left him hungry and irritable; but the menu was as much company policy as the hard deal he had struck with them. These were suppliers of cheesecakes, microwaveable deep-fried Brie balls, Kievs, cream pastries, and a whole range of "dairy-enhanced" luxury products; so naturally, they got served salad and fresh fruit. Had they been domestic greengrocery suppliers the menu would have been rich, fatty and full of obvious imports. At EdenFoods, it was policy to make suppliers feel insecure. The idea had come from Melanie Hayes. Let the bastards know that they need you more than you need them.

Later that night, properly fed and steadied by Lindy, Mark did ring his elder sister.

"I can tell you where Toby is, because he rang me from the police station."

"Oh God. Not again."

"Yes, again. Nothing much. Some party in Glasgow."

"Why doesn't he ever ring Gervase? He's used to it. He's always being rung by police stations."

"Probably terrified Gervase'll sign him on for some muck-forking with all the other young offenders."

"He's not a young offender. He's forty-three. And he'd be useless with a muck-fork. He's safe enough, the silly sod. But it isn't fair for him to call you at the office. We're more used to all that stuff. You're busy."

"Anyway," said Mark, his tone softened with sudden regard for this sister who appreciated his importance in the world of business affairs, "he did ring you, apparently, but there wasn't anybody in. Anyway, I sorted it out. Twenty pounds' fine for breach of the peace. That was on Tuesday. He said he was through with Scotland anyway, and going to stay with Topsy for a few days."

"Oh God," said Catherine once more. "That's on again, is it?"

"Sort of. I got the impression. You got the number?"

"Think so. I'll ring her. See if she's got him."

Brother and sister exchanged brief farewells. Putting the receiver down, Mark glanced through the doorway to his red-and-yellow kitchen, and saw Lindy, oblivious to the conversation, washing up the dishes. Her broad, comforting rump was encased in tight shiny leopard-print leggings, and a crop-top showed her bare midriff and nipped-in waist. Lindy had grown up in tiny houses, and always kept the central heating on high so that she could dress in December as if it were July. Mark walked up behind her and put his arms around her bare waist, breathing in comfort from her warm, scented flesh. Sixty miles away, Cat put down the telephone in the icy hallway of Knoll Farm and went back to her study, alone.

4

High over the Tottenham Court Road, three frowsty storeys above the Gimmix computer-game shop, Topsy Tanner was sitting on a kitchen chair varnishing her toenails. She was also, intermittently, varnishing quite large areas of her toes since the man lying on the unmade bed kept making her laugh, and when she laughed she shook, and the kitchen chair – the only chair in the flat, apart from bean-bags – wobbled violently. It had one leg shorter than the other three.

"Oh, stoppit, Toby!" she cried at last. "I'm getting red blotches everywhere!"

The man on the bed, remorselessly, continued his story.

"So anyway, Dunkie pulls the big chair away, and the copper sees the hole in the floor and thinks that must be where the stuff was hidden, so he gets down on all fours, right, and peers down and the rat—"

Another carmine blotch appeared on Topsy's left big toe as she erupted with mirth.

"—the rat shoots out, and the guy falls over backwards getting away from it, and Dunkie says, 'Sorry, officer, he must have eaten it all, that's why he's a bit high!'"

The girl recovered herself a little, put down the bottle of varnish and asked interestedly:

"And was there any stuff?"

"Nah," said Toby Gratton. "Dunkie doesn't do any drugs now. It was just a laugh. Only the cop got really serious, and tried to catch the rat so they could look in its stomach and see if it really had eaten a stash—"

Topsy was giggling again now, and Toby sat up, black hair

flopping forward over his high, fine brow, his eyes sparkling as he finished the story of the Glasgow constabulary, the supposedly high rat, and the disruptive Duncan. When they had both finished snorting with mirth, Topsy stretched and wiggled her drying right toes and asked in a marginally more serious tone:

"So what'cha doing here, anyway? I thought you were in Scotland for a bit. Didn't expect you hanging around here."

"Ah. Well, the booking we had in the pub ended."

"Was that the fake Irish pub you told me about?"

"Yep. Mucky Murphy's. Anyway, Dunkie got offered a bit of work for the winter, teaching schoolgirls woodwind up near Fort William, so he could stay with his Ma."

"Teaching *schoolgirls*? Dunkie?" Another blob of nail varnish flew from the brush and lodged stickily between her toes.

"Lolitas of the Lochs. Good luck to them. Then there was a bit of a row about the flat because of a party the guys had, and I ran spang bang out of money anyway, and had to get my supermarket supremo brother to pay my fine. So I came south. To you, my turtledove, my queen of hoofers, my long-leggedy beastie."

Topsy stopped twiddling her toes and fixed him with a cold stare which did not suit her snub and freckled face. She pushed back her tousled platinum-white hair with a defiant little gesture and said: "You're not staying, you know. I can lend you a bit if you want, and you might talk me into it now and again, but you're not moving in."

"Perish the thought! I said I ran out of money, but that was in Scotland. This is England."

"You've got money here?"

"Sort of. When I went up north last year I never gave my royalties agent my address, because he was a bit of an arsehole about some business with his stupid sister. And I know he's got royalties I'm owed, because the songs keep on going. So I'll go round and get the cheque, then I'm going to get a job."

"There's a bit of backstage work going at the theatre," said Topsy. "Non-union, on the quiet, sort of stuff. The show's got an extra month."

"No, a real job."

"A real job?" The girl sounded incredulous. "Ten years I've known you, you've never had a real job."

"I was a gorillagram," said Toby with studied dignity. "For six months."

"Your poor Dad," said Topsy scathingly. "All that education, and him a Lord, and the best you can do is gorillagram."

"Perhaps I should have been a Lord-o-gram. I'd be really good: burst in to the party in ermine and coronet and silk stockings, strip off the robes, introduce myself as Lord Loveaduck, do a number in suspenders—"

Topsy began to laugh again, and flung herself onto the lounging figure on the bed. Together they rolled among the tangled bedding shrieking, "Suspenders!" and "Ooh, Sir Jasper!" and "End of the peer show!" By the time they had finished what Toby called their victory roll, Topsy was late for her call and had to summon up all her dancer's fitness to run, shoes in hand, down through Covent Garden piazza to the stage door of the Imperial Theatre. Toby followed, panting, with her dressing-case.

There was an illuminated cut-out, above the shabby canopy and below the theatre's name, of a row of Topsies high-kicking in black stockings, their toes resting on giant letters spelling out THE PARIS PACK. ("A joyous knockout" – *Evening Standard*). Toby looked at it with pleasure. Looking down, he noticed that he had no shoes on, and so decided to sit on the doorstep of Gimmix Computer-Game Centre until the show ended and Topsy came home.

He did not repine. He pulled a tin whistle, in two pieces, out of his trouser pocket, fitted its sections together and busked. Between 7.00 and 10.30 he made sixteen pounds and twenty-two pence, which they spent on a large sticky pizza and a bottle of Japanese whisky. When they got upstairs with these spoils, there was a message on Topsy's answering machine about Christmas at Knoll Farm.

"She doesn't sound a bit like you, your sister," said Topsy, biting into the pizza.

"Ah, but she is like me," said Toby, wrenching off the top of the whisky bottle. "Deep, deep down." He swigged, straight from the bottle, sitting deep in one of the beanbags. "You'll see.

We're going there for Christmas, me and you." Topsy's mouth was too full of pizza to contradict him.

In the serene, humming quiet of an airline cabin high over the Alps, Lord Martindown of Ashe, a Labour peer, turned to his friend Lord Gratton of Kilmore as they put aside their papers to address their plastic dishes of dinner.

"Not a bad trip. I'm quite impressed with some of these companies that are moving into the new countries. You've got a boy with Eden, haven't you?"

"Yes. Mark. He's in the supermarkets now, but who knows."

"Your other boy in business, is he? Haven't seen him since he was a nipper when you were in Venice."

"Hmm," said Lord Gratton, taking a sudden close interest in the tinfoil cover of his *sole bonne femme*. "No, not exactly. He's a pop songwriter by trade, and he works around a lot, here and there, in the entertainment business." The foil ripped as he pulled it off, spilling sauce on to the tray. A sudden compulsion to honesty made him add: "Raffish, you might say."

"Well," said Lord Martindown, pulling the cover off his own sole in one piece with rather more grace. "We've all got one in the family, eh? My daughter's with Channel 4."

"Not bad, this fish," said his noble companion, closing the subject with natural diplomatic authority.

It was late, past eleven o'clock, when the door creaked open. Gervase looked up from his desk and smiled, a little hesitantly, at his wife. Cat crossed the faded carpet and put her hand on his shoulder with a passionless, threadbare affection. "Christmas," she said. "I worked it out. We could end up with thirteen at table, if it isn't fifteen. Does that matter?"

Gervase screwed up his face and began to count on his fingers.

"Mama, your father, Noreen – two of us, Mark and Lindy, Caroline and Alan, Toby obviously—"

"I've counted Toby as maybe two. He used to bring Topsy, didn't he? Last time round. And Mark says he's back on her phone number now, so . . ."

Gervase looked up at her, a grin suddenly transforming his

serious, ascetic's face into something almost puckish, lively in its mischief.

"I always liked Topsy."

"It's the stage-door Johnny in your blood coming out. Your father probably used to hang around theatres in the 'thirties with bunches of flowers, twirling his moustachios and waiting to have his way with Topsies."

Gervase laughed. "He wouldn't have to wait long." Cat sat on the edge of his desk, suddenly more relaxed. She smiled back at him.

"Do you remember the first time Toby brought Topsy down for the weekend?"

"She went out for a walk, and got so excited at the sight of blackberries actually growing, free on bushes, that she decided to bring some home for a surprise," said Gervase. "Only, she hadn't got a basket so—"

"She wriggled out of her bra, pulled it up through her polo-neck and brought them back in that. Said two C-cups should be enough for a pie." Cat giggled. "Then there was the business with the spiders in the bathroom."

"God, yes. Rushing round the house screaming, in a teeny towel like something in a Donald McGill postcard. Mother took days to get over it."

"She was good fun. I wish, in a way—"

"You think Toby should have married her?"

"Oh, I don't know. I mean, neither of them was remotely faithful, as far as I could tell from the conversation."

"Generally in front of my mother and poor Noreen."

"Don't remind me. But there was," Cat continued thoughtfully, "something about those two. You could see Mark was jealous of the way they were together. He never got anywhere with girls before he met Lindy. And Tobe's gone back to stay with her now Glasgow's folded up on him. They've obviously stayed friends. It might be a goer."

But Gervase seemed to have tired of discussing his brothers-in-law and their love lives, and looked meaningly down at the pile of letters on his desk. None were personal, except for a few in illiterate handwriting and oddly-coloured inks: the rest were a scatter of charity letterheads and logos. The Soil Association,

Countryside Commission, Country Landowners' Association, National Council for the Care and Resettlement of Offenders, Northamptonshire Wildlife Trust, Projects In Probation, Rare Breeds Society, Third World First. Gervase gave unstintingly of his time and energy to a dozen good causes, even apart from the boys on the farm. There was not one of these that Catherine could fault, not one pointless or undeserving labour among them. Gervase was, undoubtedly, a very good man.

She sighed, took the hint and got off the desk to begin counting on her fingers again in a businesslike way. She too was furthering a good cause, that of a united family Christmas.

"So Dad, Artemis, Noreen, Mark and Lindy, Caroline and Alan, you and me, Toby and perhaps Topsy. The kids. Then Duane makes it fourteen, or thirteen, but I've assumed the American should be here by then?"

"The WWOOFer, yes. Martin Szowalski," said Gervase, glancing down at the letters in front of him. "Coming next Friday."

"Woofer," said Cat. "That's a terrible word!"

"Working Weekends On Organic Farms," said Gervase automatically.

"I know." She was irritated now. How dare he tell her something she already knew! In that teacherly voice too, as if she were Duane. Sometimes she wondered if he remembered the difference between her and the boys. "It's just that the ones who come to us are always here for much longer than weekends, and it might be more dignified to call them just volunteers."

"As you wish." He turned back to his papers. Cat went towards the door, then turned and said: "I take it Gary *is* going to his mother for Christmas?"

"Apparently. I wish Duane would go home to his family, but he says he'd rather spend Christmas on the streets." He hesitated a moment, looking at her with a kind of appeal in his eyes, although she had already begun to turn away. "Do you mind him being here?" he said to her back. "Your Dad's birthday party and everything?"

"No," said Cat wearily. "I like my family much better when it's diluted a bit. He can have a fling with Topsy. Make a man of him."

On that small unregarded victory she withdrew, and left Gervase to his midnight oil. There was, at least, enough hot water left for a long – if spidery – bath.

"So we could be thirteen at table," said Lady Artemis Hartley, in her high disapproving voice. "You're not superstitious, then, Catherine dear?"

"'Course she's not," said Catherine's father with decision. He raised his glass to his daughter. "She grew up in so many different countries that if she took on one lot of superstitions she'd have to take on the lot. She'd be warding off the evil eye like a Venetian, keeping Hebrew festivals, believing in the *Krampus*—"

"Burying bits of meat in the garden tied up with elephant grass to cure warts," said Mark, "stamping on pomegranate seeds to abort babies—"

"That is disgusting," said Cat, reaching up to tuck a stray end of tinsel under an ivy branch on a beam. "I don't remember that one, from anywhere."

"Jo'burg," said Mark. "Mariona taught it me, in the servants' quarters. I got a lot of home voodoo lessons you never knew about. Actually, Caro—" he looked across at his younger sister – "I had a damn good go at doing it to you. I took a pomegranate seed up to my bedroom and danced round it chanting, then I stamped on you so you wouldn't be born. I didn't want a new baby."

Caroline, heavily pregnant and not in the best of tempers, glared at her brother for a moment before accepting the joke without much grace.

"It's still disgusting. Horrible little boy, you must have been."

"I was," said Mark complacently. He had arrived still rattled from the Eden directorate Christmas party the night before. Santa hats and foam reindeer horns had been handed out at the door, and he had been given horns only to find that everybody else from the Executive Two floor was wearing a Santa hat. These things mattered. Then the drive had been slow and frustrating, and ever since he and Lindy had arrived at lunch-time he had been refilling his glass from Cat's traditional welcoming saucepan of mulled wine. The glass was now horribly sticky from the sugar and his last refill was growing cold, but he sucked noisily at it and outfaced his beautiful younger sister with a stare to match her own.

Lady Artemis, curled in the better of the two fireside chairs, looked across at Caroline with condescending sympathy. Of all her son's in-laws, this beautiful cool creature was most to her taste. Boorish Mark, fey disruptive Toby, and their unspeakably common womenfolk were, in Artemis' view, not at all desirable connexions. She had originally had great hopes of Robert Gratton – a peer, albeit a mere life peer unlike her late father – and a diplomat, very nearly an ambassador. How suitable, how amusing it would have been if he as a widower, she as a widow, could have entertained a flirtation. It would have been appropriate and graceful, considering that her son rescued his daughter from the unfortunate status of deserted and penniless mother.

Yet not only, reflected the lady sourly, was the man inclined to left-wing views, but he appeared not to have the slightest gift for civilized dalliance either. So Artemis had never been such a fool as to show her hand. Now she sat a good distance from him at the Easter and Christmas gatherings around Gervase's table, suppressed her kittenish side and cultivated instead a refined aloofness. Now, gently to underline the crassness of *his* son's remark, she merely said in a cool sweet tone:

"Well, never mind the thirteen. We shall throw salt over our shoulders, as my old nanny taught me."

"It won't be thirteen, anyway," said Robert, who had been counting on his fingers. "Not if Toby brings his girlfriend and Alan gets back on time."

Artemis ignored him, to turn on the other old woman present. "Noreen, dear, you look cold. Have you had some of Catherine's hot wine?"

Mrs Noreen Lorrimer, looking older than her seventy years,

darted a terrified look at the imperious little figure at the fireside. Where Lady Artemis' hair was shining silver, hers was a dead, dirty, thinning grey; where the other woman had shrunk to a slender, aristocratic boniness, Noreen had merely sagged from middle-aged podge into elderly flab. Neither in body nor in mind could she compete; she knew that in every possible sense, when placed next to Artemis she lacked class. There was not even a moral high ground to which she could retreat. Her son, after all, had callously abandoned poor little Cathy with two babies. Lady Artemis' son was the white knight who had rescued them all three and brought them to this solid farmhouse and a life of landed security.

No, Noreen had no defence whatever against the cruel little creature in Chanel. It was a matter of unending wonder to her, indeed, that Cathy still included her in these family gatherings and wrote all year as well. Taking them in, after all, had been her plain duty when bad, bad Timothy ran off. And it had been, in addition, a pleasure. To have those children close for those precious years – her eyes filled with tears, now, when she thought of their first Christmases.

"I shouldn't really," she quavered now, but Artemis waved her objections aside.

"Mark, dear, do fill a glass for Catherine's – ah—"

This was another game that she played. She could not say "Catherine's mother-in-law", for was that not her own, Artemis', rightful title now? She could have said "the twins' grandmother" – indeed, could have asked Dave to get the drink, and said "your grandmother". Or she could just have said, to any of them, "Get Noreen a drink". Instead, she chose the small cruel barb of calling the humbler woman "Catherine's – ah." and finishing the sentence with a tinkling, silly-me laugh.

Noreen understood all this, and flushed, and accepted the sticky glass which Mark put in her hand as she had, all her life, accepted bitter cupfuls of humiliation.

But then Dave and Marianne, so long ago christened Daybreak and Mooncloud by her unspeakable betraying son, came over to Noreen as if drawn by her unspoken distress. They were fond of their grandmother: how could they not be, when from birth to the age of six they had lived in her minute house, crammed in the tiny boxroom in home-made bunks, with their mother in the only proper bedroom and Noreen on a sofa bed in the front room? The four of them had lived thus in the tiny gardenless house in Hounslow, hugger-mugger and defiantly, unjustifiably happy as the airport traffic thundered past outside and the aircraft screamed overhead taking luckier people to luckier places.

Nanna Noreen meant home to them, giggles and baking and first days at nursery and school, and Hallowe'en games involving apple peelings and Co-op marshmallows on strings and grabbing a fivepenny piece out of a mound of flour with your teeth. Of course Gervase and Knoll Farm and the animals and the green fields were an adventure, the springboard for growing independence; but the imprint of their first home was strong in both their happy, uncomplicated young hearts. The two of them bounced across to Nanna Noreen now, lapping her in welcome warmth. They had, in fact, very little to talk to her about these days; their determined careers had not much in common with her modest retired life of church and housework. But it did not matter: the warmth transmitted itself through the blandest of conversations.

"So, Nanna, give us the dirt," began Dave. "What's going on? Which evening class is it this year?"

"Upholstery," said Noreen, her smile reviving. "Oh, my, you are big! Aren't you ever going to stop growing?"

"I have stopped growing," said Dave. "Years ago. It's you, you're shrinking. But you did upholstery last year! Time you moved on!"

"Why should she?" said Marianne, who was almost as tall and broad-shouldered and simple-hearted as her brother. "You can't keep moving on all the time, you know. Some people have staying power. Perseverance. They master things." She smiled at Noreen, and gave her arm a little shake. "Don't get pushed around by these fly-by-night types, Nan. Their unhealthy sense of competition at family occasions is just another manifestation of what we psychiatric nurses call Christmas Rage. All rooted in personal inadequacy."

She looked at Dave in comic hostility, but the gibe was so plainly aimed at Lady Artemis that the latter flushed slightly, and poked a log at the edge of the big fire with a brown alligator-patterned toe. Cat was in the kitchen, hauling a shepherd's pie out of the oven and gossiping with Lindy, and Mark was too slurred to be of any social assistance. Robert Gratton, still the diplomat, weighed in with weary skill.

"Tell you something, that supper smells pretty damn good. Are we waiting for Toby and Topsy?"

"Certainly not," said Cat, reappearing. "We'll wait five minutes while Gervase and the boys check the ewes, then we'll start. Toby said he might stop off at a friend's."

"I don't get it," said Lindy, bouncing through the door behind her, a tea cloth thrown over her shoulder and her face flushed, "I thought lambs came in spring."

"They do, normally," said Cat. "But Dorsets can lamb at any time of year, and it suits Gervase to do his lambing now. That way there's plenty of work for the boys through the winter, and he's clear of it for the spring ploughing. Which he needs to be because that takes ages using horses; and we get a good price for the lamb because it's early."

Lindy listened without much understanding to this agricultural explanation. "It's just like *The Archers*, innit?" she said. "Will there be baby lambs tonight?"

"Could be. Martin reckoned one of the ewes was at it, when he went out at five o'clock."

"Brilliant," said Lindy. "I like lambs. You could have a cuddle of one for practice, eh, Caroline?"

Caroline gave a pale grimace. "I shouldn't, should I Cat?"

"Certainly not. There's a zoonosis, a disease you can catch off the animals. Enzootic abortion. Even if you don't know it's in the flock, pregnant women shouldn't go near lambing."

"Really?" Lady Artemis gave a silly, tinkling laugh. "Just as well you never had that trouble once you became a farmer's wife, Catherine dear." She had never quite forgiven Catherine for bearing healthy twins to some ghastly runaway hippy, then producing nothing at all with the impeccable Hartley genes.

"Yes, maybe," said Cat, determined not to rise to this, still less betray her own and Gervase's long-standing sorrow at that very fact. "But everyone wants to cuddle lambs, and it's always terribly embarrassing when visitors come at lambing time. You have to ask every woman of remotely likely age whether there's any risk she might be pregnant."

"Must be tricky," said Robert, intrigued. "That would challenge even a consummate diplomatic wife like your mother. Imagine asking one's middle-aged ambassadress. Or the Saudi consul-general's teenage daughter."

"You never ask me," said Marianne, demurely, twirling the ice in the gin-and-tonic she had somehow acquired in the face of the prevailing mulled wine policy.

"I *trust* you would know better, after growing up on a farm," said her mother tartly. "And it makes a useful test, every Christmas. All I have to do is say 'Marianne darling, just help Gervase in the lambing-shed' and if you won't, I'd know you're in the club. A lot of mothers would be grateful for a discreet little test like that."

Lindy, who was now perched on Mark's knee, giggled suddenly. "So if there's any chance at all . . . what do you think, Marky? Let's count back—" Mark shifted uneasily. Joyously impervious to his hinting, Lindy gushed on. "Wun't it be lovely, though? We've been trying for ever so long . . . well, six months."

"Terrific," said Dave politely. Lady Artemis made a moue of distaste for the whole subject, and rose gracefully from her fireside chair.

"Well, if dinner really is imminent, I will just withdraw for a moment or two—"

In the hall, she met Gervase, pulling off a pair of yellow rubber gloves on his way to the utility room sink.

"All well, Mother?" he asked. "Cat can dish up in a minute. Duane and Martin won't be long."

"Darling," said his mother, "are we eating with the farm boys?"

Gervase looked at her with weary resignation. Every year they had this conversation, at this time, in this hallway.

"Mother, don't be feudal. Martin is a college student taking a year out before he does a PhD in sustainable farm economics, and Duane—"

"Is Duane the one who looks mental?"

"Duane," said her son firmly, "has nowhere else to go. It's Christmas."

*   *   *

The *placement* was as tricky as any that their parents could have faced at a diplomatic dinner. With a brown envelope plucked from Gervase's desk and a stub of pencil, Cat frowned over the problem in the moments before she called them all through. It would have been natural to sit Lady Artemis Hartley next to Lord Gratton of Kilmore – clumping up the elderly nobs at one end of the table – but given their tendency to political animosity and unresolved sexual tension, Cat decided against it. Noreen must at all costs be protected from Artemis; so she was flanked by Dave, who loved her, and Robert Gratton, who had good manners. Opposite she put Martin Szowalski, the woofer, and Marianne; a distinct attraction had made itself obvious when the two first met earlier on Christmas Eve, and Cat had come to like the big young American and feel that such an attraction, however fleeting, was no bad thing for her daughter. Marianne's last boyfriend had been a sour young houseman with the appearance of an underfed and cynical rat.

Caroline, the other family member whose manners were beyond reproach, could entertain Lady Artemis at the far end of the table, with Mark on her other side. If Toby turned up he and Topsy could fit in next to Cat, near the kitchen door. Duane could sit next to Gervase, who had his mother on his other hand, and Lindy could talk at him. She never noticed whether anybody was listening or understanding. And *really* – Cat threw down her pencil in sudden exasperation – really, that was the best she could do. If Toby failed to turn up in time to eat, she herself would be a little isolated at the far end of the table, but nothing could be done about that. At this stage of the festivities she might rather enjoy a silent meal. Tomorrow, the Christmas Dinner preceded by the Christmas Morning Walk, would be time enough for bonhomous sociability. Tonight, by family tradition, a simple meal was eaten and those who were not inclined for Midnight Mass could go to bed early.

Beds. She ran through it in her mind again. The boys and Dave would sleep in the farm bunkhouse, Marianne and Noreen in Dave's old room, Robert in Marianne's, Mark and Lindy on the folding sofa in her study, Artemis down the lane with her old sparring partner the Rector. Caroline and Alan – if, as promised, he turned up later that night – would sleep in the best guest room. "Not because of Alan," she guiltily told Lindy as they drained the vegetables. "I only put them there because she's so pregnant. Normally nothing would please me more than to make bloody Alan sleep on the fold-up."

Toby and Topsy, she had resolved, could damn well doss in sleeping bags on the downstairs sofas. It would give her a certain savage sisterly satisfaction to rout them out in the morning, maybe by very loud Hoovering. Looking along the table now, enjoying the brief isolation imposed by their empty chairs on either side of her, Cat stifled a yawn and hoped that most of the party would disperse early to bed so that she could sit quietly through the Christmas midnight with her own twin children, catching up on their lives while Gervase tended the labouring sheep.

She was not left alone at her end of the table for long. Toby and Topsy arrived at nine o'clock, just as the shepherd's pie was about to be breached. They were heralded by a series of crashes, giggles and delighted squeals from the direction of the farmyard. Gervase looked up sharply at the first noises, frowned at the chorus of baas and bleats, and leapt to his feet at the unmistakable sound of a metal gate crashing to the ground and toppling a series of hurdles with it. Martin hesitated, then grinned apologetically at Marianne and followed him out. She glanced around, then muttered, "I'll give them a hand, my boots are in the hall." Dave, on a warning glance from his mother, stayed next to Noreen.

"Something escaped?" said Robert. "A farmer's work is never done, eh?"

"D'ju think I ougter go?" said Duane blankly. "Only, Mr Hartley says I aren't to go in the yard in indoor clothes."

"No, you stay. Help with the plates." Cat went through to the kitchen for the vegetables, and moved to the window to listen. From the yard came high girlish laughter, too shrill to be Marianne's, and the sound of Gervase quietly remonstrating with somebody. Metal hurdles clashed and scraped as they were reassembled to form the outdoor pen for the ewes which had not lambed. The dish of green beans in her hands grew cooler as Cat listened; at last, Toby's unmistakable drawl was heard, saying: ". . . wanted to see some Christmas animals, that's all. See if they could talk."

Gervase's voice, lower and more level, seemed to be enjoining him to come indoors. Topsy's high voice rang out again, "Woooh!" Mark came through and stood beside Cat, a lopsided smile on his face but looking less drunk – or anyway, less sullen – than he had before dinner.

"Sounds as if my big brother made it," he said. "And the amazing chorus girl."

"It's funny, isn't it," said Cat thoughtfully, handing him the dish of beans. "Fifty years out of date. These days chorus dancers are serious, superfit, ambitious, multiskilled professionals. Could turn into Sarah Brightman any day. But Toby somehow manages to find the last of the old-time high-kicking chorus girls, just when you thought they were extinct."

Mark was in no mood for cultural nostalgia. "Bloody bad manners. What are they doing coming in through the farmyard anyway?" He stumped off with the vegetables, just in time to create a distraction and abort another of Artemis' attempts to torpedo Noreen's confidence with a pointed lecture on the failure of overindulgent modern mothers to instil responsibility in their sons. "I always took great care that Gervase understood the concept of duty."

Mark's grumpy question was answered – not that he wanted an answer – minutes later when Toby came into the room flushed and grinning, pushing Topsy before him with his hands on her wriggling waist. She was wearing a very short skirt but no stockings or shoes ("Covered in sheep-shit, she fell over," said Dave under his breath to his grandmother) and giggling.

"We knew there'd be lambs," said Toby. "Wanted to salute New Life. Christmas. Congratulate a sheep, cuddle a slimy wee lamb. Very into New Life, are me and Topsy. Guess what, Dad? The long grandchild famine has become a feast. It's not just Caroline who's set to pop any day."

All eyes turned, drawn irresistibly to the girl's small waist and flat belly in the red stretch skirt, framed absurdly small between Toby's hands. He gave her midriff a shake, "Yes indeedy. A small but pukka Gratton lies within." He widened his eyes and wagged his head comically at his brother. "Bet you never thought I'd beat you to it, Grocer!"

Mark flushed to the roots of his sandy hair. "How," he asked coldly in the silence that followed this announcement, "do you know it's yours?"

Before anybody could answer, Lindy gave a piercing squeal of horror. "You never touched the lambs, did you? You'll get antibiotic abortion!"

"Enzootic," said Cat automatically.

"Boys, really," expostulated Robert.

At the end of the table Duane choked on an undercooked piece of carrot and had to be thumped, repeatedly, on the back.

6

Cat's hope of a quiet evening's talk with her son and daughter was dashed when Dave, Marianne and Martin announced that they were going for a "starwalk". The expression, however, made her smile. Dave had invented Christmas starwalks when he was seven, during his first winter at Knoll Farm. It had been a cold clear Christmas night like this one, and although church at Midmarsham was never at midnight, Dave had begged his mother to let him stay up, just to be outdoors under a skyful of pinpoint stars as midnight struck.

"Then if the animals speak I'll hear them, and if Father Christmas flies over, I'll see him." After that, starwalks had taken place for years, even on wet and cloudy Christmas Eves, with the result that a heavy-eyed mother had had to stay up until two o'clock to make sure the children were fast enough asleep not to see who filled their stockings.

The custom had lapsed, but at the end of a difficult dinner, with Toby and Topsy manic, Mark sulky, Lindy chattering nervously and Caroline picking at her food and jumping at every car engine noise from the lane, Dave's suggestion: "Starwalk? Marianne? Martin?" rang so blithe and natural over the washing-up that it lightened the whole atmosphere. The three young people went outside, with much laughing and stamping and shivering and coming back in for scarves. Duane retired with obvious thankfulness to the bunkhouse by the farmyard, and Mark and Lindy with equal relief to their attic. Toby and Topsy appropriated the chairs on either side of the dying log fire and promptly fell asleep, their mouths open, legs sprawled. With weary chivalry Robert offered to walk Lady Artemis down to the rectory, thus inadvertently rekindling certain old hopes. She had drunk quite a lot of wine, and he *was*, though left-wing, a very handsome man still. Noreen had crept up to bed clutching a hot-water bottle as soon as her drying-up duties were fulfilled. So Cat and Caroline were left alone together, both their heads swimming a little with wine and emotion, to drink a last cup of tea at the kitchen table while Gervase checked the sheep.

Cat would have begun discussing Toby's bombshell, or what on earth could be wrong with Mark to make him so chippy, but Caroline could focus only on her own baby and her own torment.

"He promised he'd be here tonight," she began immediately they were alone. "The bastard, he promised. It's Christmas Eve, there's no meeting in the world that happens on Christmas Eve. He's with that bloody woman, I know he is."

"He might still come," said Cat. "It's only eleven." She was tired, and did not want to discuss Alan any more, being far more intrigued with her brother's remarkable new status as a father-to-be. But her sister's distressful, beautiful face reproached her. Caroline's manner had subtly changed over the weeks since the night when she had first confided Alan's infidelity. She had always been too serene, too well-bred to talk of private matters in a frank, female way; but now the enthusiasm of the convert gripped her and she sought the relief of confidential chat at all hours, unconscious of her sister's busyness. The smooth veneer of her self-possession once broken, she had rung Cat incessantly, saying "it's such a relief to talk!" repeating her distress again and again, talking in circles, deciding nothing, just emanating pain and affront. Cat had listened, sympathized, and offered the most banal of reassurances; something dim but powerful prevented her from expressing to her sister anything other than platitudes. Now, reluctantly, she repeated those reassurances.

"You know he doesn't like these family gatherings. Lots of men don't when they marry into big noisy families. He's probably just holding off so he can sneak in late, get up late, have lunch and whisk you home. It's probably no more sinister than that. Do you think Dad's looking well?"

Caroline frowned, as if trying to remember who this "Dad" was who had nothing to do with her own trouble. Then distractedly she said: "Yes . . . never better . . . wonderful, really, for his age. Cat, the thing is, I've been thinking a lot, about me and the baby. It might be better for us just to admit it, mightn't it? Strike out on our own? Alan doesn't seem to care about it at all, and he was really horrible the other night when I asked him again if he was seeing Yasmin. He said I was hysterical and frigid and who could blame him if he *was* seeing her? Cat, he doesn't love me! I don't know if he ever did!"

"Maybe you're right," said Catherine heavily. "But it's too late now, isn't it?"

"Why? Why is it too late? I can see it's not going to work, it never was, he's a bastard – I'll cut my losses." She was rattling on now, on the verge of losing control, hugging herself, her teeth chattering a little despite the heat from the coal stove in the corner.

"Caroline," said Cat. "It *is* too late. The reason it is too late is sticking out from your front. You have no idea, *no idea whatsoever*, what it is like bringing up babies without their father."

"You did! Dave and Marianne are great, look at them tonight, anybody would be proud of them! And Gervase came along, and look how well you've all got on. It could be like that for me and the baby, too," said Caroline hopefully. "God knows I don't envisage any other man, right now, but people do. Meet new people. We could have another chance." She looked exalted for a moment, a woman with a high and noble destiny, a painting of Joan of Arc.

"Cat, I've thought and thought, and it's the best thing for all three of us, however hard it is. I'm going to tell him, tonight. Or" – she concluded rather lamely – "whenever he arrives."

Cat looked at her sister with irritation. Her head was beginning to ache on the left side, where her migraines always started. She felt the dim, strong inhibition within her crumble and began speaking in a low rapid voice, turning her mug of tea in her hands with nervous clicking precision on the scrubbed table-top.

"You think we were all right on our own? You really think Dave and Marianne didn't need their Dad? You think they didn't look around for their Dad, wonder about him every single bloody day? If it hadn't been for Noreen we'd have gone under."

Caroline frowned. "Yes, but you wouldn't let Mum and Dad

help you, so staying with Noreen was all you could do – I'm not saying it'll be anywhere near as hard for me, I mean financially, Alan would have to look after us—"

"It wasn't just the roof over our heads! Don't bring everything back to money!" burst out Cat. "I stayed because Noreen is Tim's *mother*. She was ashamed of what he did, but she's his mother. The twins had a right to that half of their genes. To have a life with someone who was part of their father. Noreen used to tell them about when Tim was a little boy, and she'd tell me when they did things or made faces like he used to do. When Dave built that circuit board, she told us about Tim's old crystal set. When Marianne was scared of the dark, she had stories about how her father had a nightlight till he was eleven."

Cat paused, and took a swig of tea. Her hands were shaking now. "And neither of us ever told them he was a bastard who left them. I used to fudge over why he was in America. I showed them pictures. I told them when they made the sort of jokes he liked and I didn't. We made a sort of legend of him. What I'm saying to you is that I didn't want bloody Tim back. Not for myself, not for a minute, after the first shock. But for their sake I had to pretend to think well of him and act like a grieving widow. It was hard work."

She drew a long shuddering breath and glared at her sister. "Children need a father. Preferably their real father. Your baby's got one, so hang on to him. Fuck what you need or want! Fuck all that feminist crap! That baby ought to have a chance to know its father, even if he is a bastard. Who knows? He might stop being one."

Catherine rarely made such long speeches, and generally spared her sister the strong language which came naturally after a decade of eating supper with young offenders. Caroline pouted, the wine still fogging her brain, her own trouble puffing and spreading to fill every corner of her awareness. She began again:

"But with Alan it's more of a betrayal . . . I mean, you and Tim, you were virtually students – I know I never met him, but I saw the wedding picture – you were living in a squat, there was all that impermanent seventies thing . . . you must have sort of expected—"

She checked herself as she glimpsed the expression on her sister's face.

Cat snapped down her empty mug and looked steadily across the table.

"You art restorers do learn to look at the outsides of things first, don't you?" she said slowly. "What you mean is that Tim was a student revolutionary and an anarchist and had hair down to his waist. Whereas Alan is a rich smoothie with a Saab and a big house in Kensington. You think that having pink silk knicker-blinds makes it different. It's *not* different. One louse is much like another. Tim should have behaved like a decent father and a decent human being, and so should Alan. I had a right to expect my children's father to stay around, and a duty to put up with him if he did. So do you."

She picked up her cup again and drained it. "The real difference is that Alan is still in earshot, and you have a chance to persuade him that he's got to stay with his baby and treat you halfway reasonably until it's grown up. I didn't have that chance. Tim left me a letter, in the night, and no address."

"Well, that's what I mean. They're not the same. Alan's much more guilty, 'cos he's older."

"Nah. Long-haired left-wing student louse, 1974; right-wing louse in a Kenzo suit, 1997. Same model, different trim. We were both had. The difference is, you can still fight."

"I didn't mean –" began Caroline placatingly.

"Yes you did. You've always thought I was some stupid girl who married an unsuitable sort of man and got what was coming to me, and that you were a wise virgin who made a good catch. That's what Mum would have thought. But there isn't any difference, you know. We were both stupid cows with no judgement. But you can fight. You can change things. You don't have to be a single mother."

"Well, at any rate," said Caroline, "Gervase came along, for you."

"Yes?" said Cat. "And?"

"Well, that was lucky."

"It doesn't ever occur to you that *he* was bloody lucky?" Cat stood up, and took the two mugs to the sink. "No, I suppose not."

"Well, the twins were lucky. To get a new father, and such a nice one."

"Not theirs, though. No genetic link, no tug of understanding, none of that recognition, that ability to deal with each other. Even Dad and Mark are closer than Dave and Gervase can ever be. Dad even understands Toby, though he'd rather not admit it. It's biology."

"I never knew you felt that strongly about it," said Caroline sulkily.

"Well, I do," said her sister shortly, rinsing the mugs under a jet so powerful that water spurted up and hit her in the eye. "And don't say what about adoption, what about AID babies, donor embryos, all that. I know. Lots of people make the best of it and make good families. But it isn't the same. Not the same magic." She put the mugs down to drain, and turned to dry her hands and face on the kitchen roller towel.

"Why," said Caroline, shaken out of self-absorption by her sister's strange vehemence on this unexpected subject. "Why do you feel like that?"

"Because Gervase does," said Cat, her back still turned to the table and her voice muffled, though whether by emotion or the roller towel it was hard to tell. "Because he couldn't have babies. Zero sperm count. Don't you ever tell a soul, or I'll kill you. We found out years ago. Gervase came back from the test and walked for miles, on his own with the sheepdog. Then came back and told me he didn't want donor stuff out of a test-tube. He said he'd rather be honest about it, and not even adopt. He said he'd get his stake in the next generation by using the farm and the land and the horses to help kids whose real fathers were no bloody good."

"And you agreed?" Caroline was startled out of her self-absorption. Cat tossed her head and looked steadily at her sister.

"I said yes, fine. I'd got two children already. It's not the kind of thing you argue about. We've never discussed it since. We have sheep and young offenders instead of children. Dave and Marianne have been great fun for him, but they never called him Dad. End of story, end of line for distinguished Northamptonshire landed gentry family. We let Artemis assume it's my fault for having fucked-up fallopian tubes or something. That sounds like Alan's car. Make him some tea. I'm going to bed."

When Alan Halliday came into the kitchen, shivering from the cold and anticipating a string of reproofs from his wife, he found Caroline sitting at the table, looking white and slightly shocked. But she smiled tentatively up at him. "Bad journey, darling?" she said. "Would you like some tea before bed? Nearly Christmas Day!" Bemused, he bent and cautiously, with an indefinable qualm of distaste, kissed the top of her golden head.

7

Toby woke in the armchair, cold and stiff, and saw by the grandfather clock in the firelight that Christmas midnight had passed. The house was silent but the fire had been made up again to warm the big room with its faded carpet and long beams where ivy and tinsel were wound together between years-old nails. Someone – Cat, presumably – had left two sleeping-bags and pillows on the sofa. He glanced across at Topsy. Her floss of yellow hair stood comically on end in tufts and fans of blonde exuberance as she sprawled in the other chair as relaxed as a cat.

His own body felt dense and stiff and middle-aged. He had been waking in the night quite often these past months with a sense of ageing upon him. Tentatively, he moved a leg. It creaked, he could swear it. Not yet forty-five, he was creaking. Would he ever again swarm over a backyard wall in a nightclub raid? Or drink all night, sleep on a hot beach and wake up ready to run into the sea? This ageing thing might not matter to Mark, him with his business suit and his executive villa, but he, Toby, had suited youth. He had made good use of it and enjoyed every minute. At least, since school was over and his parents ceased pestering him to be otherwise than he was.

But what he was now . . . that was not so easy to deny or discard. He wriggled in the chair, aware in the midnight chill of stale neglected muscles and the slow treacherous growth, below his belt, of a paunch.

A log fell sideways in the iron fire-basket with a small cracking noise, flaring a brighter light across the room. Topsy yawned, showing a pink mouth and sharp little white teeth like a kitten's. He roused himself from his chair and went over to her. "Bedtime," he said, and picked up her light firm dancer's body in his arms to deposit her on the bigger of the two sofas. She clung sleepily to his neck for a moment, then flopped like a rag doll, her arm dangling over the side. He picked it up, put it carefully on her chest, eased a pillow under her head and threw the better of the two sleeping-bags over her. A satisfied "mmmph!" rewarded him, as she drifted down into deeper sleep again.

He knelt for a moment, looking down at her. The only symptom of Topsy's pregnancy, in the weeks since she had revealed it gigglingly to him in a pizza bar after the show, had been this increasing sleepiness. Always a girl who fell asleep easily, she now slept even later than usual in the mornings, and had taken to dozing off backstage in a costume-hamper after her first routine, with a Post-It note on her chest saying "WAKE FOR ACT II". Sometimes, she told him with shrieks of laughter, she woke up covered in other Post-It notes written by the rest of the chorus saying "PRIME PORK", "THIS WEEK'S SPECIAL OFFER", and "THIS SIDE UP".

She also fell asleep in his arms straight after they made love. Lovemaking had been strange lately: gentler and more – more *reverent*, thought Toby, surprising himself, ever since he had known about the baby ("Definitely yours, made in Glasgow, remember – when I came up during the electricians' strike at the Imperial, and I left my sponge bag on the train"). She was no longer just another old mate, a bit of happy familiar fun, one of a dozen male and female companions of his revels in the loose world of second-string rock musicals and near-miss showbiz. Toby had been surprised by the strength of his own reaction to her news, and by its nature: no resentment, no panic, not even shock. She had told him across the glutinous pizza in the neon glare of that late-night supper, and he had taken her hand and impulsively kissed it.

"So you want it?" she had said, a little breathlessly.

"Don't you?"

"Yes, yes – I was going to say, I'm having it, whatever the girls say – sure thing." She pouted. "But I wouldn't chase you with the CSA or maintenance and stuff. Def'nitely not. Because it was my fault leaving the spongebag on the train." He had smiled then, and smiled now in the firelight, at her sturdy sense of justice.

"It's yours and mine," he said, still holding her hand. "What shall we call it?"

"I think of it as Amber. Dunno why. It's my favourite stone."

"Could be a boy. Ambrose?"

"Do me a favour!"

They had talked endlessly about it since, always in the same bantering tone, never raising such practical issues as whether they would live together, or where. Certainly not in Topsy's terrible bedsitting room over the Tottenham Court Road with the tarts down one flight of stairs and the computer games below. Nor did they discuss what any of them would live on. Toby had found £500 owed to him at his agent's, and was writing three crude songs for an aspiring boy band whose managers thought that punk aggression should make a comeback, and had turned to the old master of the genre for inspiration. It was more money than Toby usually had, and steadier work too.

But tonight, as he knelt by Topsy's side in the firelight wondering when her belly would begin to swell with his child and she would have to stop dancing, he felt the stiffening and ageing of his own body and was suddenly, unaccountably, afraid. This, he recognized, was the moment in his life to consider reversing all the decisions he took back in 1969, when he deliberately made it impossible for Radley College to house or teach him one minute longer. He would have to drop back in: but back, he saw now, into a new world which might not want to afford him a steady, income-bearing, paternal sort of job. Even if he could stand it.

He sighed, and looked at the other sleeping-bag. It was khaki and limp, and probably left over from Gervase's schooldays at army cadet camps.

"Come on, chaps!" he mimicked under his breath, pulling it over his feet as he sat on the smaller sofa. "Bivvy down, we've a five o'clock start!" He stretched out his long legs, putting his feet up on the arm rest. The sleeping-bag had a faint smell of boy scout about it, he thought as he drifted off to sleep. Poor old Cat: she might have burnt her fingers with the hairy poet Tim (Toby remembered that wedding, and the interminable readings from fake Hindu scriptures written by the groom) and he could see she wouldn't want another of those drifters. But it was a bit much to rebound onto a worthy old stiff like Gervase, and end up supporting his good works and organic sheep by boiling potatoes for sullen jailbirds and writing puling PR drivel for Eden. Poor old Cat. Toby yawned, glanced across once more at Topsy's hair sticking out from under the quilted nylon bag, and fell asleep.

Out in the farmyard, where the clean straw glimmered under brilliant stars, Gervase was on his knees beside a panting ewe. One hand was twined in the thick oily fleece of her back, and the other lifting her bloodied tail. He could see a leg, a foreleg by the look of it, just protruding from the swollen gap beneath the tail. But only the one leg. She was straining now, her flanks rock-hard with muscular effort, then relaxing into more hopeless panting. He would have to help. He let go the tail for a moment, and dipped his hand into the jar of antiseptic lubricant beside him.

Gently, he pushed the leg back, and slid the hand into the sheep. He closed his eyes, so as to feel more sensitively, and threw his head back: yes, the leg, and ah! – the other leg. Inside the warm pulsing birth canal his searching fingers could identify the head. Good. Definitely forelegs. He grasped both, waited for a contraction, and firmly but gently tugged. Both legs appeared, then a large head, eyes closed and gummy, streaked with blood and yellow mucus. With a rush of liquid, the whole lamb plopped to the ground, Gervase still holding its forelegs. The ewe was straining again now, but he turned from her to the dead-looking thing on the straw. Gently he tickled its nose with a wisp of straw, but there was no response. He lifted it and blew into its slimy mouth, to no avail. Then he stood up, wiped his hand on his trousers and picked the lamb up again, this time by the hind legs. With some violence he whirled it around his head, its forelegs and gummy head describing great circles against the stars. It worked. The little animal coughed, took a deep giddy breath, and gave a loud indignant bleat. Gervase pulled it to him, holding it against his chest, inspecting it, feeling the strengthening heartbeat in its wet woolly chest.

"Good boy! Good baby! Go on, live, live!" This moment of kindling life always moved him unbearably, even at two o'clock in the morning, even in his deepest secret depressions.

Sometimes the lamb would die hours or even minutes later, overwhelmed with delayed shock at the trauma of its coming. But this one had the mark of life on it: already its head was turning, searching blindly for its mother. He set it down on its legs and it stood, wobbling, and continued to peer around. The ewe had moved two paces away and – he saw with amused gratification – delivered the twin lamb on her own. She was licking it enthusiastically where it lay, clearly breathing, on the straw.

"Come on, girl," he said, putting the elder lamb beside her, and watching it grope, then latch on with determined greed to her teat. "You've got two. Just check –" he felt once more inside the ewe but, satisfied there was no triplet, knelt back and watched the second lamb teeter to its feet and find the other nipple.

A sound behind him made him turn his head. It was Dave, with a mug in his hand.

"Brought you tea, Gerv," he said. "Martin's still explaining the meaning of life to Marianne in the bunkhouse, and Duane's out like a light, so I thought I'd get tactfully out of the way."

"Thanks." Gervase sucked gratefully at the hot tea, tiredness welling up in him.

"How's it going?"

"Nice twins, just born."

Dave looked fondly at the lambs. "Isn't it amazing how quick they dry off, and start getting fluffy? I used to hate the slimy ones when I was seven. I thought they were really disgusting."

"You were good, though. Remember holding the torch for me, that first winter? Inside the barn, when we had all that snow?"

"I was so knocked out to be allowed to stay up, I was prepared to put up with the slime and the bloody bit round their bums. You were good, too. Couple of Hounslow kids who'd never even seen a farm animal up close, and you pretended we were a great help."

"You were." There was a definite note of finality in Gervase's voice: he was ending the conversation. Dave recognized the tone of old, and took the empty mug back from him in silence. Gervase glanced around the yard, looked through the barn door at the ewe which had lambed earlier, her sleeping young warm against her flanks, and said: "Night then. Happy Christmas."

"Happy Christmas. Shall I do the early turn?"

"No. Martin's having a look at six. That'll do. I wasn't really expecting any till Boxing Day, so this could be it for the moment."

When he had discarded his overalls and washed, Gervase eased himself into bed – his parents' old, vast, four-poster bed with springs which sagged beneath the new mattress he had bought in Cat's honour many years ago. His wife was sleeping soundly, curled in her corner. He edged close to her without touching, to feel the warmth which radiated from her evenly breathing body. He closed his eyes and pictured again the lambs rising shakily to their feet. He smiled, and relaxed into sleep.

8

The clear skies of Christmas night had clouded over by morning, and Martin's early round of the animals was done in cold mizzling rain. There were no more lambs, but he replenished the sheep's fodder, checked the three newborns, fed the horses and turned them into their own yard for the day, and carried two buckets of barley meal and water up to the pigs above the house. He could have woken Duane to help him, but decided not to bother. He liked moving about the farm, alone with his thoughts, and besides Duane might appreciate a morning in bed before he had to face Christmas dinner. Poor kid was obviously out of his depth with these people, not like that sharp-arsed Gary.

Martin Szowalski, working his way round Europe at twenty-one, had had plenty of opportunity for quiet observation of families on the various farms he helped on, and found Knoll Farm particularly striking. He admired Gervase Hartley's mission to help boys like Duane with regular work and contact with nature and self-respect and all that – but Gary, in his view, was a lost cause, a waste of space. Martin had all the unsentimental brutality of youth, about youth. Gary was a selfish asshole, and feeding pigs would teach him nothing. You could see he despised the whole thing, and Mr Hartley most of all.

Which was, in Martin's view, very unfair. Gervase seemed to him a man of high principle and an understated kindness which – as Mrs Szowalski back home would have exclaimed – was just so British it drove you wild. Martin, who had grown up amid volatile Polish-American overstatement of virtually everything, found being with Gervase a revelation. He believed in all the organic thing, he believed in social justice, but he didn't preach on about it. Just did his small bit, in his own home. Like Marianne. That was a hell of a girl: nursing mad people, obviously really into it, really caring, but laughing about it too. He hoped Marianne would stay for more of Christmas, and come back before his own time was up. He wondered whether a British family would think it presumptuous if he asked for her phone number. He might take a day or two in London.

Mrs Hartley, he was sure, wouldn't mind. Hefting the pig bucket over the electric fence, Martin reflected that Mrs H., as Gary insisted on calling her, was a hell of a lady herself. She was not much in evidence around the farm, but obviously knew a good bit; whatever she did upstairs in that study clearly preoccupied her, as did the businesslike telephone calls she took in the corner of the kitchen. But the telephone was within arm's reach of the big shabby stove, and he would watch fascinated as she stirred soup or tossed onions in oil with the receiver wedged between shoulder and chin, saying "Yes – fine – if you fax me through the layout I'll fit the copy for the NVQ piece by ten tomorrow." Or "If you need it on a floppy, you'll have to send a bike. If you can wait till Wednesday, I'll Red Star it from Northampton, and Tanya can get it printed up before the meeting. That's my best offer. OK? Great." Sometimes the calls came during the early, communal supper which the Hartleys took with the boys and any volunteers or visitors to the farm, and Gervase would frown if she answered them. But if she didn't, Martin would see her straining to hear the answering machine pick up the call in the living room next door. At times when she heard a high whining voice saying, "It's Tanya, only the DH is worried, there's a problem with the copee . . ." Cat would tend to abandon the table despite Gervase's pained look, run through, interrupt the machine and sort out the problem on the spot. Then she would come back and smile and say "Sorry!" and Gervase would press his lips together and Duane would gape stupidly, as usual, and Gary would go on eating as if there was no bad atmosphere.

So Martin would make a point of bringing up a new subject, with enthusiasm, in his relaxed Kentucky drawl. Cat would glance at him gratefully, take up his thread, and together they would cover the moment of strain with a bright web of talk.

Great lady. Martin thought – though he could not be sure – that whatever her work was, Gervase found some moral problem with it. Or at least, a problem of aesthetics or taste. He did not really want to know more: admiring Gervase, admiring his wife, the idea of such a shadow of principle between them was something he preferred to push aside. Instead, as he watched the sow and her litter splashing their noses greedily into the heavy iron feeding-ring, he let his mind wander over the equally fascinating matter of the other siblings.

What a gang! They did not seem to him to be related at all: a crazy songwriter, a cool Duchess-type, then that bad-tempered, corporate exec guy between them. And the Lord, their father, looking kind of bewildered, as if he wondered what they had to do with him. Martin's own father would never have put up with that kind of yelling-the-odds at table, even though his three brothers were all grown up and married. But Lord Gratton just sat there, with that British face. Stiff upper lip. Weird.

Cat woke at eight to find Gervase sitting on the side of the bed, stretching. Outside, the rain ran down the window-pane and the sky was leaden grey.

"Happy Christmas," she said sleepily, and he turned and kissed her on the forehead.

"Happy Christmas. Twin lambs in the night, good 'uns."

"Lovely. Did you have to help?"

"Mmmm," said Gervase. He yawned. "Martin did the early morning. I said he needn't, but he wanted to. I like that boy."

"Me too," said Cat. "Oh God."

"What?"

"I've just remembered who's in the house. Noreen, Dad, Caroline, bloody Alan, Toby, Topsy-and-a-half, the twins, Mark and Lindy with hangovers, and Artemis heading up from the Vicarage like a smart missile any minute."

"You'll cope. You do a good Christmas, I always said so."

"Aaargh." Cat winced, but it was not her houseful of guests. nor even the dankness of the unheated bedroom, which made her shudder at that moment. She had remembered the conversation, too bibulous and intimate a conversation, with Caroline. She had talked about Gervase, and fatherhood. Christ, how could she have been so stupid? Years of never letting on why they were childless, half-pretending to all her local friends that it was her, or that it was by choice. Now she had gone and told Caroline the truth, just out of irritation and to make her pull herself together about bloody Alan and the new baby. In the chill of dawn, Cat cared far less about her sister's next move. Let her go blinding off into some neurotic Kensington version of single motherhood if she insisted. She could sort her own life out.

"Oh God," she said aloud, for a second time. Stupid, rash, tipsy indiscretion! She pulled herself together and managed to smile at her husband.

"Lunch is sorted, anyway. Martin did the potatoes and sprouts, all I have to do is put them on and the pudding on. Starters are done, and the turkey's been in the slow oven all night, just needs half an hour to crisp it."

"Crackers?" said Gervase. "Nuts?"

"You can do the nuts, they're in bags in the larder. Crackers are in two big boxes in the china cupboard. Big, sealed boxes."

Gervase laughed, a more open and natural laugh than she had heard for a while. He was pulling on a sweater, but said through the wool: "Toby wouldn't do that again. He never repeats himself, I'll say that for him."

"Hmmm," said Cat. "Some things do get dreadfully familiar. When he was a little boy the whoopee cushion was never out of use for long."

"Did they have whoopee cushions in Israel?"

"It wasn't Israel, he wasn't big enough. It was Berne."

"Do they have whoopee cushions in Switzerland?"

"Is the Pope a Catholic? You have no idea how coarse the German Swiss can be. Huge hairy rubber hands. Warty latex feet. Our landlady's son Dieter gave the whoopee cushion to Toby as a goodbye present, and it was in frequent use in Washington. You can imagine how it went down with the prissy American lunch ladies."

"Not an ideal icebreaker. What happened to it? He hasn't still got it, has he?"

"Could have got a new one."

The reference to crackers went back to a time years ago, soon after Cat's marriage to Gervase, when Toby, arriving on

Christmas Eve with every intention, he said, of being "helpful", had gone to the supper table early and privately doctored the crackers, inserting mottoes of the most unlikely nature into the cardboard tube, drawn from the *Communist Manifesto*, the lyrics of Sid Vicious and the *Kama Sutra*. Worse, he had inserted his own choice of gifts. Lady Artemis, unfortunately, got the condom. Gervase (who got the pepper sweet) had been inclined to a tolerant, boys-will-be-boys attitude but Cat (who got a chocolate penis and only just managed to conceal it from Noreen) had been mortified and forcibly made the point that her brother was not a boy, but of an age to show some decent consideration for the older generation. Mark (who got the packet labelled *"powdered rhino horn, oh all right, sherbert, but a man can dream"*) had growled, irritated. Caroline had looked coolly down her nose at her brash brother and her awkward one.

Toby had merely grinned, having achieved all he set out to do by fracturing the brittle veneer of family bonhomie to bring out a pleasingly raw, salty set of emotions. Robert would have exploded with wrath but Diana, already weakening with what would be her final illness, had merely given her warring children a gentle, indulgent smile and said, "It is Christmas, dears, so let's not any of us be nasty. Cat darling, lovely stuffing."

Cat remembered that Christmas, her mother's last, and grinned in spite of herself. Bloody Toby! Still, the announcement about the baby had been a startling change of tune: and he seemed to look at Topsy with something in his eyes she had not seen before. Or not since he was a very little boy indeed, one who had to be held up by a devoted sister to see over the parapet of the Berne bear-pit when the cubs were born in spring.

She suddenly had a vivid picture of herself, too tired to hold him up any longer, plumping him down rather crossly and expecting an outcry. And Toby turning to face her, uncomplaining, eyes still shining from the wonder of the little living teddy bears, to give her a rare hug. When, she wondered vaguely, fumbling for her clothes, had the cynicism, the sharpness, the defensive manic joking set in? With prep school? Or, before that, when Mark was born and he went to that horrible American school? In France he was a tiresome brat, indeed, but she remembered an ebullient, cheerful brat who wanted you to enjoy each awful joke as much as he did. The time in South Africa – well, never mind. It was a stupid thing to wonder about. Toby had to grow up, and pray God, with this baby on the way he finally would. She gathered up a bundle of clothes and made for the comparative warmth of the bathroom.

Noreen was just leaving it, creeping apologetically down the corridor in an ancient pink candlewick dressing gown which Cat remembered from her early days in Hounslow. She smiled at the older woman, pierced by another sudden Christmas memory: of that same candlewick with one of her own babies flopped against it, flailing little fists, whimpering grumpily while Cat struggled to get a stiff terry nappy on the other twin. How dare Artemis, who had never done a thing for anybody else unless there was a lavish charity ball involved, patronize Noreen?

Noreen was a heroine. Just when she might have been enjoying some freedom as a lively middle-aged single woman with a tiny but unencumbered house, she had willingly and without reproach taken in her son's abandoned wife and baby grandchildren. She had lived a cramped and devoted life with them for six years, then without rancour or selfishness given those children up. "Don't worry about me, dear," she had said to Cat, when matters became serious with Gervase. "They'll have a much better life, out in the country. You know we're all getting too big for this poor little house, and I can visit, can't I? I'll have time to start those evening classes again!" Cat knew what it had cost Noreen, the children's second mother almost, and honoured her for it.

"Happy Christmas, Noreen," she said fondly. "Sleep well?"

"Not too bad, duckie," said her mother-in-law. She had not, in fact, slept well at all. On Christmas Eve she always remembered Tim's childhood: the few years when his father had been alive, and the years after that when she alone saved and planned for the surprises in his stocking, and crept alone to his room in the small hours to lay a heavy, gorgeously lumpy red woollen bag on the end of the bed. She had done her best all those years; yet she had done wrong. Must have done, to produce a son who would walk out on his new wife, his babies, his mother and his debts and only send one letter – a poor thing, too – explaining about his "new life" in America. Noreen did not see herself as any sort of heroine. The removal of the six-year-old twins to this distant, rather alarming place was not something of which she had ever felt entitled to complain. No, the only child she had a right to was Tim: bad, lost Tim. He was her burden, for life.

The old woman sighed, and drew the pink candlewick around her more closely as she moved down the chilly corridor.

Passing the window she looked out to see the piglets in the orchard – dear little things! – and was startled to notice amongst them, apparently dancing, two figures with tinsel and ivy twisted around their heads, presumably stolen from the living-room beams. One wore a robe improvised out of a big red linen Christmas tablecloth. That would need ironing! Noreen opened the window a fraction to see better, and the sound of singing came up to her on the cold air, one voice deep and another shrill:

> *There was a pig, went out to dig,*
> *On Chriss-um-us Day, on Chriss-um-us Day*
> *There was a pig, went out to dig*
> *On Chriss-um-uss day in the morning!*
> *We are the spirit of Christmas Present!*

As she watched, an ungainly figure walked out of the kitchen doorway and towards the orchard, a piece of bread-and-jam dripping in its hand.

"Oy!" shouted Duane. "Mrs H. says she wawnt that tablecloth back, right now!" Toby turned, rather too sharply, and caught his robe on a fence post in mid-pirouette. It whipped off and flew down the orchard on the biting wind. A tide of black piglets surged joyfully over it.

9

Cat forbade Noreen to spend the festive morning washing and ironing the muddied red tablecloth, so the Christmas table was finally adorned with a plain white one. However, so much additional holly, ivy and fir had been gathered by the penitent Toby and Topsy to make "a stunning centrepiece, I promise" and so many plates and dishes and candles covered the rest of the extended table that the colour did not matter overmuch. The errant pair, spurred by an explosion of plain speaking from Cat, had also washed up everybody's breakfast, shaken out the sofa cushions, cleaned the fireplace and put the tinsel back up on the living-room ceiling. Except for one piece which still clung to Topsy's riotous backcombed hair.

It rained too heavily, as the morning went on, for the traditional walk. Only Gervase set off heavily clothed to walk the farm and check the stock. By the time Lady Artemis arrived from church, the rest of the family were gathered in the long sitting room. Even Cat had left the supervision of the Brussels sprouts to Martin and Duane and joined her brothers and sister. The four siblings were kneeling at the hearth, drinking red wine and laughing in a rare moment of unity over some joke from a past Christmas. Alan stood a little aloof, talking international affairs with his father-in-law and studiedly ignoring the cackles and whoops from the fireside. Noreen was on the sofa, safe between the twins.

The general air of festive comfort was rapidly dispelled by the arrival of the newcomer. Artemis always liked to stand in a doorway, letting in cold air, widening her eyes so they sparkled at the company and (Toby always swore, to Cat's scandalized amusement) simultaneously clenching her pelvic floor muscles and silently saying "Brush!" to produce a hellish combination of Jackie Collins allure with a Nancy Mitford social smile. She did it now, studiously ignored by everyone present except her dutiful daughter-in-law.

"There wouldn't be a gin-and-tonic, I suppose, dear?" she chirped as Cat rose to her feet to hand her a glass of wine from the tray. "Since it *is* Christmas?" The old lady gave a little shrug and a pouting pussycat smile. "I know I'm a silly girl, but there aren't many of these modern wines I can drink without food to – er – mask them." Cat, well aware of the roughness of her supermarket dozen, tried to suppress her irritation and replied as sweetly as she could: "Oh, Artemis, I'm terribly sorry, we're out of gin."

"I drank it," said Marianne, not looking sorry at all. She had been terrified of Lady Artemis when she was a six-year-old alien from Hounslow, and now drew genuine pleasure from the fact that she no longer feared her at all. "There's some whisky. And beer."

Ignoring this suggestion, Artemis took a glass from the tray and sipped fastidiously. She glanced at Robert, but he was deep in conversation with Alan Halliday about Eastern Europe. Grimacing at the wine and setting down her glass perilously on the arm of the small sofa, she next swivelled her big, slightly protruding eyes toward Noreen and opened her mouth to speak. Cat saw this move and clapped her hands commandingly.

"I can hear Gervase at the back door!" she lied. "We're all here now! Come on, let's go through, or we'll never have finished eating in time for the Queen!"

"The Queen," murmured Artemis, foiled. "I'm glad *some* old traditions still carry on in my son's house."

"Oh, Gervase doesn't give a monkey's," said Cat, her resolve to be a peacemaker breaking down under the temptation of vengefulness. "It's me that insists on having the Queen after Christmas dinner. And Dad. And all of us. It's the old Foreign Office tradition, wiping away a tear for the Queen in far-flung climes." She held out a hand to pull Noreen off the sofa. "Remember, we expats are always the most patriotic. Ever since we were babies, home wasn't home without the Queen's picture on the wall in robes, and a certificate personally signed, saying Dad was her trusty and well-beloved Robert John Adrian Gratton." She was leading the way to the dining room now, and delivered this message over her shoulder.

"It's true," quavered Toby piously, moving to the table and pulling back a chair for Lady Artemis with rudely exaggerated courtesy. "When Mrs Queen used to say 'God bless you all' we really thought it meant *us*. Personally. We loved her. We knew that if any foreigner got on our wick she would get her Secretary of State for Foreign Affairs to request and require that Johnny Dago afford us assistance without let or hindrance or she'd have a gunboat round. It said so in our passports." He pretended to wipe away a tear and turned towards the American volunteer, who had come in rather flushed with a dishful of potatoes. "And Martin, you Yankee invader, it was a terrible thing to us when they sent us to school in Washington DC, Cat and me. They made us salute the Stars and Stripes. We felt like traitors. We were *traumatized*. You treacherous colonists, how could you have done it to nice King George?"

"That's enough!" said Robert, amused in spite of himself. "The truth is, Martin, that Toby was never remotely reluctant to embrace American culture. It was Cat who found that school a bit much. My elder son turned into the worst kind of cartoon Yankee brat in two days."

"It was a particularly awful school," said Cat hastily, feeling that her father had lacked in diplomacy. "Not because it was in America but because Mum was always a lousy picker of schools. She did it all on how good the headmistress's clothes were. Our only lucky break was when she decided nuns were chic."

"Did Mark go to school in the States?" asked Martin.

"Too little," said Cat. "He only got to suck a Popeye toy. His first school was – oh, nursery in Lille, I think."

"'*Sur le pont d'Avignon.' 'Meunier, ton moulin va trop vite,'*" said Mark dreamily. "Then I did lessons with Mum, then a year in Venice but I couldn't learn Italian fast enough so they threw me to the wolves of Haddington Hall."

"And you?" said Martin politely to Caroline, who was next to him this time.

"Oh, I wasn't born," she said in her sweet voice. "I only got born in Johannesburg. I had my first school in Venice."

"I *never* got to go to school on a *vaporetto*," said Toby resentfully. "I do not forgive you that. You and Mark got to be *bambini*, while Cat and I were beaten up by deranged Afrikaner clerics and then stuck in England eating mashed potatoes and getting rained on and having our characters formed by assorted sexual inadequates."

"You could have come out to UCLA, though," said Caroline. "When I was at school in LA I used to dream of us all being there together. I didn't have anyone to talk to but Mum, in term-time. But Cat wanted to do English university, and Toby was all over the place, and Mark was home doing 'O' levels and sending me letters about how terrible the American system was."

"Gee," said Martin. "It's like you all grew up in different worlds." Worried at the brief silence that followed this, he added: "It's a really neat way to learn about life, I bet. There's a new name for it, in corporate America when families have to relocate worldwide. They call them global nomad children, and apparently they're famous for growing up real gifted."

"We," drawled Toby, "were just common or garden diplo-brats. Who are famous for never growing up at all."

"They did warn us it might be hard for you to settle down in later life," said Robert. "But I always thought that was nonsense. Cat settled beautifully, hence this exceedingly fine meal."

"And I have settled," said Mark stiffly. Another brief silence fell, as the family looked at him without particular admiration.

Lindy chimed in: "Lovely turkey, Cath. Yum-yum!" She dug her elbow playfully into Alan, who was jammed rather too close to her in order to avoid having his legs trapped on either side of the table extension. "Innit lovely turkey, Alex?"

"Excellent," said Alan sulkily. He was furious at being seated so far from his potentially useful father-in-law. Caroline glanced pleadingly across the table at him, but met only a stony stare. She had been annoying him all morning with brightly playful but disastrously misguided attempts to please. She might as well, thought Alan sourly, spearing a sprout, have worn a t-shirt with SAINTLY FORGIVING WIFE printed on it. He turned to talk business to Mark, who was soon enthusing about his company's new in-service GNVQ training: "Not just offering staff internal progress," he said, "but a portable qualification. There was a fascinating piece in the pan-organization newsletter. Ms Raschid, at our HQ—"

Cat looked suddenly, unaccountably terrified, and Toby caught her eye and grinned. He was the only member of the family who actually knew which company she did all this lucrative copywriting for, simply because he was the only one who had ever asked.

He mouthed silently "Yours?" and Cat nodded, warily watching Mark as he quoted with reverence the words she had flung, so crossly and without commitment, onto paper earlier in the month. Toby made a zipping motion across his lips, and she smiled gratefully. He might like causing ructions, she thought through the welcome fog of wine, but he had a good heart really.

Toby had had no hand in the crackers this year, so the hats and mottoes and plastic puzzles fell from them without surprises except for Topsy going into peals of hysterical tipsy mirth on getting the motto *May all your troubles be little ones* and Gervase, who was very quiet today, getting a red plastic nose on elastic and being harassed into putting it on by a mildly inebriated Lindy. The pudding was on the table and the Queen a mere twenty minutes away when the phone rang. Gervase stood up, gravely pulling off his plastic nose.

"Sorry," he said. "I'd better. Nobody rings on Christmas Day unless it's important."

He took the call in the kitchen, learning on the stove picking absently at the turkey carcass. He listened, asked a couple of questions, said "Don't worry, I'll be over," grimaced, nodded, and hung up. For a moment he stared unseeingly at the turkey, then sighed and went back into the dining room, where somebody had tried to light an indoor firework, and in the process dripped red candlewax all over the ruins of the pudding.

"I'm *very* sorry," he said. "But I have to go to Midmarsham. That was Gary's mother. He hasn't been home since yesterday, and the police are round there searching for something. They think he might have hidden some drugs in her cottage."

"Darling, do you have to?" said his mother plaintively. "You're not these ghastly boys' *keeper*, you know." Cat flashed a warning look at her, nodding towards Duane, but he had no idea of being offended, having other things on his mind. With difficulty, beet-faced and choking down his pudding, the boy emerged from his accustomed heavy silence to say:

"Mister H.! I got to tell you—"

"Yes, Duane?" said Gervase, looking hard at him.

"Gary. I din' want to grass on 'im, but he tried to stash some stuff away in the bunkhouse."

"And did he?"

"I wun't let 'im," said Duane. "Told him that wawn't fair on you and Mrs H."

"Good man," said Gervase approvingly, and Duane glowed sheepishly. "I'm bigger'n he is," he confided to the rest of the table. "So it wawn't hero stuff." He guffawed, and picked up his glass of unfamiliar wine.

"All the same, well done," said Gervase. "But I do have to go. Gary's mother is in a bit of a state. He's probably just round at a girlfriend's, but you know . . ."

"Of course you ought to look after Mrs Bird," said Cat, briskly. "Come on, we'll go and watch the Queen."

Alan Halliday, by this time, had run out of tolerance for family life. He begged to be excused the Queen's broadcast because he and Caroline had social commitments in London. Caroline began, "Wha –?" but was silenced by a hard glare from her husband. Martin volunteered himself and Duane to start the washing-up, and the twins ("not being emotionally crippled by a diplomatic background," said Dave sweetly) abandoned the Queen to take Noreen out for a walk round the farm in the drying afternoon air. The rest moved back to the sitting room and arranged themselves around the small TV set in a silence broken by hiccups and the occasional burp.

Robert, from the end of the sofa, looked consideringly at his children. Cat looked tired, but composed; Toby, his dark hair curling untidily over his collar, as dissolute as usual but with something new about him his father could not place. It could be, thought Robert wonderingly, that this unlikely showgirl of his was going to be the woman who, at last, made his elder son grow up.

His eye rested on Mark, not altogether easily. He hoped the boy was happy: that wife of his with the ferocious Birmingham accent seemed to have made a difference. But there was always something angry about him, a lurking aggression, and the way he talked about his work had an intensity which made his father wince. In a lifetime concerned with the relations between great nations, the movements of trade and the crises of exiled individuals, he had seldom encountered the nervy passion with which Mark routinely spoke of in-service staff training modules or the importance of aisle width in supermarkets. Maybe if he had been posted to Libya, or Cuba, he would have felt more familiar with this kind of passion.

He felt sorry that Caroline had gone. She tugged at his heart, so like Diana, so likely to fall into the same traps. That husband of hers was clever enough, but clearly a bit of a shit in business. Robert hoped, staring unseeingly at the Queen's crumpled royal features, that he was not a shit in private, too.

". . . Wish you all, a happy Christmas," concluded the Queen on the screen. Toby, Mark, Robert, Artemis, Cat and Lindy rose to their feet for the National Anthem, Toby removing his paper hat with gravity. Topsy had fallen asleep. She woke, however, when Dave burst into the room saying: "Cat! Emergency! The sheep are out all over the road! What do we do? The front ones are right near the end of the lane!"

"Hell!" said Cat with feeling, and ran from the midst of her family towards the back door and the farmyard drive. She snatched the keys of the old farm LandRover from the hook above the lintel. Gervase must have taken her car to Midmarsham. Fair enough. Wrenching open the door of the sheepdog's run, she hustled the sleepy old dog into the LandRover and jumped up herself. Dave jumped in beside her.

"Top of the lane," he said, alarmed, as she shot out of the other end of the drive.

"I know," said Cat. "But I can't drive through them, can I? I'll go up the far end, along the main road, head them off."

"You've done this before, Ma," said Dave admiringly.

"Too bloody right I have. But never," Cat said with a quaver in her voice, "never this close to lambing. Christ, some of them must be virtually in labour. I hate this bloody thing, the steering's all over the place."

She was speeding down the lane now, the old vehicle leaping and juddering on the potholes, and barely slowed to swing into the main road. Dave could see ahead the half-hidden opening which marked the far end of the Knoll Farm lane, for the farmhouse lay midway on a narrow loop which left this main road and rejoined it. As Cat had predicted the first sheep were just visible, off-white noses edging forward under their woolly Dorset quiffs, hooves pattering on the damp lane. She slammed her foot down on the accelerator and shot forward, reaching the lane just ahead of the flock. Leaping out, she dragged the rear door open to release the old dog.

The flock paused, while its leaders stupidly looked at the dog and the LandRover skewed sideways across their path. For one heart-stopping moment it seemed that one bold ewe had decided to slither down into the nearside ditch, which would have given her and her followers a clear path out onto the main road. But Dave threw himself ahead of her, shouting "Gaaah!" and the ewe turned and fled back, jostling through her peers, away from the young man and the stick-waving woman and the sheepdog.

The rest of the flock took their cue from this, and fled precipitately after her, back down the lane. Cat screamed, "Come by!" at the dog, put on a burst of speed, overtook the leaders, and headed them off ("Howaaay!" yelled Cat) to the right and into the Knoll Farm front yard. She ran up the lane after them, but Duane and Martin had heard the commotion and taken up their posts. She saw them shut and secure the gates with the milling, panting flock inside.

Cat sank to her knees. "Thank Christ!" she said without a scintilla of blasphemous intent. Her heart was pounding and she drew her breath in long shuddering gasps. As Dave caught up with her he put his hand reassuringly on her shoulder.

"I'm sorry. Can't help it. It isn't just that they're about to lamb, it always gets me like this. It's the – the panic of it."

"The hysteria. The lack of control. The plain bloody barminess of them," said Dave. "I know. I always felt it, when we were little. Can you *catch* panic, off sheep? Like enzootic whatsit?"

"Gervase doesn't. He's always calm as a tree in this sort of crisis."

"Well, I know what you mean anyway. It's different with cows."

"Yes," said Cat. "When cows are running around out of control, you feel it's the exception and they'd rather be grazing quietly back on the farm. When horses go crazy, you know that *they* know they shouldn't. With sheep—!"

"They just go back to their primitive state. Brainless, aimless, suicidal panic," finished Dave. "*'The ancient panic which abides deep in all creatures'*. The great god Pan, who drives men and beasts to frenzy."

Cat recovered herself. "Are we really kneeling on a wet grass verge on Christmas Day, philosophizing about Pan?" She stood up, and rubbed her damp knees. One of her tidy Christmas-day shoes was lying near the LandRover with the heel wrenched off. She hobbled back towards it and flung it into the cab.

"I'll walk," said Dave. "Need the air. Clear my head."

Cat nodded, and started the engine. Reversing into the road, talking to herself ("Bugger this steering, Gervase'll have to have it seen to, it's really loose") she crashed the machine into first gear and proceeded slowly towards the far lane entrance. Her eyes well accustomed to the growing dusk, she did not bother to switch the lights on for the two-minute journey home.

PC Adcock and Sgt Flower were driving along the main road to pursue further enquiries into the whereabouts of Gary Bird, whose pathetically small but damning stash of Ecstasy and cannabis had been found at his mother's cottage following an anonymous telephone call from a vengeful young woman. He was, they realized, probably miles away in the company of some other young woman, and hardly likely to be tucked up in Mr Hartley's Knoll Farm bunkhouse. Nonethless, checks must be made. Ahead of them, a LandRover was turning, in rather too wide an arc, thought PC Adcock, into the farm lane. It had no lights on.

"Look at that," he said to his senior colleague. "You don't suppose—" Sgt Flower grunted. "Funny bit of driving," he said. "Christmas Day. Come on. No point wasting the whole journey."

His colleague pulled something out from the pocket in front of him, and fitted it with a tube from a sealed pack.

"Why not?" he said.

Cat had barely pulled up outside the farmhouse when the police car crunched on the stones behind her. Startled, she jumped out and found herself facing two uniformed officers, the younger of them carrying what looked like a portable telephone. Then she saw the breathing tube, which made it clear it was something else entirely. Woolly panic surged through her like a hundred stampeding sheep, as she realized for the first time that she, who never drank a drop if she were likely to drive that day, had just been in the driving seat of a vehicle on the Queen's highway with three-quarters of a bottle of Australian red inside her.

10

"The light on the box went red," said Cat, hours later. The remnants of the family were around the kitchen table, picking distractedly at the remnants of the Christmas dinner. "It went bright bloody red. And they took me to the station in Midholt, and I did another test, and that was just as positive, which I could have told them it would be." She swigged viciously at the dregs of her wine. "The young one gave me a lift back, because we couldn't get any of the taxi firms to answer. He was quite sweet. At least" – she pulled a dark brown piece off the turkey carcass, looked at it with sudden loathing, and dropped it on the dish – "one good thing is that they didn't pounce till I was on the drive. So the Landy's here, not stuck beside some road."

"Poor Cat," said Gervase sympathetically. "Did you tell them why you had to drive?"

"No. Dave did, but they repeated all the stuff about requiring me to accompany them to the police station. They were just like robots – the sergeant wasn't local, he was filling in for Christmas while the Midholt lot had leave. And then Toby banged on the roof of the police car and said they should be ashamed of themselves."

"Which didn't help," said Robert.

"Solidarity, Dad!" said Toby. "I mean, Cat was only saving the lives of woolly sheep. It's not like my pal Dunkie, in Glasgow, who does it all the time and always carries a bottle of Scotch in the side pocket and if he gets stopped, he pulls in and knocks it back so they can't prove he was drunk before."

"Does that work?" asked Cat, diverted for a moment from her trouble.

"No," admitted Toby. "He still gets banned. Actually, he only ever drives for about a month before the next ban. But there you go."

"Well," said Gervase. "I doubt you'll get banned. We'll get a decent barrister to argue that it was life and death for the sheep."

"Gordon Japhet-Menzies," said Robert, decisively. "I'll call him at home."

"Yes, he'll be good," said Gervase. "Sound, not flashy. He's got a house round here, hasn't he? The court will take the sheep into account."

Cat sucked noisily at her wine, put the glass down, drew her sleeve across her eyes and gave a long, shuddering sniff.

"No," she said loudly. "Stop organizing my defence. I'm not at all sure I *want* a defence."

The group round the messy table looked at her, waiting for more.

"I don't believe in all that," she said. "When Dave and Marianne were little and we were all living in Hounslow with the lorries going by, I was bloody glad of the breathalyser law. I think there ought to be a zero limit. I've always thought that. People who drink and drive don't deserve any sympathy at all. They kill children."

"But you were saving the sheep. You had to," said Gervase gently. "I respect what you're saying, Cat, but you weren't a danger, and you have got an excuse. Like someone going to hospital with a casualty."

"All the same, it was wrong," said Cat grumpily, "and I don't like people who wriggle out with smarmy double-barrelled barristers. I don't like excuses. I'm not bloody Gary."

"Well, I think we have to respect that," said Gervase heavily.

"I don't," said Toby. "I think you're bats."

"Don't be so rude," said Topsy abruptly, turning on him. "I reckon Cat can do what she wants."

"She was always a bit Joan of Arc," said Toby. "Father, I cannot tell a lie."

"That was George Washington" said Topsy, even more surprisingly. "And shut up. You're no help. You're all mouth, you."

"Whatever," said Cat stiffly. "I'm not defending the case. I'm pleading guilty. It'll be awkward, obviously, being banned and living here—"

"Awkward?" said Gervase under his breath. Without an extra driver, he saw in clear dismay, it would be a logistical nightmare to run the farm, and the boys' lives too. Cat did the recreational runs into town without which they grew restless, and took them to their appointments with probation officers. For a non-driver even to shop for food and farm essentials with the village two miles away and the town fifteen would be impossible. At present, the farm and the boys took all his time and more; if he had to replace her on all these runs it would be almost catastrophic.

All this chaos, a whole year of it, could perhaps be averted if Cat were to defend herself. She had only driven for a few minutes, on empty Christmas Day roads, to prevent danger both to animals and human drivers. It was not fair. Even when he turned his mind away from the coming difficulties, his head and heart throbbed with indignation for his wife's humiliation, and he longed to defend her, personally and loudly.

But he could not bring himself to argue about it. These last few years, he admitted with further silent dismay, he had been tired and she had been irritable. They had not had a holiday since the Lloyds' crash and his mother's land sale; they had not talked together relaxedly, in depth, for longer than he dared remember. When Dave and Marianne left home they had taken much of the laughter out of daily life, and now the Hartleys were scarcely more than decently behaved partners, neither lovers nor parents nor even very close friends. They respected one another's endeavours, but left each other space. Acres of empty space lay around each of them. He knew that she was equivocal about some of his human projects, like Gary: she knew, without his needing to express it, how much distaste he felt for corporations like Eden PLC, and for crafts of puffery like hers.

Yet their whole complicated, bothersome, altruistic, financially precarious life now rested on Cat's talent. Her uninspiring trade, he thought sadly, had come about because of his idealism. She churned out platitudinous copy for an aggressive and rapacious commercial empire so that he could do good for the soil and for animal welfare, and bring hope to lost and disaffected young offenders. He, Gervase, wanted to be good: Cat backed him up daily, uncomplainingly, subordinating her gifts to the production of profitable tripe. Now for once the tables were turned, and she was demanding a turn on the moral high ground. How could he argue?

Robert glanced at his son-in-law sharply, aware of something wrong. There was no colour in Gervase's face and he looked tired, worried, and oddly distant. Mark stirred uneasily and grimaced at his wife, who sat open-mouthed watching this family confrontation. Cat blundered on, determined, drunk and tired:

"Martin's with us till April. Supposing the case gets heard within about a month, it's quite quick at the magistrates' court – and suppose I get a twelve-month ban, that gives us three months of the ban reasonably covered, and when he goes we'll just have to get another volunteer who can drive. And Gervase'll have to do more, and I'm really sorry—"

Tears overcame her now, and the sleeve crossed her eyes and nose again. "Oh, sod it. I'm going to bed." Her husband looked helplessly after her, but did not move. Noreen, coming back into the kitchen with Marianne a few minutes later, found the rest of them still sitting in comparative silence, dragging streaks of ever less attractive meat from the turkey carcass. She began to clear and wash up. Gervase went outside to the lambing-yard, and the others dispersed.

When Gervase came upstairs Cat was asleep, or seemed to be. He slid quietly between the sheets and lay for a long time, his hands behind his head, staring at the low dark beams. There was not, after all, likely to be much comfort in counting sheep.

Toby and Topsy, mindful of the dreadful example made of Cat, stayed Christmas night and left sober on the morning of Boxing Day. Toby was rolled off his sofa earlier than he would have liked, because Topsy had to put in some work ahead of a rehearsal of her next high-kick musical, *Mademoiselle from Armentières*. "Nostalgia stuff," she said, "which is really lucky. No high-cut costumes. Just little skirts and awful slow choreography by that old piss-artist Mogadan. It's not like *Cats*. With a show like that I can do three months before the bulge starts to show."

"Didn't your friend Daisy dance till she was seven months

gone?" said Toby, throwing his tattered backpack into her little car.

"Yah. But she was one of the brothers' wives in *Joseph*. She only had to sway a bit."

"Nothing like Bible-wear to disguise an unwanted bump," said Toby. "Bye, then, Catto. Fine Christmas. Shame about the Old Bill."

His sister, watching from the step, smiled and raised her hand. He paused, looking at her.

"Are you going upstairs to write more scripts for Mark?" he said.

"Shh!" Cat heard Lindy, bumping down the stairs with a suitcase, and raised her finger to her lips. "Look, of course I'm going to tell him, it's just awkward finding the moment. It's his world, and you know Mark. Much better if I'm the humble rural sister who knows nothing of the big corporate jungle."

Toby laughed. "You all make things so bloody complicated, you diplomats. Me, I just get pissed and blurt everything out. Then everyone knows where they are."

"Goodbye," said Cat firmly, but smiled at him. "Topsy, look after yourself. Get some rest. It's not that easy, you know." Turning with another wave as Topsy's little car puttered into life she added in a lower voice, "Any of it." Dave and Marianne had left early, bearing Noreen off for a day out in London and one of the big musicals she loved. Without them Cat felt bereft and old and flat. Still, Marianne had looked at young Martin in a way which promised a visit sooner than usual. Who knows? thought Cat, heavily climbing the stairs to her dusty office. If that little romance went well, Martin might even stay through the summer instead of backpacking off round Europe, and her driving ban could be covered for a little longer.

The weeks after Christmas passed in the usual atmosphere of dull endurance that marked lambing-time. It was bitterly cold, and the ice had to be broken on the animals' drinking-troughs three times a day. Each night Cat did the 2.00 a.m. check of the ewes, shuddering from her bed to wrap herself in an old coat and tour the yard with a torch, peering under tails for signs of problematic labours and rounding up any lambs which had been born unattended and mislaid their mothers. Sometimes she would find one dead, drowned in a puddle or strangled by a difficult birth in the brief two hours since the last check. She would lift the small dead body and throw it beyond the fence to be dealt with in the morning. Once, a fox had killed newborn twins, and the ewe bleated over their bodies in uncomprehending distress. Often there were labour problems and she had to trudge back to the house and call Gervase; if that happened she would get up to do the pre-dawn inspection herself, and hope she did not have to wake him again.

Even so, since Martin was inexperienced Gervase worked long, taxing hours and would fall into an exhausted doze whenever he sat in a chair indoors. There was little sun, and no snow or hoar frost to throw back the paltry light from a sky which remained day after day the pale dull grey of a Tupperware lid. Cat worked upstairs for Eden and other clients, wrote a pamphlet about self-assembly furniture, a chatty exhortation about private breast screening, and a paean to a new "Time Organizer" system involving interlocking cork boards and pegs. *"Why strain your eyes peering into a computer screen?"* she wrote one morning, peering into the glowing green eye of hers. *"When you could have your whole year in front of you in vibrant optimistic colour and enhance your home decoration at the same time?"* She paused, looked at this with disfavour, and put her finger on the delete button until it vanished as far as *"Why stra"*. That, she thought, looked a bit Nordic. Perhaps it was Shetland dialect or balladeer's Scots for something. *Why stra the sheepie, quoth my luve* . . . Her head fell forward and her eyes closed.

The door behind her opened, and Gervase came in and stood hesitantly, wondering whether she were deep in thought. Cat heaved her head upright, swung round, and managed a smile.

"Hi. I'm writing about cork pegboards."

"This came," he said. "I opened it." Cat looked at the paper in his hand. It was the court summons for her drunken driving offence. It was imminent. "Good," she said. "Get it over with." Gervase stood for a moment, looking at her. She looked back at him, steadily.

"You know I feel the same as I did," she said. "Guilty, m'lud."

"Yes," said Gervase. "Fine. It's your decision."

"Martin will be here. He said the other day he might like to stay till summer."

"Can we afford him? The keep, I mean? He is useful. This new lad who's coming, the Ecstasy case, is only seventeen. The probation officer says he's nervous of animals."

Cat winced. "Ee, they do pick 'em for us," she said. "Anyway, yes, we can't afford *not* to have Martin. And think of all the money we'll save on petrol. I've told Eden I'll sometimes work by phone. I sort of pretended I was being headhunted. They were terribly co-operative then. They're wondering about putting in a teleconference videophone. Prats."

She gave a sudden bark of reluctant laughter, throwing her head back and looking more directly into her husband's eyes than she had for some time. Gervase moved towards her, put a hand on her shoulder and kissed the top of her head.

"I don't ever tell you how grateful I am," he said. "Do I?"

"No need," said Cat. She turned to her screen and read *Why stra.* "Before Lloyds," she said without looking at him, "you looked after me and the twins pretty well, for years. We owe you. And it is good, what you do. It is worthwhile. It is a bright light in a naughty world. I don't ever tell you that, do I?"

Gervase moved away, as if embarrassed. Cat wished she could summon up the eloquence she squandered every day on copywriting, could turn and stand up and take him by the shoulders and shake him and say, *"Look, I don't mind keeping us going, you work as hard as I do, just because I bring in more money doesn't mean you're worth less. Truly, truly, the more of this meretricious cheap rubbish I write for these crummy PR liars, the more I realize that even the smallest gesture towards human values is always going to be worth making. Believe me, it's true . . ."*

But she could no more have said such things to Gervase these days than fly around the room. "Talking of naughty worlds," she said, "do you have any ideas about what might make a cork board and some coloured pins into an exciting concept?"

Caroline went into hospital with high blood pressure on the same cold January day that her sister was banned from driving for twelve months. Two days later, after an exhausting and dangerous labour, Maria Annunciata Halliday was born. Alan was in Dortmund, sewing up a European broadcasting deal in the company of his former girlfriend Madeleine Minton. He received the news by fax from his father-in-law in the Whips' office at the House of Lords. It was pushed under the door of his hotel room, and he waved it towards the girl who was dressing, silhouetted prettily against the window.

"We are a father," he said. "Girl, eight pounds three ounces. You'd think they'd have metricated it by now, wouldn't you?"

"Caroline all right?" said the girl, who knew Caroline quite well.

"Oh God, yes. She's in the Portland, no expense spared."

"You flying back?"

"No, we've got to see Hauptmann again. Annie's organized some flowers, and my father-in-law's been round there, and all her mad bloody brothers and sisters are bound to pitch up. I'll fly tomorrow night as per. The baby'll be asleep, anyway. That's mainly what they do for weeks, isn't it?"

"Search me," said Madeleine, throwing on a red cashmere serape. "OK, ready."

High over Great Portland Street, in a bright private room, Caroline woke from a drugged nightmare sleep. She lay and wept for an hour, not ringing for the nurse, gazing helplessly through the clear aquarium sides of the little cot beside her where a humped, wrinkled shape lay quietly breathing under a light green blanket. "Mummy," she whispered. "Mum, I want you." At last the nurse came in, blonde and bright, with a tray of breakfast.

"All right, Mrs Halliday? Your sister's come, isn't that lovely?"

But it was not Cat, who had no lift to the station because there was a cow in labour and Martin could not be spared from the anxiety and hauling. The visitor was Lindy, bearing a florist's bunch of roses in a violent chemical pink. Caroline, who was not close to Mark and who had certainly never thought of his wife as a sister, was caught off-guard, wiping her eyes furiously on the silk sleeve of her robe and scrabbling to reclaim her perfect social manner from the snivelling ruins of the morning.

But it did not matter how Caroline looked. Lindy's eyes were all for the baby, wriggling a little now under the sterile coverings of the cot.

"Ooh, in't she *gorgeous*," she breathed. "Oh, Caroline, you are lucky. Oh, I do hope – I wish Mark—"

And she, in turn, burst into tears, leaving Caroline to mop her own face, dab her nose with powder and sit looking in helpless perplexity at this unexpected result of her childbearing. Robert had left the country again briefly; it was another day before Alan first called for a brief look at his daughter and two before Mark arrived, bearing perfume and bluff congratulations. It was Thursday when Cat managed to escape from Northamptonshire and fit in a visit after an Eden meeting.

"She's lovely," said Cat. "But I don't suppose by the look of you that *you* feel all that lovely yet."

There was at least some comfort for Caroline in Cat's dour matter-of-fact acceptance of her misery. None of the others, she reflected, brought any comfort at all. She would have liked to see Toby, just for the jokes, but for some reason he could not be contacted anywhere by Robert's faxes or Cat's telephone calls.

"Still, he always looks in at his agent's in the end," said Cat comfortingly. "He'll be in touch."

In the flurry of their daily lives, topped by the excitement of the birth, none of the family noticed a small item in the *Evening Standard*, later repeated in few words in the side-bars of the morning papers. It merely stated that a chorus dancer had been killed outright in a freak accident at a dress rehearsal, when her skull was shattered by a falling hammer. The tool was apparently left, said the newspaper, balanced on the overhead grid by a stagehand who had walked out in an earlier dispute. The man was a casual worker who could not be traced. The theatre was making no comment pending legal advice. The dead girl was named as Miss Teresa Tanner.

But none of them had ever known Topsy's surname, still less that she was a Teresa, named twenty years before by a sentimental Liverpool Catholic father in honour of the Little Flower of Lisieux.

11

Toby lay on the narrow, sagging bed high above the Gimmix computer-game shop, his hands behind his head, staring at the ceiling. He had not left the flat for three days. Two of Topsy's friends from the chorus had arrived, red-eyed, and collected some of her personal things to take up to her parents in Liverpool. They had offered Toby a lift up there in Topsy's car, for the funeral. He had lain unmoving on the bed and said: "I'm not too good at funerals. Not my thing."

He could tell they were disgusted. It did not matter. Nothing mattered. Sometimes he got up and used the lavatory in Topsy's tiny shower room. Sometimes he ate a piece of stale cheese or a biscuit from the scuffed cupboard which acted as her larder. He knew he would not be there for ever, and that he lacked the will to lie there and die. Eventually he would get off the bed and leave the flat to find more food. At that stage it was pretty certain that Topsy's landlord – who knocked occasionally and shouted through the door – would have the locks changed before he could get back up the stairs again.

That didn't matter either. A curious white blankness filled his head. He identified the texture of it: it was, quite obviously, milk of magnesia. His mother used to give him milk of magnesia when she judged his stomach to be upset. He would spit it out in long, viscous white streaks across the room, and laugh. Usually she would give up after that, though sometimes Cat would make him take it and he would obey. The other kids, in Washington and in France, had never heard of the stuff. Diana had seemed to lose faith in it later, and on holidays from prep school he never observed Mark or Caroline being dosed with it.

Anyway, here it was, in his head. Milk of magnesia, white and bland and viscous. Toby shuddered, tasting it in his throat.

Maria Annunciata Halliday fed at her mother's breast for only three sticky, hostile days. Caroline, deeply appalled by the ungainliness, the splitting and stretching and humiliating windy mess of her childbirth, wanted only to be healed, to be virginally gowned once more in crisp pure white cotton from neck to ankle. She did not want, she told the nurse hysterically, any more of this undressing and sagging and leaking. The nurse was calm and professional, and offered Caroline an opportunity to talk to a counsellor and reconsider.

"Breast-feeding really is proven to be best, you know," she said almost apologetically. "It needn't be for long, just a few weeks." But Caroline wept and stormed so that Alan flinched and sharply ordered the hospital to do as it was told. He was, after all, paying. So the nurse took Maria Annunciata away and fed her carefully and professionally from a hygienic bottle of scientifically formulated baby milk. Caroline was given neat pills on a clean tray to dry up her swollen, leaking breasts. By the time the two of them went home to the house in Kensington and a discreet, professional, careful maternity nurse, Caroline seemed her old calm self, her fair hair in a girlish Alice-band above her perfect Madonna's face.

Visiting them, Cat found Caroline alone in her studio, drawing. "Baby asleep?" she asked lightly. Her sister glanced up at her, and it seemed to Cat that the beautiful face looked sharper, the eyes unaccustomedly hostile.

"I don't know," she said. "She's with nurse. Go up if you want." She made no move to accompany Cat, but turned back to the drawing board. The older woman hesitated, then turned on her heel and went upstairs towards the sounds of activity, where firm footsteps moved to and fro and drawers were being pulled in and out in the former guest room. She found a neat round-faced woman engaged in putting away soft piles of terry and muslin nappies, and a baby with a quiff of white-blonde hair lying in a smart mahogany cradle.

"I'm Caroline's sister," she said. "You're, er—?"

"Alison Harper," said the nurse. "I'm glad to have a chance to meet you."

Cat looked away from the baby which had irresistibly drawn her attention with a small, beguilingly flailing fist and a wide pink yawn.

"Why?" she asked baldly. The nurse pressed her lips together in a dry humourless smile, acknowledging the challenge.

"I'm only here another week," she said. "I'm booked for another lady. Mrs Halliday has asked *me*" – she emphasized the pronoun, incredulously – "to interview nannies for Maria. She has asked me to make the appointment without reference to herself."

"Oh," said Cat. "Like that, is it? I thought perhaps it was just today. I hoped it was just that she was busy drawing when I arrived."

"Mrs Halliday spends a great deal of time at her drawing," said Miss Harper, with the air of one who hopes that her point will not be missed.

"And Mr Halliday?"

"It is not my place to pass comment."

Cat tired of this Kensingtonian discretion, and felt a strong impulse to shake the woman.

"Are you telling me that you think my sister has not bonded with this baby? That she doesn't like it? That she's depressed?"

The nurse made a movement of revulsion from this frankness, but fell into a more relaxed posture as Cat continued: "—because I know that already. I think she's in trouble. I thought so in hospital, and seeing her now, I know perfectly well that she is. I'm going to try and take her home with me for a while."

The professional demeanour of the nurse crumbled, and suddenly she became just a kind, smiling, confiding middle-aged woman who put down the folded nappies in a careless heap, moved impulsively to the cot and drew a finger lovingly across the baby's soft cheek. "Oh, she's a lovely baby. Really lovely. I've been so upset, I really didn't know what to do. Mr Halliday got quite annoyed when I – oh, dear."

"Mr Halliday is a bit of a bastard," said Cat conversationally. "I think that's probably part of the trouble. If she comes home with me for a while it might be better. Although I do live in a freezing tip of a farmhouse, and I am too busy to act as a full-time nanny so she'll have to pull her finger out."

"The main thing," said the woman, picking up the baby and handing her, without being asked, to her aunt, "is to get mum and baby together. To get baby properly loved. That's the main thing, isn't it? Not a pretty nursery."

"How did you ever end up as a high society nurse?" enquired Cat, nuzzling Maria Annunciata's warm floppiness.

"It's very good money," said Nurse Harper.

Lindy stood alone in her bright, primary-coloured kitchen, leaning on the smooth top of an island unit and puzzling over the calendar. The brief moment in the hospital when Caroline's baby lay in her arms, moulded to her breast and shoulder, seemed to have left her with a permanent burning imprint. The smell of newborn skin was in her nostrils and a raging unappeasable need tightened her chest until she felt she could hardly breathe. Lindy had known she wanted a baby, but not how much. Now she was counting days since her last period, not because she had reason to think herself pregnant but to find out how many more days it would be before she could allow herself the luxury of suspecting that it might be so.

The telephone rang. It was Mark.

"Cat rang me earlier, on her way in to London," he said. "She was wondering where Toby is, to see if she could drop in and tell him about Caroline's baby. She left some messages at his agent's and in Scotland, but he hasn't rung. She said to ask you if you'd been in touch with Topsy or anything, since you two seemed to be getting on well over Christmas."

"No," said Lindy, with a sharpness in her voice which made Mark, alone too at his desk, feel unhappy without knowing why. "I wouldn't know where to get hold of her."

Nor want to, she thought, replacing the phone with a snap. Topsy, stupid name anyway, was pregnant and not even *married*. Hadn't even had to *try*. No fellow-feeling there, definitely not.

When Cat came downstairs from her conversation with Nurse

Alison Harper, she was prepared to take a firm line, to bully her younger sister until she admitted that something was wrong and agreed to come and stay at Knoll Farm for a spell with the baby. She was prepared to combat any amount of bright pretence, social hauteur and plain reluctance: the sight of the baby, unloved in that sterile smart nursery, had stirred her profoundly. In the event, she did not have to make any effort. By the time she reached the little studio Caroline was crumpled over the drawing-board, sobbing her heart out.

"Oh Cat, it's Alan. He didn't ever love me, you know. I was just a trophy, I know it now. He says I'm frigid."

"Bastard," said Cat. "Oldest line in the book, the adulterer's standard excuse."

"No, but the thing is, I *am* frigid. I can't stand—"

"For God's sake, you've only just had a baby. Nobody fancies making love for weeks, months sometimes."

"I didn't much, before," said Caroline, sniffing. "Not all the long drawn out goings-on, anyway. Maybe I didn't love him, either."

"Oh God," said Cat, sitting down on the arm of a chair. This was a confidence too far. She was not up to it. Caroline turned to her, tearfully appealing.

"I know what you're going to say, I do know, Maria Annunciata needs her father and me, I have to do my duty. I will, honestly, when I can *bear* it, but every time I see her I just feel—"

She burst into a passion of tears. Cat looked steadily at her, with a mixture of weariness and compassion which was becoming all too familiar.

"Feel what?"

"Feel *raped*," burst out Caroline. "Oh Christ, it's all so disgusting!"

Cat sat looking sadly at her sister. Once, she had burned with envy of that fragile beauty, that quivering aesthetic sensibility. Even at eight years old Caroline had made her, at twenty, feel like a cart-horse, lumpish and jealous and coarse. Not any more. The tables were turned, and it was Caroline who patently could not cope with real life. Maybe, thought Cat, looking like a Renaissance statue and studying Renaissance paintings was a rather poor preparation for the actual experience of mating and motherhood. Maybe poor Caroline would have done better at both if she had specialized in Hieronymus Bosch and the postcard art of Donald McGill. Now she merely looked broken. Lucretia, raped.

But at least there was to be no trouble in transporting this marble Lucretia to the muddy world of Knoll Farm. All Cat had to do was say "Come and stay. Just while Alan's away so much, and Maria's so little. For a month or two, perhaps. It's not an imposition, you can give me the odd lift in for the shopping while I'm banned. Gervase would love it, too. He likes baby creatures."

Caroline gratefully agreed, too whelmed in her own emotion even to remember that part of the Christmas night conversation which concerned Gervase and babies, let alone notice the oddness and the generosity of her sister's making that particular remark.

They arranged for Caroline to be driven up at the weekend by the nurse, who would spend her last few days' employment settling the baby into a routine in the alien surroundings of Knoll Farm. Before she left, Cat asked: "You haven't heard from Toby?" And absently, Caroline said, "No . . . I suppose he might be abroad with one of those pop groups."

In the end, it was Mark who found the clue to Toby's silence. In his office, tapping his pen on the leather-framed blotter, he sat chilled for a moment by the unease which Lindy's sharp "No!" about Topsy had given him. The unease transferred itself to the question of Toby. His mercurial elder brother had always been more of a tormentor than a friend to slow, careful Mark. But all the same, Cat sounded worried and Cat was – in the schoolboy slang he inwardly used to himself – a good egg. Of all the family, only she was ever really nice to Lindy. And he, Mark, was efficient. He was better placed than any of his extended family (except perhaps Alan, who would never bother) to find things out. He lifted the phone and pressed the button for his secretary.

"*Mademoiselle from Arminteers*?" she said, when Mark had spoken. "Ooh, yes, I heard. It opened last night. About the war, with a lot of dancing. My friend was saying something about it being unlucky, like *Macbeth*. I'll ring the theatre. My friend knows people there."

Within ten minutes Mark knew that there had been a death, that the dead girl was blonde, young, christened Teresa but known universally as Topsy. When Cat got back to Knoll Farm (by train, long chilly wait at the station, slow local bus and two-mile walk) she found a message in Gervase's flowing italic handwriting telling her to ring Mark at home. The house was empty: Gervase was out at a Country Landowners' Association meeting, Martin was walking round the farm in the dusk checking gates and stock, and the racket from the bunkhouse suggested that Duane and the new boy Winston were comparing tastes in hard rock music. She stood by the telephone and dialled Mark's number, but when he had been speaking for a moment she sat down, suddenly, on the floor and put her head against the warm stove for support.

"Oh God, how awful. And Toby?"

"My secretary rang another friend of Topsy's, and she said he wouldn't go to the funeral but he'd been living in Topsy's flat. The phone's cut off. She gave me the address."

"I'd go there," said Cat helplessly, "only it takes half a day to get to the station at the moment, and I've got Caroline coming up with the baby for a bit because she's not feeling too good, and I'm up all hours working on some new rubbish for – for someone I work for. Oh, Mark – do you think . . . ?"

"I might not be the best person," said Mark. "You know me and Toby. Shall I tell Dad?"

"He's in Croatia," said Cat. "Caroline would be better, but she's not exactly up to much right now."

"I'll go," said Mark. "I'll come up to town early tomorrow. If there's any time Toby's bound to be in, it's early morning. Don't blame me if he bites my head off."

In the event, any of them could equally well have made the visit. The flat was empty, and the landlord, a thin seedy-looking man who inhabited the first floor alone, was volubly thankful to be rid of his unofficial tenant. "He left yesterday morning," he said, distractedly smoothing back his thinning hair as he led the visitor up the stairs to view the property. "I don't expect him back, no. He wasn't paying rent, and

Miss Tanner was two weeks behind when the tragedy happened. I wouldn't think of pursuing any claim against her family."

Mark paid, without hesitation, a hundred and fifty pounds for two weeks' outstanding rental on the bedsitter. Something about its shabbiness, exotically relieved with tattered theatre posters and a luminous orange bean-bag, touched him at a deep level he rarely acknowledged. Poor little Topsy. He did not, despite the landlord's continued hinting, offer any rent for the further fortnight that Toby had spent alone there.

That night, Mark reported back to Cat on what he had and had not found. The call was cut short by the wailing, bustling, nervously chattering arrival at Knoll Farm of Caroline, the baby, and the nurse.

Toby, meanwhile, was walking slowly through the sodium half-light of a London street, a chip-bag open in his hand. Sometimes he paused to look in a shop window, absent-mindedly pull a long greasy flopping strip of pale potato from the bag, and put it in his mouth.

As he came along the side-street near what was once Topsy's flat, he stopped in front of a grimy grocery where he and she had picked up random ingredients for their meals together. The owner was an affable Cypriot, nicknamed "Ataturk" by Topsy. On his counter was a collecting-box for change marked, in felt pen, with the words *"COMUNITY FUND; HELP TAKE LEAKAEUMIA KIDS TO DISNEYLAND PARIS"*. Toby approved of Disneylands, having served briefly as Wild West Goofy in Anaheim in 1972. He also approved of the scruffy unofficial look of the tin, and the spelling. He had often put his change in it.

The shop's front door was locked already, and the Venetian blinds half-closed. As he watched idly through the gaps, Toby saw Ataturk clearing and wiping the freezer tops and the counter. He had emptied the till into a large leather bag and now, with a practised and routine gesture, he picked up the tin, twisted off its base and without looking at its contents poured them into the same bag. He set the tin back neatly on the counter in its old place, drew the string of the leather bag tight and put it inside his padded nylon jacket before pulling down the burglar-alarm switch and vanishing through the side door.

Toby saw this from the pavement, and for the first time in the weeks since the accident he began to weep.

12

Duane and Winston, to the surprise of their probation officer Mr Willetts, would talk of nothing but the baby when they went for their March appointment. They saw him in his cramped office one after the other, their times being fixed so as not to inconvenience the Hartleys overmuch, given their transport problem. Mr Willetts privately thought it quite diabolical that the court should have disqualified Mrs Hartley, who was so careful and pleasant and had been so tolerant of generations of his troublesome young clients. That woman, he thought grimly, sacrificed her home life to a social project in a way that few wives, even farmers' wives, would consider. He burned with indignation when he thought of her driving ban and its circumstances; but the only way a probation officer could properly express such rebellious thoughts was by making it easy for her to bring the boys in for their appointments and, on occasion, offering to drive them back.

He had had many conversations, over the years, with youths who were working their time at Knoll Farm supported by Gervase and the charity. Some of his more advanced colleagues sniffed at the scheme, but Mr Willetts thought that by and large the experience – a good old-fashioned kind of social philanthropy – seemed to do young men good. Some of the town-bred boys in particular had softened into real enthusiasm for the animals and the land, chattering about it, boasting of their new dexterity with sheep-shears or piglets like the children they had never been allowed to be. Others, he admitted to himself, showed no noticeable improvement; but nonetheless they emerged with more muscle on them, and brighter eyes and less pasty faces as an effect of working long hours out of doors and eating proper food. One, to Gervase's visible horror and Mr Willetts' amusement, had become so handsome after six months' plain home cooking and fresh air that he now earned a respectable living out of modelling leisurewear for mail-order catalogues.

Only a very few, like Gary (now serving two years for dealing in prohibited substances), remained utterly unchanged and unimproved in any way by Knoll Farm, and as sullen as ever. It was a pity, a terrible pity, thought Mr Willetts, half-listening to Winston, that it had to be Gary who was filmed for that television report. Still, with luck the programme wouldn't think to follow him up a year later. If they did, it would reflect most unfairly on the record of Knoll Farm. The project, on balance, was a modest success.

Never before, though, had two successive clients spent their time in the probation officer's presence speaking exclusively of the beauty, cleverness, charm and rapid growth-rate of a baby. Duane became almost articulate in his praise of "Mary-Annie" as she now seemed to be called.

"She's really cute, yeah? She's got this little quiff of gold hair, and she's smiling all the time, big grins wiv no teeth, she's ace. Me and Winse, we do her bottle when Mrs Hartley lets us. Sometimes she gobs all over us, but we dun' mind. An' the shit is just *revolutionary*. Wicked. It's yeller, an' it actually smells OK."

Winston was more scientific in his approach. "It's ever so clever, how they learn things. Stick your tongue out, they stick theirs out back. First time Mary-Annie heard that cow mooin' out, she jumps out of her skin, all right? Next time the cow moos, she don't do nuffin. We worked out that she's learnt the score, OK? She knows it din't hurt last time, so it won't hurt this time. S'like a computer. An' she can grab things now. Just about, anyway. She can swipe."

Mr Willetts listened to this in wonderment, and later walked down with Winston to meet Cat and Caroline in the car park. The back of the little car was jammed with bags and boxes of food, and Caroline was sitting at the wheel reading the *Daily Mail*. Cat was a few yards away, studying a noticeboard about an imminent Midholt Choral Society rendering of Monteverdi's *Vespers* in the Corn Exchange. He joined her.

"This baby seems to have got the boys going," he said. "They wouldn't talk about anything else."

Cat laughed. "Yes, isn't it amazing? Martin started it, giving her a bottle on the first night while he ate his supper with the other hand. Seems he's got a little sister at home he helped bring up. The younger ones then decided on the spot that Real Men *can* play with babies, and that was it."

"It isn't too much strain, for you? Having your sister and the baby and the boys and Martin too? It's a very full house for a working lady."

She looked gratefully at the big, moon-faced, kind man she had known officially for so long.

"No," she said. "Thanks for asking. But really, the house hasn't run so well for years. I'm secretly enjoying the holiday from driving, you know. We all love Mary-Annie, she's the easiest baby there ever was, and I think it's doing my sister good to be in a busy house. She was very much on her own in London."

Mr Willetts glanced at Caroline, sitting passively at the wheel, still reading her newspaper although Duane and Winston had climbed in behind her and were laughing and pointing at something beyond the car park. She was wearing dark glasses in defiance of the season, and her smooth face had a shuttered, emotionless look.

"Good, good," he said vaguely. "Well, any problems, remember we're here. We appreciate you, you can make calls on us. And with Duane, perhaps, particularly, it might be wise . . ."

". . . not to rely on him as a babysitter," said Cat. "Oh, indeed. Still less Winston. Duane might panic, or stick a pin in her by accident, but he's restful. Winston would keep her awake all evening doing hand-eye co-ordination experiments. He thinks she's a computer game. Anyway, Martin babysits like mad, and he's practically a Norland nanny, he's so good. He's taught Winston all about zinc and castor-oil cream. We're in clover."

"And Mr Hartley, how's he taking the extended family?" said Mr Willetts.

"Oh, Gervase is a saint. We all know that," said Gervase's wife lightly, and took her leave.

When Robert Gratton came back from Croatia with much

achieved and much to think of, he found the answering machine in his London flat crowded with messages from his children. Mark's and Cat's ordered him to ring them as soon as he got back, and both asked, had he heard from Toby?

Caroline's said she was staying with Catherine and if Alan rang, please to let her know, because he was travelling a lot and calls could be difficult and her answerphone didn't seem to be working very well on the remote control.

Alan's, which followed, made no mention of Caroline or his baby or indeed of being abroad, but asked in smooth tones for more help on a business introduction Robert had mentioned at Christmas.

Then there was another one from Cat, rather peevish in tone, suggesting that she had assumed he would be back by now and *had* he heard from Toby? Robert spun the tape on, gabbling through several unconnected messages from political contacts, and reached the end of the tape. So clearly, Toby hadn't been in touch. No surprises there.

But when he listened to the rest of the tape later, after he had unpacked his neat dark leather case, he found that Toby had, in fact, rung. It was too brief to be noticed on fast forward, but between a reminder from the Chief Whip's secretary and an invitation from a charity a familiar voice, familiarly a little drunk, said: "Dad? I'm – oh, bugger it," and hung up.

Of course, Robert did not yet know about Topsy, *née* Teresa, and so it was the next day before he rang Cat and received his share of the family shock. She also, in few and spare words, filled him in on the continuing alienation of Caroline from her baby.

It stirred uncomfortable old memories in him, memories of the only bad times he ever had in his long love of Diana. As clearly as if she were in front of him he saw a fair and fragile mother, drifting around disconsolately in a big house in Washington, disliking a pale, pudgy baby Mark, looking for trouble. He felt a sudden rush of emotion for his elder daughter, a surge of pure thankfulness that she had not allowed Caroline to stay alone with the baby in that smart dull Kensington house with that smooth cold Alan.

"Can you come to lunch?" he said. "Westminster Old People's home, as ever?" Cat, slightly to his surprise, agreed with alacrity to meet him at the House of Lords. Things were easier at home, she explained, than they had been. Caroline seemed rather to enjoy driving people around, lost in her own world at the wheel, so there was no trouble about getting to the station. The household was working well, with Martin frying up American breakfasts for everybody and persuading Marianne to come up almost every weekend. Caroline, though silent and depressed, did her share of the cooking and seemed actually to prefer this to the company of her baby. Gary's mother was coming in two mornings a week for the heavy cleaning, glad of the money and the moral support now her son was in prison. Gervase had finished with lambing and was far less tired, and the two boys forever hovered helpfully around the baby. Suddenly, it was easy to get to London. She needed to fix a meeting with Eden anyway. So she would come to the House of Lords the next day at one o'clock.

"Would Caro like to come too, perhaps?" said Robert tentatively. "If there's someone to mind the baby?"

"I have no doubt she would. But she isn't coming, and don't tell her. She can come on her own another time. We've got things to discuss."

By the time Cat stood waiting for Robert under the low stone arches of the House of Lords' lobby, she had one thing more to talk about. Walking out to the car that morning ahead of Caroline, she had intercepted the postman in the lane to see if there were any late amendments from Eden on the spring staff magazine. There were, as she suspected, five bothersome pages of quibbles to read through on the train. But there was also a postcard from Toby.

Standing now near the security desk in the mellow light of the vaulted stone lobby, she pulled it out again. Her father was in sight, but deep in conversation with a thin-faced man in a blue suit. A lord of incredible antiquity shuffled past her, his old back bent, murmuring "Beg pardon, m'dear". His arms did not take to being raised above shoulder height, and he began to make lunging unsuccessful attempts to get his coat on the hook which bore his name. Like nursery-school, really, Cat thought. She stepped forward to help him, dropped the postcard as she did so, accepted his courtly snuffling thanks, and turned to find

Toby's card trapped beneath the tiptoe shoe of a stout peeress. When she retrieved it there was a clear pointed toeprint across the text, which annoyed her immoderately.

She looked for a moment at the picture of Dover harbour, then turned it over again and re-read it. When Lord Gratton extricated himself from the conversation of Lord Gilbrand (with whom, things being tight in the lobby, he shared a coat-peg) she was frowningly intent on the trampled slip of card.

"Lo, darling," said her father. "Sorry to keep you."

"No – it's fine," said his daughter distractedly. "I've been trying to make something out. Toby's writing."

"Oho!" said Robert with something like joviality. "So he's surfaced! Good, good!"

"Not quite," said Cat. "Come on, for God's sake let's go through, before I get trampled by any more of these dinosaurs." Irritably, she hunched her shoulders, jerking her head towards the latest group of elderly men and women arriving for a subsidized Palace of Westminster lunch. "I'm sorry, I know you all do good work and all that, but it gives me the creeps."

"Why, especially?" asked her father, amused. He led the way beneath the vaulting and turned left. "Not that it doesn't take me the same way, some days. But why does it get you?"

"Oh, because of the boys on the farm, I suppose, and how hopeless it is trying to do anything about the way their lives go," said Cat, looking with distaste at a particularly florid hatchment. "Because of Noreen in Hounslow all these years with the planes flying overhead, and Marianne earning peanuts in that psychiatric ward, and Dave having to crawl to some Omani foundation to get his research funded. Just *because*! This building is so fusty I want to turn a hose on it."

"Child of the sixties," said her father fondly. "It isn't turning a hose on things that makes them into new shapes. It's drip, drip, drip that does it. We drip and drip on Parliamentary bills, we improve them, and that improves things for all your Noreens and Garries."

"Oh, I don't too much care about Gary," said Cat, as they turned into the dining room. "You can turn a hose on him, anytime. Do you know his mother got pulled in on Boxing Day for questioning, on suspicion of knowing about his drug stash? Gervase was down at Midholt station with her half the day. She was in tears."

"He's a good man, Gervase," said Robert. "I have no idea how he got that way, given Artemis as a mother. Do *you* know, she spent all that walk to the Rector's going on about how homeless was only a trendy modern word for "feckless"? On Christmas Eve?"

"Gervase is still rebelling," said Cat. "The world probably owes Artemis a great debt. If it wasn't for her, he'd probably be an ordinary country gent with no imagination."

"What was his father like? Does he ever say?" asked Robert, interestedly.

"Oh, you know. Bless the squire and his relations, and help us keep our proper stations. All that. But look, Dad, I want to talk about Toby. And Caroline. But especially Toby."

She pushed the postcard across the table to him, and he put a pair of wire-rimmed glasses on his nose and frowned at it for a few moments.

"Hmm. Postmark Dover. Picture of Dover. That seems clear."

"It ties in," said Cat. "Mark rang his agent, Louis or whatever his name is, and apparently Toby turned up looking pretty dirty and a bit manic, and asked if there was any money for him. There was two hundred and fifty pounds due, so Louis advanced him that. And he picked up his passport."

"What was that doing there?"

"Apparently he leaves his passport at the agent's, and a few documents – birth certificate, all that stuff Mum made us each take over when we were twenty-one. Toby says he'd only lose them, so he leaves them with Louis."

"So Dover, and a passport," said Robert. "You reckon he's gone abroad?"

"I'd say so. But the thing is, Dad" – Cat's head went forward and her voice broke a little – "none of us have seen him or spoken to him since Topsy – God, that was awful."

Her father looked at her with melancholy understanding. Diana, he reflected, had seen this eldest child as hopelessly prosaic, but as a repressed, discreet diplomat himself, he had always known that behind her calm exterior Cat – like him – suffered from a vivid dramatic imagination. He had hoped she would be an artist or a writer; but maybe the deliberate repression of her romanticism was the reason for her success in writing glib, catchy copy.

Muffled now, her words confirmed his suspicion that she, more than any of them, had suffered some moments of pure horror in the days since she learned about Topsy. "Things falling on your head. I've always been terrified about that. Won't walk under scaffolding. Poor Tops."

"She couldn't have known a thing," said Robert comfortingly. "Not if it fell straight from the overhead grid. There'd be no sound, no rush of air even."

"I think you'd know. A second before. Eyes in the top of your head. You'd know."

There was a silence. The waiter brought them water and took the order. Cat began again: "Anyway, it's Toby I worry about now. I know he and Topsy weren't exactly conventional, but I think he was excited about the baby. He didn't just do his big announcement at Christmas to shock Artemis and annoy Mark."

"Although that was part of it," said Robert gently. "But yes, I know. I wish he'd rung you, or one of the family, when the accident happened."

He looked down at the postcard again, folded up his wire glasses, sighed, and pushed the card back towards his daughter.

"Well, he's an odd one. I remember Diana saying when he was six or seven, when we were on the way to France from Washington, that the reason Toby was so tiring was that you never knew how he would react. You'd be expecting him to be upset and he'd make a joke, and seem quite unconcerned. Like when that dreadful hamster died, in Lille. But at other times, when you thought he'd join in the fun he suddenly wouldn't. Just sit and stare as if he'd seen a ghost."

"I wish he'd rung. I wish he'd come to us," said Cat.

"Yes, but what would he have said, poor devil? He wouldn't have the vocabulary to express something like that. He was never much of what Lord Norwich calls a 'feelings-discusser or a shoulder-leaner-onner'. People like Toby don't start acting conventionally just because conventional tragedies happen to them."

As he delivered this insightful remark, lunch arrived: shepherd's pie for Robert, roast beef for his daughter. They began to eat the comforting nursery food in a gloomy, companionable silence. After a few moments Cat said: "Well, I think he's gone abroad. The postcard."

"It could mean that," agreed Toby's father. "We'll have to think about what he means in that last line. Come back to it. But the other thing. You said Caroline was in trouble?"

Cat had meant to tell him everything, in the hope that her father's concern would be explosively brought to bear on Alan, the son-in-law who admired him – or at least, hoped to trade on his peerage and his influence. She found herself, however, hesitating and qualifying everything. She seemed unable to describe Caroline's problem directly, as she would have to a woman. In these masculine, lordly surroundings, with elderly men of the Establishment tucking into steak-and-kidney pudding all around, it was peculiarly difficult to talk about something as painfully and intimately female as this particular depression and alienation. She stumbled, quite unlike herself, and accordingly became cross and terse.

"Oh, I suppose it's nothing. I daresay she'll be all right. She talks more to Gervase than to any of us. They play chess."

Robert put down his knife and fork and wiped his mouth. "I used to play chess with her in Venice. I taught her when she was five, and we played with the glass pieces Diana bought at Murano." He picked up his glass, and swirled the dregs of the red wine in it.

"What you're saying," he continued after a pause, "is that she doesn't seem to care about the baby."

"I wouldn't put it –" began Cat defensively. Spoken in the House of Lords, masculinity heavy on the air, his words sounded like a harsh condemnation of her sex. "It's sometimes very difficult for new mothers."

"Look," said Robert. "I _know_. I lived with it. Diana really couldn't be bothered with Mark for two years. In Washington. You may even remember that, if you cast your mind back."

Cat flinched. "I remember she cried a lot. And she was always cross. And we had Conchita to help."

"Conchita did all the mothering," said Robert. "It took me a year to realize that. When I tried to talk about you children, your mother always came up with Toby's latest misdeed, or how well you were doing at school. She hardly ever mentioned Mark. Called him 'the baby'. She used to say those words," he continued, after a pause, "rather accusingly. As if he was all my fault."

Cat stirred uneasily. Perhaps, in this new age, one was supposed to talk about these things even with one's own father. Devilishly difficult, it was. Especially cold sober, in the middle of the day. She wished she had arranged to meet him for a drink at his flat. She demurred: "Well, it might have seemed like that. But she had a lot to do. I'm sure she didn't really—"

"She had nothing whatsoever to do," said Robert. "Except cocktail parties in the evening, and spooning with that damn Hungarian count all afternoon."

Cat's embarrassment grew. She steered the conversation back to her own generation.

"It worries me that Caroline was so adamant about not feeding Mary-Annie herself," she began, wildly, although she had not meant to bring this detail up. Robert looked at her and gave a dry, mirthless bark of laughter.

"Diana wouldn't feed Mark. In that Swiss hospital, she took one look and said no. They gave her pills to dry it up. She told me on the phone, after my plane landed in Washington. She'd fed Toby for eleven months. Later on, she fed Caroline for six months."

"Did she feed me?" Cat asked unwillingly.

"Two months. Then she said you were so big you needed solids, you'd wipe her out with the amount you sucked."

Cat could stand this intimacy no longer. She looked at her watch. "Dad, I've got to fly. I've got a work meeting."

Robert, suddenly looking old and tired, reached out a hand and held her arm as she tried to stand up.

"Darling, I wouldn't bring any of this up if I didn't think it might be helpful. I want to know if I should talk to Caroline about all of it, whether it would help her."

"Why might it?"

"Because your mother and I were very happy for ten years, and then again, even happier really, for twenty-seven years.

But there were two years in between the good times which were pretty dreadful. If it had been today, we'd probably have divorced. But people didn't give up so easily, then. I was busy in Washington. I know I didn't do enough for Diana when she was off the rails. We talked about it all, years later. All I'm saying is that Caroline could well be having the same sort of interlude. A new baby, a husband who isn't around or isn't very sympathetic. That's enough to throw someone off the track for a bit. She's lucky to have Knoll Farm, instead of a big stuffy official residence and a Mexican girl."

"But it's different, she's only just married." Cat could not go on. A parallel between her mother's bad time and Caroline's could not be made; Diana had had, and fed, two babies already, and surely, *surely* a well-married woman could not suffer the kind of neurotic physical revulsions which Caroline, almost nightly now, expressed in tears to her sister over their final private tea-drinking session in the kitchen. She looked at her father and blushed. Come to think of it, after three children in seven years there had been a gap of another seven between Mark's birth and Caroline's. Oh God. Why were these things so hard to think about?

In her anxiety to get clear of all this, Cat had lied to her father about her appointment time. When she left the Palace of Westminster, she had an hour and a half to kill before going to Eden, and spent it in a flyblown sandwich bar off Piccadilly, watching skin form on a nasty cup of coffee and re-reading Toby's postcard.

"*Tell Caro best of luck to her and the baby,*" it said. Then in slightly less tidy handwriting: "*Can't seem to get comfortable. Best to go back and start again, I think. Toby.*"

What did he mean? She tried to think of Toby, to think like Toby; she conjured up his floppy dark hair, untidy over the collar and treacherously greying round the ears; his humorous, mobile mouth, his arched brows and occasional camp fluttering of the eyelashes to defuse a particularly devastating joke. Because of the uncomfortable talk over lunch, though, this mental Toby kept shrinking and being replaced in her mind's eye by other Tobies. There was the sixth-former, hair down to his shoulders, nonchalantly telling his parents the news that Radley did not want him back at any price but that he had organized a job with Diego at Long Beach. There was the schoolboy Toby who had crossed Europe with her on those rattling, whistling trains, bound for home in Venice; he had once got off at Basle for a dare, and been left on the platform, his white face looking up at her half-scared and half-triumphant in the moments before she pulled the communication cord and started a row with Swiss railways which it took all Robert's diplomacy to cool down ("Herr Hartley, we must insist, if these English children are not fit to travel unaccompanied at this age, you must make other arrangements"). There was Toby in Johannesburg, beaten up at school for telling his Afrikaner classmates that in America and France and "proper countries" black people were considered just as good as white ones. Only Cat knew the reason for the beating-up, and had agreed with Toby that they would not tell their parents because it would only lead to their both being sent straight to English boarding-schools. To avoid this separation brother and sister had conspired to pretend that Toby's fight was precipitated by the usual annoying Toby behaviour. Diana and Robert had accepted this as only too likely.

Sitting at the chipped counter, fiddling with packets of sugar, Cat thought fondly of that Johannesburg Toby. It proved he did have principles, no matter how heavily disguised they might be. Then she thought of him with the nuns, in Lille: cherubic, reciting his nightly *Fable de la Fontaine* by heart, making up the bits he forgot with such panache that sometimes he was not caught out and deprived of his bread-and-chocolate at break-time. She remembered him in Washington, in his Yankee brat baseball hats, running wild and cheeking visiting senators during Diana's bad time; and then saw, as perfect as ever, the moment when she had held the little boy up to see the baby bears in Berne.

God, what a mixture of childhoods they had had, he and she together! What richness of scenery, what poverty of outside friendships, what a crazy claustrophobic bubble they had bounced around the world in, never belonging anywhere! What had he said at Christmas dinner? Something about diplobrats never growing up at all.

Well, she had grown up. If there was one thing her early

motherhood and the poor days in Hounslow had done it was to make Cat renounce childish things. Gervase was grown up, too; that was what she first liked about him when they met. He had lived his childhood, said a polite goodbye to it, put aside play and self-indulgence and shouldered adult responsibilities with a will. She liked that. And Mark had at least covered his continuing childish sulkiness with a façade of dull mercantile respectability, the opposite of his brother's fey irresponsible enthusiasm.

Caroline hardly counted; her life had been different from theirs. Her first memories would be of Venice and she was in Los Angeles until she was eleven; but after that she had become a standard English home counties schoolgirl and then a schoolgirlish habituée of the genteelly English world of art galleries. Caroline was settled, rooted; she belonged clearly in a certain class and in certain very English settings. Not for her that enduring sense that word could come from Whitehall and change your life any day; that nothing would last beyond a three-year posting so you might as well not get too involved.

Cat, fiddling with a plastic spoon at the drab Formica café table, felt a spasm of irritation at her sister. What did she know, her and her day-school friends who spent seven, eight years together and could stay in touch now if they wanted? The effect of foreign postings and a cosmopolitan boarding-school was that the friends of Catherine's childhood and teenage years were scattered across two hemispheres: she had come in and out of their lives like a ghost, and nobody but Toby shared her memories.

Probably, she thought, that lonely fact had actually made her anxious to settle down. She was sometimes conscious of a queer, absurd exultation when somebody – Mr Willetts at the probation service, or Noreen's brother in Hounslow – made a careless remark that indicated that she and they "went back a long way together". She cherished every proof that she, Cat Hartley, had a history of her own now. A personal history, not dictated by the files at the Foreign Office.

This wool-gathering ended as she glanced down again at the postcard, which now bore a dribble of coffee from the unwiped counter as well as the peeress's footprint. *Can't seem to get comfortable. Best to go back and start again.*

But where? Cat drank the cold coffee in front of her, grimaced, and set off reluctantly through the darkening afternoon to where, in some neon-lit committee room, the Eden Corporate Outsourcing Motivation Working Party awaited her.

13

"Where?" asked Caroline. "Start again where? What does he mean?" She had been unusually animated since Cat showed her the postcard, with pink spots in her cheeks and a shine in her eyes. "It's such an extraordinary way to express it."

Gervase, Caroline and Catherine were sitting round the kitchen table after supper. The chessboard was out, but for once neither Gervase nor Caroline showed much interest. Cat had work to do upstairs, readjusting her newsletter to be, as the chief nuisance at Eden HQ put it, more "dynamically motivational". Shorter sentences and more buzz words should do the trick, Cat reflected. Perhaps "buzz" itself would be a good buzz word. But she could not bring herself to go up to the study and wrestle with that just now. Caroline and Gervase were anxious to talk. They had both, slightly to her surprise, been fired by Toby's cryptic message into curiosity, compassion and a lust for activity.

"I think he must need help," said Gervase, after first reading it. "You were quite right to talk it over with your father. Where do you think he means when he says 'go back'?"

Caroline chimed in, equally curious. "Do you think he means back to Scotland?" she said. "He met Topsy there, didn't he? When she was up with some Fringe show he wrote, three or four years back?"

"I think so. It was a punk tartan leg-show. KILT WITH KIND-NESS, or something. But that wouldn't explain Dover, would it?" said Cat. "Even Toby wouldn't go to Glasgow via Dover."

Caroline giggled. "He might."

"It's funny," said Gervase. "Here we all are, really rather

worried about the poor sod, and we keep ending up with these surreal Toby jokes."

"It's what he's always been most at home with," said Caroline. But her eye fell on the card, and *Can't seem to get comfortable*. "Poor Toby," she said softly. "It's as if he's never done grief. Doesn't know how to handle it." Cat looked at her sister in surprise. It was the first time she had heard her express pity for somebody else ever since her tearful collapse that night in Kensington.

"How was Toby," asked Gervase awkwardly, "when your mother died?"

Cat frowned, and shrugged. "OK. Fine. Came to the funeral, stayed over with Dad, stayed sober. Didn't say much. He was going around with that group that did his 'Jack and Jill' record, being a publicist I think. Or a roadie, or something. To be honest, I never talked to him about it. You know funerals. All busy and dutiful."

Caroline had risen from the table, and was rinsing the coffee mugs in the sink. She set them to drain and was gone without a word. Gervase looked alarmed. He arched his eyebrows at his wife questioningly.

"*She* was off work for nine months," said Cat quietly. "Remember? You probably don't. We were very busy, we had the bunkhouse full, five boys, everything running full tilt. But Caroline was so devastated when Mum died that she gave up her flat and went to live with Dad in the cottage for nearly a year."

"Oh God," said Gervase. "I put my foot in it just now."

"No," said Cat. "Mark and Dad used to go around carefully not mentioning Mum at Christmas or anything, but I think we ought to. She's always needed chivvying out of her Victorian vapours. She only went back to work in the gallery because Dad got fed up with having her trail around like a pre-Raphaelite maiden, so he sold the cottage and got himself the little flat in Westminster."

Gervase looked unhappy. "Still, poor girl," he said. "It's all a lot to take. Do you know –" his fine features crinkled in concern – "I don't think Alan's really behaving very well. I even wonder if he's the right chap for her."

"Bravo! Give that man a coconut," said Cat rudely, getting up. "I'd better do some work before bed. It's funny, every time today I talk about Toby, in about three seconds flat the subject gets round to dear Caroline's troubles."

She went upstairs, really very angry. Toby was alone somewhere, his lover and unborn baby dead, and still he kept becoming a joke, because Toby had always chosen to be a joke. Whereas Caroline, about whom nobody would dream of joking, had a choice of homes, a beautiful baby she ignored and a rich handsome husband who – Cat disloyally let herself think – she had driven away with her stagey, posed aesthetic coldness. Yet both Robert and Gervase dismissed Toby and fell over themselves to pity and understand Caroline.

"Pah!" said Cat savagely, punching the button on her old word processor. "What I have got, old friend Amstrad, is compassion fatigue. I was a nice person, and no longer am so."

Half an hour later, from along the corridor below her room came a thin, high infant wail. Cat hesitated, then resignedly got up from her desk and went to investigate. Last time she had left Caroline to attend alone to one of the mercifully rare night alarums from the baby, she had followed her into the little bedroom ten minutes later because the screaming did not stop. She found her sister standing over the cot, graceful as an angel in her pure white nightgown and a cashmere shawl, tearfully pleading: "Do be quiet, it's night-time, honestly." Caroline had neither picked up the child nor so much as smoothed the rucked, sweaty sheet and blanket.

Cat had picked up the baby without a word, cuddled her to her tatty flannelette nightshirt and dried the tears. Caroline, also without a word, had vanished back to bed. Something, a sort of horror mingled with a feminine solidarity and reluctant pity, prevented the older sister from telling Gervase about this. But ever since, she had gone to Mary-Annie at night herself.

Cat had no idea how it would all resolve itself. This time the baby, as it happened, only wanted brief assistance to deliver a massive burp. Cat laid her down, kissed the top of the downy head and slipped out of the room. At the end of the corridor the shadowy figure of Gervase was saying goodnight, solicitously, through a doorway to someone who must be Caroline.

Toby walked along the streets of the small, exhausted town,

in the general direction of the Western Docks. His old habit of glancing into shop windows yielded little excitement here in Dover. There was a chip shop, a tired looking wool and haberdashery shop, then two charity shops, another reeking chippie and a heavily barred window behind which radios and cassette machines lay, their casings bleached by too long an unsold exposure to the daylight. Sleet was falling, but he paid little attention to it. He was thinking about death.

He had known deaths in his forty-three years: who could escape it? He faintly remembered a grandfather, seldom seen but mourned at home in an official, embarrassedly British way. News had come to Lille of that death when he was seven, and his mother had taken the three of them to light a candle in the church of Saint-Maurice. "I know it's papist, darling," he had heard her say to his father, "but we expatriate Prods just don't have the rituals available, do we? What do you suppose the Chaplain would recommend? That we drink a glass of sherry in Pa's memory?" Toby had liked lighting the candle and had behaved surprisingly well, hardly needing Cat's restraining hand on his shoulder as they knelt in the side chapel afterwards. Two years later, walking home one evening from the convent, on the corner of the Grand'Place he and Cat had seen a tight crowd and a pair of legs sticking out sideways on the pavement in their midst. The gathering was under a big neon sign of a humped, running ferret which always fascinated him, an advertisement for something called *Le Furet du Nord*. It was Toby who remembered the bang they had heard a moment earlier and tugged Cat's arm.

"Hey, someone's been shot. I bet it's an Algerian." It was a time of Algerian terrorism; Cat's judo lesson with Sylvie and her brother Chrétien was often cancelled because M. Derain was off on a *"cours de déplastiquage"*, learning to defuse the new plastic bombs.

Toby was right. It was an Algerian, a suspect bomber, shot dead moments before by the police. Cat had hurried him past, but the dead feet stayed in his mind. Not unpleasantly: excitingly. Like something in a film.

He walked on. Death as excitement, what a joke. Who could ever have thought that? He, lyricist of the punk anthem "Jack and Jill they kill for thrill", saw now with awful and private clarity that there was nothing exciting at all about it. Life was exciting. Death just stopped you dead. The triteness of the thought made him suddenly laugh aloud, and the sound of his own laugh frightened him. He would be shouting philosophical thoughts at passers-by next, like a bag lady.

There had been other deaths. Later, half a world away, Miguel had died. His father Diego knew that Miguel and Toby were beach friends. In fact Toby – a dark, elfin-faced boy who could in a dim light pass for the paler sort of Mexican – had briefly lent Miguel his British passport when the cops came, and thus averted his deportation. That was why Diego and his brother Pablo gave Toby the job on the burger stand when Miguel died of the sickness. But that death had not shaken him much, either. At nineteen, friends come and go for a dozen different reasons, especially when you have never lived anywhere for more than three years in your whole life. Miguel had, simply, moved on. Toby realized with a shock that he had always half expected to meet the young Mexican again. Probably in a bar in Glasgow. Most of his old semi-detached friends seemed to turn up there eventually: it was that kind of city. A hot city, a resurrection city. Like Los Angeles.

Death, death. It squatted on him now, an idea not so much horrifying as plain boring. Cat, he knew, believed in something afterwards, in some sort of ultimate justice, an eventual sorting out and levelling up of old deserts and old scores. His mother, Diana, had quite explicitly believed in heaven. "Otherwise, why would there be all those paintings of it?" she had said flippantly in the nursing home. When she died, he had not managed to be as upset as he knew he ought to be; it seemed so obvious that she had merely moved on to some exquisitely civilized otherwordly setting, probably a version of the Accademia or the Louvre only with softer chairs.

But as for himself, he was not sure what he believed or where Topsy was now. *Whether* Topsy was, now.

Toby found he had stopped again, and that tears were springing to his eyes. He had no words for this, no words for grief. Grief was not something in which he had ever had any interest. Girlfriends had frequently and strongly told him he was an "emotional illiterate": especially when he burst out laughing at intimate or highly-charged moments in their relationship. Many had left him precisely because of this tendency. The joy of being with Topsy was that there never had been a wrong moment to laugh. She always joined in on a high, glad shriek of merriment.

Toby walked on towards the docks, and the tears on his face mingled with the falling melting sleet. He had obviously missed out learning something, years ago. Whatever thing it was that made other people able to deal with these disasters. That was why he couldn't get comfortable. Best to go back, and start again.

Alan arrived at Knoll Farm one Saturday morning unannounced, his big Saab crunching heavily on the shingle drive. He knocked perfunctorily on the kitchen door and walked in to find a black youth with dreadlocks and scruffy farm clothes playing with a blinking baby in a bouncing chair, which was set in the middle of the large scrubbed wooden table. The boy glanced at him, said, "Hi, man," and continued swinging a red-painted cotton reel on a string just within the baby's reach. "Go on – swipe – yesss!" he crowed. "An' again – backhander – ah, shame!"

"Is Mrs Halliday in?" asked Alan, irritably. This baby was presumably his daughter, although he had only seen her in her first fortnight of life, and mainly asleep.

"Mrs Hartley? Nah. She's gone to Midmarsham, wiv Martin, in the Landy," said the boy, turning his attention back to the baby.

"Not Mrs Hartley. My wife. Mrs Halliday. The mother –" said Alan pointedly, "I presume, of this baby."

"Oh, *Caroline*. Why din't you say?" said the boy. "She's in bed, I s'pose. Mrs H. got the baby up, and I did her breakfast. She's on a bit of mushed-up stuff now," he added informatively, "only we don't give her eggs because of allergies and bacon's too salty and sausages got additives. So at breakfast she has just milk and a bit of Farex when she's on a growth spurt."

Alan did not reply, but walked through the kitchen, down the stone floor of the corridor and up the back stairs towards the guest bedroom he had occupied at Christmas. Here he found Caroline, apparently asleep. She lay sprawled on her back right across the sagging double bed, her golden hair fanned around her tranquil face, one hand theatrically resting on her breast, and the white broderie of her nightdress parting to reveal a chaste, pale triangle of soft skin at her neck.

He sat down on the bed, heavily. Caroline stirred and rolled her head away from him. Fury filled him, sour and black and sudden. "For Christ's SAKE!" he shouted. "Wake up!"

Caroline hunched, stretched, rolled her head back towards him and opened her eyes. He saw them widen in shock. Heart pounding, she hefted herself up on one elbow and said: "Wha – what 'you doing here? I didn't know—"

"I came to ask you what the hell you're playing at. Seven weeks, you've been here. Do you want a divorce, or what? Your father's been on the phone, it's bloody embarrassing. We're just both making ourselves look silly."

"How you can sit there, after staying away all this time," exploded Caroline, drawing the neck of her nightdress closed, "and coolly ask me if" – she mimicked him "'I want a divorce or what' – you are a shit!"

He glared at her, infuriated by her bleating. "Well, do you?"

"Yes. Since you ask. It hasn't been much of a marriage, has it?"

"Whose fault is that?"

"Yours," said Caroline, promptly. "You only wanted me as a wife for show. Nice blonde art gallery girl, Lord's daughter, suitable for Kensington-stroke-Knightsbridge man on the make. I'm surprised you didn't just order a wife from Harvey Nicks."

"I might as well have," said Alan scornfully. "It always was rather like fucking a shop-window dummy."

"Ohhh!" Caroline fell back on the pillow, tears springing to her eyes. Over the weeks of vague indulged depression, of Gervase's courtly sensitivity and the boys' guileless enthusiasm, she had forgotten how abrasive life with Alan used to be. "I suppose you never thought it was your fault?"

"Couldn't be," said Alan, smugly. "Never had any complaints from anyone else. Still don't have. You've got the problem, sweetie, not me."

"I've had your baby," said Caroline, sniffing.

"Oh yeah. I like your new nanny, by the way," he said sarcastically. "Does he let my daughter chew his greasy dreadlocks?"

"Maria Annunciata is perfectly well looked after," said Caroline.

Alan snorted. "Well, I wouldn't know. Bloody typical of you not even to be able to have a boy."

"I want a divorce!" screamed Caroline. "And you'll bloody well maintain me, and her, and keep away from us!"

"That," said Alan coldly, "will be no hardship."

As he passed back through the kitchen, Winston was solemnly peering at the baby over the top of a tin baking tray which he raised and lowered in irregular rhythms. "Peek-a-*boo*!" he said, whereupon Mary-Annie's face broke into a broad, gummy grin and her voice into a crowing explosive laugh. Alan saw only the mess of Farex still hardening on the table, the unwashed breakfast mugs, the wooden stand of socks and underwear airing in front of the range, the cobwebs in the corner, and the scruffy youth making idiot noises at the dribbling infant. He walked past it all and out into the drive. Near his car there was a cloud of snowdrops on the verge and a few crocuses, edges of vivid colour just unfolding from the pale green shoots. He did not see those either, but accelerated his car sharply and drove it hard towards the motorway, London, and his lawyer.

14

As the grass began to grow, the work of the farm changed. The grazing animals could at last be turned out to fend for themselves, instead of having their food brought to them in heavy bales and buckets. On the other hand, the laborious spring ploughing demanded Gervase's daily attention, and with Martin he walked some ten miles a day up and down the furrows behind the big horses. The two boys, Duane and Winston, could not yet be trusted with a plough except during their two hours' individual daily lesson with Gervase; otherwise they spent the lengthening days mucking out the deep winter litter of the yards with the help of the oldest and most forgiving carthorse. Every two or three days they would break one of the shafts of the cart, and have to stop and mend it. Winston, at least, had been taught carpentry remarkably well at school, so Gervase could leave him to it. All four men came in groaning at five o'clock in dire need of their tea and rest. Martin, whose spirits were high and level, taught them to eat peanut-butter-and-jam sandwiches, and to call the jam jello.

At the beginning of April, Gervase confidently decided there would be no more frost, and made decisions accordingly. After each day's work the three horses were turned out not into the dull yard, but to gallop and roll in soft freedom on the growing grass. The pigs were cleared from the orchard they had reduced to a muddy swamp, and allowed to dig over the turnip and mangel fields for forgotten roots. One of Gervase's small sentimentalities was that he would never ring his pigs' noses to deprive them of the pleasure of digging. The sheep were transferred, in the usual woolly wave of irrational panic, from the barnyard to the hill field.

Cat would take a half-hour break to walk up there in the morning and visit the flock with Mary-Annie on her hip. Every year since her arrival at the farm with her own young children, she had been fascinated by the progress of the lambs. Newborn, they were unsteady and dependent, and stayed close to the mother ewe. Within a week or so, they began to play, jumping on top of the hay in the feeding-rings, butting one another, balancing upon their mothers' placid backs on their sharp little hooves like children on a pile of wobbling foam cushions, legs tense with the effort to stay upright.

Liberated into the field a few weeks later, they would race around in gangs, leaping one another and playing random games which looked deceptively complex. Dave and Marianne used to throw a football in amongst them and watch the group of lambs surge to and fro, knocking it, looking as if they had goals to score. Cat watched the mothers: generally, one or two ewes stayed near the lambs and the others congregated at the far end to graze peacefully in company, ignoring their progeny except when they sauntered back one by one to suckle. "A sure sign," the eighteen-year-old Dave had said when he was considering teaching as a profession, "that school is, in fact, a wholly natural institution."

Then, every year, there suddenly came a day when the lambs stopped frisking. It was as if, Cat thought, the lambs each in turn woke up one morning and said, "Hell, I'm a sheep." What triggered the change she did not know: perhaps it was increasing body weight and the need to feed longer, perhaps the heaviness of a growing fleece. At any rate, when this moment came the young sheep would no longer waste valuable energy in play, nor get stuck in ditches and tangled in wire. Instead they dropped their heads dutifully, grazed, and put on flesh as the farmer would wish.

Their lives, henceforth, would be ruled not by whimsicality or spontaneous surges of life force but by the usual dull ovine exigencies of hunger, panic, flock solidarity, and flight. This regime of dull or frightening imperatives would be, at least for rams and ewes, leavened occasionally by sex; but there was nothing remotely frolicsome about that either. Cat had once been vastly amused by an article entitled "Homosexuality in Farm

Animals: some findings", which she had chanced upon in one of Gervase's more arcane magazines of alternative agriculture. The American researcher opined that there were probably a great many lesbian sheep: but that it proved difficult to gauge because when a ewe is willing for sex, her behaviour is to stand stock-still so as to be available for the ram. "So there could," Cat concluded to Gervase at the time, "be a whole field full of ewes standing stock-still, lusting after one another and doing nothing about it. How sad."

Gervase had been passingly amused by the thought – this was back in the days before the extra land was sold, when things amused him rather more often than they did now. But Cat had remembered it, enough to giggle to herself whenever she passed a field of torpid, stock-still summer ewes. Toby had liked the joke when she proffered it; Mark seemed slightly shocked. For some reason she had never felt like telling it to Caroline.

This year, Gervase's lambing had begun so early that several of the first lambs had already graduated to being mere sheep. A few, however, were still young and light, and frisked close to Cat when she came into the field, unafraid and curious, thrusting their white noses against her leg. On one such morning, she knelt upright and set the baby on the grass, supporting its back against her thighs: the lambs came closer, and allowed their ears to be assailed by the small fat fists. Cat knelt there for a while, enjoying the sight of this instinctive baby-to-baby communication and warding off the bigger lambs from butting the child. Hearing a sound by the gate she turned, and found Gervase looking down at her.

"Hi. Look – new stockperson."

He smiled, and stooped to pick up the baby with a practised movement. Maria Annunciata grasped his nose and ear and blinked approvingly as he settled her on his arm. It was a warm day: his shirt was rolled up, and the baby's bare fat leg lay against his brown, scarred arm. His face, streaked with oil from the seed drill he had been setting up in the yard, had more colour and animation than usual. Cat looked at him with a love which was mixed with a little too much pity. The sight of Gervase and the baby always filled her with warring emotions.

He should have had one; poor Gervase. He should have let her have one artificially: bloody Gervase.

Her own feelings about the sanctity of natural fatherhood, never as deep as she loyally pretended, had undergone a good deal of change since the outburst of Christmas night. Having Mary-Annie about the house, chuckling and grabbing her toes and beaming toothlessly and falling asleep in positions of comical abandon, had altered all of them to a startling degree. Winston was talking of going to the Midholt FE college to get some GCSEs and study child psychology; Duane seemed to have put on twenty points of IQ in the past month. Martin's repertoire of American hushabye songs was a constant source of general amusement.

Gervase was less effusive about the baby, but took more than his share of her care with ease and grace. He looked younger, and laughed more. Cat herself could bear her work far better now that she could turn gratefully from writing glib management bulletins to the solid benevolent reality of the baby. She no longer saw any attraction in those isolated nights in the London hotel, and only went up by the day, every two or three weeks. Home was where Mary-Annie spent much of the day propped up near her desk, or rolling on a rug, stretching out for rattles and garish plastic squeakers with small, delighted gurgles.

As for the absence of the real father – since his early morning visit to Caroline Alan had sent one cold letter, confirming his wish for a divorce – the loss of him bothered nobody, least of all the baby. The blithe easiness of Mary-Annie's temperament amazed Cat, who remembered the chaos of her own first months with the twins. Indeed in private thought, she had admitted to herself that her passionate Christmas Eve speech in defence of biological fatherhood owed less to rational thought than to her own long-buried resentment of those abandoned days. Tim had left, and there was no man to cheer her and the babies up, only a tearful, staunch but shocked Noreen. Now history had repeated itself and Alan had left; but things were very different. He was replaced by a houseful of men, each more delightedly appreciative than the next, and the baby was thriving on it. Perhaps biological fatherhood was not, after all, so important.

The only cloud over this blessed baby's life, thought her aunt, was that of all the household Caroline was least interested in the child she still formally referred to as Maria Annunciata. She drove her to the local clinic, recorded her weight on the chart provided, and made polite bland conversation when the health visitor called. Beyond that she preferred to spend her day reading, driving around, shopping, helping round the house or drawing at the board she had set up in the guest room. Since the night when Cat had tacitly taken over control by picking up the baby, she had become acutely sensitive to the fact which nobody else in the besotted household had noticed: that Caroline avoided touching Mary-Annie at all.

One evening the sisters had gone together to a free concert by the Midholt Choral Society, where a new arrangement of the medieval carol "I sing of a maiden that is makeles" had been performed. Cat tended to doze in concerts, her mind floating free, solving problems on its own. When the choir sang with sudden a capella clarity the words:

> Maiden and moder
> Was neer none but she
> Wel mote such a lady
> Goddes moder be

Cat had jumped, physically jerked, in her seat and turned to the quiet rapt beautiful face beside her. Maiden and mother. Caroline, she suddenly thought, was virgin. This business of not touching the baby's skin, the revulsion she had unguardedly expressed at the birth, was something deeper than mere depression. It was unnervingly odd. *Maiden and mother*. Much could be forgiven a woman whose husband was brutally, insouciantly unfaithful and rejected her so cavalierly at such a time in her life. But all the same, Alan was not the whole explanation. If Caroline had picked the baby up and shaken it, screamed at it, then collapsed in sobbing hugs of remorse Cat could have understood. In all her years of involvement with Gervase's disturbed youths and their womenfolk, she had met across her own kitchen table plenty of stressed mothers. Remembering the worst days in Hounslow, she had been able to sympathize unaffectedly with their mixed feelings about their children.

But this was new and unnatural. Dangerous, even. Caroline should somehow be helped. Often Cat had thought to tackle her on the subject; always her nerve had failed her. A sister was not a good cause, or a client, or a case. And apart from anything else, if they were to quarrel, Caroline might leave and take the baby with her and all this strange new contentment in the farmstead would be gone.

Now, up in the quiet sheep meadow, Gervase finished nuzzling and talking nonsense to the baby and handed her back to his wife as she stood up.

"I was down there loading the pigs," he began. "You know, Sally's litter. They're off, I'm afraid."

He always disliked sending young pigs to the butcher; but these were five months old, and ready. "I kept back one sow, lovely girl, and one pig who might make a boar for Fred Ainsly at Midmarsham."

"Those were the piglets who ran over the Christmas tablecloth," said Cat. "Remember?"

"When Toby and Topsy did their ritual dance? I missed that. I was up the farm."

"I wish we knew where Toby was," said Cat. "I'm still not easy about it." It was the first time in weeks that she had mentioned her brother; Alan's swoop on his wife had taken their attention from the earlier drama. Mark had written to Duncan care of the pub in Glasgow, and received a phone call saying that there was no sign of Toby, but that just after Christmas he had rung up about some clothes and mentioned that he was "shacked up and having a baby". His agent Louis had heard no more since the taking of the passport. Cat thought about him a good deal, but in public the subject had somehow lapsed.

"That's what I came up to talk about," said Gervase, surprisingly. "That and Mary-Annie. It was while I was loading the pigs, Caroline came out to help—"

"She *what*?" Cat was startled. Caroline had never been near the farmyard or any of the animals except to pat a horse cautiously in passing, or admire one of the cleaner-looking lambs.

"Well, she came out just as Martin and I were getting them up the ramp, and I gave her a pig-board to hold."

"Wonders never cease," said Cat. "But what's that got to do with Toby? Or Mary-Annie?"

"Well, I was loading those pigs," said Gervase. "And remembering when they were born, and this year's lambing, and Caroline expecting Mary-Annie. And thinking about young creatures growing up, and – and everything. And it came to me. It's obvious."

"What?" said Cat, although a fluttering, sinking sensation in her chest gave her reason to think that she knew.

"Alan's gone. Caroline's got a lot to sort out, and she isn't well in herself. Alan's put the Kensington house on the market. Suppose Mary-Annie and she just – stayed on here? As their base?"

"With the emphasis on Mary-Annie?"

"Well, yes. Actually, that's what Caroline was really coming out to say. She wants to go to Los Angeles."

Cat moved the baby onto her other arm, and began to walk across the damp grass, towards the gate. Gervase walked with her.

"My sister," said Cat, "wants to go to Los Angeles? Leaving her baby with us. With *me*. Just like that."

"With us. All of us. She's only going for a week or two. Initially, anyway. There's some Gulbenkian Trust museum conference, and she's got a friend out there who says there could be restoration jobs. The baby would be better off here. Gary's Mum could help. Martin wants to stay till harvest, so he could do the driving while she's away."

Cat was breathing rather heavily. Gervase stopped, reached out in a mute offer to help, and took the baby into his own arms again. Walking on with his long stride down the grassy headland, he continued, half to the baby: "We like having her, don't we? Don't we, beautiful?"

"Of course we do," said Cat at last. "But really, it'll get out of hand. The whole thing, it's weird, it's not right—"

Gervase stopped and turned, barring her way. His face was alight, boyish and pleading, altogether unlike himself. Or, at least, the self she had known for the last decade. So were his words:

"Cat, we made a mistake. I made it. I thought that if I couldn't have a child of my own, and there weren't any babies to adopt, it was more honest and dignified to put all that energy somewhere else. I decided very high-mindedly that I would put all the effort I would have given my own child into helping other people's lost kids. I thought the project and the farm and the charities would be enough."

He eased the baby up his shoulder and rubbed her back. "I thought it would be better to do something honest and useful than having a pretend baby by some pretend scientific method out of a test-tube."

"You're saying you were wrong?" said his wife, slowly.

"I'm saying that there's no such thing as a pretend baby. If the sperm had been from Jack the Ripper, or Robert Maxwell, the baby would have been just as glorious. This one, if you think about it," he kissed Mary-Annie's fat cheek, "is Alan Halliday's. And look at her."

"Yes, but she's not ours," said Cat. She felt dizzy and afraid, not least of her own emotions.

"No," said Gervase. "But she could be." He turned away and began walking down the hill, so fast that Cat, after a moment's astonished paralysis, had to run stumblingly to catch him.

"No!" she said. "We can't adopt a baby! She's Caroline's! Caroline's got to take responsibility! It really is time she thought of somebody other than herself!"

"Oh, she has," said Gervase, slowing down a little as they came within earshot of the yard where Winston and Duane were forking smelly straw into a cart. "That's the point. That's the other thing I was going to tell you. She's also going to Los Angeles because she's convinced that Toby's there."

Just as Gervase reached the bottom of the hill, there was a cry of indignation and alarm. Another shaft had broken on the cart, and Duane was blaming Winston. The conversation between husband and wife ended abruptly as Gervase intervened to calm the two boys and the horse. Cat took Mary-Annie back indoors for her nap and returned to her desk. Here, putting aside shock and confusion, she worked steadily at the text of an Eden Welcome pamphlet designed for the induction of young hotel staff. It was to be built, at the Personnel Director's personal insistence, around the buzz phrase: "The Eden Smile".

The Eden Smile tells Eden customers that Eden hotels try hard to be home, she wrote glumly. *Eden people are proud of it: and that pride translates into warmth, consideration, and pro-active efficiency on the customer's behalf.*

She pushed her old kitchen chair back, stretched her arms out as if crucified, and stared critically at the screen. "Translates" would never do for them. Too literary. It would have to go. Pride "turns into" warmth? Or "from that pride springs a warmth", etc?

That might do. On the other hand, the phrase "pro-active efficiency" repelled her so much that she had to avert her eyes from it; but it was the Personnel Director's latest buzz, and must be included. And the pamphlet itself was an extra, paying an extra £500 over and above her retainer. She had insisted on this, in an unwonted burst of commercial hawkishness a few days earlier. Abandoning her normal policy of obliging subservience to paymasters, she had cut up rough, made demands, refused to come in for a meeting and delivered her financial ultimatum blithely, by telephone.

Surprisingly, they had met her every demand without a murmur. Probably she had been undervaluing her services to Eden for some time, as anxious dependent freelance contractors often do. It seemed to Cat, however, more as though she had been magically fortified for the battle by having Mary-Annie on her knee at the time, pulling at her cheeks and pushing small intrusive fingers up her nose. Somehow the baby's closeness had dispelled fear and self-deprecation, and made even dealing with Eden headquarters into a joke. A surreal, Toby-ish joke. She had almost said at one point: "I'm sorry, I can't take under five hundred pounds, I just have too many fingers up my nose." But the departmental sub-head would probably have thought this was another of the latest snappy management metaphors, like "running things up the flagpole" or "going belly-up". In no time, Eden departmental heads would have been snapping at one another: "Sorry, JB, scrub round the Stuttgart option – too many fingers up my nose." Toby would have liked that idea.

"So what the hell," said Cat aloud, squinting at the screen. She must think of the money and put up with the verbal infelicities of Eden HQ. She pushed back her dishevelled hair and typed on, turning out seamless credible glib rubbish, fortified by an infant niece's innocence and a vanished brother's wayward humour.

Later that day, downstairs in the kitchen, Caroline was scattering prawns lavishly onto a fish pie. She had offered to make a financial contribution to the housekeeping, but the Hartleys had refused it, saying that her willingness to drive the car was reward enough for her modest keep. Gervase had added that the small charity which supported the project could always do with help, if she felt like it.

Cat's housekeeping, however, tended of necessity towards the plain and plentiful. So it was not long before Caroline had taken over aspects of the bi-weekly food shopping and begun – with a personal financial subsidy which was never mentioned – to introduce her own tastes to the table. Baby corn and mangetout would appear as vegetables alongside the garden cabbage; stews would be laced with wine and puddings with Cointreau and double cream. Cat made fish pies once a week with coley and a great deal of potato: Caroline would volunteer to help, and sneakily insert beneath the potato a layer of fresh giant prawns, sometimes even langoustines, from Tesco's in Midholt. Martin and Gervase would eat the result with enthusiasm, Cat with mild irritation. Duane and Winston would say nothing but just leave their giant prawns on the side of the plate to be devoured later by the aloof, unsociable barn cat.

This particular fish pie, however, was a Caroline creation right from the start: cod, salmon, prawns, mussels, half a bottle of wine, and unseasonal fresh coriander, flown in to the chilly flatlands of Midholt from God knew where. Caroline hummed happily as she made it, for she was thinking of California. The note from her old tutor at the Courtauld, grudgingly forwarded by Alan, had seemed to open a shimmering arch to freedom. Suddenly she realized that from this damp uncertain English spring she could fly in less than a day to all the things she had left at eleven years old. To the dry heat, the long beaches, the palms and the Pacific; the gorgeously arrayed hotel doormen and the general sense of being lapped in relaxed Californian wealth.

She could go now – tomorrow – next week anyway – and be there again, as if the years had never happened. City of the Angels!

Those who knew her in London, through the galleries and the small world of fine-art restoration, would have been astonished to know the fervour with which the refined, gently-spoken, English rose they knew was thinking now of west coast America. They would have understood it better if Caroline had yearned for Prague, or Venice, or Paris. Indeed, she sometimes did: Venice had been the backdrop of her early childhood, and its alleys and prospects and gentle peeling grandeur still lay deep within her and at the root of her career. She had frequently been back there as an adult, first of all at twenty-one as part of her course at the Courtauld, when she gained gratifying kudos among her fellow students for having once properly lived in a flat near the Arsenale. Venice was a continuing part of her life. She had never been back to Los Angeles, or even thought of it.

Yet she thought now that it was LA she had been missing all the time. LA had been the route out of childhood into freedom and a growingly triumphant sense of self. In Venice she had been just the little English girl, obedient to the nuns, kindly treated but not seen as anything remarkable in that city of wonders. In California from the age of seven she had been an exotic: admired and fêted, indulged and listened to. "Hey, honey, sing us that Eye-talian song again! Did you really ride in a gondola?"

In LA it had always been sunny. It had been relaxing, too, to be the only child at home in term-time (except for Toby, somewhere in Long Beach with his illegal Mexican friends). Robert had been busy and important there, so in the house on Las Palmas Avenue she and Diana had become not mother and daughter but sisterly friends, conferring together in cosy girlishness as to how each might best enhance her beauty. There, drifting around the big stores, peering into the windows of Gucci and Cartier and Geary's, Caroline had learnt all kinds of things from Diana: how pale natural blondes should wear black – always with enough glowing skin bare at the neck – how to drape a scarf, how to pause for a heartbeat so that a man could open the door, and smile your thanks without speaking. Here she had absorbed the lesson that a woman, however good her body, looked far, far classier in a one-piece than flaunting it all in a bikini. Here she discovered the woman she would shortly become, a work of art and grace. The child Caroline found a serious joy in the prospect.

That elegant dream had faded with the family's return to the grey UK, and her own enrolment in the dispiritingly prosaic school in Sussex where she wore a hateful grey skirt and square blazer and was expected to play hockey. California became no more than a memory, an atmosphere, a remembered mood. It had never once occurred to her to go back to Los Angeles, any more than it would occur to her that she could be ten years old again. Indeed, it had almost come as a shock, opening the letter so clearly datelined by Marie-Claire, to realize that Los Angeles was still there.

Caroline pushed the pie into the oven, and began to clear up the pans and implements ready for supper. She would go to LA. It would not be self-indulgence; because of course, as she had said on impulse to Gervase, Toby was absolutely bound to have gone there too. In her suddenly exalted mood she knew absolutely that anybody who had once lived in golden California would flee back there if they were in trouble on the other side of the world. Europe was too close, too difficult, too intricate, too unforgiving. California was big and wide and easy. Toby must have gone out there, and got involved as he always did in the rock music business. Marie-Claire lived with a guitarist; she would help to find him, healing his grief by the ocean. Just as she, in that sunny shining place, would get over her own unhappiness. Banging the pots around in the sink, for the first time in months Caroline Halliday began to sing.

Cat came down, pale and stiff from an afternoon at her computer screen, carrying the baby chair and its yawning occupant to the kitchen for her six o'clock milk and stewed apple.

"You sound cheerful," she said. "Have you mixed up Yannie's milk, or shall I?"

Caroline looked down at her baby with hooded unreadable eyes. "Yannie, now?" she said, sombreness overtaking her again. "Yannie?"

"Sorry. It gets shorter and shorter, doesn't it? The boys keep calling her that. Winston says it stops Martin always thinking everybody's talking about Marianne."

"Martin and Marianne. They're quite an item, aren't they?" said Caroline lightly, turning away from the baby to stack some pots in the cupboard while Cat reached for the milk powder and the sterilizer. "She's been up here on nearly all her days off lately. What do you reckon?"

"Well," said Cat, spooning milk into the bottle, "I can tell you one highly significant thing. She's told him her real name."

"Gosh. You mean – er – Mooncloud, wasn't it?"

"Yup. And do you know what he told her in return?"

"No?"

"He told her he is actually christened – wait for it – Martinique. His parents conceived him on a Caribbean cruise."

Caroline straightened up and began to laugh, a carefree new Los Angeles laugh which gave Cat, despite her unease about the baby and the weeks of growing irritation with her sister, a rush of hope and gladness.

"We have to encourage this!" said Caroline. "*I, Mooncloud, take thee, Martinique, to be my lawful wedded husband . . .* wouldn't it be wonderful? Bring the church to a standstill."

"Sssh!" Cat heard the three young men stamping their feet on the scraper outside the kitchen door, and the sound of boots being noisily discarded. She picked up the baby chair and put it on the table. Duane was first in, skidding a little on the lino in his eagerness.

"C'n I give Yan her bottle, Mrs Hartley?"

"Yan, now," said the child's aunt, relinquishing the bottle. "Shorter and shorter." Caroline pretended not to hear this exchange, but concentrated on pulling the film off an expensive pack of imported baby courgettes.

There was no opportunity to talk alone to Caroline that night; she went to bed early, before Martin had gone back to join the boys in the bunkhouse. In any case, neither of the Hartleys wanted to start discussing her future or the baby's before they had talked in private. Gervase abandoned his Rural Housing Trust committee paperwork early to come up to bed when Cat did. She was sitting up against the pillows, waiting for him.

"Did I dream it," she began, "or did you make an extraordinary suggestion up in the field this morning?"

Gervase was silent, pulling off his slippers and socks with exaggerated care.

"Did you," his wife continued remorselessly, "try to suggest that we adopt Mary-Annie as our own?"

"I never said adopt," replied Gervase stiffly, kicking off his trousers and hunting around for the old towelling robe he wore to the bathroom. "I only thought, since it's going so well – blast, where's the belt?"

He struggled for a moment with an inside-out sleeve then resumed, not looking directly at his silent, waiting wife.

"Look, Cat, all through history people have been brought up by their uncles and aunts and grandmothers and cousins. Nineteenth-century novels are full of it. It happened in the war. In Africa nobody thinks twice about it. The Inuit do it. They've got fifteen different words for different degrees of adoption, apparently. All I'm saying is that Caroline needs some time to herself to get straight, and the baby's well off here, and, anyway . . ."

"Anyway?"

Gervase threw his trousers onto a chair and said rather rapidly, staring at the window whose curtain was never drawn. "I was looking at the pigs this morning, and remembering how fast they grew and how important every hour in that orchard had been to them, digging around, having a good life. I thought we ought to do everything we can *now*, for Mary-Annie. She's growing so fast, she's taking everything in. She needs concentrating on. And we—"

"We can do better for her than her own mother?"

"I wasn't going to say that," said Gervase, sharply. "I was going to say, we love her."

Cat was silent for a moment, then: "Yes, we do. I do too. She's the light of my life, if you must know. But it's wrong."

Gervase made a movement but she stilled him, raising her hand and speaking louder. "It won't always be like this. She'll grow up, need to go to school, need all that support. We're both going to be fifty before she's been at primary school a year. We're old farts, Gervase. We're empty-nesters. We're not even all that hot financially, and I don't see Alan paying us child support, do you? Or you taking it, for that matter? And we'll be tired and broke, and she'll be a teenager. It's all just impossible. Caroline is twelve years younger than me."

She paused for a moment, looked at his averted head, and said more softly: "But I do know what you're trying to say about the way she is with the baby. I do love Mary-Annie, and I fear for her. I want to talk about all that."

Gervase grunted, and headed for the bathroom. Cat lay with her hands behind her head, waiting for his return and his reply. When he reappeared, however, she spoke first.

"The thing is that I don't see Caroline staying like this for good. She's had a baby, for God's sake. I don't know what's wrong with her, but she's in some sort of trance. Shock over Alan, probably. Some day the penny's going to drop and she'll want to be a normal mother. Then if we'd virtually adopted Mary-Annie, where would that leave us?"

"Bereft," said Gervase simply. "But it might have been worth it. Specially for Mary-Annie." He pulled back the quilt on his side, and slid into bed beside her, not touching her.

"I didn't tell you," he continued, "but when she said she was going to LA, she had this idea of hiring a Norland nanny and installing her and the baby in this flat in London that Alan's buying her. There's plenty of money."

"Oh, no!" said Cat with real horror. She rolled onto one elbow, looking down at him with widened eyes. "She's just going to – to buy the baby a home and a mother, is she, and bugger off?"

Gervase began to protest, but fell silent. Caroline had in fact made it quite clear that she felt her duty to the baby would be adequately fulfilled by this chilly arrangement. This had shaken him, but for reasons as complicated as Cat's own previous reticence on the subject, he did not want to discuss it.

"Well, if so, she's got us over a barrel," said Cat. "I'm not sending that baby off to some bloody service flat with a hired nanny. We'll formally invite Miss Maria Annunciata Halliday to stay on here. For a bit. As a guest."

"Thank you." Gervase leaned across and kissed her on the temple. "That's as much as it's fair to ask. I am a very foolish fond old man, as King Lear would say. There's something about a baby that is very nourishing, after all these years of young offenders. Perhaps it's the way she doesn't have a probation officer."

"You had Dave and Marianne," said Cat. "They didn't have probation officers."

"No," said Gervase, turning out the light. "But they weren't mine."

Cat opened her mouth to say that this baby wasn't either, but closed it again. She lay awake for some time, listening to her husband's soft regular breathing.

Caroline flew to Los Angeles a week later, having successfully evaded all Cat's attempts to talk seriously to her by a cunning combination of nervous prattle, queenly silence, and sudden gushes of gratitude ("You are super, so kind to look after me like this, I don't deserve it"). As the ground fell away beneath the great aeroplane, she in turn seemed to cast the fetters of earth. It butted through clouds, which skimmed the windows in a confusion of racing mist; then rose triumphantly above them into clear sunshine. Caroline sat back in her club class seat and smiled. Here, up in the sky above the fluffy mattress of cloud, she was whole and pure and clean again, *Maria Assunta*, assumed into the heavens.

Gervase, who had driven her to the airport in Cat's old Renault, was back on the motorway by then and heading for Knoll Farm, her baby and his wife. He found Cat in her attic room, typing furiously with the baby rolling and stretching on a rug alongside. Without turning round, she picked up a postcard from her desk and passed it back over her shoulder to him. It was in Toby's untidy scrawl, bore the words "*Found the way. One way, anyway. Love to All*" and was postmarked Calais. He read it, studied the picture on the reverse, and put it back on the desk.

"What do you think?" he asked doubtfully of his wife's back.

"I think," she said, still typing, "that Dover to Calais is not the most obvious route to Los Angeles."

16

That week, Eden talked of another special commission at a special rate, but could not be diverted from demanding a face-to-face "brainstorming" meeting. Mrs Bird, Gary's mother, volunteered to spend the day at the house so that Cat could go to London without, as she put it, "the whole farm going to rack while a pack of daft men fought over that baby". When her meeting was over, Cat rang Mark on an impulse and asked him to come for a drink with her after work.

They met in a cavernous, mirrored pub two streets down from his office. Mark was looking tense and thin after a period of worsening conflict with Dean Hayes and Melanie Harwood. This time the issue was over whether Eden should emulate Tesco and get the Salvation Army in to run in-store Sunday schools, or whether they should steal a march by employing their own chaplains, in company livery, to counsel shoppers. He was openly contemptuous of Caroline's theory that Toby had gone to California.

"He only had two hundred and fifty quid," he said. "And he hadn't been out there for years."

"Nor had Caroline," objected Cat. "And *she* seems to have decided that LA is the place for her to get over the business with Alan. She's sort of homing there. It hasn't really got anything to do with Marie-Claire's museum conference. Maybe she's right. Maybe Toby went there too."

"Well, I quite liked school holidays in LA," said Mark. "But I certainly wouldn't rush back. If I was going anywhere, I'd go to Johannesburg."

"Good God. Why?"

"See the Kruger National Park again, I really missed those wart hogs when I was back at school. Anyway, I wouldn't go to LA. I don't think Toby was all that smitten with it, either."

"Well, he worked there," said Cat. "Remember all the row about the Mexican boy and the passport?"

"You mean when he was selling greaseburgers? He left that to go and be Pluto. No, Goofy. Didn't he get thrown out of Disneyland?"

"Yes," said Cat fondly. "Disney characters aren't supposed to speak to people when they're in costume. Specially they're not meant to call the customers ignorant arseholes."

There was a faraway, reminiscent, affectionate smile on the sister's face. In the moment's silence which followed this memory, Mark too smiled, but forcedly: the dry mirthless smile of the prodigal son's brother, aware that you are less remembered, less loved, for merely being well-behaved and helpful than you are for being wayward, difficult and charming.

"Well," he said flatly, "for one thing I don't know how Caroline thinks she's going to find him with no clues and no leads, in ten thousand acres of Southern California. She'll probably hardly look. I wouldn't hold my breath waiting for any news. For another thing, I don't think for a minute he's gone that far. He's probably back in Glasgow by now."

"He's not," said Cat bleakly. "I rang Duncan again. Anyway, there was a postcard from Calais."

Mark shifted restlessly on the hard pub bench, and gulped his lager. "Look, Cat, I know you're worried, and I am too. A bit. But he's always been one for wandering around. He's been out of touch for longer than this."

"Not after something like – Topsy dying."

"No." Mark shifted again, embarrassed. "But what can we do?"

"What I wanted to ask you," said Cat, "because you're a bloke, I suppose, is where do *you* think he'd go? Out of all the places we lived?"

"Why would it be somewhere we used to live?" asked Mark.

"Because that's what Caroline did," said his sister firmly, swirling the ice in her whisky. "And the more I think about it, the more I think that's what any of us would do if we were in trouble. We'd run for somewhere we used to live when we were kids. When Tim went—"

Mark looked at her, astonished. Never once had Cat discussed with him the defection of her husband. He thought she never mentioned it.

"When he left, I dreamed about moving to France. To Lille. I kept seeing the old courtyard, and the stone lions, and thinking of the twins in pinafores with the nuns, like me and Toby. I remembered Sunday skating with Sylvie and Chrétien and Thierry and the old gang. It was a sort of hallucination. Sometimes in the night when I was really tired, it felt as if I'd never stopped living in Lille. Just been home on leave."

"You never did go back there, though."

"Never had any money. And I knew that Hounslow was real life. Running off into the past is just a fantasy. I'm a plodder. But Toby isn't, is he? I mean, if he had an idea like that, he'd go."

"Gosh," said Mark noncommittally. "Diplobrat therapy, you reckon? Run back to your favourite post? Tough, if you were in Yugoslavia."

"It's a theory," said Cat stiffly. "Do you want another drink?"

"No thanks," said Mark. "I must get home. Lindy's got the neighbours round for dinner." He stood up.

"Mark," said Cat, as they walked together towards the Underground station. "Where *would* you go? If you ran away?"

"I wouldn't run away," said Mark with finality. "I'm not just home on leave, like you lot. Me and Lindy, we live here."

Their trains went from opposite platforms. Cat turned from his farewell rather brusquely. She crossed the footbridge and moments later looked at him across the grey gap, standing trim and composed in his dark suit and overcoat, waiting for the train home.

As Mark had predicted, there was no word from Caroline, nor any further cards from Toby. Almost a month later, when she had settled the baby after her supper-time romp, Cat was back in the kitchen contemplating the washing-up and picking listlessly at the carcass of an elderly duck culled by Gervase, cooked by herself and eaten without noticeable enthusiasm from anybody. Caroline's exotic enhancements of the farmhouse diet were still missed. The telephone rang and she answered it flatly: "Knoll Farm."

"Hi, it's Caroline!" said a high, distant voice. "How are you all?"

"Fine," said Cat. "Long time no hear."

"Yes. I'm sorry," said Caroline's voice, oddly light and happy. "Only, my therapist said it was better not to. Ring anybody, I mean."

"Your therapist?" Cat snapped the wishbone of the duck, hard, between her greasy fingers. "What therapist?"

"I've been seeing someone. Adeline McGilligan. Marie-Claire knew her. She does this one-month shock programme, not long Jungian stuff. Three sessions a day, and bomb-doses of vitamins. She told me to live inside myself for one month, and make friends with myself. I know," said the tinny voice apologetically, "that it sounds a bit naff, but it's worked. I've even rung Alan, to say I'd like the divorce to be friendly and constructive."

"Christ," said Cat rudely. "What did he say?"

"Well, not much," admitted Caroline. "He just said to talk to the lawyer about the money and leave him alone. But I wanted to say sorry to you, too. I must have been awful to live with all those weeks."

"No need," said Cat, formally. "Glad you're better." Then, on an impulse that had more than a little nastiness in it, "Any sign of Toby?"

Over three thousand miles came a long exhalation. "No. It was a stupid idea. I did put ads in the local paper, the first week. I even had one on the local television, and Marie-Claire's chap has friends in Venice Beach and places like that. But nobody'd heard a thing. The real reason I know he's not here is that there is one guy who knew him, from years ago, and he was positive he hadn't been in touch. He was sure that Toby would have come to him."

"Would Toby have been able to find him?"

"Yes. It's a café. The same one this guy always ran, in Laguna Beach. Toby worked there too. We'd forgotten. And he even wrote occasionally, apparently. He'd written about how he was having a baby. A postcard."

"Oh well," said Cat heavily. "That's that, then. Are you staying out there?"

"No, of course not!" said Caroline, laughing down the wire. "I'm coming home! I'm dying to see Mary-Annie!"

"Oh," said Cat. "Good."

Replacing the telephone, Caroline looked around her at the light, bright, luxuriously simple interior of Marie-Claire's family-room in Pacific Palisades. She would make her new home like this: polished floors, good rugs, Tiffany lamps, no fuss or clutter or stifling British establishment mock antiquity. Los Angeles had not been as rosy as she remembered, not at all: the miles of scruffy run-down housing, car-body shops and hoardings had eclipsed much of the pleasure of seeing Saks again and taking trips to the ocean and the mountains. She had rented a car, remembering happy runs with Diana in the sunshine, but given it up very quickly. She found herself terrified by a new savage aggression in the driving around her: a sense, as Marie-Claire put it, of a handgun in every glove box. She had gone downtown with her friend to the headquarters of the finance company which was backing the museum conference, and hated the glare and the glassiness and the acrid hooting heat of it.

No, she certainly did not want to live here, not geographically. But oh! She did want to live in the private atmosphere which despite the tension on the streets, she had found here. Her newly lightened spirit stretched and basked in a confusion of orange trees and wealth and optimism and expensive simplicity. Her baby, like the Californian babies she had seen, would have a pale carved oak crib on rockers, and simple streamlined cotton clothes, and real diapers for the sake of the planet. Light would flood into their house and their lives. She would paint again, and listen to music, and raise Mary-Annie – she liked the name now – by the precepts of the current buzzing Californian book, *Hey, Baby!*. Phrases – used half-ironically by her Paris-born hostess and more seriously by the therapist Adeline – came to Caroline like clear trumpet calls, summoning her to a simple but rich happiness. *Laid back. In touch. Shiny, happy people*.

She thought with a momentary pang of Cat, up in her cobwebby study at that old computer, supporting a life filled with muck and straw, bounded by intransigent animals with filthy bottoms and marred, inarticulate young men. She thought with a shudder of her own Kensington life, of the stifling traditional pomp of her ill-fated wedding a year ago, of the pointless profusion of General Trading Company knick-knacks in her kitchen, the overcareful clothes in her cupboards and the snobbish chic of Alan's long sitting room. She was out of all that now: renewed, fresh, new from the New World.

Then she thought of Gervase. Oddly, she did not associate her brother-in-law with the muck of the farmyard and the ungainly young men in the kitchen, but with the chessboard, the bookshelves in his study, a restful certainty and quietness, a kind monastic face. Yes, Gervase was in touch with the important things in life. He would understand her transformation. He would be interested in Adeline's book. She would take him one. Cat might laugh at the therapy, but Gervase would not.

Caroline picked up the telephone again to book a flight home. To the new home that she would build, and surprise them all.

17

On a shining Monday morning in May, Martin Szowalski drove the old Renault through the winding lanes that enmeshed Knoll Farm and protected it from the howl of A1 traffic. New green cowparsley brushed against the wheels when he pulled in to let a tractor pass, and the giddy smell of the whitening hedgerows blew through the broken ventilation grid beneath the dashboard, making him sneeze.

Martin felt light-hearted, pleasantly jolted from a long sober routine. Apart from weekend bike rides with Marianne and the regular duty runs to Midholt and Midmarsham, he had not left the farm since Christmas. Mrs Hartley had teased him about it. "You're turning into an Amish recluse," she would protest. "If you want to go to London, or the coast, or Scotland for a few days, for God's sake do. You're a volunteer, not a bondslave. You don't want to spend your whole time in Britain pegged out on the same few acres of Midlands mud."

But Martin never wanted to leave Knoll Farm. For one thing the work entranced him. He had spent months doing hard and mundane tasks on organic farms across Europe, but never before encountered the archaic eccentricity of one worked with carthorses. He was a serious young man, interested in Gervase's theories about how horsepower and human-scale farming could help young offenders regain social balance. He had come to observe this and contribute to the project, but he had stayed out of mere delight. Martin had found a talent: a growing, concentrated, sober pleasure in the big horses, their harness and gear and their time-worn traditional tasks on the land. Never mind what carthorses might do for Duanes and Winstons; they were doing wonders for him.

To begin with he had been allowed only to handle the old horse, Nelson, and a simple waggon: a tumbril, they called it here. But now Gervase let him go harrowing and even ploughing alone with the young pair. He had drilled a field of wheat, four acres of it, assisted only by Duane to fill and check the hoppers as the horses drew them over the prepared soil.

"We'll know exactly how straight you drove them, when that comes up," said Gervase. "The plants will show up every wiggle."

"There'll be a big kink in the line by the hedge," said Martin honestly. "Prince veered off when a pheasant came up under him." He had liked the imputation that he would still be there on the farm, still welcome, in the months when the corn began to sprout. Now, weeks later, there was little doubt that he could stay as long as he wanted, earning pocket money and his keep. Winston was still afraid of the horses, although he would lead the quietest of them if he had to. Duane had improved beyond measure from the gawping idiocy of his earlier self, but was still too prone to panic and confusion for Gervase to risk leaving him alone with a working animal weighing nearly a ton. So Martin evolved into Gervase's head horseman, and took a lot of work off the farmer's shoulders.

His favourite moments came when he was alone under a coppery late afternoon sky, his hands on the plough handles, feeling the living power of the great horses through the smooth worn wood, his arms responsive to every quiver and sway of the willing bodies as they moved along the furrow. At such moments, Martin wanted to stay forever suspended in time, happy in his increasingly ragged working clothes, wedded to these damp brown acres and magically forgetful of the dull realities of finding a living in the late twentieth century. At other times, aware of the financial tightrope the Hartleys walked, seeing Gervase's lined ascetic face bent over his paperwork calculating feed prices and falling markets, he would be chilled by the realization that there were no longer any simple farming idylls. "There never were," Cat would tell him. "Farmers have starved since the beginning of time. Especially small farmers."

But there was Marianne, too. She was on a course, and came home nearly every weekend now. Martin knew, from odd remarks dropped by her mother, that this had not always been so. He and she would talk for hours, casually, out by a hedge or in the barn while he worked. On Saturday he had been laying out sacks and hurdles ready for Monday's shearing, and Marianne had helped him all afternoon. They had hardly touched hands, but both knew that slowly, satisfyingly, things were moving on between them.

Exhausted from stacking hurdles, she had collapsed back on him in the barn, laughing like a comrade, her long hair wild and damp from the drizzle outside. He had set her on her feet and held her shoulders a moment longer than was necessary for balance. When she twisted round to face him she was smiling. He smiled now, thinking how his friends at home – and probably, her friends in London – would despise such a laggard old-fashioned courtship. But for the moment, in the Arcadian dream of those weekends, the pace suited them both very well. "Summer's coming," Marianne had said, stretching and shrugging her thin shoulders. "It gets warmer every day." And she smiled again as, perfectly understanding her, he said, "Yeah, I like the way the warm times come on slowly here. All the better. Back home, the hot wind comes and the land gets scorched, real quick. I like this way best."

As they built the pens of hurdles in the barn, Martin fully expected to be on hand when the shearers came. But on Monday morning Mrs Hartley had opened a telegram, clicked her tongue in exasperation and said: "Caroline's flight gets in this afternoon, two-thirty-five at Terminal Four, she says. I suppose that means she expects to be met."

"Did you say we'd meet her?" asked Gervase absently. He was leaning on the stove and eating a piece of toast while he read a set of committee minutes.

"Not on the phone. But I think she must be expecting it. Come to think of it, I shouldn't think she's ever arrived at an airport in her life and not been met."

Cat was irritable: the baby was teething early, and nights had been disturbed. They moved the cot into their own bedroom so that she and Gervase could get to the child faster; notionally they took turns, but in fact Cat woke at the first whimper and Gervase only at a full-blown wail.

"I'm really sorry, but I think it must be biological," Gervase would say in the morning, waking fresh and untroubled when Cat had been up four or five times, walking the fretful baby up and down the corridor.

"Doesn't matter," she would say. "You've got the farm. I can always nap when she does and catch up on work in the evenings." But she grew daily more tired, and felt her years. Eden were using her services constantly at the moment, squeezing out all her other clients; they were undergoing some kind of corporate restructuring, and Cat was part of the effort to sell the new systems and teams to the fretful workforce. She was earning twice as much as usual, but with the freelancer's insecurity she did not quite dare to turn down any of their demands. Caroline, she thought crossly, could perfectly well take a train up as far as Northampton. Or hire a car and drive to Midholt. On Alan's alimony she could afford a taxi. But instead she sent this peremptory telegram, naming her flight and expecting somebody from a busy household – made extra busy by *her* baby – to drop everything and drive a hundred-and-fifty-mile round trip to collect her and her Gucci luggage.

"Bloody hell then," she said, crumpling the telegram in her hand. "So who's going?"

"We've got the shearers coming at ten," said Gervase. "I really ought to be there. You know how touchy Gerry is, and he's the only one round here who'll do small flocks."

"How many catchers do you need in the barn?" asked Cat. "I'd really rather not get involved with the shearing, if you can spare me. I've got a lot of work I could get done while Yannie flakes out this morning."

She hated catching ewes for the shearer anyway, and Gervase knew it. Cat resented the dreadful irrationality of sheep, the way that right to the end of the shearing day each ewe fought as if her life depended on it, a woolly bundle of panic refusing to be dragged over to the shearing stand even though she could perfectly well see that her sisters had not been massacred, but merely shorn of their uncomfortable coats and left safe and white in the outer pen.

"Oh, don't worry," said Gervase. "Duane and Winston can do it. Then Martin might be so kind as to go and fetch Caroline."

"Winston won't like catching ewes," said Martin. "You know him and animals."

"Sheep won't hurt him," said Gervase. "He can't go on refusing to get to grips with stock."

Duane, who was washing up the porridge-pan, guffawed. "Bet 'e can."

"He can make an effort," said Cat, laughing at the big stolid boy's small joke. "You've all been too soft with him about it. He still says he wants to do NNEB and work in a nursery, you know. There might be rabbits, or hamsters to deal with. Let alone toddlers. He can practise on the sheep." Through the window, she could see Winston's long black clusters of plaits swinging as he carried the baby round the garden, crooning, bouncing her up and down, pointing out colours. "What about you, Martin? It's a boring drive to Heathrow."

"I'd be glad to help, if you think Mrs Halliday wouldn't mind my not being family," said Martin.

"Lucky to get anybody," Cat snorted.

And so it was settled, and later that morning while the baby slept in her carrycot by Cat's desk and Winston nervously eyed his first sheep, Martin drove southward to collect Maria Annunciata's mother from the airport.

The road held no terrors for him, nor the geography of Heathrow airport; but as he came closer he began to feel shy of what he would say to Mrs Hartley's beautiful, cool, distant sister. Despite her friendly condescension to the boys, there had always been something about Caroline which Martin found forbidding. It was a bit like he imagined talking to the Queen. In the kindness of his heart he was quite ready to ascribe all her little coldnesses, even towards the baby, to the bad shock she had received over her husband's leaving. Nonetheless, he did not feel at home with Caroline Halliday and began to wish as the miles reeled on that he had not volunteered so readily.

What would they talk about on the long drive back? Or would she sit silent, criticizing his driving? Should he offer to let her drive? She would have been better off with Gervase. They could talk about chess and art and all that stuff. Even better, of course, with her sister; but then, poor Mrs H. was still banned from driving.

He stood uncomfortably behind the rope barrier as the flight emerged from the baggage hall. Caroline moved towards him, gliding as smoothly as her trolley across the crowded concourse, and after a moment's hesitation recognized his face.

"Malcolm!" she said. "How sweet of you to come!"

"It's, um Martin," he said stumblingly apologetic. "Sorry, but Gervase couldn't come because of the shearing, so I, I—"

"But it's so sweet of you! I wasn't expecting to be met at all!"

Oh huh, lady! thought Martin in sudden rebellion. Oh, huh – so that's why you sent the flight details? Guys who really aren't expecting to be met just say what *day* they'll arrive. Not which *terminal*. This rebellious thought dispelled his uncomfortable sense of awe. Feeling much better, he hefted her two suitcases with a guilelessly friendly grin.

"A OK! Let's get these out to that car park." Caroline followed him, looking around with her new, shiny, happy positive attitude at the ranks of throbbing square black taxis, the pale May sunshine and the faded check shirt across the young man's broad shoulders. She was going home. Home to the country. How comfortable that sounded: she, Caroline, was through with Bond Street and Knightsbridge and crocodile shoes and Alan's dinners in restaurants with the powerful. Off with the old! She was even, she thought, glad for the moment to be away from echoing museums and the thick soundless carpet of Mayfair galleries. She had lived at second-hand for too long: been too fastidious, too frozen. Adeline had told her this and she saw it to be true. Now she would live calmly with her child: near some water perhaps, where she could paint the changing light, heal her inner child and quietly find wisdom, Gervase's kind of wisdom, the balanced pleasure of a simpler, plainer life.

The sight of Cat's old car shook her slightly. Never an elegant vehicle, it had been used this year by a number of drivers – even by Duane, once he got his licence back – and bore traces of farm and family life which jolted her fresh, bright, newly Californian sensibilities. Next to the baby seat (found by Winston for £1.20 at a car-boot sale and dreadfully scuffed) Gervase had left a leather head collar, a drift of files from one of his meetings, and a large spanner. There was evidence on the floor that a feed sack had at some stage split and leaked its floury contents. The outside was spattered liberally with spots of rust and streaks of mud, some of which had unaccountably found its way onto the dashboard. The glove box hung open, spilling cracked cassette boxes. Following her glance, Martin suddenly saw this familiar car with new eyes and flushed.

"Hey – I'm sorry we didn't clean up the car a bit. We only heard this morning."

"No, it's *lovely* to be home. And lovely to be met. I feel as if I was back on the farm already. Mmm, lovely horsey smell." While Martin put her smart suitcases in the boot (with difficulty, as there was an overlooked horse collar and a broken flywheel there already), Caroline surreptitiously dusted the passenger seat with her silk scarf, then slid in, to turn her serenely smiling eyes on him as he climbed in.

"Well!" she said chattily. "Tell me all the news!"

As he manoeuvred from the airport to the motorway, Martin did his best. He began with halting items of farm news, because he felt embarrassed about mentioning the baby, seeing that she had left it behind. Then Caroline gaily asked:

"And how's my daughter? Yannie, you call her, don't you?"

"Uh – yep. She's great. Bigger every day. I guess," he ventured daringly, "she'll be glad to have her Mom back."

Caroline swivelled her big eyes to look at the boy's profile as he drove. Adeline McGilligan was still strong within her as she said: "You must think I'm a terrible woman, leaving her like that. But I needed to get myself strong. Strong inside, so I could be strong for her. I've done that now. I'm ready to be a parent. No pain, no shame, just hope and new beginnings."

This frankness gave Martin considerable discomfort. He had absorbed a good deal of Gervase's reticence along with his farm-lore. Still, it did not seem to need an answer so he drove on silently. After a moment, Caroline began again, apparently without embarrassment: "I can accept your feelings. You're bound to have a residue of your feelings that's hostile to the way I was when I was in grief." She pronounced the word *hostel*, as her therapist so often did. "That's healthy. To reject the manifestations of grief. People in grief give off negativity and danger. But it fades. My job is the same as all of yours: to accept the faults in the person I was, and build on them. None of us is perfect."

"No," bleated Martin, hating this. "Hey, do you mind if I have the *One o'clock News* on? There's some sorta conference about BSE transmission."

"Go ahead," said Caroline, and smiled at him again as he fumbled, rather desperately, with the radio.

When they got to the farm the shearers were packing up their electric tools and stands, and the boys were lugging huge buoyant sacks of fleece up to the end of the barn. Gervase and the old dog could be seen in the middle distance, running the flock of shining white sheep down into the more sheltered of the meadows for their first night of lighter, cooler summer life. The afternoon sun slanted beautifully across the red tiles of the farmhouse roof, and there were pale delicate leaves around the back door. Caroline stood by the car, surveying it all with pleasure.

"Isn't it just gorgeous?" she said. "A place of peace and healing." Martin, who might before that morning have felt much the same way himself, although without saying so, could manage only a surly grunt as he pulled her cases from the boot. "Shall I take these up?" he asked. "Only, I don't know . . ." He lived in the bunkhouse with the boys and, although the rule about not going beyond the kitchen and big sitting room did not strictly apply to him, he rarely penetrated upstairs in the house.

"No, no, you've got work to do, I'm sure," said Caroline graciously. "The lobby will be fine." So she walked alone, through the kitchen and up the stairs, to find her sister and her child.

18

Cat was asleep on the floor of her study, head on a rolled baby blanket, when the car pulled up. Next to her was a battered plastic carrycot which the boys had found at yet another car-boot sale. There were four of these now, each equipped with a clean ancient flannel sheet and a light cellular blanket from the WI craft market; Cat hated carrying baby furniture around, and found it easier to have a number of bases scattered through the house where the infant could safely be put down to doze. As long as she had her muslin square to clasp to her face and suck, Maria Annunciata did not seem to mind a frequent change of bed.

She slept on now, muslin clutched in her small fat fist, while her aunt raised herself on one elbow and shook her head, trying mistily to make sense of the sounds on the attic stairs. On the desk, the old Amstrad screen burned with the words which had sent Cat to sleep:

*Pro-active courtesy, pro-active efficiency – these are the bnechmarks of Ened service provisio@ £$^*

The footsteps on the stair became louder and closer, and Cat sat up, rubbed her eyes, and ran her hands through her hair. The door opened and she saw her sister: tanned, crisply dressed in a white blouse and pale linen skirt, golden-haired, clear-eyed and serenely smiling.

From the door Caroline saw a middle-aged woman in a tattered tracksuit, with bags under her eyes, her hair a dull brown birds' nest streaked with grey, sitting on a threadbare carpet by a cluttered desk and a grimy old computer. Next to her was a carrycot, its inner walls clean enough but its exterior a battered nightmare of peeling, fading, hideous orange plastic.

In it, half covered by a clashing blanket in lime green and cherry red, slept a baby dressed in a well-worn towelling Babygro suit, a rag in her fist. Jammed into the corner of the carrycot between the cardboard stiffener and the torn plastic was a twig with many branches, from each of which hung a thread bearing a silver foil milk-bottle top which turned and twisted in the draught from the doorway.

Caroline was silent for a moment, and even through her sleepiness Cat saw why, and was suddenly and deeply angry. It took all her genetic history of circumspect diplomatic repression to say merely: "Hello. Good journey?"

"Fine, thanks," said Caroline, with equal social self-possession. "How is everything?"

"Fine," said Cat. "I was just power-napping. Mary-Annie should be waking up any minute."

"Lovely," said Caroline. Now that she was here, the baby at her feet filled her with frightening, unsayable mixed emotions. She bent with difficulty towards the carrycot, and peered at the small face.

"She's grown."

"They do that," said Cat.

Caroline made a rapid brave decision, went on one knee and picked up the baby, blanket and all. She was not as inept as she might have been before LA: Marie-Claire's best friend in Pacific Palisades had a boy of much the same age, and Caroline had warily handled him a few times as he was passed from one doting woman to another. Besides, she had re-read that encouraging manual *Hey, Baby!* twice all through on the aeroplane.

Upright against her mother's shoulder, Mary-Annie blinked herself awake and burrowed her face, a little snottily, against the white linen of Caroline's Saks blouse.

"That's the girl," said Caroline. "What a big girl!"

Cat watched, half-angry and half-relieved that the baby did not cry at this stranger's embrace.

"Thanks for looking after her so well," said Caroline, not letting her eyes stray to the terrible carrycot and twig. And carefully, step by step, she carried her baby out of Cat's attic and down the stairs.

"She has milk at four o'clock," said Cat to the retreating back.

"Everything's in the kitchen." And, as an afterthought, "Winston will show you where."

The baby was used to many faces, many bodies: from Cat's warm female solidity to Winston's bony energy, from Duane's slow, careful, freckled arms to Gervase's lean tanned ones, from Mrs Bird's dishevelled doughy gentleness to Martin's bristling beard and wiry arms, she knew and rejoiced in the diversity of people. It was rare for her to offer any of them less than a toothless beam of welcome. The smooth, cool, lightly scented bosom of Caroline was new to her but nonetheless agreeable; besides, on reaching the kitchen she found herself in earshot of familiar deep male voices and promising smells of food, and began to crow contentedly.

So it was that Gervase and the two boys, coming in with wisps of oily wool stuck to their jackets and a great thirst for tea, were met by the sight of beautiful Caroline, her face transfigured by a smile of triumphant relief and dawning love, and in her arms little Mary-Annie: grinning and gurgling and waving her fists in an ecstasy of general approval of the world, the company, and – so it seemed to Gervase in particular – her new found mother.

He paused in the door, the boys behind him, and looked at mother and child standing in the dappled sunlight. Then: "Welcome back," he said, and crossed the floor to kiss her smooth cheek with deliberate measured courtesy. "Welcome home."

Cat, descending the back stairs to the kitchen, stepped through the door just in time to see their two bright faces bent together over the baby's head. Looking beyond them, she saw something like dismay in the eyes of Winston and Duane. Things were changing at Knoll Farm; an era ending. Everybody knew it except Maria Annunciata.

The changes were rapid, too rapid for Duane's slow wits to understand. He had never seen much of Caroline except at meal times in the depths of her cold depression, and gaped at this new, swift-moving decisive woman with her steely smiles and cool politeness. She had, being not insensitive to atmospheres, rapidly given up talking like a therapist since the first car ride with Martin, and reverted to her old dainty reticence. Except sometimes, alone with Gervase, when she talked as to a father confessor and he listened gravely.

On the day after her arrival she entrusted the baby – with a slightly absurd formality of gratefulness – to her sister and Mrs Bird, and borrowed the car to drive to Birmingham. In the following days, carriers and parcels arrived in bewildering profusion: a smart new pale walnut cot – "She's outgrowing the carrycots," a modern car seat with a handle, a highchair and harness adjustable for either reclining or self-supporting babies, a changing chest beautifully painted with roses and butterflies, and a snowstorm of new clothes.

Duane had never seen clothes like them. Most were white and many bore discreet frills or embroideries; a few were larkily multicoloured, like tiny chic rugby shirts with strange Italian labels on the chest. There were little silk knitted sweaters and elegantly chunky sheepskin bootees. Some of them did not fit, since Caroline had not taken the baby with her when she bought them; but there were enough good guesses there to transform his familiar little Yannie into another baby altogether. A Kensington baby, beautifully packaged. He would not have attempted to change a nappy now, not with these unfamiliar garments to contend with. But then, he would not have dared anyhow. The baby had suddenly become too close an associate of the awe-inspiring Caroline. He could as soon fumble with her immaculate clothing as with this child's.

Winston was less shy. He was, after all, street-sharp, opinionated, and buoyed by his new ambitions in professional childcare. On the third day after her arrival Caroline came into the kitchen one evening – having left the baby to her sister's care while she collected a mended head collar from the saddler in Midmarsham – to find the boy with the long dreadlocks and the single earring spooning puréed apple into her daughter's wide, enthusiastic mouth. A gobbet of it was trickling down her chin, not onto one of the new starched bibs Caroline had bought but onto an old tea towel from Cat's kitchen drawer, which Winston had expertly tied around her neck as he always did.

"Hi," said Winston, concentrating on his task and unable to see the mother's face. "Mrs H.'s gone up the paddock to sort out a sheep. She asked me to do Yan's tea. I usually do anyway."

"Yes, well, I'll take over, thank you," said Caroline.

"S'all right. She's nearly finished, and I've done the milk for after," said Winston, oblivious to nuance. Caroline, however, picked up a white piqué Italian bib from the laundry basket in the corner, and came to stand so very close to him that in a moment he rose, backed away and left her the spoon. Mary-Annie had a second spoon in her hand, with which she was enthusiastically conducting some invisible orchestra, and a third one lay on the table. Seeing the mother's momentary bemusement, Winston kindly explained:

"She likes to 'old the spoon, yeah? In 'er and. So I give 'er one in each hand, and I use the third one. She nearly gets her own ones in 'er mouth, so I dip it in the apple so she gets the idea. She'll be feeding on 'er own in no time."

Caroline did not reply, but went on spooning apple into the baby's mouth, wiping the dribbling lips fastidiously between each mouthful. When the bowl was nearly empty, Winston picked up the bottle from the stove, whipped off its cap and tested the temperature of the milk on his thin dark wrist.

"S'fine. Here you are. She likes to hold the bottle, but she's not too good at it, so you have to watch all the time."

Caroline looked at the white bottle in the boy's black hand, hesitated, then took it and plugged it firmly into the baby's mouth, supporting it with her hand, still not speaking. Only the eager glugging and sighing of the child broke the quiet of the kitchen. Winston watched critically.

"Oughter be tipped up more. Or she gets air in, and burps."

At this point Cat came in to the kitchen, stamping her feet on the mat and shuddering with theatrical distaste. She was holding a bottle of cooking oil.

"I hate capsized bloody sheep. Why can't they get up by themselves? Lying there with their legs in the air. It's a design fault."

"Woss the oil for?" asked Winston, momentarily diverted from supervising mother and baby.

"If they get bloated up from being on their back, you force oil down their throat and it makes them belch and fart."

"Please!" The cry from Caroline was involuntary, and she flushed immediately and pretended to carry on with the baby.

"Saves their rotten life, doesn't it?" said Cat truculently. "And it's all right, it isn't the same bottle of oil we use for cooking." Caroline shuddered. The baby sucked the last centimetre of milk and looked hopefully, dribblingly around for more.

That evening, when the boys had retired to the bunkhouse and Gervase was in his study, Caroline caught her sister alone, peeling potatoes, and said: "Cat, I came into the kitchen tonight and Mary-Annie was alone with that drug boy."

Cat looked at her in genuine astonishment.

"You mean Winston?"

"Yes. The farm boy, the delinquent. He was feeding her."

"He usually does. Him or Duane. They're very careful. They adore her."

"I thought," said Caroline, "that if I left my baby with you . . ."

"That I'd never allow anyone else in the household to touch her? Come off it. You lived here for eight weeks, while we all took turns."

"Well, you and Gervase. And Mrs Bird. I never realized that the farm boys *fed* her."

"They even do her nappies," said Cat brutally. "Always have. If you'd ever bothered to be around your own baby, you'd have known perfectly well that we all help. And don't call them farm boys. You sound like Gervase's mother."

Caroline bridled. Cat had not spoken to her so unkindly since Christmas Eve.

"I really don't think it's unreasonable to be surprised that you leave a four-month-old baby alone to be fed – *God knows what* – by a convicted drug dealer."

"Oh, give me strength!" exploded her sister. "Winston is as safe as houses. Safer than some neurotic anorexic bloody Kensington au pair, I shouldn't wonder. What do you think he does? Spikes her Ostermilk with crack?"

"He's a convicted criminal. Drugs!"

"He has a suspended sentence," said Cat, as if to a three-year-old, "for selling a tab of Ecstasy to an undercover policewoman in a club in Northampton."

"Well? So that makes him suitable to feed my baby?" Caroline was fired up now, angry at the contempt in her sister's voice.

"No," said Cat steadily. "But the person he is now, the person he has become and always was underneath, is a person to be trusted. Within reason, he can be trusted to rejoin mainstream society. That's what we do here. Mary Annie has helped." *Unlike some*, said her tone.

The two women glared at one another, then Cat turned to the stove and, with her back to Caroline lest she be tempted to slap her, continued:

"Do you know how that boy has lived? His mother lost her cleaning job at the steelworks at Corby when it closed. She went on the game and got murdered. He spent three years in a children's home, then was chucked out at sixteen and became a runner for drug dealers. He got caught in his first week and sent to a young offenders' institution. When they let him out he did it again, because he didn't have any other way of affording anywhere to eat or sleep. Mr Willetts the probation officer says he used to look after some of the other younger kids on the street, buy them chips. He's the gentlest thing on earth."

Caroline made a small, dissenting noise. Cat went on, almost pleading now.

"He won't even get tough with the horses, so they haul him all over the place. He's worked here for four months and been good as gold. He's been provisionally accepted at the Midholt FE college to do a course in social care of children. He wants to be a nursery nurse."

Caroline had absorbed Adeline McGilligan's views about the need to be unaggressively assertive. She said, controlledly:

"Well, we shall have to agree to differ. I'm very grateful for all you've done. I won't impose on you much longer. But I am afraid I have a right to say who feeds my baby." Too late, she realized she should not have said "I am afraid". But Adeline, she felt, would have said it was not a bad try.

When Caroline had gone upstairs to check her baby, Cat turned her face to the kitchen door and cried into the roller towel.

19

At bedtime, Cat kicked off her old corduroy slippers and told Gervase: "Caroline says Winston isn't to feed the baby."

"She's doing almost everything herself now, isn't she?" said Gervase. "I suppose that's a good thing."

He had been quiet, over the few days Caroline was home. His brief dream of the baby had faded when he saw her in her true mother's arms. He felt a little ashamed of it: this new Caroline was so clearly, so beautifully, the mother. He now felt a chivalrous desire – almost a hunger – that things should go well for her in her state of single motherhood. When they sat together over the chessboard she did most of the talking, her lovely face newly animated, her hair shining in the lamplight. He listened gravely, admiring and supporting her resolve to live well with the child. Now he said to his wife:

"Mary-Annie seems to be doing rather well on it. She's looking very bonny. Caroline says she's slept right through, these last two nights."

The baby's cot was now set up in a separate bedroom, linked to Caroline by a sleek space-age baby alarm system. During Mary-Annie's daytime naps, she carried the receiver clipped unobtrusively to her blouse. She looked (thought Duane privately) just like a TV policewoman waiting for the summons to an affray.

"It's not some magic mother's touch," said Cat, irritably. "The baby's just stopped teething for the moment, that's all. It was very early anyway." She swung her legs onto the bed, wincing at the coldness of the sheet. "If Caroline had been back last week she'd have found it a different game altogether. But never mind that:

what I'm trying to tell you is that she doesn't want poor Winston even touching the baby. Even playing with her. It's because he's black, and he's what she calls a delinquent."

"Oh no," said Gervase, shocked. "I'm sure you've misunderstood. Caroline's really keen on the project, on everything we do here. She was talking about it only tonight. That American doctor seems to have helped her understand a lot of things."

Without answering, Cat lay down on her own side and pulled the quilt around her ears. They did not speak again until morning. But then, Gervase had always been prone to long periods of restful, contemplative silence. It was one of the things which had attracted her to him years before, after living for six years with the nervous chattiness of Noreen and the prattle of the twins. She had loved his quietness, as she loved the quietness of her part-time job at the library. That quietness could harden into silence had never, in those noisy days, occurred to her.

The next day he went out early to the farm as usual, and Cat decided that she should talk to Winston before breakfast. His habit was to walk Mary-Annie round the garden while her bottle was made up, holding her up in his strong dark arms and teaching her the names of plants and colours according to the precepts of the infant development video which Cat had got him from the Midholt library. This excursion must be forestalled, for today at any rate. She must prevent a direct confrontation between the boy and Caroline. If Winston was to take this new situation well, it must be presented to him well, and without exposing him to the reality of the mother's distaste.

When she came down she saw that Caroline had been up since the baby's early milk feed and was in the kitchen, rinsing spoons and frowning at the label of an expensive little jar of organic muesli. Mary-Annie, in her new chair, examined her bare toes and made loud, sociable yarring noises. It seemed to Cat, in her state of heightened sensitivity, as if the baby's eyes kept turning, hopefully, in the direction of the bunkhouse from which every morning her teenage admirers had been wont to emerge, racing to greet her. She nodded briefly to her sister, pushed her feet into rubber boots and went out into the yard to waylay the boys.

It had taken some hours of the night to work out how to put the situation to them. Cat Hartley was no sentimentalist, but in the years of bringing up her own Dave and rubbing along domestically with Gervase's changing entourage of young offenders, she had formed her own view of what lay beneath the showy superficial toughness of the adolescent male. Winston, she felt and feared now, was softer-centred even than most.

Generally, she reflected as she loitered near the bunkhouse door, it was a girl who uncovered the inarticulate warm gooey centre behind a young man's brittle street-wisdom. Sometimes it was an animal. One eighteen-year-old had been on the verge of being sent home as too angry and intractable even for Gervase, until by good fortune a calf had been born too weak to stand. The boy, Mikey, had ended up sleeping in the straw next to the weak animal, while its mother roamed distractedly in the shadows of the barn nearby. He begged an alarm clock from Cat, and four times a night he would milk the cow of colostrum and feed it to the calf through a tube pushed over its rough tongue, while the cow licked the back of his jacket gratefully with her rough tongue. The calf lived; Mikey did not change overnight, but after that he worked his time out at the farm, and left in a better state than he came.

In Winston's case the baby had wrought the change; and to deny him contact with her now seemed a thing more cruel than Cat liked to contemplate. Duane, she thought, would be all right about the prohibition: his obsession with Mary-Annie had faded to a more casual brotherly affection since he began to lavish his inner gooeyness upon the stout, shy new barmaid at the Midmarsham pub. Winston had no girlfriend, and seemed for the moment not to want one.

He erupted out of the bunkhouse, a tall skinny dark figure, and hesitated when he saw her. He glanced back towards Duane who stood, in an ungainly questioning stance, in the doorway. "We late or what? The clock said—"

"No, I wanted to catch you two," began Cat. "It's about Mrs Halliday. Caroline. My sister."

Winston looked suddenly defensive. Maybe, thought Cat, he had understood more of her sister's attitude than she knew.

"She leavin', then?" asked Winston abruptly. "Lives in London, yeah?"

"Not yet," said Cat. "Soon, I daresay. Actually, she's decided to look for a cottage not far from here, rather than go back to London."

The boy's face lightened. Cat dragged herself unwillingly back to the point. "She was ill when Mary-Annie was born, and couldn't look after her much. So she's got a bit of catching up to do. Mothers have to be with their babies a lot."

"Bonding," nodded Winston, more comfortably. "Yeah, obviously." This had been much featured on the video.

Cat looked at the boy's bony, intelligent face and called up all her reserves of the family talent for emollient presentation of hard truths. It was considerable: a talent bred in a dozen diplomatic residences, hammered home from childhood as the central principle of courtesy, and honed on Eden corporate newsletters.

"She's decided," she said brightly, "that we ought to change the way we do things. A little."

The boys looked at her, expectantly. Cat wavered and continued, lying bravely:

"She knows how well you've helped me look after Mary-Annie, and she's really grateful. But now she thinks that it would be better if nobody else did things for the baby – feeding, playing, carrying her around even. Just for a while. So they can get really used to each other. As Winston said, it's a matter of bonding."

It was a brave attempt which fooled nobody. Not even Duane, who looked at his feet and said: "Not even you an' Mrs Bird and Mr H.?"

Cat was thrown.

"Ah – well, mainly – not any of us."

"What about while she does the driving?" persisted Duane, his freckled face creasing in puzzlement. "Shops, an' Mr Willetts an' that. Yan doesn't like being in the car more'n ten minutes, unless it's nap time, an' even then—"

Winston turned on him and broke his silence. "Don't be a stupid dickhead. She just dun't want us two yobs touchin' Yannie, thass all. Innit?"

His challenge was so direct that Cat capitulated.

"OK, all right, that's partly it. She's a bit old-fashioned," she continued wildly. "I suppose she thinks only women should handle little babies."

At that moment Gervase emerged from the kitchen with Mary-Annie cuddled on his arm and Caroline laughing behind him.

Winston turned to Duane and said flatly: "C'mon, dickhead. We'll do the pigs before breakfast." Before Cat could speak again, he had vanished into the shadows of the feed shed.

There had been no family gathering back at Easter, because Lady Artemis was staying with friends in Gstaad and Robert was at an aid conference in Rome. Cat had been glad of it. Although Toby had frequently missed family reunions, his absence on this occasion would have had a poignancy she dreaded. Instead, Noreen had come up in Marianne's car, and Dave had turned up for Easter Sunday lunch and fallen as much in love with the baby as any of them. Despite Caroline's frozen listlessness it had been an easy, relaxed Easter. Cat had an obscure, guilty feeling of having somehow got away with it: got past another landmark of the traditional family year without trouble.

Artemis, however, always found that after a gap of a certain number of months her maternal compass-needle fluttered irresistibly back towards Knoll Farm and another visit to her son. This she announced, her high confident voice ringing down the telephone, on the sunny May day after Cat's painful interview with Winston. She was surprised at the unaccustomed warmth with which her daughter-in-law received the notification of her visit.

"That'll be nice," said Cat with sincerity. Indeed, she longed for any dilution of the difficult atmosphere at mealtimes. Winston had spoken to nobody, except in the way of work, since the prohibition. He ate rapidly and left for the bunkhouse. Gervase was believing – or pretending – that there was no problem, and when the baby was at table, exchanged his usual social courtesies with her while Duane and Winston glowered powerlessly, not feeling they could even play peek-a-boo under the cool eye of Caroline. Martin did not really understand any of it, but sensed the new atmosphere of constraint and did not smother Mary-Annie with giggles and tickles or throw her aloft as he had been used to do. Deprived of the element of whoopee in her life, the baby was a little more grizzly than usual; but she was a good-natured creature, and was at least constantly tended by her mother with scrupulous, if slightly mechanical, carefulness.

Only Caroline seemed entirely at peace: in the evenings she sat glowing with such untroubled inner serenity that her sister wanted to shake her as a dog shakes a rat, and with much the same fatal result. Or so she told Marianne, her only confidante in this matter, on the phone one night.

Marianne sympathized wholeheartedly, but could not come to Knoll Farm for several weekends more because of her work. Cat had tried to get Noreen to come, but she was on a coach trip to the Dutch bulbfields. So Artemis would have to do. Any visitor would, at least, provide a diversion. Cat told her:

"Caroline's back. She'll be thrilled to see you. You haven't met the baby yet, have you? She's a darling. Maybe Dad's free too. That would be fun." Robert was indeed free, and when his elder daughter rang him to demand that he help entertain Artemis, he willingly agreed. And on the Friday evening, Lindy rang, sounding a little strained, to ask whether she could come up alone for Saturday night and meet Mark at the farm on Sunday, after his presentation to a sales conference near Kettering.

"Wonderful!" said Cat. "Full house, how nice. Dad'll give you a lift if you don't want to drive."

Caroline had already been to Midholt and bought a great deal of expensive cheese and bread with dried tomatoes embedded in it, and the ingredients for *canard à l'orange*. Gervase had killed and plucked two of the floating population of farmyard ducks and requested this dish, since duck had always been his mother's favourite fowl.

However, when Caroline saw the two grim, scrawny carcasses left for her on the stone slab in the larder, their legs untidy and their skin bagging, she quietly went back to Tesco on Saturday morning on the pretext of dropping Duane at his girlfriend's. Here she bought two corn-fed, butter-plump, oven-ready birds from the Auvergne, rosy and neatly trussed on clean white trays. The old sheepdog was more than pleased to dispose of Gervase's birds and only Martin, passing the kennel, noticed what had happened. Brits, he thought, were sometimes really strange.

None of the visitors was expected before lunch-time. The late morning sun was slanting in through the kitchen window where Caroline stood chopping onions for the *canard*, as Cat came into the room and found herself for the first time in days alone with her sister.

It was a pretty scene, the older sister had to admit to herself. Mary-Annie, in a pale blue smock, lay back in her new soft white padded chair, big-eyed, sucking on an equally new teething ring with bells on it. It was made of some soft smooth plastic but modelled on a Victorian ivory piece. The kitchen was unaccustomedly tidy, and Caroline had found enough primroses to fill a little jug which shone from the centre of the scrubbed table. She herself was wearing jeans and a pale knitted silk sweater, and humming softly as she worked. Her eyes were as big and blue and clear as the baby's.

Cat stood in the doorway for a moment, reluctant to break the picturesque peace of the moment. Then she said:

"Caro." She used the baby name, as she rarely did. "Caro, could I have a word?"

"Of course. I'm just getting the smelly bits of the cooking over with. These onions are strong, aren't they?"

"Organic," said Cat. "Gervase is very pleased with that lot of seed. Small but deadly. Totally pest-resistant."

"They're wonderful," said Caroline warmly. "So are the potatoes. Goodness, they've kept well, haven't they?"

Cat wished that they could continue discussing vegetables and leave it at that. She recognized in herself a strong inhibition against upsetting Caroline, and had decided with dry resignation that it must be a legacy of their youth. When Caroline was the new and precious baby, she, Cat, was a big girl twelve years older who must be gentle and considerate. Even today she could advise and support, counsel and suggest, but rarely rebuke her baby sister. You must not risk making her cry. Old refrains ran through her mind: *She's only little. You should know better! Fancy making poor Caroline cry. Look after Caroline.*

Contemplating beautiful Caroline, beautifully and tearlessly chopping onions, Cat rubbed her forehead in a moment of perplexity. It was a terrible thing, she thought, to recognize an irrational inhibition in yourself and still be its prisoner. Caroline was nearly thirty-three years old now. Not a baby. She had a duty of consideration to other people. She was behaving like a selfish cow. Something had to be said. Cat drew herself together and began:

"I wanted to talk to you about the boys. Winston. And Duane. And this business about Mary-Annie."

"Oh?" said Caroline, not looking at her, chopping with precision.

"I understand about your wanting to look after her yourself mostly. That's great. It's natural. You had a difficult start, you need to make up time." Cat realized that she was repeating to Caroline the half-truth she had concocted for the boys. Well, it would do. She continued:

"But it would be a great help to us – to Gervase's work" – ah, fiendish, diplomatic cunning! – "if you'd just sometimes hand her to one of the boys, quite casually. To Winston, especially. Just for ten minutes. Ask him to take her round the garden, or give her a bottle. He got very fond of her while you were away. And before that, while you were low. Gervase and I think it really helped his growing up to know that we all trust him with something so precious."

It was not entirely true about Gervase. Cat had tried to raise the subject with him once or twice after the first failure, but he had merely spoken gravely about Caroline's need to feel secure about everything connected with the baby, and her right to have reservations about outsiders of a type with which she was unfamiliar. "We're used to these boys. She isn't." As to the effect on Winston, he said, the lad was doing fine as far as the farm went, and had always been a bit moody. He would come round. Attention would make it worse. Meanwhile, he was sure that Caroline did not mean any slight to the boys by her attitude. One must remember she had had a terrible shock, over Alan.

Cat had given up. Gervase, without ever intending to, had a way of making other people feel mean and small-minded.

Now, since Caroline was still chopping and not speaking, she continued: "Winston really is very careful of her. He adores her."

The baby, bored with the rattle, dropped it and began to whicker with frustration. Cat bent to return it.

Caroline put down the knife, and turned, hand on hip. All

Dr Adeline's carefully implanted assertiveness rose to order as she said, in a calm and sweet voice: "I'm afraid I don't think it's appropriate."

Oh God! thought Cat, looking at the beautiful face before her, framed in sunlit, smooth golden hair. Oh God in heaven, was there anywhere a worse torment than being rightly and justifiably infuriated by somebody, so much that you longed to smack her and berate her, and yet to be inhibited from speaking your mind by a lifelong fear of upsetting her? She shuddered a little, put a hand for strength on Mary-Annie's small chubby leg, and said, averting her eyes from her sister's face: "What do you mean, 'appropriate'? You sound like a social worker."

"The other day," said Caroline, "you said I sounded like Artemis. She hardly sounds like a social worker, does she?"

"Let's not fight."

"I'm not fighting," said Caroline, and pulled another peeled onion towards her. The glinting little knife sank into its flesh, and it wept sharp tears onto the board. "I am making decisions about the care of my child. I'm sure Winston will turn out very well, but I don't think it's appropriate or healthy for a boy from that kind of home, with that kind of record, to be handling a baby." She paused. "A baby girl. Or 'adoring' her, frankly."

There was a moment's silence, then Cat, startled by the emphasis of the last words, said in a voice that rose uncontrollably to a squeak: "Are you saying he's some sort of sex abuser?"

The inhibition was fading. She wanted to pique Caroline now, to make her deny any such absurd suspicion, to explain herself. But Caroline only gave an almost imperceptible nod, and pushed a neat pile of onion shavings to the corner of the board.

"She can't speak for herself," she said. "It's up to us to protect her from – emotional abuse and inappropriate relationships. I'd have thought you'd see that. You read the papers."

"She's not five months old yet!" howled Cat, her control now quite gone. "You stupid bloody dirty-minded prig, what fucking nonsense *have* you brought back from America now?"

"I wouldn't have thought," said Caroline, still calm, still chopping, her voice still sweet, "that you'd be so naïve about the things which can happen to children. At any age."

"Winston is *not* a baby-molester!" said Cat. "Ask Gervase! You always seem to believe every bloody thing he says!"

"Gervase agrees with me," said Caroline, "that it's healthy for me to make decisions about Mary-Annie. He doesn't question my judgement. I'm sure nobody questioned your judgement, when the twins were small."

Cat wanted to turn and walk out, but suddenly saw a saving vision of Winston, lanky, bony, grinning whitely at some trick of Mary-Annie's as he expertly tested the heat of her milk on his wrist. He was worth one more try:

"Suppose I promised that I'll always be in sight of him, always in the room, while he plays with the baby? Just to let him down lightly. He's only here another month or so."

"I'm sorry," said Caroline. "I've given it a lot of thought, and anybody who knows about these things" – she meant Adeline, and the author of *Hey, Baby!* – "says that when you're not easy about a relationship in a child's life or an adult's, a clean break is far better."

"But Caro – relationship isn't quite the word—" Cat was still trying, although now she hated herself for it. She ought by rights, she thought, to have thrown a plate at her sister and walked out, telling her to pack her bags and take her dirty prim little mind elsewhere. "Caro, this is a *baby*. She doesn't do relationships yet. She does cuddles and jokes and feeding and pointing at things."

Mary-Annie dropped the rattle again and began to whimper, in earnest this time. Caroline rinsed her hands and dried them carefully on some of the kitchen paper (she used a whole roll every two days in her pursuit of hygiene). The whimpering increased in volume. She crossed to the chair to pick her child up.

"I'm sorry," she said again, "especially as I am a guest in your house. But nothing's changing. Anyway, the boy seems to have lost interest, doesn't he? I don't know what all the fuss is about. I've hardly seen him for two days."

20

If – and there was no sign of it in her behaviour – Caroline was dismayed by this encounter with her elder sister, the approval she received an hour later from Lady Artemis would have been more than enough to soothe any ruffled feelings. Gervase had sent his mother a Polaroid of his new niece a while back: it showed Mary-Annie staring beadily at the camera in a grubby towelling Babygro and a crudely knitted red woolly tank-top made by Mrs Bird. Artemis had not been attracted by this picture, particularly since the uncleared breakfast-table was all too visible in the background. Anyway, thanks to Martin's camera technique the child appeared to have one ear larger than the other.

She was, therefore, quite unprepared for the beaming beauty and refined wardrobe of this Maria Annunciata. The baby took her unawares, ambushed her with downy wisps of golden hair, wide uncertain smiles and fat waving fists. The old lady capitulated, even risking her immaculate suit by kneeling on the hearth rug where the baby was doing push-ups in the manner of a seal.

She cried, "What a duck!", almost said, "Coochy coo!" and bestowed upon pretty, gentle-mannered Caroline a more wholehearted smile than her own daughter-in-law had ever seen. Cat, after all, had brought into the distinguished Hartley family no such beauty of a baby. When she arrived as Gervase's bride sixteen years earlier, she had been leading two shy, pasty-faced six-year-olds who wore – Artemis shuddered to remember – dreadfully common anoraks.

"Isn't she a gorgeous little one?" she continued, chucking the complaisant Mary-Annie on the cheek. "Looking so pretty! I do love proper broderie. Is it Swiss?"

"Austrian," said Caroline. "I'm afraid I do like little girls in dresses."

"Oh, of course! Sometimes these days you just can't tell, can you? All the children in these *shell suits*."

Martin came in, shyly, with a basket of freshly split firewood. He was uneasy around Caroline, although since the first effusions of the car journey she had been less ready with the psychobabble. He did not know what had happened between her, Cat, Winston and the baby, but disliked the changed atmosphere. Even the horses were little comfort now that something was askew in the homestead. And Marianne was away on duty for three successive weekends. As for old Lady Artemis, she terrified him. Martin dumped the log-basket and asked diffidently: "Shall I build the fire up a bit?"

"Why not?" said Artemis expansively, turning her big green eyes on him with frightening charm. "Keep us all and baby warm. What a duck!"

"I'll tell Mrs Hartley you're here," said Martin, and immediately regretted it. He sounded like some kinda Jeeves! Why was it, he thought resentfully as he slipped back into the kitchen, that he could be on terms of perfect ease and familiarity with Gervase, Cat, the twins, and everyone else he met in this place from Mrs Bird to Lord Gratton, but still feel like a hick and a stumblebum whenever he was round Caroline or Lady Artemis? No way were they better than the others, not by anybody's standards. Not cleverer, not kinder, certainly not more useful. It was just that in their presence his stature seemed to shrink and his hands and feet to grow huge and unwieldy.

Cat was in the utility room, rinsing out some milk bottles. She looked tired, and her eyes were a little red, but she smiled at Martin.

"Gervase's mother's come," he said.

"I know," replied Cat. "I'm hiding for a moment. You know how it is. Some people make your feet go all enormous, and you just know you're going to be rude."

"Yeah," said Martin, comforted. "Me too."

"I'll go through in a minute," said Cat. "I just had a bit of a shock this morning, that's all. I need a while to get myself ready to face Artemis. It'll be easier when Dad arrives, and

Lindy. You remember from Christmas, Mark's wife. Dad's giving her a lift."

Suddenly she leaned on the drainer, using her two hands to steady herself, and her head fell forwards with a shuddering breath, as if she had been stricken by pain. Martin looked at her with real concern now.

"Shall I get Gervase? He's only cleaning out the vet. cupboard."

"No," said Cat. She straightened up and turned to dry her hands, and Martin saw that she was crying. He started towards her, his hand outstretched to touch her shoulder, then thought better of it. Alone like this, with the colour gone from her cheeks and her hair fluffed out, she suddenly looked too vulnerable – and strangely, too damn pretty – to risk touching. With a small embarrassed "Uh, OK," he backed out of the utility room.

Alone in the room Cat went on staring at the toy which had caught her eye. It was a rag-doll clown with a Velcro tab on it to fasten around a baby's wrist. Winston had bought it at the Midholt toy shop for Mary-Annie, who had spent many hours waving it enthusiastically on her arm. Caroline, although she did not know its origins, had banished it because *Hey, Baby!* said that tied-on toys discouraged babies from correct development of the grasping reflex. Now it was lying, damp and discarded, on top of the pedal-bin with the other rubbish.

In the living room, over a glass of sherry, Artemis solved the problem of Caroline's future dwelling.

"You're absolutely *right* not to go back to London," she said. "It's a *frightful* place to bring up a little gel. What you need is a cottage, and put the rest of your settlement away to pick up some interest for when you and Maria need it most. There are things," she spoke with the wisdom of a woman whose friends numbered many ageing and querulous ex-wives of wealthy men, "things you never *can* get a man to pay for. He'll do school fees, obviously, but there are things like ponies. And decent ski-ing."

"I like the idea of a cottage," said Caroline. "But I haven't seen anything to buy or rent round here, and I'd like to be near my sister and Gervase. I can still help with the driving, then." She smiled, the image of a princess in a story, as kind as she was beautiful.

"Why not the Rectory Cottage?" said Artemis. "Mr Dallway would let you have it for hardly anything. It can't be sold because of some trust or other, and being right against the churchyard. But as rector in charge he's responsible for upkeep, and it's a terrible worry it standing empty."

"Is it up for rent?" said Caroline, interested. "I never knew." The cottage in question, two miles from Knoll Farm on the edge of Midmarsham, was well known to her: tiny, dilapidated pale-pink, with beautiful old oak window frames and a sagging roof of mossy red tiles.

"He had a tenant for ten years, a potter woman, but she left and Mr Dallway just can't bear the idea of putting it on the open market to rent. Not when it's so close to the church. And the Rectory. People have these *sound systems*, you know . . ."

Caroline laughed. "Not me. I like silence. It would be perfect if I could rent it for the moment. Just while Alan and I sort out the money, and I think about the long term. Shall I ask the vicar?"

"No," said Artemis. "*I* shall *tell* him."

She did so before dinner that very evening, making Robert drive her and Caroline down to the Rectory as soon as he arrived, and bursting in on her old friend Mr Dallway's modest evening meal. "All settled then," she said, half-an-hour later, getting back into the car.

"He needs to clear it with the diocese," protested Robert, who was hungry and not a little cross.

"He will," said Artemis. "And it'll be *lovely* for Caroline to have her own little place with her own little baby. I might," she said kittenishly, "come and stay! In that *lovely* little back bedroom!"

"That would be lovely," said Caroline politely. "No, really lovely." Robert, tired of all this ladylike loveliness, put his foot down and sped up the lane to his dinner.

"When shall you move?" asked Gervase later, tackling his duck. "Is the cottage habitable?"

"Perfectly," said Caroline. "Just some decorating, which won't take long, it's so tiny. I've imposed on you for so long, I really feel I should get out of all your hair now, so I'll decamp as soon as possible."

Cat, still quiet and red-eyed, looked sharply at her sister but could detect no other meaning behind this. Robert said: "Well, you'll be close at hand. I trust you'll carry on as chauffeur."

"Of course!" said Caroline. "Oh, we'll be in and out of one another's houses all the time! Very Jane Austen! Lovely!" She was gay tonight, a flush in her cheeks, smiling like the little girl Robert remembered. He smiled back. Then his eye caught his elder daughter's face, tired and tense, and he raised an eyebrow in her direction in gentle query. Cat avoided his glance and turned to Lindy, who was also strangely quiet.

"Everything OK?"

"Lovely," said Lindy mechanically, but her enthusiasm was but a pale echo of Caroline's. "Lovely duck. Is it from the farm?"

"Yes," said Gervase, innocently. Martin glanced at Caroline, but she continued demurely to dissect her own portion. He wondered whether it was possible for anybody else to use the word "lovely".

"Lovely and plump," said Lindy to the duck, trying to sound more enthusiastic. "Super."

She fell silent again, and this time Cat made no effort to draw her back into conversation. Robert embarked on some story from his UN aid conference, about a scheme for raising fowls in the Ugandan highlands. Martin asked intelligent questions. Caroline began talking nursery furnishings to Artemis. It was Gervase who looked around, his first hunger assuaged, and enquired: "Did Duane and Winston eat earlier?"

"Duane's at the pub with his girlfriend," said Cat. "Having chips. Winston said he wasn't hungry. He'll be in the bunk-house."

"I don't think he is," said Martin politely. "The lights are off."

"Perhaps he went to the pub with Duane," said Gervase. He looked at his watch, hesitated, frowned, then explained to the company at large:

"He is supposed to be in by nine, under his probation con-ditions. Until the end of the month, anyway. Then he has a month without curfews, then he's clear."

"I don't know how you live with all this crime business," said Artemis, shuddering. "You must admit, it is rather sordid."

Cat stared at her plate, and the wave of misery which had hung above her all day broke and overwhelmed her. This particular overture from Artemis had been familiar for the whole of her married life. Normally she would have answered, taken issue with the old monster, challenged her on Gervase's behalf while he smiled dryly in his corner. He rather liked being relieved, by his wife's voluble loyalty, of the tiresome need to defend his vocation from his mother. That was the pattern of their relationship as mother and daughter-in-law, and it had been for years a comfortable joke between Cat and Gervase. Years ago Gervase used to laugh about it at bedtime: "Forty-fifteen, I think. My darling, I can't tell you what a relief it is to have you take over the job of arguing social policy with my Mama. I've been doing it for twenty years to absolutely no effect." Cat used to laugh too, and say "You set me up, you bastard. One day I'll teach you a lesson. I'll crack, and agree with her that it's all just too sordid and that they should be locked up and the key thrown away. You wait."

This time, however, she could not respond to Artemis. Tonight the Knoll Farm Project did seem sordid, and pointless, and hopeless. Winston, as she knew perfectly well, had gone to the Midmarsham pub with Duane in her car. He would certainly not be back by nine. It was his first breach of the probation condition since a couple of rebellious evenings early in his stay. Before Mary-Annie came. It would not be the last truancy for Winston was suddenly alone and so – Cat thought with crushing misery – was she.

For it was Gervase's job to keep Winston on the rails, sober and well-governed and up to his work: but only Cat understood the terrible thing which had been done to the boy, and only she feared the terrible consequences. Gervase, for some reason, was wilfully blind to the danger; he could see only Caroline's problems and Caroline's rights. Cat pressed her lips together. She should be angry, but the sensation in her was more like fear. After all these years of living with volatile, angry, damaged, awkward boys and never thinking twice about it, she had for the first time a sense of foreboding.

She realized, with a shock of unwilling admiration, that the reason this sense of dread was so new to her was that Gervase had, quite simply, never been wrong before. He had had failures, like Gary. But he had never misjudged a situation so badly. She, and all of the changing, rolling population of boys and volunteers, had sheltered for sixteen years behind his wisdom and unerring instinct. If his judgement had deserted him, they would all be bare to the winds.

Somehow, nauseous and frightened, she got through dinner, joining in the ebb and flow of spiritless conversation. Once, a dustbin lid blew off outside, and with a twisting pain she remembered Christmas Eve and the racket Toby and Topsy made in the lambing pens. She longed for Toby now as never before. Not for comfort or understanding, for these had never been the currency between them. Rather Cat wanted Toby to bring a joke, a diversion, an outrage; to splash a rude half-brick into the stagnant, reeking pond of family life. But God knew where he was, or whether the sister who wanted him most would ever see him again.

She stood alone in the kitchen at ten, stacking dishes in the sink for Martin to wash up after he had checked the livestock. Winston was not back. Duane was, which made this even more worrying; he had come in for a mug of cocoa and volunteered the information that Winse was "off with some blokes he knows". Robert, Artemis, Gervase and Caroline were gathered round the fire. Lindy, who never spent more time in a room with Lady Artemis than she had to, wandered in to lean on the kitchen stove.

"C'n I help?"

"Martin might like someone to dry for him, in a minute," said Cat shortly. "I'm going upstairs early, got a bit of work to finish."

"Well, the thing is, I did want to ask you something." Lindy twisted girlishly, grinding her pointed toe on the floor, cocking her head on one side.

"Mmm?" said Cat interrogatively. She was scraping some bones into the bucket, not the pig-bucket but a newly installed bucket which fed a green plastic conical composter which Gervase was testing in the orchard on behalf of a recycling campaign. She noted with irritation that there was only one sachet of accelerator chemical left. Why was the simple life so bloody complicated? "Ask away."

"It's about Mark," said Lindy. "I wanted to know if you knew anything about him and kids. He's being funny about our having a baby."

"Ah, babies," said Cat obscurely. "Babies! Cup of instant?" The good coffeepot had gone through to the party in the living room. Gratefully, Lindy received a mug of the powdered variety and sat down.

"I really, really want us to have kids, like really soon," said Lindy. "We've been trying. I've been off the pill for a year."

"And Mark?"

"I thought he was fine at first. But now he won't talk about it."

"Perhaps he's afraid he's infertile? Men really don't like that idea," said Cat. She wondered what she had done to deserve this. Every family gathering ended with her sitting here, looking at poultry bones, drinking nasty coffee and discussing reproduction with a series of distraught female relatives.

"He won't go for tests," said Lindy. "But I don't think he's afraid of firing blanks. I think he's quite bloody *pleased*." The end of the sentence rose: her Birmingham accent and her language always became stronger as she grew more animated. Cat stared at her.

"You mean you think he doesn't actually want a baby?"

"That's it! He doesn't! He went along with me trying, but he keeps saying, ever so cheerfully, that sometimes it just isn't meant to be, and all this fertility treatment is against nature, and how kids aren't everything."

"I suppose they aren't," said Cat slowly. Lindy swept on:

"Then I thought back, and the thing is, he always did go on a lot about me and him being – you know, everything. He always says how he only needs me in the world." She blushed. "He once said his mother never even liked him, and I was the first woman who understood him and so he needs all of me. He doesn't even like me being on the phone when he gets home. I have to be at the door, all lovely-dovey."

Cat, recipient as usual of one confidence too many, squirmed a little. "What I'm getting at, Cathy," said her sister-in-law, banging her mug down on the table for emphasis, "is, I think he might have done something, know what I mean?"

"Er—" said Cat. "No, I don't quite get—"

"I'm almost certain," said Lindy, "that sometime, I dunno when, he had the snip!"

"A vasectomy?" said Cat, incredulous. "Why?"

"To not have babies, ever!" said Lindy. "That's why people have it done, right?" And she burst into noisy tears just as the back door opened to admit an instantly embarrassed Martin.

21

Gervase woke early on Sunday, and found himself looking around the gloom of the curtained bedroom for the baby's cot. Then, shaking off the last soft rags of sleep, he remembered reality and went through his morning drill of composing his mind carefully to understanding, acceptance, and generosity.

Dear little Mary-Annie: she was best with her own mother's arms around her. Her mother, in turn, must be upheld and protected by the family, as all mothers should be supported and encouraged by the wider society. Each of us depends on all the others: the principle of chivalry, the courtesy of the strong to the weak, underlies all civilization. To be in a position to offer protection, support and comfort to those weaker or less fortunate is not a burden but an honour. We share the earth, and owe it, too, a certain courtesy.

Naturally, Gervase did not enunciate all these thoughts and principles as he lay beneath the lumpy duvet beside his sleeping wife. They merely gathered themselves around him, the daytime garments of conviction which he had worn ever since he had found them as an eighteen-year-old student volunteer on a London soup run. He had no need to preach sermons to himself or anybody else. It was not difficult to know what was right.

Sometimes there was even a melancholy beauty in doing right and thinking right, against your own more selfish inclinations. The baby had woken last night and Caroline had brought her down. Seeing them together, both so beautiful in the last flickering firelight, Gervase had been transfixed with an intensity of chivalry he had rarely felt. Or at least not since the day he first saw Cat, coping gracefully with her twin children at the gate of a mean and scruffy West London school where he had come for a City Farms committee meeting.

Cat stirred now, and rolled towards him. Gervase turned and smiled, then laid a hesitant hand on her shoulder. Her eyes snapped open.

"Uurgh," she said. Then, sitting upright, "Oh God. Did Winston get back?"

"Not by the time I came up," said Gervase. "With luck he's here now. I won't ring the Probation service over his breaking one curfew. He's been doing really well."

"You know why he isn't doing well any more, don't you?" said Cat.

"I doubt if it's as simple as you think," said Gervase. "You know my view. Winston's got to respect Caroline's wishes, the same as we do. It's part of learning how to grow up."

"Why shouldn't Caroline respect Winston a bit?" said Cat, wearily.

"I know it's hard for him," said Gervase. "But there'll be plenty more babies for him to play with. A new mother is vulnerable, and deserves support."

"I'm surprised you can't see anything wrong with Caroline's reasons for banning him from the baby," said Cat. "They're very Kensington, you know. Very Artemis."

"I don't presume to know her reasons. You have to make allowances for new mothers. Everyone has to, including Winston."

Cat climbed out of bed. "Well, I put it down to sex," she said rudely. "You can't think of anything but protecting Caroline, and I can't think of anything but how badly she's messing up poor old Winston."

"She can't be expected—" began Gervase, but his wife cut him off.

"No, you're right. She can't be expected to behave like anything but a selfish, snobbish cow. Till last night I never realized who it was your mother had reminded me of, all these years."

Gervase did not answer. It was not in his nature or within his principles to brawl with his wife.

Caroline had provided supermarket part-baked French rolls and croissants for breakfast, and Duane, seeing the prettily laid table, took fright and removed himself and his porridge to the garden on the pretext that it was a beautiful morning. Artemis, admiring the stiff white bib Caroline was tying on the baby, remarked that it was the most civilized breakfast-table she had seen in Knoll Farm for years. Martin, feeling more than ever like some kinda Jeeves, made the coffee. Robert had been out early to collect the Sunday papers from Midholt station and engrossed himself in the foreign news.

Cat picked up the business section and was reading about the corporate reorganization inside the Eden empire: it was a far less flattering version of the new structure and system than she had been writing for their newsletters over the past weeks, and she found herself cringing slightly at her involvement. Just as well Mark was not here until mid-morning to catch her reading it. Lindy was sleeping in, recovering from her cathartic, if inconclusive, storm of tears the night before. Cat, against her will, had promised to ask Mark the big vasectomy question, and was now cursing herself for this excess of helpfulness and wondering whether she could get out of it. Gervase came in from the farm just as the telephone began to ring.

"I'll get it," he said. Then: "Yes. Yes, it is. Oh dear. Are you pressing charges? Good. Shall I come over to collect him? Yes, obviously, the Probation service. Doug Willetts, at Midholt. Speak to him myself. About an hour. Thank you."

He came back to the table. Cat handed him a chipped mug of coffee, without comment. To the company in general Gervase said: "That was the police. I have to collect Winston"

"Really!" tinkled Artemis, mainly to Caroline. "Just like Christmas Day, isn't it dear? Do you *never* get a meal here without the police ringing?"

"Which station?" asked Cat. "Midholt?"

"No," said Gervase glumly. "Much worse. Northampton. He was in a club. It got raided."

Cat rubbed her eyes with the back of her hand. "But no charges?"

"No," said Gervase. "Only the sergeant did say he was apparently back with his old crowd. Two of the men with him were found in possession, and one has been charged with dealing. Luckily he was clean."

"I knew this would happen," said Cat. As Gervase left the room she looked across the table at Caroline, who was spooning apple into the baby's mouth with a neutral expression on her face.

"You did this," she said suddenly. "Caroline, you pushed him back onto the slippery slope. Poor bloody kid."

Caroline put down the spoon, and wiped Mary-Annie's mouth. The child was looking around beadily for the milk which should follow, and gave a little *yarr* of impatience. Caroline reached for the bottle.

"I hardly think that's fair," she said. "I was unwilling to let a farmhand with a drug record associate with my daughter. This morning's news isn't very likely to change my mind, is it?" She shook the prepared bottle of milk, and flipped the cap off.

"He wouldn't have *gone* back there," said Cat, between her teeth, "he wouldn't have *needed* his old friends, if he hadn't been so snubbed. Warned off going anywhere near a baby he'd loved and helped look after for most of her *life*. You did it, Caroline. Whatever happens to him now, you're involved."

"You're entitled to your opinion," said Caroline. "Look, sweetie. Bottle!"

Robert and Artemis found this exchange mystifying, and stared in open-mouthed astonishment at the cold fury which had fallen across this civilized breakfast-table. Martin, however, was overwhelmed by understanding, at last, what was going on. In the bunkhouse Winston had been sullen and angry all week, Duane oddly embarrassed and avoiding the family. He himself had exchanged no more than passing smiles with Mary-Annie, but only because he felt politely constrained in her dazzling mother's presence. The heat rose under his collar: was he, too, banned? Even without criminal convictions, he was, he supposed, a "farmhand".

Gervase reappeared, looked harassed, and saved him from the rising tide of embarrassment. "Martin, I've obviously got to drive into Northampton. Would you mind taking over? Just the horses to do, then the antibiotic shot for that ewe that had the prolapse. I put her in the isolation box. Give her more blowfly spray as well, just in case. There's a lot of stuff round her back end." Artemis shuddered and pushed away her croissant, but Martin gratefully said: "Yep. I'll go right now."

Cat left the table and threw her mug into the sink, where the handle broke off. "I'll be outside," she said to nobody in particular. Then she walked up alone to the meadow where she used to go with Mary-Annie on her hip. There was no frolicking up there now: the last lambs had given up, and become dully grazing sheep.

So solid was Gervase's principle that all should eat together that even on this Sunday, at one o'clock, ten adults were once again grouped around the table eating roast chicken, cauliflower cheese and peas as if nothing were amiss between them. Winston did not speak a word: Cat had tried to talk to him before lunch and got nowhere. Duane gobbled his food and sat, poised for flight, waiting his moment to make an excuse and cycle down to Midmarsham and his girlfriend. Mark had arrived, looking anxious and miserable and unable to keep his hands off Lindy, who fended off his clumsy caresses rather snappishly and flirted with an ever more embarrassed Martin. Artemis and Caroline talked about pelmets and rugs; Robert took in the atmosphere with dismay and escaped between courses, carrying a pile of greasy dishes, to confront his elder daughter in the kitchen.

"What *is* going on?" he asked plaintively. "I'd rather mediate in Sarajevo than your household just now."

"Caroline," said Cat savagely, "is what is going on. And, bloody soon I hope, she is going down the road."

"But I thought she was getting on well," said Robert with a plaintive, injured masculine obtuseness which irritated even his favourite daughter, not least because she knew him capable of better understanding. "I was so pleased when you said she was looking after the baby at last. And she's well rid of that dreadful Halliday man. Did I tell you he still rings me up for contacts? The nerve. Surely everything's on course, now? As far as it can be, with a divorce. Poor little Caro."

"Well, you're wrong. It was better the way it was before," said Cat, taking the plates from him. "Caroline the frigid monster-woman was a bloody sight less trouble than Caroline the Perfect bloody Madonna and child. Believe me. The sooner she goes, the better. I'm sorry Dad: I've had it."

"Well, well," said Robert soothingly. "Diana always said it was asking for trouble when women shared a kitchen. Especially sisters. You've done very well."

His elder daughter made a noise very like "Bah!" Robert continued: "And what about Mark? Does he always come home from sales conferences and maul his wife in public? And why is *she* so grumpy?"

Cat looked at her father, wondering whether to explain the whole thing to him. That day in the House of Lords he had shown unexpected subtlety of understanding: maybe she ought to lay out before him as patriarch all the twisted feelings that lay between his children and their households. But no: she herself could not bear it. That lunch had been embarrassing enough, without her now plunging into some lurid account of suspected vasectomies, quixotic adoption attempts, misplaced chivalry, psychobabble, wilfully provocative designer babywear and an orphan boy betrayed back into a Dickensian life of crime. Instead she just said sadly:

"Sorry Dad. All your little lambs have just grown up and turned into sheep. It happens."

Across both of them, at that moment, fell the shadow of Toby, the black sheep and now the lost one. But neither mentioned him. There was nothing to say.

The task of challenging Mark was not easy. After lunch, he sat next to Lindy on the sofa, holding her unwilling hand. After twenty minutes he finished the last of his coffee and said: "We'd better be off home."

Lindy made a face to Cat and said, "Yeah, OK. I'll get my case—"

"I'll come up," said Mark.

Lindy threw an appealing glance at Cat, who nodded and said: "No, just come through a minute – I've got something to show you."

Unwillingly, he followed her through to the kitchen. Here, weary of diplomacy and subterfuge, she turned to him and said crossly: "Have you had a vasectomy?"

Mark stared at her and took a step back, hitting his head on the low beam by the cooker.

"Why do you ask?" he said stiffly, when he had recovered himself.

"Because Lindy's upset she isn't getting pregnant."

"She could have talked to me about it. These things take time."

"Oh, for God's sake!" said Cat. "I don't want to get involved in your reproductive strategies, I'm sick of the whole bloody subject, for certain reasons I will not bore you with. But Lindy has been weeping half the night about it, and she suspects you're not telling her something. Just go on, spit it out, let's be honest for a change. If you won't tell me, at least have it out with her. Bloody, bloody families!"

She sniffed and, to her horror, began to cry. Mark stood thunderstruck, then seemed to realize that this let him off answering her question, and gave a curious, tight little smile. Cat did not see it but Lindy, who had been lurking behind the door to the backstairs saw the smirk and stepped out to confront him.

"I should've asked you myself," she said. "Cat, I'm ever so sorry. I think I know now, anyway, dunni?"

He was silent. She said again, her voice thick and rough and angry, "Dunni? Mark? S'true, innit?"

"I've already been to the clinic," he said stiffly. "About getting it reversed. They say there's a good chance."

Lindy stared at him a moment, then threw her arms around his shoulders and hugged him.

"Marky! You old fool!" she said. Her tears damped his crisp conference shirt, and she shifted her grip to cling with both hands to his grey suit lapels. "Why din't you tell me?"

Cat recovered herself and said, "Look, you two, get in your car. Drive down the lane, then stop and talk about all this. You don't want Dad and Artemis and Caroline all involved."

But it was too late. Caroline had drifted through with the coffee tray, and to Cat's horror she had lying next to the coffeepot a proof copy of a pamphlet called *Eden PLC and the Millennium: The plan, the prospects, the people*.

"Look," she said innocently. "Artemis found this down the back of the sofa. Don't you work for Eden, Mark? We thought you might be interested."

22

On a grey morning in late June, Caroline moved into the Rectory Cottage. She and Artemis and a bevy of cowed workmen had transformed it from fusty and chintzy neglect into a simple but beautiful interior of Shaker austerity, in keeping with Caroline's new mood of West Coast spirituality. The plank floors were sanded, polished and covered with soft knotted Indian rugs, the sofas draped in expensive cream wool, the matchboarding painted pale blue, the kitchen furnished with two traditional dressers and a deep old stone sink. It was the same sink, but looked quite different now that it was surrounded not by chipped Formica but by a solid oak worktop shaped and cunningly dropped over the previous surface.

"No point spending money on things you can't take away. Not in rented property," said Artemis masterfully. Cat, still low in spirits and reeling from a long, crazy letter from Mark about breach of trust, professional duplicity and wanton conflict of interest, had been glad to have Artemis stay on to help Caroline. Her mother-in-law had at least the gift of being a useful surface irritant, which distracted everybody from deeper pains. During some of her more absurd tirades about the way modern youth "simply don't care", even Duane caught Cat's eye once or twice and almost giggled.

Only Winston remained wrapped up in himself, silent and morose. Martin told her that he had asked for one of the Polaroids of Mary-Annie, and kept it in his pocket. The baby herself he avoided, bolting his food at meal times and leaving early. Cat tried to talk to him once or twice, but whatever softening of his angry nature the baby had brought about, it had not yet taught him how to confide.

Thanks to Artemis' relentless bullying of the workmen, on moving day only the extractor fan in the kitchen remained to be fitted, everything else being neatly and beautifully in place. Caroline had not wanted to bring up any household equipment from Kensington: Alan, she told Gervase with an air of dignified sorrow, had actually moved in one of his girlfriends. Accordingly she fetched only the rest of her clothes and a few personal things in four smart suitcases, and equipped the cottage kitchen from new. Alan had agreed to settle upon her, in addition to the maintenance he paid for Mary-Annie, a capital sum amounting to half the value of the Kensington house. Large Kensington houses were doing rather well that spring, and Alan's stockbroker had organized her investments. Caroline would be comfortable, even without work.

All that had to be done on moving day was for her and Artemis to bring the cases and Mary-Annie down the lane in Cat's car, and for Gervase to drive the baby's bulky, awkward-shaped mass of new equipment in the LandRover. That night Caroline ate supper and slept in her own cottage home, with her sister's mother-in-law for company in the spare room.

The weather cleared during the day; at dusk, while Mary-Annie gurgled herself to sleep in her new pink room and Artemis telephoned her friends to relate her triumph, Caroline wandered out into the overgrown little garden next to the graveyard.

The sky was turning to darker blue above the last red smudge of sunset, and against it one star shone bright and alone. As she stood there gently thoughtful, relishing the damp fragrance of the garden, a footstep crunched on pebbles beside the lane and made her turn. Gervase stood there, apologetic but smiling, with a framed picture under his arm.

"I forgot to give you this," he said. "Housewarming." Caroline took it: behind the glass was a spotted, faded Victorian print, obviously one of a series of allegorical exhortations to morality. The picture showed a hooded and skeletal figure at a chessboard, opposite a young knight; at least, the human player was attired as a knight but the face was sexless in its purity, and fair hair waved down its back. Beneath the picture was the legend: *Against the pure, no evil shall prevail.*

"It was in my bedroom when I was a child," said Gervase. "I found it a very reassuring notion. I thought you and Mary-Annie might like it, especially as you'll be teaching her chess before long."

"We'll both teach her." Caroline smiled up at him in the dusk. "But even before that, she's going to need her best uncle nearby. Thanks for everything. It feels funny moving out. But do come and see us. Often."

"I will," said Gervase.

With Caroline and the baby gone, the next few days saw Knoll Farm returning to a semblance of its old normality. Winston in his present surly state was no pleasure to be with, but no more trouble than many other boys had been down the years. Duane had been offered a job on a production line making kits to convert cars for the disabled in a rural industrial unit not far from the Midmarsham pub and his girlfriend. They were, he confided to Cat, keen to "start a family". Cat flinched, but only told him he had plenty of time. A new boy, Terry, was coming in July. Winston's curfew had been extended for another month by Mr Willetts after his escapade in Northampton, but he too was due to leave soon.

Caroline continued to do driving errands and shopping by day, picking up a daily list without much conversation with her sister. Marianne came down for the weekend, to Martin's delight, and the two of them went for a five-hour walk and came back glowing and subtly changed. Next time she came there was no chance for anything but working at Martin's side in the hayfield; haymaking, at Knoll Farm, was deliberately done in an old-fashioned and laborious manner without machinery so that during the weeks of June the farm became hectically busy. The horses were out every day turning or raking the sweet-smelling piles of drying grass, and sweating men built stacks with pitchforks as they would have done a century before.

The idea, as Gervase often told journalists (who ignored it) was not olde-worlde picturesqueness, but to practise his ideas about the dignity and healing qualities of simple manual labour. Nonetheless, amateur photographers and camcorder enthusiasts appeared, as usual, alongside the hedges to record this pastoral poppy-strewn scene with stooks and stacks and horses. One man asked Winston to move out of shot because, being black, he "didn't quite fit. No offence, mate".

Cat, who rarely helped outdoors at this season because of her hay fever, continued desultorily at her desk with the window tightly shut. One morning Gervase came upstairs with her post and stood by her chair holding a letter of his own.

"How about this?" he asked. Despite Cat's visible depression since the affair of Caroline and Winston, his manner towards her was the same as it always was: level, gentle, respectful.

"Just a mo," she said, slitting open her bank statement. "I just want to check this." She looked down at the figures before her, incredulous. "Gosh," she said. "Ta-ra! I'm rich."

Gervase walked over to the window and looked down at the fattening sheep across the lane. Cat continued to stare at the print-out. Since the upheavals at Eden and the removal of her driving duties at home, she had been doing a lot of extra work and logging it hastily in her account book. She had not realized, however, that she was doing so very well. Each month her account automatically fed £750 into the shared account; after she had put away tax money, this rarely left her with more than £120 a month against which she could draw her infrequent personal cheques. Now, although it seemed that the joint account had received its monthly boost, Mrs Catherine Hartley's Private A/C showed a credit of £1893.97. Moreover, another Eden payment was due any day and could well be even bigger than the last few.

"Yup, I'm rich," she said again. Then, looking out through the dusty window at the sunshine: "Shall we have a holiday, for once?"

Gervase began to pace around the room. "You know how I'm placed in summer," he said. "Hay, then harvest. We could go away for a long weekend in September, if I could get cover here and stand down the boys for a few days. I can't just walk out."

"Yes. Silly idea," said his wife, still staring at the statement. "You wouldn't miss me, though, if I went?"

"You do what you like. You work too hard," said Gervase automatically. Then, brandishing his own envelope: "But look at this. Morefield Youth Trust."

"Oh, that bequest thingy? It was in the papers. The millionaire with the druggy son who died?"

"That's him. Anyway, they're really interested in what we're doing. Their senior Trustee is the Prince of Wales. Apparently he told them he was coming here on a private visit. They want to do a fact-finding trip around the time he comes."

"That's nice," said Cat vaguely. "Have they got any spare money?"

"Heaps. But what puzzles me is that they seem to think the Prince is visiting us during haymaking, because they're asking about photography."

"He'd have to get a move on. There's only about a week left, isn't there?"

"Yes. What do you suppose is going on? Do you think they're considering actually supporting the project?"

"Search me," said Cat. She was still looking down at her bank statement. "Interesting, anyway. Well done."

When he had gone she opened the next envelope, the Midholt Choral Society newsletter, which against all reasonable expectation seemed to surprise and interest her almost as much as the bank statement.

At lunch-time she came downstairs. Mrs Bird was dishing out leek and potato soup; she had diffidently asked for more hours' work to cushion the effort and worry of visiting Gary, who had been moved to Littlehey Prison. Cat gladly agreed: there had still been pleasure in cooking when Mary-Annie was all hers, sitting in her bouncy chair, grabbing at her feet and crooning to the birds outside the window. Since she had gone the meals were once again a dull, repetitive chore and she had resolved, at any cost, to pay Mrs Bird and avoid the kitchen.

The boys were already sitting at table, elbows sprawled, eating lumps of bread. Gervase was on the telephone in the hall, but came through, looking almost excited.

"Next Wednesday. It's definite. The visit."

"What visit?" asked Cat, who was reading the Choral Society newsletter again.

"What we talked about. Upstairs. He's coming."

"Old Bat Ears?" said Cat, incredulously. "Here? Wow!"

Sometimes, thought Gervase with a flash of unwonted irritation, his wife sounded just like a cheeky teenage boy. His fault, perhaps, for surrounding her with teenage boys for so many years. Or maybe it was some obscure gesture of solidarity with her favourite, her missing, brother. He recovered his aplomb and frowned meaningly, jerking his head towards the three young men and Mrs Bird.

"Yes. The – er – conservation, bat people. To look at the barn," he improvised. "They think we've got a rare species. Of bat." Cat stared at him in turn. Gervase very rarely lied. It consorted ill with his usual dignity.

Later, alone, he chided her. "We have to keep it quiet," he said. "It's not on the official register of Royal engagements. The boys can know on the day. It's all supposed to be very low-key, but it ties up with the possibility that the Morefield Trust will be quite a lot of help to the project. Financially."

"Aha," said Cat. "Money. Beats royalty, any day."

"They're coming on Monday to look us over," said Gervase. "And if they decide to put themselves behind us, they'll announce it on the day of the Prince's visit, to invited press. It could take a lot of pressure off us financially. Off you."

"Then I'll be even richer." Cat was in a frivolous mood, so strong a contrast to her recent depression that her husband was puzzled.

"Are you OK?" he asked.

"Never better," said Cat. "But I shan't be here to press the royal paw. I'm going on a little holiday. A mission, actually. I'm going to France. I might even track down Toby."

It was curious, she thought in later years, that despite the months of wondering about Toby, and even the abortive discussion with Mark on whether he might have gone to one of their childhood cities, it had never occurred to her to make the journey herself. Partly, it was her habit of dour pragmatism. Cat, since early adulthood, had gone to some lengths to suppress romantic notions in herself. She recognized in her heart a treacherous desire to think of Toby as having fled the world to purge his grief; perhaps to turn up years later like Sebastian Flyte in *Brideshead Revisited*, as a lay-brother in some peaceful Mediterranean monastery. On identifying this wishful, wistful train of thought she had firmly quashed it. Grief or no grief, she cruelly told herself, in spite of the haunting oddity of that postcard Toby was more likely to be off somewhere with another woman, or women, and a great deal of booze. When Caroline had made for Los Angeles claiming to search for Toby, Cat had half-envied and half-despised her sister. It was obviously nonsense: nobody ever found a wilfully missing person just by wandering around looking for them in the right few thousand acres of the globe, even if they could guess where that was. The idea of following the Calais lead had come to her, but been quashed as ridiculous and self-indulgent. There was, after all, Mary-Annie to look after. Then.

The other reason, she saw now, was that in lives such as theirs a kind of curtain fell at the end of every posting, cutting you off from the past. Diplomatic families seemed to know by instinct that it was better that way. None of the Grattons had been back to Lille, nor to Berne or Tel Aviv. Caroline had gone to Venice, but only as part of her fine-art career. Robert travelled to Washington, but once admitted that even then he steered clear of the old house and the old street. Caroline had gone back to Los Angeles, but only because of her abnormal state of emotional turmoil. No, thought Cat: in the ordinary way of things, diplomatic and military families rarely go back. Perhaps they are afraid to acknowledge that they are forever incomplete: that they have left torn-off roots in too wide a spread of alien soil.

But then again, maybe it was this very sense of taboo which had made her wonder if Toby had. Of all of them, he with his perennial perversity was the most likely to break unwritten rules, to whisk aside the curtain and disappear into some corner of the family past. He always liked forbidden thrills. Caroline had shown symptoms of hectic, almost guilty excitement over her return to LA. Now Cat herself was finding that the idea of going to Lille – only an hour beyond Calais on the motorway, for heaven's sake – brought a surprising frisson of joy and fright at her own temerity.

Even the windfall money might not have tripped her into it, were it not for the Midholt Choral Society newsletter and the boxed announcement on the front page.

TWINNING CONCERT WITH SAINT-OMER:
FAURÉ REQUIEM AND CHANSONS CYCLE

We are now travelling to Saint-Omer via the Channel Tunnel! Three 12-seater minibuses will make the journey on 14 June, returning 16 June. On the return trip we are full, as six of our twin-town choristers are coming to swell the numbers for the Verdi Requiem at the Corn Exchange. This means there are six spare seats outbound. Anybody want a one-way ticket to fabulous Flanders? High quality on-board singing guaranteed, a snip at only £22. You could always take the Eurostar back from Lille! and make the whole round trip for £50. We leave at noon on the 14th and get there for dinner and a run-through.

CHOIR – REMEMBER YOUR MUSIC THIS TIME!

Cat was a long-lapsed member of the Choral Society. She had not known about the twinning. So it was thirty-three years since she had read the name of Saint-Omer.

It brought back a cluster of other names on signposts long ago: Béthune, Lens, Douai, Ypres, Roubaix, Armentières: signs from the centre of the northern city of Lille, signs to suburbs and towns of the Pas-de-Calais, long ago and far away in flat homely Flanders where she had been a child. The odd word *Tourcoing* sprang into her mind: where was it? A lit sign on the front of a tram, that was it: *Tourcoing*, suburb of Lille. Her friend Marie-Noelle came in from there, to school with the *bonnes soeurs* at 66 Rue Royale. Cat really liked Sylvie better, and they both came ice-skating on Sunday mornings with Cat and Véronique, her very best friend; sometimes their brothers Thierry and Chrétien came too. Sylvie was the best skater of all, and swung around the rink to the strains of the "Blue Danube" or – better! – Edith Piaf singing "*Je ne regrette rien*". Cat, at twelve, came alone to the *patinoire* by tram with her own money and her own skates in a smart white plastic boot-bag. By the end of her time in Lille she was enjoying heady freedoms: allowed to walk home from school, alone or in charge of Toby, and to buy a hot *croque-monsieur* in the Place Général de Gaulle on the way. In Lille she found her first near-adult freedoms.

Now she closed her eyes, and saw again for the first time in years the humped, scampering red neon outline of a ferret on the far side of the Grand'Place. Why was it there? Ah yes, the bookshop and stationery supplier where she bought her neat school pencil cases. *Le Furet du Nord.* Why should a ferret be the symbol of a bookshop? Was it still running and writhing up there today?

Lille! God bless it. She would go there and try out her long forgotten French again; she would not kid herself that she would find Toby, but you never knew. Maybe the best way to find a runaway was to run away yourself.

However, as an acknowledgement of the dull middling English-woman she had become Cat would cross the Channel humbly, in a spare seat on the choir bus. All this she had decided, upstairs in her room before lunch. Nothing would now deflect her from it.

"But are you sure you don't want to put it off a few days?" asked Gervase, a little bewildered. "It's not every day we get . . . well, a royal visit."

Cat turned to him and he saw that she was smiling: a mischievous, younger smile. Like her brother Toby's.

"Ah, come on," she said. "You know you're better at selling the project than me. That's why I keep out of these PR things. I'd only say something negative, or flip, or let on about Winston's little outing the other night. Do you really want to let your copy-writing cynic of a wife loose on His Royal Highness's innocent idealism?"

Gervase looked helplessly at her. "Will you at any rate see the Morefield Trust with me on Monday?" he asked. "Please? You are part of the project. For the boys. The family side does matter as well as the work."

"Yes, OK," said Cat. "I'll be good. Whether poor old Winston will be is another matter."

23

Winston, in the event, behaved perfectly, although without much enthusiasm. Perhaps he already knew that the Monday of the Morefield Trust inspection was his last at Knoll Farm. Later that night he went for a walk after supper, hitched a lift into Midholt, and drank six cans of lager with some old acquaintances who by ill-chance he found sitting on the horse trough outside the Corn Exchange with their feet in the Council's prized floral arrangement. He rode with them in a battered Ford van as far as Northampton where, in the clubs and on the streets, he spent the next few days before being picked up by the police in possession of several smiley, sticky dots of Ecstasy and a wad of unearned money.

Cat went to see him in the remand centre on the day before her trip to France. It was a concession, wrenched from the system after several days' hard work by Mr Willetts. He had high regard for Mrs Hartley, and firmly believed that any request she made must have some reason behind it.

"Hello," she said. Winston sat, looking smaller and more defenceless than usual, on a cold plastic chair opposite her.

"Hi," said Winston. He looked away, apparently studying the peeling paint on the small room's door.

"I just came to say something," said Cat. "Do you want to know what it is?"

"Advice to yobs? Come on boy, get yo' act together, society expects it?" said Winston. "OK, might as well."

"No," said Cat. "Not advice to yobs. Three pieces of information. None of them will be any use when your case comes up, but you might want to know them."

She wanted his attention, and was uncertain whether he had taken any of the fuddling drugs his friends dealt in. She paused, watching him, until unwillingly he dragged his eyes back to her; eyes which, she saw, were perfectly clear and undrugged. He said: "Yeah? What?"

Cat smiled. She had him listening now. She raised three fingers, and counted off her points on them with the other hand.

"Fact one," she said. "My sister, Caroline Halliday, is a silly, snotty, spoilt little cow. None of her opinions on anything – except perhaps Renaissance altarpieces – is worth wasting five minutes on. Got that? She's a silly bitch, and I often want to slap her one."

Winston stared, his attention riveted. Cat continued:

"Fact two. You, Winston Maliba, are one of the best, carefullest, gentlest, most intelligent men with a baby that I have ever known. You are better than an awful lot of women. Your own kids will be really lucky to have you. So will any kids you work with. You did a lot for Mary-Annie, when her bloody mother wouldn't play with her and I was too busy to do much. All the fun that you had together will stay there, inside her, for all her life. Believe me. I know about babies. She'll be a happier and better grown-up because she had you."

Winston sat silent, staring at his thin dark hands on the table in front of him. He was very still. There was a silence.

"Do you want to talk any more now?" said Cat gently.

He shook his head, and a tear fell onto his right knuckle.

"OK," she said, getting up. "So I'll just tell you Fact three. You haven't blown it. Not for always. Even if they send you down, there's life out there waiting. See you."

"That was quick" said Mr Willetts, outside.

"All we needed," said Cat.

The big man sighed. "I've been talking to the solicitor. We might get him another non-custodial sentence. That's what I pray for. If he does time now, he's had it."

"Keep praying," said Cat.

The second minibus in the Choral Society's convoy held five baritones, two basses, four sopranos and Cat. More than half of them had been with her in the choir, for lives did not change fast in Midholt. It was strange to be among them again, and reminded her of more light-hearted days before the Lloyds disaster and the land sale.

When she was first married to Gervase he had a full-time helper on the farm, a woman to cook, and the bunkhouse held five boys at a time. Cat did some part-time copywriting for an advertising agency, raised her own children, and had leisure enough to spend two evenings a week singing in this good-spirited innocent neighbourhood choir. As they teased her now for her desertion, she felt soothed to be among them. They were people from a rare, brief time of undemanding ordinariness in her life: quite different from her spiky cosmopolitan family, from the boys on the farm project and their social workers, and above all from the savage, neurotic working world of Eden PLC. They were kind people, unimaginative, comfortable, sensible provincials who ran shops and banks and builders' yards and channelled their romanticism into the eternal yearnings of song.

"Don't know why you ever left, Mrs Hartley," said the leading bass, gallantly. "Top C's never been the same without you."

"Oooh! cheeky!" said two sopranos in unison. "Not that we don't miss you, love."

"Well, someone has to be in the audience," said Cat. "I'm a very good subscriber."

"Saw you with that sister of yours a month or so back," said a baritone, owner of Midholt's leading fruit-and-vegetable shop. "Gor, that's a beautiful woman. Nearly made me lose my place."

"Pretty, but not flawless," said Cat. "Cracked notes, there. Dissonant intervals." The others laughed. The last musical director had referred to all faults of character by musical similes. Then they teased her until, half-unwillingly, she led them off, hesitant but true, into the verse from *Dido and Aeneas* in which she had led the women's chorus thirteen years earlier:

"*To the hills and the vales*," sang Cat to the speeding traffic on the grey unrolling road,

> "*To the rocks and the mountains*
> *To the musical glades*
> *And the cool shady fountains.*"

The bus filled with sound as the rest joined in, the men improvising themselves a deeper part beneath the soaring sopranos:

> *Let the tri-hi-hi-hi-hi-hi-hiumphs*
> *Let the tri-i-i-umphs*
> *Of love and of beauty be shown."*

Bowling down the A1 they sang on through their common repertoire, the driver – a non-singer, only there for the *hypermarché* beer – smiling indulgently as the women's notes soared and swooped around his ears, and the men's boomed deep enough to rattle the windows on the hired bus.

Back at the farm, Duane and Martin sat a little disconsolately over their mid-morning mug of tea in the bunkhouse.

"Just us, now," said Martin. "And the boss. Weird, huh?"

"I'm off next week," said Duane. "New job an' all. You staying on?"

"Gervase asked me to," said Martin. "I can do some of the driving, and I suppose I'm quite handy with the horses now. We'll have to teach the new boys. I don't need to be home till September."

They looked up as Gervase loomed in the doorway. It was rare for him to come to the bunkhouse unless to sort out a fight: this place, in his system, represented the boys' own territory, a rehearsal for living their own lives. He was smiling.

"Some news. Good news. We are going to be taken over. It's partly thanks to the good impression you gave last Monday."

"Whassat?" asked Duane. Martin, who had taken in more of the import of the Trustees' visit, said:

"They're giving you a grant? The Morefield Trust?"

"Better," said Gervase. "They're employing me. At a salary, to run Knoll Farm more or less exactly the way it is now. Only with a full-time trained care assistant, so we can take people with learning difficulties on day programmes. And we get funding for four places at once in the bunkhouse. And a volunteer, on pocket-money, when we can get one."

"Does it all change, then?" asked Duane, stupidly.

"No, that's the beauty of it. They want the farm to run the way it does now. It's just that we can have more lads. We always used to. And someone to cook."

"Will it still be your farm?" asked Martin. He wondered whether he ought to have asked that; Gervase looked embarrassed. But he answered readily enough.

"I make the land over to the Trust," he said. "The house stays mine. The contract is firm for five years, then if I want I can train a successor, sell them the house at market value and sever the link. Or sign for another five."

"Sounds neat," said Martin. "I don't see any farmers back home handing over fifty acres just like that, though."

Gervase laughed, looking twenty years younger.

"I daresay I wasn't ever really cut out to be a landowner," he said. "And I've no one to leave it to but Cat, and she wouldn't want what she calls a load of old mud."

Martin smiled with him, but inwardly marvelled at the unworldliness of some Brits. It was, he knew, quite possible and even likely that the odd, fierce, likeable Cat Hartley would not object to her husband's handing over some hundred thousand dollarsworth of land to a charity in return for being allowed to carry on working as hard as he did now. But he wondered whether Gervase had had a chance to ask her.

Later that day, Gervase took the LandRover past Rectory Cottage, and on an impulse, stopped. Caroline was kneeling on the grass making a daisy-chain. Mary-Annie was sitting up, surrounded by unbleached canvas cushions and wobbling slightly, but nonetheless unmistakably sitting under her own power.

"Look!" said Caroline. "She's almost safe to leave sitting up now. The clinic says her lower back muscle tone is excellent. Really advanced for six months."

Gervase looked fondly at the baby. "Clever girl," he said. Looking up at him, with her lifelong enthusiasm for men, the child crowed and stretched her fat arms skywards. He bent down and scooped her up before the excitement could make her forget her muscle tone and collapse onto the cushions.

"Ooza girl?" he said. "Ooza beautiful girl?" The baby lunged towards him, mouth pursed in goldfish style, to attempt one of her newly-learnt wet sloppy kisses. Gervase grimaced and bounced her in his arms, facing him. "Great lump you are," he said. And to Caroline: "How are things? Settled in?"

"Blissful," said Caroline. "I never knew how good it could be, living somewhere small and quiet with a child to look after. I feel as if my whole life has been too complicated." She looked up at her brother-in-law and smiled, and even with her big eyes screwed up a little against the afternoon sun she was beautiful.

"I suppose you think I'm a complete escapist. I mean, my life hasn't achieved nearly as much as yours, and you're still out there fighting all the dragons."

"No," said Gervase. "I do what makes me happiest. And I honour your idea of living simply and quietly." He glanced at the open door of the cottage. At Knoll Farm the view inwards through the back door showed a jumble of heavy coats flung over hooks, of rubber boots and boxes and baskets and sometimes the wheel of a bicycle or a horse collar waiting to be mended. Looking through Caroline's door he saw only a pale clear scrubbed flagstone floor, a stark Japanese vase with an arrangement of dried grasses, and a plain but spotless rug in pale restful blue. It might have been a photograph in an interiors magazine. It was a door to step through and find rest.

"You've made it beautiful," he said.

"Just a little beautiful. I don't need anything else," she said, quiet as a nun. Gervase bent down and placed the baby, tenderly, in her arms. There was a moment's charged silence before it was rudely broken by a loud burp from Maria Annunciata.

The three buses stopped at last in front of some tall white gantries and a row of paybooths. Cat had dropped out of the chorus somewhere on the M20 motorway, when the men began illustrating a new craze for barbershop harmonies which they had adopted in order to annoy the chastely minded Musical Director. To a background of "Shine on Harvest Moon" she looked around at the Le Shuttle terminus in bemusement. Holidays with Gervase had been brief and generally Scottish, but years ago she had crossed the Channel often, on trips from school to home in Venice or from Lille to grandparents in England. She knew the Channel crossing: it meant docks, ferries waiting with wisps of steam coming from their funnels, cars rattling up ramps, foot passengers walking up gangways that swayed, passport and boarding card in their teeth. It meant jokes about the rough crossing, going on deck to see the white cliffs, being glad you were not sick.

This cool sterile efficient approach felt like an anticlimax. "How long does it take?" she asked as the little bus trundled into a steel box of a carriage.

"Twenty-five minutes or so," said the driver casually. "We should be on the Calais bypass by six, well on the way. You want dropping at Calais, though, don't you, love?"

"Mmm," said Cat. She was strangely shaken by this encounter with the prosaic efficiencies and flat unromantic hurry of this modern terminus. It was not a railway station nor an airport nor a harbour, but something new. A processing station for submarine voyagers, each cocooned smugly in their own car, free from the rude jostle of fellow travellers.

It was odd, too, to be sitting in a car seat that swayed and juddered like a train. She had never thought about the safety of the tunnel, regarding the news of its arrival two years earlier as just another echo of a distant changing world, nothing to do with her. Now, forty-five metres below the Channel waves, slightly nauseous from the odd motion caused by the train's swaying and the vehicle's suspension working together, she shuddered for a moment. Had Toby come this way? No, he couldn't have: no foot passengers except on the train, and the train did not run from Dover to Calais and conveniently stop for postcards. He could, of course, have got a lift from somebody in a car. But Topsy's friends had said he would have nothing to do with anybody.

She wrenched her mind back to the present. "Is it easy to drop me at the station, at Calais?" she asked the driver.

"Certainly is. No trouble."

"You're very welcome to come on for the night with us," said Lesley Berrett, a soprano who used to stand next but one to her. "I'm sure the host families would find you a room. You don't want to be jauntering around France in the dark, alone, do you, dear?"

Oh, I do! thought Cat secretly. That is exactly what I want. To jaunter around France in the dark, alone. To be responsible for nobody, to visit my childhood. I shall be in Lille tonight, I shall buy a *croque-monsieur* and take a tram and find a hotel for a couple of nights, and not think of Eden or Winston or Caroline, or babies or meals or family aggravation, or everyone going into a flat spin over Prince Charles coming to frown thoughtfully at muck heaps with Gervase. Instead of all this, she thought with a surge of joy, I am going to jaunter round France alone, in the dark.

Now she was anxious to get out of this coach with her light bag and be clear of these cosy Midholt people whose history had nothing to do with hers. She read the Franglais signs which flickered across the display over their head. *Vous arrivez au destination . . . close sunroofs and vents . . .*

In another moment, the train emerged from the strange subsea hole, the minibuses rolled onto French soil and the driver kept his word and dropped her, fifteen minutes later, at the Calais station. Outside it, though, the first thing she saw was a coach labelled LILLE – ARMENTIÈRES.

She spoke briefly to the driver, surprised that the French words came without effort, and swung her tartan bag over her shoulder to climb up the coach's high step. Catherine Hartley, née Gratton, was on the way home.

24

The coach was three-quarters empty. Cat sat near the front, enjoying through the driver's open window the faint farty, cabbagey smell of French drains. No, surely not drains, not these days. Calais harbour, maybe. Or the chemical plant.

Signs said NORD – PAS DE CALAIS and she smiled, remembering arguments with seven-year-old Toby about the absurdity of calling a region "Not Calais". Or, as Robert more accurately translated it to tease them, "*pas de Calais* – none of that Calais". Then he explained that the "*pas*" had more to do with a step, or a "*passe*", but the children were not listening by then, but shrieking "None of yer Calais!" and swinging on the wrought-iron banisters.

She leaned her head against the vibrating windowpane and watched the signs go by. *Dunquerque*, said the first. How odd, she thought, that she should have heard so many times from Artemis the story of how Gervase's father and his uncle took their little boat to Dunkirk to get the troops off ("Never a thank you, mind, from the common soldiers"). Never once, half-listening to her mother-in-law, had she remembered that once, to her, it was spelt Dunquerque. It was the place where you drove from a camping weekend on the beach at Wissant, to buy the things the little shop did not stock. There was irony in having heard so often of Dunkirk, the episode of British history, and forgotten Dunquerque the peaceable Flemish port town.

Happy, bemused, floating above herself, she leaned back and sat relaxed as the bus thundered on across the great industrial and agricultural plain of Flanders. She read battlefield names which were also childhood Sunday drives: Ypres, St-Omer, Menen. Soon the sprawling industrial conurbation of Lille embraced them. She peered out into the gloom, where rain was beginning to fall. There, there indeed, were signs to *Tourcoing*: that odd name which had come to her when she opened the choral society newsletter in the tumbled attic study so many miles and moods away.

Another name: Lambersart, for heaven's sake. Surely Sylvie Jacob lived at Lambersart, and her brother Chrétien? He came to skating and Judo Club and called her *Chatte*, for Cat, when she was trying hard to be "Catherine" to her schoolfriends. She had retaliated by naming him "Crétin", and to his disgust the name had stuck, as the children swooped and skidded and threw up tinkling showers of ice-scrapings, week after week at the rink.

The coach stopped in the Rue Nationale, and Cat alighted onto the damp glistening pavement. Looking across the road, she felt another jolt of recognition. Above a pharmacist's shop there was a green neon sign: a pulsing, growing then decreasing viridian cross of light. It was a symbol unchanged, somehow overlooked by the bustling decades since she had left Lille. Other forgotten, unimportant signs ambushed her wherever she turned: *La Voix du Nord, Stella Artois, Boulangerie Paul, Défence de cracher*.

Slowly she walked towards the central square: Place Général de Gaulle by name, Grand'Place by popular appellation. Childishly, she very much wanted to see the neon ferret; but stepping out into the pedestrianized square – where were the cobbles? – she saw that while the bookshop was there, vast and prosperous, newly themed with a high artificial rock wall down one side, there was no neon ferret to be seen. What cultural and historic forces, she wondered hazily, preserved a flashing green cross for chemists for a third of a century, yet swept away the clever ferret?

And there was a Metro station. A metro! In Lille? Unbidden, there sounded in her mind's ear the clang of a tram and the rattle of its iron wheels through ankle-twisting tracks in cobblestones. She had not thought of trams much since childhood, but once all postings divided into tram and non-tram cities. Trams in Berne, trams in Lille. No trams, back in London. Trams in Sheffield, though, where Diana's mother lived in a retirement home for her last two years, and where her reluctant grandchildren were once dragged on a visit, only to be consoled by the trams. No trams in Los Angeles – although one holiday trip to San Francisco had caused both her and Toby an adolescent pang of nostalgia at the streetcars. No trams in Venice, obviously. Robert had always promised to take them to Vienna, where the trams were still running in the same rails he had ridden with Diana during their courtship; but they had never quite got there.

So the world Cat grew up in had always divided nicely into the two kinds of cities, trammed and tramless; there was something shocking in seeing that Lille had crossed the divide and proved unfaithful to the clattering lords of the city. No more would their spindly arms draw strength from mazy wires, or flash bolts of escaping electricity against a wet winter's night sky between the tall houses. No more would child Tobies and Catherines swing themselves arrogantly aboard to traverse the city at swaying speed, cutting through the mundane motor traffic. She looked down: the rails must have been long since ripped up, together with the old cobblestones.

Cat stood, feeling queer and cold, looking at the fountain in the centre of the square. Then she slowly turned her head, raised her eyes, and with a rush of relief saw the great vainglorious absurd-ity of the sky-gesticulating sculpture, the neoclassical stone riot which stands proud of the façade of the Lille Opéra. Yes. She looked around again at the wet stones, the glowering Flemish roofline of steep then shallow pitched housetops with red tiles, like giant cottages. She took in the grand, swaggering, bourgeois confidence of the square and the steamy windows of bistros, *Stella Artois*, *La Voix du Nord*, *Le Furet du Nord*, luscious sculptured piles of bread in the *Boulangerie Paul*. The city fell into place again around her, the same old city. It had evolved, that was all.

As she had, too. A grown woman now, with no tea to hurry home to, Cat walked into the first hotel she saw, checked in and rose in the shaking lift to the fourth floor. Opening the door of her room she was met by the stifling tinny smell of old heating in a shuttered room, and looked with recognition at the radiator with its sharp flanges and chased decoration blurred with decades of repainting. The house at Rue du Lombard used to smell like that. There were rounded edges on the dusty panelling of the lobby that led to her shower, and peeling shutters on the windows which she flung open to the damp night air. By the shower was a rectangular and cracked bidet with an elaborate pattern of crazed white enamel foliage around its base.

Recognizing everything, back in the snug idiom of shabby bourgeois grandeur that she knew and had forgotten, Cat smiled through the cloud of irrelevant memory and the long-forgotten props of childhood. Home! The hot, dusty smell of the room mingled with the damp warm breeze that smelt of pavements and dog-dirt and toasted cheese and garlic. She was a little hungry but did not want to go out again. Kicking off her shoes, she lay down on the bed, stretched, and yawned.

Irresistible, inarticulate, more memories closed in. With her eyes shut this could be her bedroom at Rue du Lombard. The year she had the jaundice, perhaps. Any minute M. le Médecin would call with his gold-rimmed specs, speak darkly of the perils of liver ailments, and prescribe vast brownish suppositories and jugs of unsweetened lemon juice. Not a golden memory, exactly, but enough to drift her happily off to sleep.

In the morning, Gervase once again came early to the bunk house. "May I have a word?" he asked, punctiliously. "We've got a bit of an event here today. I wasn't allowed to tell you before."

"Is it about the new lads, Terry and Spider?" asked Duane. "Only we know they're coming on a visit for the day, to see the work, like. Mr Willetts told me at my 'pointment."

"Not just that," said Gervase. "Though actually, we fixed their visit for today for a reason. We wanted to have more of us around to meet our visitor. The Prince of Wales is coming here."

"Cor," said Duane. Martin stood silent at this new turn of events.

Gervase continued:

"He's been interested for quite a time. It's basically a private visit, but there'll also be a couple of press people. The Morefield Trust is going to announce that we are becoming one of their key projects, and that they plan to have more farms."

"Will Mrs Hartley be back?" asked Martin. "I mean, it's a big thing, OK? Wouldn't she be sick to miss it?"

"Oh," said Gervase. "She had something important to do in France. Anyway, it's the farmwork they're coming to see. And you, Duane. Since Winston isn't with us. The Prince will probably want to talk to you about what you feel about being here."

"It's good," said Duane judicially. "But it was more fun with Mary-Annie to look after."

"Well," said Gervase. "Better not go into that with him, perhaps?"

He ran briskly through some arrangements, mainly for animals to be fed later than usual for the photographers' benefit, and asked Martin to look out a particular set of horse harness. There was little else to be done. The security check had been completed yesterday while Martin drove Cat to the bus and Duane to his probation appointment. Gervase would have scorned to do any further prettification of the premises; the farm was, at any rate, always kept neat and workmanlike as part of his ethic.

He paused on the drive and hesitated before going back into the house. It would not be restful in there. Mrs Bird had been summoned early and was cutting bread and emitting little helium squeaks of loyal excitement at the prospect of offering the heir to the throne an egg sandwich. Maybe he should go down to the cottage and ask Caroline if she would like to come up for the morning.

Cat woke to find dusty sunlight streaming through her open hotel window. She lay for a moment and remembered where she was. It felt strange to have no household around her, yet no Eden meeting to go to, either. There was nothing to stop her lying here all day, except that she was very hungry. She had not taken sandwiches on the coach, nor had she bothered with supper. A *café complet* on the corner of the square would do nicely. She sat on the edge of the bed, stretching and looking with disfavour at her travelling clothes, a pair of crumpled, chintzy cotton trousers, grey knitted cotton sweater and black lightweight wool jacket. Very dull, very English. Rooting in her equally dull and English tartan bag she found that some saving instinct had made her throw in a black skirt and green silky blouse. All her clothes came from mid-market mail order catalogues: decent, pleasant, nothing noteworthy, plenty of natural fabrics. Next to Mrs Bird's draggled acrylics she looked almost chic; next to Caroline, irredeemably provincial. Neither of these comparisons had ever bothered her for a moment. Now, however, almost for the first time since her second wedding Catherine Hartley gave ten minutes' serious thought to her wardrobe and decided that at the very least, a trip to *Printemps* could be justified by the health of her bank balance.

First, breakfast. Then a walk. She sat in a bar on the corner of the Rue Neuve and fortified herself with two croissants, half a baguette, and a bowl of *café-au-lait*, remembering how at school breakfasts on Mass days she had learnt to dip the buttered bread casually into her coffee, leaving an oily slick and floating flakes of crust. She did it now, and noted with approval that the barman brought over the jam in a jar and the butter not wrapped in tiny sweaty foil portions, but on a plate with a knife. This homeliness was probably illegal under EC health regulations: it was good to see that France, her almost forgotten second homeland, had not advanced too far along the road of neurotic hygiene. Maybe, after all, it *was* the drains she had smelt through the bus window at Calais.

Looking out through the window, she thought for a second that she could see Toby. But it was another man: as dark as Toby, fine-featured, in a long business overcoat with his hair flopping over his forehead. He was laughing with a square blond friend in an anorak as they walked towards some office with their briefcases. No, nothing like Toby, really: smaller, and smarter. But there had been something. Cat returned, thoughtfully, to her croissant.

Caroline was only too delighted to come up to Knoll Farm for the visit of the Prince and the Trustees. "It's marvellous!" she said. And "I can quite see why you weren't allowed to tell me earlier. How thrilling!"

This, perversely, made Gervase feel guilty that he had not told her. Still, she smiled at him without a trace of offence taken, and put an eager hand on his forearm, on the warm skin beneath the rolled-up shirtsleeve. "Would it be all right if Mary-Annie came up? You know how quiet she is."

"Of course," said Gervase, and smiled down at her. "Nothing's complete without Mary-Annie."

Martin, driving up the lane with the two extra bottles of milk Mrs Bird had demanded he fetch, saw them standing in the cottage doorway, her light hand on his tanned arm, smiling into one another's eyes. He did not like it.

25

Cat spent all morning walking, refreshed at eleven by more coffee and a *tarte aux fraises* at the *Boulangerie Paul*. She walked to the church of St-Maurice, where she had long ago seen her Catholic schoolmates confirmed by a magnificent purple-and-gold bishop in a waxy haze of candlelight and incense, and envied them in the secret romantic depths of her heart. The smell was unchanged: a cool intoxication.

She stood aimlessly for a moment then lit a candle, knelt before a dim-lit Virgin in a side chapel and improvised a prayer for Toby. He was not here; he never had been. She could feel it. An old priest emerged beaming from the confessional box to greet her as she rose; they exchanged a few words. The old man seemed puzzled and unable to place her, and after a few moments she realized how strange she must sound. She had not been in France for decades, yet in these surroundings her accent and grammar and intonation returned to the old, instinctive, schoolgirl bilinguality while her vocabulary remained comically rusted by years of disuse. She found herself voluble and fluent, thinking in French constructions, dropping slangy, childish French exclamations yet frequently groping for the right word even for simple things like candles – *comment dit-on? flût! aaah . . . oui, les cierges* . . . To the priest, she must have seemed not like a struggling Anglophone but a French amnesiac. Or a drug-taker.

She walked to the Place de Béthune, and looked for the row of cinemas where she had gone with Toby and Robert on every possible Saturday night, searching out films with English soundtracks and French subtitles. The only one she could remember was *The Long Ships*, a recreation of Viking times so absurd that she and Robert had laughed about its horned hats and fur loincloths all the way home. Toby, still only seven, had been thrilled by the adventure and took offence at their levity.

She walked to the Jardin Vauban and then back to the Grand' Place following a street map, but then decided to fold the map and let her feet take her where they would. After a moment's hesitation she found herself on the Rue Anatole France, heading towards the station and moving purposefully into a quarter of the old town peculiarly rich in sex video shops.

Rue de Roubaix. *Ciné Sex*. Why was she here? Much was unfamiliar, or merely similar to the rest of the town she had walked in all morning; there was a wholly unfamiliar black-glass building, modern and unseemly, in the foreground at one point and yet, sometimes, a smell, a corner, an angle of leprous stone would strike her so forcibly that she gasped.

In a few minutes she turned right at a rusting dark-blue road plaque saying *Rue du Lombard*. This explained at last why she was here. She had meant to visit the old house later, but had convinced herself that it lay over to the west of the Grand'Place. She looked at the great wrought-iron gates of No. 1, and read the newly cleaned plaque on the wall outside, in honour of M. Scrive-Labbé, who *"au péril de sa vie"* brought the first carding machine from England to Lille and founded, presumably, his city's textile supremacy.

How on earth had this crumbling merchant palace, or a corner of it, been acquired for rent by the Foreign Office of the very nation which presumably had imperilled M. Scrive-Labbé's life in the attempt to keep its carding machine? Maybe, though, it was his compatriots who had imperilled his life, in a spirit of machine-wrecking Luddism? Or perhaps it was in a fit of post-Occupation solidarity and gratitude that Madame its owner had permitted M. le Consul Britannique to inhabit it, and his shrill English children to climb on the little stone lions in the centre of the court?

Except that, come to think of it, playing on the stone lions was one thing most definitely not permitted. They were deemed fragile, and Madame the landlady would be out shaking her stick, within seconds of Toby's most furtive approach to them. Cat peered in through the gate. Madame must have been right about the fragility because the lions were gone, only twisted iron fastenings remaining. The place was clearly some government building now: she hesitated to go in to the courtyard, and retraced her steps a little sadly to turn the corner and look for the sweetshop which sold the chocolate mice and Caram'bars. It was the *Video Sexy*. Ah well, evolution.

She walked back, past the Opéra and across the Grand'Place, aiming to go up the Rue Esquermoise past the old Consulate, and beyond it to the Rue Royale and the big wooden doors of the convent at No. 66. How lucky she and Toby had been, compared to her own children with their long dull country school runs by car! She had walked to school, sometimes with her father coming half the distance, to his office, and she had generally walked home. Never mind that there was no garden at Rue du Lombard, and only the forbidden lions for outdoor amusement. That, she supposed with maternal hindsight, must have been hardest on Mark, who was little. But for her and, in his last year at least for Toby, the old city had been freedom itself.

She could not find the Consulate or remember the number where it had been. Baffled, she halted for a moment outside the Banque Jacob. It was Sylvie Jacob's father's bank, as established and honoured a fact of Lillois life as the adjacent Banque Scalbert. When she was going home for tea with Sylvie, they would walk down here together and sit, scuffing their feet and giggling, in the marble foyer while M. Jacob finished his day. He would appear flanked by deferential underlings and wearing a long, smart woollen overcoat, greet the girls politely (*Mademoiselle Gratton! Enchanté!*) and drive them home to the bourgeois decorum of the Jacob townhouse in Lambersart. She looked in: the foyer was lightly modernized now, but the floor she had shuffled her school shoes on was exactly the same. So were one or two of the men's overcoats as they sauntered out for lunch, coats as long and dark and fine as Papa Jacob's used to be, worn even in June in defiance of the age of the anorak.

Watching the men emerge, she saw again the one she had momentarily taken for Toby when she looked through the bar window at breakfast-time. Nothing like Toby, and yet familiar.

It was an idle observation, and she only stood still a moment longer because her feet were tired from long unaccustomed walking on city streets. She did not notice at first that the dark man had turned and was staring at her. Only when he called, his voice echoing in the marble hall, did the shock of full recognition come on her.

"*Chatte!*" said the man in clear, confident tones. "*Chatonne! Méchante Chatte Anglaise! Que fais-tu ici, hein?*"

She stared back from the broad entrance doors. "*Dieu!*" she said, the forgotten exclamation forced from her. "*C'est toi! Crétin!*"

Heads turned in interrogation. The chic receptionist raised a hennaed eyebrow; a young man stiffened as if to hurry to his master's aid. In a second, though, these observers saw that M. le Directeur was laughing delightedly, holding out both hands and advancing on the woman in the doorway. The receptionist gave a tiny shrug and glanced at the younger man. If M. le Directeur was happy to be called a cretin by a rather dishevelled, pink-faced foreign woman of a certain age, that was his affair.

He had her hands now, held firmly in his own. "Where are your skates?" he asked. "Where is your horsetail?"

"Ponytail," said Cat, looking at him with incredulity. "*Dieu*, it really is you! Where is your sister? Sylvie?"

"Bruxelles," said Chrétien Jacob in tones of the profoundest disapproval. "She is a big Euroboss, imagine. Married to an even bigger Euroboss. She was more clever than me, and older, but she would not come into the bank. My father was disgusted. He wanted to make a big modern gesture and be succeeded by his daughter, not his son. But you see how it has ended. Sylvie rejected the Bank, I did not go to St-Cyr, I did not become a general after all. I studied economics." He said the word with vehement comic disgust: Cat could see the boy of thirteen behind the man, and a laugh broke from her. His eyes danced. "Yes, I am Monsieur le Directeur and life is very dull, for a General. It would have been better to stay *un gosse*, with you and Sylvie and Véronique at the ice rink. In fact, even that has closed. There is a trade Expo there now."

He turned to the young man and spoke rapidly. The boy nodded obediently, made a note in a small book, and scuttled off back into the interior of the bank. Chrétien, still firmly holding one of Cat's hands, turned back to her.

"*Voilà*. Everything is arranged. I have no important business lunch engagement any more. *Madame*" – he had glanced foxily down towards her ring finger and noted Gervase's narrow smooth gold band – "would you do me the pleasure of accompanying me to lunch, in some place where my business contact will under no circumstances see us? A *croque-monsieur*, perhaps, and a bag of *frites* in the Jardin Vauban?"

"A sausage," said Cat, laughing back at him. "A hot-dog *Americaine*, with English mustard to make your eyes weep."

"Ah, memories of childhood," said M. le Directeur, sentimentally. "But I think I can find somewhere with tables and chairs and a cellar. Viens." The receptionist looked after him as he swept Cat out through the brassbound doorway into the street. Not at all his usual kind of little friend. English, too, from one or two of her words. That would explain the terrible hair.

By this time, events at Knoll Farm were moving along nicely according to plan. The Prince and the chairman of the Morefield Trust posed with a cow, then with Gervase and some sheep. Then the Prince picked up a body brush and groomed a horse for a while, with Duane; Caroline watched, and was introduced, and had Mary-Annie duly admired and the importance of "family atmosphere" spoken of approvingly by another Trustee. More flashguns crackled for informal pictures. The Prince left. Then Gervase and the others went to the farmhouse to eat Mrs Bird's egg sandwiches and talk to the two reporters with notebooks, and Caroline went with them. Martin said to Duane: "I dunno, it doesn't seem too right. Mrs Hartley not being here."

"Her sister looks at home, don't she?" said Duane. "Imagine, little Yannie meeting a Prince."

"I don't like it," said Martin. He did not mean Yannie's exalted social encounter. He went off to unharness the horses.

Cat had forgotten them all. In a smoky little bistro with her schoolfriend's brother she was plunged in joyful mutual reminiscence, each of them capping the other's memories, forgetful of the present, revelling in detail.

"Remember the Judo tournament?"

"*Re!*" said Cat, and bowed across the table.

"*Hadjimi!*" he replied, and lunged to grab the collar and one lapel of her jacket, knocking over the salt as he did so. "Then I move in – so – and sweep you off balance with a *deuxieme de pied—*"

"But I am too quick for you, and do a Sacrifice," said Cat. "I put my foot in your chest, roll over on my back, and you do a forward roll to the corner of the mat."

"And roll back onto my feet, plunge down, grab you in a neck-lock," said Chrétien, "and immobilize you until you tap—" Cat tapped the tablecloth twice, with a flat hand "For surrender. *Hélas*, superior strength and cunning have defeated you again."

"You never could skate backwards, though, could you?" said Cat. "You used to fall on your head."

"A very necessary apprenticeship for a Lille banker," said Chrétien. "It dulls the sensibilities. *Ah, mais!* It is so good to remember, so dull to be an adult."

"What is your adult life?" asked Cat, attacking a portion of thinly beaten steak and chips. "Do you have a family? Do you live in Lille?"

"I married a Belgian. She lives now in Belgium," said Chrétien carelessly. "I have two sons rising in the Bank, in Calais and Dunquerque, a daughter married, and a little daughter at the Sorbonne. I live mainly in an apartment in Vieux-Lille, not far from M. le Consul's house at Rue du Lombard."

"Oh, I'm sorry," said Cat. "I mean, that your wife—"

The dark man laughed. "After twenty-five years of marriage," he said, "wise married people understand one another very well. *N'est ce pas?*"

He picked up her hand with its wedding ring.

"Where is your husband? I do not see him."

"In England. In Northamptonshire. He is a farmer."

"With sheep?"

"Yes, and cows and pigs and horses."

"Good. He is in England with sheep, you are in Lille. Why?"

"I don't know," said Cat, in genuine astonishment at herself. "*Voyons*, that is true. I don't know. I just got a chance to come."

"Destiny called you," said Chrétien. "*Comme c'est gentil.* Tell me, what does destiny call you to do this afternoon? Does it call you to take a promenade with me, and accompany me to a very poor performance at the Opéra, and dine in some place better than this?"

Cat was silent for a moment. The red wine and the food were making her dazed, groggy and happy and irresponsible. It was a long time since she had wasted a whole day on a whim.

"Yes," she said. "Yes, I feel it calling now."

"To destiny!" he raised his glass.

"To destiny," she said.

She looked across, suddenly uncertain, wondering if she had been misunderstood. French men were famously unschooled in the subtleties of political correctness and sexual harassment. But no! This was no stereotype Frenchman: this was Chrétien, spirited teasing-partner of her childhood, always after her to gang up with him and play jokes on Sylvie. She knew, deeply and instinctively, that she could slap down any silly ideas he might have without even jeopardizing their refreshed friendship. She could keep Chrétien at bay.

If she wanted to.

By mutual silent consent, both fell to talking of other people and places they had known. Chrétien gave her news of Sylvie, of Véronique (now a mother of six living in Orléans, married to a banker he knew slightly). He told her how the Sacred Heart sisters left the convent years before, and how M. Derain the police sergeant who taught them Judo was killed in an Algerian terrorist bombing the year after Cat had vanished to Johannesburg. He told her how the last trams went in the 1980s when the Metro was built, how proud the new Lillois were of their improvements at the centre, how high the crime and poverty rates had grown in the sprawling conurbation all around.

"Could a girl of eleven, as I was, still walk to school?" said Cat.

He considered. "Yes. I think so. In the centre. But too many go by car."

"Could a little girl cross the city to go skating on a Sunday morning?"

"Yes," said Chrétien. "But there might be rude boys. Or rude girls."

"I'm sorry I called you Crétin, in the bank," said Cat, for the first time feeling the awkwardness of that public moment. "I didn't know you were Monsieur le Directeur."

"Pah!" he said. "They have no respect anyway. They know my view of banking. My deputy is excellent, but by great ill-fortune for him and good fortune for me, his family name is not Jacob."

"I didn't recognize you, not completely, until you said my name," said Cat. "How on earth did you recognize me, from a twelve-year-old girl?"

"Round face, English skin, hair that jumps from your head, big green eyes, an expression of hopefulness and worry, a tendency to peer through doors." He reeled his list off, deadpan, then smiled. *"Une petite mine gentille, quoi. Ça ne change pas."*

"You haven't changed either," said Cat. "You're like my brother Toby, that way."

They wandered out into the afternoon air, and Chrétien asked "What would you like to see? The country, or the town?"

"Town," said Cat. "I wanted to see the old house, but it's a ministry now. Ministry of Culture."

"Pas de problème." He began to walk rapidly down the Rue Anatole France where her hesitant, remembering steps had taken her that morning. "We shall see and appreciate everything. Surely that is the meaning of culture? I have not been inside Numero Un since you left. Anyway, I know exactly how to effect an entrance."

He did. He and his impressive card were greeted with comradely scepticism by the official in charge when he explained that an important client of his bank was Mlle Gratton, who wished to inspect her father's old residence. Together they walked in through the iron-and-glass double doors, together stood for a moment dumbstruck at the way the hall was unchanged even to the way the back stairs oddly began almost next to the grand main staircase. Then they turned with one accord through the curved panelling of the door to their left.

"The playroom! I had forgotten!" said Cat, looking into a dusty meeting room with utility chairs and tables and flakes of plaster off the ceiling. And Chrétien peered in behind her, demanding: "Where is baby Mark's train? The one you can sit on?"

"I expect," said the Ministry official drily from behind them, "that it was considered surplus to cultural needs. This is a monument, *monsieur*. An historic building. Groups come especially, by appointment, to view the remarkable ceiling of the small salon."

"What ceiling?" asked Cat, puzzled. "Oh hang on – a girl sitting on something?"

Together they passed through into what had been Robert and Diana's grandest dining room of all postings.

"Good grief," said Cat. "How could I have forgotten that?"

"No eye for art," said Chrétien. They stared up, Cat wrestling with another wave of the mixed sensations which had assailed her all day. To remember things and then go back and find them a little different, a little smaller, was normal. To be suddenly confronted with things you had utterly forgotten was strange and unsettling. It pushed you helplessly down a slide towards other memories and feelings. Nostalgia, she saw, was not necessarily cosy or voluntary. She was glad that nothing deeply traumatic had happened in her childhood. If it had it would surely rush back now, along with all these other feelings.

Passing back through the double doors to the small salon, she suddenly remembered hiding with Toby in the dark dusty space between the two sets of doors, eating the miniature sausages off a cocktail plate during a party.

Chrétien's best pleadings could not get him beyond the first floor landing: he had, he said, once written *MERDE* on the ceiling of the third attic room by shooting air-pistol pellets into the plaster. It was during a visit when Sylvie and Cat were being dull, with dolls. He wanted to see if it was still there. The official was obdurate, and they left, laughing, pointing at the place where the lions had been and at the cross concierge's little stone hut.

"Extraordinary place to live," said Cat as they passed the barrier into the road. "Scruffy, bit magnificent, all those grand rooms but no garden. The opposite of anything English."

"Not very like my own house," said Chrétien ruefully. "My wife has always been fond of *le style scandinave*. Me, I have an apartment above Rue Neuve, which is entirely Lillois, magnificent and impossible to clean, with shutters which are painted, not naked Scandinavian wood."

"What is Sylvie's house like?" said Cat, wanting to move the subject away from his apartment.

"Rootless Belgian style. Eurosmart. Terrible," said Chrétien, and took her hand. "Now," he said, leading her at a fast pace down the road, "we must understand one another. Speaking of my apartment has made you nervous. You are an English woman now, very respectable, and you think that because I am a French man, I wish to dress you in fur coats and make you my mistress in the middle of the afternoon. You think this. True?"

Cat pulled her hand away, pink-cheeked, and tried to protest. He continued, blithely: "I know this, because my father gave me books to read by Nancy Mitford. He said it was important to understand what English women think about French men, or I would make terrible *bêtises* with the new style of English clients, who are important bank ladies and do not think of making love with business contacts in the afternoon. I know that English women think French men are very, very dangerous and consider themselves invited to bed at all times. This is a very nice idea. But if you think I am an occasion of sin, we shall not have a very amusing afternoon, reliving our youth."

"Hmm," said Cat, recovering her aplomb. "Be honest, then. Be like the chevalier Bayard, without fear or fault. Are you the dangerous Frenchman we are warned about?"

"I am harmless," said Chrétien. He stopped, and turned to face her, grinning. "I promise you. Today I am harmless. In return for my docility, I need stories and conversation and memory. It is terrible, in the bank. Even the women are dull. They want to be respected as bankers and yet admired as women. English women are excellent. They never expect to be respected, and certainly they do not care whether you admire them or not. You can tell by the way they dress. All I want, dear Madame, is to hear the story of your life. It would be delightful if you could include the great influence I had upon you, and the fact that you have never been able to forget me for the last thirty-three years. But, *voyons*, since I had quite forgotten you, I cannot insist on that. *Venez, Madame!* We will walk in the park and you will tell me everything."

26

Hours later, Cat and Chrétien sat opposite one another at a small table in a bistro at the corner of the Grand'Place, laughing. They had abandoned the Opéra after the first act, Chrétien remarking that it was surely enough for a bank to sponsor dreadful modern performances without its director having to watch them. The long-suffering young male secretary was telephoned – he was still working at the Banque Jacob building, apparently – to come "with any woman you can find" and sit in their places so that nobody should remark on his dereliction of duty.

"We shall dine in peace," he said. "And then at eleven o'clock I shall return to the Opéra and mingle with the other sponsors for five minutes." Cat – who had during the afternoon made a hasty dive into Printemps for a black dress, stockings and pumps – pretended to deplore this defection and told him that no Englishman would consider such behaviour.

"You lie," he said tranquilly, breaking his bread and dipping it in the juice of his Chateaubriand. "They are even worse than us. But not as rude and boorish as Belgians. But go on, allez! More of this saga."

He had by degrees persuaded Cat to tell him every detail of her recent life. Her fluency grew every minute and she found the act of relating Knoll Farm's domestic travails to this mocking, amused outsider increasingly exhilarating. Chrétien, unaffectedly delighted and entertained, egged her on:

"So he is a philanthropist, a saint, your husband? He cares for vauriens and makes young robbers into good citizens, by the care of sheep and pigs? But he earns no money to maintain his beautiful wife? The English! I despair! Then he goes off and looks after *vauriens* while you bravely rescue his sheep from death, and are persecuted by the police. *Aie, aie aie!*"

"No – no," she would protest, laughing at his theatrical display of horror. "It isn't like that. It was my fault about the driving licence. I wouldn't even contest the charge. That was my decision. As for Gervase and me, everything is –" she hesitated, looking for the right word, and hit on the universal French expression – "*bien arrangé*, between us. It works very well. His work with the boys is not unusual, either. You have people here who do the same kind of work, in Paris and Lille."

"Yes," he said smugly. "But they are generally priests, with no wives to distract their attention and make a division of duty. We are more logical, you see?"

Cat had not enough ammunition to argue, and felt too good-humoured and tipsy to protest at the rain of insults he flirtatiously continued to pour on all those who, in his opinion, were failing to look after her properly. She laughed and shrugged her shoulders. The black dress, soft and sheer and short, made her feel like a creature who should, indeed, be looked after. She faintly remembered feeling this before, this relaxed warm sense of being a fragile woman, a precious responsibility. But not for a long time.

Chrétien, more vigilant than his debonair manner betrayed, saw the change in her and enjoyed it. Women, he thought, should be able to slough off this terrible modern omnicompetence, and allow men sometimes to treat them like gossamer. It was an old game, which too many of them (especially Belgians) forgot how to play. Either they refused all care, or began to think themselves entitled to an excess of it. Occasionally, to make Cat laugh even more, he veered off into a description of his own distant wife's exacting standards and material demands, and contrasted them woefully with the neglect women plainly suffered in the wilderness of *l'Angleterre*. Outside the window, it had begun to rain: the neon signs of the Grand'Place reflected in the wet glistening flagstones, making their table seem even more of an intimate island.

On his bantering insistence, she had explained about Caroline, and Alan, and the baby, and the upset over Winston, and how it had all distressed her. Strangely, it was easier to express her own outrage and worry because at this, Chrétien wisely expressed no particular sympathy.

"So – I will just make sure I recapitulate correctly. You see what a good careful banker I have become. I could write a full report on this shocking affair. One: your sister did not like her baby, so you arranged for some criminals to help you look after it. Two: she went to California and a woman called Adeline told her that naturally, she did like the baby after all. Three: she has come home and taken this very important baby away from the criminals, and Monsieur the Saint, your husband, says this is good. Four: you say it is wrong to prevent criminals from feeding babies, and he refuses to listen."

"You make it sound like a bad film plot," protested Cat.

"It is a bad film plot," said Chrétien. "So, to continue: on the side we have another plot, an opera this time, quite terrible enough for the Banque Jacob to sponsor. Your brother Mark has no babies, and his wife suspects he has been cut, so she comes to complain to you. You confront your brother, he admits everything, and they make up the quarrel. End of Act One. In Act Two he discovers that you secretly write a newspaper for this horrible Eden – did you know they have a hotel at Roubaix? Disgusting place, just like America, iced water and no bidets. Because you work for the same company as him he will not speak to you and vows to send his troops to kill you unless the baritone, *votre père*, can prevent him. Correct?"

"More or less," said Cat, pouring herself more red wine. "Except for the troops. And that my father does not play the patriarchal role you suggest. I sometimes think he is still a light romantic tenor at heart."

"Is there a *grand'mère*?" asked Chrétien, interestedly. "In French family battles there is normally a grandmother to arrange things in the end."

"Only Artemis," said Cat. "I suppose she arranged Caroline's house."

"Could she arrange Mark? And the young criminals?"

"No," said Cat. "And don't keep calling them criminals."

"As for the missing Toby," continued Chrétien, "he is obviously the missing voice, the voice from off the stage. Your sister pretends to think he is in Los Angeles because she wanted to go there to cure this strange disease of hating babies. You pretend Toby is in Lille, because your instinct tells you that your fate is to come here and have dinner with a handsome bank director from your distant past. I think this is a very convenient brother." He said thoughtfully, "I wish my sister would disappear, then I could go and search for her for many months – where? The Maldives, perhaps. Or Seychelles. I enjoy scuba very much, did I tell you? I think I could persuade myself that I must search for her on tropical islands. She would, for example, definitely not be in Belgium."

"You have spent so long retelling the opera of my life," said Cat, looking at her watch, "that you have left yourself only two minutes to get back to the Opéra and pretend you enjoyed the real performance."

He glanced at his own watch and jumped up. "Wait!" he said. "I will be back. I will tell them that my important client from England felt faint and had to be escorted to her hotel. I would like a *café noir* and a *Cognac*, and tell Madame Olin that I require petits-fours, not the ones the tourists have, but her own. Then you shall explain properly to me, who is Martin? And why do Monsieur le Saint's sheep need an American as well as all the criminals?"

The rain was heavier now; he hurried across the square, his overcoat held over his head, and Cat looked after him as he ran.

Gervase and Caroline sat either side of the fireplace in Rectory Cottage. Mrs Bird had made Duane and Martin a high tea, while Gervase took one of the Morefield Trustees back to the station. He returned to find them both gone to the pub, and only a crusted portion of shepherd's pie left under an inverted soup-bowl for his supper. He looked at it, but Mrs Bird had a heavy hand with food. The pie failed to tempt his appetite. So he walked out into the warm evening, still elated from the events of the day, and found his steps taking him along the lane towards Midmarsham. There was a light in Caroline's front room, and a welcome met his hesitant knock.

"I wanted to thank you for helping out today. Mary-Annie really broke the ice," he began, awkwardly.

"I was honoured to be asked," said Caroline. "Have you eaten? I was just going to make an omelette."

So, four hours later they were still there, the chessboard between them but the game abandoned, sometimes talking, sometimes falling into warm companionable silences. The apple-wood fire was sinking into low, fragrant embers. Both were sleepy but neither chose to break the peace of the moment. Caroline was filled with a deep sense of contentment. This was her home, her own place; her child slept beautifully upstairs, and the fire she had lit burnt clear and warm and flickered on Gervase's thin, wise, ascetic face. He was deep in thought; a log fell and flared suddenly, and he started out of his reverie and smiled at her. Caroline smiled back, and no words were needed.

Up at the farm Martin made a last tour of inspection of the yard and paddocks, checked the electric fencing round the pigs, and looked despondently at the darkened farmhouse. None of his business, OK? He went to bed, but lay for a long time sleepless, waiting for the sound of a footfall on the drive.

Chrétien came back from his foray to the Opéra after what Cat severely told him was a shamefully short time.

"I told them I was so troubled and moved that I needed time to think alone about the message of this new work," he said. "And I promised them 40,000 francs to fund a feasibility study for an application to Brussels for – for some thing. It was a cheap escape. Now. My coffee? Les petits fours?"

When they could no longer extend their evening by one drop more of coffee or one more sugared grape, Cat reluctantly said:

"I should go to my hotel now. I have had a very long day."

"Indeed. We shall take a little promenade, though. I will show you the new restoration work on the balconies behind the Rue Neuve. See? The rain has stopped. Lille smells and feels at its most beautiful at night, after summer rain." He held out a hand to help her to her feet. "Even that is not terribly beautiful," he admitted. "But it will do."

27

The sympathetic and responsible newspaper which had been invited to take pictures of the Prince's visit to Knoll Farm was not quite so serious-minded as to ignore the potential effect of blondes and babies on circulation figures. Accordingly, the night news editor took one look at the posed pictures of Gervase, Duane, assorted sheep and the Prince of Wales and pushed them aside with a sigh, to spread out the three more informal pictures which the photographer had left on the end of the film. In one of these, the Prince was leaning towards Caroline; in her arms was Mary-Annie in a white puff-sleeved dress and a broad grin, reaching both fat hands towards the red cow which Gervase, laughing, held on a rope halter.

"Aaah," said his secretary, wandering past the desk. "He should have had a little girl, poor old Charles. Look at his face!"

The news editor looked at the enchanting picture, which he now perceived to be full of equally enchanting subtext. Then he looked at the one which lay next to it, the best of the rest. It was a static study of the Prince with his hand on a sheep's head, Duane with his mouth open looking moronic, and Gervase caught at a bad angle and visibly in need of a haircut.

"No contest," he said. "The baby's not really the story, though, is it? Presumably it belongs to the guy who runs it, that Addams Family geezer there. We're doing two-fifty words on the farm and the young offenders, aren't we?"

"Room for five hundred," said his colleague, punching a keyboard. "One or two nice quotes about family life. Tie in with the baby. Family values. All that."

"Great," said the night news editor, and put it from his mind except for the brief, wistful observation: "She's a gorgeous bit of stuff, that wife of his. Wonderful face. Like a statue."

Cat decided to spend the morning on those few things she had promised herself to do to verify that Toby had indeed not been in Lille. The day's and night's events had cleared her mind, and hardened a resigned belief that her search would be useless. Whatever obscure tug of memory and unreason had brought her here was no more likely to be shared by Toby than the motive which had taken Caroline to Los Angeles. Out of their kaleidoscopic early memories each child of the family would have formed a different, private interior pattern, not to be discerned by any parent or sibling. If Toby were alive, he would come back to her one day. If not, she would never know where it was that he travelled after Calais.

Yesterday morning she could not have confronted that thought without succumbing to despair. Today, she could. *"Can't seem to get comfortable. Best to go back and start again"* he had written on the Calais card. At least she knew, now, what he meant by "getting comfortable". She hoped he had succeeded as well as she had, and found the same queer, unexpected peace by going back. She smiled at certain memories of the day before.

During the morning, though, she did the duty she had promised herself to do. She visited every major police station and three of the hospitals, leaving with each the photograph and details about Toby which she had photocopied in Midholt before the minibus left. It was a pointless, lonely task; with a guilty sense of relief she hurried back across town to meet Chrétien for lunch at *La Chicorée* (*"Non, non* – I do not have a business lunch appointment. If I do, it will regrettably be cancelled due to a secret crisis on the Bourse which only I can avert").

Pausing outside the *Furet du Nord*, she saw that the newspaper shop had some English press. She went in and reached for *The Times*, but as she did so glanced down at one of its rivals and saw above the fold the words:

CHARLES BACKS FAMILY FARMS FOR FELONS.

Smiling, she picked up the paper. So Gervase had got his bit of publicity, and presumably his Trust deal as well. Good. She paid for the paper and walked on down the square to the bistro.

Chrétien would not be there for ten minutes; she would sit with a drink and browse idly in the newspaper. Feeling the sun on her back Cat wriggled voluptuously and smiled. The waiter who was laying outdoor tables smiled back, raising an eyebrow.

Wine and good bread on the pavement, diversion in idleness, sunshine, company, male admiration: these were simple pleasures long forgotten. For years she had not had occasion even to flirt, because Gervase was the least flirtatious of men, besides being her husband. Eden meetings were all with men like Mark, their passion focused exclusively on the corporate game and the conquest of markets. At home, living with a volatile floating population of troubled teenage boys had taught her to be consistently wary of giving off the slightest sign of feminine teasing. Out here in the sunshine amid the French smells, such careful inhibition seemed as distant and irrelevant as the dusty Amstrad, the messy kitchen and the skinning of coley fillets for fish pie.

When she had settled down, facing the square across which Chrétien would walk to meet her, Cat unfolded the newspaper. For a few moments she stared at it: then turned it over, took several deep breaths, and turned it right side up again for another look.

It was a long look. Chrétien had crossed the square, entered the restaurant's enclosure and placed both hands on her shoulders before she noticed him. She felt the warmth of his hands through her blouse and turned to him, smiling in spite of herself. When he sat down she pushed the newspaper across, still speechless.

Chrétien, whose English was less good than her French, frowned for a moment or two and then began to laugh.

"Ah, *bien!*" he said. "This is a very good opera now. I begin to enjoy it even more. The younger sister steals the elder one's identity and the husband is wearing an ass's head – no, a sheep's head perhaps – and does not notice. The Prince is deceived."

Cat snatched it back. "You make everything into a joke!" she said, heatedly.

"Everything is a joke, *ma belle*," said Chrétien tranquilly.

Gervase saw the paper at lunch-time, because Martin, back from shopping, had laid the front page accusingly on the table where he could not miss it. He glanced down at the picture, beguiled for a moment by Mary-Annie and irritated by the headline, but stiffened as he read it through.

"CHARLES BACKS FAMILY FARMS FOR FELONS," it said. And under the picture of Mary-Annie lunging for the cow and being laughed at in her lovely mother's arms by the Prince of Wales, the caption:

Mr and Mrs Hartley and their baby daughter demonstrate to the Prince of Wales the family values of Knoll Farm, the latest social project to receive the backing of the Morefield Trust for Youth Reclamation.

The rest of the story was unexceptionable: explaining the takeover of the land, quoting Mr Willetts on the value of Gervase's work and experience, and the Trustees on their pleasure that this innovative social project would at last be put on a secure footing after living for so long from hand to mouth through the efforts of the Hartley family and a small local charity. It even quoted Duane, saying that living in a family and doing a useful job of work had changed his outlook and set him on a new path (Cat, reading that, instantly recognized the coaching of Mr Willetts. Gervase was merely touched).

Martin watched Gervase reading it. When he had finished the young American said: "Whaddya think of that?" and his tone was challenging, less than usually friendly.

"It's a fair account. But a pity about the picture caption being wrong," said Gervase. "Very embarrassing. I must apologize to Caroline for not making it clearer who she was."

Martin, who had not for one moment troubled himself about the embarrassment of Caroline, was momentarily speechless. Then in a queer, rough voice he said: "I need a break. Is it OK if I take off for a coupla days? You did say—"

"Yes, of course," said Gervase absently, still looking at the picture.

"Next week?"

"No," said the boy harshly. "Today." And, an hour later, he left. He did not borrow Cat's car nor the LandRover, but rode the old black bike all the way to Midholt station. It had begun to drizzle: cycling fast through the damp air, pressing the pedals down at each stroke with a controlled, vicious fury, Martin took comfort in one thing only: the prospect of telling Marianne and asking her what the hell to do?

Once Cat was over the first shock she did not know whether to be predominantly angry or amused. Chrétien, addressing his lamb cutlets with gusto, thought the whole thing vastly entertaining.

"This baby which has given 'family value' – what does this mean? – family value to the criminals, and met your future king. This is the same baby which, in truth, is not allowed to be touched by the criminals, because your sister went to California and was cured of hating it?"

"Oh, more or less," said Cat. "Yes, that's a fair summary. Do you think I should be angry?"

"Anger – *un petit colère* – is very good for the complexion. My wife says so," said Chrétien. "It brings up the blood and purifies the pores. *Vas-y*. Be angry." He pulled a mobile telephone out of his pocket and switched it on. "You see, I am truly a modern European banker. Internationally linked at all times." He peered at the display, which seemed unfamiliar to him. "Anatole, my secretary, makes me bring it even to lunch. Go on, ring the saint husband and ask why he is pretending to have another wife. Make 00 44 before the number."

Cat dialled Knoll Farm, giggling slightly. The first glass of wine had begun to work. The answering machine was on, but Mrs Bird picked up the telephone halfway through her message.

"Oooh," she said. She had not seen the newspaper because Gervase had taken it down to Rectory Cottage. "I just took a message for you. That's lucky you rang! Natalie, she said her name was, rang from your office you work for. Eden Pee-elsie, or something. I said you were in France with the music club, and she got very excited and said where? And I said I thought it was right up in the north, not too far, and she said good, because they need a profeel of their new hotel there in a place called –" she checked the message pad again – "Lily. She said they were in a rush, and would you ring her about doing the profeel as an extra?"

Cat thanked Mrs Bird, switched off the telephone and gave it back to Chrétien. He was painstakingly deciphering the news-paper story again, and she waited while he finished.

"I think," he said eventually, "if I am not mistaken, that the opera has gained another new twist. Is this correct, that your husband has given away all your land to this charity for drug-sellers and *vauriens*?"

"Yes," said Cat. "But I'm not at all interested in that. I knew it was on the cards. We keep the house. It's nothing to do with me, the land. It belongs to Gervase's family."

"Then it is your inheritance!" said Chrétien, scandalized. "Wars are fought over land!"

"Not by me," she said. "I pay my own way. Actually, I've just heard I've got a piece of work I can do here, right here in Lille, so I'll feel less guilty. I can even claim my travel expenses back."

"*Fantastique!*" said her companion. "Now you can stay some more days, and we will go back to the Ministry of Culture and this time absolutely demand to look at the ceiling in the third attic."

Caroline gazed down at the newspaper which Gervase brought to her, and looked up at him with beautiful, starry tears in her eyes. "Oh God," she said. "I'm sorry, but seeing it here in black and white like this, all I can think is *why not*? Why does everything work out the wrong way round?"

And she began to cry in earnest, so that Gervase had no choice but to take her in his arms and murmur, to her soft hair, words of comfort. Over her shoulder his eyes were wide with recognition and a look very like horror. Mary-Annie, oblivious to this pretty scene, emitted a loud raspberry, and threw the wooden train she was gnawing into the cold hearth with a crash.

28

It was a week before Cat came home. She eventually rang Gervase, who sounded constrained and uncommunicative. Despite Chrétien's teasing prompts she did not mention having seen the newspaper, nor did she ask after Caroline. The Eden job provided a good enough reason for her sojourn, a reason which seemed welcome to both of them. Gervase did say, haltingly, at the end of the brief conversation: "I hope you're – having a rest, as well. You deserve a holiday, Cat. It's going to be much easier for you now. Financially."

"Oh yes," said Cat. "Don't worry about me. I'm a new woman."

Putting down the phone, Gervase wondered whether he ought to have told her that Martin had gone for good. He had sent a letter, postmarked (if only Gervase noticed such things) from the street corner nearest Marianne's flat in London. It said that "all things considered" he had decided to go back to the States a month early, and hoped this would not cause difficulty. The clothes he had left in the bunkhouse were all worn out, so it would be fine to burn them or throw them out. The bike was at the station. In formal terms and without warmth, he thanked Gervase for giving him the chance to gain experience with working horses, and said that it would be very relevant to his future career as he had an opportunity to do an anthropological project with the Amish as part of his higher degree. He sent his best to Duane, and to Winston if anyone should see him.

He did not mention Cat. Gervase assumed that, as they had seemed to be good friends, Martin would be writing to her separately. It was a nuisance, he reflected, to lose the lad just now: especially with Cat's driving ban and two new boys, Terry and Spider, arriving any day. But that was the way with volunteers. They always stayed a longer or a shorter time than they originally planned. There was a New Zealander who wanted to come in September and who had ploughed with horses before. As for the driving problem Mrs Bird, who had in the past week been almost continuously at the farm making obscure pickles and rearranging saucepans, had offered to take on the shopping too, if she was given a proper list. Maybe now they could afford more of her time. They always used to have a cook, in the early days of the Project.

And then there was Caroline. But he avoided thinking about Caroline, because it was complicated, and distressed him, and he was too busy organizing the Morefield handover to deal with the implications of it yet. Gervase had always been good at setting priorities. He filed Martin's letter, forgot it, and pulled out a folder marked *IACS returns: 1995–6*.

Eight days after her arrival in Lille, Cat stood with Chrétien, in his long overcoat, on the station platform. She had been back to *Printemps* a couple of times, and was wearing a cotton dress, straight and severe in line and vivid pink in colour, with a white cotton jacket. "*Jolie chatte*," said Chrétien, approvingly, as she came back from buying a magazine. "You look very young. Twelve years old, at most."

"Crétin," replied Cat. "You lie. The very best we can hope is that I look like my mother looked when we were children, and you look like your father. Life does not stand still."

"No," said Chrétien, his arm on hers. "It dances!"

Together, slowly, they walked towards the Calais train. All around her Cat saw other options, blazoned on locomotives and signboards with the devastating casualness of a big continent whose very trains can promise you the world: *Bruxelles, Basel, Strasbourg, Berlin, Milano, Venezia*. Two doors slammed somewhere, echoing under the arches, and another train moved off.

"Are you sure you would not rather take the Eurostar?" said Chrétien. "My London colleagues say it is a marvel."

"No," said Cat. "I'll take the ferry, like we used to. One last indulgence of nostalgia."

She smiled up at him. They had talked themselves out during the first few days: she knew about his formal, property-led marriage, his many mistresses, his arid relationship with his children, his boredom at work and determined frivolity away from it. None of it dimmed her liking for him, only overlaid it with melancholy for the loss of the spirited, hopeful boy he had once been. They had spoken less these last few days, but in the silences between them lay an understanding of one another and of their impending farewell. Only when too much meaning fell into that silence did Cat deliberately stir him to theatrical indignation, generally by mischievously pretending to extol the merits of the Eden-Lille hotel she was profiling.

"*Alors*," he said now. "This is your train. This is your bag. I think that now we will say *au revoir*."

"*Adieu*," said Cat. "A long *adieu*. We agreed that, after international discussions."

"No, *au revoir*," he said. "There will come a time when even English women will understand how to conduct married life."

Cat leaned across and kissed him, gently, on the mouth. "In another thirty years then, *peut-être*."

"I shall pass the time in dreaming of your eyes," he said in painstaking English, and bowed theatrically over her hand. "That was a good line, *hein?*"

"Go," said Cat. "Go back to your office! Little Anatole will be worried."

This time Chrétien only raised his hand in ironic farewell, turned, and walked rapidly along the platform. Cat turned also, to climb the high step of the train. When she looked out of the window he was nowhere to be seen.

Mary-Annie was cutting another tooth: it made her angry and fretful, and drove her sleepless mother close to despair. One day, Caroline walked up to the farm with the pushchair in an attempt to pacify the baby, and found not Duane or Martin but two strange boys, with almost shaven heads and enormous boots, staring gormlessly at her from the yard.

"Is Mr Hartley here?" she asked.

"Nah," said one of the boys. "Gonta Mid'olt. Mrs Bird's in."

In the kitchen, Caroline found Mrs Bird scrubbing new potatoes. Mary-Annie began to cry the instant the pushchair stopped, and Caroline almost as soon.

"There there!" said Mrs Bird, flapping round the table in her floral apron. "It can take you hard, looking after a baby all by yourself. You sit down and I'll make you a nice cup of tea. Come on, little darling, none of that noise."

Here Gervase found them, Caroline tear-stained but now composed, Mary-Annie sullenly rolling potatoes round on the floor, Mrs Bird mothering them both.

"Cat's back today," he said baldly. "She said she'd take a cab from the station, since she's on expenses. Could be any time." And Caroline, stumbling to her feet, muttering excuses, stuffed the baby rapidly back into the pushchair with a potato still in her fist and took her leave. Gervase looked helplessly after her and Mrs Bird said, "Well! Making heavy weather of everything today, poor lamb!"

Cat leaned over the rail of the ferry, staring unseeingly back at France. There were new memories there now, three decades newer and many layers shallower than the powerful childhood ones. Petits-fours and laughter; walking on wet pavements at midnight holding a warm dry hand; morning sunshine through shutters, high above the Rue Neuve, and the sleeping body of a man with whom she had no deep or lasting bond nor ever would have.

She wondered why she felt no guilt, she who had always championed fidelity and self-control. Maybe it was part of middle age. Perhaps when you were past child-bearing and knew the value of a long, accommodating, accustomed partnership, these things of the body genuinely could come to mean nothing important. Just an extension of friendship and shared memory, a few nights' defiance of the ageing and stiffening world. "What a Gallic way to think," she said aloud, to the rain. "It must be something in the water."

Turning, she thought for a moment that she saw Chrétien's back vanishing into a staff doorway; but it was another dark, darting figure, one of the stewards by the look of his jacket.

Cat sighed. She would see M. le Directeur, she suspected, a few times more out of the corner of her mind's eye before his image finally faded.

As, of course, it must.

29

Artemis swooped on Midmarsham again the day after Cat came home, and invited Caroline to accompany her on a visit to Gervase's uncle in Scotland for a few weeks.

"You're looking peaky," she said. "And Mary-Annie ought to meet the rest of the family. Heaven knows Gervase is remiss enough about keeping in touch." She seemed, marvellously, to have forgotten that the delightful Mary-Annie and her pretty, well-mannered mother actually formed no part of the Hartley blood line. Senility, as Cat tartly observed to Gervase, is at times a great blessing.

At any rate Caroline gladly went, and Gervase seemed more relaxed after her departure. Cat was in high spirits, fonder and more playful than usual, keeping even Terry and Spider in fits of laughter at meal times with her account of the day when at last – with permission direct from the Minister of Culture herself – she and Chrétien had penetrated into the upper reaches of Rue du Lombard and found the "*Merde*" which the boy Chrétien had spelt in air gun pellets on the plaster ceiling of the third attic room. The punch-line, much appreciated by the boys, was a lively description of the moment when Chrétien had dived behind a water tank, and come up with his dark business suit whitened with plaster and streaked with cobwebs, brandishing the actual gun itself.

"It was not mine, I never said so," he had announced to the surprised and lightly scandalized man from the Ministry. "It was Toby's."

"Toby was never allowed an air pistol," objected Cat. "For heaven's sake, he can't have been more than eight."

"Toby never asked for one," said Chrétien. "He exchanged it for his old ice-skates, at the boys' Epiphany party down at the Jesuit school. How he must have missed it, when I threw it behind the tank."

Whereon he had fiddled with the cocking mechanism for a moment, slipped in a pellet from the old-fashioned holder in its handle, and to everybody's surprise induced the gun to work.

"Pellet went right through the side of the water tank," said Cat. "Mercifully, just on the very top of the water level. But it did drip quite a bit." The boys guffawed. Gervase was quiet, wrapped in his own thoughts.

Marianne rang after a few days, asking whether she could come down for the weekend. Cat was so pleased at the prospect of seeing her daughter that she met her on the drive; the day was fine and they left Marianne's bag in the car and walked together up to the top pasture. When they were a good distance from the house Marianne said: "Mum, two things I have to talk to you about. The first one is me and Martin."

"Yes?" said Cat, with what she dryly recognized as breathless, middle-aged maternal anticipation.

"We're getting married," said her daughter. "We would have liked to tell you together, because I'm going to the States with him, to work wherever he ends up. It might not even be nursing. I've said I don't mind, it'll be an adventure. But he wouldn't come up this weekend, because of the other thing."

Cat frowned, not understanding. "But it's wonderful. He's a nice boy, a gem, just right for you. You know my views on early marriage and I suspect you do right to ignore them. I would have loved to see him and tell him that. Does he think Gervase and I are going to disapprove?"

Marianne flopped down on a convenient log. "Oh no, no. It isn't that. It's worse. It's something he's got a bee in his bonnet about. About Gervase."

"Oh?" Cat was still at sea. Marianne drew a deep, rough breath.

"About Gervase and Caroline. While you were away. He thinks Gervase and Caroline . . . oh, you know. He was so angry that he left. He thinks the world of you, Mum. He did think the world of Gervase, too, but now he's just spitting mad about it all."

Cat was silent, taking it in.

"Well," she said finally. "I'm really touched that he cared that much. But I don't believe it."

"I don't know what I believe," said Marianne cautiously. "But I promised him I'd tell you. He says he saw them, more than once, looking exactly as if . . ."

She avoided her mother's eye but doggedly continued: "And he says that one night Gervase wasn't back until the small hours. He was angry because it was just after you went away, after Caroline moved to the cottage, and it looked as if it was planned. Gervase didn't have supper with the boys. He wasn't here most of the night. Martin lay awake. He's from a very moral Catholic family."

"Marianne," said Cat. "I have lived with an unfaithful man before, remember. I know the scenery. I really don't think I'm living with one now. And I don't think Caroline would do it either."

There was a pause, then:

"I do," said Marianne flatly. "She's been jealous of you and Grandad all her life, hasn't she? Because Grandad prefers you, even though she's prettier. It could have been a great chance for her to steal an older man, a father-figure-type, off you. To prove she can beat you."

"You," said her mother, "have been mixing with psychiatrists for too bloody long. Get out west with Martin and rope some steers, why don't you?"

But later, when Marianne had gone upstairs with her bag, Cat sat down suddenly at the kitchen table as if she had been winded.

On stage, for dramatic convenience, people tend to confront one another immediately about such allegations. In real life it can be harder to find the moment. Cat, at any rate, so steadfastly did not believe that her husband had slept with her sister that she was inclined for a while to ignore the whole thing. Caroline, after all, was in Scotland; all the evidence suggested that Gervase was actually much happier since she left. He was busy with the paperwork for the Morefield Trust handover, and kept optimistically, and rather touchingly, she thought, returning to the fact that with farm costs paid and himself on a small salary, her own financial responsibilities would dwindle.

"You could write something of your own," he said hopefully. "Not always have to do commercial work."

Cat only laughed at him. "I'm not a thwarted poet, you know. There isn't a burning work of art in me, waiting its chance to get out. It's nonsense about all copywriters having a novel in their bottom drawer: some of us are just copywriters."

"But you must want to do something of your own," he would persist, disappointed.

"No," she said. "Sorry. No soul, you see. The only thing I quite fancy is doing some soap opera scripts. Winston and I used to have some great ideas about what to do next in *Coronation Street.*"

She was unsure, even as she spoke, how much of this statement was manufactured for the sheer pleasure of seeing his shocked face. Fleetingly, she thought of Toby.

There had been a postcard from Artemis at the end of the first three weeks saying that Caroline was a "huge success" and that Mary-Annie was being taken on long moorland walks with her mother by a neighbour, a distant cousin called Roddy who carried the baby in a backpack and was teaching Caroline to fish, up at the Castle.

"*Roddy,*" said Cat. "Wouldn't you just know that Artemis would find someone called Roddy, in a Scottish castle, and foist him on Caroline? That woman belongs in a P G Wodehouse novel. Aunt Agatha."

"It sounds as if it's doing them all good," said Gervase, flatly. "I think it was time Caroline got away for a bit."

Cat hesitated then, as if to speak; but in fact it was another three weeks, and the eve of Caroline's return, before she at last raised the matter of Martin's suspicions. She had come back on her old black bike from a visit to the doctor's Friday afternoon surgery in Midmarsham. Mrs Bird had gone home early, and Terry and Spider were cutting thistles in the lower pasture. She found Gervase in the workshop by the yard, shaping a new shaft for a tumbril. As usual he straightened, put down the spokeshave and gravely saluted his wife.

"I don't know how to lead up to this," she said. "But Marianne has told me why Martin left. It was because he thought you were having an affair."

Gervase looked at her in silence, impassive. "An affair with Caroline," she continued. "And Gervase, we're both grown-up people. We've been through a lot together, so it seems simplest if I just ask you, and we can go from there. OK?"

He did not answer, but went on looking at her, troubled.

"Is it true? Have you slept with Caroline?"

Gervase cleared his throat.

"No," he said. "No."

"Did you want to? Was it going to happen? Is it going to happen?"

He hesitated, searching for words: "No, it wouldn't have happened. Ever. I mean, not for me. I am afraid that Caroline may have got the wrong idea."

"I see," said Cat, remembering Marianne's theory, and pressing her lips together. Gervase saw her expression and hurried on:

"She has been in a vulnerable state. It was probably all my fault. I am naïve about women, I always have been. You know that."

"Did you make yourself clear?" asked Cat.

"Yes," he said in a low voice. "It was a dreadful thing to have to do. I never knew that doing something right could feel so cruel and sad. But the truth is, I have not been unfaithful to you. Not ever."

"Ah," said Cat. "I didn't really think you had, actually. But it makes it harder for me."

"Why?" asked Gervase. Suddenly the infuriating innocence of his look was too much for her: the same look, she thought suddenly, that a far younger Gervase had given her on her wedding day. She ducked her head, and hurried on blindly, wanting it all over and done with, out in the open, whatever might be the result.

"The reason it makes it harder is that I have to tell you that *I* have been unfaithful to *you*."

The stableyard was quiet. A bird twittered suddenly; a horse, inside the shelter, scraped an iron-shod hoof on the concrete.

"I'm not as honest as you are," said Cat. "And I probably

wouldn't have told you, because it meant nothing important. But I have to, because I'm now pregnant."

Gervase looked at her incredulously. His first thought was for her protection: she was cracking up, suffering delusions, and it was his fault for imposing such years of strain on her in this odd life. His fault for not being able to give her babies.

"Sit down," he said, pulling over a low workbench. "You're tired. It's my fault."

"It's not your fault, you *gummock*!" said Cat, who read his reaction only too well. "And I'm not a crazy menopausal woman. It's true. I had a brief fling in France. With a childhood friend. The one who found the air pistol behind the water tank, remember? I was telling the boys the story at supper when I came back. It never occurred to me I could get pregnant. Not for a minute. I must have been out of my head."

The corroborative detail about the air pistol seemed to clear Gervase's perception, and he looked at her with new eyes.

"You'll have to forgive me. It'll take a while to sink in," he said formally. And then, in a different voice, which shook a little:

"Are you sure you're pregnant?"

"Yes. I did a test two weeks ago, and the doctor's done an official one. He says it's a bit late over forty, but everything's fine and there's no reason I shouldn't have it. No physical reason."

Gervase picked up his spokeshave again and began stroking the wood of the cart-shaft.

"Are you going to go?" he muttered. "To France? Are you and the baby going to live with him?"

"No!" shouted Cat. "I told you, the affair was irrelevant. It was – I don't know, think of it as therapy. Like a health farm, a massage, physiotherapy, all mixed up with childhood friendship and old jokes and a couple of good dinners with too much wine." She ran her hand through her hair, half-embarrassed, half-perplexed.

"It was just very French, the whole thing. I can hardly believe it now. It's not real. Except that there is this baby."

"He'll want it," said Gervase in a low voice, scraping the wood. "Of course he will."

Cat went over to him, took the tool from his hand, and led

him to the bench. Her arm was round his shoulders, his head in her neck. She felt his tears warm on her skin.

"No, he won't," she said. "Anyway, tough shit if he does. It's ours, Gervase. Ours, if we want it. I do."

They sat for a long time in the yard together, and their talk was quiet and private and deep. When at last they came indoors, Terry and Spider were finishing their high tea under the eye of Mrs Bird, and there were two messages on the answering machine. One was from Caroline, in a high, light, happy voice, announcing her return. The other was from Artemis, who usually refused to use such machines, saying in conspiratorial tones that Caroline had some very good news to tell them. Gervase must, she said, ring his mother straight away once Caroline had explained, and she would fill in all the background. It was perfectly suitable, she said, and he need not worry.

"It'll be about *Roddy*," said Cat. "I bet you."

It was about Roddy, inevitably. Caroline shyly told her sister all about it the next day when she arrived home, and asked her to tell Gervase. If all continued to go well, she would probably move to Scotland.

Nothing more was said between them about what could have happened during Cat's trip to France. The sisters returned gratefully to their old status of non-confiding but vaguely benevolent relatives, each with her own busy and perfectly satisfactory separate life. So did Lindy, who rang up a few weeks later with some anodyne chat and said brightly to Cat, as if none of the awful intimacies of past months had ever been shared:

"Mark and I are thinking of starting a family, did I tell you? I had a bit of trouble, but I've been to a clinic and we've got the all-clear now."

Cat, the diplomat's daughter, responded with suitable surprise and pleasure, just as if the subject had never been raised between them before. Mark, said Lindy airily as she rang off, sent his love. Cat conveyed hers back in an equally light tone, wondering as she did so whether she had destroyed the crazy accusing letter Mark had sent her or whether it still lay incriminatingly on her desk under a grimy pile of Eden faxes and induction leaflets. She must look it out and destroy it. Every home should have a shredder, she thought. There was no point in preserving the past if it was only going to cause trouble.

Toby Christian Hartley, immediately nicknamed TC, was born in March. He weighed seven and a half pounds and looked, all the family said, startlingly like his uncle and namesake: dark, elfin, with a weirdly amused air even on his third or fourth day of life.

His uncle Mark stood as godfather, and spent most of the ceremony gazing tenderly across the font at his own pregnant wife. Gervase stood as close as he could get, maintaining a jealous vigilance as his son – oh yes, his son! – lay whickering in protest in Mark's unskilful arms. The service was Anglican, traditional and soothing; outside Midmarsham church a gale bent the trees and blew stinging sleet and occasional hailstones. Mark and Lindy had wanted to delay the gathering until spring and were backed up by Artemis, who detested travelling in winter; but Cat had insisted on an early christening so that the baby's half-sister Marianne could be there before her departure to Texas. Caroline invited her Scottish cavalier, who came rather shyly because it was his first appearance at a Gratton family gathering.

After the ceremony, they drove through the darkening gale in their various cars to a tea at Knoll Farm laid out by Mrs Bird. Roddy lugged from his car a christening present of a case of vintage port. This, said Roddy, would come of age in the same year of the 21st century as Toby Christian did.

"If it's lucky," Cat muttered. She had eschewed all alcohol in her pregnancy, and was beginning to recover a taste for it. Gervase laughed, and assured Roddy that the port would be properly hidden from the owner's mother.

"Well," said Cat. "It'd only be family tradition if I did drink it. Dad, isn't it true that Mum borrowed my silver-and-glass christening necklace I got from my godfather in Murano, and lost it?"

"That's right," admitted Robert. "She lost it at a cocktail party in Tel Aviv. She was conscience-stricken. She bought you a silver spoon instead."

"Which she also lost, in the move from Washington," said Cat. "Nothing like a good grudge, is there?"

Robert had grown suddenly old, bent and small, with a new translucence to his skin: a winter of chest infections and stiffening limbs had given him what the French would call a *coup de vieux*. In spite of it he felt now a sense of completion, of resigned contentment. He was tired and had scaled down his public work, so that the family seemed suddenly to have swum into clearer focus. They were more important to him than at any time since Diana's death. And the family, with one exception, seemed to be flourishing.

The dimness and conventionality of Caroline's new man friend had shocked him for a while, but now he reflected that perhaps the best régime for his younger daughter was precisely what Roddy could offer: uncritical adoration and rolling acres. She seemed calm and blooming, if a little chilly towards her brother-in-law Gervase. Mark was less tense than usual, his wife pink-cheeked and clinging; and above all, this new grandchild filled him with particular joy. Looking around his burgeoning family the old man said quietly to Cat:

"Happy day. But you mustn't think we've all forgotten who's missing. Do you know, Mousie, I sometimes work out how old Toby and Topsy's child would have been now. About eight months, I reckon."

Cat was touched. "Oh Dad!"

"It's another grandchild of mine," he said gruffly, touching the new baby's cheek. "And of Diana's."

Cat looked down at her infant lolling off to sleep in a wicker basket at her side. She fended off Mary-Annie, who was crawling to investigate her squashy new cousin, and as Caroline hurried up to suppress her daughter, she turned back and said abruptly to Robert:

"Do you think we ought to stop hoping now, Dad? Admit that TC here has only got one uncle?"